those Splendid memories

PREVIOUSLY BY THE AUTHOR

Come Sing With Me My People

Colour Sergeant Chesney V.C.

Battling Spirits And Kindly Hearts

Love Across The Decades

Available from www.bookguild.co.uk

those
Splendid
memories

Steven Baker

The Book Guild Ltd

First published in Great Britain in 2018 by
The Book Guild Ltd
9 Priory Business Park
Wistow Road, Kibworth
Leicestershire, LE8 0RX
Freephone: 0800 999 2982
www.bookguild.co.uk
Email: info@bookguild.co.uk
Twitter: @bookguild

This work is entirely fictitious and bears no resemblance to any persons living or dead.

Typeset in Aldine401 BT

Printed and bound in Great Britain by CPI Group (UK) Ltd, Croydon, CR0 4YY

ISBN 978 1912362 448

British Library Cataloguing in Publication Data.
A catalogue record for this book is available from the British Library.

For the brave and adventurous

One

Russia 1892

"Anatole! Anatole wake up," his father called out. Viktor Luchenya was a kind man with a slight stoop and strong features which made his innate Jewishness clear. He was immensely proud and loving of his children. "Wake up, my boy. Today we begin our journey to America." The boy stirred in his sleep and yawned.

It was four o'clock in the morning and absolutely ice cold. Outside it was pitch black but in the stark, barren countryside of bare brown trees and uncultivated land, there was movement. People were leaving their villages and heading to various destinations. They had been ordered to do so. The soldiers would soon be coming to move people out. Some were already there on horseback watching the departing populace. It was a poignant sight: people leaving, driven out by virtue of their faith. Sad-looking Jewish families limped past in the darkness.

"Wake up, my son," Viktor said gently. He raised his boy from the bed and tousled his hair. "Come. Wash now. Your mother and sister are waiting."

Anatole left the bedroom and went into the next room where his mother, Ekaterina, was waiting with a bowl of water to wash him and his two-year-old sister, Mariska. Viktor began to put his son's clothes into a bag and he looked around this stark bare room where Anatole had slept for the six years he had lived. It was time to leave this house and the grim, grey surroundings of a sad, cold, inhospitable landscape.

The house was bare with little furniture and material possessions. It was a cold wooden structure, more like a shelter than an abode, yet it had been home to the Luchenya family for some time. Viktor and Ekaterina

1

had done their best to make it a good home for their two young children. The nights had often been bitterly cold in this house with little to choose between the temperatures outside and in. The rural community they had been part of was dying.

When the edict came from the government for all Jewish families to be moved, Viktor knew that if they remained they would be persecuted. America seemed to offer a glowing alternative. Viktor was a tailor, a master of his trade, and in America he felt sure that his family could lead good lives there. He was in his forties but he looked like an elderly man because of the bitter cold that had seeped into his bones and face. His wife, Ekaterina, was in her late thirties, but she too looked much older. Her hair had turned prematurely grey and she had a tired, lined face. She looked constantly sad. However, when she smiled her whole face lit up. This morning was the start of a new life for the Luchenya family. Both parents hoped that the road ahead would not be one of fear or trepidation, but one of optimism and happiness.

Viktor put several bags of clothing and belongings on a wooden handcart, which he would have to push for many miles until they reached their ultimate destination: the docks. From there, they would take a boat to England, work for a while, and then take another boat departing from Liverpool and arriving in New York.

When Victor had packed his son's clothing, he took one last look at the small bedroom, then left closing the door for the last time and he walked into the main room. His daughter, Mariska, was sitting by her mother who was brushing Anatole's hair and smartening him up ready for their long journey. At two years of age Mariska was a pretty little girl who looked around her with confusion. With a child's sense of the unexpected she was aware that things were changing.

"This house, it has been home for so long. I cannot bear to think of us leaving," Ekaterina said quietly, her eyes betraying sadness and fear at the thought of an uncertain future.

"We must go," Viktor replied. "We will make another home – a happy home. In a place where our people will not be fearful or wary." He pushed the handcart to the door indicating it was time to go. "Are we ready Ekaterina? My children?"

"We are," she said, rising from her chair and both children, without any prompting, held her hands.

"Come, my family," Viktor beckoned, and then his voice took on an unexpected note of optimism. "There is a bright future for us all in America. Let us join our friends." He pushed the door open. There in front of them were the sad-faced villagers passing by. Families carried their belongings and were followed by their children, and even grandparents. Viktor left the house first and he stood until Ekaterina and the children were by his side. "We go now." He began to push the handcart and in the darkness, they joined the moving throng of people. Soldiers of the tsar's army rode past. They began the long walk.

There was one thing common to every house they passed: the front door was always open. It was possible to look right inside and see a barren, empty house where a family once lived. When each house was vacated, a soldier would ride up and check inside to see if any family member remained.

Viktor and Ekaterina did not look back. They did not want to. It was too painful for them to think about. The house had seen the birth of their two children, Mariska and Anatole. For them it had been a happy home. But now the whole community was leaving.

Even in the darkness of night, it was possible to see the pain in the eyes of their fellow travellers. Red-streaked eyes gave the indication that the uprooting of their lives had been a deeply emotional experience. They walked for several miles across flat, coarse land until they came to a forest. Walking through the tall trees that rose everywhere, Anatole looked up in childish fear. The trees in the black of night took on twisted and contorted facial shapes, like fearsome gargoyles glaring with angry eyes at unsuspecting victims. Anatole looked frightened. This did not go unnoticed by his mother.

"It's all right, my son," Ekaterina reassured him.

They continued walking until they came to a clearing. Once through this they saw a train line and a small station ahead. The villagers clambered onto the platform and, within minutes, a train could be seen approaching. Thick grey steam followed on from behind like a faded streamer. On the platform, no one said anything. They stood there, cold, shivering, emotional and in silence. It was still dark and inhospitable. Viktor looked at his wife and children lovingly. Then, as the train pulled into the station, the group of Jewish people picked up their belongings and boarded the carriages. There were not enough seats and most people, including the Luchenya family, stood. They waited in silence for what seemed ages and then all of a sudden the sound of the engine moving into motion could be heard. The train was on the move. An aura of relief fell across the passengers.

Viktor and Ekaterina looked out at the passing countryside knowing they would never ever again set eyes on it. In the next twenty-five years, there would be a revolution in Russia and the tsar would be gone. They could not have predicted this, of course. The world was changing in preparation for the new century and with it, their own lives.

In the far off distance, red flames suddenly surged into the night sky; Anatole and Mariska were jarred out of their drowsiness by the sight. Houses were burning. Soldiers were riding past. Viktor looked on in horror. Ekaterina turned inwards to her husband. It was their village in the far away scene that was ablaze. The tsar's soldiers were burning the now empty villages.

"Our home is no more," Viktor said in a quiet whisper to his wife. Anatole watched with horrified fascination. Viktor put his hand on his son's shoulder and gripped it. Mariska held her mother's hand tightly. From within the safety of the carriages, the Jewish people looked out at the fires that blazed in the distance. It was as if the fires were burning not only the places that had once been their homes, but also the bridges that bound them to the land of their birth. For both the young and old who looked out, tears were evident in some and pretty close in others. Anatole would never forget this day for as long as he lived.

Two

Leeds, Yorkshire, England, 1892

The Luchenya family had arrived in England in the middle of 1892. They had been pleasantly surprised to be greeted with warm sunshine and cheerful faces when the boat had docked at Grimsby. There was something else they could sense about the place they had come to. A person couldn't see it, taste it or sense it, but they knew from now on it was something they would miss were it ever to be taken away from them. It was that sense of freedom; the feeling that there was no hostile authority that could suddenly force them to move on. They had arrived in a country that was free and where the people were almost always cheerful and optimistic, no matter what their circumstances were or how changeable the weather could be.

They had travelled across to Leeds where Viktor had found work in a textile factory in Harehills. Close by they had rented some rooms. Their plan was to work there for a few months and then catch the boat from Liverpool to New York. Ekaterina looked after Mariska and Anatole. The green of England and the beautiful parks in Leeds filled her with peace and serenity. Sometimes she would take the children into the city centre of Leeds and gaze in awe at all the fine goods displayed in the shops. The English were polite and courteous mostly, but the clothes the Luchenya family wore immediately marked them out as émigrés and sometimes people would stare or make a whispered comment. To all extents, they were still outsiders, yet they felt happy. In fact, Viktor had contemplated the idea that perhaps the family might want to stay in Leeds.

Many of their fellow countrymen had decided to stay in Leeds where they had settled in areas like Chapel Allerton, and found work in many of the local factories. Yorkshire people were hardworking, productive and full of enterprise. This was an attitude that suited Viktor. He was skilled at his trade, earned good money and he worked long hours. There was something else about the work he carried out. He enjoyed it. The results were good. The materials he worked with were of a good quality and there was camaraderie amongst the workforce. Whereas in Russia he had been self-employed, here in Yorkshire he was part of a large factory which respected his skills and conscientious approach to the work.

At night Viktor would make his way home along the cobbled streets to the terraced house where the rooms they lived in were situated. Ekaterina always had a meal ready for him, together with her homemade cakes she had specially baked. After he had recited the Kaddish, the family sat round the table enjoying the warmth and love that is only ever really felt in the early years of childhood.

Although their conditions of living were austere, there was something safe and secure about the concept of working hard and coming home to a peaceful household, good food and the love of a family. It was a way of life Viktor never took for granted. Truly there was heavenly bliss in the most humble of circumstances. How wonderful it was to lead a life without fear. They liked the Yorkshire people with their geniality and easy-going affability. He began to question himself if it was in his best interests for the family to make the big journey to America.

✳✳✳

One Sunday afternoon the family sat in a pleasant park in Roundhay. Viktor and Ekaterina watched their children playing. It was a peaceful, sunny day: people strolled arm in arm, loving couples gazed adoringly at each other, families were having picnics, ladies in colourful dresses with bustles and beautiful hats strolled by with admiring gentlemen in their Sunday best. People looked happy and laughed together. Viktor and Ekaterina could equate the sight that afternoon with just one word: happiness. It was that blissful state of being which they both absorbed like the warmth of the sun.

"We have known good days in the time we have been here," Ekaterina said. Viktor nodded and smiled in agreement. "Are we still going to America? If you want to stay here I will understand."

Viktor did not answer the question directly. "The English are nice people. Very different to how I imagined. But I notice the big divide. There are the rich. The very rich – the upper class, they call it. Then there are the well-off or the comfortable. Of course, there are the poor. There is poverty here, a different type of poor to what we knew. To advance ourselves will be hard. I am not the young man that I was, my dear. Perhaps in America we will not be bracketed. There may be real opportunities, not just for us, but our children." He smiled at the sight of Mariska and Anatole playing together. "Look how happy they are."

"And you think that they will be better off in America?" Ekaterina asked. "It is civilised here. People are polite. The children are beginning to pick up words of English. Soon English will be their language. Their own language."

Victor contemplated Ekaterina's words. A short way from them was a bandstand. Some military figures with instruments began taking their place for a Sunday afternoon concert. Shortly the people in Roundhay Park would be entertained by these musicians.

"America is a young country," Viktor finally answered. "It is a growing country. Something new. In the twentieth century who knows how it will evolve? It is exciting too. New cities, plains, forests and wide beaches lapped by oceans. New industries. This country is good, but it is an old civilisation. If America doesn't turn out to be what we hope, perhaps we could come back?"

"Perhaps," said Ekaterina. "You speak with such certainty. Then, we go to America and all will be well." Before Viktor could answer, Ekaterina pointed to another Jewish couple coming across the park. "Isn't that… Mr and Mrs Shezevion, from the boat?"

"Of course, Anna and Kristov." They both waved and the couple came across to them, embraced and shook hands. The band started to play. Mariska and Anatole stopped to listen to the music. Both couples engaged in small talk and caught up on what they had all been doing during their time in Leeds. Anatole appeared fascinated by the band. Mariska turned and ran to her mother who cuddled her.

"Your children are beautiful," said Anna.

"They are my jewels," Ekaterina declared.

"Look at your boy. He loves the music," Kristov said, pointing to Anatole who was beginning to move in time to the beat and rhythm.

Perhaps a psychologist might have interpreted the six-year-old boy's sudden fascination of the music as being the first stirrings of his soul, and an interest awoken in performers. In his brief childhood, Anatole had never heard a note of music. The only time in Russia he had heard anyone sing was his mother when she had sung a lullaby. He turned around and joined his family, who were happily laughing with Kristov and Anna.

"It is good to catch up with you both," Kristov said delightedly. "You know our son Alexander is getting married to a lovely girl called Maria. They both met on the boat when we were all coming over." He looked at his wife quickly to seek approval. "We would like you both, and your children, to come to the wedding."

"Yes. We would be happy for you all to be there," Anna agreed.

"We would love to come!" Ekaterina said with a genuine enthusiasm.

***

At their place of lodging in Harehills, Ekaterina schooled her children in the English language. Her late father had once been a seaman who had brought back books from foreign parts. Some were of the English classics by Robert Louis Stevenson, as well as picture book stories, all of which had been voraciously read by Ekaterina. From these she had learned the basis of English and together with Viktor they had grasped the fundamentals of the language.

Here in Yorkshire while her husband was out working long hours, Ekaterina taught her children to speak English. She would use pictures and objects, and describe them carefully to Anatole and Mariska. Slowly but surely they began to speak sentences in a somewhat halting fashion.

Ekaterina would read out aloud from books such as *Treasure Island* and *Oliver Twist*. The children would listen avidly, trying hard to understand and, when they did, their mother would explain things even more. In every way Ekaterina demonstrated her love for her children as a teacher, disciplinarian and with a deep kindliness that was constantly on show in her eyes as she gazed at both Mariska and Anatole. Her children were everything, and as she was so often fond of saying, they were her jewels.

Whenever they walked down the cobbled streets of Leeds, Ekaterina always proudly strolled with Mariska and Viktor. On one such day a neighbour had told her that Queen Victoria would be visiting – a rare public appearance by the widowed monarch. After a luncheon with leading citizens at the Town Hall the queen would then be driven in a horse-drawn carriage to the railway station. By the time Ekaterina and the children arrived in the city centre, the crowds were already gathered. They stood there amongst the enthusiastic onlookers, although their traditional Jewish attire set them apart from the rest.

A little boy in the crowd turned around and studied them with curiosity. He looked up and down at their clothes and their faces, somewhat rudely, but not deliberately so. Mariska and Viktor looked back at him, not understanding why he stared at them in such a strange manner. The boy's mother turned around slowly and caught sight of Ekaterina and the children. She was very well-dressed in colourful clothes and a lovely hat. Her face was one of beauty and serenity. The lady was obviously one who was frequently termed as 'well to do' or 'one of the gentry'. Almost without expectation the lady beamed a warm smile at Ekaterina and the children and said, "It's a lovely day, isn't it? I do hope you enjoy it."

Diplomatically and perhaps with an element of warm surprise at the lady's kind remark, Ekaterina responded by saying, "Thank you. You have a nice boy. You are beautiful and you dress so fine."

Somehow Ekaterina's accented English and genuine sincerity didn't seem out of place. The lady, who was slightly taken aback by the remark, nodded appreciatively. It was the first time someone had spoken directly to Ekaterina. There was some background noise and it was clear that something was happening in the distance.

"Here she comes," someone said. It was a remark that was repeated several times by different people in the crowd. The queen and her entourage were approaching. The sound of cheering grew louder and louder until finally her carriage came into view.

"Look, Anatole! Look, Mariska! It is the Queen of England!" Ekaterina exclaimed. She picked Mariska up so that she could see this once in a lifetime event. Ekaterina's immediate thought was that, on first sight, Queen Victoria appeared to be a little old lady who looked as if she had been on an expensive shopping trip, rather than the empress who reigned over half the world and who often admonished such influential towering political figures as Disraeli and Gladstone. The queen wore dark clothes, waved briskly but seemed a grim, unsmiling figure.

Just as quickly as she came, the queen was gone. The crowds began to disperse almost immediately. Ekaterina would have liked to have spoken to the lady with the kind face, but she too had disappeared quickly with her son in tow.

That was one of the things about the English that puzzled Ekaterina. On first meeting them they could be gracious and polite yet they seemed to have a sheet of ice around them that needed to be penetrated before one could really get to know them and become friends. Was it her faith? Was it her class? Perhaps, even, did their cut of clothes isolate and separate them? Ekaterina could never work out the answer. In America she wondered if they would still stand isolated?

At the tailoring factory in Harehills, Viktor was getting a good reputation as a worker. Not only was he a skilled cutter, but also a highly productive one. The truth was, he enjoyed his work. He loved everything about textiles, cutting, measuring and designing clothes. Soon, though, Viktor would have to make the decision to tender his resignation, and let the manager know that he and his family would be emigrating to America. Frequently one of his supervisors would stop and look over his shoulder and make a comment.

"Good work, Mr Luchenya. Where did you learn your trade?"

Viktor never feigned false modesty. He was always as honest as the day was long and humble in his manner. "I am self-taught. I learned from practice as a young man in Russia."

"Aye, and a lot of practice too," the supervisor remarked in a broad Yorkshire accent. "I wish all my cutters took the time and trouble you do to produce real quality."

It was an art, no doubt about it. Good tradesmen never learned their profession overnight. Years of practice, patience, precision and endurance paid dividends. Viktor also was acutely aware that a good tradesman never rested on his laurels, or resisted change, by emphatically insisting that the old ways were best. New methods. New ideas. New tools. These were what kept the old trades alive and brought them into the modern world.

Viktor knew that the move from Russia to Yorkshire had been an upheaval and had taken courage to do so. It was the next leg of the journey to America which would require nerve and tenacity to undertake. For a while he had self doubts about going to this new and great country, but something was beckoning him. Something was guiding him.

Three

In late 1892, Viktor tendered his resignation with regret to the manager of the textile factory who expressed his sadness at losing such a good employee; however, he wished Viktor and his family good luck in their new life in America. He also said that were he a few years younger he would have tried to take the same opportunity either in America or one of the colonies of the British Empire.

Before the Luchenya family left Yorkshire, they had a wedding to attend. Their friends, Kristov and Anna Shezevion, had invited them to see their son, Alexander, marry his fellow expatriate Maria. The wedding was held in a part of Leeds that over the years had effectively become something of a Jewish area.

It seemed as if everyone of the faith or even someone with the remotest link or trace with it was there. The ceremony and festivities, as with all weddings, was a joyous occasion. The happy couple both in their early twenties had met on the boat to England, and, in their own words, had fallen in love at first sight. Alexander was a handsome young man whose eyes shone in adoration when he looked at Maria. Kristov and Anna could not hold back with tears of joy and contagious smiles. That was one thing about the Jewish people which was so obviously evident: their deep love of the family unit. They were also an emotional race, demonstrative in their show of love and affection, and passionate in all respects.

Outside the synagogue, as Alexander and Maria emerged, the guests and onlookers gazed on admiringly. Viktor and Ekaterina stood proudly with their children. The glow and warmth of the bridal couple's happiness generated similar feelings to the guests.

"Oh what it is like to be young and in love with it all before you," Viktor mused. Ekaterina smiled at his reflection on the past.

11

"But we still have it all before us," she reaffirmed. "We are still young in our minds."

Viktor looked down at the children and smiled in a loving way at Ekaterina. "The children will keep us young."

The wedding reception was a happy and boisterous occasion. There was much singing and dancing, with everyone joining in. Even the young children mimicked the adults. Anatole and Mariska began to join in from the sidelines. It was a blur of dancing and faces passing by, with musicians playing with zest and enthusiasm. To Anatole's six-year-old eyes, the music and dancing stirred his young heart. He moved forward and started to copy the movements of the adults.

Viktor and Ekaterina looked on with an element of surprise at their son's sudden display of extroversion. Then to add to the initial surprise little Mariska grabbed her brother's hand and started to dance with him. For a few minutes it was as if all eyes were focussed on them. Then smiles seemed to break out all round. Without realising its Anatole and Mariska at their tender ages had in their childhood precociousness become entertainers of the moment. The music was intoxicating. The happiness of the occasion was contagious. The atmosphere of the wedding reception was pure joy.

Alexander and Maria sat at the dining table surrounded by friends, relatives and well wishers. The music changed and the tune changed to one of a slow dance. It was the signal for Alexander and Maria to take to the floor followed by other couples. Mariska and Anatole stood to one side flanked by Viktor and Ekaterina, Kristov and Anna came across to them.

"Thank you for coming," Anna said sincerely. "It's been so nice that you came."

"It has been a wonderful day," Kristov agreed, and there were tears in his eyes. "We are just getting to know you and now you are leaving for America. We wish you and the family well. May God watch over you."

They hugged and embraced. There could not have been a happier note to depart on, than a wedding amongst friends, and fellow Jewish migrants. It is a strange fact of life that when someone leaves a place on a positive note of happiness, prosperity and good will the future looks optimistic. To leave on a note of negativity, austerity and unease, the future looks foreboding and worrying. Viktor was the eternal optimist.

A week later they were in Liverpool to board the boat for America.

Liverpool at the time was a thriving port from which passengers sailed to all parts of the world. Cargo boats came from all over to load and unload merchandise. It was actually a very grey day when they arrived, with fog hanging over the port. The sea air was cold and stung the cheeks. The queue to board the ship seemed to stretch on and on. The immigrant ship would soon be full of men, women and children from the industrial North, bound for what they all hoped would be a better life in the United States. Many of Viktor's countrymen, who had been working in the cotton mills, and textile industries of Lancashire and Yorkshire, were also aboard on the next leg of their journey.

When the ship departed from Liverpool, many of the English passengers leaned over the rail taking one last nostalgic look at their homeland. It was a moment of poignancy and sadness for many of them, as they would probably never ever return, not even for a visit. Viktor, Ekaterina and the children gazed at the coastline as it faded into the distance. Even though it was not their country, and they had only really been there for a period of working transition, they felt sad. It was as if in the brief time they had been there the family had developed a sense of belonging. They would take away with them memories of cheerful people, cobbled streets and terraced houses, manufacturing industries, hard work, affluence alongside poverty, beautiful parks and the Yorkshire Dales.

Perhaps, because of the easy familiarity of the place, it felt like home. For the rest of their lives Viktor and Ekaterina would remember their time in Yorkshire with affection. It had been the time in their lives where they had enjoyed an unrestricted freedom to do as they wanted, when they wanted.

The boat put down at the Irish ports of Belfast and Dun Laoghaire for Dublin, where more migrants came aboard. Then, the vessel sailed out into the Atlantic Ocean. On board the various groups of migrating passengers sang songs that were traditional to their homeland and danced on deck when the mood took them, and the weather allowed them to do so.

Just over a week later the boat sailed into New York harbour. All the passengers lined the rail looking out at this rising new metropolis that gleamed in the early morning sunlight. It had been a long journey since the Luchenya family had left Russia. One early morning they had watched from the train the fires enveloping the village of their past life. Today, on this early morning, the passengers watched as the sun rose over the city of their new life. And what a city it was! Young, dynamic, with gleaming white buildings which seemed to emit waves of energy and enterprise. Victor put his arm around Ekaterina tightly.

"It has been a long journey," he said in an innocent understatement. "We have finally arrived."

Ekaterina added quickly, "In the land of the free."

Anatole and Mariska looked on. Their eyes were shining.

Four

New York, USA, 1898

There was a big parade in the centre of the city that bright spring day. New York was a city that seemed to hold parades at the drop of a hat; that was one of the things that twelve-year-old Anatole Luchenya liked about this city. He considered himself a real American boy now, not just an immigrant kid. The crowds were gathered for this parade. It wasn't one of huge flotillas, carnivals or cowboys on horseback. This one was a military parade of American Civil War veterans – those who had fought in the blue uniform of the Union.

Anatole stood amongst the crowds waiting for the proceedings to begin. He wasn't sure why this parade was taking place thirty-three years after General Robert E Lee surrendered the Confederate Army, and the war *1865* had come to an end between the North and South. He just knew this was something strong pertaining to America's history. Anatole was constantly learning about this country, the one which he had called home for the last six years.

The sound of a military band suddenly hit the air with a lively rendition of a marching tune. This was the signal for the people lining the street to break out into a round of thunderous applause and flag-waving in a display of patriotic fervour.

Heading the parade were policemen on horseback. Immediately behind them marched police from almost every precinct. They were predominately Irish, a mixture of first and second generation. Behind them came a US Army band with fresh-faced young men, already professional musicians skilled on pipe, brass and drum. The loudest cheer came for the group of men who came afterwards.

They were proud middle-aged and elderly men wearing the original blue uniforms of the Union. Anatole removed his cap, as others did in the crowd of onlookers, as a sign of respect. Once they had been the young men who had gone off to fight a war which had resulted in the deaths of almost half a million Americans. The southern states, once rich and prosperous, were besieged by poverty, as the northern states' ultimate aim was the abolition of slavery.

It was a piece of living history that Anatole absorbed that day. For these men had fought in campaigns in places that belonged in the military history books, such places as Gettysburg, Bull Run, Vicksburg, Chickamauga. It was hard not to be awed by the sight of these veterans who in every crevice of their faces evoked the experience of what they had been through. Who knew what tragedy, heartbreak and misery their tired eyes had once seen on the blood red battlefields of long ago?

When the parade was over Anatole put his cap back on and quickly walked away into the crowds. It was a bustling Saturday afternoon. Everywhere people were going somewhere. There was no school today and he was on his way home to the drab apartment block in the Bronx where his family lived. His ma and pa would soon be home and getting the evening meal ready. Always for his father, Viktor, it was work, work, work. Never did he seem to stop since he had formed his own business. Both he and Ekaterina dreamed of moving to a home of their own. Even after six years, the dream seemed so far away.

During the week, Anatole sold newspapers from a pitch near the city's main railway station. Straight after school, he headed back into the city to earn money for the family household. Already his father had impressed on him the importance of the work ethic. Viktor emphasised that when he tailored beautiful suits he always created deep pockets. This, he said, was to ensure that they would always contain plenty of money.

Anatole was heading through the city when he started to notice the various hawkers and street musicians who seemed to proliferate everywhere. There was one entertainer who suddenly caught his eye. He was a well-dressed black gentleman who, accompanied by a banjo player and a mouth organist, danced in a tap dancing style. The man was tall with a broad smile, lithe and rhythmic, and he moved in such a way that it was compelling to watch. The tune that the man danced to was one Anatole had once heard someone sing: 'Way down upon the Swanee River'. He twirled and rotated, gave little leaps, tapped his shoes and swayed and stretched. It was the kind of dancing that was more likely to be associated with the southern states in its demonstration of skill, and style, and was hugely entertaining to watch. Only a few watched. Anatole was a captive audience, appreciative and enthused.

When the tune had come to an end Anatole applauded prompting the others to join in. The dancer winked at him and smiled. People threw coins into a box by his side. Anatole did the same.

"Thank you, son," he said in a deep voice.

"How did you learn that, mister?" Anatole asked him.

The dancer looked at both the musicians quizzically and then replied, "One hell of a lot of practice, boy."

"Could you show me how to do it?" Anatole surprised the man who looked at him with surprise. "I want to be a dancer, Mr…"

"The name's Jess Reubens. Now why does a kid like you want to dance? You want to make a career out of it?" He had a big smile and a friendly nature. "You want to see a guy who can dance? There's a fellow called Eddie Foy appearing in a theatre round the block. That's a dancer."

"But you're good. I like the way you dance."

"I'm a black Southern boy. It's in my heart and soul. Those civil war veterans who marched today… I owe them my life. I was a twelve-year-old slave boy, separated from his parents and beaten by his masters. God bless old Abe Lincoln. I felt like dancing ever since I was freed and I ain't never stopped. It's freedom, boy. I danced all the way up from the South and I won't stop until the day the good Lord up above sends for me and says, 'Jess, I want you to sing in my heavenly choir'."

"You sing too?" Anatole queried.

"Sure. I sing spirituals, Negro spirituals. You want to hear singing like an angel choir? Well, there's a church in Harlem you want to visit tomorrow night if you've got time. Boy, when they raise a note together it reaches the heavens."

"Will you dance again? Now? Please, Mr Reubens."

"See that box there?" Jess pointed. "The boys and I want to eat tonight. Throw a nickel or a dime in there and I'll dance up a storm."

Almost automatically onlookers threw coins into the box. Anatole rummaged in his pockets and found some money, which he added to the trio's collection. Jess Reubens and the two musicians immediately went into their act. This time the performance brought more onlookers, fascinated by the dancing style of this smiling man. To the tune of 'Camp Town Races' Jess once again lit up the sidewalk with a display of dancing that bedazzled the city folk that Saturday afternoon.

It didn't stop there. Once he finished that number to big applause, and more coins added to the box, Jess started to sing a sad and mournful song. It was called 'Poor Old Joe' and it began:

> *'Gone are the days*
> *When my heart was young and gay.*
> *Gone are my friends*
> *From the cotton fields away,*
> *Gone from the earth*
> *To a better land I know.*
> *I hear their gentle voices*
> *Calling "Poor old Joe".'*

The song was sad and reflected on the plight of a black man looking back on a life that had been spent as a slave. To Anatole it was almost too sad to listen to and he continued on his journey. Music rung in his ears. He knew that his father, Viktor, wanted him to learn the trade of a tailor but Anatole had other ideas. The thought of a life on the stage was far more appealing than long hours spent in a tailoring business. He knew his father spent fourteen hours a day at work every day of the week. Perhaps it was because Viktor was brought up on the theme that hard work is virtuous. Hard work led to affluence and riches but along the way many sacrifices were made. Time spent with the family for example. There were times when Anatole felt he didn't really know his father.

Viktor was fifty now but he had the appearance of a much older man. The little hair he had left was silver and was carefully covered by a yarmulke, which he wore most of the time. A pair of thin glasses covered his red-strained eyes. A silver beard protruded from his chin like a direction pointer. He was stooped, and his back seemed to have a permanent arch in it. If anyone didn't know his real age, he would have been mistaken for a man of seventy and more.

This Saturday he had been particularly busy. He worked alone and looked forward to the day, hopefully soon, when his son would join the family business as an assistant. He felt sure that the pair of them would be a great working team. Viktor felt tired, overly tired. The long hours had been catching up on him. He was a poor sleeper too. Often he lay awake worrying about work and money. In all of the years of his life he had never learned the art of relaxation.

"Oy… oy… oy… I am tired," he said to himself putting a hand to his head. He stopped measuring fabric and sat by the window looking out at the busy Brooklyn thoroughfare where his business was situated. Well-dressed people passed by in horse-drawn carriages. A couple of US sailors walked by, laughing raucously. A group of youths passing a ball to each other rushed past. *New York on a Saturday afternoon*, thought Viktor. *Full of life. Everyone is always going somewhere.* Viktor turned his head from the window to a mirror on the desk next to him. He gazed at his appearance almost in dismay and disbelief. He spoke aloud to the vision in the mirror. "Viktor, my boy, you are an old man now before you've been a middle-aged man." He felt a slight twinge on his chest and rubbed it. He felt short of breath today. Perhaps he would go home slightly earlier tonight and spend more time with his family.

Ekaterina was busy preparing the evening meal. The Luchenya apartment was at the rear of a tenement block and three flights up. From the kitchen she could look down at a small courtyard between the blocks where the children played. She smiled at little Mariska, who was playing hoops with another little girl. Mariska was now eight years old, a very happy child with fair hair and an engaging smile. Even though the family lived in relative poverty, it had no effect on the children who never questioned their lot in life. Mariska looked up from down below and waved to her mother who smiled and waved back. *That one would surely break hearts when she grew up*, thought Ekaterina.

The apartment block was grey and drab with outside stairs that wrapped around the building. Although it was newer in comparison to the rooms the Luchenya family had lived in back in Yorkshire, it lacked the cosiness and warmth of that place they had called home. Compared to their wooden house in Russia it was infinitely superior. But to Ekaterina it was a sad, tragic place of people who came and went, and barely acknowledged each other. They were all of a mixed background. At night she could hear voices speaking with Irish, Sicilian, Greek, Polish and Italian accents. Whether they had come from Naples, Dublin,

Warsaw or Palermo, they were all equal here. Equal in their level of poverty, perhaps?

Anatole came to a road near Central Park and he stopped at the corner just to watch the city life in all of its forms pass by. He leaned against a lamppost and surveyed the scene. A policeman with a tall helmet, resembling a London peeler more than a precinct cop, strolled by just appearing to fill in time. A classy gent in a bowler and a three-piece suit stopped to check his pocket timepiece, at the same time catching the glance of two dazzling ladies in wide showy hats and carrying parasols. He turned his head to admire them. To his delight they had also turned to look back at him and smiled. He pinched the rim of his bowler and smiled at them. An elderly couple walked hand in hand. Anatole was surprised. He thought it was only young couples who held hands in that first heady flourish of love. He didn't realise that a good strong love can last a lifetime, and that the old are still capable of mutual adoration.

From across the road drifted the voice of a young boy singing a melancholy song. More music to listen to, like a moth drawn to a flame Anatole was at once attracted into the magnetic field of the singer. Avoiding the various hansom cabs and horse-drawn carriages, he crossed the road to investigate. Just before the entrance to Central Park, there was a shoeshine boy anxiously looking around for customers. His prayers were answered when the man in the bowler Anatole had noticed crossed over and indicated for the boy to clean his shoes. A few yards away stood another boy with an open bag at his feet filled with coins. He sang a song called 'I'll take you home Kathleen'.

What an afternoon for entertainment, thought Anatole. He had seen a veteran's parade, a talented black man dancing, and now a boy solo singer around about the same age as Anatole.

The words of the song were sad. They were about a dying woman called Kathleen being taken back to a place where she was once happy. Anatole listened carefully. It seemed strange that a young boy of twelve or so could sing an adult song that could only really be understood in later years, after going through the heartbreak that life often brings. Beneath the cap the boy wore was a thatch of dark curly hair and an expressive face with bright blue eyes. His voice was crystal clear and every word came across clear and concise. Several people gathered as they always did with all the street entertainers who performed on weekends. The usual round of applause followed. Anatole was always curious about the talent other people displayed and in his growing ambitions he was always keen to pick up tips that he might use at some later stage.

"Whose song is that?" Anatole asked him.

"It's my song. What's it to you?" the boy retorted in a sharp Irish accent. He was obviously a belligerent so and so, but Anatole pressed on anyway.

"Where did it come from? That's what I mean," he pursued.

"I don't know. It's an Irish song. That's all I know," the boy came back.

A voice from one side of them intervened sharply: "It was written right here in America, kid." Anatole and the Irish boy looked to where the well-dressed gent was having his shoes polished. He grinned at the surprised look on the boy's faces. "That's right."

"How do you know?" the Irish boy asked, clearly annoyed.

"Because I'm a music publisher, kid. It's my job to know such things. The Irish might have adopted it, but the Americans gave birth to it." He paid the shoeshine boy and came across to the young singer. "What's your name, kid?"

"Jack Clancy," he replied.

"I'm Paul Kapsia. I know the music industry backwards. You've got a good voice, kid. What are you going to do with it?"

"I'm just singing to get a few coins to take home to my mother. My father died a while back. It's been a struggle for my ma." Paul Kapsia looked sympathetic. Jack added as an afterthought. "I'm going to be a boxer when I grow up."

"With a voice like that? Ah, you're wasted! Not only do I publish music but I'm also an agent. I might have booked you a few years down the line for a show. If you ever change your mind, come and see me. I've got an office on 42nd Street." He shook hands with Jack. "I enjoyed the song." Paul Kapsia moved off watched by the shoeshine boy, Jack and Anatole.

"Sorry about your father," said Anatole with genuine sympathy.

"Don't be," Jack responded. "He was a bully and a drunk. He used to beat my ma when he got plastered. He got into a fight and somebody bumped him off in a bar. End of story. Don't want to talk about it anymore."

There was a silence as the boys seemed embarrassed and bewildered as to what to say next. Finally the shoeshine boy decided to introduce himself.

"I'm Jake Mahoney. My friends call me Slugs. I'm a Mick. My

grandparents came from Cork. My great grandfather died in a penal colony in Australia. How about that then?"

This didn't impress Jack or Anatole in the slightest. Instead, Jack asked him, "Why do your pals call you Slugs?"

At this he put up his fists and shadow boxed. "See? I'm a slugger! Any kid in the neighbourhood who tries to take me on, I'm ready for them."

"Bronx or Brooklyn?" asked Jack.

"Bronx of course!" Slugs replied. He was round and pugnacious looking. "I'm a neighbour of our friend here." Anatole looked at him curiously. "I've passed you and your old man in the street now and again. You never gave me a second glance." Unbeknownst to them, a camaraderie was beginning to evolve between the three. "Say, boys. You like singing, right?" The others nodded. "Well there's a barbershop quartet performing at four right here in the park. Why don't you stick around and we'll see it together?"

"Sounds good to me," said Anatole.

"Let's give it a go. Why not?" Jack agreed.

"Got any money?" Slugs asked, rummaging in his pockets with the takings from his job as a shoeshine boy. "Don't worry if you haven't. I'll buy you both a soda. Come on, let's go"

The barbershop quartet performed at four o'clock exactly on a small stage set in Central Park. Quite a crowd had gathered. Slugs, Jack and Anatole sat down amongst the audience. Anatole had never heard singing in harmony before. The singers were masters of blending their voices together in such a way that the notes of the song came together with the unison of an orchestra. Totally unaccompanied by any musicians the barbershop quartet made their voices sound as skilful as finely tuned musical instruments. Not only did they sound good but they looked good too. With their bowler hats, and striped shirts, their presence was ignited by each others laughing smiling faces.

They sang songs about happy days in the summertime, sweet girls who had captured their hearts and the joy of love. It was music that made people feel good. All around people had smiling faces and, in the glowing sunlight of that Saturday afternoon in May 1898, there was this feeling of good times and happiness. The pugnacious Jake 'Slugs' Mahoney appeared mesmerised. Jack Clancy, a streetwise Irish kid with an unhappy past and a belligerent nature, felt calm and happy and enjoyed the show. Anatole, for whom the day had been one long entertainment, was entranced and thrilled. He knew in his heart that he loved music and dancing more than anything. Somehow he wanted to make a life where he could combine these two things.

Just when Anatole and his two new friends thought the afternoon couldn't get any better then this barbershop quartet stopped for a moment and sprang a surprise on the audience. In their act up until now they had been singing the traditional popular songs more familiar to Tin Pan Alley. This time to the amazement of the audience they began to sing a song from an opera that was currently drawing in big audiences in New York. The song was normally performed as a duet. In fact it was called the Pearl Fisher's Duet. The barbershop quartet disregarded this fact and all four sang the song not in the operatic style for which it had been fashioned, but as if it had been written for them. It didn't lose the original impact the song had in the Opera House but out here in the park the magic seemed to reach everywhere. It was spellbinding for everyone concerned. Perhaps, none more so than for Anatole. — *AGED 12*

Today had been a good one for him. Apart from the entertainment, he had made friends who would figure in his life for years to come: Jess Reubens, Paul Kapsia, Jack Clancy and Slugs Mahoney. The three boys left the park together and, before heading off in different directions, they agreed to meet up again.

BLACK DANCER *x* *MUSIC AGENT* *x¹* *SINGER* *x²* *SHOE SHINE* *x3*

"I'll look out for you around the Bronx," said Slugs to Anatole. "Gotta go now, I'm meeting my old man in town. Nice to meet you, Jack." Off he went, swaggering as he walked. Even at the age of twelve, he was full of confidence. A bruiser. A boy who had no fear or ever gave away any sign of concession.

"He's sure of himself, isn't he?" Jack remarked, watching Slugs walk away.

"Confident," agreed Anatole. "Where are you going now?"

"I'm going to take the dough I earned from singing home to the old lady in Brooklyn." A shadow seemed to appear out of nowhere on his face. "She's not been too well lately. I'm worried about her."

"I'm sorry to hear that. You've had a rough race," Anatole said in a low voice. He could see unwept tears in Jack's eyes. "What's your ma's name."

There was a pause before Jack replied. "Kathleen." The same name as in the moving song Jack had sung. No wonder he sung with such emotion.

"Look after yourself, buddy." Anatole surprised himself. It was the first time in his life he had ever used the word buddy. He was becoming more Americanised than he ever realised. For some reason beyond his own understanding he was both sympathetic of Jack's situation and empathic too.

Neither of them could ever have predicted that they had both embarked on a friendship that would interweave in each others lives for a very long time in future years.

Five

Viktor felt run down and tired on that May Saturday in 1898. He had decided to go home earlier much to Ekaterina's delight. Tonight he was determined to enjoy the company of his family who he realised with dismay that he really didn't spend enough time with them. He sat at the table with Mariska and Ekaterina waiting patiently for Anatole to return. Then the door opened and in came a smiling Anatole eager to tell the family of the events of the day.

"Hiya Momma, hi Pa …hi Mariska!" His voice was full of enthusiasm and happiness. "I've seen a parade! People singing. A barbershop quartet! What a day! Wow!"

"Listen to that," said Ekaterina with a touch of irony in her voice. "'Hiya Momma,' he says! He is becoming an all American boy."

"Not bad for a boy born in Russia, who spent time in Yorkshire, and is being raised in New York." Viktor looked at his son almost admiringly. The boy was only twelve yet he was filled with an eagerness and interest in all things. Anatole was at that wonderful stage of life where there was a world out there to explore, he hadn't been tarnished by failure, and he was too young to be cynical.

"Go and wash now. Tidy yourself up. Then we will all have supper together. It is not often I am home early enough to sit down with my family."

"Sure, Pa," Anatole said removing his cap and scratching his head. He went into his bedroom and removed his jacket. The room was bare. From the window he could look across to the other tenements and the area where the children played in between the buildings. It seemed a good place to practice the dancing style he had seen Jess Reubens perform. He looked at himself in the mirror and started to emulate Jess's movements. It all felt so natural. He was so carried away that he didn't see Mariska enter the room.

She looked bewildered at her brother. But in a minute she was following him dancing in co-ordination as if she was being pulled by invisible strings. Anatole smiled at his sister.

"Where did you learn that?" Mariska asked him, pausing for a moment. Anatole stopped and turned to her.

"I saw a black man called Jess Reubens dancing in town. I want to dance like him when I grow up."

"You want to be a dancer when you're older?" Mariska exclaimed. It was the first time Anatole had revealed his ambition to anyone. "Pa wants you to be a tailor like him."

"I know," he sighed. "Maybe I will, for a while. Anyway we better get ready. Ma and Pa are waiting."

The next day Viktor took Anatole to see his place of work. It was a quiet Sunday morning and it seemed a good idea for Viktor to find a place where he could really talk to his boy. This intention wasn't just to introduce Anatole to the trade. There was another troubling concern. For a few months Viktor had been feeling ill. He had really been struggling at times. Breathless and on edge, headaches, exhaustion – these symptoms had coincided with the fearful thought that he may not live long enough to see his children grow up. He would talk to his son in such a way that he would expound kindness and love for him to remember always.

"This is my place of employment," Viktor said with a flourish. He stood amongst his tools of trade, work desks, cutting machines, steam presses and piles of materials. Anatole looked on. He had never been to his father's firm before. "Look at this fabric." Viktor held out some examples of the material he worked with. Anatole felt it. "From these I make beautiful suits for the businessmen, the affluent, for men getting married wanting to look their best on the happiest day of their life. Each one I tailor to suit the individual. People come in all shapes and sizes you know. People have different tastes. Some are fussy." He smiled at the thought of some of the difficult customers he had met. "If you can handle the moods and temperaments of people then you can handle anything." He sat down and waved his hand to indicate Anatole to do the same. There was something about his father that struck home that morning. Viktor looked so much older than his years. His skin was wrinkled and lined, almost leathery in fact. He eyes were red and strained. There was an air of a deep melancholic sadness about him. Anatole felt alarmed at his father's appearance. "Well this is my little kingdom," Victor continued, and then his voice changed with a note of concern apparent. "You know, your old father Viktor is not a well man. I am much tired, my boy. I am short of breath and I don't move too good these days."

"Is there anything I can do, Pa?" Anatole asked. He was concerned, but in his childhood naivety he had guilty feelings almost as if he was responsible for his father's ill health.

"If anything happens to me give your mother all the help you can and look after little Mariska. See that she never comes to any harm. Promise me that."

"Of course, Pa. I promise that. You're not going to die are you?"

"No sooner than I have to my son. That is my promise to you. Yet I have to prepare you for such eventualities. I am fifty years of age. I feel – I feel – so much older. Life in Russia for the Luchenya family was always hard and had it not been for the fact that our families were ordered from their homes, then we would probably have stayed. We had both of you late in life and it is my deep regret that we did not have you earlier so I could have spent more time with you and your sister. You understand, Anatole?"

"You had to work hard. I know that."

"Your mother would have liked for us to have stayed in Yorkshire. Tell me, do you think I did the right thing in bringing the family to New York?"

"This is all I know, Father." Anatole suddenly became more respectful, dropping the word Pa to replace it with the more traditional. "I was too young to remember anywhere else."

"I know," Victor said quietly. "Some fathers say that when they look at their sons, they see a mirror image of what they themselves were like when they were at that age. That may have been true of my father and I, but not you. I sense you are growing up to be a different person with ambitions and hopes of your own. When you came home yesterday you spoke of parades and the music you had heard. Your eyes were shining. You were enthusiastic. You were bursting with a love of life yet to be lived." Anatole thought to himself that his father was wiser and more keenly astute than he had previously appeared to be. "That is good. Never lose interest in life. I would like you to help me after school sometimes. Even if this is not what you want to do in the long term, I would like you to get to know the work that I do and learn the trade."

"I'll do my best," Anatole assured him.

"Now, my boy," Victor said, rising from his chair and feeling the small of his back, "you have seen where I work. But I am sure you don't want to be here on this sunny day. And, I don't want to be either. Today I shall rest and spend it with my boy. How about I buy you a soda and some lunch somewhere and we take a walk around town afterwards?"

"That would be great, Father," Anatole replied. "Could I ask if we could do something else as well?"

"Certainly, my boy. What is it?"

"Yesterday I spoke to this dancer in the city. He said that there is a church in Harlem where they sing Negro spirituals. I wonder if we could call by there this evening. Just stop outside and listen for a while."

Viktor looked perplexed. "Harlem? Negro spirituals?"

"I know we don't worship in the same way they do but the man said they sing like an angel choir."

"Spirituals. An angel choir?" Viktor shrugged his shoulders. He didn't quite know what to make of this request. Finally, he said, "An angel choir, you say? This I must hear also."

***

This was a day Anatole would long remember. Other than the normal father and son talk at home, they had never really had a long in depth conversation. Viktor opened up about his life in a way that he had never done so before. He spoke of how he and Ekaterina had met when they were young and of their upbringing in Tsarist Russia. They sat on park benches and talked of all manner of things. They looked around art galleries and museums. Through it all Anatole listened carefully to his father's reminiscences in such a way as to memorise every detail in case they never talked in this manner again.

Anatole was unsettled though. Seldom had his father talked so deeply and displayed such an innate kindliness to him. It was as if Viktor had a premonition that his days were numbered. Yet, if this was so, Viktor had a glow about his face, his normally sad eyes filled with good humour and warmth, and for a man who seemed to permanently wear a mask of sadness, as if it were a prerequisite of his very being, he smiled and laughed a lot that day. There was a hidden side to his character that seldom revealed itself and for just a brief time Anatole had been given a glimpse into the hidden facets of his father. It was a side he liked.

Viktor kept his promise and stopped off in Harlem with Anatole. They found the church that Jess Reubens had told Anatole about. In fact, they could hear the singing as they were walking down the street. So powerful was the singing that it seemed to flood the night air with the effect of coming down from the heavens in the manner of Jess Reuben's observation – like an angel choir.

"I think we have found your heavenly voices," said Viktor. Immediately outside the church there was a bench where he took the weight off his shoes and sat down. The door of the church was open and Anatole peered through.

From within came the amalgamation of voices of all levels beautifully blended together to create the kind of singing that left the listener spellbound. Anatole looked at the totally negro congregation who sang and worshipped in a far more expressive and demonstrative fashion than he had ever imagined. For someone who had been brought up in an orthodox Jewish family he was remarkably open-minded about the manner of worship carried out by other faiths. Here in this church in Harlem the voices of the black people produced a sound that was filled with joy, sweetness and an aching poignancy, yet, at the same time, a sense of freedom at being able to express themselves so happily in song. Only thirty-three years before the American Civil War had ended and slavery had been abolished. Perhaps that was why they sang with such joy. They were still thankful to be free.

The congregation sang 'The Battle Hymn of the Republic'. Anatole listened with a thrill in his heart. He cast a sideways glance to his father, who sat quietly on the park bench. Viktor smiled back. He too enjoyed the heavenly voices. The next song that they sang was a spiritual called 'We are climbing Jacob's ladder'. Never in his short lifespan had Anatole heard such singing. It was the essence of a spiritual song that it could move the listener to the point of balance between tears and joy. The faces in the congregation were young and old. The voices were of every level. But it was the coming together of the singers that truly moved the spirit.

A familiar face turned around from within the church. Almost straight away he recognised Anatole at the door. Jess Reubens smiled. Anatole turned around and returned to his father.

"Not even in heaven will I ever hear such singing," said Viktor. He was about to get up to go when Jess Reubens emerged from the church. Jess came towards them, offering his hand to shake Anatole's and then Viktor's.

"Father, this is Mr Reubens, the dancer I told you about," he proudly announced.

"Very pleased to meet you, sir," said Jess. "May I join you?"

"Of course," replied Viktor and Jess sat down with them. He was courteous and well mannered. "I am not of your faith Mr Reubens as you obviously gather, but I never fail to be impressed by the worship of God and the way they sing in the church. Such deep reverence. Your people sing with such emotion and joy. Yet, were you not slaves and the children of slaves not so very long ago, until Mr Lincoln issued the proclamation of emancipation? Does that not sadden the hearts of your brothers and sisters? Is not your heart still heavy with the grief of such that was once suffered?"

Jess's eyes seemed to cloud over. He at once recognised in Viktor similar traits to his own, although their backgrounds were vastly different.

"I ask you then, sir, is it not a Christian act to forgive? And forgive I must. I don't forget the pain that I and my brothers and sisters endured. I cannot live with malice. But when you ask me is my heart still heavy with grief, I reply that it is. Yet I sing with my friends in the church to thank the Lord for the life that I have and the freedom I enjoy. No man could ask for more."

"Forgiveness is a remarkable thing, Mr Reubens. I am of a race too that has been persecuted down the ages. When one gets to my age there is much to forgive. One learns that in life you don't make peace with your friends, you make peace with your enemies. That is a great thing. The spirit of reconciliation is much alive in America. I wish it were so in other parts of the world."

Anatole listened with interest. He had not been previously aware of the hidden depths of feeling his father held. It was a surprise to him to see how Viktor and Jess could speak on such a subject. Here in Harlem on this beautiful clear night Anatole learned how people of such a different background could have an amazing rapport. There was Viktor, a Russian Jew who had known poverty and persecution on the one hand. Immediately next to him was Jess Reubens, a former black slave, who had known deprivations and beatings. Yet the contrast between them did not conceal their mutual kinship. It was a lesson to Anatole that every man has a story of their own and that in this world everyone is equal in some way or the other.

"You wouldn't believe what the old South was like once," Jess said in a reflective tone. "Huge cotton and tobacco plantations. And grand old houses. Fields full of workers, and slaves." He paused. "Yes, slaves like me. My momma and papa were slaves. They were both sold to different owners. When I was twelve, I was sold too. I was taken to an auction to be sold like a piece of cattle. I was told to stand naked while owners checked me out. Then I was hit with a stick and told to jump up and down to see how fit I was. My face was slapped to see if my teeth were okay. To the people buying slaves, we were treated as if we weren't human. One man finally said, 'I've seen better but he'll do for now until we get a better one'. That's how it was in them days."

"Your owners… did they treat you well?" Viktor asked, curious about the man's story.

"No sir," came the reply. "Almost as soon as I started there, the overseer… he used to beat me. To make matters worse the overseer's son used to come and beat me sometimes. He was not much older than me and he used to laugh when he did it. I didn't know too much about the war other than the young men started to wear grey uniforms and disappear to fight. Many of them didn't return. They died on bloodstained battlefields in towns and villages I had never heard of. When Mr Lincoln issued the emancipation proclamation, a group of us slaves walked out from the plantation as soon as we heard the news. A few former slaves, who I knew, joined the Northern Army. One came back with his fellow soldiers of the blue and killed the overseer. When it was all over and our country was at peace again, I was determined that I would celebrate being free every day of my life and thank God that I could walk this earth in any direction of my own choosing."

Anatole who had been quietly listening to the conversationally finally asked, "Did you ever see your parents again?"

"One day, many years later, when I was a young man in my twenties. I was working on a Mississippi riverboat as a deckhand when we put into a port north of New Orleans. We stopped there to pick up a cargo of flour from the mills, as I recall, and it was a dry old town, not too much there – wheelwrights, blacksmiths, general store, factory and saloon. That was about it. It was a real hot, muggy afternoon and I saw a group of freed

31

slaves sitting under the shade of a big tall tree with branches outspreading everywhere. I went over to say good afternoon and there was one particular black lady who looked real familiar. She had a sweet face and beautiful smile. And I said to her, 'Are you my momma?' She looked up at me and she says, 'Are you my boy, Jess, all grown up?' and I says, 'Are you my Momma Winifred?' Oh, it sure was a happy day for us both."

"What about your father?" Anatole pursued.

"He died on the plantation. Some sort of fever." Behind them, the congregation started to leave. Jess waved to some of them amiably. "My momma was one of the first freed slaves. Well, I stayed on in that town, took a job in the flour mill, and I took care of my momma. Six months later I came home from the mill and she was sitting in her favourite spot under the tree. Momma was smiling. She was at peace. Her son had come home. But Momma had died. She was just forty-four."

"Such a sad story," Viktor said sympathetically.

"No sir," retorted Jess. "That's a happy story. I found my momma again. She knew she was loved by her son. Momma died free… a happy woman. Momma died peacefully on a day filled with sunshine in her favourite place, beneath the big old flowering tree. Many slaves never saw

their kinfolk again. I was one of the lucky ones."

"Well, Mr Reubens, we must go now," said Viktor, rising from the bench. "It has been a great pleasure to meet you. In fact, sir, it has been a great privilege too."

"And you, sir," Jess said shaking his hand. "God bless you both."

Anatole smiled at him. The two of them moved off after what had been a very happy day. It was just as well that Viktor had decided to have a special day with his son. His premonition had been proved correct. Less than a week later Viktor was found dead from a heart attack in his workplace. He was just fifty years old.

A week later Ekaterina also died. Mired in grief, she fell asleep at the kitchen table and never woke up. Her heart had also given out. If a doctor had written as cause of death 'died of a broken heart' no one would have disputed it. Viktor and Ekaterina had been devoted to each other. Their subsequent deaths meant that Anatole and Mariska became orphans. They were swiftly taken to Oakwood Children's Home where they would spend the rest of their adolescent years.

Six

Mariska looked through the wrought iron gates of the Oakwood Children's Home. Her eyes were filled with tears. At eight years of age she had lost both parents and it was too much for her young mind to take in. How she yearned for the home life that had existed only weeks before, and the warmth and love of her gentle but ailing parents. It was as if in the suddenness of an instant, Mariska had been wrenched from the security of a family to the loneliness and fear of the future felt by so many orphans.

Anatole felt the same way. In the dormitory he sat by the bed with his head bent low. When he raised his head tears rolled down his cheeks. There was a feeling of such loss within him. He thought of the special day he had spent with his father and how they had talked in a way that they had never done so before. His heart ached for his mother. Ekaterina had been such a gentle presence in his life, always there with kind words and a soft nature yet concealing a hidden strength that gave constant support to Viktor.

Now they were both gone and even though the children's home was warm and clean, Anatole's heart was still in that poverty stricken tenement in the Bronx that had been the Luchenya family home. He decided that he could not sit in the dormitory any more and that he had to find his sister. Anatole rose and walked through the rooms and corridors. All through the building orphan children played and talked together. *Life could be cruel*, thought Anatole. All these children had parents once. Now they were all alone.

He found Mariska where he expected. The very sight of her at the gates crying alone tortured him. Anatole walked up to her. His face was wet with tears. Mariska turned to look at him. Her pretty young face was a picture of sadness and despair.

"Mama… Papa…" she murmured softly.

"I miss them so much too, sis." They both held each other and cried. "Don't worry, I'll look after you." It was no good though. The grief they both shared overwhelmed them. It tore through their hearts. The loss of one parent was enormous. To lose both parents was devastating.

***

Beyond the gates in the real world, the newspaper billboards were full of stories about the Spanish-American War in Cuba. Ably promoted by the newspapers of William Randolph Hearst, the United States government had decided to intervene on the side of the Cuban rebels in their struggle against Spanish rule. Now the emphasis was on the victories at San Juan Ridge, gained by Theodore Roosevelt and the Rough Riders.

None of this was important to the children at the orphanage. Least of all to Mariska and Anatole, for them their world had stopped. It was as if the teeming crowds of New York City had become depopulated by the passing of Viktor and Ekaterina. Above all at their young ages, they learned the harsh and brutal fact that yesterday has gone. Nothing is going to bring it back. Nor will the people who were alive then but are dead today ever come back. Never in their lives until their own passing would Anatole and Mariska ever have closure on the death of their parents.

Anatole knew he would have to be strong for Mariska but deep inside he felt a hurt beyond physical pain. At night he would lay awake in the boy's only dormitory just staring up at the ceiling. How could two good people like his parents be taken away so quickly? Anatole may have thought that he had become a tough knockabout New York boy. In reality he was a sensitive kid with a veneer that concealed much. He so much wanted to talk to his mother and father. It was as if he desperately wanted to reach out and grab the time back when they had all been together. They were here, alive, real and a strong warm presence. Then they were gone. Totally absent and a mere memory. Only voices and images in the mind.

The orphanage was full of children from a variety of backgrounds. Each of them had different stories to tell of how they had ended up there. In time Anatole got to know many of his fellow orphans. Many had come from broken homes where one parent had died and there were no other relatives for them to go to. Several had seen a violent father murder a mother. Thes who had performed these crimes were executed leaving the children of these unions without parents, and traumatised for life. They were usually withdrawn isolated children who stood alone in corridors and the corner of rooms unable to mix with the others. In their eyes were varying degrees of fear, hurt and anxiety. Some would never recover from their ordeals and it would affect the way they lived for the rest of their lives.

Terminal illnesses, poverty, alcoholism and industrial accidents had claimed the lives of various parents. Many of the children were of migrant families who had no next of kin in America, and for them they were on their own completely. Anatole and Mariska were not the only children who found themselves in this predicament. Others had come from Italy, Sicily, Germany, Ireland and various European nations.

Depending on the character of the individual orphans, the children's home could indirectly influence the course of their lives. Some who had only ever experienced poverty and the restrictions imposed on them by the Oakwood home became determined to rise from the low level they had been reduced to. They would go on to work incredibly hard expecting little but achieving all that was possible in America; good careers, happy marriages and their dreams of being independent, often becoming entrepreneurs and business people. Others were not so lucky or lost the willpower to take this route. There were some orphans who, when they reached adulthood, took the road into crime and in later years found themselves in another home, the state penitentiary, where they would serve long sentences. A couple of them were convicted of murder and their lives ended in the electric chair.

One boy was so profoundly moved by the plight of orphans that he resolved to do something about it when he grew up. After years of hard study for Law he entered politics, becoming a respected congressman and a leading spokesman on poverty in America. At one stage he was considered by his party as a possible candidate for the Presidency but was beaten by a few votes. He later went on to become an Ambassador in Europe and a representative for the League of Nations.

The one thing that united all the orphans was the determination to break free of the circumstances that shackled them. Anatole dreamed of the day he could become a dancer in Vaudeville. One day he would turn up at Paul Kapsia's office on 42nd Street with Mariska in tow and audition for a part in a musical show. For now though he and his sister were still in mourning over the death of their parents. It would be many months before they could even move on just slightly.

It was about a year later that fate, along with coincidence, intervened in their lives. In the interim period before that they had continued with their schooling. Neither had much enthusiasm for education. Their parents had been the driving force behind them, especially Ekaterina, who had taken so much trouble to teach them English. More than likely, Anatole would leave school at fourteen and learn some sort of trade. With his background, someone at the orphanage would almost certainly try and find a company of Tailors who would employ him. For Mariska she had several more years of school to go before she made any big decisions or they were made for her.

One day Anatole and Mariska were walking in the grounds of the Oakwood Children's Home when they noticed a boy staring out through the big iron gates. There was nothing unfamiliar about this. It was always possible to tell when a child was a recent arrival. They could usually be found in tears looking at the outside world wondering how their lives could turn so dramatically that they had ended up in this home. There was something however very familiar about the boy. Anatole and Mariska approached him. The boy turned around revealing a tear-stained face. Anatole recognised him immediately.

"Jack?" he gasped in amazement. "Jack Clancy?"

"That's me," Jack said ,struggling to speak through his tears. "I lost my ma."

"I'm so sorry, pal," Anatole said, trying to console him. "This is my sister, Mariska."

"Hi Jack," she said shyly.

"Did you lose your ma and pa?" Jack asked, wiping his face.

"Papa died at work," replied Mariska. "Then Momma died a week later at home."

"Ma was all I had. She was too young to die." Jack's face was full of pain. "Why? I don't understand. Why?"

"You think we do?" Anatole responded. His voice too was tinged with despair and frustration at the predicament. "You think we understand why we lost our mama and papa in the same week? They were both here and then they were gone."

Jack broke down in tears. Mariska and Anatole put their arms around him. The little girl looked up at the sight of this tough little Irish boy showing all his vulnerability and pathos.

"We'll look after you," she said. It was almost heartbreaking for the other two boys to hear this for they knew only too well that Mariska was missing her mother badly. "We'll be your family too."

Jack looked at her through his tears. What a caring little girl she was. Anatole forced a smile and nodded his head in agreement to give his friend some reassurance.

***

That night all three lay in their dormitory beds thinking of their family members. The magnitude of their loss was enormous and very, very painful. It had been a year since Ekaterina and Viktor had died. Mariska wanted to wake up and find it had all been a dream and that her parents were still alive. But each morning that passed proved to her that life was going on without the presence of her parents. Mariska lay back and in the night darkness she remembered a day with her mother when they had spoken in the kitchen one morning. For a moment it was as if Ekaterina was looking at her through kindly eyes.

***

They were seated at the kitchen table of the apartment in the Bronx. Ekaterina poured her daughter a cup of steaming hot coffee. She looked at Mariska with pride and smiled.

"Make your old mama and papa very proud," Ekaterina said in her warm accented honeycombed voice. "When you grow up be a fine lady, be kind and gracious."

"Like you, Mama?" Mariska asked, not realising she was paying her mother a fine compliment.

"Better than me!" Ekaterina exclaimed. "You know in the time we have lived in New York I can see great opportunities for a young lady. There is a rich life to be had here that I could never have imagined when I was a young Russian girl."

"What was it like when you were young in Russia, Mama?" Mariska asked. She was then eight years of age and showing signs of a childlike curiosity in most things.

"Not like this. Not like it is here in America. But then our people never knew anything else. When I was a young girl in Russia, we led a very simple life. Your grandfather was a seaman, often away on voyages to Scotland, Ireland and England. He always brought back books and presents for your grandmother and I."

"What was he like?"

Ekaterina smiled at the memory of him. "He was big, with a huge laugh that came right from his belly. We didn't see a lot of him but he always looked after us. He died at sea when he was thirty-seven, younger than I am now. And your grandma... there was a fine woman. How I miss her. Your father took care of me soon after she died and I know he doesn't say it, but we have raised a nice family in you and Anatole." She paused to smile at Mariska. It was a smile that warmed her little girl's heart. "I love you both so much. You are my treasures."

Ekaterina reached out and hugged Mariska, who responded with equal warmth. A good mother's love is truly a head start in the race of life for any child. To know that feeling of warmth and the emotions of maternal love were a gift of life beyond measure. Ekaterina's eyes brimmed with tears, as if she knew something no one else did. Perhaps she felt that maybe her life would not be a long one and that every moment spent with her precious children was a golden time that would not come again. Better now to tell a child that they are loved than never at all.

***

Mariska wiped a tear away and rolled over in her dormitory bed. She missed her mama so much. But as she lay there in the darkness, yearning for the love of her mother she would never know again, Mariska made a promise to herself – not just to herself but also to the souls of her late parents. One day she would grow up to be that fine and gracious lady. Mariska would make her mama and papa proud wherever they might be.

***

Anatole looked up into the darkness from his bed. Perhaps it was his senses playing havoc with his consciousness, but coming towards him were Ekaterina and Viktor. They were arm in arm, younger than when he had last seen them. Ekaterina stroked Anatole's forehead and Viktor appeared to bow his head slightly in acknowledgement.

"We are sorry to have left you so early, my son," Ekaterina was saying. "We will meet again one day."

"But until then," Viktor added softly, "you are the man of the house now. You are the master of your own destiny."

"Look after Mariska," Ekaterina said in a gentle, compassionate voice. "She is only little. I am not there to see her grow and develop into a young lady. I cannot influence her. I cannot teach her. I can only shine my mother's love on her from afar. It is up to you my son." Ekaterina paused and then added, "My very good son. I love you both."

"Your mother would talk all night," Viktor said with a hint of humour in his voice "I shall… *we* shall never be far from you. We must go now to a place of shining light, pure crystal waters, rolling green, peace and such love, indescribable love. Farewell, my boy."

They both waved. Anatole blinked and then rubbed his eyes. Had he been dreaming? Had his parents really been there? He just could not distinguish fact from fantasy, a dream from reality, but whether it had happened or not Anatole lay there, thinking of the impression the vision had made. He lay back, closed his eyes and fell asleep. Even though he was deep in slumber, a tear rolled down his cheek.

***

Jack Clancy had been through a lot by the age of fourteen. His brawling, drunken father, who regularly beat his mother, had been murdered in a bar after misjudging an opponent. Afterwards Jack had got money any way he could to help his ailing mother. Jack had done a newspaper round, delivered milk, helped out in a butcher's shop, sang on street corners and learned all the skills of boxing at an early age, of which he was convinced he was destined to become a champion. Jack fancied himself as the Irish kid from Brooklyn who would rise to be a respectable man from the proceeds of the fight game. Now he realised he was only really interested in boxing to make money for his late mother, Kathleen. He remembered a conversation he once had with her at home.

"Ireland. I often think about it," she said wistfully. "The green countryside, and the farms. I don't suppose you remember much, do you?"

"Hardly anything at all," the ten-year-old Jack replied.

"Sometimes, I think I would like to go back now that your father…" This would always be a different area to speak of and Kathleen moved swiftly on. Her son understood anyway. "How would you like to go back if we could find a way of raising the fare?"

"I don't know," Jack said honestly. "I know I'm Irish but I feel American. Whatever you want to do."

Kathleen was only in her thirties but already there was an air of a tragic faded beauty about her. When she had been young in a coastal village in County Wexford, all the young men had eyes for her. However, when she met the local publican's son, Sean Clancy, her heart had melted. He was dangerously handsome with a strong emphasis on the word dangerous. While he was normally a hardworking carpenter with a jovial nature, once he started to drink he didn't stop until he was incapable of holding a glass straight. During these binges he became violent and didn't care who he loosened his fists upon. It was the tragedy of Kathleen's life that she had become intoxicated with this man who brought her nothing but pain and misery.

Coming to America was supposedly a new start for them and their marriage. It didn't last. Sean Clancy was a man of a restless spirit and roving eye. For Kathleen and Jack his presence was one of unsettling times. His end had come suddenly and dramatically leaving Kathleen in impoverished circumstances and poor health to bring up her son. She had worked as a washerwoman and waitress but it was a struggle. Many times Jack caught sight of his mother gazing out of the window with a wistful look in her eyes. Jack knew that she was dreaming of going back to Ireland and walking the beaches and country lanes of her youth.

"There were lovely empty beaches I used to walk on when I was a little girl," she said with a faint smile broaching her lips. "I used to love listening to the roll of the waves and the sea crashing down on the beach. The fishermen were always out early. I was happy then, happy there in my home village with my mother and father, sisters and brothers. The fields were deep green. It's not called the Emerald Isle for nothing, you know. Oh… and I just loved the country lanes, seeing the people at their doorways and smiling as I walked past."

"Why did we leave?" asked Jack, who was listening intently to his mother.

father

"It was your who wanted to go. Not me. You're named after your Uncle Jack. He was in the British Army in India. Died at a battle there. Your father always felt he had to live up to him. America seemed a good idea. But I want to go home. I want my family. Our family. To drink a glass of fresh Irish buttermilk and hear the waves break on the beaches I knew as a child and to see the lobster potters again."

***

Kathleen never saw her homeland again. One day at work, she was carrying a bundle of clothes when she began to cough up blood. Within minutes she had haemorrhaged and the stomach cancer she had been suffering from claimed her life at the young age of thirty-four. Jack had lived through much tragedy in his life and these experiences made him cynical beyond his years. He would fight life's battles on his own terms from now on.

***

Life continued for Anatole, Mariska and Jack as they came to terms with the heartbreak they had all suffered. Each gradually began to look to the future. In time the three of them formed a camaraderie and looked out for each other.

Sometimes Anatole would see Mariska dancing with other girls in the playroom. Life would never be normal for her again without her parents but it was slowly taking on a different direction. Jack could be seen sparring with other boys yet he also showed that in his character there was both a mixture of toughness and sentimentality. He and Anatole would occasionally sing old Irish songs together. Whenever they could, the pair of them would sneak away from the children's home and make some money by singing on street corners.

This was to be the pattern of their lives over the next few years until one day the three of them decided to pay a visit to Paul Kapsia's office on 42nd Street.

Seven

1904

Paul Kapsia sat at his desk looking through sheets of music and newly written songs that had been offered to his company. Some of the material was the usual Tin Pan Alley stuff he had seen so often. There were a few songs though he felt sure he could use in a new show he was staging. With the right arrangement and a vocalist who knew how to interpret lyrics, he was certain he had a winner here. To Paul Kapsia, a good song was like a woman. Treat it right and it could create waves of passion.

He walked across the office and sat at a piano, gently tinkling the keys. On the top of the piano were two photographs mounted in frames of his two daughters, Anna and Karen. They were two beauties who performed as dancers in his various touring shows. For a moment Paul Kapsia forgot about the current crop of songs he had and he began to sing an old ballad called Lenora. It was a tune that must have been played in a thousand saloons across the Wild West and on a thousand stages in every American city. The song didn't date despite the passing of the ages. Paul was desperately trying to find some new songs to put into a musical he was planning.

A sudden knock on the door caused him to stop playing and he turned around. The door swung open and the smiling face of one of his best dancers greeted him. The man looked smart and well suited. Paul grinned back at his friend Jess Reubens.

"Hey Jess! When did you get back, old pal?" Paul exclaimed in delight. Jess was one of those people who just by his mere presence made others feel happy. The two men shook hands.

"Just this afternoon, Paul. Say, you wouldn't believe it: the show's been a sell out in every city we played. From Chicago to 'Frisco, we've packed them in." Jess was very enthusiastic. He had been signed up by Paul Kapsia's agency to appear in a minstrel show and for Jess it had provided him with opportunities this former slave boy had never dreamed of.

"That's just terrific, Jess," Paul said with a smile beaming out. "The money keeps rolling in. That's what I like to hear. How about you give me a quick display of your dancing. Let's see how good you are."

"Sure boss," replied Jess, and he launched into a quick routine spinning around and dancing from wall to wall.

"Yep. That's good. Keep it going like that on the stage and get the customers in. Well, Jess, I figure you've earned your supper. How about I stake you for a bite to eat around the corner at Mandolino's restaurant and we'll discuss this show I'm putting on?"

"Another show?" gasped Jess. "The day I signed with you my luck changed forever."

The two men left the office and walked out into the cold night air. New York in 1904 was a buoyant busy cosmopolitan city full of life. The wind blew icy cold. Both men who had the appearance of successful businessmen, more than men in the entertainment industry, wrapped themselves up. Round the corner in Mandolino's there would be warm Italian food, full of flavour and herbs, served by singing waiters, with background musicians who would play romantic tunes about Sorrento and Naples. But before they got there they could hear two strong voices in harmony drifting up from the street corner.

A smile broached Paul's lips. "Listen to that?" he said.

The two men stopped and listened. "Kinda sweet, ain't they?" Jess remarked. They walked a bit further along. At the corner there stood two eighteen-year-old boys with caps and working clothes that implied impoverished backgrounds. Anatole and Jack had grown considerably in years since Paul Kapsia and Jess Reubens had last set eyes on them.

"I recognise those kids," Paul said in a whisper to his friend.

So too did Jess. They stood and watched as the two rough and ready boys from the Oakwood Children's Home sang the 'Rose of Tralee' in a beautiful harmonious style. At their feet was a bag where passers-by threw coins in. They were amassing themselves quite a pile. Some people stood by and watched while others, on their way home from work, cast a backward glance at the two eighteen-year-olds who had such a strong presence.

"I like those kids. They've got something. I don't know what it is but it could sell millions. Let's go and talk." Paul was not for missing the main chance.

"I know what they've got," suggested Jess. "They can sing. They look like ordinary working guys."

When the boys had finished their song Jess and Paul approached them. They recognised each other immediately especially Anatole who remembered the time he had introduced Jess to his father outside the church in Harlem. It had been six years since they had last met but the impression of that time lingered on. They all shook hands warmly.

"You've grown young man," sad Jess to Anatole. "How's your father?"

"Dead," a stony-faced Anatole replied. "Jack here lost his ma and ended up in the same Children's Home as me."

"Sorry to hear that," replied Jess. "Your pa was a grand old man. I liked him when we met that time."

"And you," Paul said to Jack, "you're the Irish kid who didn't want to use that great voice of yours and wanted to be a boxer instead. Have you still got that ambition?"

"To be sure," Jack replied with a smile. "I'm training down at Sammy Rosen's outfit. He's got a lot of young boxers there. Sammy's trying to set up a bout for me."

"How about that?" Paul said. "Sammy Rosen's an old pal of mine. We went to St John's School together. If there's a few bucks to be made I might promote a fight for him. I'll have to get together with Sammy." Then he turned to Anatole. "I remember you. The last time I saw you, you were watching. Now you're singing. You've got a good voice."

"I want to learn to dance like Jess and be in shows. I've got a little sister who can dance too. Can you help us?"

Paul looked across to Jess as if he was seeking inspiration or was it encouragement? "OK, young fellow, I'll give you a try. Bring your kid sister with you to the office sometime and I'll see what we can do. I'm in the Enterprise building on 42nd Street."

"Where are you boys living now? What are you doing?" Jess pursued.

"We're working down on the docks unloading cargo," Jack answered.

"My sister's only fourteen. She's still at the orphanage. But Jack and I… we're living at a boarding house round the corner."

Paul raised the bowler he always wore and smoothed back his hair.

He always looked smart and dapper. Sometimes in manner of speech and attitude he appeared casual. This in fact masked a cunning shrewdness and an eye for the main chance. He knew that both of these boys had something that separated themselves from the crowd.

"Well boys, Jess and I have got to go. There's a meal waiting for us at Mandolino's." Paul flicked some coins into the bag. "Go get yourselves something warm to eat. I'll catch up with you."

Jess gave a friendly salute and then walked on, while Paul, Anatole and Jack looked down at their hoard and smiled. This amount would top us their wages just nicely from their labour at the docks.

***

A few weeks later Anatole and Mariska turned up at Paul Kapsia's office. Paul was impressed by the dexterity the two Luchenya's displayed in the dancing skills they showed him. They were self-taught. However, he knew they had a long way to go before they would be ready for any gruelling stage shows. Paul knew that for them to perform well they would have to undergo a regime of fitness, flexibility and intensive dance instruction.

In this he was not to be disappointed. Anatole and Mariska were model pupils. They picked things up quickly and embraced everything with enthusiasm. Paul had them trained at a dance studio where he sent his potential chorus line and solo stars too. He was particularly enamoured with Mariska. If ever there was a real star in the making, it was her. Although only fourteen, all the potential was there. Paul also knew if Anatole and Mariska were to go on tour because of their young ages, he would have to be not only their manager but their guardian too. This wasn't a problem with Paul. He enjoyed going on tour with his shows along the length and breadth of the United States. There was one problem, however, that daunted Paul. He wondered how the names of Anatole and Mariska would go on a bill. The more he thought about it, the more he thought that his young protégés should be given a new stage name, especially if they were to become a double act.

Paul watched from the sidelines as his dancers trained and rehearsed. Anatole was learning the mastery of tap dance; his mentor was Jess Reubens, who showed him every trick in synchronising movements and creating a rhythm in dance. Mariska was learning how to twirl, how to be part of a chorus line and, more importantly, how to dance solo on a stage dominating it entirely through her own presence. Not quite fifteen, she was in that stage of transformation from being a pretty girl to blossoming into a beautiful woman radiating an aura of good health and wellbeing. The constant dancing exercised on a daily basis gave her an eye-catching figure and every day she improved her posture.

What fascinating luck to work in such an industry, thought Paul. He had brought shows on to the stages of various theatres in New York which had then gone on national tours of the United States. During the course of his career he had published tunes by budding song writers that people everywhere would soon whistle on their way to work. He had nurtured talent and promoted then in such a way that they would soon become headliners. Paul himself was the son of a migrant who had found his way from Bratislava to the New World where he had made a living as a wet fish salesman before opening up his own market store. From that background Paul Kapsia had risen to his present wealthy status in life and he was enjoying every minute of his success.

One day Paul had a masterstroke of an idea. He remembered the day he had played the tune 'Lenora' in the office. This was an old time ballad that was wide open to interpretation and adaption. He decided to incorporate it into a show he was currently staging at the State Theatre. It was always best with a spartan accompaniment of a lone piano. But why not use two pianos? One at one side of the stage and another on the opposite side. Then he would have the song displayed as a mini-show with a male dancer attempting to woo a female dancer. This was ideally suited to Anatole and Mariska. Anatole would dance towards Mariska who would be dressed like a well-to-do lady with a bonnet, bustle and parasol. Anatole would be clad in a bowler, waistcoat and good trousers. He would dance around her, mock proposing while she would turn away shyly and coyly, dancing in an almost ballet-like fashion. The pianists would blend their notes together and play in a dramatic manner that would mesmerise the audience.

While watching them train one day, Paul decide to put the idea to them and at the same time he would suggest a new stage name for them that would make their act more easily identifiable to audiences as they grew in stature and fame.

"Hiya kids," Paul said amiably as he approached them from one side of the studio. "I'm really impressed by how you're coming on. How would you feel about doing a show at the State Theatre?"

"Wow! You mean a real live show?" asked Mariska, clearly amazed.

"Sure I mean it," growled Paul. "I've got a great idea for you both to make your stage debut. It would mean a lot of rehearsal. What about you, Anatole? Are you in? Or is it too soon for you?"

"I'm ready!" replied Anatole. "I've been ready since I was twelve. I'm nineteen soon. I can't wait to quit the docks and get into vaudeville."

"Steady, kid!" Paul warned him. "One step at a time. You've got to learn to walk before you run. This business is riddled with broken dreams. Take it as it comes. Go gently with the flow and it will all come good. OK, so you're both in – that's great. But now I've got to list your names on the bill. For a potential vaudeville and stage show act, Anatole and Mariska Luchenya doesn't exactly roll off the tongue. Do you know what I mean, kids? If you're going to make a career in this business you need to have a name folks are going to easily remember."

"What's wrong with Anatole and Mariska?" the bemused Anatole asked.

"There's nothing wrong with the name… if you both were a pair of Russian ballet dancers. Let's face it Enrico Caruso is a great name for an opera singer. It wouldn't sound quite right if he was singing Stephen Foster songs in blackface in vaudeville. You keep your real names on all the official documents, of course, but on stage you appear under a name strictly for show business purposes only."

"If you say so," said Anatole halfheartedly.

"That's the ticket, son," Paul said with a smile. "Well now, young lady, if you weren't called Mariska, what would you have liked to have been named?"

"The other girls at the children's home say Mariska is too hard to remember so they just call me Mary. I don't mind that."

"Mary it is then for the stage. What about you, Anatole?"

"I like Nat."

"Nat? Let me think." Paul rubbed his chin. "Nat for short. Nat sounds OK. Sounds good for show business. How about we go with the name Nat?"

"So I'm Nat Luchenya on stage?" asked Anatole.

"Not exactly," Paul said, indicating a change of surname too. "Luchenya is hard to remember and pronounce for some. I need to change that." Then

Paul's eyes twinkled. "Lucky... yes. Lucky. How about that then? Nat and Mary Lucky?"

Anatole looked at Mariska and smiled. "Hi Mary," he said with a cheeky grin.

"Hi Nat," she responded with a grin of equal proportions.

"Of course, you'll still get your pay cheques made out to Anatole and Mariska Luchenya. I've got ideas for you both. First of all... Nat, I want you to perform a tap dance routine with Jess Reubens. Then, Mary, I want you to dance and sing solo. After that... Nat, get used to being called Nat. I want you also to do a dance and a solo. Finally I want you two to do a particular number I've got in mind for you."

"All that?" Mariska exclaimed.

"My word, young lady," Paul said and he added with relish, "I am going to rehearse you and rehearse you until you can dance the routine upside down in your sleep."

***

Sammy Rosen was studying the form of his young boxers at a gym in the centre of the city. He watched Jack Clancy with a professional eye. At nineteen Jack had developed into a fit and muscular young boxer. All the potential was there but Sammy felt he needed to stretch his energies out and become a fighter who could last the distance rather then be a scrapper aiming for a quick knockout. Jack was due to take part in his first major bout very soon.

Paul Kapsia and Sammy Rosen had been friends since they had been at St John's School together. Both were virtually self-made men. They were both the sons of European migrants who had followed their own ambitions, diversifying their business interests over a period of time. Sammy was a stout six-footer with jet-black hair. By day he ran his own carpet and furniture store. At night he devoted himself to boxing. He had once been an aspiring fighter himself but now he had dreams of producing a champion. For some reason known only to him there was something about Jack Clancy that made him think he had found what he was looking for in a boxer. He couldn't identify the special ingredient Jack had that separated him from his other contenders. Sammy just knew Jack had that special something.

"How's he doing, old pal?" a friendly voice said to him from behind. Sammy turned around to see who it was. Paul Kapsia stood there.

"Paul! How's it going?" Sammy responded.

"I'm fine, Sammy." Paul looked up at the ring where Jack Clancy was sparring with an opponent. "The boy's fast. Light on his feet. He would have made a great dancer. He can sing, you know. Did you know that?"

"Sure I know. He's a street corner crooner. The only time I want to hear him sing is when he wins. Then he can sing the 'Battle Hymn of the Republic' for all I care. He's a good prospect."

Almost as if Jack had eavesdropped into the conversation, he suddenly sprang into life. He moved forward with a sense of menace. His eyes blazed. His energy level was up high. Jack neither smoked nor drank and he was naturally fit as well as being well trained and exercised. There was a certain star quality about him. Not only was his technique as a boxer something to be admired but in equal measures he was tremendously entertaining to watch.

Paul Kapsia had identified this when Jack was a boy singing on street corners. In the ring he was the epitome of the idealised Irishman except he was now more Brooklyn than Cork. He was toned, dark-haired and in his movements it was easy to imagine him doing an Irish jig in the middle of fast flowing punches. Jack was an attacking boxer. He wasn't going to be pushed onto the ropes by anyone. Always moving forward he gave the impression of the street fighting kid that never took a backward step and faced aggression and confrontation head on. Like many men of charm he could also be a dangerous opponent.

"Yes, my friend, I figure we have a real good fighter," said Sammy, relishing the prospect of nurturing a future champion. Jack stopped fighting and shook hands with his opponent. He turned and grinned at Sammy who beckoned to him to step down from the ring. "Hey kid, over here for a moment."

Jack wiped his forehead with a towel and came across. "Hiya Sammy. Hiya Paul. Have you got something for me?"

"Sure we have," replied Sammy. "We've got a fight fixed up for you next Saturday night. How do you feel about that?"

"Ready as I'll ever be," Jack responded. "Who am I up against?"

"An old pal of yours by all accounts," said Sammy. "A very confident young fellow with a bit of a swagger." Jack searched his memory quickly. "Claims he knows you from way back."

"Think of a cocky Bronx kid that used to shine my shoes," Paul reminded him.

It suddenly dawned on Jack who his opponent was going to be.

"Slugs?"

"That's him," Paul said with a smile. "Jake Mahoney."

Jack allowed himself a smile at the irony and coincidence of it all. "Now that's going to be quite a fight," he mused. "Stick around for the whole show, fellas."

"You bet your ass we will, pal!" Sammy retorted. We've got more dough riding on you than a bread loaf on a stallion!"

Eight

The following Saturday night arrived after a week of intensive physical training for Jack. Initially he had thought himself to be confident enough to win this bout. He thought because he knew Slugs Mahoney this immediately gave him the measure of the man and, so he thought, an advantage; however, as each day passed, Jack became more and more nervous. On the Saturday of the fight, Jack was on edge. The adrenalin was surging through him. His nervous energy was beginning to jettison him to an explosive state of mind. Once in the ring and up against a formidable opponent, he would be a whirling dervish. The tension was building up.

In his dressing room Jack was sparring and working himself up for his first major fight. Sammy Rosen and Anatole looked on and tried to get him to calm down. The roar of the crowd anxiously waiting for the commencement began to get louder and louder.

"Hear that, kid!" Sammy said. "That's the sound of your boxing career beginning."

Jack became more and more anxious. He moved round the room jabbing and punching thin air. The countdown was beginning.

In another dressing room, Slugs Mahoney was doing exactly the same thing. Shortly two young men would literally set fire to the atmosphere when they met in the ring.

Then after moments of nerve-wracking tension it was time for the two fighters to make their way down to the ring. Jack was determined not to lose momentum. Flanked by Anatole and Sammy he bounded down the long corridor punching and jabbing with a spring in his step. He was puffing and blowing but only in mock practice.

Along the front row of the audience Paul Kapsia and Jess Reubens sat in apprehension of the coming fight. The audience was building up as the excitement mounted and then as the two fighters came into the ring a roar went up that almost took the roof off. Cameras flashed. Cheers of approval and boos rent forth in the highly charged atmosphere. For the first time in his life, Jack realised the enormity of appearing before an audience. It was a breathtaking, overpowering feeling knowing that the performance he gave in the ring that night would be greeted with heroic applause or a chorus of disapproval.

With their entourage taking up their positions at the opposite end of the ring, the two men came together for the first time in years. Each had grown into physically strong eager young fighters. Slugs and Jack stared hard at each other challenging and defiant. But Slugs dropped his guard briefly and gave him a quick grin.

"Never thought we'd meet like this again. Eh, Jack?"

"No hard feelings, Slugs, but I'm going to beat you tonight."

"None taken, friend, but this one's mine."

Jack and Slugs were equally defiant. It was definitely a case of the irresistible force against the immovable object. Both of them were boxers that led the attack rather than defend and land the odd blow here and there. This was a gladiatorial battle in the making.

Within minutes of the introductions and announcements to the spectators, the fight was underway. It was as if the moment Slugs stepped into the ring his whole persona changed. From being the amiable knockabout kid on the block, he became a mean, ferocious man with only one intention in mind: to demolish his opponent in the shortest time possible. Not so for Jack. His aim was to keep his opponent second-guessing and to avoid as many blows as possible while sneaking in as many sly punches that he could.

Slugs knew he had a real opponent and was merciless in his onslaught on Jack who, in turn, proved to be resilient as a cliff face. The spectators were enthralled. The two men were determined to hold their own and not give an inch to the other. Round after round followed and both fighters slammed and thumped each other. Neither would yield to the other.

"I can't pin the guy down," Slugs said anxiously to his trainer at the end of one round.

"I can't get that lucky blow in," Jack said to his trainer with a similar tone of anxiety.

They stared across at each other. Yet amidst the tension and the tumult of their fight Slugs suddenly smiled and winked at his opponent.

Amazingly Jack did the same. The warmth between them was undeniable but once facing each other in the ring with their fists raised the battle royal continued. This time there was real ferocity in their actions. Punches flew backwards and forwards furiously. Each chased the other around the ring. Then once at close distance they hammered into each other. The crowd went into a frenzy.

Then suddenly Jack got one lucky punch in. The one he had strived to get in. Slugs came towards him and left his face unguarded for a split second. Jack broke through and delivered the hardest punch he had ever thrown in his life which sent Slugs keeling back onto the floor of the ring. The referee moved in and begun the count.

"One! Two!" Slugs raised slightly. Jack had won this one. He was sure of it. "Three! Four!" Still no sign of Slugs rising to his feet.

"C'mon, kid. Off your ass!" Slugs' trainer called out.

"Five! Six!" Slugs leaned up. He rubbed his chin and slapped his face. "Seven! Eight!"

Slugs was on his feet. He was dizzy and staggering slightly but with all the energy he could bring to himself he came back into the fight. Being a good-humoured rough diamond, he managed to wink to the spectators. His bruised face and perspiring forehead did nothing to diminish the fact he was back in the game.

"Lucky punch, kid! Bronx kids don't cry. They just get back up again. Old Slugs is back in town, Jack!"

Jack knew he had little time and energy to win this fight. Slugs was like a dynamo regenerated. In the next round he was squaring up from every direction. Jack was no longer the attacking boxer, he was on the defensive, under siege from a man who would not, and could not, relent.

The audience was baying for blood. Standing up, cheering, booing and yelling. Paul Kapsia and Jess Reubens looked around. The ferocity of the fight seemed to set the audience ablaze with excitement. From the sidelines Sammy Rosen and Anatole looked on anxiously waiting for that crucial defining moment when the fight would come to its sudden climax.

Then it was all over. A near-exhausted Jack averted his eyes for one moment. Slugs seized his moment. A long punch came across striking Jack sharply. He was spinning and then he fell. It was only on the count of ten that he began to stir. Above him he was seeing stars and flashes, people and lights, and in the background the roar of the crowd rose as someone shouted "and the winner is the Bronx's own… ladies and gentlemen I give you Jake… Slugs… Mahoney."

Slugs basked in his moment of fleeting admiration and fame, raising his fists above his head. A generous opponent he pushed his way through his surrounding entourage and reached out to Jack.

"On your feet, buddy." He helped lift Jack to his standing position. "Alright, kid?"

"I'll live to fight another day," Jack mumbled.

In the centre of the ring, Slugs raised Jack's hand as if he was the winner instead.

"This here's my buddy Jack Clancy. Let's hear it for a grand opponent! I may have won the fight but he sure as hell gave me one."

At this the spectators gave a loud cheer and Slugs and Jack stood for a moment, soaking up the appreciation. There is nothing like the roar of the crowd and their shining faces for boosting the spirits and egos of a man. No wonder politicians and entertainers let it all go to their heads. Slugs whispered in Jack's ear. Jack nodded in agreement. Slugs motioned to the crowd with his arms for quiet. Then when it was almost silent Jack and Slugs, two bruised, very sweat soaked boxers began to sing the song 'America the Beautiful'. All round the ring the spectators began to join in.

Sammy Rosen and Anatole sang as loud as they could. Paul Kapsia and Jess Reubens sang with beaming smiles across their faces. This was some life thought Jack when he realised how spellbinding it is to have power over the crowd. This thought was not lost on Anatole who was shortly due to make his stage debut with Mariska.

"Not bad for two Micks eh!" Sammy said to him.

"Not bad! Hell they were good!" exclaimed Anatole.

***

The show business careers of Anatole and Mariska began in earnest soon after in a small New York theatre. The state theatre not only marked their debut as performers but also the venue where they learned every aspect of stagecraft. Mariska was only fourteen, while Anatole was nearing nineteen yet their confidence on stage made for entertaining watching.

On stage, they were Nat and Mary Lucky. Outwardly, they had the appearance of all American hoofers: they tap-danced. They sang. They mimicked, but above all, in classic vaudeville fashion, they entertained. Each did a solo spot. Anatole sang Stephen Foster songs like 'Weep no more my lady' and 'Poor old Joe'. In one number he was joined on stage by Jess Reubens. The two of them danced up a storm, bringing the house down. When Anatole came off stage he could feel the adrenalin and nervous energy flowing through him.

Mariska came on straight away after Jess and Anatole. At only fourteen she possessed all the ingredients that make a true star. There are some people who are born for the stage by virtue of their sheer personality, charisma and magnetism. Mariska had all these qualities yet they were combined by her fresh-faced innocence. When she sang an old time love song her voice resonated across the theatre. Normally a difficult, tough, and hard to please audience, the New Yorkers took her to their hearts. Several rounds of applause later Mariska ran off the stage to greet Anatole.

"Did I do well, brother?" she asked.

"Babe, you and I are going places!" Anatole replied, thrilled at the reception she had been given.

***

Going places was definitely the right expression. One year later Paul Kapsia organised a travelling vaudeville show that was to take them across the length and breadth of the United States. Anatole and Mariska looked on in excitement at all the fascinating places they visited. America was rich, diverse and ever changing.

Under their stage name of Nat and Mary Lucky, they performed in small theatres, on board riverboats, in open air shows and on the sidewalks of provincial cities. America in 1905 still had something of the hell for leather, rip-roaring frontier spirits, that had so entranced its forefathers, and which had attracted immigrants from all parts of the world.

There were times when the trains they travelled in pulled into stations that still had a romantic link to the Wild West. Sheriffs and Marshalls still held sway. Cowboys of an age gone by still rode into some towns and tied their horses to the rail outside rough-looking saloons, where the jingle of pianos being played badly intermingled with loud, masculine voices and hysterical laughter of men and women who couldn't hold their drink.

Sometimes the train would pull into a glittering town like Pittsburgh, Boston or New Orleans. There the vaudeville show would play to a smartly dressed audience. Then they would play to a frontier town where the audience would be raucous and loud, and the entertainers would have to be strong enough to stand the inevitable onslaught. A river boat show on one of the many rivers in the United States would give the vaudevillians a captive audience. Jess Reubens was smart enough to know that often audiences didn't just want to listen. They also wanted to participate. Jess would beckon to the audience to sing along if they knew the words and, happily, they would join in. Passers-by on the riverbank often saw a paddle steamer making its way at any time of the day with a huge chorus rising up to greet them. These were glorious halcyon days of discovery.

Across the plains and prairies of America, the train would pass herds of Buffalo and itinerant Native Americans roaming with their families. Travelling never ceased to fascinate Anatole.

"Look at that, kid," he said, nudging his sister, who would often fall asleep on long journeys.

"What am I looking at?" Mariska asked drowsily, stretching her arms and then stifling a yawn.

A herd of buffalo raced past. Anatole's eyes were gleaming.

"America, kid," he replied. "America. This is one hell of a country!"

Mariska smiled at him and gazed out at the splendour and grandeur of it all. It was a long way from her Russian birthplace.

★★★

San Francisco was the final destination of their America wide tour. Jess Reubens had been there before but he had lost none of his enthusiasm for this colourful city. He had boosted the excitement of Anatole and Mariska by telling them all about this metropolis overlooking the sparkling Pacific Ocean. In a sense, it was the largest great city on America's West Coast. The next major city and seaport was Sydney in Australia on the other side of the Pacific.

The reputation of the notorious Barbary Coast had preceded itself. When Anatole was told that the women were free and easy there, his imagination went wild. He was also told that the men went wild and that many vices including gambling and showgirls were available.

What the hell, he thought? He would taste all sides of life. Sure he would like the grandeur of the buildings and the scenic views but he would also engross himself in living life to the full gracefully or disgracefully. There was plenty of life to choose from.

San Francisco was a melting pot of many races. It had a mixture of Irishmen, Italians, Spaniards, Jews, Russians, Japanese and Chinese. It still had the buzz and energy of the gold rush days about it. In 1905, Paul Kapsia's travelling show came to its final shows before the entertainers would return to their homes. With its sweeping views of the Pacific, its winding streets and rickety roads, of all the cities they had visited for Anatole and Mariska this was probably their favourite place. From the balcony of their hotel in Market Street they gazed down at the bustling crowds.

"You know what, sis? I think I'm going to have the time of my life here," Anatole said, his eyes shining with delight. "This is a beautiful town."

"You watch yourself," Mariska replied. "I hear there are some dangerous places you wouldn't want to visit on your own."

"Sure, I'll be okay," he said winking at her. "Tell you what. Tomorrow night when we open at the Palace, we'll knock them dead. We'll be the best show in town."

***

True to his word when the vaudeville show opened at the Palace Theatre, the troupe gave the performance of their lives. Jess Reubens danced up a storm. Anatole's renditions of Stephen Foster's songs had the audience mesmerised but the biggest applause came when Mariska took to the stage. She sang and danced solo. Then she performed with Anatole when he sang the old traditional song 'Lenora'. Mariska danced in graceful moves, spun round almost like a ballet dancer. A star was born that night and all who watched had no doubt about it.

***

One night Anatole decided to visit the rougher side of San Francisco. He visited saloons and gambling houses, his eager mind keen to take in the potpourri of the cosmopolitan population, particularly the women. If there was one thing that set his pulse racing, it was the sight of a glamorous woman. Anatole was getting slowly drunk as the night wore on, and then he caught sight of a dazzling attractive woman, well-dressed but with a figure suggesting she could have been a showgirl. He half smiled at her and she gave him an acknowledging one in return. At a rough guess she could have been six or seven years older than him. Out of curiosity, Anatole followed her along one salubrious street of the Barbary Coast. Drunken sailors passed by. Loud, raucous voices seemed to come from every side street. A brawl took place in the street and people passed by as if this was commonplace.

The woman turned around suddenly. There was a look of amusement in her eyes. "Honey, you've been following me. What are you? Eighteen?"

"Nineteen – nearly twenty."

"Sure you are," she said with admiration, looking at his good cut of clothes. She felt the cloth. "Mmm. Nice cut. What do you do, handsome?"

"Show business. I'm in vaudeville at the Palace. I'm from New York. From Russia originally, but I grew up in the Bronx. My name is Anatole."

"Is that right? I'm Christina. Yeah, I was a migrant kid too. The folks brought me over when I was six. Why don't you buy me a drink in there?" She pointed to a saloon called The Horseshoe. "That's a nice bar. We can talk about our travels in there."

Anatole didn't hesitate. He was keen to get to know this lady both socially and physically. They entered the saloon together. This 'nice bar' was in fact a place of ill repute to the extreme. It was smoky and crowded. There were roughnecks, big built seamen with tattoos drinking liquor, gamblers played at corner tables, scantily dressed showgirls danced on a stage displaying long beautiful legs, cowboys from the Wild West strode confidently through the crowd with their guns clearly visible beneath their jackets.

Looking around Anatole saw girls stop and talk to customers, usually by discreetly whispering in their ear. The next moment they would be heading upstairs. He was pretty clear in his mind about what was going on there. Quickly he turned to talk to Christina who in turn asked him about his life. Drinks seemed to appear out of nowhere and Anatole, who drank whatever was put before him, found himself drifting into a haze of uncontrollable laughter and dulled senses. Behind him a Chinese man spoke to a couple of tough-looking sailors and nodded in his direction.

Such was his drunken state that Anatole failed to realise he was talking to himself. Christina had mysteriously disappeared. He stood up from his chair to look for her. Oh gosh, he felt unsteady on his feet. His mind was racing. There were blurred images and raucous laughter. That was the last thing he remembered that night.

Nine

Mariska was very concerned. Anatole had not returned to the hotel the previous night and when she knocked loudly on his room door there had been no reply. The first person she had spoken to about it was Jess Reubens. He at once reported to the concierge, who had not seen Anatole come or go, and neither had the man at the reception. This was a serious worry. Jess, who had performed in San Francisco before, knew of its reputation and how the temptations of the Barbary Coast could lead men seriously astray. Mariska and Jess immediately set off to find the nearest police station to report that Anatole was missing.

But what had happened to Anatole? The harsh fact was that he was no longer in San Francisco but on a boat in the Pacific Ocean. In the Horseshoe Saloon, Christina Ehlert had, under instruction from her masters, surreptitiously slipped a potion into Anatole's drinks all night, rendering him paralytically drunk. Christina vanished, looking for her next victim and Anatole had been effectively shanghaied.

Police Sergeant Jurgen Zielinski was sympathetic to Mariska but there were many similar cases he had dealt with before. He watched Mariska and Jess leave then turned to his colleague Constable Ray Pedler.

"Well what d'ya think? That fella went for a drink on the Barbary Coast and went missing."

"Quite a few have gone missing. Five in the past few weeks."

"And many more who have not been reported," Zielinski came back.

"Ray, get a few of the boys together and get some answers from as many saloon bar owners as possible."

"Yes sir," Ray replied. "Oh, Sergeant Zielinski! Do you want us to bring in the usual suspects?"

"You do that! And find out what boats have left Frisco in the past few days and where they're heading." Zielinski slapped his truncheon in the palm of his hand and frowned. He had his suspicions about what had happened to Anatole and others who had also disappeared. A little more proof and he would take pleasure in putting the saloon out of business.

***

In a park overlooking a bay Mariska and Jess sat looking out across the water. "What could have happened to him, Jess?"

Jess's eyes showed concern. "It's real serious, I tell you that straight. But you gotta keep the faith, young lady."

"It's not like him to go missing," Mariska said quietly. "Oh, he thinks he's a toughie and can handle anything, but he's just a kid. We've been through so much together, coming from Russia as children and being orphaned. If anything happens to him I don't know how I'll keep going."

"You'll keep going because you have to," Jess affirmed. "And what is more you will go out and do the best show you can tonight."

"Without Anatole?" she asked. "How can I do it? Why should I do it?"

"Do it for him," Jess replied.

Mariska looked at him tearfully. What else could she do? Money had to be earned to eat. The cast of the show were relying on her. Besides, to go on and perform tonight would motivate her to apply her concentration elsewhere. Tonight Mariska thought she would overreach herself and give the performance of her life.

***

Out in the Pacific Ocean Anatole found himself to be a shanghaied crewmember aboard a less than comfortable vessel called *The High Priestess*. He had woken from his drunken stupor along with other unwilling recruits to find himself en route to China. Now he was swabbing deck and taking orders from some fierce-looking oriental sailors. Why he had been kidnapped was a mystery to him. No one told him. All he knew was that if he tried to mutiny against the crew he would probably be thrown overboard. The object of the voyage was also a mystery and just exactly what was the secret cargo they were collecting in China?

The answer came several days after the ship passed Hawaii. Anatole lay back on the wooden bunk one night. His muscles were aching from the toil of working for hours at a stretch and he was truly exhausted. A Dutch-accented man in the next bunk spoke to him.

"I'm Harry Van Der Gruys," he said amiably. "Which bar did you get plastered in?"

"The Horseshoe," Anatole replied. "I'm Anatole."

"Funny. I thought you were Nat Lucky, the dancer I saw at the Palace. You danced with a lady called Mary. A good show, my friend,"

"I am," Anatole said with a brief smile. "Nat Lucky is my stage name. Mary is my sister. How in the hell did I get here?"

He looked down at the full length of the crew's quarters. One long room contained many dishevelled and bemused-looking men. It suddenly dawned on Anatole the brutal truth of just what was happening. Harry Van Der Gruys was quick to pick up on this.

"You are wondering if all these men came voluntarily, eh?" Anatole nodded realising the obvious answer would be no. "We are all – to coin a phrase – in the same boat. We were kidnapped and laid low by drink. We are now on our way to China – Shanghai – to pick up a cargo of human life who will be made to work on the wild side of 'Frisco," Anatole looked at him, concerned. "Women – Chinese women – to work for their masters. That is the cargo we will collect and then they will dump us in Shanghai to get back on our own."

"What if we take over the ship and shoot the bastards?" Anatole asked him in a voice clearly intent. "I'm not going to be part of a filthy business like that. My parents brought me and my sister to America from Russia to be free. Didn't they have a civil war to end slavery?"

"Take over the ship!" Harry Van Der Gruys chortled. "Who do you think you are, Long John Silver?" He nodded in the direction of the gaolers. "They are the real pirates. No, my friend, we will steal this vessel when the time is right."

Anatole stared down at the crew and whispered to Van Der Gruys. "Give me the sign when the time is right." Almost as soon as he had spoken the lights went out and Anatole lay back, contemplating his escape plan.

Long, gruelling days at sea followed. The Chinese captors were by their very nature tough, unrelenting and verging on the sadistic. The men who had found themselves unwilling crewmembers were an assorted bunch of roughnecks, hoodlums and ordinary upstanding citizens who had just happened to have taken one drink too much in the wrong bar.

The captain of this vessel frequently stood on the top deck watching his unlucky sailors hard at work. He had a sinister look and an evil glint in his eyes as if he was a man totally lacking any humanity. He also had a rifle strapped to his shoulder. There was no doubt he would use it. Once, long ago Anatole's mother had told him that there was good in everyone. No one was completely bad. Looking at the captain and crew, Anatole had his doubts about that.

Harry Van Der Gruys was an amiable enough companion. He was about forty with a strong build – a sailor from Amsterdam since he was fourteen. He was not a man to be trifled with and, although on the surface he seemed jovial and friendly, Van Der Gruys was in fact the veteran of many a brawl and skirmish. His history in his maritime career had not been pure. In his time he had been a gunrunner to the Boers in South Africa, smuggled diamonds, transported illicit cargo and taken paid passengers of dubious character to new lives abroad. He was not above performing any sort of skulduggery as long as he was paid handsomely for it.

There was another shanghaied crewman whom Harry Van Der Gruys and Anatole became close to. He was eager to get his revenge on his captors and awaited the moment Harry Van Der Gruys was ready to strike. Jim Cope was an Australian from Ballarat in Victoria, who had sailed on merchant vessels from Melbourne and Sydney right across the Pacific. He had been to every port from Saigon to Yokohama and on the other side of the Pacific he had sailed from Vancouver to Cape Horn. Jim Cope signed on and off ships wherever the mood took him. Young and restless he felt duty bound to no one but himself.

"Just say the word, you blokes," he said amiably to Harry and Anatole as they swabbed the decks. "I'll back you up as soon as you say go."

They all looked up at the sinister captain who never said a word but whose silence spoke volumes. There was one member of the captured crew who was bursting to break free. He was a tough, big-muscled, shaven-headed American who looked like a wrestler. For some reason he was nicknamed 'Irons' by the crew, and he too was a silent man, not given to talk. He was pushing a crate on deck when he caught sight of the captain. Irons stopped what he was doing and stared hard and long at the captain as if he was silently challenging him. The two men seemed to have no fear of the other.

Watched by the entire crew they were spellbound as Irons began walking towards the captain. The Chinese crew, well aware that something dramatic was happening, began to close ranks. One of them suddenly drew a whip and moved forward to face him. This didn't dispel Irons. He moved forward one pace, gave the man a look up and down, and then turned around and walked back. The captain gave a signal and in the next instant several crew members surrounded Irons and attempted to take him down below.

This was a big mistake. All hell suddenly broke loose. Irons was far stronger than the Chinese crew realised. He kicked, punched and lashed out at his captors. Anatole, Jim Cope and several others started to move forward ready for a violent scuffle with the crew. Shots suddenly rang out above their heads as the Captain fired his rifle. Within minutes Irons was struck over the head from behind and taken below. The rest of the crew started pushing and whiplashing the other men to carry out their duties.

"Don't worry about Irons too much," Harry whispered.

"You know him?" Jim asked.

"Sure I do," said Harry, and he added, "So do the police in California. He was arrested for killing three men and escaped from jail only to be kidnapped and brought on board."

"We're keeping good company on this voyage aren't we?" Anatole said with a hint of cynicism. "Well I'll be dammed if they will keep me a prisoner! When the time is right I'm going to break free whatever it takes. Be ready, fellas."

Ten

The hotel lobby in San Francisco was bustling that morning. Mariska sat composed and serene, watching the melting pot of people coming and going. Her colleagues on tour were heading back east today but Mariska wasn't going. She had decided not to go with them in the vain hope that Anatole would turn up. Jess Reubens came down the stairs smartly dressed, wearing a broad hat and carrying a suitcase. On seeing her he walked across and sat down beside her.

"Are you sure about this, honey?" he asked. "Do you really want to stay here on your own? Don't you want to go back home?"

A rare smile broached Mariska's lips. "Where is home, Jess? When I'm on tour with Anatole, that's the only home I know."

"Sure I understand that, Mariska, but Anatole's a big boy now. If he returns and you're not here he'll find his way back to New York. You're fifteen, kid. Kinda young to be on your own in this wild city. What are you going to survive on? Fresh air?"

"I'll get work as a dancer."

"You're still too young to be on your own," Jess said firmly.

"I seem to recall you telling me that when slavery was abolished you walked free – and you weren't much older than I am," Mariska pointed out with some relish.

"Well I guess I can't argue with that," Jess replied, realising it was useless to try and convince her otherwise. He reached into his jacket and handed her a wad of notes. "Take this to look after yourself. I'll see you back in New York when you're ready."

"With Anatole hopefully. Bless you, Jess, you're a real friend."

Mariska embraced him. Jess smiled at her, turned on his toes and walked out of the hotel lobby. She watched him go and as the door closed the stark realisation came over her that for the first time in her life she was truly alone. For a moment Mariska pondered what to do next. It would have been easy to sit there all day just watching people come and go. Real life had to be faced. This morning she would find an agent and a theatre. Getting work would be a priority. Then this afternoon she would find lodgings. Picking up her case she walked outside into Market Street. A horse-drawn carriage passed by. Men were hurrying to their offices. Ladies in big hats and carrying parasols strutted by. Policemen riding horses, looked keenly about them. A breeze blew down from the seafront carrying with it the unmistakable smell of fish. It was time to get walking and begin knocking on a few doors.

***

Faraway on the other side of the Pacific the coast of China came into view. It was the first time the crew and its unwilling victims had seen land since San Francisco. Always on approaching land the scent of new places filled the air. Junks and fishing vessels sailed by. All of the kidnapped crew looked at the distant coast with breathtaking uncertainty. What would be their fate now? Almost as soon as they had drifted off into thoughts of freedom the sound of cracking whips could be heard. The captors came round lashing out at individuals spurning them back to work. At once they returned to their duties. Harry Van Der Gruys looked at this sight with distaste.

"Tonight!" he said quietly to Anatole and Jim. "We go tonight!"

In fact, things were already hotting up. Below decks, in the hold, Irons was getting angrier and angrier. In chains he felt as if he was part of a work gang in some out of the way obscure prison. A triple murderer who had no conscience, sense of guilt or even humanity, Irons had worked out in his own mind how to escape despite the restrictions placed on him.

He waited for one of his gaolers who would bring him his next meal. Anxiously he prepared himself for that intense moment of fury he would unleash. The wooden boards on which his chains were attached had been badly affected by damp and were splintering. A very red-faced and enraged Irons exerted as much pressure as he could on the boards. He pulled and pushed until the perspiration dripped down his face. Then, when he least expected it, a board broke and he had one hand free. Quickly he secured release from the other chains and began to scramble around, seeking a way out of the hold. Looking around he saw several crates and chests.

Piling them on top of each other he climbed on them and moved towards the hatch door. A draught of air came through the cracks. Irons tried to work out a way of prising it open.

Up above, the press-ganged crew were also stirring. For weeks now they had been at the mercy of their captors. Now their anger which had been simmering was boiling. A Chinese crewman approached them with a whip and, as he prepared to bring it down on the back of an unsuspecting victim, Harry Van Der Gruys caught sight of it and signalled to Jim. This was the spur for reprisal that both men had waited for. Both of them rushed forward and overpowered the man. Jim gave him several punches and, with Harry Van Der Gruys' assistance, promptly threw the man over the side. Open warfare began on the boat as the furious sailors suddenly rushed their captors and took their revenge.

Below, Irons hacked away at the hatch door until it eventually broke. He pushed upwards and scrambled through. Dashing along the passageway, he found himself confronted by two crewmembers. Two blows delivered were delivered in a sledgehammer, bare-knuckle style, knocking them out instantly. Irons seized their rifles, went through their pockets for money and valuables and ran up on deck where the mother of all fights was taking place. Using the butt of one of the rifles he struck out at the hated crew. He tossed a rifle to Harry Van Der Gruys and the two men took aim at their captors.

There were fists flying and bullets whizzing. Irons spared none of his tormentors but his revenge was short-lived. A bullet struck him and he lurched perilously close to the side. Another bullet struck and he went over into the sea. In the meantime Anatole and Jim fought furiously together, backed up by the other press gangs. Anatole had never been in a fight like this in all of his life. There were people coming from all directions and several times he thought it was all over. Van De Gruys saved his life by firing at the attackers. He also packed a dynamite punch.

Jim meantime moved to where the lifeboats were situated and began to untie them. Van Der Gruys decided to scramble below deck and steal money. Grabbing a rifle he shot and punched everyone that tried to obstruct him. Van Der Gruys had no conscience about taking what he wanted.

Up above, the shanghaied crew had the upper hand over the legitimate crew, who of those that remained, were disarmed. Jim, Anatole and the other Americans started to move to the lifeboats. Van Der Gruys found a stash of cash in several lockers and promptly cleared them out. He also found opium, spirits and other trinkets of value he knew he could sell to raise money. Swiftly, he piled them into a sack and started to make his way out. He immediately found his path blocked by a fierce-looking sailor. It was clear neither man was going to give way. The sailor suddenly flashed a knife at Van Der Gruys, who dropped the sack and swung his rifle. To his horror, he found the ammunition had run out. There was nothing else for it but to fight it out. Both men were strong and well built. The man parried and slashed at Van Der Gruys who in turn used the butt of his rifle to send back return blows. It was a gladiatorial battle.

In the lifeboats Jim was running out of patience, as were the other Americans. He looked at Anatole and then cast a glance at the deck.

"We better go, cobber," Jim said reluctantly. Anatole nodded in agreement. Then the boat started to descend into the harbour waters of Shanghai.

Van Der Gruys was still in the fight of his life. Like a boxer and a wrestler he was doing everything in his power to survive. The tremendous fight between the two men reached full pitch when both of them lost their weapons. The knife went one way and the rifle in the other direction. Van Der Gruys delivered a stunning blow to his opponent, grabbed the sack and tried to get away but the Chinese sailor wasn't done yet. He kicked the door of a cupboard down which contained explosives for what dubious purposes only he knew. Quickly he flicked a match in the cupboard and raced after Van Der Gruys. The sailor grabbed Van Der Gruys leg as he tried to ascend to the upper deck. Van Der Gruys turned sharply and swung the sack at the sailor causing him to fall back. There was no time to waste.

Van Der Gruys ran across the deck only to find the lifeboats were now in the water below. He had no alternative. Either face the wrath of the defeated crew on deck or brave the waters. Clutching the sack he climbed over the rail and jumped into the harbour in a bid to reach the lifeboats.

Jim spotted him and stretched out to bring him on board the boat. No sooner had he been pulled into the safety of the lifeboat than there was an almighty explosion as the vessel, that had effectively been their floating prison for weeks, went up in fire and flames. The crew leapt from the *High*

Priestess into the harbour. The sheer pandemonium that lay before them was an awful sight of death, and the end of a chapter.

For a moment the flames soaring into the air reminded Anatole of when he had been a boy in Russia. From the train he had seen his home village go up in flames. He had never wanted to be part of such a thing again and he grimaced at the sight of it. Van Der Gruys took the oar, indicating for the others to start rowing. They would have a lot of explaining to the authorities about how they had come to arrive in Shanghai.

***

Mariska had stayed on in San Francisco as she had intended to do. By day she worked in a dress shop and several nights a week she was in the chorus of a show in the Phoenix Theatre. Her anxiety about Anatole stayed with her each day. In her heart she feared that she would never see her brother again. He had been gone for several months in that year of 1905 and the harsh but realistic thought struck Mariska that if no trace of Anatole could be found then it might make sense to return to New York. There Paul Kapsia could continue to manage her show business career and she could turn to Jess Reubens for fatherly advice.

Beautiful women came into the shop to look at the array of clothes on display. In addition to costumes for every occasion, some customers would ask for measurements on wedding outfits. Mariska smiled as potential brides eyed up a particular dress. For the first time in her life she wondered when and if she would ever meet a man who would be a good husband to her. All that seemed a long way off for now. Mariska knew that she was still a teenager and there were stars in her eyes for other things such as her show business career. In this she had an all consuming passion. It just wasn't the same without Anatole and she kept thinking about where he might be.

In the time Mariska had worked there, she had become good friends with the manageress, Mrs Joan Gale. Mariska found her good company. Joan was a Chicago girl originally who had moved west in the 1890s. Although she was in her mid-forties Joan Gale was still very attractive but she had an air of wisdom about her.

"Are you dancing tonight at the Phoenix Theatre?" Joan asked amiably.

"Yes. I've got two shows tonight," replied Mariska.

"You'll wear yourself out, young lady," Joan said with a laugh. "Well you better get going soon. I'll lock up tonight." She looked across at a girl admiring a wedding dress. "She's got dreams, Mariska. I was like that once."

Mariska glanced at her. "Weren't you happy when you got married?"

"Twice! Each time I got married I was thrilled. Then real life set in and boy did I get it wrong! Take a tip from me, Mariska, when you find the number one man for yourself, make sure he's not a long shot."

Mariska smiled and glanced at the clock. "Is it okay, Mrs Gale, if I make a move now?"

"Why not?" Joan replied. "Business has been slow today. Maybe it'll pick up tomorrow. By the way, ask your boss if he wants any costumes made for any of the shows at the Theatre. I better start to expand my trade a bit."

"I'll put a word in for you," said Mariska. She promptly attended to the customers before finishing her day job. Then it would be a dash to the theatre and two shows at the Phoenix Theatre in the chorus line. The show was a musical western and her part was a high kicking saloon girl. When they closed Mariska made her way home to a small room in a boarding house where she would retreat to her bed exhausted after a long day. By the side of her bed she had placed a photograph of Anatole in a frame. She missed him so much. Terrifying thoughts went through her mind. The thought of being totally alone in the world frightened her. Her parents, Viktor and Ekaterina had died seven years before. Now her brother had gone missing. Would she be strong enough to carry on alone? Where on earth was he?

***

Shanghai was a city that seemed to encompass all the mystique of the Orient. The harbour was filled with junks, fishing boats, steamships from different parts of the world, and rickety old houseboats on which whole families lived. Sailors and vagabonds haunted the waterfront, while rickshaw drivers looked forever outwards, eager for their next passenger. Grey buildings loomed in the background surrounded by swirls of fog or mist with the sun trying desperately to shine through the crevices. There were hidden narrow streets with outdoor cafes serving unusual delicacies such as chicken and sea slugs or sharks fins and yellow fish. Secretive-looking buildings with coloured balconies and shutters seemed to be tucked away from main thoroughfares, containing mysterious wealthy residents who may have been merchant traders or affluent businessmen. Cosmopolitan figures in western dress, who wore broad-rimmed hats and smart suits easily intermingled with the local population in traditional Chinese attire.

It all seemed to be an extraordinary place, a pot-pourri of fascination and oriental mystery with a dash of danger in certain parts of the city, where definite boundaries could not be crossed unless a person had business to be done there.

***

What an adventure this had been! Anatole could not believe it even now. He gazed down at the busy city from his hotel room. Commerce and trade were carried out frantically as the local population scurried around industriously. In years to come this would be a wild story he could relate to any eager listener. But so far in his short life of nineteen years, he had gone from Russia to England, on to America and then unwillingly to China. For a moment he smiled at the irony of it all. Where else would the journey of life take him?

When the press-ganged crew had escaped from the *High Priestess* vessel they were immediately arrested at the docks by the Shanghai police and promptly locked up. They were each questioned over and over again until they were worn out. The police were particularly interested in why the vessel had blown up on the harbour which no one could shed any light on. Finally, they were released pending an interview with their respective consulates and allocated to a ship that would take them back to their home shores.

Their captors who had dived into the harbour waters had mysteriously disappeared and vanished into the busy streets of Shanghai probably never to be seen again. The Americans who had been kidnapped had been sent to various hotels and told to stay there until their identities had been recorded and travel documents approved.

The exception was the Dutchman, Harry Van Der Gruys, and the Australian, Jim Cope. They had no such inhibitions about roaming around the city. Neither man liked being told what to do and had no compunction about defying authority. In fact that was very much part of the make up in their character. Van Der Gruys was loaded with money having stolen much from the *High Priestess* before his escape.

There was a knock on the hotel door and Anatole opened it to find Harry and Jim there. Harry had a sack with him and Anatole immediately recognised it as the one his friend had when he had swam to the lifeboats.

"How are you, my young friend?" Harry asked, settling himself down into a chair.

"I'm alive. That's more than Irons is," he replied. Then a thought struck Anatole. "Tell me about Irons. You seemed to know more about him than anybody."

"Yeah, I'd like to know too," said Jim, taking in the view before sitting down.

"What is there to say?" Harry said casually and then added, "He was a wild man. He had a history behind him. In San Francisco he came to my ship and asked me to take him on my next voyage to Europe or Australia. One of my crew recognised him from a wanted police poster. He was a jail escapee."

"We probably owe him our lives," said Jim pensively.

Harry nodded solemnly in agreement. "I think as soon as we get our travel documents sorted it would be best if we got out of China as soon as possible. That ship, our floating prison, belonged to a Chinese warlord and it was carrying weapons – rifles, guns, dynamite, gunpowder and ammunition – all of it from their suppliers in California, mainly based on the Barbary Coast. In return women were transported to work in... well... shall we say, unpleasant places in San Francisco."

"We get the picture," Jim stated.

"What our captors didn't bargain for was our escape," Harry continued. "Nor did they expect the entire vessel to be blown up in Shanghai Harbour. Just as well. It was a rat-infested boat, unfit for human habitation. You know if you really want to describe it, I would call it a slave ship. Enslaved crew like us to be dumped here. Then the voyage back would have a different crew together with a group of poor women who were treated no better than slaves to work for masters who took all their money for favours to men on the Barbary Coast. There was another cargo they carried." He paused for a moment, thinking about what they had been involved in. "Opium. Freight loads of it. Backwards and forwards between China and San Francisco. Quite a lucrative trade by all accounts gentlemen and we were in the thick of it."

"With all that on board why did they blow the ship up?" Anatole was sure that Harry hadn't told them the full story.

"When I went below I found cash in lockers and boxes," Harry smiled. "Dollars, American Dollars." He pulled the sack into the centre of the room and tipped it out. "Thousands of American Dollars." Jim whistled at the sight of it. "I also took opium and whisky, some stuff I sold on the waterfront for information. I was involved in a fight below and the man lit the fireworks. Let's put it that way. That's when I raced to the top with the spoils and jumped over the side. The word on the waterfront is that the warlord's men are looking for us. Are you seeing the American consulate tomorrow Anatole?"

"At eleven o'clock tomorrow morning," replied Anatole.

"We better come with you, mate, and keep an eye out for you," Jim said, and then he turned to Harry as if a sudden afterthought had flashed in his mind. "You mean to say, Harry, that while we were fighting for our lives on the top deck you were below looting as much cash as you could get your hands on and stuffing opium and whisky into that sack like Santa Claus on a Christmas shopping trip!"

"That's right!" replied Harry. "Look at all that money. Think of it as our wages."

"Our wages!" exclaimed Jim. "More like a death sentence!" Jim was beside himself now. "So the warlord was expecting money from dirty dealings in San Francisco and a whole supply of guns and rifles. You took the money and the ship goes up in flames with all the weapons in the harbour! Bloody hell, cobber, the surviving crew who swam to the shore will be after our blood!"

"Suffering polecats!" muttered Anatole. "I just want to get back to San Francisco. But I wouldn't place any bets on us getting out of here that easy. Surely they'll be watching the waterfront."

"On that point I agree with you," Harry conceded. "The ships to San Francisco are booked up for weeks. Our best bet would be to travel overland to Hong Kong."

"Well I'm not going back to America," said Jim. "I'm going home to Australia. I'll go and see my folks in Ballarat and then maybe I'll get another ship in Melbourne. What about you blokes then?"

Harry looked up from counting his money. "The ship I was Captain of, will have sailed from San Francisco by now. The crew were under instructions that if I went missing to return to my home port of Amsterdam and that is where I shall be heading. If I can get a ship home from Hong Kong I shall sail on that long route through the Suez Canal." He looked at Anatole. "That only leaves you. Are you going to sail back with the other Americans, which could take weeks, or travel with us?" He tossed wads of money across to him and Jim. "It's up to you."

"I can't take this money," said Anatole. "It doesn't seem right."

"Well I bloody can!" snapped Jim. "They got it by dishonest means. This is our fare and wages. Don't get too fussy, mate. Forget your scruples. They didn't show us any when we got dropped through a hatch and taken away."

Anatole stood up and looked out of the window. He realised he was in a difficult predicament because of Harry, but at the same time he felt excited. Perhaps it was because he had discovered an adventurous spirit that he hadn't been aware of before, and he was suddenly enjoying the unpredictability of it all.

"Now that you put it like that, Jim, maybe I'll take this in good faith," he said in an upbeat mood. "If I come down to Australia with you, can I get a boat to San Francisco from there?"

"Of course. Anywhere you want to go."

"Well if you two come with me tomorrow and I get my documents sorted I'll be ready to leave when you are."

Eleven

The early morning sunlight streamed through the shutters in Anatole's hotel room bathing him in warmth. He rolled over in the small springy bed and contemplated just what the day would bring. Rising from his bed, he stood naked and gazed through the shutters at the bustle and cacophony of the streets.

Amazing how strong sunlight soaking into the drab grey buildings could enhance everything and make the colours so much more vivid. Soon Harry and Jim would call round for him and then together they would head off to the American consulate. He opened one of the windows slightly and the scent of mixed spices rose up to greet him. The spray from the harbour waters seemed to blow with a gentle breeze, and the combined noise of birds squawking together with the sounds of livestock created a curious atmosphere. Chinese voices involved in different conversations only added to the mystique of Anatole's first taste of the orient.

Anatole took a bath and dressed in some presentable clothes. Outside Harry and Jim were waiting. Each boarded a rickshaw and then headed off along the busy streets to the less than imposing building that housed the consulate. For some reason unknown to him, Anatole felt nervous. Several times a face in the crowd would give him a fixed stare. At first he put it down to being a westerner. Then the more sobering thought occurred to him that perhaps they were members of the crew of the *High Priestess* on the lookout for him and the others who got away. He could only speculate. In an alleyway, had Anatole looked more carefully, he would have seen one face that he would have instantly recognised. It was Irons, alive and well!

At the consulate building he left Harry and Jim outside while he entered. A well-dressed lady greeted him and took him to an office where on the door was the man's name Mr Robert Gover. The American lady knocked on the door and a voice from inside indicated for Anatole to enter.

"Good morning to you, sir. I'm Anatole Luchenya."

Mr Gover was wearing a beige suit and blue tie; he had dark hair and wore thin glasses. Anatole presumed him to be somewhere in his middle forties.

"I'm Robert Gover," he said, pleasantly rising to meet him ands shaking hands with a firm grip. He studied Anatole's appearance curiously. At nineteen, Anatole was just under six foot with black shiny hair and blue eyes; he had strong features that did not suggest ethnic origins other than that of a homespun America.

"Take a seat," he beckoned to Anatole. On his desk was a file, which he opened and browsed through. Several times as he read it he looked up and glanced at Anatole.

"Will this be a long meeting?" Anatole asked betraying a slight nervousness at being interviewed by a figure of authority.

Mr Gover didn't answer the question. Instead, he said, "Forget about the Robert, I prefer Bob Gover. Bob Gover to my friends." He looked at the file the Chinese authorities had passed on to him. "Interesting." Then he looked hard at Anatole with suspicious eyes. "Tell me, young man, who is the President of the United States?"

Anatole gave him a quizzical look in return. "Why Theodore Roosevelt, of course."

"Who is the secretary of war?"

"Look, what is this? I'm not too interested in politics. I'm a song and dance man," Anatole protested and then added, "Is it William Taft?"

Mr Gover nodded that it was and then pursued him with a further question. "What is the name of a recently constructed building in Fifth Avenue, New York?"

"The Flatiron building?" Anatole replied, making it sound more like a question than a response.

"Who was the general who died at Little Big Horn?"

"Custer!" Anatole responded.

"Name me a famous American poet, a composter and a legendary Wild West figure?"

"How about Walt Whitman? Stephen Foster? Buffalo Bill?"

"Fine," said Mr Gover. "I just needed to know that you're the genuine article. So far so good. I've got in front of me the file the Chinese authorities handed me. Your surname is Luchenya. What is that... Polish?"

"Russian." Bob Gover rubbed his chin and looked at Anatole, anticipating further clarification. "I was brought up in America."

"And you say you're a song and dance man? What sort of song and dance man?"

"Vaudeville. I did an act with my sister. We reached San Francisco after a coast-to-coast tour. I went into a bar and I had a drink or two and…"

"You woke up at sea," Mr Gover finished the sentence for him. "Young fella, and you are a young, naïve fellow, no doubt charmed by a seductive woman and bamboozled by strong drink somewhere on the Barbary Coast. Do you know how many Americans I get passing through this office in a similar situation to you? You wouldn't want to try counting. If America went to war and the opposing army was made of dazzling eager women in bustles soaked in perfume and carrying bottles of liquor, we would lose every time." Mr Gover's remarks brought a smile to Anatole's face. "Well, young man, I will provide you with travel documents. Come back to this office in a few days time and I'll have everything ready for you. In the meantime take a look around Shanghai. It's a fascinating place." He put his hand on Anatole's shoulder like a father about to dispense wise advice, and showed him to the door. "While you're here, Mr Luchenya, watch your back and don't talk to any strange women unless they're young, beautiful, look like they've got a million dollars, and they're with their mothers!"

"Knowing my luck, Mr Gover, I'd probably end up with the mother! I'm grateful for your help. I'll see you in a few days' time."

Anatole emerged from the office a few minutes later, where Harry and Jim were waiting for him. They chatted for a while, unbeknown to them that from behind a street seller Irons was avidly watching them. The three of them started to walk to take in the sights of Shanghai. With the money Harry had stolen he had bought some European clothes for each of them. Harry had equipped himself with naval clothes and a Captain's cap. He looked every inch the part with his broad frame fitting perfectly into a naval blazer. He was possessed of a huge personality, an amiable face but had a shrewd mind and was first and foremost a business man with an eye for the main chance.

In contrast Jim was a relatively simple man. He was a homespun Australian of a basic give-it-a-go nature who was, in all respects, a down to earth working man. Jim had no understanding of flowery phrases or long-winded sentences; plain, simple language was all he knew. Dark-haired, brown-eyed, with a working man's build, he got on with life, often working between ships as a docker or mill worker.

The three of them with their different backgrounds had a good camaraderie though. It was a lesson to Anatole that often people who seem to have absolutely nothing in common sometimes can become the best of friends when circumstances bring them together.

There were a lot of eyes on them that morning. They walked through markets which sold jade, food, trinkets, birds, clothes and textiles. Hot food was boiled in pans while hungry customers took small dishes away to eat the contents with chopsticks. People looked at them curiously. Westerners were normally in some sort of uniform. Only a few years before the Boxer Rebellion of 1900 had taken place, some international forces had remained with the intention of maintaining peace should another uprising take place. A few French sailors and British soldiers were dotted amongst the crowds.

From one side of a narrow street lined with market stalls a thin bespectacled Chinese man beckoned to them to take a look in his shop. It was in fact a small photographic studio. The three men went inside, more out of courtesy than anything, and looked around. Examples of the photographer's work lined the walls. It was a real eye-opener. There were portraits of various people who had passed through the city of Shanghai over the years. There were well-dressed travellers who may have been diplomats or men and women of wealth and affluence. Old sepia photographs depicting scenes of Shanghai's streets and markets adorned some shelves. Anatole bought a couple of these pictures and indicated to the owner he would like a shot of himself together with Harry and Jim. The photographer immediately set the camera up and organised the three to stand together in a fitting pose. When several shorts were taken Anatole paid the man and scribbled a note. He asked that the note together with the photographs could be sent to his sister, Mariska, care of Paul Kapsia's office in 42nd Street, New York. Hopefully Mariska would receive these and relax in the knowledge that her brother was still alive albeit a long way away.

The three of them continued their walk through the maze of streets. Following at a safe distance was Irons, keeping himself well concealed from them. Irons too had found the resources to equip himself with new clothes.

His muscular build and shaven, bald head earmarked him as an imposing figure but he had a certain look and presence about his person that others sensed. He could be a dangerous and volatile man when riled. But at that moment in time he had no malicious intent. He was following his friends more out of a protective instinct than anything.

Jim turned to Harry and smiled. "You reckon we ought to keep our heads down and there we are getting photographed."

"I think we are pretty safe," replied Harry. "What purpose would it serve for them to come after us?"

He had tempted fate with this remark. In the flash of an instant as they turned into an alleyway, they found themselves surrounded by half a dozen sinister looking men. Anatole recognised a couple of them as being crewmembers of the *High Priestess*. They were well armed with knives and cutlasses. Escape was impossible. The three of them were pushed and shoved towards another alleyway that led towards a junk on the water. Anatole had a display of fear in his eyes. He looked around desperate for some way to escape this dilemma, only to be pushed forward. They weren't simply being taken away. There was some definite unpleasant destination they were heading for. Each of them was fearing this predicament with dread.

Irons turned into the alley and looked round. Where had his friends gone? He went down the alley in panic, accidentally knocking over a stall. Then from a distance he saw a small group of Chinese sailors herding Harry, Jim and Anatole onto the junk. There were too many for Irons to take on. He looked at the situation with despair. Hiding behind a wooden pillar on the waterfront, he watched as the junk set sail. What on earth could he do? He looked around. This was a dark part of the harbour with a few junks berthed close by. Then he gripped his side. He reached down beneath his shirt and felt blood seeping through. In his haste to reach his friends, he had strained on a self made bandage he had placed across the flesh wound he had received when he had made his escape from the *High Priestess*.

Ripping his shirt he tore off a strip and wrapped it tightly around the wound. Irons was struggling though as he staggered towards a small houseboat. Almost as if on cue a swarthy man of European descent emerged. He looked at Irons in shock at the sight of blood.

"Monsieur! What has happened? The blood…"

"Help me," groaned Irons. The man immediately came across to him and helped him onto the boat. Irons had virtually collapsed when the man helped him onto a bunk. The Frenchman immediately started to attend to his wounds.

"You have been shot, my friend!" he said making a definite observation. Irons just moaned. "It has torn your flesh. Any deeper and you would be a dead man." He reached for a nearby bottle of something very strong. "Drink this. It'll ease the pain."

Irons swigged it back sharply, spluttered and coughed. "What the hell is that? Rotgut?"

The Frenchman gave him a lopsided grin. "Old Chinese remedy." He soothed Irons' injury with some ointment, tied a long strip of cloth over it several times and pulled it tight. "You must rest a while here. What are you? American? A fugitive perhaps?" He looked at Irons laid low by injury. At close examination he was clearly a Frenchman of mixed origins. There was a hint of North African strain in his appearance. "So who are you?" he asked Irons again.

"What do you think?" Irons growled in reply.

"I would say you are a fugitive from America." Irons appeared to nod slightly. "The east is full of fugitives big man. From Shanghai to Java, Saigon to Bali, there are many people wanted for criminal activity, an endless line of individuals due to spend the rest of their days wandering from port to port."

"Including you, eh, Frenchie?"

"Especially me. What is your name, American?"

Irons rolled over on the bunk and took a sip from the bottle. "Call me Irons. Who are you?"

"Michel Nessler. And I am French-Algerian. Raised in both countries and living on the back streets of Marseilles at fourteen, until I joined the Foreign Legion and fell into bad company."

"Can you go back to France?"

Michel should his head: he couldn't. There was a momentary flash of sadness in his eyes. "No. To do so would mean the guillotine or spending the rest of my days on Devil's Island. Neither is an appealing prospect."

Irons paused at this revelation and then changed the subject dramatically. "I need your help. Now."

Twelve

Once on board the junk Anatole, Harry and Jim had been tied up and put in a separate part of the boat. They were furious at being captives again. Anatole began to wish he had gone back to his hotel and waited until all the travel paperwork had been completed. The faces of the men who had captured them were instantly recognisable as familiar crewmen of the High Priestess who had survived. No one had told the trio where they were heading. Not a word of dialogue had passed between them. They sat there in silence not knowing what to say. Then the door slid open and at once they recognised the sinister face of the captain of the *High Priestess*. He looked at them for a moment as if he was trying to stare them out. Then he turned away and went back outside, closing the door behind him.

A few hours passed. Every so often a member of the crew looked in. Without any indication of where they were going it became more and more frustrating for them. Through a slit in the cabin walls Harry peered at the passing coastline.

"What can you see, Harry?" asked Jim.

"Trees. Forest. We're a long way from the city. It's getting dark too."

"Can you see any other boats?" Anatole asked fearful of the future.

Harry looked harder. "A couple of fishing boats I think. I can see lights on the coast. I've a pretty good idea of where we're going though."

Beneath them the pace of the boat began to slow to the point of drifting. This did not go unnoticed by Jim. "We're slowing down. I reckon we'll pull in somewhere." Then his eyes shone as if he had a brainwave. "Harry old mate I've got an idea." He looked at the broken wood of the junk and, lashing out with his boot, he kicked it until it splintered and a jagged piece stuck out.

"What are you doing?" Harry asked in surprise.

"Shift your fat carcass across the door. I'm going to cut the rope on the wood." Harry did as he was told, a first for him in his life, while Jim managed to manoeuvre himself into a position to rub the ropes behind his back against the wood until they frayed and were looser. He did that for about five minutes and to his amazement, he had managed to sever the knot so that the rope fell away. Quickly he began to loosen the ropes of both Harry and Anatole. "I'll leave it loose, fellas, until we're ready to make a break. Keep your nerve, you blokes. You don't know what that mob has got in mind for us."

He got back into position with the others and sat there as if they were still tied up. Harry gazed through a slit again and he could see a lantern by a small landing wharf. To his horror he could see several men in dark oriental clothes waiting there armed with rifles.

"We have problems, gentlemen," he murmured. "We have a reception waiting for us with guns."

"Oh hell fire!" snapped Jim. "How the hell do we get out of this one?"

"For a starter, make sure your ropes remain behind your back and are still loose," replied Harry. He nodded to Anatole. "Push that broken wood back. We don't want to give our captors any clues."

Anatole immediately kicked it back into place. Inside his stomach was churning. As the youngest of the three he was probably feeling the fear more than the others.

The junk slowly drifted towards the small wharf. Then it came to a sudden abrupt halt. There was silence during which Harry, Jim and Anatole sat with trepidation for a few heart-stopping moments. The silence was broken by the sound of raised voices speaking in Chinese. To the three captives they couldn't understand a single word of dialogue. Occasionally the intonations and aggressive tone seemed to suggest it was far from an even-tempered conversation. Before they could even translate a hint of the words flowing back and forwards the door opened and a crewmember with a rifle beckoned them to stand up and come towards him. He immediately went behind them and prodded each one to leave.

The Aussie was really up in Jim that night. No slouch where fisticuffs were concerned, he wanted to belt the man but he curtailed his angry instinct. There was no telling what might happen. Harry, who was also a bad opponent to cross, felt the same way. He too decided to bide his time.

Once out of the junk they walked up a ramp leading towards some rural countryside and were met with a group of armed men. One stepped forward and immediately tied blindfolds around each one so that they would not see where they were ultimately heading. They were then pushed and prodded forward by their antagonisers, one who made a habit of shouting the same Chinese word over and over again, which Anatole presumed simply to be 'move!' Every so often if one of the three captives stumbled or slowed down one of the men would fire a rifle in the air near them frightening each man to get up and move quickly. The journey up a steep hill and then down into a small plateau seemed to take about half an hour.

Then they were made to stop and their blindfolds were removed. For a moment as they adjusted their vision to adapt to the night sky, they tried to take in their surroundings. A few huts were set amidst some rural ground with oxen and goats quite nearby. A water carrier made his way past them while some women and children looked on at the spectacle of the three Westerners shepherded into the tiny village. Each of the prisoners looked at the other with bemusement. What had they been brought here for?

From around the corner of one hut the answer came. A number of men, forty or more perhaps, appeared with rifles. They were all uniformly dressed as if they were some sort of rebel group. Then Harry, Jim and Anatole were marched to a small house watched over by the men. A man with a rifle opened a door and the three were pushed inside with the door slammed behind them. Two guards stood immediately behind making it abundantly clear escape was not an option.

Inside the room a couple of joss sticks flickered. There was a scent of spices in the air and some spartan furniture dotted round the room. A side door opened and a man of a relatively ordinary presence entered. There was nothing dynamic or charismatic to set him apart from anyone in a crowd. He gazed at the three foreigners and studied their appearance from top to bottom. His face was soft and sympathetic, but this was a delusion. In reality he was a warlord with a following and in control of criminal activities that stretched from one side of the Pacific Ocean to the other.

"I speak English," he announced softly. "You are English?"

"No bloody fear, cobber!" Jim retorted. "I'm Australian."

"And I'm Dutch," came back Harry.

"I'm American," Anatole said, almost proudly. "Actually, I was born in Russia but I was brought to America as a kid."

The warlord looked at him squarely. "And you are still a kid!" he said in a soft voice. "You are a mere boy playing the part of a man." His face began to show signs of anger. In the flash of an instant the softness they had initially seen in the man had turned to one of menace. "You have all meddled in something you know nothing about! You have lost me thousands and thousands of dollars! American dollars! And much more besides! Who blew the boat up?"

"One of your own men," replied Harry.

The warlord sat down and looked at them intently. His face took on a composure of calm again. "Explain!" he said.

***

Somewhere along the coastline, another boat made its way towards the landing wharf close to the warlord's village. In the darkness it was only the glow of the moon that seemed to emit any light. The moon's reflection in the water was like a lantern guiding the vessel on its voyage. Inside Michel Nessler steered it on a course while keeping an eye open for the junk that Irons had seen earlier. Irons darted from one side to the other eagerly looking for it then he joined Michel at the helm.

"There!" he exclaimed suddenly. "That's it." He pointed to the junk berthed at the wharf.

"Are you absolutely certain?" Michel Nessler asked.

"No doubt about it, Frenchie," he replied. The nickname Frenchie was beginning to stick.

"Alright, my American friend, we will berth two coves up ahead." The French-Algerian man looked concerned. "The territory we are in is mainly controlled by Huang Cho-Li. He is a warlord dealing in opium, slavery, transportation of Chinese women to California, import of weapons and various other mercenary activities. Get the picture?"

"He's a tough customer. And we'll be lucky to survive." Nessler nodded. "What the hell have we got to lose, pal? Both of us are facing the death sentence in our home countries."

Meanwhile in the warlord's village the interrogation was still continuing. Huang Cho-Li fielded questions at the three luckless captives. It was Harry who most impressed the warlord. He stood there fearless, his composure never dropped and when he answered questions he would lean forward to answer without fear.

"We were taken prisoner. We have no interest in your affairs. The boat blew up when one of your men tried to stop us escaping." Harry stood waiting for the next question. Instead Jim seized the moment and barged in like a rampant bull.

"Listen here, mate!" he exploded. "I don't give a brass razoo what you do. Each of us were minding our own business getting plastered in bars in San Francisco, eyeing up the sheilas, and the next thing we know we're all waking up as bloody slave crew members on a bloody boat bound for China. We didn't ask to flaming well come here, sport. We couldn't even walk round Shanghai without your mob coming after us"

A glint of humour appeared in the warlord's eyes at the anger rising in Jim. The two guards stepped forward slightly, aware of the potential fight that seemed about to occur.

"The same story here, pal!" Anatole added. "And I don't like people like you telling me I'm a mere boy playing the part of a man! Who the hell are you taking us prisoner! You make me want to…"

"Steady," Harry said, grabbing Anatole's shoulder and almost in a protective manner he moved directly in front of his two friends so that he was face to face with the warlord. "What is it that you want from us?"

Huang Cho-Li moved forward and looked at him directly in the eyes, and in a quiet voice asked, "You are a captain… of your own ship?"

Harry indicated that he was. "You carry a mixed cargo of people and goods?" Harry looked hard at him. What on earth was he driving at? "And a lot of money passed your way? What is the main currency you are paid in?"

"Dollars. Pounds. Guineas. Francs. Whatever," Harry replied. He was one step ahead in thought of the warlord. "Are you looking for someone to trade for you?" Huang Cho-Li had a way of saying 'yes' or 'no' simply by flicking his eyes upwards or a tilt of the head forwards. "What is it that you want?" The silence waiting for the warlord to answer was deafening. "Ammunition? Guns? Weapons."

"Can you or your friends here supply us?" Huang Cho-Li asked.

"For what purpose?" Harry who was stern now. "To use against who?"

"That is for me to decide. I take it that you cannot provide… or will not."

Jim was getting nervous at the way the conversation was going. Behind his back he began loosening the frayed ropes around his wrists. He looked at the two guards and considered the options of taking them both on.

Then in a flurry of courage and foolishness, he turned round sharply and rushed the guards suddenly. He knocked each man out with sharp punches and head butts, grabbed their rifles tossing one across to Harry who promptly shoved the barrel in the warlord's face. Anatole immediately used the ropes they had been previously tied up with, and bound and gagged the men. Harry looked for a way out. One door at the side, from which the warlord had entered, seemed the obvious escape. He tried it, looked outside and saw a route that led into the undergrowth behind the village. Harry nodded to Anatole and Jim to move quickly while he held the rifle up at the ready. Then he moved out after them.

They ran into a forest that was illuminated by the light of the moon. Softly and quietly they paced themselves as they tried desperately to get away from the village. In the distance they could hear shouting and three shots being fired into the air which they assumed to be a signal for the warlord's men to begin the chase. Obviously the warlord and his guards had been discovered. There was absolute pandemonium as the sound of men running and shouting could be heard. Then there was the sound of bullets striking against the trees.

Harry signalled for them to duck down quickly. Hiding behind some bushes they could hear firing. Looking from side to side, the three of them were puzzled as the bullets were coming from both directions.

"What's happening? Where are the other shots coming from?" Jim asked. His face was a picture of confusion. Anatole looked bewildered. It was like being in a war zone with ammunition flying all around them. The bullets seemed to ricochet off the trees surrounding them. The noise of rifle fire went on for what seemed an interminably long time but in reality lasted mere minutes.

Their questions were answered when a figure stepped into the spotlight bathed by the moon's rays. With his newfound friend Nessler, stood the unmistakable figure of Irons. They gasped in amazement at the sight of this robust man.

"I thought he was a goner," Anatole started in a voice tinged with shock. "It's Irons!"

The three of them rose to see him. At once he indicated to them to follow him back down towards the waters edge. "This way! Move it!" While they followed him Michel Nessler reloaded and kept firing at the warlord's men. They all began to run as fast as they could. Never in their lives had each man run so fast. Harry, who carried considerable weight, found that in dangerous circumstances he was embroiled in a new energy which propelled him forward.

Nessler and Irons held their ground and kept firing while the others ran down towards the coast. Then a clearing came into view. They were just about to dive into the water when a further shock greeted them. A United States Navy gunboat was clearly visible and several boats of sailors armed with rifles approached the shore. The sailors disembarked quickly and ran towards them.

"Are you the civilians who were kidnapped?" one of them asked.

"How in the hell did you find out?" Anatole exclaimed in amazement.

The sailor didn't have time to explain. "Get to those boats quickly." No sooner had the three of them boarded the rowboats, than Jim looked round and asked, "Where's Irons and his mate?"

They were nowhere to be seen. The US sailors who had gone ashore continued to wage a conflict for a long time. Anatole, Jim and Harry boarded the United States Navy vessel. They watched from the safety of the boat as the warlord's men were effectively rounded up and their activities curtailed. They never quite knew all the details of what had happened that night. It was only a few days later when Anatole went along to the American consulate that he learned more.

***

Mr Gover sat opposite Anatole in the American consulate and looked at him like a stern school teacher about to admonish a wayward pupil. There was a spark of latent humour about him though and some sympathy for the position he found himself in. A secretary came into the room with a try on which neatly placed was a pot of coffee, milk, sugar and two cups.

"Help yourself, son," said Mr Gover. Anatole gratefully poured them both a cup. It had been some time since he had tasted good American coffee.

"Tastes good. The first decent cup I've had since San Francisco," he smiled.

"Well, Mr Luchenya," Bob Gover continued, "through no fault of your own you and your friends were inadvertently caught up in an international incident. Trouble seems to come looking for you. At the docks someone sent a message to us here at the consulate that three Europeans had been taken by force aboard a junk. Any idea who sent that message?"

"Not a clue, sir." Anatole was genuinely baffled.

"The US Navy has a permanent presence in these waters. Peace keeping, you understand? Well as soon as we got the message another one was relayed to the ship Pennsylvania. They were heading down the coast and heard the shooting. Quite a show young fellow. How you and your friends made an escape was the stuff of boys tales. You said two other men were with you?"

He was referring to Nessler and Irons. "They came ashore as we were escaping and held the warlords men off while we were taken to safety. When we were aboard the Navy vessel they had disappeared."

"Hmmm. That's a mystery," Mr Gover mused. "I've had to make a full report of everything that's happened. One account I have from the men on the *High Priestess* is that an American was shot and went overboard in Shanghai harbour during the scuffle that ended with the boat being blown up. Can you tell me about the man?"

"Not a lot. He was quiet. Kept himself to himself. He was as broad as a redwood tree. He saved our lives when we were trying to escape. The man had guts. I'll say that for him."

"One of the crewmembers who was kidnapped recognised him. He was wanted for murder in California." Anatole knew this from conversations he had with Harry but listened attentively. "He was a triple murderer. Normally I wouldn't discuss the private details of anyone but since he's passed on – to describe it gently – I am curious to know how much you got to know him."

"Like I said," reiterated Anatole, "he kept himself to himself."

Mr Gover adjusted his spectacles and looked directly at him. "His real name is Pete Slattery. Back in the 1880s, he was widowed and he and his teenage son bought a cattle property and land in mid-California. However, a crooked lawyer called Ian Stephenson, a nasty man, who was acting as a vendor for the sale, decided to resell the land on false documents and after he had done this, he embezzled the money and disappeared. The other family, also a widower with two sons, came to the land and insisted to

Slattery that it was their property now. He told them to go back to their own lawyers and see the sheriff to see if they could track down the crook."

"He had a bad deal then?" Anatole said stating the obvious.

"Very bad!" retorted Mr Gover. "When Mr Slattery was away in town the man and his two sons returned to the property, shot all his livestock, shot his son and a hired hand, who managed to escape and was a witness to what happened. Then they burnt the homestead down."

Anatole was aghast. "What a terrible thing to happen."

"And then," Mr Gover continued, "understandably Pete Slattery went mad. He went looking for the three of them and shot them dead. He's been on the run for seventeen years before he was captured in San Francisco, and then escaped only to be kidnapped and to die in Shanghai harbour. Some story, eh, Mr Luchenya?"

"Like something out of an old Wild West story," Anatole murmured.

"If there's nothing you can add I shall send a message to the police force in San Francisco telling them of Mr Slattery's passing."

"Nothing at all," replied Anatole.

For a moment Mr Gover looked at Anatole with a look of doubt in his face and then he reached in a drawer. "I have your travel documentation available for you." He handed it across to Anatole. "Have you worked out what you'll do next?"

"Yes sir. I intend to take a boat to Australia, sign on as a deck hand, and then return home."

Mr Gover stood up and Anatole rose from his chair. He gave him a warm handshake. "If there's anything you need call by. Good luck, son."

"Thank you," Anatole said and he walked out of the office to enjoy the taste of freedom again. This time he had no fear of retribution. His life so far had encompassed experiences that had toughened him up. He walked along the bustling streets of Shanghai proudly and with an air of confidence. Now that he was no longer a prisoner or restricted in his freedom of movement, the mysterious city of Shanghai suddenly revealed itself to be a place of beautiful buildings and pleasant avenues.

Thirteen

Jim Cope and Harry Van Der Gruys were waiting for Anatole. They had arranged to meet up at the Bund and make arrangements for their outward voyages. While walking from the American consulate, Anatole stopped to look at the panorama of the harbour. It was full of all types of seagoing vessels: yachts, steamboats, clippers, junks, barges and windjammers. The sky above was a clean mid blue with sunlight streaming across the American settlement with the Episcopal Mission Church standing out from the other traditional buildings that stretched across to the mouth of Hong Kou Creek.

A Chinese artist sat at the water's edge painstakingly reproducing in an almost photographic style a perfect image of the scene. Anatole watched with fascination at the Artist's brush strokes and colourisation of each detail. By his side there were many pictures of this scene and others of Shanghai's city streets. The artist, realising Anatole was behind him turned his head, revealing a friendly face of an elderly man with thin horn-rimmed spectacles and smiled at him. Each painting was a composition of a mixture of oils. Anatole looked with admiration at each one and considered how much he would like to buy some as a souvenir of his sojourn in China. The artist, realising he had a potential buyer hovering by him, indicated on his fingers how much each one cost. Anatole reached into his pocket and to his surprise found himself walking away with two of these paintings which one day he would hang on a wall hopefully in an American home of his own.

On the way to the Bund he kept stealing a glance at the pictures. He was impressed by the style of the artist and in his mind he began to contemplate if a talent for painting was God-given or could it possibly be developed?

Arriving at the Bund Harry and Jim were sitting at an open-air café looking out across the waters. Anatole strode into the café carrying the two pictures he had acquired. He looked different that day. From a European tailor, in the central district, Anatole had bought a cream suit and Panama hat, and looked more like a visiting businessman than the scruffy dishevelled sailor he had arrived as. Anatole sat down with his friends and ordered tea.

"We've tracked down Irons," Harry said in a low whisper, quickly looking from side to side to see if anyone was listening.

"I've got some good news for him," Anatole was quick to respond. The others looked at him sharply. "The American consulate have declared that he died. They're going to report back to the police in San Francisco that he was shot dead when we made our escape from the High Priestess."

"We found Irons down at the Harbour," said Jim. "We've found a boat we can sign on. Irons is staying on a houseboat with a French-Algerian man he befriended. He was trying to get aboard as a crewmember on a rusty old vessel called the *Kota Java*. It's our ticket out of here. Are you game?"

"Where's it headed?" asked Anatole.

"Quite a voyage," Jim replied with a smile. "Down to Hong Kong, Saigon, Singapore, Java and then to Australia. From there we will all take different ships to whatever destination we want to go to. You and I could board another boat to Sydney and then you can get one there back to San Francisco."

Anatole sipped his tea and thought it over for a minute. "That's fine by me. Let's do it then."

***

A horse-drawn carriage took them to where the ship *Kota Java* was berthed. They passed it and went down a bit further where there were some houseboats. Harry pointed one out to the driver and the carriage stopped beside it. The three men got out and approached the boat. Harry told them to stay outside while he entered. Then after a minute or so he came out and nodded for them to go inside.

The interior of the boat was bare and spartanly furnished with a couple of bunk beds, chairs and tables. Irons rose clearly bandaged around his midriff. Michel Nessler stood by with his hands on his hips and acknowledged the men with a smile.

"Lucky for you we came when we did," Nessler said. "If you wonder where the American Navy came from I told a yank sailor on the waterfront that there had been a kidnapping. My friend, Irons, here followed you three men through the town."

"I got shot in the side," Irons explained. "Another bullet grazed my forehead. The next thing I knew I was in the harbour. I was rescued by a fisherman and then our buddy here came to my rescue again. When I collapsed at the dock the boat took you away up river."

Harry, as always, took the lead in every situation. "You are dead now, my friend. Officially, declared so by the American consulate no less. Isn't that right, Anatole?"

"Absolutely! One of our crewmates recognised you from California. You are Pete Slattery. That is your real name?" Irons looked grave and serious. Anatole continued quietly and cautiously, unaware of how Irons might react, "The consulate told me the full story of how a crooked lawyer stitched you up over a land deal and sold your property illegally to another family who tried to force you out. Then went ahead and… you know the rest. So do we now."

"Technically, you're free, mate," added Jim.

"I'll never be free," growled Irons. "They murdered my son, destroyed everything I had and I got my retribution but it will up here in my conscience!" He tapped his head. "Up here swirling around in my memory what they did! I committed murder! I'll never be free of that. Do you know what it's like to run away, crawl and hide for years? It's like being a prey for the hunter. I just want to take a boat and go somewhere and live a civilised life like a human being. I'll be haunted by it 'til the day I die! Before all that happened I was a peaceful homesteader minding my own business taking care of my boy after my wife died. Then I'm running and running…"

For a moment it looked as if Irons was about to break down in tears. It was inconceivable that this hard man who appeared to be totally devoid of feelings could show such a completely different side of his character.

"Don't you want to go back to America? To live anonymously now, perhaps? I have means of providing you with a new identity." Harry was quite sincere in what he was saying.

"I'll decide where I'll go," Irons said sharply.

"Sign on with us on the *Kota Java* then," Harry said. I've already met the captain. His name is Nick Collis-George. I'll explain that you were brought here against your will." Irons nodded in agreement and then he looked at his friend Nessler. "What about your friend here?"

"Count me in, monsieur. I need a new identity too. My hope is to get to Africa… eventually."

***

In the few days before the *Kota Java* left Shanghai, Anatole spent his time making sketches of the local populous and street scenes. In the back of his mind was the thought that perhaps when he returned to New York he could embark on a second career as an Artist. One day he would reproduce the images on to a large canvas and paint with oils. Anatole surprised himself by showing real talent as a draughtsman. He was proud mostly of his sketches of a Chinese carpenter, engineer and labourer, on the waterfront. Pictures of market stalls and street scenes made up his portfolio, which he could show round to his friends back home.

The day arrived when they set sail from Shanghai. The skipper of the *Kota Java*, Nick Collis-George was of a similar nature to Harry. The two men got on famously. Nick was a broad, muscular man with red hair, a matching beard and eyes that sparkled with amusement. A gregarious character with a booming laugh, he was a Scotsman from Glasgow who had first gone to sea as a boy harpooner on whale boats before joining the merchant fleet. Something of a rogue with a jovial nature by his own admission he was not averse to making a crafty quid if it meant taking a contraband cargo of 'mysterious strangers' to places with strange sounding names.

It was time for the little group to take their final farewell look at the developing city of Shanghai. A hundred years later Shanghai would become one of the economic powerhouses of the twenty-first century. Few would have ever predicted it then. Anatole, Jim Cope, Harry Van Der Gruys, Irons and Michel Nessler stood at the rail inhaling all the sights and sounds of this exotic place. Beneath them they could feel the throbbing of the engines. The *Kota Java* was leaving. From behind them they heard the booming voice of Captain Collis-George.

"Take your last look, gentlemen, and then join the rest of the crew. There's plenty of work to be done."

This time as a volunteer sailor Anatole thought to himself that he and his friends would be paid a decent wage for their efforts. Furthermore he thought to himself there would be good food served up in the mess. The voyage now would be like a pleasure cruise compared to the one that had brought him to China. At least that was what he thought. But Collis-George, however jovial on the surface he appeared to be, was a strict disciplinarian when it came to the running of his ship. He made sure that he got his money's worth from each man in terms of the work that they did.

Irons found himself working in the engine room. A practical man by nature who, in his previous life before being a rancher, had done all sorts of heavy duty labouring. It was thought by Collis-George he could handle the pulsating engines. Irons had worked in a mine, a foundry and steel works, hence the nickname. In the engine room it was a permanently perspiration soaked oily atmosphere with temperatures that left him drained at the end of each day.

Nessler who never spoke of his past as a legionnaire and a member of a gang of crooks in Marseilles was given a job in the hold of the ship. Below decks he loaded and unloaded cargo at every port they docked.

Collis-George who was a perceptive person when it came to judging a person at first glance considered Nessler a shady character. He decided the best way to keep him in line was to give him permanently physically exhausting labouring jobs in the hold that rendered him worn out every day. All Nessler wanted to do when he had finished his days work was to sink back a bottle of beer, go to sleep and dream of the beautiful girls he had once known in his youth in Paris and Marseilles.

Nick Collis-George had great respect for Harry Van Der Gruys. Both men had similar traits of character. The old saying that familiarity breeds contempt did not apply in this case. Two larger than life personalities worked well on all aspects of steering a ship in terms of navigation, keeping one step ahead of judging the variable weather conditions that were so diverse in oriental seas, and making sure that every crew member on this cargo laden boat were active. Frequently, the two men laughed together and were also serious about what they were doing. To them a life at sea, foreign parts, establishing contacts wherever they sailed together, with the asides of mystery and romance that were occasionally thrown up, gave them exciting memories to cherish in future years.

Jim Cope and Anatole worked on every task possible that Collis-

George found them. He didn't spare them in any respect and made sure they earned their passage to their chosen destination. A very hard taskmaster Collis-George had Jim and Anatole working wherever necessary. They helped out in the hold with Nessler, cleaned out cabins, washed bed linen and clothes, served on tables, waited on the few paying passengers on this cargo boat, swabbed the decks, assisted in the sweltering hellish depths of the engine room, and painted parts of the boat that showed considerable signs of wear. There was never a minute on board the *Kota Java* when a job of work couldn't be found for them.

The surprising thing for Anatole was that he rose to every task and enjoyed it. Apart from helping his late father, Viktor, at home with occasional tailoring jobs the only real work he had done since leaving the orphanage was a brief stint as a dock labourer. His whole life had been in the make-believe world of show business as a dancer and singer. Not for one moment had Anatole ever considered any other career option. He had found show business a compulsion, an addiction, intoxicating like that forbidden first drink that would tip an alcoholic into an unending binge with an uncertain future. Being shanghaied in San Francisco and all the other events that had taken place since then, had brought him down hard with a bump.

Each port they docked at was a thrill to behold. The crown colony of Hong Kong had its own indefinable magic. Sailing into the harbour, Mount Victoria soared high in the back ground, beneath which areas like Kowloon and Aberdeen were teeming with life and bustle. Along the busy streets Chinese and European residents hurried along to their destinations. Rickshaws and horse-drawn carriages passed by. The British influence was to be seen everywhere. Army officers wearing monocles strode along the streets, often exuding arrogance, a self assumed superiority, and an unattractive patrician air. How different they seemed to the ordinary folk Anatole had remembered from his brief childhood sojourn in Yorkshire.

On the harbour there were Royal Navy vessels, ships belonging to the American fleet, Dutch and French merchant boats, sampans, junks, cargo boats, trader barges and yachts. It was a mass of colour and spectacle. Hong Kong was exciting and bedazzling. There were so many scenes that entranced Anatole. He was quick to sketch pictures and get photographs taken that were duly despatched to his sister, Mariska, care of Paul Kapsia's office in New York. This was a routine he followed at every exotic port that the *Kota Java* docked at.

Anatole often thought of Mariska. He wondered how his sister had coped without him. In fact he seriously misunderstood how strong and independent she had become in the few months since they had been apart. Back in San Francisco Mariska carried on performing at night as a dancer and by day she worked hard in a dress shop that specialised in wedding clothes. Through the manageress, Mrs Gale, she had organised to provide some of the local theatres with costumes for shows. Business was in fact taking off. Mariska smiled often at the thought she wasn't a tailors daughter for nothing. Her father, Viktor, if he was watching from some celestial paradise, would surely be proud of her.

***

The camaraderie aboard the *Kota Java* was developing too. The mixed bunch of shipmates in their separation from the mainstream of real life had a good rapport with each other. There was a recognition amongst them that in any other place or time they would have had little in common, but here together there was at times a candid honesty about their situations.

Captain Nick Collis-George, himself a rogue mariner, sat with them often in the crew's dining room. One night he voluntarily began speaking about himself. Van Der Gruys regarded their nightly conversations in this room as something of a confessional centre. On the basis that none of them would ever see the other again once the voyage had ended in Australia, they talked a lot about their past lives. All, that is, except Michel Nessler who spoke of his years in poverty in Paris, but never of his time in the Foreign Legion or a period of his life when he frequented 'Les Gangsters' in Marseilles. This time remained a mystery to his crewmates.

"Well we're a mixed group, are we not?" Nick stated, pouring each of them a glass of rum. "I've done this run for a wee while now and it never fails to thrill me. Aye, it's a long way and a long time since I was a wee lad sitting on the banks of the Clyde looking at the ships coming and going. I went to sea on a whaler when I was in my teens you know and since then I've worked on vessels of every kind. I shall never forget seeing a whale for the first time. A truly magnificent creature rising from the depths. What about you, Mr Van Der Gruys? What is your story? Do you have a tale to tell?

"Do you mean, Captain Collis-George, that I am something of a rogue?" Van Der Gruys asked in a laughing voice. "I could be arrested for some of the things I have done to make money. The more daring the escapade the more money I've made. I've smuggled goods of every sort. Travelled with villains and princes. Maybe my career choice doesn't appeal to everyone but I wouldn't have it any other way. I live an interesting, sometimes dangerous, life."

"You two are lucky," came the surprised response from Irons, who was normally a strong silent figure, perceived by others as a cold unemotional man. "My life's work began in coal mines and steel works and hot, blasting places, so hot all the colour of your face drained away... and your arms and legs ached all over. That was when I decided to buy a homestead." He paused for a moment to sip his rum and his face was grave as if he was being swamped by bad memories. "Who knows how things work out? I was an ordinary man from the Mid-West, a widower trying to do my best for my boy... a fine boy who would have grown up to be an even finer man. Then... Then it was all taken away from me."

There was silence in the room. Irons wasn't the sort of man it was easy to show sympathy for. He was too strong a character and gave the impression of being someone who didn't need anyone. It was Jim Cope who managed to supply the right comment to ease the situation.

"Your loss makes me think how lucky I am to have a family near Melbourne to go back to. My old man loves to spin a yarn about his life in the bush as a young bloke. I don't think I will ever moan about his spinning the bull again. He's always on about when he knew Ned Kelly."

"Who's Ned Kelly?" Anatole asked innocently.

"Ned Kelly! You've never heard of Ned Kelly?" Jim Cope was genuinely amazed. "Oh mate, Ned Kelly was a bush ranger. He was like Billy the Kid in the States Ned Kelly was the son of an Irish convict who went on a bit of a rampage in Victoria. My old man remembers him well."

"My old man was a fisherman," Collis-George added to the conversation. "He used to sail along the coast of northwestern Scotland fishing in ice cold seas. I always wanted to go to sea but I longed for tropical warm seas. Aye, and I've certainly found them."

"My old man was a church-going wheelwright," Irons butted in.

"Straight as a ramrod. Honest as the day is long. Good working class stock. I never imagined…" He broke off in mid-conversation. "What's the next port of call?"

"Manila in the Philippines," Collis-George replied. "The ladies in Manila are quite an eyeful."

"I know. I have been there," said Nessler with a wicked grin.

"And then on to the delights of Saigon… and a few other ports before we make it to Australia," said Collis-George.

"Where do you live?" The normally quiet Nessler asked. "Are you a resident of the orient now or do you go home to ice cold Scotland?"

"I've not lived in Scotland for a wee while now. And it's not always ice cold, Frenchie. Out on the highlands, the moors and the lochs, the air is fresh and clear. When the sun breaks through it enhances the colours of the countryside, the old fortresses and the granite buildings. I was a poor Glasgow boy though living on the pittance my father made from his earnings as a Fisherman. There was a wider world out there for me. I've shivered on ice cold seas when I was on the whaling boats and I've sweltered on the tankers and rustbuckets and tramp steamers from Bombay to Brisbane. My home is in Sydney now from where I've sailed often but my regular sailing route is between the southern ports of the antipodes and the ports of Japan and Hong Kong."

"You're quiet about your life, Mr Nessler," Anatole said.

"I have much to be quiet about," he retorted with a smile.

"We're good listeners, pal," Anatole responded. "We can afford to be honest with each other. Once this voyage is over we'll all be going to different destinations never to see the other again. Everyone has a past."

Nessler was suddenly on the defensive. "There are some things people with a past never talk about. The orient was a good place to run away to."

"Didn't mean to be intrusive," Anatole said, realising he might have overstepped the mark.

Nessler just nodded and smiled. For the rest of the voyage he remained secretive about his life. The truth about his life was quite startling. In his mid-forties Nessler was a dishevelled, shifty man, yet in a strange way he was a charismatic person. His father had been a Parisian watchmaker who had gone to Algeria and married a local woman. They had then returned to Paris where their two children, Michel and Joelle, had been born. The father died at a young age after being knocked down by a coach and horses. Almost immediately the mother and the two children returned to Algeria. Until Nessler's teens the family lived fairly happily but he had a restless spirit and at the age of fourteen he worked his way to Marseilles on a fishing boat There he lived rough on the streets before becoming a gang member involved in various criminal activities. In the roughhouse atmosphere of the underworld in Marseilles there had been a confrontation between two rival gangs over territory which resulted in the deaths of several men. Nessler was recognised by an over enthusiastic gendarme and was immediately incriminated. But he was too fast for the police. Using an alias, Michel Nessler joined the French Foreign Legion, and soon found himself stationed in Corsica before beginning a long stint in North Africa. Ten years later when he took his discharge from the Legion, he didn't return to France. Instead he made his way across to Alexandria where he boarded a boat for the Orient. For years he drifted from one port to the other. Now his destination was unclear. He half committed himself to the thought of living in Algeria. Time would only tell.

Each member of their little group had something of a past. No man was untainted or had led a normal conventional life. Perhaps that was what made it all the more interesting.

The *Kota Java* continued on its voyage southwards. Anatole sketched as many interesting scenes as he could. In Manila in the Philippines he drew scenes of a palm-fringed coast and a beautiful woman who walked barefoot along the beaches, like a silhouette in the distance. He did the same in Saigon where the city's architecture had a strong French flavour about them. Every port of call that followed fascinated Anatole. Still only twenty years of age he marvelled at the sights of Singapore, Java, the temples and paddy fields of Bali, and the frontier atmosphere of Port Moresby in Papua New Guinea where steamy jungles and mountains seemed only a few moments away.

The night before the *Kota Java* was due to dock in Palmerston the Captain, Nick Collis-George, decided to hold a ceilidh. A proud travelling Scotsman who had been away from his home country for many years, Collis-George still held its old traditions dear. This was to be a farewell party to his crew and he persuaded them, or perhaps rather ordered them, to wear kilts. At first Irons looked at Collis-George with an expression that bordered on amazement and then for the first time ever since he had been shanghaied in San Francisco he broke out into a smile. The idea of a roughneck Frenchman like Nessler wearing a kilt also seemed highly improbable. But after a bit of friendly persuasion, he too decided to join in on the festivities.

On the night of the ceilidh, Irons, Nessler, Anatole, Jim Cope, Harry Van Der Gruys and Nick Collis-George all came on the deck together. It was a sparkling sight. The men in kilts and plaid were a dazzling sight. Jim leaned across to Anatole and said, "Geez if only we had a few sheilas to impress. We're a handsome bunch of drongos dressed like this!"

True. Kilts and plaid made each obviously a very masculine man, just a little bit more manly. Especially Irons and Harry, who looked like the idealised highland warriors who in another generation might have fought alongside Rob Roy. The crew made up of Chinese and other nationalities had somehow learned to play the bagpipes. Not only could they play but the sounds merged together like a professional orchestra playing a concert at a major venue. Everyone looked happy. The atmosphere was vibrant and colourful. They sang 'Loch Lomond' and drank Scotch whisky. When they went to toast each other as the glasses clinked a ships photographer duly recorded the scene. The pipes played 'Auld Lang Syne' in a spellbinding way that entranced the audience. For a moment it seemed as if tears were not that far away. Not even Nessler and Irons, the hardest, cold-hearted men aboard, seemed exempt from the emotion of such a finale.

In the silence that followed each man looked at their fellow crewman. After the adventures in the Pacific and China, it really was the end of a colourful chapter in each of their lives.

Harry raised a glass to them. "Well, gentlemen, this has been quite an experience. We may never meet again and I bid you good tidings. Tomorrow we part in Palmerston where we will go to our separate destinations."

***

It was a sweltering hot day when the boat arrived at Palmerston which would one day be known as Darwin in the Northern Territory, Australia. How amazing to be in this relatively great brown land. There was something so awe inspiring about being in this country that in the year of 1905 was an unknown quantity few people knew much about or was rarely featured in international news.

The little group comprising Nick Collis-George, Irons, Nessler, Van Der Gruys, Jim and Anatole stood at the rail of the boat looking out at the shabby wooden port buildings of Palmerston while a heat haze shimmered in the distance. Beyond these buildings lay the beating heart of Australia and endless miles of desert and bush. The country was so vast with few settlements between Palmerton and Adelaide on the southern coast. The next stop for Anatole was still to be determined. His ultimate aim was to get back to San Francisco and to be reunited with Mariska.

They disembarked from the *Kota Java* and agreed to meet up in a bar in Fanny Bay once they had made arrangements for their onwards journeys. The heat was unbearable. Walking through the streets was as if they were pushing against a sea of humidity. Anatole and Jim stopped every so often to down a cold beer, to fortify themselves against the onslaught of the heat. Finally Anatole could stand it no longer and retired to a saloon bar resembling something from the Wild West, while Jim braved the elements to find a shipping office. While he was waiting, he was joined by his fellow travellers. There they sunk beer after beer, and so hot was it that day, that none of them got drunk. They stayed sober much to their own surprise.

Anatole listened to the broad Australian accents in the bar. Apart from Jim Cope he had never met an Australian before. It was fascinating listening to their conversations. The men spoke of cattle drives and auctions, the bush and the usual topics of women, who were always referred to as 'sheilas'. Anatole considered for a moment that the women would have to be made of strong stuff to survive in this harsh environment.

A while later Jim returned carrying with him a list of sailings. He walked into the bar, removed his broad rimmed hat, mopped his brow and luxuriated beneath a ceiling fan swishing backwards and forwards.

"Strewth, it's sweltering out there," he said cooling off rapidly. Van Der Gruys handed him a glass of beer which he managed to down in virtually one gulp. "My word, I needed that!" He placed the sailing lists on the table. "There you go, fellows. Cast a glance over that. Bloke in the shipping office tells me boats to Sydney are booked up for a few weeks. Plenty of boats going on to Ceylon and India, through the Suez to Europe, apparently short on crew too. So sign up for a voyage if you need to."

"That will do for me," Nessler said with a smile. Irons nodded in agreement.

"And me too," Van Der Gruys agreed.

"I'll wait here," said Collis-George. "I've got some business to attend to. I'll get a boat to Sydney when I can, which leaves you two gentlemen. He looked at Jim and Anatole. "What are you going to do?"

Jim rubbed his chin. "Well I got talking to some bloke up the road and he told me about a cattle drive to the gulf country. From there we could get a boat down to Sydney and Anatole can get a vessel across to San Francisco." He looked at Anatole. "What do you reckon mate? Do you want to sign on?"

"A cattle drive?" Anatole seemed to be thinking hard. "To the…"

"The gulf country," Jim added. "We can get a boat from Cooktown to Sydney and then the world's your oyster. You can catch a boat there to San Francisco." Anatole seemed to be having difficulty making up his mind. Finally, Jim pushed him. "Go on, mate, it's an adventure."

"I have never ridden a horse," Anatole protested.

"Oh mate! Nothing to it! You'll have a sore backside for a while!"

"Okay," Anatole agreed. "Let's do it. What's a sore backside after all we've been through?"

Fourteen

For anyone visiting Palmerston in 1905 it would have been hard for them to visualise that some day in the future when it was renamed Darwin, it would become a major trading port and a place of strategic importance. At the top end of Australia it was a town in its infancy, still developing, still spreading and on the edge of desert and bush land that still contained mysteries yet to be discovered.

At the dock it was a time of farewells. Van Der Gruys, Irons and Nessler had all signed on a westward-bound vessel which was headed in the general direction of Europe. Collis-George, Anatole and Jim shock hands with their departing friends and watched them board a passenger steamer where they would work their passage.

Each of the three men leaving had a different life to lead. Van Der Gruys would return to Amsterdam, and hopefully another ship, where he would resume his captaincy. It would be different stories for Irons and Nessler. Both men on the run would begin new lives with identities that would never indicate who they were originally.

Michel Nessler stayed on the boat until it docked in Colombo, Ceylon. From there, he caught a boat to Reunion Island in the Indian Ocean. He lived the life of an itinerant beachcomber for a few years, often in a state of penury, but with a certain amount of peace and solitude. Occasionally he would take a Creole girl as his lover and share the comforts they would offer him. Eventually he grew restless and knew he wanted to move on. One day a Madagascan fishing boat docked in St Denis. The boat was bound for the Somali basin and eventually Aden, which suited Nessler as it provided him with the perfect jumping off point for his eventual return to the places he knew so well in North Africa. In Aden Nessler left the boat and set off walking on his own, hitching lifts on carts pulled by oxen, jumping trains and joining nomadic tribes and camel trains that made their way across the endless expanse of the Sahara Desert from Egypt, through Libya, and finally to Algeria.

By the time Michel Nessler arrived he was no longer a Westernised traveller but had reverted to his origins wearing typical Arab clothing and becoming an obscure figure in the souks and bazaars of Algiers. After years away he was just another stranger in the crowd. To his surprise he found his mother still alive in her eighties, and his sister happily married to a businessman who promptly offered him a job in a textile factory. Nessler never returned to France. He was haunted by the possibility that even after twenty years a gendarme might recognise him, arrest him, try him in a French court, find him guilty of a crime he didn't commit and sentence him to death by the guillotine.

In the circumstances it seemed that Nessler's lack of faith in the French judicial system may well have been justified. In 1894 a captain in the French Army called Alfred Dreyfus had been found guilty of treason. It was alleged that he had been passing secrets to the Germans, a charge he strenuously denied. A secret court martial sentenced Dreyfus to solitary confinement for life on Devil's Island. However, the writer Emile Zola mounted a campaign to free Dreyfus convinced that the evidence against him had been forged. Eventually freed in the following year of 1906 Dreyfus was officially cleared, reinstated as a major, and awarded the Legion of Honour.

Sometimes Nessler would go to the top of the factory and look out at the minarets and turrets, and the flat white buildings of Algiers. His eyes would twinkle and he would smile with delight at how far he had come. He was free of his life he lived with the secrets of his own personal turmoil. The shady establishment he had frequented in his gangster years known as Café Tangier would one day become a venue for resistance fighters in the Second World War. Nessler never returned to his old life and instead became an unlikely but hardworking businessman.

***

The story of Irons, or Pete Slattery as he was really known, took on many twists and turns. He disembarked from the boat at Naples in Southern Italy. He had visited a local vineyard and suddenly acquired a fascination for the development of wine. Although he couldn't speak a single word of Italian he found himself a job there and got to work amongst the towering grapevines and distilleries. It was a huge change from the life he had once wanted to lead as a peaceful homesteader in mid California yet, for the first time in years, he found a new challenge. There was something alluring, intoxicating, even thrilling about working in the wine industry. For a man who had worked in his younger years in the sweltering soup hot atmospheres of blast furnaces and irons works, to be out in the sun picking grapes while his Italian co-workers sang as they toiled was like a taste of heaven. The hardness in his soul, and the coldness in his heart, began to dissipate. He began to feel something he hadn't felt for a long time, a sense of happiness at what he was doing, and a feeling of useful purposefulness.

Irons was sharp though. He realised that in every life a state of happiness is often only temporal. Almost certainly something will happen that disrupts those moments of near nirvana. The rumbles of a war in Europe were beginning to gain momentum. Much of Europe eyed Kaiser Wilhelm's rearmament programme in Germany with suspicion. Irons decided to move to the vineyards of Northern France. After working there for six years he took a boat to Brazil.

Rio de Janeiro was a breathtaking city with an undercurrent mixture of sensuality and excitement. Irons was by nature a lonely man, but he did not feel that way in Rio. With his new identity that he had travelled on since he left China, he felt a different person from the haunted man he had been. Here in Rio his strong physical build drew many admiring looks from the Carioca women. He had let his hair grow back again and, with an almost permanent tan, his appearance suggested he might have been a wealthy American visitor. For a time he worked as an odd job man around the beaches of Copacabana and Ipanema. He loved the easy-going nature of the city in which the inhabitants seemed to almost drift along in the sunny climes with the enchanting backdrop of Sugar Loaf mountain, and Mount Corcovado in the distance. Irons did some building work in Petropolis high in the hills above Rio. One of its attractions was the Summer Palace belonging to the Brazilian Royal Family. But it was a visit to the fishing village of Itacuruca that impressed him. Taking a saveiro for a sail on the peaceful waters of Sepetiba Bay he fell in love with the nearby banana and coconut plantations that proliferated along the coast.

It was there he found work, rising to become a plantation overseer and eventually a manager. He stayed there for many years, making his home in Brazil.

Some years later locals in a Californian town housing a large graveyard were surprised to see flowers and a message placed on the headstone of Peter Slattery junior. The message came from a loving father who missed his son always and mourned for the loss of a decent young man. It was signed by Peter Slattery, a proud father. No one saw him face to face. One graveyard attendant remembered seeing a smartly dressed man in a broad-rimmed hat visiting the grave. Every few years he came but Irons was always elusive.

***

Jim Cope and Anatole joined the cattle drive at a junction just outside Palmerston. The other drovers were tough, leathery, hard as granite men, who for the most part were the strong silent types of legend. Robin Pacholke, the head drover, was tall and rangy with a sardonic sense of humour. In his late thirties, he sat on his horse while occasionally squinting his eyes from beneath his battered drover's hat and giving orders to the small band of people busily preparing for the drive ahead. He caught sight of Jim and Anatole coming towards them. Behind him there was a massive herd of cattle, a covered wagon containing stores and belongings, a motley band of drovers including two Aboriginal jackeroos who rode their horses feverishly.

Robint Pacholke shook hands with Anatole and Jim. He then introduced them to a couple of other drovers. "Welcome boys," he said amiable. "Meet my mates. This is Colin Palmer and Tony Rasmussen"

Colin pinched his hat and smiled. He was dark-haired and dark-eyed. On the surface he seemed easy-going but he had ambitions to one day own and run his own cattle station. Tony was about five-five of slight build and a genial, sunny nature. There were a number of other drovers they were introduced to, and some who introduced themselves in time. Doug Evans was a chain-smoking, fearless rider who tackled any job without question. Peter Reynolds was a true man of the bush. In his late forties he had spent his entire life in the outback. Over four decades of life the ever-present sun had bleached his hair, wrinkled and dried his skin to the extent it was like leather. Terry Clout was a bully and a fat-necked oaf who seemed to take a perverse pleasure in running down the humbler of the jackeroos. He would fight with anyone given the chance, but as with most bullies, once someone fought back he would turn away and look for another victim.

The cattle drive was to take them all the way to the abattoirs of Longreach, Winton, Charleville and the coastal ports of the Gulf country. Once at each of these places, the meat would supply the cities of Cairns, Brisbane, Sydney and southwards to Melbourne and Adelaide. Also much of it at the seaboard harbours would be transported for export across the world.

Anatole and Jim were part of this great cattle drive. It was hard not to be enthralled by the spectacle of it all. It was early in the morning when the drovers waited for a sign from their leader Robin Pacholke to start the drive. He called out to Colin Palmer.

"Col! Over hear!" Col rode up quickly. "How are you on tallying?"

The leathery-faced Col wiped his brow. It may have been early in the day but it was still quite warm. "I'm pretty accurate. Reckon I can tally within a hundred or so."

"Off you go then," said Rob. "Give me a figure approximately and then we're on our way."

There was a wide boundary gate that when opened would allow the mob of steers to begin the onward trek to the Gulf country of Northern Queensland. Col Palmer rode around the mob getting a good idea of the size of the herd. The rest of the drovers and the cook in the wagonette sat in silence while the count took place. A short while later Palmer rode back with a broad grin on his face.

"Seven hundred and fifty-three, boss."

"Yeah. That's about it," Rob affirmed. "Let's take them to the Gulf. Open the gates and let the brutes out, and start cracking the whips!"

Palmer rode off quickly and he and the boss opened the gates. The cattle began to stream through. Robin Pacholke raised his hat and waved it to the rest of the men to start moving forward. The result was instantaneous. Dust flared up in the air as the cattle drive began. Jim Cope pulled a bandana around his face to protect him from the red dust which rose like a cloud from the onrush of the cattle. Anatole dug his boots into the stirrups and the horse moved forward. The very long journey had begun. The thought went through his mind. Where would this experience take him?

The cattle drive had begun in earnest. In just a few minutes it had become a swirl of movement and noise. Anatole could not believe how in his own short life span he had managed to fit in so much. It was as if some extreme forces of an unseen nature had picked him and thrown him from country to country, experience to experience. The thought occurred to him. When he eventually returned to America who on earth would believe his story?

Australia had never figured much in his thoughts at all. After all a young boy who had come from Russia to America with his parents and sister at an early age had considered that a vast journey. Now that he was in the bush of the huge brown land down under in sweltering temperatures, it was a completely new learning experience for him. His fellow drovers were of mixed Irish, Scottish and English stock. They were basic men who kept themselves to themselves, spoke mainly about their work, and little else. This suited Anatole, who didn't want to talk of his life as a dancer. That time, although only recent in the light of all the events of the past year, seemed a long time ago,

The scenery as the drive progressed rarely changed. Hot big distances, the smoke from the embers of camp fires, and the endless restlessness of the herd, seemed to sum up what the cattle drive was really all about. It was hard, gruelling, perspiration soaked work at times, attempting to keep the herd together but with the stony isolation of the bush there was a kind of peace that was hard to define. Beneath a wide deep blue sky of panoramic proportions, it was as if the band of drovers and the cattle were the only living creatures in the world.

***

Far away in San Francisco, Mariska was in her dressing room preparing for the evening show at the Phoenix. Tonight she was doing a solo spot with some particularly spectacular dancing involved and as a result she was on edge with excitement. There was a knock on the door. Quickly she tidied herself up, checked her appearance in the mirror and opened the door. To her amazement she found herself looking at the smiling, reassuring face of a kind man whose friendship she valued immensely. It was Jess Reubens.

"Hi honey," he said with a sparkling smile. "Got a hug for your old friend Jess?"

Mariska stood up and embraced him. "Jess, this is such a surprise. I thought you were back east. What are you doing here?"

"Sit down, young lady," he said happily. She did as she was told and looked up into the warm face of Jess. "I am the bearer of good tidings. It's about your brother, Nat." Mariska looked apprehensive. "He's fine, Mary."

"He's alive!" Jess nodded that he was. "Where is he?"

"It's a long story. When are you due on stage?"

"Oh gosh!" Mariska exclaimed. "In about ten minutes. I am doing a solo spot."

Jess looked at her approvingly. "Well, honey, you had better go out and knock 'em wild. I'll watch from the wings. When you come off stage, we'll have a meal and I'll tell you the story. Mary, it's one hell of a tale too."

The audience at the Phoenix were always tough and hard to please with no respect or sensitivity to the acts that performed there. Mariska knew this but she had no qualms about her appearances. She had to eat and besides in her dreams it was all good rehearsal for the better venues that one day she would perform at.

Jess watched from the wings as Mariska performed that night. What a skilful entertainer she had become. With a group of dancers behind her Mariska took the stage by storm. Her voice was strong now. She had the power to move an audience to tears or laughter. Jess watched with fascination as he marvelled at how his young protégé had developed. There are some people who just gravitate to the limelight and once there they positively glow. Mariska was one such person.

She could sing a Stephen Foster song and make it her own, or she could get her voice around an English Music Hall ditty. When Mariska was at her peak, her eyes sparkled with humour and warmth. It was when she danced that Mariska bedazzled the audience. Jess could not resist it. Knowing every move she was making he danced out of the wings, on to the stage, and ripped the show right open. Jess and Mariska together were spectacular together. The normally cynical, hard nosed and sometimes jeering audience were on their feet cheering and applauding. It had been one of the best nights Mariska had known on stage.

***

"And that's the full story," Jess was saying to Mariska. "Your brother got taken to China and now he's on his way back. Eventually."

They sat across a table from each other in one of San Francisco's loveliest restaurants. In the background a string quartet played a soft romantic melody.

"It's quite a story, Jess."

"Anatole sent letters and pictures to Paul Kapsia's office in New York. He sent me across to take you home, if you want to go." Jess looked at her wondering if she was ready to leave. Mariska really had matured and become quite independent.

"Where is he now?" Mariska asked.

"Somewhere in the Pacific," he replied, only knowing that Anatole had sent letters from Hong Kong and was last known to be heading south on a steamer. "Do you want to go back home? Paul Kapsia's got a new show in preparation with a big part for you if you want it?" Mariska seemed to be considering her options. "Or do you want to stay? To wait here for Anatole."

She thought about it for a moment. "I'll wait, Jess."

"So be it then. I guess I'll stick around for a while too."

Fifteen

Surprisingly to Anatole, after the sweltering heat during the day, the nights in the bush were sometimes still and cold. At night the stars glittered like Christmas lights. He lay back on his blanket roll and gazed up at the sky. The camp was quiet beneath the purple blackness of the outback sky. The herd were motionless. Smoking embers from the campfire streamed upwards. Most of the drovers were asleep in makeshift beds on the ground. Those that weren't luxuriated in the peace of it all taking short drags on their cigarettes or sipping beer from a bottle.

A smile crossed his face as he realised that every inch this cattle drive moved was closer and closer to the time he would board a vessel in Sydney and sail across the Pacific to San Francisco where he would be hopefully reunited with his sister, Mariska. What a time he had! How could one man be swept along in life by a mixture of circumstances, fate and opportunity? The old saying 'you can have your plans but the Gods laugh' was never more true. How can anyone ever make plans in life without due thought to the unexpected accidents, obstacles or diversions that all go to ensure one certainty – there will always be unpredictability.

Anatole had not expected Australia to be so rugged and sunburnt. He could not make comparison to anywhere he had been. It was brash, brazen but still a fledgling nation, little known to the outside world. Like a younger America, perhaps, although waiting for an influx of migration in 1906 for new settlements and trade to be established.

All along the drive from Palmerston, which would one day be renamed Darwin, the land had been undulating and dusty. At the end of each day, Anatole found his clothes covered in red dust. If he took a wash at the rare billabong he found it in his hair and all over his body.

The drovers were a mixed lot with language liberally laced with swear words and phrases he had never heard before. Strangely enough he did not take offence. Different country. Different accent. Different dialect. Different dialogue. Except for Terry Clout, who seemed to go out of his way to look for fights that he lost, the rest of the drovers were just hard faced working men who did what they did because it was more than a job. To all extents the cattle, the bush, the environment and their language was a way of life.

Laying there that night contemplating the future, Anatole looked towards a ridge a short way off. To his surprise there was a silhouetted figure virtually blending into the blackness who stood alone and erect. Anatole blinked his eyes and stared hard at this lone man who looked like a sentry alert for anything unexpected. He turned to Tony Rasmussen who lay back sipping beer.

"Tony... Tony." The man stirred. Anatole pointed to the figure. "There's someone watching us."

Tony smiled. "Nah, he's not watching us. It's an Abo. He's asleep."

Anatole looked up in surprise at the lone Aborigine who stood resting on a spear. He stood up and then began walking towards the ridge. Jim and Tony followed him. At night the rocks and crevices took on a luminous effect. They walked for a while until they came close to the Aborigine. Before they got that far they stopped at a flat level. In front of them there were a group of Aborigines sitting around chanting something. Anatole went to take a step forward to have a closer look but Tony put his hand on his shoulder and nodded his head to indicate he should go no further.

Almost at that very instant the Aborigines seemed to spring up and start dancing in a spellbinding but eerie fashion. During his travels across America Anatole had seen various Native American tribes such as the Sioux, the Mohawks and the Apaches perform their various dance rituals and ceremonies. He had never seen anything like this before.

"Do you know what this is mate?" Tony whispered. "This is a corroboree."

"What is that?" Anatole asked in a quiet hushed voice.

"Traditional Aboriginal dance. Better not let them see us watching too long."

Anatole watched for a while. He was fascinated by the ritual and chanting. The markings on their ebony skin seemed something mysterious, a secret known only to them. He cast his eyes around the small camp. Several of them sat watching. One man with a long white beard seemed of a lighter shade to the rest of them. His skin did not appear to be the natural complexion of an Aborigine. It was more like that of a white man's who had spent years in the sun. Almost as if he had realised that Anatole was watching him with curiosity he raised his eyes towards him. They were the bloodshot eyes of an older man. His face was lined and tanned but there was no doubt he was unmistakeably a man of anglo-saxon origin.

"C'mon, mate," Jim reminded him, and the three of them moved back to the drover's campsite. Sleep came in fitful bursts and the early morning sun soon rose. The cook served from the waggonette. There was a tasty bread called Damper that was made from flour and water over a fire. He didn't have a strong appetite at that time of the day. All he really wanted was a strong mug of tea.

In the mornings the men always moved cautiously and quietly. Cattle stampedes could start at the slightest thing. Cutlery falling on a tin plate. A broken branch. Once panic overwhelmed the cattle the herd would scatter in different directions. During the course of the drive this happened several times and the tumult and chaos took ages to control.

Before they moved off Anatole looked up at the ridge. The lone Aborigine had gone. He walked back to where the corroboree had taken place. The group of Aborigines were at rest now. He took a long gaze at them and then turned around to find himself facing the bearded man. They both took a long silent look at each other. It was Anatole who broke the silence.

"Who are you?" he asked in a low voice. The man just continued to stand in silence but there was a momentary flash in his eye as if he had realised his cover had been blown. "Do you understand me?" The man looked towards the tribe then back to Anatole. He appeared to be looking directly into Anatole's eyes.

"You're a white man, aren't you?" Anatole asked again quietly. After yet another silence he asked finally. "You don't belong here, do you?"

To his amazement the man spoke in response. "No. I am a white man. Living with an Aboriginal tribe."

"Why? Where do you come from? What are you doing here?"

"I am an Englishman," he replied. "From Cornwall, forty years ago and more. Transported to Australia for my crimes of robbery... and worse... a convict... of foul nature and temper... handy with a knife, and dangerous to all who crossed me." Anatole was stunned. He had known that English convicts had been transported. He hadn't realised there were some still alive in 1906. "I am Edwin Hyde from Cambourne in the West Country. Now I am of no particular place. I roam with the tribe."

"This place is so barren... so empty. Why does an Englishman – a Cornishman – roam with Aborigines?"

"Because I'm free. There are no chains to hold me. No guards to beat and whip me. No enforced starvation. I fled from the south and took sail to the north. Then I walked across the wilderness. My clothes ragged. My spirits at rock bottom. I was found near naked and burnt by the sun." He pointed at the tribe. "They were my saviour. I have no need of city life or the false fruits of civilisation. They showed me how when it is cold you sit and freeze. When it is warm you soak the heat. I learned how to find moisture and water for drink where others would perish. I took up their ways and loved their women. I ate the food we hunted. No foreman or inspector inflicts humiliation and orders on me. I am my own man. A stranger amongst strangers, in a harsh and unyielding wilderness. Here I am not Edwin Hyde of Cambourne, Cornwall, but a white refugee adopted by a tribe who lives according to the rules he alone subscribes to, and not the tainted justice of an Old Bailey judge and jury seeking to be vindictive to a poor misguided fool turned violent and thieving by the fates that be so cruel to battling folk. The young man that I once was and the old man that stands before you are two different souls with no resemblance to what was and what is. An angry roughneck of a man that I was has evolved into a man of aching bones and a rainbow maze of memories. I answer only to myself and my conscience."

There was something almost biblical about the way Edwin Hyde recounted his tale. His speech was peppered with phrases and an almost poetic way of speaking that belonged to a man of another age and era. It was as if he was an ancient figure resurrected in the modern age of the early years of the twentieth century but still set in the ways of a bygone age.

"You will stay with this tribe for the rest of your days?" Anatole asked, already assuming the answer.

"I have no reason to wish otherwise."

"Not even to see Cornwall again?"

"Cornwall!" Edwin Hyde smiled at the mention of it. "My young soul belongs there to the ruggedness of rocks crushed by wild surging waves and fierce winds blowing across the moors. The places of a childhood lost like an island shrouded in rain mist never to be returned to. I could never tread the moors as I did. But I went to London thieving and pick pocketing trying to beat hunger and working for a pittance for tyrannical, despotic men who were mean and miserly, and had no compassion for the common man. In time I became a felon and the judge said transportation to Botany Bay."

"And now you're a man of this rugged place? An exile?"

"Not an exile," Edwin replied. "I'm a free soul. I must go… to my family."

Anatole looked at him fascinated by Edwin's history. He watched as he walked away to rejoin the other members of the tribe. Anatole walked back to his own camp. The drovers were packing their blanket rolls and cutlery into the wagonettes.

"You speak the same language as the black fella's eh?" Terry Clout said with a sardonic smile. "I never thought you were up to much the first time I saw you'se. I always thought you were a bit of a cissy drongo. You'se has never been a working man in your life."

Jim Cope at once saw red. "Why you… low life bastard, Clout. My mate Anatole has got more sense than you've got in that fat backside of yours."

"Yeah… what are you going to do about it?" Clout came back, spoiling for a fight. A silence fell across the camp as the others realised a fight was in the making. Robin Pacholke and Colin Palmer descended from their horses in a bid to stop the brawl from beginning. They were too slow.

Anatole walked up to Clout whose response was to stick his chest out. His momentary resistance was met by a fist from Anatole who surprised himself by sending a punch down on Clout's chin which amazed him more than anybody.

"Strewth! Where did you learn a knockout punch like that?" Jim asked in half admiration – half in awe.

"The Bronx," Anatole replied, remembering the fight between Jack Clancy and Slugs Mahoney.

Robin Pacholke intervened quickly. "When you gentlemen have finished your tea break we'd like to get moving." He stared at Terry Clout, who was getting up rubbing his chin. "As for you, another fight and you'll be out, Clout! Understand! Now get on your horse and move it!"

The drive continued and it took several weeks to cover the distance to the coast. For the entire journey, Anatole found himself developing an affinity with his horse. *Trust your horse. Rely on your horse.* This was the advice from the grizzled old time stockman Robin Pacholke and Colin Palmer, who carried authority without imposing it too much. It was hard not to admire their characteristics of leadership. By mere demonstration in the manner in which they rode their horses and controlled the cattle especially the straying beasts who tried to break away from the herd, the two men set an example that others followed.

Fondness for their horses was apparent. They may have ridden them hard but at the end of each day every horse was looked after as if it was a prize winner in the races in Melbourne and Sydney. Their hooves were checked by a drover who doubled up as a blacksmith and vet. The harnesses were removed and the horses enjoyed their leisure by rolling in the dusty sand. It was not uncommon and often heartwarming to see the toughest of drovers stroking and talking to their horses.

Doug Evans and Peter Reynolds constantly checked the route and were given the job of assessing the water supplies and resources. They reported back to Robin Pacholke and Colin Palmer, keeping them informed of the trail which the cattle should take. One thing Anatole could remember is that the drovers kept talking about the cattle route being taken close to the rabbit proof fence.

The route took them past sandy ridges, dried out creeks and billabongs, across the mulga and seemingly impassable plains. Some days the trail would pass by a remote township where the local pub would experience boom time as the thirsty drovers assuaged their thirst. Sure enough there would be at least one fight when Terry Clout picked another one only to end up being flung out of the pub. Across saltbush plains and stark desolate land with gleaming white ghost gums, the cattle drive came within sight of the coast. A short time later the trail came to an end at a railhead where the cattle would be distributed to the main cities of the south.

Along the way Anatole had drawn sketches of many of the scenes he had encountered. The herd at rest. A drover and his horse. From memory he had drawn a picture of the Aboriginal corroboree. He could not forget the face of Edwin Hyde, the convict from Cornwall who had become an Aborigine. His face of streaked grey wispy hair, sharp features yet red-streaked eyes dulled by the passing of age and squinting because of the fierce Antipodean sun, and a long white beard. In all of his travels so far Edwin Hyde was the most fascinating of characters he had ever met.

While Anatole and Jim Cope celebrated the end of the drive in Cooktown, far away in the purple-black night of the bush, Edwin Hyde roamed with the other tribe members. When it came time to rest, Edwin sat at the edge of a billabong and thought of his encounter with Anatole and the conversation they had. He did not live in the past. Nor did he mourn for a lost and perhaps wasted youth. But something had been reawakened within him. He closed his eyes and in reflection he thought of the wild and rocky West Country. The Cornish accent he was so familiar with came into his memory in the guise of people he had once known: the rugged fishermen, the blacksmith, the furrier, ordinary villagers. He smiled at the memory of it all and lay back peacefully. He thought of the stern Old Bailey judge and the punishment of transportation he was given that did not fit the crime he had committed. That was nearly fifty years before when he had come over in a boatload filled with cut-throats and villains. His survival was a miracle. How many of those other convicts could have endured and lived long lives against the odds? Edwin Hyde had. That was his proudest achievement.

In Cooktown Anatole and Jim boarded a steamer bound for Sydney. This really would be the final farewell for the two friends. Before Anatole returned to America they would enjoy all the fruits of this burgeoning metropolis which one day would become one of the great cities of the world. The steamer *SS Prince George* sailed from Cooktown down the eastern seaboard of Australia with short stops in Cairns, Brisbane, Port Macquarie, until one day they entered the glorious heads of Sydney Harbour between Manly and Watsons Bay, where many a tea clipper had sailed.

The steamer entered Sydney on a blustery warm day with the bluest of skies and bright sunshine, enhancing the green of the harbour bank sides. Through the harbour the *SS Prince George* passed the suburbs of Vaucluse, Neilsen Park, Rose Bay, Double Bay, Rushcutters Bay and Woolloomooloo before arriving at Circular Quay. Anatole and Jim looked out from the top deck at the city that lay before them. It was a flourishing settlement, growing and developing, but it gave no hint to the magnificence that would come when a huge span of bridge would link both North Shore and the opposite side. One day the bridge would be affectionately known as the 'Coathanger'. Until then ferryboats flickered between the two shores bringing commuting passengers into the city for work and leisure. Nor did the Fort Macquarie tram depot at Bennelong Point suggest that this was the possible venue in which a sparkling but oddly shaped and controversial building, the Sydney Opera House, would open to great fanfare in 1973. Anatole and Jim saw before them on that gloriously sunny day the sister city of San Francisco, young, bustling and bursting with expectation of things to come.

They found lodgings in the North Shore suburb of Mosman Bay where they soaked up the sun at nearby Balmoral Beach. The days were spent swimming at beaches like Manly, Nielsen Park, Bondi and Dee Why, where two young men like Anatole and Jim, both in need of sex and passion, chased the suntanned girls at every opportunity. At night they drank in pubs in the Rocks district and the city bars.

Anatole took a shine to a dazzling dark-haired beauty called Sarah Lunn who worked as a waitress in Mosman. Her brown eyes at times could flash degrees of sensitivity or deep anger as the mood took her, but in Sarah Anatole found the deep passion he had yearned for and when he held her in his arms and kissed her he felt love and lust surging through him. They would undress each other slowly and then Anatole would pick her up naked and carry her to the bedroom where they would entwine themselves and make love with a fervour and a red hot excitement until they would sink into each others arms as the early morning rays of sunshine flickered through the windows illuminating their soft skin. Passion was such a beautiful thing yet it could be fiery and breathtaking.

Sarah and Anatole would walk hand in hand across the beaches of Sydney and dive into the sparkling blue sea as the surf crashed down on them. When she was soaking wet and glistening Sarah, looked extraordinarily beautiful – a girl whose figure and bearing were intoxicating to men, but none more so than Anatole. When they kissed, her soft lips pressed and teased, invigorating so much that Anatole didn't want to stop. When they were in bed and Anatole plunged inside of her, Sarah's face lit up with excitement and thrills, and as they completed their journey of love, she would let out a sigh, close her eyes in ecstasy and smile so warmly.

Just as quickly, as it had begun Anatole's brief romance came to an end without hard feelings, as it was time to take the boat to San Francisco. The young city of Sydney had proved to be the best place he could have ever chosen for rest and relaxation, passion and romance. He would never forget it for the rest of his life. From the time he had been shanghaied in San Francisco to the day of his departure from Sydney it had been an extraordinary journey. Jim Cope came to see Anatole off at Circular Quay as he boarded the *SS Morning Sun* which would take him on the North bound route to San Francisco.

"Well, mate, we've met a lot of characters and been to many places," Jim said. "We won't lack for stories to tell any grandchildren we might have."

"Who would believe it?" Anatole replied with a broad smile.

"This is really it then. Just one thing left for me to do. That's to wish you a long and happy life."

"You too, Jim." Anatole shook hands with Jim and walked up the gangplank. He wanted to say more but somehow he felt choked inside and couldn't find the words. Jim felt the same way too. They had both found a friendship borne of the strangest circumstances. It was the type of friendship found in battle or a chance meeting at some foreign outpost where two people of entirely different backgrounds forged a kinship that could never have been possible in normal day-to-day life.

The last memory Anatole had of Jim was of him standing on Circular Quay waving his broad rim hat as the *SS Morning Sun* pulled away. They would never meet again. Jim returned to his family at Ballarat in Victoria and didn't go to sea again. He took up a position as a sheep shearer at a nearby property where he worked until the outbreak of the Great War in 1914.

He became an infantryman and in 1915; he sailed with other Australian forces to Gallipoli in the Dardanelles. There the soldiers fought against the Turks, who were Germany's allies. Jim went over the top with his fellow infantrymen only to be mown down by Turkish machine gunfire in the interminable slaughter that followed on a blood soaked battlefield. He lost his life fighting for the mother country alongside the lives of so many young men and in doing so became part of the Anzac Legend.

***

The *SS Morning Sun* sailed out into the wide blue Pacific Ocean. A brief day's stopover followed in Auckland, New Zealand. This handsome leafy city with Mount Eden in the background looked more like an English county town and compared to the outgoing open feeling of its near neighbour Sydney, Auckland was quiet and introverted. From there the ship sailed north to the exotic islands of Samoa.

This place had a particular fascination for Anatole. When Anatole was a child on the first leg of the Luchenya's journey from Russia to America, in order to pay for the fare to New York the family had worked in Yorkshire for a while. His dear mother, Ekaterina, had taught Anatole how to speak and read English. On freezing cold nights she had read him the stories of Robert Louis Stevenson such as *Kidnapped* and *Treasure Island*. In his childhood he had been thrilled by such adventure stories.

Robert Louis Stevenson had spent the last years of his short life in Samoa at a grand house called Vailama in the shadow of Mount Vaea. He was only forty-four years old when he died. The local Samoans called him Tusitala, which meant 'Teller of Tales'. While the *SS Morning Sun* was berthed in the port of Apia, Anatole paid a visit to the long terraced house called Vailama. He gazed at it in awe, spellbound that he was actually here looking at the house of the illustrious author who had created such characters as Dr Jekyll, Long John Silver and Alan Breck.

At Vailama Stevenson had lived with his wife Fanny Osbourne and her sons from a previous marriage to a civil war soldier. There on the long terrace the Feast of the Loving Heart had taken place when Stevenson had dined with Samoan Chieftans and their families. It felt simply magical to be there in the presence of the spirit of this giant of literature. From there it was a short walk to Mount Vaea where Anatole followed the winding, twisting mountain path to the top where Stevenson's tomb was positioned midway between some trees swaying in the breeze. *Home is the hunter, home from the hill,* thought Anatole, recalling the words of one of Stevenson's poems. The port of Apia lay far below, where steamers, schooners, tugs and ships were berthed.

What a paradise this lush green island was with big friendly muscular men and beautiful, smiling well-rounded women. There were long golden beaches where the warm Pacific waters rolled in. Palms with all kinds of tropical fruit fringed every lane and valley. Waterfalls with creamy water cascaded in deep ravines. It would have been so easy to stay here forever thought Anatole. Surely outside of heaven this place must have been the closest to the real thing.

From this glorious place the *SS Morning Sun* sailed north to Hawaii.

A few days were spent there and Anatole concluded that the Pacific Isles were the most beautiful places on earth. Finally the boat left for its ultimate destination, the United States of America. Anatole was excited at the prospect of returning to America. He had been gone from there for the best part of a year during which time he had seen more of the world than he had ever planned to in his entire life.

Then early one morning the clouds lifted suddenly and the sun's rays streamed out over a port that looked welcoming and hospitable. Anatole smiled great beams of happiness. He was overjoyed. Once more he was home again in a land that he had wondered if he would ever see again during the course of his recent adventures.

He was home in the land of the free, on board a ship entering one of the great cities of the Pacific, San Francisco. How great it was to see that rumbustious, noisy, spectacular town again. Anatole couldn't wait to get ashore.

Sixteen

San Francisco was bustling on that morning in 1906 when Anatole disembarked from the *SS Morning Sun*. The streets were full of horse-drawn carriages. The ladies in their hats and suits never looked so attractive. Businessmen smoking cigars read the latest newspapers as they walked, glancing quickly at their pocket watches anxiously as if they were late for some important company meeting. Policemen in helmets guided the traffic and kept watch for the occasional villain. Otherwise, it was business as usual in downtown San Francisco.

How good it was to be back on American soil. Anatole clad in a broad hat and good suit felt quite the man about town. There is nothing like that first homecoming. To return to one's homeland worldly wise and full of experiences that he would hopefully regale to any interested listener. He strode through the town confident and bursting with enthusiasm.

First of all he had to find a hotel to stay in and then he would travel on to New York where he naturally assumed Mariska would have returned to. Nearing Market Street Anatole stopped to buy a paper and he was surprised to see the Great Caruso was appearing there. Caruso. The greatest opera singer in the world was appearing in San Francisco. What he would give to see this star, who had risen to celestial heights in the opera world from the back streets of Naples.

Anatole decided he wouldn't spend the next few nights in a rough place for fear of being shanghaied again. He chose a first-rate hotel at the corner of Powell and Market Street and booked himself in. After all he was a man of the world now. He had been to China, Hong Kong, Australia, Samoa, Hawaii and had lived to tell the tale.

In the hotel lobby Anatole watched the comings and goings of the people. He couldn't explain it but he felt different. He was not the young naïve man who had been forcibly kidnapped and taken away on the high

INTENTS

seas. To all extents and purposes, he felt sophisticated and as if he could hold his own in any company, anywhere, rich or poor.

By jingo, he thought to himself, how he would love to go to see the concert Caruso was appearing in. He went to the reception desk and pressed the bell. A tall man came to the desk.

"Hey buddy," Anatole asked without pretension, "do you know where I could get a ticket to see the *Great Caruso*?"

The man appeared to be looking down his nose at Anatole, who responded by staring directly into his eyes and moving slightly forward, hinting a touch of aggression that indicated he was very much his equal.

"Well as a matter of fact, sir," the desk manager said, slightly startled at Anatole's forward manner, "the hotel has reserved a few for its guests."

"A wise decision," Anatole agreed. "Okay, how much is the starting price?"

Surely this young whippersnapper couldn't afford it? The snooty desk manager misjudged Anatole very badly. For all the years he had worked in hotels he was obviously no judge of character.

"They are rather expensive. Can you afford…?"

"How much, bud?"

"Well. Sixty dollars."

"Sixty bucks, eh?" There was a pause. Anatole put a cigar in his mouth and reached into his pocket. "Give us two, buddy."

The desk manager looked on in amazement as Anatole reeled off one hundred and twenty dollars in succession. He handed Anatole two tickets from behind the desk.

"You did say two tickets, didn't you, sir?" he asked.

"Sure," replied Anatole, putting the tickets inside his jacket. "I've got my eye on that dame sitting alone over there. She'll go with me."

The desk manager glanced quickly at an attractive young woman on the other side of the lobby. Anatole strode off confidently towards her. He approached her with a huge smile.

"Hullo lady," Anatole greeted her. "How would you like to see the *Great Caruso*?"

***

On the warm spring evening of 17th April 1906 Enrico Caruso played the role of Don Jose in Bizet's Carmen at the Grand Opera House in San

Francisco. At first glance, Caruso did not only appear to be a handsome Italian of legend, but he also cut a fine dash. He had that indefinable quality great performers have in spades, which distinguishes them from the main stream. Magnetism. Charisma. Stage presence. Call it whatever. When he sang it was the purest, richest voice the audience had ever heard. It was a spellbinding performance that would set the precedent for the opera singers to come. Opera was like a fine wine. Rich in flavour and tone.

Anatole could hardly believe his luck in being there. Especially his luck in finding a new acquaintance in the lobby of his hotel. The girl was called Jane who was from Squam Lake in New Hampshire and had been visiting her Aunt in San Francisco. She was as surprised as anyone to be there watching Caruso. They were seated amongst high society in furs and diamonds. This was the life. Anatole smiled to himself. Here he was with a beautiful young woman sitting amongst the big shots watching Caruso, the greatest opera singer in the world. He was only twenty years of age but he had been a singer and dancer, and travelled everywhere.

There would be few nights as memorable as this at the Grand Opera House for many reasons. Caruso took standing ovation after ovation as the San Franciscans applauded this legendary figure. Anatole and Jane stood up amongst the affluent and the millionaires to lead the applause. When Caruso left the theatre that night with his entourage he was greeted with a blaze of flashbulbs and photographers. He was staying in the swish Palace Hotel in Market Street, only a stone's throw from the one Anatole was staying at.

"How about a candlelit supper, Jane?" Anatole suggested. "Don't worry I'll behave like a gent and get you a cab home. What do you say?"

"Sure. Sounds good to me."

***

They found an Italian restaurant which was by a coincidence the same one Jess Reubens and Mariska dined at from time to time. There they sat amongst many of the diners who had also been to see Caruso that night. These nights are so rare Anatole thought to himself. This night would be a golden memory he would surely remember all his life. He was right but not for the reasons he thought. Something unpredictable was about to hit

San Francisco in a matter of hours. He looked across at Jane. She was a well-dressed nineteen-year-old New Hampshire girl, wholesome and blonde, and as traditionally American as mother's home made apple pie.

"Have you ever been to New Hampshire Anatole?" she asked.

"New Hampshire? No. I've been everywhere else. It sounds pretty."

"It is. I come from a small town near Squam Lake on one side and Lake Winnipesaukee on the other. I think it's one of America's beauties."

"So are you, honey," said Anatole making her blush, "and I've seen ladies all over the world!"

"You're a well travelled man," Jane said quickly, changing the subject and trying to get him to enlarge on their initial conversation. At this point, directly behind Anatole, she saw a man come into the restaurant, weaving his way between the customers. He was smartly dressed with a sense of *joie de vivre* but he had obviously 'had a few' and was in search of a table. Anatole was unaware of the man behind him, who was eavesdropping into the conversation.

"Sure I'm well travelled. I've been across the States as a singer and dancer with my sister in a double act. Then I've been to China, Hong Kong, the Far East, New Guinea, down to Australia and—"

"Did you say Australia, young man?" the handsome stranger asked.

"I did as a matter of fact to my girlfriend here," Anatole replied without rudeness.

"Ah young man, I am soon to leave this fine city to take a boat there for a theatrical tour. I heard you say you were a singer and dancer. I am a thespian you know. I've acted in Shakespeare and Oscar Wilde plays."

"You don't say. Are you somebody important?"

"I'm going to be famous, young man! I'm going to be as famous as Caruso!" he responded adamantly.

"Okay, fellow. What's your name? I'll put it in my book for people I once met who are going to be famous."

"My name is John Barrymore. Remember the name." He went on his way and a waiter showed him to a table.

"John Barrymore, eh?" Anatole repeated.

At the end of the evening Anatole behaved exactly as he said he would. Like a true gentleman he showed Jane to a horse-drawn cab and paid the driver her fare in advance to take her to her aunt's home in the Haight-Ashbury district.

"Look me up in New Hampshire if you get up that way." She handed him a note with her address on. "Here's where I live. Thank you for a wonderful evening."

"Thank you, Jane." He looked at the note with Jane Galyer's address on and watched her depart. "Honey," he said under his breath. "If I ever get to New Hampshire I'll marry you."

He felt so happy that night. Apart from being back on American soil for a year he had seen Caruso at the Grand Opera House and fallen instantly in love with a girl called Jane. He was so happy and lightheaded he could have sworn the earth moved beneath him. Then he made his way back to the hotel happy in the thought that tomorrow he would be heading back to New York, hopefully to have a happy reunion with his sister, Mariska, who he was completely unaware had been living and working in San Francisco, waiting for his own safe return.

***

Mariska could not sleep that night. She was so buoyed up by her performance at the Phoenix Theatre and yet so tired from holding a day job at the costumiers; she found it impossible to relax. There was something in the atmosphere that night which seemed to keep her awake. Horses in a nearby stable kept whinnying and neighing all night. The early morning birds seemed to be making louder noises than ever before. There was also the feel of movement like a rhythm or a beat in the air as if a drum was being played. She was sure she felt dizzy. It was five in the early morning and her bed felt for a moment like it was on a sea. The walls vibrated a little bit. Mariska rose up quickly to dress and look out of the window. There was a sudden knocking on the door. She opened it to find Jess Reubens there who was staying at an apartment down the hall from her.

"Something bad is happening, Mary. The walls are vibrating and the telegraph poles are shaking."

"What the hell is it, Jess?"

"Honey, I may be knocking on and feeling the strain of the years, but I'd say it's some sort of tremor."

"You mean an earthquake!"

"Get your stuff together, Mary, and let's get the hell out of here!"

At the market's district, Police Sergeant Jurgen Zielinski was doing his early morning rounds around the city when he noticed cattle in a corral were behaving strangely. At five in the morning the city was busy waking up. Fruit store holders were getting their daily produce set up for the day's trade. Fishermen were bringing their catch to the stalls. Lights were going on all over the city as San Franciscans woke to a new day. But there was something different about it. The extra sensory perception of the animals hearing picked up vibrations in the atmosphere. The cattle were uneasy, so too were the horses tied up in the livery stables as their owners tried to gently ease them out to their carriages or carts.

Zielinski smiled at the stallholders but as he looked around him he too felt nervous. In the half-dark half-light of the early morning he suddenly felt the ground below him shake.

"What's happening here boys?" he bellowed, and in mere seconds he saw nearby buildings shake. The stallholders looked up in amazement as entire blocks of offices began to shake. In the commotion a telegraph pole broke away from its foundations and toppled over across the road.

"Earthquake!" yelled Zielinski. "Take care of yourselves. Now." At once the men began to move off. To their horror the main road literally split open right down the centre leaving a gap of four to five feet between the cracks. Zielinski sprung into action and ran around the stalls.

"Move it! Now, everybody! The city's having an earthquake. Get out now." He cupped his hands and yelled directions. "This way! Hurry! We don't know when the next one will spring up."

No sooner had he said that his eyes froze in horror as a building began to slide and shatter with screaming occupants inside. There were half dressed people gazing out of the windows as the building disintegrated. One man jumped. Another fell to his death. In minutes it was as if the city was self destructing. There were people taking to the streets and running and running. Horses broke out from the livery stables and stampeded aimlessly in all directions. So did cattle in the corrals. Soon the streets were filled with frightened people and livestock all running to save their lives. Telegraph poles fell. Offices and houses all over began to topple and slide as if they were on the sea rather than supposedly firm ground. Mayhem broke out all over San Francisco.

**

Mariska and Jess ran from their apartments in Nob Hill. There was nowhere that seemed safe. In San Francisco, a city of hills and twisting roads, if they could make for the higher ground, they might find some sort of sanctuary from the devils work that was taking effect.

Jess, who was not a young man by any stretch of the imagination and well into his fifties, pulled Mariska by the hand as they ran through the suburbs. More and more people joined them as they ran, who knows where, to find some safety. Roads cracked. Buildings fell. A Fire Service vehicle went storming past. Several times they narrowly missed being hit by falling bricks and escaped horses racing past.

It was terrifying. A road split and Mariska lost her footing. It was only Jess's pull of her hand that prevented her from falling into an abyss where the road had cracked and pulled back to reveal a fall of about fourteen feet. He pulled her up and she sighed with relief.

"You'll live, young lady," Jess said trying to be good-humoured. "You've got a show. Paul's counting on you being in back in New York. Let's go!"

They continued to run with the ever-growing throng of people who fled from their homes and apartments. Policemen joined in to try and control the crowds but their cries to the people to calm down were met with a stampede who couldn't have cared less for law and order at such a crucial time as this, and some of them were knocked over and crushed by the fleeing masses.

***

Anatole wasn't hanging around either. This wild and wonderful city of San Francisco had seen him shanghaied to China. Now it was putting on an earthquake beneath him! He wondered for a moment if he had done something to upset it! All this and after seeing Caruso perform and meeting John Barrymore who would one day become a Hollywood star!

He looked on in horror as buildings slid into each other with a definite loss of life in each of them. It was a terrifying spectacle. The ground shook and trembled. Splits in the road appeared everywhere without warning. Cracks appeared in buildings giving notice that the foundations were about to crumble and moments later cement, bricks, glass, furniture and people were ejected in a cloud of dust and smoke onto the street.

Anatole could not bear to look at it. He wanted to run away as fast as his legs would carry him, away from the spectacle of horror that was happening around him. All he knew was that he wanted to find somewhere safe that was not being affected. What can a man do in such circumstances but keep on running? The fear drove him to run faster than an Olympic athlete. Several times he narrowly missed death. A chimney came crashing down seconds after he had passed the spot. A stampeding group of horses charged in front of him. A fire service vehicle shot out from a side street. Fire hydrants sprayed up unexpected geysers of water. The road split in two then closed just as suddenly forcing him to change direction suddenly, only to see a building come down in front of him caking him in cement and smoke. Heavens to Betsy, where was he to go? He climbed over the rubble of what had been a derelict lot apparently with no loss of life and continued on his way to find the higher reaches of the city.

All over San Francisco roads were split and buildings damaged – even City Hall. At the Palace Hotel a pyjama-clad Caruso, still basking in the adoration of his audience at the Grand Opera House, reluctantly left his room with the entourage that always accompanied him on these tours. He was heard muttering, "Hell of a city. Hell of a city."

It might have been hell that day but there was far more to come. In the hours that followed after the earthquake had abated, and the wreckage of the city was observed at close hand, many people headed for a park in the Northern part of the city where the Red Cross was attempting to help the newly homeless.

Anatole wandered around the city for ages washing himself down with water from a burst pipe and taking a sip to drink. He was totally and utterly exhausted. He found an alleyway between two broken buildings and lay down on the rubble. The noise in the background was one of people hurrying by, horses pulling carriages and carts, babies and children crying, women sobbing, men shouting, buildings retching and crumbling. He wanted to get up but he couldn't find the strength to do so. In the next few minutes he closed his eyes and passed out. He lay there for hours as the blackness of night fell across San Francisco's longest day.

***

Mariska and Jess woke up early the next morning in a park where makeshift tents and a soup kitchen had been established. All around them were homeless people recovering from the day before. More were arriving every hour while the overworked Red Cross were hard pressed to attend to the increasing numbers. President Theodore Roosevelt had ordered the army and Emergency Forces into San Francisco to assist in this natural disaster that had most unnaturally decimated the city.

From their vantage point at the park Mariska and Jess had seen the smoke rise from the fire that had spread across the city. All sorts of dire thoughts went through their mind about what had happened there. Rumours about the number of deaths and devastation began to spread amongst the people at the camp. They seemed to get more and more wilder as newcomers arrived.

"There's no reason for us to stay now, is there, Jess?" Mariska asked him.

"Best to leave as soon as we can," he replied. "Right now, Mary, New York looks pretty good to me. San Francisco is going to take a while to recover from this."

"I need to check out the folks at our apartments and my boss at her shop and the staff at the Phoenix Theatre. When I've done that I'll be ready to go."

"I understand, but we better hold out here until the authorities say it's safe to return.

***

Anatole began to stir. He was awoken by the sound of gunfire. Someone was shooting in the main street. Quickly he got to his feet, rubbed his sleepy eyes and moved to the corner of the alley. There were a number of dead bodies laying in the street. Some were obviously casualties of the earthquake while one or two had bullet holes and blood-soaked jackets. Anatole stared left and right. There were police obviously trigger happy in the streets.

"Dam looters," said one and from his pocket he pulled out a bottle of liquor and swilled back the contents.

One man ran from a side street carrying a bag and looked extremely nervous, as if he might have been faced with an onslaught of police carrying guns.

"Hey, you, stop!" cried out one of the policemen. The man panicked and started to run in the other direction. A policeman raised his rifle and shot him dead without finding out whether the man was a looter or not. A terrifying scenario was building up.

After the stark terror of the earthquake the streets were now becoming a no go area. A man suspected of being a looter could be shot on sight whether he was or not. Anatole wasn't going to risk being shot in the street by a drunken cop. He turned around and made his way down the alley and across the rubble. He pushed bricks from side to side and scrambled out into the street on the other side only to be met by a policeman with a gun.

"Stand there!" he shouted and slammed Anatole up against the wall. "Where are you going, fella?"

"I'm trying to get to safety! Where the hell do you think I'm going?"

"You could be looting! You look like a looter to me, you son of a bitch!"

"Hell fire, copper! Do I look like I'm looting? Are you stupid?"

The policeman's response was to strike him with the barrel of the gun drawing blood from Anatole's chin. He went down on the floor semi-conscious. The man frisked his jacket and pockets. Bad mistake. Anatole shot his arms out around the man's throat and head butted him unconscious. He could have killed him for all he knew. Anatole took the rifle and discharged all the ammunition and threw the bullets into the rubble. Quickly he moved off and instead of running he began to walk slowly judging every step he took, and carefully looking up ahead for any signs of vigilant reprisals.

Behind him he could hear shooting. There was still random shooting taking place of suspected looters. San Francisco was not a safe place to be on the streets that day. Sometimes Anatole saw soldiers and policemen grab men on the streets and give them spades to start digging out the rubble. He moved on slowly and cautiously, hiding behind anything he could find if he suspected foul play up ahead.

Ambulance men carried out bodies from buildings and beneath the ruins. It was a grim sight as corpses were laid out on the sidewalks. There were some miraculous stories of survival that day. Many people with varying injuries had been pulled out alive from beneath the rubble and were able to carry on leading their lives. The resilience of the San Franciscans was not to be underestimated. This fine city would be back in business big time.

Groups of people seemed to be heading in the same direction. Too many for the soldiers and police force to stop and search individually. Anatole joined the throng and followed them to wherever it was they were heading. He walked alongside a man who swigged from a bottle. Noticing Anatole licking his lips he offered him the bottle to take a sip. Anatole gratefully took it and sipped a mouthful. It was ginger beer but on that morning it tasted like champagne!

Whole families with frightened children walked together that day. Aimless individuals stunned by the happenings followed in a dazed stupor. Anatole still had his wits about him. Once this was over he was determined to get back and pick up his old life on the stage again. Thoughts of the girl he had met kept going through his mind. He wondered if she and her Aunt had survived that terrible day. How sad that such a special night could be followed by hellish devastation. Keep walking. Keep going. Always in his life did he seem to be running from something. Little did he know this would be the pattern of his life for years to come.

***

At the hill park the camaraderie between people was growing. The previous day's disaster had united folk of all kind and classes. Looking around them Mariska could see citizens with looks varying from tired and drained to anxious and nervy. Rather than sit around waiting for things to happen Mariska and Jess had joined the army of volunteers and assisted in handing out soup and food. They were waiting until the authorities gave the all clear that it was safe for them to return and find out if they still had homes to go to.

Anatole began walking up the hill to the park. He was dazed and beyond tiredness. Once he saw the people camped out he knew that he would put his head down on the grass and go to sleep for hours at a stretch. All these people lay before him. The scale of the disaster was hard to comprehend. Where had they all come from? Where would they go? How would they be re-housed? That was a massive problem for the city's Mayor and his colleagues. The human cost in this disaster could not be underestimated.

Jess handed out some soup to a family and then in an instant his eyes froze in amazement. He could see Anatole in the distance about ready to collapse. For a moment he stopped what he was doing and walked closer.

There was no doubt about it. Jess was looking at Anatole who sat down on the grass and buried his head in his hands. Jess turned and looked for Mariska who was also handing out food. He approached Mariska and gave her a look of concern. A look that spelt words without saying anything.

"What is it, Jess?" she asked.

"It's your brother, honey," Jess replied softly.

"Anatole?"

"He's over there," Jess pointed to him, "he's alive."

Mariska's face changed expression suddenly. She looked toward Anatole and the tears fell from her eyes. Slowly she walked towards him until she was facing him. Anatole was sitting with his hands over his head, unaware his sister was right in front of him.

"Anatole. Where the hell have you been this past year?" she asked in a voice cracking with emotion.

For a moment Anatole thought he had been dreaming. Was it his wild imagination or had he just heard the voice of his sister? He looked up in disbelief as he recognised Mariska. Virtually devoid of all energy he raised himself and embraced his sister,

"Oh Anatole," Mariska said in relief. "I can't believe you're here. Where have you been?"

"You will never believe me," Anatole croaked in reply. Behind them Jess smiled gently at their reunion. At least some good came out of this disaster. A brother and sister had found each other again.

Seventeen

New York, May, 1906

Paul Kapsia was waiting anxiously at ~~this~~ HIS office today. He knew who was coming to see him and he felt excited at the thought of seeing his young protégés again. Anatole and Mariska were like his second family. Not only was he their employer but he took a fatherly concern in their lives. At his office he had photographs and sketches that Anatole had sent from the many foreign lands he had visited. Paul looked at them with absolute fascination. He could hardly believe where Anatole had travelled to in the past year. Not only that, he was impressed with the new artistic talent that Anatole had demonstrated in sketching scenes and people.

Always with an entrepreneurial mind Paul was forever on the lookout for new ways to make money. He considered the possibility of Anatole's sketches and photographs might be worthy of an exhibition if he could persuade a gallery owner of their merit. At the very least when it came to promoting one of his shows Paul could use the exhibits in a newspaper article demonstrating that his young dancer not only had talent in abundance but backbone too.

He was abuzz with excitement. Mariska and Anatole had come a long way since 1898 when he had first encountered them. Now they were two professional performers bubbling with talent and confidence and, damn it all, he thought, Mariska was still only sixteen while Anatole was a cocky, know-it-all twenty-year-old. What a future these two had.

The door opened suddenly in his office and the smiling face of Jess Reubens looked through.

"We're back, boss!" He could hardly restrain himself from the thrill of it all. "And look who I've got with me!"

He ushered Mariska and Anatole into the office. Mariska looked like a debonair young lady in a flowery hat and Anatole had a dashing, man-about-town appearance that gave him real presence. Paul embraced them both while Jess looked on, beaming a happy smile.

"You will never know how glad I am to see you two kids again," Paul said without bothering to conceal his own personal happiness. "Let me look at you. My god, you've both grown!" Then for a moment his expression changed quickly. "When I heard about the earthquake in San Francisco I don't mind telling you I was worried. What's it like?"

"The place has taken one hell of a battering," Anatole replied.

"I was happy there too," said Mariska. "I made some great friends and did real well at the Phoenix Theatre. It's gone now. The earthquake took it away."

"Too bad. Too bad." Paul knew of the theatre and loved the city from his own visits there. "And the San Franciscans…?"

"They'll build a new San Francisco," Jess added. "And it'll be better than ever."

"Let's hope so," Paul said with concern. Then he motioned them to take a seat. They each sat down. "It's so good to have you back again. Life goes on. We've got shows lined up for the next few years. Not only here in the States but in South America and maybe even Europe. I'll tell you this, Nat, – no bars and strange women for you!"

"Don't worry, Paul. I've got my eye on a girl from New Hampshire."

"I like your artwork, kid. Maybe we can use it sometime. A display perhaps? An exhibition? Now let's talk about some shows I'm planning in South America…"

***

Rehearsals began soon afterwards. This time the act of Nat and Mary Lucky took on a new dimension. It became a more sophisticated dance routine at a complete variance to their vaudeville performances. Paul Kapsia was keen to establish his entertainers on the South American theatre circuit and he was a professional down to his fingertips. He knew that songs about the old South and the civil war would not travel well. The old show business world of the stage was changing in the twentieth century. New dance movements were being created. Cinematography was in its earliest stages, but it hinted at a whole new entertainment industry to come. Everyone who was involved felt a sense of excitement at the ever-changing world of their field.

Anatole and Mariska were hungry enough to develop their talents. Not content with being hoofers or tap dancers, they were keen to embrace the intense smouldering and sensual passion of Latin American dance movements. The Tango dance was in its infancy and it was intimate, suggestive without being blatant, skilful, entrancing and hypnotic both for the audience and the participants. In order to perform it well dancers needed to be lithe, agile and capable of showing a restrained passion before unleashing a sensuality that took one's breath away.

Paul knew that it was a huge responsibility asking Mariska and Anatole to head the show up on their own. He devised an act where the usual chorus line he employed on his various shows would back them up. The result on stage would be a massive friction of tango dancing on stage giving way to Anatole and Mariska emerging from the sidelines to take centre spot. The act went into immediate rehearsal six days a week for hours at a stretch. There was no doubt that the smouldering passions it ignited in the dancers, was a sure fire hit for the audience too.

New Yorkers enjoyed a dry run at the State Theatre where they had their first taste of the sensualities of Latin American dance. Musicians were recruited from amongst the South American and Spanish migrant communities. In his search for talent to back up his new show Paul Kapsia even found a flamenco dancer from Southern Spain whose dancing prowess could set audiences ablaze. He immediately gave this new discovery a solo spot which added and enhanced the colour of the show. This dry run, as Paul Kapsia called it, turned out to be a long running show which gave cast and musicians gainful employment right through to 1908. By that time the members of the show would be more than ready to tour South America.

While the show became a runaway success in New York there was a sadness to come in 1908. Jess Reubens was in his late fifties now, and with the passing of the years, his fitness was being called into question. He lived for dance. He loved his profession. But his body didn't have the agility and quick recovery after a dance session that it did when he was a younger man. One night after a show he went to sleep in his dressing room, and didn't wake up. Mariska and Anatole felt they had lost someone who was more than just a friend. He was a warm fatherly figure who represented a time gone by yet he was also a remarkable young person in outlook. With his broad smile and cheerful nature, he had the habit of making people feel good about themselves and celebrating the life they had.

***

"Our brother Jess has gone to the Promised Land," said the preacher at his funeral. He addressed the congregation of a sea of black faces, and everyone he had worked with during his long show business career. "Jess was such a man. Amen. He was born a slave and died in liberty – a free man who loved to dance and entertain. He was not yet sixty years of age but he ran the race of a man who had lived one hundred years! From the old world of the Southern States and confederacy to the United States that we are all proud to be part of, he came with those twinkling eyes. That great smile would warm a thousand chilly hearts and those dancing feet took him from ocean to ocean and across it to perform in the great cities of London and Paris. Jess was a generous man. A man who loved people, and those who were dear to him." At this point Mariska's eyes began to shed tears. So too did Anatole. Paul Kapsia put a steady arm round each of them. He too had lost a dear friend. "Yes my good friends," continued the Preacher, "Jess Reubens was such a man. A good man. The best of men."

When it came to the time to commit Jess Reuben's coffin to the grave, the black members of the congregation began to sing. The song they sang was an old African American spiritual called 'We are climbing Jacob's ladder'. The voices reached an harmonic crescendo and Mariska considered, as she wiped her tears away. *How Jess would have approved.*

Anatole remembered how a decade before in the summer of 1898 he had first seen Jess dancing on the street in New York. It was because of him he had fallen in love with the idea of becoming a dancer himself. He realised he had lost a link with his own father, for one memorable night at the same church in the same year Jess had met Viktor and the two men were both kindly souls with a real story to tell about their lives.

Mariska thought how well Jess had trained her in the field of dance, and how on tour he had more or less become her unofficial guardian always looking out for her and ever the gentleman. When Anatole had gone missing in San Francisco, and Mariska had decided to stay on, Jess, unbeknown to her, had given her virtually all of his fee for the tour to bide her over. Jess had been a generous man and the fatherly advice he had dispensed was something she would always cherish. It was a puzzle to Mariska and Anatole why such a good-looking man with a loving heart had never married and had children. There was a rumour by one of the less cautious cast members that Jess once had a woman and child in the old South, but nothing came of it. The truth was Jess had the greatest love for his profession. He loved to entertain. That was what he lived for.

***

Soon after the long-awaited, much-heralded tour of South America began. The cast members boarded a boat in New York Harbour bound for Buenos Aires, Argentina. It was not going to be a luxury cruise though. Paul Kapsia made sure of that. He had his show business team out on deck every day, rehearsing and rehearsing. At night he had them entertain the passengers in the lounge. There was no room for complacency in one of his shows. Perfection was the name of the game as far as Paul Kapsia was concerned. The only time the cast really got to rest was when the boat made brief day and night stops at ports such as Miami, Havana, Nassau, Caracas, Sao Paulo, Rio de Janeiro and finally Buenos Aires.

Paul Kapsia ensured that this show was to be a definite money-spinner. He had taken a huge risk in the departure from the usual vaudeville musicals to the exotic Latin American display that he was now touring with. No venue was avoided. Shows were performed in Royal Palaces, Presidential Mansions, open air theatres and arenas, shady half lit nightclubs where millionaires sat amongst the workers, and glamorous women smoked cigarettes in a sensual manner.

The new flamenco dancer stopped the show with his dazzling display of footwork. Some of the cast members might have even thought that, like a cunning burglar, he had deliberately set out to seal the show. Never the less his presence drew the audiences in. Anatole and Mariska, who were still billed as Nat and Mary Lucky, held their ground and when they took to the centre of the stage to dance the ever growing popular Tango, they performed the routine in such a professional manner that even the Argentinians could not distinguish them from their own countrymen.

The tour took them all over South America. Originally scheduled for only Buenos Aires, the bookings came in thick and fast. The cast moved north to the exciting city of Rio de Janeiro. With a background of Sugar Loaf Mountain and Mount Corcovado, and the exotic beaches of Copacabana and Ipanamena, the buzz of life and the infectious enthusiasm of its inhabitants soon rubbed off on the cast who found it a city for living life to the full. It is a strange fact of life that sometimes when a person is taken out of their usual safe home environment and works and lives in a new place, their character takes on new facets of personality – so it was with the cast. The spark of new venues in different places always thrilled them, and for the price of this travel all they had to do was keep the audiences entertained to the best of their ability.

***

From Brazil they toured in Paraguay, Bolivia and Venezuela, always playing to audiences ranging from the poor to the elite, of which there were a distinguishable amount in the various classes of South America. What had originally been intended as a six-month tour turned into an eighteen month sojourn. The entire cast finally arrived home in New York harbour in the early part of 1910.

During all their time touring, neither Mariska or Anatole ever found time to have relationships in their private lives which might possibly lead to an engagement or marriage. Anatole was not adverse to having dalliances with showgirls or a glamorous girl in the audience if she gave him sufficient eye contact. After the disaster he had experienced in San Francisco he was naturally cautious and always made love to the lady in his own private dressing room.

Paul Kapsia was always looking ahead to his next show. Even on the boat coming back to New York he dreamed up a new idea of a Wild West show in which two men would bid for the heart of a country girl. The songs would be ones in which the audiences would be asked to join in. Always a high-risk strategy, but one that usually paid off as the audiences would go home feeling happier than when they came in. This time he had his eyes on the theatres of Europe. If Buffalo Bill could tour in the romantic cities so could Paul Kapsia's shows. Europe was interested and fascinated by the Americas. Now instead of them coming to the United States he could take it to them.

A short rest followed in New York. Then it was back down to business. The show did not get off to an easy start. The original plot did not stand up on stage and the story had to be rewritten several times before it held good to an audience. The songs did not gel either. Paul Kapsia, who had another interest in song publishing, found some up and coming lyricists. They could weave a story into their compositions. Rewriting and rehearsing took months and months to prepare before it was ready for its New York debut in 1911.

Where had the years gone? Anatole was now twenty-five and Mariska was now a very eligible twenty-one-year-old. Already both of them had packed a lot into their short lives more than many people could have ever dreamed of doing in an entire lifetime. But Mariska was beginning to wonder about just where life was taking her. Thoughts of marriage entered her head. She loved her brother dearly yet she could not rely on him for support forever. Already she was quite independent and confident in herself. She still missed her parents, Viktor and Ekaterina, a great deal. They had a good, strong marriage and were devoted to each other. Even in their forties, although appearing much older, they looked at each other with a deep love and affection. Mariska wanted something like that for herself although she shied away from telling anyone her own personal thoughts. Anatole was slightly restless and he too began casting his eye around for someone who could become a permanent fixture in his life.

What of the past though? Soon after the San Francisco earthquake, Anatole had tried to find Jane in New Hampshire but his letters were returned unmarked. He had lost contact with his boyhood pals Jack Clancy and Jake Mahoney. Often he wondered how the course of their lives had run. Another alarming thought went through his mind. How long would his show business career last? What would happen if bookings dropped or his act no longer became entertaining to audiences? What would he do? The whole fantasy life he had been living was beginning to turn into reality now. He was beginning to grow up too. In every life there is a price to pay at some stage.

The later part of 1911 took the show to Europe. For Mariska and Anatole it was like going home again after years of being away. They would see England again with a show in Leeds where they had once briefly lived. The tour took in the great cities of Vienna, Budapest, Rome, Milan, Monte

Carlo, Paris and London, from whence they travelled on an extensive tour of England.

Here in this green and pleasant land the show received the best notices and true to form also their best audiences. Birmingham, Manchester, Liverpool, Portsmouth and Blackpool all featured on their itinerary. In Leeds Anatole and Mariska relived old memories going back to their old rooms on the cobble stoned pavements of Harehills, where on cold nights Ekaterina had read them the stories of Robert Louis Stevenson's novels.

Not only did they play in the major cities but also the provincial towns of the Home Counties too. Places such as Oxford, Cambridge, Winchester, Canterbury, Horsham and Brighton. After playing in these lovely old towns, the show was invited to perform at the Drury Lane Theatre in London, a prestigious venue at which they were invited to a party at Claridges held by the British music hall artiste, Marie Lloyd.

London had been welcoming to Anatole and Mariska. In fact their whole tour of England had been like coming home. It was not the land of their birth. They had only lived in Yorkshire as children for a matter of months. Yet once they had landed at Tilbury Dock it had felt as if they had arrived home. They had been impressed by the cheery patter of the people and the olde worlde buildings dating back centuries with interesting history attached to them. The warmth and good humour of what were still deemed as the working classes, although many of them toiled for a pittance, while the aristocracy and dukedoms lived a life of affluence beyond anyone's wildest dreams.

The two Luchenya's enjoyed walking through St James Park, looking at the views across the River Thames to Westminster and Big Ben, studying the exhibits in the British Museum, seeing the bustle of the markets in Petticoat Lane. They enjoyed also taking a sip of mild beer in an oak-beamed pub with a friendly 'gaffer' who could talk the hind legs off a donkey, regaling any unexpected patron with stories of his adventures in the Sudan and India. In teahouses they would listen to the chatter of folk often speaking in a cockney accent, so different to the cut-glass voice of legend. In this beautiful but still class-ridden country distinctions and accents varied wildly. It was hard not to love it. For reasons they could not fathom, they felt safe and warm here.

At Drury Lane the show had received great notices and a good box office return. The Brits, it seemed, were still fascinated by the good old

Wild West. Paul Kapsia who kept an eye on proceedings added tunes to the repertoire if they were able to enhance the show. He brought back the old love song, 'Lenora', which Anatole sang to Mariska It never failed to make its mark on an audience.

Marie Lloyd was a chirpy fun filled darling of the music hall who audiences and public loved immensely. Back stage at Drury Lane she went to congratulate the cast, particularly Anatole and Mariska, who she promptly invited to a party at Claridges.

When they entered the gathering they found themselves amongst a group of dinner suited, bow tired, ballroom gown wearing, tiara wearing people, the like of which they had never encountered this side of the Bronx. Marie Lloyd introduced them to various entrepreneurs, agents and people on the fringes of the show business world such as writers, actors and producers. Then to their amazement they were introduced to a member of the Royal Family who was charm in himself.

"Anatole… Mariska…" she began. "May I introduce you to the Prince of Wales." Marie Lloyd continued, "Sir, these two fine people are from across the pond in the good old USA and they've been performing at sell out shows across the country."

"Well, I'm very pleased to meet you both," he said in a casual manner, not betraying any sign of class or even a hint that one day he would be king and heir to an empire. "I believe your show has been a good musical portrayal of your country. I have a ticket for tomorrow night. I shall watch with great interest."

"We hope you enjoy it, sir," said Mariska, emerging from her shell. She was suddenly aware of the man the Prince had been talking to who stood quietly in the background. His eyes were fixed on her as if there had been an immediately attraction.

Almost as if he was aware of it, the Prince decided to introduce him to them both.

"I'm forgetting my manners," he said with a slight smile. "This gentleman is Lord Bernard Shervington. Lord Bernard…. Anatole and Mariska here have been entertaining our country folk up and down this land."

"Very pleased to meet you," he said, shaking Anatole's hand first and then when he greeted Mariska he felt the softness of her hand and looked deep into her face as if the mutual attraction had been borne of an instant.

Marie Lloyd was acutely aware of the signs and she indicated to Anatole he might like to meet more people. The Prince of Wales was much in demand as people clamoured to speak to him, leaving Lord Shervington deep in conversation with Mariska. Anatole glanced back as he was introduced to dukes and earls. It was the first time he had seen his sister so enraptured with a potential suitor.

Lord Bernard Shervington was about five-feet-ten-inches tall with brown hair and a fresh face as yet unlined for a man of thirty-two years of age. He was still single but not for the lack of trying. His career had been as an engineer in the army, during which time he had built bridges in India. Now he was working as an architect restoring old buildings into a new perspective using modern materials. He came from a good Sussex family but his social and professional life took him to London often. Gazing at this Russian-Jewish girl from the Bronx he was instantly smitten, and he was determined to take this new association as far as possible.

He became a regular at their shows when they appeared in Portsmouth, Horsham, Worthing, Brighton and Eastbourne. Always he would call backstage to see Mariska and the romance began to blossom. Instead of going walking accompanied by her brother, Mariska went out with Lord Shervington. They would sit on a bench by a lake or a river and hold hands. Anatole was aware of the direction Mariska's romance was taking, but he simply assumed as the tour was winding up it would simply burn itself out and they would be on board a liner from Southampton bound for New York. How wrong he was.

***

One day in a theatre office in London they were seated opposite Paul Kapsia discussing how well the tour had gone. There had been no pre-empting of any announcement to come. In fact it had been a typical business as usual conversation. Outside the sun shone brightly on the London streets enhancing the buildings with colour and light. What a wonderful city London is when the sun shines! The English tour had been the best so far in their careers. It was also to be Mariska's last tour.

"Lord Bernard Shervington has asked me to marry him," she said quietly. Paul Kapsia and Anatole looked at each other dumbstruck and totally lost for words. Neither had imagined a scenario as this one evolving.

"You never mentioned it to me, kid!" Anatole at last replied in surprise.

"I wasn't sure I was going to say yes then." Mariska gave a positive indication of what she had decided.

"Are you sure about this, Mary?" Paul waded in. "You've got a hell of a good future in the business. Both of you! When we get back to New York I could find you work in the movies. How about a trip to Hollywood? You could be up there in a film with Fairbanks, Chaplin or Pickford?"

"He's right," Anatole was quick to agree. "Besides you're only twenty-one. You haven't met that many fellas. Don't you think you ought to shop around until you're really certain?"

"Like you?" she giggled. "Don't make me remind you of a girl in San Francisco who ensured you got a free trip to China."

"Don't remind me. But what about your career? What now?"

"All these years I watched you develop into a fine performer." Paul was quite concerned. "I know you had it tough as kids in the orphanage and I love you both like you were my own. I'd just hate to see you make a mistake Mary. Does this mean you're giving up on your career to become… I guess if you marry a lord that makes you… a lady… Lady Mariska Shervington?"

She looked up suddenly and nodded with a smile, as if she had only just realised this.

"Are you really prepared to give up the stage for marriage?" Paul asked.

"I've thought about that." She was quite serious now. "I could get work here in London on the stage. I could even come back to the States from time to time. But that's all for the future. I'll finish the tour with you."

"We've got bookings until the end of February 1912," Paul confirmed. "I'll be grateful if you see the run through."

"I will. We intend to get married in March next year."

"I guess I'll stick around a bit longer Paul," added Anatole. "I'll take a later boat back to the States – and then figure out how I pursue a solo career. It'll be hard without you kid. I'm going to miss you."

Mariska looked at him and her expression was enough of a reply in itself for Anatole to realise she felt the same way.

***

Lord Shervington took Mariska to meet his family in Sussex over the following weekend. He collected her in his open top car and proceeded to drive from London to the wilds of West Sussex, except that it wasn't wild. It was full of lush green meadows and pastureland, little villages with cricket ovals, and farms where people were bailing hay and tending to livestock. It had a charming ambiance about it. Mariska had always imagined England to be a land permanently drenched in rain or fog but they had been lucky to enjoy warm summer weather. In her mind she began to think how much she was going to enjoy living here. The pretty villages of Sussex were a long way from the tenements of New York.

They eventually arrived in a village called Storrington where Lord Shervington's family lived in a mansion high above the Sussex Downs. Driving through Storrington it seemed to be a pleasant rustic place with not a lot of activity apart from a few horse-drawn vehicles, some riders and villagers stopping occasionally to chat; and a local pub called The White Horse that looked like a tempting ale hostelry to while away the hours and get to know the locals.

At the Shervington estate the car drew up. Shervington Manor was a grandiose Tudor-built home with a spectacular view of the agricultural countryside below which incorporated dairy farms, cornfields and meadows stretching between villages such as Amberley on one side to Pulborough on the other.

"Are you nervous, my dear?" Lord Shervington asked her before they got out of the car.

"More nervous than when I go on stage," Mariska confessed.

"Don't be. My aunt's a softie when you break through the surface."

Lord Shervington opened the door for Mariska and escorted her inside the house. The interior of the house was like entering another world. It reflected a bygone era of colonial times. The walls of the hallway were adorned with paintings of rural India and portrait pictures of army officers. There were statues of Indian goddesses and a tapestry of dancers entwined in movement.

At the end of the hallway there was a long leather chair at the foot of a spiral staircase with highly polished banisters. A butler walked down the stairs and smiled at Lord Shervington.

"Good afternoon, sir. Nice to see you back," he said amiably.

"And you Bobby." The man was elderly and had been with the

Shervington family for many years. "Would you be so kind as to bring my fiancée here some tea while I go upstairs and see Lady Shervington?"

"Fiancée, sir?" Bobby Grey beamed with delight. "How marvellous! Congratulations, sir. I'll fetch the tea."

"My name is Mariska. Pleased to meet you."

"Mariska from America. America. My word, you have come far. Well I wish you much happiness. It's been a long time since we've had a wedding in the family. Will the marriage take place at St Mary's Church?"

Bobby hadn't realised there was a different faith between them and that in all probability it would be a civil wedding in a London register office.

"We haven't decided on a venue yet, Bobby," Lord Shervington replied. Turning to Mariska he said, "If you wait here, Bobby will bring you the tea and I'll go upstairs and see my aunt."

Mariska was surprised at how formal it was in the house. In her easygoing American ways she hadn't realised how rigid manners and tradition were maintained in English country houses.

Lady Bernadette Shervington was working in her study upstairs. She was a well-dressed lady with shiny grey hair that had once been a striking natural blonde. Now in her early seventies she still had an elegant poise about her and her mind was as sharp as mustard and capable of keeping control of the various family interests. Lady Bernadette was the widow of Captain Rex Shervington who died in battle in India while serving with the 25th Queens Light Northern Regiment. Lord Bernard entered the room and greeted her with a smile.

"She's here Aunt Bernadette, my intended. She's waiting downstairs to meet you."

"Tell me more about her Bernard," she said putting her quill pen down and closing a ledger book. Bernard sat down in front of her. He knew that this line of questioning was really about her suitability to join the family ranks.

"Well... she's American. Actually... no... she was born in Russia but taken to Leeds when she was a little girl, and then the family moved to New York where she was orphaned, and later formed a dance partnership with her brother that's toured the world together."

"Mariska? You say that's her name?" Bernard nodded that it was. "A dancer? That's very different to your usual society girl. Are you certain?"

"I think she'll make a great family member. Mariska is unstuffy. She's warm. She's polite and well mannered… and she's willing to give up her profession."

"But are you certain Bernard?" Lady Bernadette repeated. "You know your late parents always wanted a good match for you. It's a strange combination, an architect and a dancer. You couldn't be more poles apart, and then there is the question of the faiths between you. That rules out the traditional St Mary's wedding day. A London registry office I take it?"

"Followed by a wonderful reception, of course, at a top London hotel"

"Of course." Lady Bernadette stood up. "We'll have lunch in the garden, shall we? Let's meet this lovely lady of yours then."

★★★

Lady Bernadette was not stuffy either. Beneath her formality and dignity there was a latent spark of humour and a warm nature. The three of them sat at a long table in a garden with well rolled green lawns and an array of highly coloured flowers in surrounding beds. The sun was warm and the view over Storrington village was clear and vivid. Bobby brought them lunch consisting of kippers, baked potatoes, kidneys, carrots and turnips, followed by a blackberry and apple pie and Indian tea.

The conversation between the three of them was very amiable. Lady Bernadette talked pleasantly to Mariska yet with a polite cunning to discern any note of something hidden. Bernadette, with the wisdom that the years had brought, was able to observe something about Mariska. To her she may have been a professional dancer who held no fear of audiences on a stage, but privately she was still a lost little girl yearning for love. If she would give up fame and acclaim for love then this would be a good match.

From a distance Bobby, the family butler, walked back to the house carrying a tray and beaming a big smile. The cook, a lady called Mrs Price, was working hard, already preparing the main meal for the evening.

"What are you looking so happy about, Bobby?" she asked him.

"Lord Bernard's got himself engaged to an American lady."

"Really! That's wonderful news!"

"Yes. Been a while since there was a wedding in the family. A great day to come."

Mrs Price stopped what she was doing and went to the window of the kitchen to look out. There she could see Lady Bernadette, Mariska and Bernard all laughing together. They did look a very happy group that day.

Eighteen

Mariska and Lord Bernard were married in a registry office in Chelsea, London, in March 1912. Anatole had stayed on after the cast had departed for New York. He looked on at the ceremony with a mixture of sadness and happiness. In truth he wasn't sure about Lord Bernard. He wasn't sure at all about the man and whether he was truly the person to make his little sister happy or not, but it wasn't his choice. Mariska had made her choice and now this sparky New Yorker had an English brother-in-law who was a peer of the realm. How curious the hand of fate.

The reception was held at Claridges. Who were all these guests? Who were all these well-dressed fashionable chic people? Anatole was like a fish out of water here. He felt he didn't belong to his sister's new world, and this was the start of a new life of independence for him. Rather than join in as dancers took to the floor, he found himself on the sidelines watching the whole thing like a member of the audience at a silent movie.

A female voice resonated in his ear suddenly, almost stunning him senseless.

"Are you a friend of the couple?"

He turned to find himself facing a well to do young lady with the bluest of eyes he had ever seen.

"You could say that," Anatole said with a wry sense of humour. "Actually the bride is my sister."

"Ah… I thought as much," she responded. "The Americans… the dancing Luckies. You'll be dancing on your own now then?"

"Looks that way, honey."

"How about you dance with me here now instead?"

"Sounds good to me, young lady. Let's show them how it's done."

Anatole and his new companion took to the floor and began to dance. To his surprise he found she could match him step for step.

"You're a professional dancer?" he exclaimed.

"Had you fooled, eh? Yes, I dance in a chorus line."

From the back of the reception, Mariska caught sight of Anatole on the dance floor. She turned to Lord Shervington and smiled.

"Look at that, my brother's found a new partner already!"

"Either that or a new lover for the night," he replied.

"Pity he's leaving for the States soon," Mariska said sadly. "But he'll be thrilled when he learns of our surprise gift to him. A voyage on a new liner."

"Yes," said Lord Shervington and he added without premonition, "At least it will be a voyage he'll never forget."

***

The gift to Anatole was a voyage home to New York on a remarkable new liner built by the British shipping company White Star Line. The new ship was 882½ feet long, 66,000 tons displacement, and capable of making a speed of 25 knots. It was made to magnificent specifications all except for one poor safety aspect. Such was the misguided confidence of the ship's owners that they pronounced it to be 'unsinkable' and for a full compliment of 3,000 passengers they had only provided enough lifeboats for a small proportion of these travellers. It had almost been damned from the start. The liner was called the *Titanic*.

Nevertheless when Anatole was driven to the docks at Southampton by the new Lord and Lady Shervington, he gazed up at the sight of the *Titanic* in awe. It was 10 April 1912. It was a grandiose vessel with private promenade decks, cabins with Turkish baths and gymnasiums. Everything smacked of riches including the passengers who collectively were worth around several hundred million dollars. They included tycoons, controversial journalists, high society, buyers and merchants, lawyers and business people of all industries in First Class. The luxuries that the First and Second Class passengers enjoyed however was not extended to that of the third class where only two bath tubs were provided for 700 passengers.

Anatole had been accorded a berth in First Class through Lord Shervington's generosity and he intended to enjoy every minute of his voyage home. However a dark cloud hung over his head at the thought of returning to America without his only family member. He took his suitcase and walked with Mariska and Lord Bernard to the foot of the ship. The *Titanic* was a hub of activity with passengers and cargo being loaded while people said farewell to loved ones at the gangplank. At the bottom Anatole stopped and put down his cases for a moment.

"Well I guess this is it," he said apprehensively to his sister. "Mariska… this is really hard to say goodbye, not knowing when we'll meet again. I'm not good at this."

"Neither am I," she agreed.

"Bernard. Look after her." Anatole shook Lord Shervington's hand.

"You can be sure I will do," he responded.

For a few painful moments Anatole took a last close look at his little sister. Mariska would always be his little sister even though she would be known as Lady Mary Shervington from now on. Her life would be as a Lady of the Manor in the little Sussex village of Storrington, while his would continue in New York as a solo performer. Anatole put his arms around her and embraced her.

"Make sure you're happy, kid, and always come out on top," he said, and then picking up his cases he smiled at both of them and made his way up the gangplank to sail on the maiden voyage of the *Titanic*.

Whenever a ship sailed from Southampton water to a far-flung destination, its departure is always something of an emotional experience to watch. For many of the passengers would never ever see their homeland again. Given the massive publicity of the *Titanic*, photographers and early newsreel cameramen were out in force recording this exciting scene of departure of the unsinkable liner. Just a few days later there would be an added poignancy about these scenes.

***

Once on board Anatole became his old self-confident, cocky personality again. Here he was amongst the big shots able to hold his own and to speak confidently and perhaps boastfully of all the places he had seen. He didn't feign shyness or modesty – it wasn't in his character to do so. He may not have been in the same money-bracket as the rich guys but his lifetime experiences were million dollar memories. Things that even money couldn't buy.

For once in his life Anatole felt no joy about returning home. It was a suspect future with his career prospects in doubt and family life apparently at an end. Well-dressed in a smart suit and hat, he confidently strode around the deck smiling at the elegant ladies and making conversation with passengers. However, beneath all the bravado he suddenly felt more alone in the world than at any time in his life since he had been a child in the orphanage. He gazed out at the sparkling sea and took in the scent of salt spray. What would be the next crisis in his life he wondered? In just a few days he would find out.

***

Mariska meanwhile was becoming acquainted with her new role as Lady Shervington. In this her mentor was Lady Bernadette. The two women, who were both very different in character and nature, were surprisingly compatible. In truth, Bernadette, who in her younger years was a flirtatious head-turner, had in her dotage become the essence of a genteel English lady: well-mannered, courteous and not judgemental, biased or xenophobic against anything foreign after years of living in India.

"I'd like to know who all these people are," Mariska said to Bernadette one day in the house, gazing at all the portraits in the manor house.

Bernadette smiled. "Curious to know the familiarity of all the Shervingtons? It's quite a story. You'll get to know it in time. That distinguished-looking man was my husband, Captain Rex Shervington. He died in India during an uprising many years ago." Mariska looked up at the painting. "He was quite the epitome of the British soldier in the last century."

"You must miss him, even now," Mariska said with some sympathy, realising how much Bernadette spoke well of him.

"Yes I do but I can't live in the past. He was a hero. Revered by men… and loved by women." Mariska interpreted a double meaning. "Oh, yes, women always found him fascinating," she added quietly, indicating that he had probably been unfaithful. "Even when he was married to me. Perhaps he was like a magnet to women. Some men are."

They moved on to the next painting of another officer. He wore the uniform of a Crimean War soldier. His hair was white and he had a matching moustache.

"This is Major Gideon Shervington. Hero of Crimea. I remember him as a white-bearded old man always speaking of the past and his wartime glories. He lived in the past you know. Anything modern he didn't want to know about. He was rather the traditionalist. Much preferred the old ways. Brusque in manner, gruff, but always impeccably turned out, as if he was going on a regimental parade. A Galahad to women – like his son, Rex – and equal on all terms with men. As far as he was concerned, no man was above or below him. He was equal as far as he was concerned, but I have to say for all that he often acted as if he was their superior."

"Sounds like a complex man," Mariska remarked.

"All men are a puzzle sometimes," said Lady Bernadette.

The two women looked at each for a moment as if neither knew what to say next and then Mariska glanced up at a picture of an Indian-looking gentleman dressed in the uniform of a British Boer War soldier.

"That's Ravi," Lady Bernadette pointed out. "He came from India to work for us. Originally he worked at the Officers Club in Calcutta and when he came here he became one of our most valued staff members. A good manservant and butler. His father was a British soldier." She paused and gave a swift glance towards the picture of Captain Shervington, which Mariska assumed meant Ravi was Rex's illegitimate son. He was. There was quite a story attached to Rex and Ravi but that was to be saved for another time. "Ravi joined up in 1899. He served in his father's regiment. The 25th Light Northern Sussex Regiment. Sadly he was killed on the battlefield in South Africa."

"I'm sorry."

"Yes. I was too. He was engaged to a housemaid we had here called Jessica. Poor girl was broken hearted. She left soon after,"

"Is it still traditional for all the Shervington men to join the…?"

"The 25th Light Northern Sussex Regiment?" Lady Bernadette nodded. "No. The Regiment was absorbed into the Sussex as a whole a few years later. Each county has their own. The Surreys. The Gloucesters." She pointed to a large regimental photograph in a frame mounted on the wall. "That is what the 25th looked like at Fort Valaka in India back in the last century. This photograph was taken in 1885, not long after my husband died. There were some great characters in that picture. Good men who died in action soon afterwards."

"A very interesting history," said Mariska. "If you don't mind me being direct, you must wonder how I could fit into all this. Me... being an American... an orphan child of New York."

They walked through to the lobby and sat down.

"Don't underestimate yourself, Mariska," Lady Bernadette remarked in an equally direct fashion. "You're far more than just an American orphan child. Russian born. Cosmopolitan. A traveller. A performer. An all round entertainer. I have travelled east of Suez. I have lived in India and I have been as far as Rangoon in my life but you... you have been to and seen more of the world than I have. At such a young age too. The Shervington family have their own history. Yours is still beginning. I think the military history of the Shervington's is over now, at least until the next war."

"The next war?" Mariska was surprised. "Do you think there will be a war?"

"It's possible," Bernadette said quietly and then added with a bit more certainty, "Probable I would say. The German kaiser has re-armed his country with weapons he's itching to use to stress his imagined superiority. Armaments create jobs and the people who work in the factories that make them don't realise the extent of what they're part of. Europe is a tinderbox at the moment. The Balkans. Old Empire's teetering. Any trouble and Britain is bound by treaties to intervene. That means war. I sincerely hope it doesn't come to that, but one never knows these days. When I was in India I saw the effects after battles and I remember the Boer War soldiers coming home ten years ago. Still we don't want to talk about all that do we? I wonder how that brother of yours is enjoying the voyage on the *Titanic*."

"If I know my brother, he's probably at the centre of things aboard ship."

***

Anatole was still absorbing the opulence of the luxury liner, *Titanic*. Although he was nowhere near as rich as some of the illustrious passengers, he had, as predicted, held his own in conversation with the people he had met. His cocky self-assurance and confidence put aside many of his feelings of monetary inferiority. He happily chatted to passengers like John Jacob Astor, Henry Harper of the famous publishing firm, and Archie Butt, who was President William Taft's military aide. There was no class as far as he was concerned. Only degrees of money separated people. Wealth and poverty could happen to any man. It didn't make them less superior in his eyes. It was the way a man handled his circumstances.

One man Anatole enjoyed talking to was a controversial journalist called William T Stead who was also something of an evangelist, social reformer and someone who believed strongly in spiritualism. Another man Anatole found good conversation with was an elegant, enthusiastic elderly man called Albert A Stewart, who had a long association with the famous Barnum and Bailey Circus. He had talked amiably to the ship's commander, Captain Edward J Smith, who at fifty-nine years of age was in the sunset of his long maritime career.

The voyage had so far been too good to be true. Already Anatole had started to think of his future as a solo performer in New York. He was sure Paul Kapsia would continue to represent him and find him work. It was a temporary reprieve however. On 14 April 1912 a crisis was about to engulf the *Titanic* which would make headlines around the world.

While the passengers luxuriated in delectable cuisine and distinguished company, there were six lookouts who kept a sharp eye out for anything unexpected that might distract the ship from its smooth voyage. It was a clear night with twinkling stars, with a freezing, ice-cold wind and hints of snow and icebergs in the distance. It was a relatively calm sea on which the *Titanic* ploughed across at the rate of 22½ knots. At 11.40 pm on Sunday the 14th April 1912, one of the lookouts, Frederick Fleet, was startled to see a sizeable iceberg loom out of the darkness. Instantly he rattled the crow's nest bell several times and spoke on the internal phone to the bridge warning the gentlemen at the other end of what he had seen.

"Iceberg ahead, sir," he said, with some trepidation as the ship approached it ominously. It got closer and closer, to the point that a gigantic crash seemed inevitable. Then the boat suddenly veered to one side, narrowly avoiding the ice. Fleet blew his cheeks out in relief. It had been a close run thing.

At this stage none of the passengers had been aware of the near disaster that had just been averted. Many were already asleep while others were preparing for bed. Anatole was restless as if he had a sense that all was not well and he sat in his cabin smoking a cigar almost nervously. Then suddenly there came a powerful grinding jolt which seemed to last for a few nail-biting minutes. This wasn't part of the normality of the throbbing of a ship's engines. The inconsistency indicated that something was vitally wrong. Anatole leapt to his feet and ascended quickly to the top desk.

A sailor raced past him with a worried look on his face.

"What's happening, I heard a…?"

"The ships hit an iceberg, mate," said the sailor in a matter of fact manner then added with a wink, "Don't worry, she's unsinkable, ain't she?"

A well-dressed man standing nearby heard the sailor's remark and glanced at Anatole. The look on his face suggested disbelief.

For sometime afterwards the *Titanic* lay inert in the freezing cold sea. There was an aura of danger which gradually began to seep into the minds of all the passengers. In the starry cold night steam surged upwards from three of the four funnels. Various passengers began to congregate on board deck to see what had happened. Strangely enough there was no sign of urgency. When passengers asked how long it would be before the ship resumed its course, stewards and crewmen advised this was just a temporary problem. But the passengers knew better than this. The aura spread.

Upstairs the captain was informed that the vessel was sinking. He had been told in no uncertain terms that the *Titanic* was about an hour and a half before it began to sink. He was ashen faced. This was his final voyage in his career and he was now in all probability in the last hour and a half of his life. Not for one moment had he ever envisaged that the *Titanic* could possibly sink. After all, this outstanding vessel had been promoted as unsinkable by the White Star Line. Now the builder, Mr Andrews, was informing him that it was sinking. Even more horrifying was the little known fact by the crew that of the 2,207 passengers on board, the lifeboats combined only had capacity for 1,178 people.

The word went around very quickly to the passengers. Stewards informed them to vacate their cabins and go on deck with their lifebelts on. Anatole had returned to his cabin only to receive a knock on the door shortly after entering. He opened the door to find himself facing the steward.

"Very sorry to trouble you sir," he said amiably, "But everybody is to go on deck with lifebelts on, at once."

"At once?" queried Anatole.

"Yes, sir, just as a matter of precaution."

"We're in trouble aren't we?"

"As quick as you can sir." The steward was professional to the last detail.

Anatole needed no further prompting. His sense of drama told him that turmoil was about to happen in a very big way. The passengers began to leave their cabins and head up to the Boat Deck. For some of them they approached the situation with good humour and made jokes amongst themselves. Perhaps it was a reaction to a grave predicament about to occur, but the people seemed to be putting up a wall of self defence disguised as stoic humour.

The sight before Anatole was a mingling throng of people in all sorts of attire. On board the Boat Deck not only were the passengers gathering, but so too were all manner of crewmen joined by the firemen, catering staff, waiters and administrative staff. The urgency of the situation became immediately apparent to everyone as staff on the Boat Deck suddenly started to organise the *Titanic*'s sixteen lifeboats. This was no simple exercise or emergency precaution. This was the evacuation of passengers from the liner that had previously been thought of as unsinkable.

For a while the passengers had been serene and good-humoured, but they quickly began to look on in a mixture of confusion and concern as the crew began preparing the lifeboats. Canvas covering each boat was removed and each small vessel had lanterns and foodstuffs placed inside.

Anatole seriously began to question his luck. He had been shanghaied in San Francisco only to return to get caught in the 1906 earthquake; now he was on an unsinkable liner that was about to sink. He watched the action taking place around him. The lifeboats were being slowly swung out ready for the passengers to board. Curiously, for a state of emergency, the ship's band assembled on the Boat Deck and began to play. Not for them did they play serious music. The music was happy foot tapping ragtime. The band were professional, playing to their captive audience on an icy cold night in the North Atlantic as if they were performing at an outstanding concert venue. The bandmaster, Wallace Henry Hartley, was a man of the old show business school who believed the show must go on. His fellow musicians were Jock Hume who played the violin, Roger Bricoux a cello player, pianist Theodore Brailey, bass violinist Fred Clark and others who made a total of eight.

The image that would be forever ingrained in Anatole's memory was of the faces of the passengers on that night. They were a mixture of fear and anxiety. Some were shivering with the cold. Well wrapped up children huddled close to their mothers. Couples, both young and old, held hands. All around the Boat Deck there was a hub of activity. The crewmen worked frantically to prepare the passengers for their imminent departures on the lifeboats. In the freezing cold temperatures tempers began to fray in some quarters, while in others they remained peaceful and resolved to whatever their destiny would be.

Down below the compartments of the *Titanic* were beginning to fill with water. Gradually each deck would fill and then the ship would sink. Captain Smith had asked the wireless operator to send out distress calls to the nearest ships at sea. Messages were sent to the Carpathia, the Frankfort, the Californian with various acknowledgements of the ship's plight. In those early days of wireless telegraphy, the range that messages could be sent was restricted, and once they were received they were often indistinct. The hapless wireless operator on another ship may have had difficulty interpreting a distress call due to an extremely faint signal, and sadly this was the case with the *Titanic* on that dreadful night. The dire prospect ahead was of the surviving passengers, drifting in lifeboats on an icy sea without a ship coming to their aid.

Captain Smith was desperate with worry now. He decided that distress flares needed to be sent high into the blackness of the night sky. With luck one of the vessels nearby would recognise the signs. The captain summoned the quartermaster and ordered him to send out rockets every few minutes.

Anatole looked up at the night sky and watched the flares light up the night sky. In the background the music of the ship's band played. The passengers grew uneasy and started to push forward in anxiety as the crew tried to quell their worries. When the cry had gone out for women and children first to enter the lifeboats, Anatole felt sure that this was the final curtain.

Nineteen

19 April, 1912

Mariska and Bernard sat in the dining room of Shervington Manor in Storrington. The expressions on each one's face was of disbelief and shock. Before them on a table lay a copy of the *Daily Mirror,* dated 19 April, 1912. It was hard for them to absorb the news about the sinking of the *Titanic*.

"But they said… she was unsinkable," Mariska spoke in a hushed voice.

"And to think we thought we were doing him a favour," Lord Shervington said with a voice that betrayed his anxiety. He stood up, walked to the window and gazed out at the Sussex Downs. "Not enough lifeboats!" He turned around to face his wife. "Can you imagine it? The world's greatest liner and they didn't have enough lifeboats! What kind of madness is that?"

Mariska looked at the *Daily Mirror*'s headline, "Why were there only twenty lifeboats for 2,207 people on board the ill-fated *Titanic*?" The story accompanying the headlines made for very grim reading. Captain Smith had shot himself on the bridge, and the chief engineer had also committed suicide. The death toll had reached nearly 1,600. Passengers had stampeded to the lifeboats only to be turned away as each one was filled to its full capacity. Some men had taken a chance and dived into the icy-cold waters. When some male passengers had attempted to enter the lifeboats to be with their wives and children, sailors threatened to shoot them. Reading these headlines in a country village far away, the scenes on board were unimaginable.

Scanning down the list of surviving passengers, Mariska could not find her brother's name. She put her head in her hands with despair. Lord Shervington came across to her and put his hand on her shoulder. He looked at the newspaper under the column with the headline *'Women's vigil for news of dear ones'*. Many had waited at the White Star Line offices in Cockspur Street, London, all day and night for news of their male relatives.

"What could have happened to him?" Mariska said in a soft, tearful voice..

"I am afraid we must prepare ourselves for the worst," her husband answered. "I wish I could be optimistic but reality tells me otherwise."

***

The reality of that night was far worse than they could ever have imagined. Along with the other male passengers Anatole had watched as the women and children boarded the lifeboats. The icy windblast roared across the *Titanic's* decks intermingled with the chilly cold sense of fear experienced by the individuals who felt death was imminent. Some of the women were frightened by the prospect of entering the lifeboats and the crew had to cajole them into going. Husbands had to escort their wives, who were reluctant to leave. One elderly lady ran from the lifeboat but a kindly man persuaded her to go back. Children said goodbye to their fathers in tearful mode. It was all too tragic to watch as the events of the night began to unfold.

Anatole looked at the departing women and children, and then cast his glance across the Boat Deck at the men who were remaining aboard. He then turned his view towards the cold blackness of the sea and considered what his chances of survival would be. If anything he would risk his all. He was too young not to try. Around him people watched as each lifeboat was lowered and began to move away from the sinking ship. The slant of the *Titanic* was obvious now as the boat tilted upwards.

While other passengers seemed resigned to their fate Anatole was having none of it. He began to panic. All the lifeboats had gone and it was as if the several hundreds left were simply waiting to die. What was the matter with all of these people? Weren't they going to at least try to survive even if it meant a desperate swim in the icy black sea? It was amazing to him that members of the crew were carrying on working as if normal service was about to shortly resume. Looking around he even saw two men laughing and joking together despite the imminent doom that was about to engulf them all.

Finally he could stand it no longer. He raced round the deck looking for some way of leaving the ship. Then, in the corner of the Boat Deck, he saw his escape. Several deck chairs stood deserted, almost ghostly empty, as if people had vacated them through sudden death. Nearby was a rope coil and close by were two lifebelts that looked as if they were tossed aside by passengers not daring to risk the elements. His escape was looking back at him. If he took the two deckchairs, opened them flat out and tied them together, and separately tied the two lifebelts at opposite ends, it might possibly make a floatable raft. With his own lifebelt tied around him as a backup he could lay on the raft and paddle his way from the sinking ship. There was no time to be lost. Immediately he set about his work and frantically strapped up his makeshift raft. A couple of passengers looked at him amazed not realising just what he was doing. Anatole ignored them and carried on tying the chairs and lifebelts as securely as he could. The only way he was going to survive this traumatic ordeal was by his own volition. No one else was going to look after him.

When he was certain that the deck chair raft had at least a semblance of floating he raised it vertically and walked to the rail of the ship. His head was throbbing with excitement. In his ears he could hear the blood pulsating through him. He was trembling with both fear and the intense cold, and yet he was also perspiring with fear. Emotions of stark terror and nervousness were going through his mind. Then the ship began to tilt even more alarmingly. There was absolutely no time for hesitation, it was now or never. He picked up his raft and ascended the rail, and then leapt into the darkness of the inhospitable icy sea to an unknown fate of life or death.

It was almost as if it had only taken mere seconds to come crashing down on the sea. He came down flat on the raft and for a moment it plunged below the sea but just as quickly it bobbed back up on the surface. He couldn't look back. To do so might dispel him. He had to start paddling away as quickly as possible to avoid being caught up in the suction of the ship as it began to sink rapidly. The sea was icy cold and his arms felt strained. Like an athlete making that last rapid charge to win a gold medal, he exerted all his latent energies to keep track of the lifeboats up ahead. His face showed the absolute strain of it all. Ringing in his ears was the sound of the ships band. For a moment he contemplated the unmistakeable fact that they were playing right to the bitter end. The wind blew stingingly cold in his face and it was as if the water on his face was turning to ice. In the pitch black, only the stars, illuminating the sky like crystal chandeliers, added some guidance on this tragically dark night in maritime history.

Back on board the steadily inclining ship, many passengers simply waited for the inevitable. John Jacob Astor stayed deep in thought in reclusion. The New York and Philadelphian socialite group took on an air of stiff upper lip and steely resolve, while various jumpers fearing the consequences of waiting too long began plunging into the sea to take their chances.

Down in the smoking room Thomas Andrews, *Titanic*'s builder and the managing director of Harland & Wolff Shipyard stood grim-faced and alone in the room, facing a large portrait called 'The Approach of the New World'. This voyage should have been the pinnacle of his career. He had joined this trip in order to do a reconnaissance of the workings of the ship on its maiden voyage. Mr Andrews had kept technical notes of every part of its operations from engineering to passenger service. Now it was all coming to an ignominious end. He was sunken in spirit and mystified that the unsinkable liner he had created was rapidly sinking.

"Aren't you going to try for it, Mr Andrews?" a steward asked him quietly. There was no reply. Thomas Andrews just stood in disbelief at the whole terrible situation.

On deck the band continued to play. People prayed in a small group with the Reverend Tomas Byles. Water gradually filled the lower decks. The *Titanic* inclined even further. The waves got higher. Furniture slid all over the boat. Chandeliers broke. Breaking glass could be heard. Bottles of spirits and beers broke. Flowerpots and vases broke. Doors broke off their hinges. Gradually, by the forces of nature, the ship was being torn apart piece by piece.

Up above, the funnels of the ship began to topple off the boat striking swimmers escaping below. This was the last chapter in the short life span of the *Titanic*. The chaos was terrible to watch. Such was the incline in the ship now, people were unable to hold their footing, and slid down the decks into the sea followed by ropes, furniture, deck chairs and broken planks from the deck. People had no choice but to try and swim for it,

Out at sea it was a horrifying spectacle to be witness to. For over two hours the *Titanic* had been sinking and now the end was coming closer than ever. The passengers in the lifeboats found it distinctly hard to watch. On the raft Anatole rested his aching limbs and drifted for a while. He looked back at the boat. The screams and shouts of the remaining passengers on board drifted back in the wind and the dark. There was a massive creaking sound. Then the boat slanted and began to subside very quickly. All the tumult and noise suddenly dissipated as the sea rolled over the *Titanic*. The silence that followed was shattering.

Anatole's eyes froze with fear. Only seconds before the very same passengers had been alive. Now they were all fatalities. The cold tore right through him. He shivered with the cold and he shivered with the fear of what he had just seen. Turning away from the dramatic sight, he looked up at the lifeboats ahead. He couldn't dwell on what he had just seen and he had to catch up. Reluctantly, and with sadness in his heart, he turned away from this scene of horror and with every piece of strength he could harness he began to paddle frantically.

Within a quarter of an hour or so he found himself directly alongside a lifeboat of traumatized passengers. They sat in stony frozen silence while a ships officer sat at the helm.

"Hey buddy!" Anatole croaked in a broken voice. "Got room for me?"

The officer looked around at his shivering passengers and shook his head grimly – there wasn't.

"Sure there's room for this young man!" boomed the voice of an American lady.

"I'm in charge here, madam," the officer retorted angrily, but the robust American lady was made of sterner stuff. She stood up in the lifeboat and put her hand out to Anatole.

"Don't argue with me, buster!" she said to the officer with fury in her eyes. "We're talking life and death here. There's room for another. Here, young man, take my hand."

Anatole gratefully took the lady's hand and clambered into the lifeboat.

"What's your name, miss?" he asked.

"Honey, I'm Molly Brown," she replied confidently.

"I'm grateful to you, Miss Brown," he said, easing himself into a space between two passengers. Then he turned around to see his raft floating away. He gazed back at where the *Titanic* had been and grimaced.

"Don't look back, young man," said Molly Brown.

"All those passengers…." Anatole said quietly. "Lost… because there weren't enough lifeboats."

The lifeboat's officer began to row the paddles. It was a slow quiet drift on a freezing cold sea. A couple of the ladies began to cry. Anatole held his hands to his face and when he removed them they were wet with tears.

***

Some hours later the Carpathia appeared with the dawn as a saviour to the lifeboats. For all the surviving *Titanic* passengers it had been the longest night of their lives. They gazed up at the decks of the Carpathia. Shortly the nightmare of what had happened would temporarily vanish from their minds as thoughts of hot coffee and warm beds entered their heads.

Soon after the Carpathia arrived in New York, the post mortem on the *Titanic*'s demise and the after effects would begin. Almost like an ominous sign from the heavens a total eclipse of the sun cast a shadow over the crowds of people who waited for information about their relatives at the White Star Line Office in Liverpool. Quickly the popular press, thriving on the drama of such a tragic event, nicknamed it 'The *Titanic* Eclipse'. The human tragedy of this disaster outweighed all other considerations why this supposedly unsinkable liner had plunged to the depths of the Atlantic Ocean. Never again would a ship be so ill equipped for a potential disaster as this one had been. The safety of passengers would be uppermost in the minds of ship designers from now on.

Twenty

1914

The open-topped chauffeur-driven car with Mariska and Bernard in made its way along Church Street in Storrington. It had been a sombre morning. Lady Bernadette Shervington had passed away peacefully, and that very morning she had been laid to rest in the graveyard of St Mary's, the beautiful old church she loved so much.

"She was a grand lady," said Bernard, fighting back the tears. "After my mother died, she became my closest relative. I loved hearing her stories about her days in India and Burma."

"I thought she was warm and sweet like honey, especially when I first came to the house." Mariska smiled at the memory and held her husband's hand warmly. "I shall miss her too."

The car eventually pulled up at Shervington Manor and with its arrival came the realisation that Mariska was now the only titled lady of the house. The affable chauffeur, Tom Mollomby, stepped out of the vehicle and opened the doors for each of them. Tom had been a boy soldier who had gone on to serve in the Sudan, in India, later in South Africa during the Boer War.

"A sad day for us all, sir," he said sincerely.

"Indeed ,Tom, but life goes on," Bernard said quietly, the hurt evident in his eyes.

They both entered the house and were greeted by the butler, Bobby Grey. In the corridor were a number of parcels wrapped in brown paper. The stamps on each signified that they came from overseas.

"What's all this, Bobby?" Mariska asked.

"A delivery from America, m'lady. Came this morning by special post. Here's a letter for you too, also from America."

Bernard felt one of the parcels. "Feels like picture frames."

"Must be some of my brother's painting." Mariska opened the letter and read it quickly. "My goodness, Nat has been in Hollywood. He's made films with Chaplin"

"First time in a year since you've heard from him," Bernard pointed out.

"Well it took him a long time to get over the *Titanic*."

"True. That must have been a very traumatic experience."

Mariska read on. "He says that his contract with the studio is due to expire and that he is going back east to New York to try for a part in a stage show with Al Jolson," she paused. "I'm sorry, darling. I've forgotten what this day means to you."

"It's alright, Mary," Bernard always called her Mary. "We needed some good news to brighten up this day." He had opened up several of the paintings. "These are very good. He has paintings here of China, New Guinea and Australia, of all the magical places your very adventurous brother has been. Why has he sent us these?"

"It says that Nat is always on the move and wants us to look after them. He has had them exhibited by Paul Kapsia in New York and hopes to do so in London one day. Well what about that?"

***

Hollywood had indeed been another exciting experience for Anatole. After the disaster of the *Titanic* he had arrived back in New York somewhat shattered by what he had been through. He was getting used to the unpredictable in his life. His whole life had been a series of chapters. He realised that with Mariska's marriage and new life in England, he was completely on his own now

For a while he drifted around New York lost in his own thoughts and unsure about his own future until he finally decided to turn up at Paul Kapsia's office. After his travels in Europe Anatole felt restless. The double act with his sister was over now. Paul Kapsia had recently been out to Hollywood and returned with letters of introduction. The next thing he knew, Anatole was heading out to California.

The casting directors were impressed by this young man with a pleasant singing voice and extraordinary dancing skills but in this era of silent movies these talents did not transfer to the screen. The need was for charismatic and photogenic personalities who, whether they played drama or comedy, could almost leap out of the screen and into the audience.

Stars like Douglas Fairbanks, Charlie Chaplin, Mary Pickford and Fatty Arbuckle all had one thing in common apart from talent in their field. They knew how to play their roles to the camera. Every expression had to make up for the loss of dialogue and actions counted *FAR* for more than words. Anatole found himself as a much-employed extra working in films with all these famous names and although he enjoyed his work he was well aware of their vanity and gigantic egos.

It was a small price to pay to work in Hollywood in its infancy. Los Angeles was yet to be tarnished by freeways and the advent of smog brought on in later years by petrol guzzling vehicles. It was truly a sunshine city and life was good. In nearly two years in Hollywood as an extra he had played the parts of a Roman Centurion, one of Mary Pickford's suitors, been part of a sword fight with Douglas Fairbanks, a foil for Fatty Arbuckle, a comedic policeman being outwitted by a mischievous Charlie Chaplin, and a distant admirer of Mabel Normand.

When his contract came up for renewal Anatole wondered whether his chances of stardom were more likely on the New York stage than in Hollywood. The competition was certainly strong. From all over America and the World it seemed that the most beautiful girls and handsomest men were heading for the studios in a bid to become starlets of the silent screen. For Anatole, his looks did not guarantee him a lead role. He was a song and dance man, and until sound was introduced, there would be no place on the screen for him. Two of the biggest stars of the stage, Al Jolson and Sophie Tucker, hadn't been able to demonstrate their talents in films. Their time would come later when 'talkies' arrived.

While he had been in Hollywood Anatole had taken photographs of California and the studios. He had also drawn sketches from memory of the stars he had worked with and, in the quiet of his apartment, he had enhanced his pictures with oil colours. When they were completed, together with the photographs, he sent them to his sister in the leafy Sussex village of Storrington.

An idea entered his head. With his newfound talent for painting, he considered the possibility that if his show business career floundered, and even if it didn't, he might be able to make a living as an artist. The thought struck home when on his journeys across America there were wonderful landscapes and diverse scenery that would make great paintings. Another important factor of a nation is the people that inhabit it. The United States had a colourful population of immigrants, Native Americans of many tribes, and people working in every trade. Anatole decided that on his return trip to New York he would jump on and off trains, stopping off at various places, to paint the scenery and the people.

In Nevada, he captured scenes of the desert at different times of the day. The sunsets were particularly beautiful. A combination of red desert, golden sun dipping on a horizon line flanked by a purple-blue sky. Simply magical. He drifted across to Arizona where he studied the apaches and their history with fascination. So many Indian tribes in America, he thought. Where had they all come from? Anatole rode the rattlers, sometimes hiding in a goods carriage and not paying his fare, often discovering he was not alone. He met hobos and itinerant workers doing the same thing as himself. Just drifting from one place to the other searching for that unattainable pot of gold at the mythical end of the rainbow.

Anatole meandered along. He would hitch rides sometimes in lorries or private vehicles ending up in places as diverse as Phoenix and Tucson in Arizona, El Paso, up to Albuquerque and Santa Fe in New Mexico, and then down into the wilds of Texas. One day he jumped aboard a rattling old train not realising, apart from the driver and firemen, that it carried only freight. The last station that it called at was a dusty outpost that looked to be hardly a town but a small settlement with a few homes scattered around. There was a saloon where a few Mexicans, clad in sombreros, stood outside. Some men in overalls unloaded the freight from the train. In the distance he could see what appeared to be a monastery and further on a general store. He decided to walk through what there was of it. This was the town of San Castillo. *Hardly a town he,* thought. He would find a bed for the night and hitch out the next day.

After about a mile and half Anatole espied a structure on the very outskirts of the town. He couldn't be sure just what it was exactly and moving closely he realised it was an oil well, probably manned by some wildcatters eager to pump up the black gold and become millionaires. This was the stuff that American legends were built on. He had to get close to see it in work.

A fence cordoned the oil well all around. Looking over it he could see the pumps going up and down while several men checked its mechanism. One man stood on the top of the derrick gazing down and issuing instructions. A Mexican labourer handed them tools and wiped his brow. It was already hot in the mid-morning sun. Anatole looked on in admiration at these men. One of them obviously had faith in the project that oil would be found. More than likely he had convinced a sceptical bank manager that this was a sure fire hit worth financing and had mortgaged himself to the limit. The leader of this project would either soon be enjoying untold riches or facing bankruptcy.

To Anatole's surprise one of the men stopped what he was doing and walked across to him. He was a big broad man around about thirty-five, suntanned with an open friendly face.

"Impressive huh?" he said nodding towards the rig. Anatole nodded and smiled. "I'm Joe Donahue. This is my baby and I'm waiting for her to ooze champagne."

"Champagne?"

"Oil, son. Champagne is what me and the boys will be drinking when the well comes in. This is hard work. Grease, perspiration and aching muscles. Sixteen hours a day gruelling in the hot sun. Passing through fella?"

"That's right. I'm drifting across America, drawing and sketching as I go along."

"A draughtsman? Maybe you can sketch me a picture of the rig right there. I call her Ole Caroline after my mother."

"I'd be glad to." Anatole sensed this conversation was leading up to something.

"I need an extra hand on the job. Would you be interested? Free lodging. I've got huts right over there." He pointed them out. "I pay by the hour. The more hours you put in the bigger the pay… and when the well comes in everybody gets a bonus. How about it? What do you say?"

This was a surprise to Anatole. He hadn't expected an offer of work like this. "Well… this is not my usual line of work. I once worked as a docker… I was a seaman… I worked with cattle…"

"Can you use a spade… fetch and carry… use a wrench… tighten a few bolts… keep watch on the pumps… drive a truck to bring supplies and tools back for the boys… grease the machinery?"

"When do I start?"

"C'mon I'll introduce you to the boys."

"That was one hell of a quick interview," Anatole quipped. In his mind he considered that he could work here for a few months earning a good living. Then he could head back to New York with good money in his pocket and attend the auditions later in the year for the Al Jolson musical.

Amazingly for such a big oil project, Joe Donahue only employed including himself five regular workers. He took on an extra labourer when he needed to. Anatole was one of a long line of labourers who came and went as they were required.

Joe was undoubtedly the leader of this small group. He was friendly and warm but as Anatole found out later, Joe was the hardest man of all in a group of hard men. On the surface he was a good old boy but he had nerves of steel and an unwavering determination to find oil. No stranger to bar room brawls, he preferred to use his brain now. He had read deeply on the subject of oil drilling and after years of manual jobs he was now wildcatting. This meant drilling on previously untapped land outside of the usual company owned oil resource rich territories. It was a hell of a risk but at that time many Americans were embarking on ventures like this.

Anatole was introduced to Joe's small team. Red Diamond was an athletic looking Texan who spoke quietly in a soft drawl and was an industrious worker. He seemed to concentrate on the mechanics of the rig. The pump and beam needed to be constantly adjusted and Red was always on hand to see that things were working correctly.

River Orville was an amiable African American somewhere in his forties. The grandson of a slave he was a jack-of-all-trades who helped out wherever he was needed. Mainly his tasks were as a tool dresser.

The final member of Joe's team was a Mexican called Juan Pertezco. In his fifties with streaks of grey hair he was the eldest of the group. He was the cook for the group. When he wasn't preparing meals for the boys he ran errands and carried goods to the rig. Often he would climb up to the beam and hand tools to Joe and Red as they grappled with the movement and accuracy of the pieces leading to the drill bit.

Over the next few months the five of them worked well together. It was clear that this project was having difficulties. There were so many problems: the rig wasn't steady, the drill bits were not right and needed replacing, the makeshift road to the rig needed clearing and resurfacing for vehicles to get to and fro. When Anatole had been asked if he could use a spade, he had not bargained for digging a road. He and River found themselves employed on constructing a road for a while. Anatole allowed himself a smile from time to time on these perspiration soaked days. He was earning more money now than when he had been employed as an extra in Hollywood making eyes at Mary Pickford.

He was quiet about his past when he talked with the boys. All he would make reference to was his time working on the docks or as a seaman but he didn't let on that he had been press-ganged. For all intents and purposes he passed himself off as a drifter and a working man.

"Old Joe is real worried," said River to Anatole one day when they were surfacing the road.

Anatole looked towards the rig. "Why? He's likely to strike oil any day, isn't he? He could be a millionaire any time soon."

"It's taking a long time, friend. He's thinking that it's dry. Maybe he even built it at the wrong place."

At that moment Joe and Red stood by the rig reading a report. Joe had a concerned look on his face.

"The geologist's report seemed pretty certain. Do you reckon we've got a chance with this? You've worked on other rigs, Red. Have I blown my dough? Be honest as you can. I can take it."

"It takes time. I've worked on rigs that took months to even get started. We've got to keep going. There's oil down there somewhere."

"What shall I do now, Red?"

"Pack up for the day and let's have a couple of belts with the boys at the bar." He put a reassuring arm on Joe's shoulder. "It's a pretty tough old surface. It's not as if its porous or clay. We need to get some fluid into the piping and try and get some of the rocks to flow up to the surface. That will, I hope, give us some idea what exactly we have to drill through. We may have to look at the size of the drill bit."

"The bank's nervous about this investment." Joe took a letter out from his pocket. "They want to know when the well is coming in. If we don't get a gusher in the next six weeks, they'll go ahead and foreclose. I'm already extended to the limit. There will be just enough to pay the boys to then and that's it… busted… broke… bankrupt. I tell you, Red, if necessary I will work twenty-four hours a day in any weather to get that oil well up and running."

***

The saloon in San Castillo was doing good business that evening. Anatole went to the bar to buy a round for his co-workers and he looked around at his surroundings. It was easy to imagine this room in the bad old days when shootouts were a regular occurrence in what passed as the main street. In one corner Juan Pertezco was talking to a couple of cowboys. The others were sitting at a table waiting for Anatole to return. They were engrossed in a debate when he brought the drinks back. Red was making a good case for the future of Texas.

"I've got great faith in this state. What do you think, River? You never say too much."

"Every day I learn something different. Where there's cattle, where there is water and maybe somewhere down below there is oil." He said it with a smile.

"You tell me where it is, River and we'll start drilling tomorrow," Joe responded in good humour.

River continued, "People here talk a lot about the past. I don't know whether it's pride in this state or there's just a lot of talk about. The Alamo. Valley Forge. Bunker Hill. I guess they should look to the future more. The state has a lot going for it."

Juan returned to the table and sat down with them taking a sip of the beer Anatole had bought him.

"We're just debating Texas," said Red.

"It is a good place to be," Juan agreed. "When I look at what is happening in my own country. Mexico is in turmoil… you know… Pancho Villa and the revolution and now there is trouble in Europe."

"Europe? What is happening there?" asked River.

Juan pointed to the men he had been talking to at the bar. "Some of the boys are saying that an Austrian Archduke has been assassinated by a member of something called the Black Hand."

"Sounds like war," Joe said with firmness. "They've been sabre rattling."

"If there is a war in Europe, will America go in?" asked Juan.

"Let's not speculate," replied Joe. "Anyway it would be a European war. Not our concern. Let's concentrate on making our fortune here." A thought suddenly struck him. "If America went in, do you know what they would need?"

"Oil. Oodles of it," piped in Red. "To drive the machinery and the armaments. We better get those drills and pipes checked out, eh, Joe?"

"First thing tomorrow. Another round, fellas?" He got up to buy some more leaving the little group quiet for a moment.

"What did you do before this, River?" Anatole asked more or less to change the conversation from the downbeat topic of imminent war.

"I worked on the railway in three states. Then the Klan came calling at my last place and I figured it was time to move on and do something different. I never ever reckoned I'd be working in the oil business. I've enjoyed it. I feel like I've been working in something real special for the benefit of America."

"Nor me," agreed Juan. "I worked with horses on ranches in Mexico and picked berries and fruits. I cooked meals. Now in the hot sun I dig roads and assemble the rig. When that big gusher comes I don't think I will fully believe it myself until I am black with oil."

"It's coming," Red stated with certainty. "And when it comes it'll be big."

In the weeks that followed, the team concentrated on working very hard on getting the oil rig in good working order. The events in Europe could not have been further away from their minds. With a time limit of just six weeks to produce a gusher, the men worked late into the night. The rig was strengthened. The pumps were re-aligned to drill at a different angle. The drill bits were changed. Now when the fluid in the pumps pushed up rocks to the surface, Joe and Red knew just what they were up against. Once they got through the upper layer, the pump could press down harder allowing the drill bit to get further and further down until it could make that first strike.

There were times when the project seemed never ending. Finally the road to the rig was ready. A new fence was set up around the perimeter of it. The pump was restarted this time applying more pressure in its downward thrust and a new drill bit was boring down fiercely. Surely a strike wasn't that far away now.

At time it was an exhilarating and exciting experience to be part of. Oil exploration was a vital part of America's economy in the early twentieth century. Anatole was determined to stick around to see what an oil strike would be like. Ole Caroline, as Joe had named it, was a sight to see on the outskirts of San Castillo. Anatole carefully sketched it one day and decided to enhance it with oil colours. The locals watched the progress of it with interest. If the well came in big there would be employment for many people and big wages to match. Many took bets on just when that would happen.

In the centre of town a rickety old wood hall doubled up as a picture house. The Charlie Chaplin films were particularly popular and regularly played to packed houses. One night a Douglas Fairbanks swashbuckler was being shown and Juan, River and Anatole decided to go along. When they arrived at the venue Anatole realised with dismay that it was a film he had appeared in as an extra. For one moment he considered making an excuse not to go in but, never actually having seen the movie, he changed his mind and entered the building. Once inside he took his place with the others on the long hard cold wooden benches that passed for cinema seats. The men and women came from miles around to see this cinematic event, leaving their horses tethered to wooden rails and their vehicles, if they were lucky enough to have one, parked in the main street.

The magnetic charisma of Douglas Fairbanks lit up the screen. He was all things to everyone. Athletic. A swordsman. Macho before the word was invented. Sparky and with a sexual aura to the women who sighed in the audience. No one with the charisma of Fairbanks ever visited San Castillo. Anatole smiled and laughed with the audience. Watching this film here in this rough old town with grease stains on his fingernails he could hardly believe only a short time ago he had been part of that fabled and magical world. Then all of a sudden the scene he had been involved in crept up on him. There was a dramatic swordfight where Douglas Fairbanks had demolished several opponents with a swift parry and thrust.

Then the camera had swooped in for a close shot on the faces of the other swordsmen. Anatole paused for breath as his own face seemed to fill the screen in that wooden hall. Without saying anything, Juan and River turned to look at Anatole. They were lost for words at the realisation that their co-worker had been in films.

Back at the hut where the three of them had bunks he got round to explaining things. Red and Joe had another hut which they also used as an office. Juan, River and Anatole each lay in their bunks quietly. Finally Juan broke the silence.

"You are a man of many talents, senor."

"I'm a drifter," Anatole responded. "I take work where I find it." This was half true at least. "I worked on the docks in New York. I was a sailor on a boat to China. I was on a cattle drive. Yeah… I was an extra in Hollywood. Now I dig and grease on an oil well. So what the hell? It all makes for an interesting life."

"What next?" asked River. "That is when this work is over."

"I haven't thought that far," he replied and then he added, "of course if there is a war in Europe and the Yanks go in then I guess I'll join the boys in uniform. It might seem far off at the moment but you never know."

"I hope not," said River. "My grandfather joined the first black regiment in the Union Army back in the Civil War. He told me stories of what he had seen. War sure is terrible. I want no part of it. If a soldier is not killed on the battlefield or suffers some terrible injury then he is maimed in mind by having seen his friends die. I see no glory in war. No adventure in battle. There are still big issues in peacetime to be settled."

Juan and Anatole had listened respectfully as River had espoused his view. There was a definite sense of expectation that the world was on the brink of war. Anatole took a drink of water from beside his bed and lay back.

"I feel like I've been drifting all my life," he said. "Do you have family Juan?"

"I have a woman and children in Mexico. The children are grown up now. I have not seen them for some time. And you, senor?"

"Family? A sister. She lives in England.

"Before you ask," interrupted River, "I have no family.'

"So we are all orphans," said Anatole.

"Not quite, senor," Juan added. "We have today and tomorrow. We best get some sleep now. There is work to be done. Who knows that oil strike may come tomorrow."

Twenty-One

Lord Bernard Shervington wondered if the project he had been working on would be completed before the expected war. In his profession as an architect he was rebuilding an historic church that had virtually been destroyed by fire. It was located in a hamlet near Horsham in Sussex. During its existence it had served as a focal point for the community. In its lifetime whole generations of families had been baptised there, sang in the church choir, and married between its once sturdy walls. Now the new minister, the kindly Reverend Peter Nowlan wished for it to be restored to its previous glory.

It was quite a challenge. To begin with the original brickwork and stained glass windows were of another age. They would be difficult to replicate and after an extensive feasibility study an application was made to completely rebuild the structure. A local charity for the church construction was established, and the Member of Parliament for the constituency made a successful application for additional funds. Using old photographs and paintings of the church Lord Shervington had draughtsmen draw up plans with specifications based on the original measurements. Artists were hired to design paintings to be used on stained glass windows. The project was gradually taking shape and looked very promising. It was a modern church with an old design now

Reverend Peter Nowlan and Lord Shervington walked around the framework of the church. The carpenters and bricklayers had produced a sturdy job. The reverend ran his hands over the brickwork.

"Like a phoenix rising from the ashes. The structure is new yet it all resembles the original. How on earth did you get the bricks to match? The originals were made a hundred or so years ago."

"That's easy. The Shervingtons have a number of companies. One of them is a brickworks. I just gave them some of the originals and they did the rest."

"This is going to be a wonderful church in one of the most beautiful parts of England. I am looking forward to conducting services here. Tell me, Lord Shervington, I know architecture is your career but I know from our previous conversations you are from an old military family. What is your impression of these most distressing events in Europe? Do you think war is imminent?"

"I am sorry to say I think it seems inevitable. I regret to say it but I think the politicians are talking it up."

"Let us hope it does not come to that and by God's grace there will be a swift solution. Well, sir, I am very grateful for the work so far. I cannot wait for its completion."

They walked out into the sunshine where Tom Mollomby, the chauffeur, was waiting in the family car, a shiny Bentley. Behind them was a flurry of activity as carpenters and labourers went about their work.

"This has been one of the most worthwhile projects I have ever worked on," said Lord Shervington. "I can't estimate an exact time scale for you at this stage. Hopefully, baring any unforeseen circumstances no more than a few months."

BARRING

"By unforeseen circumstances you mean if there is a war, all the young men will go, such as those who are working so actively on the church."

"Possibly." Lord Shervington thought about that for a moment. The tradesmen all seemed to be young, eager and fresh faced. He stretched out his hand to the Reverend. "Sir, I will see you soon." He walked to the car where Tom held the door open for him. "Let's go to Chesney's Teashop in Horsham."

He had earlier arranged to meet Mariska there when he had finished his days' work. Restoration of old buildings was a satisfying career for Bernard, but he knew in all probability that soon he would probably be donning a uniform again. The war that was imminent looked set to be a strange complex one in which many nations would participate with a devastating loss of life.

How had it all begun? The trigger for the First World War began with the assassination of the Archduke Franz Ferdinand and his wife, Sophie, on 28th June 1914. The fifty-year-old heir to the Austro-Hungarian throne was shot as he and his wife were driven in an open-topped car in Sarajevo. Their assassin was a nineteen-year-old Bosnian Serb nationalist called Gavrilo Princip. He was a campaigner for release from the Austro-

Hungarian Empire – this event created tension between Austria and Serbia, and their respective allies. Germany supported Austria and Russia backed Serbia. France, which had suffered from earlier Prussian invasions, found itself at odds with Germany. Prussia had led the German Empire into an alliance with one of the Austro-Hungarian Hapsburg powerbases. Now as the Germans began mobilising their forces in Belgium and France, Britain found itself drawn into the war by its commitment to a number of treaties. No one could have predicted just what a terrible war this was going to be.

In the general atmosphere of things that day people went about their normal routine without any thoughts of the coming events. Men baled hay in the fields. People were out in the orchards picking fruit. Cows grazed peacefully. The green of the Downs and the trees looked lush velvet against a lustrous blue sky. Bernard indicated to Tom to pull over at a spot where there was a particularly scenic view.

"What is it, sir?" asked Tom.

"That view. England. Don't you just love this country? I would fight to the end to protect it from Kaiser Bill."

"If I were a younger man so would I. Finest country in the world. I've seen campaigns in Sudan and India. There is something about this fine green land that brings us back. I wish we didn't have to go to war. There are people in this land living in dire poverty, in appalling conditions with bed bugs and vermin, and children going hungry. Sometimes I think we need to fight for them."

"You have strong feelings then, Tom."

"Aye that I do, sir, and I had no right to say that to you. Especially with you being my employers."

"You had every right to say that," Bernard reassured him. "In this country we have the right to free speech. I happen to agree with you. As it happens, Mariska was born into poverty in Russia and raised in a tenement in New York. I once did a planning job in Limehouse. I saw enough then. I'm not a socialist. To be frank, I probably don't even know the true meaning of the word. But I think once the urgency of the crisis in Europe is over there will be firebrands battling for the under privileged and the poor. I may well join in the clamour if my status as a Lord gives me a right to do so." He paused. "Let's get to Chesney's Teashop. I'm meeting Mariska there at four o'clock."

The owner of the Teashop was Harry Chesney. He was a former

Colour Sergeant in the 25th Light Northern regiment in India who had won the Victoria Cross in an earlier campaign. Chesney had served with Captain Rex Shervington, and had brought the officers illegitimate son, Ravi, to England. After leaving the army, Chesney had become a tea planter in India and had made his fortune. Upon returning to England he had opened up a teashop and warehouse in Horsham. The teashop had become a thriving enterprise and was now the place to meet in the afternoons. Through Chesney's association with the Shervington family he had found Ravi employment as a butler at the house in Storrington. When the Boer War came in 1899, Ravi had enlisted in his late father's regiment only to die tragically on a battlefield in the Veldt. The Shervingtons, as with many families, had their secrets but with Lady Bernadette's death, and Mariska's arrival, they had moved on to a new generation. Now it seemed with the advent of war Bernard was about to follow the family tradition and rejoin the army. Almost certainly it would be a Sussex regiment.

Inside the teashop there were many well-dressed ladies enjoying the scones and cakes that were on offer. The walls were adorned with pictures of India and photographs of the regiment that Chesney had served in. Lord Shervington arrived and made his way into the ornate surroundings. Harry Chesney had done a good job in converting a run down building in the centre of Horsham to making it a plush venue for the local people. Mariska duly arrived shortly after and they sat down together to enjoy a Devonshire Tea of scones, clotted cream, jam and a pot of the finest brew that Chesney imported from Darjeeling. It was the calm before the storm. They both knew that these golden moments would be few from now on. A soldier and his lady passed by their table. Soon the sprinkling of service uniforms would be everywhere.

"What's the latest on that brother of yours?" Bernard asked. Anatole was always a good subject for conversation as he was so unpredictable.

"He was heading back to New York to try the stage again. It seems he got waylaid in Texas and is working on some oilfield in a place I've never heard of called San Castillo."

"I imagine you are both getting further and further away from your show business days. Do you miss it?"

"To be honest, I miss the whole razzamatazz. It was good while it lasted. Nat and I… well we went all over the world, met many famous people. Did I ever tell you Teddy Roosevelt came backstage once in New York?"

"No, I didn't know that."

"He sure did. Imposing figure. Real American legend. Yes, it was a great life. My agent, Paul Kapsia, wanted me to go to Hollywood. That was before we got engaged. Do you know something though, honey?" Bernard looked on. "I would rather be here with you than anywhere else in the world."

"Why? You had a great life on stage. Sometimes I feel I took you away from all that applause and adoration that goes with the show business world. The green and quiet of Sussex is a long way from a starring role in musicals and you were good at it – magnificent, in fact. Are you really happy? Do I make you feel good?"

Mariska squeezed his hand. "Bernard. I've got you. You are my rock. I was an orphan girl back in the States, remember? I took it bad when I lost my sweet and loving parents. The truth I guess is since then I have just wanted to belong somewhere. To be loved. When I was on stage the applause… the ovation…. the stage door Johnnies… if you don't know how to handle it… well you can get carried away by it all. I thought that being loved by an audience or by your fellow cast members would be enough. But at the end of the day I wanted something else. A home. A husband. Maybe I will go back at some time to the stage. Not for some time though."

"You know I will be joining up again?"

"Yes. We will be waiting for you." Mariska smiled to herself, wondering if he would understand her hint.

"We…?" he queried.

"That's right. I am going to have a child."

Lord Shervington's face lit up like a beacon. "How absolutely wonderful! I can't believe it. How long? When?"

"Three months. The doctor confirmed it this morning. Let's fact it, we've been married two years now. I was getting worried for a while. But no we're fine now. Happy?"

"Blissfully," he replied in a soft voice. "Sometimes the best of couples no matter how much they want children aren't blessed with them. My goodness we are lucky, aren't we? An heir to the Shervington estate. For a while I thought I would be the last in line."

"So you see, my darling, my return to the stage is going to be some way off. Since you're likely to be away at war for some time – and let us pray to God that it is all over quickly – and I'm going to be at home with a babe in arms. I would really like to get involved more in the family business. I know I can sing and dance but I have a brain too. My parents were hardworking. Pa was a seven day a week worker. It's not in my nature just to be a lord's wife. I want to do more, contribute more. I mean Lady Bernadette was an astute manager of the family affairs."

Lord Shervington appeared to ponder over what she had said. He was still learning something different about his wife every day. Mariska certainly had a strong will, no doubt inherited from her industrious Russian roots. The nation would be embroiled in war shortly and it would be a good time for her to become familiar with the Shervington companies.

"That makes sense," he agreed. "Not only are the Shervingtons a family steeped in military tradition, we are also entrepreneurial. I became an architect because my early army career consisted of me deploying men to build bridges in India. I broke away to be my own man. Besides Lady Bernadette was very much in charge of administrative things. The Shervingtons have invested in a garden nursery at Findon, a brickworks in Thakeham, stables in West Chiltington, two fishing boats – one in Worthing and the other in Littlehampton. I studied at University after the army and set up my own Architectural company with a strong emphasis on restoring old buildings. I'll have Tom drive you round the various companies and introduce you. How does that sound?"

Mariska smiled and nodded. The facts were that she wasn't so much as driven but curious and interested in the new world that she had entered. It was an eagerness to fit into the Shervington family enterprises. Each company basically managed itself with skilled workers in their respective trades. The Shervingtons had been instrumental in providing the finance to get each business started and, as investors, they audited the books from time to time as Lady Bernadette had done. The returns from their investments were enough to keep the manor house in Storrington well funded.

On the way out Lord Shervington was greeted with a warm smile by the proprietor, Harry Chesney. In days long gone he had been a regular visitor to Shervington Manor. On one occasion Lady Bernadette had invited him to a dinner party where King Edward VII and Rudyard Kipling had been the star guests. It was something of a surprise to all concerned that this ruffian son of the workhouse and Victoria Cross winner had more than just held his own presence in such distinguished company. He was a fascinating character. Mariska and Bernard spoke to him for a while. Then they walked out arm in arm into the sunshine of a beautiful summer's afternoon when everything looked glorious.

In the bandstand located in the centre of the town a military band played. They stood amongst the throng of well-dressed people and listened to the proud marching tunes. The band played 'Land of Hope and Glory', 'Soldiers of the Queen' and 'D'ye ken John Peel' There was something warm and wonderful about that splendid afternoon. The news that Mariska was expecting had only served to enhance this time.

On the eve of the First World War, 14th August 1914, the Foreign Secretary, Sir Edward Grey, announced, *"The lamps are going out all over Europe; we shall not see them lit again in our lifetime."*

Twenty-Two

Juan Pertezco prepared breakfast for his fellow co-workers on the oil rig. These were crucial days for the project leader, Joe Donahue. Each man knew it and the tension to produce the gusher was nail biting. In a week or so, unless he could get a credit extension from the bank, the oil rig would cease operations. Then they would all be out of business.

They all sat round the breakfast table as Juan served up sizzling bacon and eggs, freshly made biscuits and hot coffee. Joe leaned forward as if he was about to make an announcement. Red could sense what was coming.

"It's not good news, is it?" Red anticipated him.

"Three days, boys. I can only pay you to then, unless we get a strike, of course."

"Boss, I've got faith in you," River cut in quickly. "If you can't pay me I don't mind staying on a bit longer without my wage… as long as Juan keeps making breakfasts like this and my tummy is full, I won't complain."

"That's very good of you, old friend, but the bank is putting the handcuffs on me in five days' time, and more than likely they'll move their men in to take possession of the rig. I don't want to do this. I have to let a couple of you go today."

Anatole swiftly volunteered his resignation. "Let me finish my shift today, Joe, and I'll save you the trouble. You only brought me on for a while. I understand that."

"I'm obliged to you, Nat, and thanks for getting your hands dirty."

"I'll go too," said River. "I might try the railways in California."

"Thanks to both of you. Well let's enjoy this breakfast and get the days work done. I'll have your wages ready for you this evening."

"I'm sure there's oil there, Joe," Red assured him. "If we try and increase the pressure on the pump more we might get a breakthrough."

"Give it everything you've got then," Joe responded. "Tomorrow I'm driving to Dallas to see the bank manager for more time. You're in charge, Red." He turned to Anatole. "I'll be sad to lose you and River. Are you heading east? I could drive you to Dallas if you want a lift."

"What is there in Dallas?"

"Plenty of places to spend your hard earned dollars, and a lot of pretty women."

"You talked me into it." Anatole smiled. He was going to try not to waste any money on women. He had made that mistake before. But he knew he would fail on that intention.

***

The men worked hard that day. In the short time they had been together, they had established a good working relationship. Each man helped the other when necessary. They didn't say anything to each other but the general feeling was that Joe had drawn a blank. The project they were working on was almost certainly a dry hole without the prospect of an oil gusher. By the end of the day the machinery was in good working order. Everything was fine. If there was oil down below it would only be a matter of time. However, it was time for Anatole and River to say goodbye and to have a farewell drink with the boys at the saloon in San Castillo. During the months that they had worked at Ole Caroline the team had got to know many of the townsfolk. Grease monkeys and roughnecks mainly. Good ole boys who enjoyed themselves once they were free of the sweatshop conditions they worked in.

Drinks flowed like waterfalls that night. They sang 'The Yellow Rose of Texas'. Juan and a fiery senorita with flashing eyes danced in Mexican style in the saloon. To their surprise Anatole joined in. His dancing expertise held him in good stead. He hadn't toured South America with Paul Kapsia's outfit for nothing. Then all too soon another chapter in Anatole's life came to an end.

The next morning Anatole gave Joe an oil painting of Ole Caroline as he had requested. Whatever happened now it would serve as a reminder of a very difficult project, which so far was unyielding. Anatole had wanted to be there when the gusher came. He almost felt a failure for not being part of the winning team. These were the cards he had been dealt with this time. River shook hands with each of the men and then made his way to the rickety train station at San Castillo where he would soon be bound for a job on the railways in California. Joe and Anatole drove away to Dallas. In Joe's absence, Red and Juan remained behind to watch the progress of the pumps. Red was already hatching a plan to bring oil to the surface.

It was a long drive to Dallas, dusty and hot. The prairie and desert looked scorchingly hot. Occasionally a spiked cactus like a lone symbol of the Texas desert broke the monotony. Surprisingly despite the brutal heat a wind seemed to blow, and as it did balls of something resembling cotton fluff called mesquite was thrown up in the air.

Joe drove carefully. Hardly a vehicle passed them by. Sometimes there would be herds of Longhorn steers grazing in the distance and cowboys on horses rode close by. Anatole noticed Joe was strangely quiet. It was make or break time for him now. Joe had waged a fortune on this wildcatting venture and in the next day he would find out if he had a reprieve, at last temporarily.

"When do you see the manager at the bank?" Anatole asked.

"What's that?" Joe was caught unaware. "Oh, we won't get into Dallas until late tonight. Tomorrow morning I expect. I hope the guy is in a good mood when I see him. Neither of us will be laughing much. Still it's not your worry. What do you have in mind? Any plans?"

"I guess I'll head back to New York. You know, Joe, I really hope you find oil on Ole Caroline. It's been a hell of a challenge. A tough bet for sure."

"Well it's up to Red now. If the bank doesn't allow more time then that's it. That's the simple truth of the matter. A wildcat oilman's life is always a long shot."

The way Joe had spoken there was a sense of resignation about him. He was normally a positive man who had no time for sensitivity and caution in business. A total commitment and involvement was the only way to achieve big things. Now it seemed as if his hopes were dashed.

***

Red meanwhile was working hard back at the rig. He and Juan had put the rig mechanism on full strength. The wheel went round at a much increased pace, almost to danger levels, thereby maximising the pressure on the pump. The drill bit was going further and harder down than before. Night was beginning to fall and still the wheel was rotating more and more.

In the darkness a nervous Red stood perspiring. The tension and stress was beginning to take its toll. Juan handed him a bottle of beer and the two men knocked the contents back while keeping an eagle eye on the proceedings. Faster and faster the wheel turned. The pump was going up and down with great rapidity.

"If this doesn't work, I'm going to put nitroglycerin down there!" Red exclaimed and anyone else who listened in would have known he was serious.

"If you do that, senor, then you will blow the oil well to smithereens," Juan pointed out.

"There's oil down there. I can smell it. It's in the air." Red spoke with an absolute certainty. It was a hot night and the fury of the pump threw red dust up in the air. Juan's serape and sombrero was covered in a sprinkling of it. "Let's go back to the hut, my Mexican friend, and while we're waiting for the big oil strike I know that's going to come, we'll have a few bottles of this beer and if the whole goddam place goes up in blazes, we'll be too plastered to notice or to give a damn!"

The two men sat in the hut swilling back bottles of beer. Red was anxious and red-faced. Perspiration dripped from his brow. His shirt was soaking. For a moment it looked as if he was about to burst. Juan looked at him concerned, not knowing what to do or say. In the background the pump had been primed to maximum effect and the rig was making worrying noises. The fear each man had was that the well would be blowing wild before long

Meanwhile in Dallas, Joe and Anatole had shaken hands and parted. Anatole had immediately found a willing truck driver who gave him a lift up north. Joe checked into the Lone Star Hotel and after a couple of drinks in the bar he retired for the night. Soon he would be speaking to the manager of the bank asking for a stay of execution as far as foreclosure was concerned. Dammit, Joe was a proud man! The idea of virtually pleading with a jumped up nobody for more time was anathema to him. Hellfire! It was men like Joe who had risked everything to help build America. The bank manager had probably never had grease under his fingernails in his entire life. There was little he could do now but lay back on the bed and *LIE* hope a solution to this desperately troubling issue could be found the next morning.

Joe was a hard man who had made a living doing manual labour all his life. He had carried bricks, worked on construction sites, dug roads, laid pipes and erected telegraph poles. Anything dirty and difficult requiring muscle, brawn and sheer bloody mindedness was no stranger to his way of life. He wasn't used to dealing with the big shot money men and the legal niceties of solid contracts. Joe used to joke that he tackled work in the same way he made love to a good woman, with vigour, energy, knowhow and always learning new methods.

At three-thirty in the morning with only a few hours to go before his meeting with the bank manager, the sound of heavy rainfall bearing against the window woke him up from his slumbers. Texas was often a drought stricken state. Not so tonight. There was a sense of foreboding about the downpour outside.

The same noise struck the huts by Ole Caroline at approximately the same time. So powerful was the force against the windows that it seemed as if the hut was shaking. Both men had drunk themselves into a stupor and lay on the floor surrounded by empty beer bottles. It had been a hell of a party. Juan was the first to be roused and as he opened his eyes the first thing he noticed was that the walls were vibrating. There was the sound of something throbbing loudly and spluttering from outside. A whooshing sound combined with a roar suddenly hit the air. By now Red too had been woken and he listened momentarily to the mixture of noises. The hut was shaking so violently it felt as if it was likely to collapse at any second. They looked at each other in shock and without saying a word they rose to their feet and dashed outside.

The sight that greeted them shook them rigid. The well had come in big time. Black oil soared up into the starlit night sky. The huts were covered in oil. Red and Juan stood there gazing up at the gusher as if it was a firecracker on the fourth of July. Pretty soon their clothes were covered in it. Red moved forward to take a clearer look. The wheel on the pump was rotating at record speed. Any faster and the whole mechanism would collapse. "Juan, old fella, it's payday! The biggest payday we'll ever know!" He wiped the oil from his face. "First thing tomorrow we'll send a telegram to Joe's bank in Dallas and let them know."

"Before we do anything else, Red, don't you think we better slow things down?" Juan pointed to the pumps.

"Sure thing," he replied and went across to ease the pressure. So, after many agonising months 'Ole Caroline' named after Joe's late mother came in big. They didn't go to bed that night. The pair of them worked on the rig until seven o'clock in the morning. Then they cleaned themselves up and went for a hearty breakfast. Virtually as soon as the telegraph office in San Castillo opened Red sent a telegram to the manger of the bank in Dallas. By the time Joe went to plead for the extension of his loans, the manager would know of the strike.

**

Joe went to the bank the following morning. He walked in just after nine o'clock with a sense of dread. There was a secretary sitting close to the manager's office. He approached her and removed his hat.

"Morning, m'am. I'm here to see the manager, Mr Tooley."

"Your name, sir?" the secretary asked without looking up at him.

"Tell him Joe Donahue is here."

"Ah," she murmured and then looked up at him. Her eyes had lit up. "Mr Tooley is expecting you."

"He is?" This was news to Joe who had called without an appointment.

The secretary knocked on the bank manager's door and entered. A period of silence followed. Joe stood there wondering what he would say. Then the door opened quickly and the secretary emerged.

"Please go in," she said.

Joe walked in and Mr David Tooley stood up to greet him. He was a small rotund man with a contagious smile that surprised Joe. What on earth was he smiling about? Was he about to take a morbid pleasure in foreclosure? Mr Tooley shook Joe's hand warmly. What the hell was about to happen next?

"Congratulations, Mr Donahue! That is one hell of great news! Take a seat." Joe sat down with a quizzical look on his face.

"Excuse me for not understanding you, Mr Tooley, but why in hell are you congratulating me? Your secretary said you were expecting me. I've come here to plead, against my instincts to do so, for the bank to extend my credit. I'm missing something here, buddy. Are you taking a rise out of me or something?"

"This, Mr Donahue!" He waved a telegram at Joe. "Read it!"

Joe read the telegram. His eyes widened with amazement.

"Strike...! At three-thirty this morning." Joe looked across at the bank manager who was smiling back at him. "Ole Caroline came in after all!"

"I have to say, Joe... may I call you Joe? I was saying the bank were worried... real worried that the well wasn't coming in the way we hoped but I can't tell you just how pleased and relieved we all were when your associate Red Diamond sent the telegram to our office this morning. Me and a couple of the boys from the bank will come down to see your operation in San Castillo in the next day or two. Is that fine by you? Rest assured the bank will extend the deadline. We hope that you and the bank will have a long and very profitable association."

Joe smiled to himself. It is amazing how, when a man gets a winning streak, the bank are his best friends. When he is losing they are quick to admonish a guy like a misbehaving schoolboy who has been caught behind the wall with a pantry maid.

"I look forward to that, sir."

"Now I expect you have a payroll to meet. The bank will help you there. Any other likely oilfields you plan to wildcat?"

"Let's get this one fully operational."

"Sure." Mr Tooley shuffled through some papers. "I need you to sign these for the continuation of funds from the bank to ensure the future of your enterprise. Have you considered a name for your company?"

Joe contemplated for a moment. "I guess the Donahue Diamond Oil Company for the time being." He read through the papers and signed them. There was a smile on his face as he realised, by a stroke of luck, he had defied the odds.

***

The Donahue Diamond Company or DD Oil as it was later referred to was officially formed that day. It was a fruitful partnership that led to another eighteen oil wells being established in Texas over the next twenty years. The company became one of the major suppliers in the United States. It grew and prospered so much that it eventually became the dominant player in the cartel. Twenty years later after the establishment of DD Oil, Joe Donahue occupied a large office in Dallas. Hanging on the wall of the DD

Oil headquarters boardroom was the painting of Ole Caroline that Anatole had given to Joe. It remained there for many years afterwards even when the oil company's founders, Joe and Red, had passed on.

***

Anatole arrived back in New York some weeks later. He immediately went to see Paul Kapsia to find out about any parts going in any of the city's stage and musical shows. Al Jolson had been scheduled to appear in a show in which Paul had hoped he could find a role for Anatole. The show had now been postponed until further notice. There was a further shock to come for Anatole. Paul had announced he was quitting one side of the business as an agent to concentrate on his other role as a music publisher. It was a short-lived exit for on his way home one night Paul stumbled, fell over and died of a heart attack. For some time now he had been juggling the business of being a booking agent, show business entrepreneur, and music publisher. He had loved his work wholeheartedly which was why at the age of seventy-two he still felt compelled to carry on. An earlier health scare had convinced him it was time to offload some of his huge commitments and concentrate on his first love of music publishing. However, the decision had come too late. Now he was dead, leaving his beloved daughters, Anna and Karen, bereft.

For Anatole it was a double blow. Paul Kapsia had taken him and his sister, Mariska, under his wing at an early age. He had not only been their manager but a close friend and confidant often dispensingly concern. Anatole felt a deep loss at his passing. First of all it had been Jess Reubens. Now it had been Paul Kapsia. With Mariska in England Anatole's world had changed with a heart stopping suddenness. All three companies that Paul had run were now being wound down.

There was no one to represent Anatole now. Once more he was on his own. In order to survive he took a job waiting on tables in a sidewalk café while considering what to do next. He would read the papers on a daily basis to find out how the war in Europe was progressing. A terrible carnage was taking place. Already there were rumours in the press that President Woodrow Wilson would be called upon to commit American troops to the conflict.

One evening in the restaurant where he worked two soldiers came in and began discussing the probability of America's involvement in the war. They were convinced the call would come soon. Anatole, who cautiously eavesdropped into the conversation as he served them, decided what his next move would be. He would enlist in the army.

It seemed that his show business career was well and truly over now. After Paul Kapsia's death he considered finding another agent. The truth was that he would never find one with whom he could have such a good professional relationship as he did with Paul. His heart was no longer in the business. He and his sister had been a great dancing act but that was in the past now. Without guidance he was a lost man.

A premonition told him America would enter the war. How could they possibly stay out? The newspapers were urging involvement. For Anatole, he began to think of himself more and more as a professional adventurer rather than the dancer he had once been. He had a hunch if he joined up now he would have a good chance of becoming an officer. Never in his life had he lacked courage or nerve. This was to be the next major chapter in his life.

The next day Anatole went to an army recruiting office. There were a lot of men in the queue that day. It seemed many others had the same idea as he had, that a world war was imminent rather than just an European one. Close to home, American troops were already involved in another conflict. In Mexico the government had enlisted the aid of the United States military to wage battle against the rebel forces of Pancho Villa. It was more than a strong possibility that Anatole could find himself there. He wasn't worried. Whatever happened it would be another adventure.

Finally after a long wait a burly sergeant indicated to Anatole to join him at his desk. He was unsmiling, with a very serious face.

"I want to join the army," Anatole said confidently.

The Army sergeant looked him up and down, wondering whether he was a suitable recruit for uniform. "So tell me, son, why do you want to join the army? What makes a city slicker like you think you would be a good soldier?"

Twenty-Three

1915

Mariska gave birth to her first child at a private hospital in Worthing, West Sussex, while her husband was away at the front in Northern France. It was a boy who was named Alexander James Shervington. Her joy was only tempered by the sadness that Lord Bernard could not be there. He was a Captain in the Royal Sussex Regiment firmly entrenched in the muddy blood soaked battlefields near the French-Belgian border. This was a war like no other. The loss of life was not only staggering, it was frightening.

Captain Shervington had served in the army in peacetime. This time he was a leader of men at the height of constant bombardment from shellfire. The rain fell heavily as soldiers stood waist deep in water within the trenches. Nerves were frayed to breaking point. Constantly under siege by the Hun, Captain Shervington endeavoured to keep the morale of the men in good stead. Oh, how he loathed this war! The carnage in the battlefields was in the multitudes.

Here in the trenches, the tunnels were extended and widened to drain some of the water. It involved many of the men digging frantically to ease the severity of the conditions. The mud, cold, hunger, lice and general discomfort sapped the energies of the soldiers who always faced each day with the proximity of death ever near. They had been stuck firmly behind the trench lines in what seemed to be a tense waiting game broken suddenly by shelling and sniper bullets, and the fearful whizz bangs that soared past with devastating effect.

The stress of these events and ceaseless danger played on Captain Shervington's nerves. He was determined for as many members of those under his command to survive. A stoic reserve was one thing, but to lay in wait in the trenches for the inevitable advance by the German soldiers was no longer an option. In his bid for survival he stripped away any notion of vain glory on the battlefield. He needed to get his men up and out of the trenches, and across the German lines as quickly as possible, dismissing many of the enemy fatally. There were wire fences to get through as well. He was eager to develop a strategy; one that would not fail.

Down below in the trenches, in a room that passed for a study, he sipped from a mug of tea and with a pencil he sketched a scenario for a line of attack. It was lonely making a decision that if it were wrong could prove catastrophic for the lives of his fellow soldiers. He knew it was a matter of urgency and after much argument with his own conscience he came up with a plan. He immediately left his room and ascended a ladder to the top of the trenches

The rain had eased now and the sky was looking clearer. He sought out one of the most dependable soldiers he was serving with. Major Chris Sury was checking 303 rifles and munitions when Captain Shervington approached him. He had a pair of binoculars with him and looked across at the German lines. Then he handed them to Major Sury.

"Have a look and tell me how many machine guns you can see."

The major studied the other side in great detail. He could see the movement of the German soldiers through a tangle of barbed wire fences. They were doing virtually the same things as their British counterparts. Rifles were being checked. A haughty looking officer examined the guns. Machine guns were being reloaded and large field guns were being rolled forward. It was a grim sight. A further heavy bombardment was obviously imminent. He lowered the glasses slowly and turned to look at Captain Shervington in a direct manner. "Probably about seven or eight… that are clearly visible at least. There are the larger cannons too. If our men aren't mown down by machine gun fire then we'll be shelled as well."

The captain's response was instantaneous. "We're going over the top tonight. Get our best marksmen ready. I want the machine gunners taken out quickly. Let's go down below and we'll discuss strategy."

Major Sury was uncomfortable with the decision but as a military man of long standing he knew time was running out in the trenches. It was clear the enemy were planning an all out attack. Just when the strike would take place was anybody's guess. Captain Shervington hazarded a guess and considered the likelihood of an early hours attack. He decided to pre-empt the Germans."

"Do you have children, Major Sury?" They were beneath the lines now in preparation for the onslaught.

"Yes, sir. A boy aged eight and a girl of five."

"My wife may have given birth as we speak. I want to get home to see them urgently. I expect you're eager too, aren't you?"

"Of course, sir. And so is every man in the trenches who has a family."

"The thing is, Major, if we stay here waiting, the odds against us surviving are overwhelming." He glanced at his watch. "It's six o'clock now. I am proposing an attack at eleven o'clock tonight. That gives us five hours to prepare ourselves. I might be wrong in my estimation – and God forgive me if I am – but the way the enemy are conducting themselves, I suspect they are getting ready for an early morning tirade against us. We need to get in there even earlier and hit them with everything we've got. If we strike with some ferocity now our men stand a greater chance of survival and at the same time we can stop the advancement of the German lines. Should we lose this battle not only are we consigned to history but there will be no stopping the Hun. They will be ceaseless in their pursuit of our troops. They will be unstoppable. We cannot allow them that movement. Are you ready to go over the details now?"

"Sir, may I ask a question?" Captain Shervington nodded. "Do you estimate many casualties?"

It was a frank question that deserved an honest answer. "This is war, Major Sury. Yes, there will be casualties… and I may well be the first. I intend to lead the men." He pointed to a box on the table beside him. "In there are ten stopwatches. Issue them to ten good marksmen. They should set their watches for eleven o'clock tonight. Each man is to go out separately on patrol at ten-thirty tonight to reconnoitre where the machine guns are and take up position. At ten fifty-five they are to take careful aim. The moment the watches show eleven o'clock each man is to take out the gunners as far as possible and unleash a volley on the German lines. At the same time, precisely at eleven o'clock I will lead fifteen carefully selected men – and I want you to handpick them. Each of us will be carrying wire cutters and we will cut through the barbed wire. Then as we pass through we will lob grenades and dynamite at the heavy guns. Following on from that the rest of the troops can come in at all angles, and we will fight with gun, pistol, bayonet and our own bare hands if necessary. It will be bloody and it will be ferocious. But as long as we have the edge on the enemy casualties can, I hope, be kept to the minimum." The captain stopped to think for a moment. He looked directly at the major. "In the event of my demise, I think you know what to do. Your responsibility will be to lead the men to safety. I don't want to predict heavy losses Major. You may want to tell the men – if they haven't already done so already… to write letters to their loved ones in case… well if… I have already written one to my wife. I suggest you do the same to your wife and children. Tell me your thoughts on my plan. Don't hold back, Major Sury, I know you're an ambitious officer."

"I think it's a dangerous, high-risk strategy. I also think it might work. It's the field guns that worry me. They have the capacity to destroy great swathes of our troops. There's a need to get there quickly and blow them up. On the ground, face to face with the Germans, the combat may prove to be very rough indeed. It's not an understatement to say that it worries me."

"Have you thought what the only other option that is open to us? To literally sit there in the trenches with the lice and the rats in the filthy mud while Fritz slowly shells us all to oblivion. I don't know about you but I would rather go out fighting and, as company commander, it is my responsibility. On top of the safety of the men the only way to win this war is to force the enemy back. Should France fall to the Germans, then it may only be a matter of time before they cross the English Channel. If you're ready Major, I would appreciate it if these orders could be carried out immediately."

"Yes, sir. I do have one question, Captain Shervington. It's on the subject of prisoners."

"Prisoners? I know what Command are saying. The enemy has to be genuine in its surrender. A misjudgement could cost the lives of our men. Any doubt and I think we all know what we must do." He paused becoming pensive and thoughtful. "The enemy must be treated humanely if they lay down arms in good faith. They are soldiers fighting their cause, however misguided it may be. If they raise arms after volunteering surrender that is a treacherous act and we must do the necessary. We have to get through the night first of all Major. That will be difficult enough. Will you let me know when everything is set to go?"

"Yes. It's going to be a long night, isn't it, sir?"

"Maybe the longest night of our lives." The major turned to go. Captain Shervington quickly added an afterthought. "Oh, Major… I hope we can see our respective families very soon."

Major Sury left and returned to the lines to organise the attack. It was lonely for the captain, having made one of the most crucial decisions he would ever have to make in his life. Like a man awaiting execution the hours would tick by slowly. He absorbed every passing minute in the lead up to the coming battle. His conscience troubled him. The responsibility of his decision weighed heavily on him. He wished he could go back to being Lord Bernard Shervington following his career as an architect, and living in the quiet village of Storrington.

Lord Bernard Shervington was a man who possessed great qualities of courage, sincerity and loyalty. He had a rich, warm-hearted voice that endeared him to those he met. In addition he was authoritative with a commanding presence. Basically he may have come from a military background but he was a peaceful person by nature who found war unpalatable. He only viewed his present position as having to do his duty and carry out distasteful tasks in the short term. Once this was all over he would happily return to his peacetime occupation.

A number of officers and men came to see him to discuss tactics. Then when they had gone he quietly said the Lord's Prayer in the sanctuary of his private room below the trenches. He took out of his backpack a photograph. It was of him and Mariska on the Sussex Downs. For Bernard it was the most beautiful place in the world and Mariska had been the crowning glory of his life.

Up above there was a sombre, reflective mood amongst the soldiers as they took up their positions in preparedness for the tumultuous battle that would take place. In this war 'to end all wars', each side was cautious and in readiness for the surprise attack that they were always ready for. Whether it had been with Gordon at Khartoum, against the Zulus at Rorkes Drift, or in Mafeking, the British soldier had always shown exemplary courage. Tonight would be no exception.

A bespectacled Tommy played the tune of 'Greensleeves' on his mouth organ. In the silence before the coming storm, the tune seemed to rise above the sombreness of the battlefield to the extent that even the Germans paused to listen. In the British lines on a cold, wet, uncomfortable night it was a reminder of the green land of their birth, and the loved ones they might never see again. Reflected in the eyes of each man was the mirror image of something that meant love or nostalgia. Their eyes were either red with the immense tiredness or resilience against constant battle, or the agonising thoughts that this could well be their last hours. Even the most hardened man could not avoid the tears from welling up. Crying was just for babies some might have thought. How wrong they were. It was also for men not scared to show their emotions and loving feelings.

One young soldier climbed one of the ladders in the trenches and dared to look across the parapet, taking a daredevil risk to avoid a sniper's bullet. To his amazement he saw a German soldier doing exactly the same thing. The young man mouthed the words "Hullo Fritz". Further to his surprise the German soldier touched his metal helmet and appeared to mouth back "Hullo Tommy". Even more surprising was the fact the German soldier smiled at him. The soldier returned the smile, winked at him, and then descended down the ladder back down into the trenches. *Poor bloke. We'll be trying to kill each other tonight and I've nothing personal against him*, thought the soldier.

Captain Shervington duly joined the lines. The men took up their positions and the feelings of nervous anticipation swamped them. At exactly ten-thirty his specially chosen marksmen began to filter quietly out of the trenches crawling carefully to their allotted positions. It was a long wait until 10.55pm when they would carefully aim at their respective targets. A thought suddenly entered the Captain's head. He turned to the soldier who had been playing the mouth organ.

"Son, what's your name?"

"Private Billy Ward, sir."

"Play that tune… 'Greensleeves'… up to eleven o'clock as the men leave the trenches… and good luck, son."

"I will do. Good luck to you too, sir."

The tension was unbearable. Private Ward began playing the tune. 'Greensleeves' floated above the silence. The marksmen took aim. The countdown to eleven o'clock began. The soldiers in the trenches began to get ready like runners at the starting point. The stopwatches ticked more quickly now it seemed. Five, four, three, two, one. Then there was a massive chorus of 303-rifle fire. The German machine gunners were dispensed with almost immediately. Several just slumped back without awareness of what had happened to them.

Captain Shervington raced forward with his team of men who cut their way quickly through the tangled mess of the barbed wire. It was definitely a race to the finish line. The marksmen kept up a continual barrage of bullet fire for as long as they possibly could. No sooner had the barbed wire fences been cut than the soldiers ran through tossing grenades and sticks of dynamite at the huge cannons. In the next instant the British soldiers used every weapon at their disposal. The confrontation was fierce and horrifyingly violent. Behind the Captain's men the rest of the soldiers poured across the German lines gradually overwhelming the enemy. The fighting raged on for what seemed an interminably long time. It was a terrible friction of bullet and bayonet.

Never in his life had Bernard Shervington been in such a tussle. He seemed to fight man after man and still survive. He stopped seeing the faces of the enemy whether they be young or approaching middle age. All he saw was the German uniform and he struck out regardless at it. Then he lost his footing in the mud and he was on his back as a soldier of the Kaiser's army came towards him with a bayonet. His gun wouldn't fire and the mud was so slippery he couldn't get to his feet. That was it. It was all over. From one side Private Billy Ward shot the man with his pistol and took on several others immediately afterwards protecting his captain from the onslaught. Quickly he threw the captain his pistol and picking up a fallen rifle he shot and bayoneted his way through the enemy soldiers. Bernard was on his feet and fighting again. On and on he went managing to survive this most dreadful of battles.

The British had won through on this skirmish. It had been no easy victory. The loss of life on their own side had been incalculable. This triumph had come at a terrible cost but for the Germans it had been disastrous. From seemingly what had been a certain victory they had not only lost virtually all their troops, but their fierce fighting artillery had also been destroyed.

In the early hours of the morning as the dawn broke over the French countryside the scene was one of smoking wreckage and smouldering embers. The stench of the dead and the flames still flickering from the ashes of the field guns that had been blown up was grave and unforgiving. An army padre prayed with many of the men. Medical orderlies attended to the wounded. In a bid to bolster the confidence of the men, Captain Shervington walked around thanking as many as possible and in particular Private Billy Ward who had certainly saved his life that day. He spoke to the wounded and dying, a task he tackled head on realising that his own risky decision was the reason for their outcome. Inside he was grief-stricken but on the surface he tried to be controlled and unemotional. He came face to face with Major Sury. The two men looked at each other not really knowing what to say as they surveyed the battlefield. Finally it was the Captain who broke the ice.

"How many more of these battles must we go through, Major, before it's finally over?"

***

Mariska had been woken up early by the baby at Shervington Manor. Looking out of the window from her bedroom she could see that the Sussex Downs were shrouded in mist. She opened the window to take in the early morning air which was so pure it was like fine wine. There was a wind blowing up which seemed to carry the faint sounds of thunder breaking in the distance. Mariska looked up at the sky. There were no signs of rain clouds. It was a peculiar phenomenon. She listened carefully. Surely it couldn't be. Then she realised with dismay that the noise she was hearing wasn't that of thunder. It was the sound of cannon fire being blown across the English Channel all the way from Northern France. Her heart felt saddened. Those poor boys over there. What hell they must be going through. She thought of her husband. Would he survive to see his newborn son?

There were photographs in frames of Bernard, Anatole and her late parents on the occasion they attended the wedding in Leeds. Mariska picked up the baby and gently rocked him. She walked across to each of the photographs that were mounted in different places around the bedroom.

"This is your daddy, Alexander," she said softly. "He is a good, brave man and I want both of you to meet very soon. I love him and you so much. My mother once told me that my brother and I were her jewels." Mariska stood holding her baby by the photograph of Viktor and Ekaterina. "This is my mother, your grandmother with your grandfather." She sighed with sadness. "All these years on I miss them with all my heart. They were such kind, gentle people." Moving on a bit further to a dressing table she came to a picture of her and Anatole on stage as the Dancing Luckies. "And this is my brother, Anatole. Your Uncle Nat who you will hopefully get to know one day." She spoke quietly to herself. "Just where he is now, I have no idea."

Unbeknown to her, Anatole was also at war. He was serving with the United States Army in Mexico. His battles were against the raucous but highly disciplined rebel army of Pancho Villa.

Twenty-Four

1916

Mexico was a rugged, passionate, dramatic land that contained elements of beauty and squalor. It was a mass of contradictions. On the one hand it had poverty to the extreme and on the other it had riches unattainable to even the most hardworking and entrepreneurial of citizens. There was an undercurrent of violence yet somehow the country remained fervently religious. Even at this time of revolution, the majority of people seemed peaceful and well mannered. Fiestas regularly took place ignoring the day-to-day battles between government troops and Pancho Villa's rebels. This was a defining time in the history of Mexico.

The image of the swaggering hombre and the dazzling señoritas was very much in evidence. It was clear that the country had not lost its confidence and pride in itself. Nor had it lost its sense of merriment. The people carried on with life regardless.

José Doroteo Arango Arámbula was known better by the pseudonym of Francisco Villa but it was the nickname Pancho Villa that brought him notoriety. He became one of the most charismatic and legendary revolutionaries in Mexican history. Like some sort of twentieth-century Latin-American Robin Hood, the myth surrounding his exploits seemed to outstrip the reality. Amongst the peasant population, Villa and his loyal followers reached heroic status, robbing the wealthy patrons, and subsequently taking back the vast acres of hacienda land which were then handed over to the poverty stricken masses. While the United States government led by Woodrow Wilson had been broadly sympathetic to the rebel cause, they had now given their support to Villa's rival Venustiano Carranza who they considered could establish a far more stable administration.

Villa had lost credibility when a group of his supporters had ambushed a train near Santa Isabel, Chihuahua, which resulted in the loss of American lives. A further attack by the forces of Pancho Villa on the town of Columbus, New Mexico took place. This time the 13th Cavalry were attacked and military provisions were stolen. More Americans were killed in the ensuing battle. This prompted President Wilson to take drastic action in a bid to resolve the dangerously escalating crisis.

General John Pershing took command of 5,000 US Army troops who were specifically brought into Mexico to bring Pancho Villa to heel. If they managed to capture him they could break the morale of the revolutionary forces and effectively end the opposition to the Carranza regime. Almost as a rehearsal for America's entry into the Great War, heavy artillery, including tanks and aircraft, were employed in their search for Villa. Across a fierce and blistering terrain Pancho Villa managed to remain an elusive invisible renegade undetectable even by the most advanced military force.

When Anatole had joined the army a little over a year before he had imagined, expected even, that the United States would have found itself embroiled in the European War by now. This hadn't happened as President Woodrow Wilson went to great lengths to keep the nation out of the war. Now they were in the Mexican campaign.

Conflicts were breaking out all over the world. The war in Europe raged on with a terrible loss of life. For future generations the tragic battlefields of the Somme, Reims, Ypres and Passchendaele would pass into military history. In the Middle East a sensitive, emotional, tough and highly intelligent English officer, T E Lawrence, became something of an unlikely and enigmatic hero. He showed immense skill and organising ability in uniting warring Arab tribes against Germany's principal ally, the Turks, who had something of a stranglehold in that region. Lawrence not only led the Arabs into battle in a warrior-like fashion but he showed diplomacy at the highest level. Thereafter he would forever be known as Lawrence of Arabia. His story would be retold for years to come.

At Gallipoli a generation of brave Anzac troops including Anatole's friend Jim Cope lost their lives in a disastrous military misjudgement. For the British their problems were further compounded by the troubles in Ireland and the Easter Uprising. They were fighting now on two fronts. On the fields of Flanders and the Irish mainland, young men were laying down their lives. In Russia a fierce revolution took place in which the tsar and his family were executed. It seemed as if war would never end.

It was all a long way from Mexico where reports of the war regularly came through to the serving troops. Some had relatives and friends there, particularly those from immigrant families who expressed concern for their loved ones caught up in the maelstrom of war.

Anatole had found the army tougher and more rigorous than he had ever imagined. He had undergone his basic training under the near sadistic auspices of a career sergeant who was verbally abusive to every new recruit without exception. Somewhat narcissistic he was full of his own self-importance, thinking of himself as a superior being to the mere mortals who he considered were play-acting at being soldiers. He drilled them to near exhaustion, double marched them at every opportunity, exercised them to the extent that they were physically fit and able to show great endurance in the toughest of all conditions. Constantly he criticised each man personally until his harsh words began to flow off them like water off a duck's back. By the time the recruits had been trained, they were lean, hard and resistant to the cruellest of words. They were also crack shots trained to hit long-distance moving targets. It came as a relief to some of them to be sent to Mexico. Surely action in the field would be easier than the training they had just gone through! Many of the troops would go on to serve in the Great War. They would be more than ready for that conflict by then.

The war did not have entirely unanimous support from all Americans. It was the same story with most wars, that sometimes men would fight for a cause and not necessarily the nation. There were American mercenaries and medical staff who were employed by Villa. They fought against the Mexican Army rather than the troops of their own nation. The result was that Americans on both sides of the war would lose their lives in Mexico.

The camp where Anatole was based consisted of rows and rows of cone shaped tents. Several of the officers had larger tents where they also had desks and tables from where they planned their next strategy. The camp was situated some way out of town where it had been deliberately sited on open ground so that they were not easy prey for an ambush. To be too close to a major town would pose other difficulties. The people of Mexico were not happy at the presence of US troops in their country which some considered tantamount to an invasion. Most of them looked forward to the earliest possible resolution to the political turmoil that began in 1910 and would drag on for another ten turbulent years to 1920.

There was one lieutenant who managed to project leadership and the strong silent character associated with the heroes of American legend. He went to great lengths to assess the individuality of his troops. Tall, lean, firm in making decisions and commanding in every sense of the word, he was also ambitious. In time he would go on to become one of the most famous generals in the military history of the United States.

It was a surprise to Anatole when one day the adjutant came across to see him in his tent and told him to report to the lieutenant. Anatole was now a corporal and wondered why he, in his lowly rank, was being called for. When he arrived at the lieutenant's long tent he recognised another soldier he had become friends with. Sergeant Gerry Valentine was also waiting there.

The lieutenant looked both of them up and down, responding in turn to their salutes. "Stand easy, men." He unfurled some maps on a long table. "You are both wondering why I've called you over. I've got a mission for you. I have been asking for details on suitable men for the job I've got in mind, and your names came up. Sergeant Valentine, I understand you've worked with horses and you speak several languages. Is my information correct?"

"Yes sir. I was raised on a ranch just outside of Miles City, Montana, and I was a professor of languages at University in California." The lieutenant had the unnerving habit of staring right into the person's eyes he was talking to. Gerry Valentine wore thin-rimmed glasses, looked more Swedish than American, and appeared very academic.

"Why did you join up, Sergeant?" asked the lieutenant.

"I figure America will be in the European war at some stage. On the other hand, I reckoned on getting a head start."

"A wise decision. I hear you're good at tracking."

"That is correct, sir. My parents had a cattle ranch and a lot of rustling went on in those parts of the country. From my father I learned how to follow trails and survive in the open. He also taught me how to find direction by using the stars at night."

"How's your Spanish?"

"It's my strong point, particularly Catalan. I can speak it fluently, read and translate without too much difficulty."

The lieutenant then turned to Anatole. "You're a Rusky. Is that correct?

Anatole wasn't quite sure about the lieutenant's reason for asking the question, but assumed the man may have harboured suspicions of foreigners serving in the US Army.

"I was born in Russia, sir, but my parents took me first to Yorkshire, England, when I was six and then on to America. I am an American citizen."

"You've had something of a mixed career, Luchenya." The officer glanced down at his notes. "Entertainer. Shanghaied to China. Worked with cattle in Australia. Spent some time on an oil well in San Castillo, Texas." He paused to see his reaction. Anatole was surprised. The lieutenant had really done his homework. He continued, "San Castillo has quite a large Mexican population. Did you ever hear the revolution mentioned in conversation by any of the residents?"

"Only briefly, sir," Anatole replied. "The local Mexicans were just itinerant peasants. They worked in factories. The sweatshops. One worked with me on the rig. I hardly heard a mention of it."

"You were an artist too. Good at sketching. A draughtsman."

"Yes sir. That was another string to my bow."

"Good I can use all those talents, gentlemen. I want to use both of you in a scouting capacity. Take a seat." There were two chairs behind the long table with maps. They sat down and the lieutenant sat on the opposite side. "Pancho Villa has gone to ground. No one has set eyes on him and we want to find him. He is not to be underestimated. He's cunning and ruthless. Our intelligence sources suggest he may be hiding out in Durango, possibly in the Sierra Madre Hills where he was once a bandito. My gut instinct is that it may be a ruse and in fact he could be leading his army south. Villa has won a significant number of battles at Chihuaha, Ojinaga, Torreon, Saltillo amongst others. Some Americans who worked for the American smelting and refining company were killed in the train ambush at Santa Isabel. Villa and his men left Columbus in ruins. There have been further attacks in Texas at Glenn Springs, San Ygnacio and Fort Hancock. Before all this I met him at Fort Bliss in Texas and I can tell you now, despite the legend and the support he enjoys from a vast majority of Mexicans, he is not a loveable bandito. He was once a shrewd governor of Chihuahua and a skilful general. I want both of you to head down south and check out all his trails and tracks to give us a general indication of just where his men may be heading." He leaned across to a map on the table and pinpointed a position. "I had an army cartographic draughtsman draw up this map with an emphasis on high and low ground. I believe some of his men may be hiding in the hills. This is where you come in, Sergeant Valentine. I want you to put your tracking skills to good use."

"Where do we start, sir?" He leaned forward to examine the location.

"We're here." The lieutenant pointed to a spot on the map. "I want you both to head down about seventy miles in one direction traversing a combination of high ground and low areas returning a different way so that you cover a large radius. Look hard at the tracks, Sergeant Valentine. Very hard. Examine for heavy wheel tread. That suggests cannons and field guns perhaps. Light tracks may mean covered wagons. These may contain rifles and other forms of arms. Horse tracks by the dozen indicate that Villa's army is on the move. A few riders here and there could well be individual riders who might be scouting ahead for US Army patrols. Make notes on this map of what you find. Don't skimp on any detail. The more information you can provide the more we have to work on. Any questions Sergeant?"

"Yes sir. If we encounter any of Villa's men… presuming we don't have a shoot out and they put pressure on us…"

The lieutenant was quick to interrupt. "Don't take any chances. His boys may play rough. Use your knowledge of Spanish as a diplomatic linguist to bargain, extract information or, if you get close enough to a camp, to listen in and translate a conversation. Just one shred of information you can come up with may be enough to help us influence a military manoeuvre. Make sure you have plenty of ammunition, spare rifles and pistols, everything you need if you are in a very tight spot." He reached into a case by the side of the table and produced several photographs. "These are recent pictures of Pancho Villa. This one was taken at Fort Bliss, Texas, where I was General Pershing's aide. Villa is in the centre between General Obregon and Pershing. The other shots are of him more recently put out by his own people. If you come up close to anyone with the slightest resemblance to him, I want to know about it and just where you saw him. Should you be on high ground and see from a distance a band of armed men moving at long or close range, this is where your abilities, Corporal Luchenya, will be needed. I want you to sketch what you see in the finest detail, the men, horses, weapons if you can make them out. Draw anything that you think may be useful. Where a camp has been. Wagons. Carriages. That's it, gentlemen. Get everything you need and be ready to move out in an hour. Take this map. Be back when you can… safely."

"Yes sir," they both replied in unison, standing up and saluting without any prompting. Gerry and Anatole immediately walked out of the tent into the bright sunshine. When they had gone a fair distance away from the earshot of the lieutenant, they stopped to take stock of their orders.

"He didn't miss a beat, did he, Gerry?"

"Thorough to every last detail."

"What was his name again?"

"His name? Patton. Lieutenant George S Patton."

***

Gerry and Anatole left the camp fully prepared within the hour. There was a strong element of tension about their mission. The risks were huge. Right from the outset of their journey Gerry examined every trace of a hoof, boot print or wheel groove. He was a consummate professional who took his tasks very seriously. In his youth in Montana Gerry and his rancher father had frequently tracked down rustlers. Now he was employing those same skills in pursuit of a rebel Army.

It was a hard and gruelling trail. Lieutenant Patton had been right to be selective in his choice of men for this mission. Both Anatole and Gerry may have worked in professions light years away from soldiering but underneath they were tough cookies who could roll with the punches. Each man's background equipped them with a granite nerve able to withstand tremendous pressure. While Gerry studied the track for telltale traces of groups of soldiers, Anatole would ride up ridges and steep inclines always keeping a vigilant eye for any rebels lurking in hiding waiting for a potential ambush.

The first town they came to was Corsuva which was set like a lone fortress in the desert. It bore all the hallmarks of what was perceived as a typical Mexican settlement. Decaying adobe buildings gleamed against the backdrop of a deep wide blue sky and red sandy plains. Knowing that this was likely to be the last major town they would encounter for many miles to come, the temptation to stop was irresistible. Even sleepy towns had their secrets. No stone was to be left unturned. It was just possible that hidden behind these unappealing walls the revolutionary leader they were seeking may well have been staring out through a crack. For two American soldiers entering Corsuva was a rehearsal for suicide. Their uniform engendered hostility. The American presence in Mexico no matter how well intended was barely tolerated. But Gerry and Anatole did not lack courage and decided to show defiance by riding into town.

Corsuva was a ramshackle dilapidated poverty stricken town that showed no signs of ever having been a prosperous place. It was too hot and humid for the locals to be angry. Malnourished Mexican Indians sat by the side of the road as if they weren't sure how to spend the day. Goats roamed freely and aimlessly, as did a few steers. Vaqueros stood in the shade watching suspiciously as Gerry and Anatole rode by. Market sellers glanced upwards quickly. Old women squinted their eyes in the sun while the younger ones took longer looks at the strangers in their midst. A crumbling Spanish mission stood at the end of one street. In another a Catholic church with stained-glass windows in pristine condition appeared to be the most carefully preserved building in the town. Perhaps it was the sanctity of the place. The whole town was all too quiet and peaceful to be believed. Maybe it was Gerry and Anatole's inbred cynicism that anywhere could, on the surface, appear so calm.

They brought their horses to rest outside the church. For a moment both men stood and looked around them. It was hot, dusty and quiet. Hardly busy at all – in fact there hardly seemed to be anyone around. There was always the possibility of the sly gunman who would suddenly emerge and take them by surprise leaving them no chance at all. Gerry looked around for the glimmer of sunlight that might be sparkling off the gun-barrel. Anatole looked around nervously. His fingers were at the ready in case he urgently needed to reach for his gun.

"These people are dirt poor, Nat," said Gerry. "No wonder there's a revolution here. There are gold and extravagant palaces in Mexico yet the poor live like this. If I was a peasant I'd be backing Pancho Villa."

"I wonder what the hell they eat."

"Probably grasshoppers and beans. The food we eat back in the States would be considered a feast here. Looks quiet enough to me. There's nothing in the trail to this town that suggests Villa's men have passed through. I just want to go inside the church for a moment."

"I didn't realise you were a religious man, Gerry."

"Only when I need to be. Keep watch. Be careful."

Gerry entered the church. There was an aura of peace and something so calm about the interior that it eased any tension he felt. He was not a man given to displays of emotion or someone who spoke openly of his religious beliefs. To him prayer was a private thing. In the church there were a handful of people. Several old women sat on their own space at infrequent distances. A young woman sat with her head in her lap. It was hard to work out if she was just resting or in silent prayer. Two old men sat close to each other, saying nothing and just staring straight ahead. Another man sat on his own with a sombrero pulled down so that his face was not discernible. He pushed his hat up slightly and watched Gerry kneel down in prayer. There was nothing about the man that gave rise to suspicion. He just seemed to be an ordinary peasant taking out time from his daily chores for private worship. Nothing in his appearance set him apart from anyone else in the town. Such was his normality it would have been hard for anyone close by to grasp the fact that this man was Pancho Villa. While Gerry and Anatole examined the trails for his location, the very man they were looking for was just yards away. The atmosphere in the church was so quiet it was possible to hear the sounds of one's own breathing. Always it seemed that the spiritual presence of a divine deity could be linked to that of prayer in thought and solitude.

When Gerry had finished his private worship he rose to his feet and walked out gently. There was something about the beauty and rigid religious values of the Catholic Church that the people attending always moved around quietly. Outside Anatole was waiting patiently. His eyes flickered around constantly. Although he couldn't see anybody in the nearby buildings he felt he was being watched. He was anxious to leave. Gerry came out into the sunshine and untethered his horse.

"I was about to ask you what you were praying for," said Anatole. "But I guess if I did you'd say I was sticking my snout in where it doesn't belong."

"Yep. I could say that. I'm more polite though. Let's go, Nat."

They mounted their horses and rose off slowly. From behind a market stall a lone man aimed a rifle in their direction. He raised it and began to pull the trigger. Before he could fire a hand shot out and gripped his shoulder hard, forcing the man to spin around in anger. He found himself glaring into the face of Pancho Villa who nodded his head.

"No my friend" Villa said in Spanish. "We have no quarrel with the individuals. It is armies we oppose."

The man brandishing the rifle lowered it and watched them ride away. Villa nodded his head in one direction and said, "Come! We will join the men,"

Unbeknown to Gerry and Anatole the Army of Pancho Villa's army was regrouping only a few miles away behind some hills in the distance. Had they gone on a different trail they could well have ridden straight into Villa's army. If Gerry and Anatole returned by an alternative route they would almost certainly be facing Villa's guns.

While the two soldiers rode away, Pancho Villa and his friend mounted their horses and rode quietly out of the town, apparently unrecognised by the local people. Such was Villa's appearance he seemed to blend in with the ordinary peasant worker making his identification from the mainstream an extraordinarily difficult task. His revolutionary group had been hiding in the hills near Corsuva where they had a secret cache of weapons. These included a batch of 7mm Mauser rifles and carbines. Shortly Villa and his men would start moving south as Patton had predicted.

A few miles outside Corsuva Gerry and Anatole passed by a creek which in the stark barrenness of the Mexican desert was not so much a stream but a mere trickle of water, where there were a number of peasant women filling up water buckets and washing clothes. They looked up disapprovingly at the soldiers. Anatole attempted a smile at them in a charm offensive. It failed to break down the barriers. An old woman moved forward and spat at them.

"Go home, Yankee! Let us solve our own problems. You are not wanted here!"

For a moment Anatole feared the wrath of the women more than an encounter with Villa and his militia! They upped the pace of their horses and rode back out onto the central trail they had earlier been following. For several more days they rode lonely desert routes, checking foot and hoof prints. Anatole sketched a burnt-out camp, but it didn't appear to be that of many men. Probably lone riders or banditos. Not once in three days did they encounter a single rider. Nor did the tracks yield anything other than the fact that no one seemed to have passed that way for some time. Soon it would be time to start riding back to their own camp following the route on the hills and high ranges that Lieutenant Patton had highlighted on the map. It had been a fruitless mission so far. Neither man wanted to return devoid of information. They needed something of substance to show their officers. Very shortly they would have just that.

Twenty-Five

Travelling through Mexico on horseback was one of the best ways of seeing this scenically diverse country even at a time of revolution. From the dusty harsh plains and scrubland they had now begun the return journey on high ground. The night was beginning to fall and the two men decided to pitch camp on the heights. It was still quite warm as they settled down for a few hours before continuing their mission. The horses rolled on their backs in the dust. Gerry and Anatole eked out their remaining rations. Another worry that they had was that their horses were beginning to tire. Soon they would need to rest by one of the waterholes indicated on the highly detailed map they carried.

Beyond their military duties neither man had really talked to each other on a social basis. At this stage in the intense quiet and humidity Anatole decided to talk to his fellow soldier about something more than just their pursuit of Pancho Villa's men. Gerry Valentine was not an easy man to get to know. So far he had just been a dogged professional.

"I guess our first priority tomorrow morning will be to go back down there and find the waterhole for us… and our horses."

"Yes, Corporal Luchenya, that would be right. We'll go at first light in just a few hours time. I just checked Patton's map. It's only a mile or two away. I don't know about you but I'm concerned we haven't got anything to deliver to Patton back at the camp. He won't be happy if we've nothing to report."

"We'll find something. I'm sure of it. For a country in the midst of a revolution tearing itself apart every thing we've seen so far seems mighty quiet. In Corsuva the town was pretty subdued. When you went into the church to pray I was surprised that as a serving hard-nosed soldier you had such a strong faith."

"Oh, we have faith in those fine horses of ours that have carried us across the harsh extremes of this country. We have faith in those guns of ours that we will probably need to use. Some people ask how can you have faith in something you can't see? The invisible. Well that's the real test and it's that which I lean on. Get the picture?"

"Sure I do. It's a private thing. I respect that. I live in hope that one day I'll see my mother and father in another life. I lost both of them when I was a kid. I might be a grown man but I still miss them. Maybe I'll see them sooner than expected if I don't get through this, or if we go to war in Europe. I was there a few years ago on tour as a dancer. I went to Berlin on that trip too. Have you been to Europe, Gerry?"

"Yes indeed! I taught over there. I was in England and Italy for a while. Fell in love with a beauty of an Italian girl I met in Florence. Great Days! Now that the old folks have gone maybe I'll find my way back over there again."

"It's a funny thing but when you told Lieutenant Patton back there that the reason you joined up was because you believed America might be in the European war, that could have been me saying exactly the same words. Patton didn't even bother denying the possibility. He said a wise decision. Do you think he knows something we don't?"

Gerry suddenly turned quickly. "Shh… I can hear voices. The sound of horses." He rolled to his rifle and looked about him quickly. In the silence of the night a horse whinnied from down below. "Get ready pal. I think we've got visitors… trouble perhaps." Anatole grabbed his gun. The two men looked down from the ridge. Sure enough down on the escarpment below five Mexicans wearing bandoliers were making camp for the night unaware of the two US soldiers gazing down at them. Their horses were grazing by a clump of trees.

"They're Villa's men alright," said Anatole. "They're well armed too."

"The question is what to do now?" Gerry whispered. "Get sketching while we've got them in view. I'm going down there behind those trees to try and listen in to their conversation. I need to get an idea of what they're up to. If they catch sight of either of us, get firing like you've never fired before. They could well be scouts too. Perhaps they were sent ahead to check out the opposition."

Anatole quickly grabbed some paper and started to draw the indolent figures below. Gerry watched the men who spoke loudly.

"I'm going down," he said in a whisper. "Keep me covered. You know what to do. Dump the artwork and start shooting otherwise we're both gone."

Gerry quietly began to descend the rocks. The night shadows had fallen and he moved at a stealthy pace like an animal about to pounce on its prey. He manoeuvred his way along a narrow ridge that led its way to the trees. Once off the ridge Gerry began to crawl along the ground clutching his rifle for dear life. He was so close now he could see the Mexican revolutionaries from behind the trees. They were big smiling laughing men but probably highly dangerous. Their conversation ranged from the humorous to the serious. Gerry listened carefully from the seclusion of his vantage point for the best part of twenty minutes. The things he heard, he translated and memorised. So intently did he listen that any fear of being discovered he promptly pushed to the back of his mind. When the men decided to retire for the night Gerry made his way back carefully.

Anatole had done some lightning sketch work and he pushed the drawings into his saddlebags. An ashen faced Gerry returned and sat in silence for a few moments as if to digest all that he had listened to. He looked up at Anatole with a concerned look.

"Well… what did you hear? You look dumbstruck." He spoke in a voice of a tone barely above a whisper.

"Villa and his men are coming this way in the next day or two. They have rearmed with weapons supplied by the German government, would you believe?"

"What has Germany got to do with a war in Mexico? It doesn't make sense. They're too busy in the wholesale slaughter in Europe."

"I translated as best as I could and I picked up a thread in their conversation. Germany is supplying arms to the rebels in Ireland so that the British are having to lose some of their troops in France to deal with the uprising there. The Germans have got the same idea about here. They reckon by providing arms to Pancho Villa's boys, America will be so wrapped up here it will delay our possible entry into the war in Europe. That's not all. They are saying that if Germany wins the war they will assist Mexico in winning back Texas, New Mexico and Arizona."

"That's horse-dung! They'd have the whole of the States down on them."

"That's what I figure too." He quickly looked over the ridge. One of the men below was sitting up holding his rifle. "We'll have to let Patton know the full details. Let's have a look at those sketches."

Anatole showed him the drawings. "That's the best I can do."

"Pretty good Corporal. We've got something for them back at the camp. The question is: What do we do now? See that fella sitting there with the rifle. I reckon one sound from us and he'll be taking pot shots. No sleep for us tonight. We wait. And as soon as they move off we'll head first for the waterhole, then we will make our way back to camp."

***

They didn't sleep that night at all. For hours they sat poised by their rifles. The Mexican rebels didn't wake up early. They slept quietly by a smouldering campfire. The one man who had sat up all night on guard stifled a yawn. Both Gerry and Anatole were tired now to the point of exhaustion. They had both been on a humid, sticky, uncomfortable trail for days now and neither man had got a proper night's sleep in all that time. Both of them were nervous that had they fallen asleep one of the rebels would have found them. The man who had been guarding the others stood up and stretched his arms. He looked up at the ridge for a moment then at his friends who were beginning to rise. Gerry's horse suddenly made a noise and in the silence of the early morning, the sound carried.

Suddenly all the men were awake and they grabbed their guns quickly. One man pointed to the ridge. They stood up and gazed upwards. A man grabbed a long blade and started to move forward. Gerry glanced quickly at Anatole. Both of them raised their rifles and started to prepare to fire. Perspiration started to run down their faces. Any second now and they would have to fire.

Then without warning several shots rang out. Each of the men below lay dead. Neither Gerry not Anatole had fired their guns. Anatole had moved forward quickly to see who had been doing the shooting. Gerry swiftly pulled him back. They waited for a few minutes. The silence in the aftermath of the killings was chilling.

From the side of the escarpment a group of rough-looking men on horseback rode through the trees. They dismounted and walked over to where the bodies lay. There were probably a dozen or so. They wore no recognisable uniform. Their general appearance was unkempt and ragged. For a moment they surveyed their kill and then they started to strip the dead men of anything they could lay their hands on. Money, valuables, weapons, boots, and ammunition. These men had no scruples or loyalties, they were cold hearted savages without mercy or compassion.

"Bandits," muttered 'Gerry angrily. "Look at those sons of bitches slobbering over their spoils. I bet those bandits are neither for or against the revolution. They probably don't give a damn for anyone but themselves."

In the distance there was the sound of an aircraft engine. The bandits looked round sharply.

"What the hell is that?" Anatole looked to the sky. An army aircraft was flying down low towards the escarpment. The pilot wearing goggles was clearly visible and there was a soldier in the rear seat at the helm of a machine gun.

The bandits started firing at the plane. Before Gerry and Anatole could do anything the plane swept down low over the men. The sound of the machine gun could be heard. Within the space of a few minutes there was not a single man left standing. The scene below resembled a blood bath.

It had all happened so quickly that the two soldiers were left frozen in shock. The scene was horrific and a scary introduction for both of them to the frightening aspects of war. A few hundred yards away the aircraft descended as if they were about to attempt a landing but the surface seemed so rugged the pilot quickly flew away.

"Let's get the hell out of here, Nat," said Gerry in a voice betraying anxiety.

"We need some proof from down there, don't we? However distasteful it might be," Anatole pointed out. "Another thing, what about the bodies? Wouldn't it be uncivilised to just leave them there rotting in the sun?"

"I agree but do you want to stick around for Pancho Villa's men? If they see us looking over the mess down there including those dead outlaws who did the dirty deed then we won't make our thirtieth birthdays. And where did that plane come from? Who ordered the plane? They sent us out to scout."

"We're wasting time here, Gerry," Anatole said with a hint of frustration in his voice. "Shall we go down and see what we can find?" He took out a pair of binoculars and looked first into the far off distance, and then at the carnage below. "You're a horse-loving man, aren't you? There's a few running loose down there."

"What say we take one of the horses with us and have some ammunition and arms placed on one? We check through the saddlebags on the others. Once we've done that. We toss the bags to one side and let the horses run free."

"And we vamoose very quickly."

"Let's go then, Nat. We'll return to the high ground after we've been to the waterhole and follow the trail back that way. If we stay down there we might meet Villa's boys head on."

***

The two men swiftly packed up everything and made their way down to the horrific sight below. It was the men's introduction to the sheer dreadfulness of war. Far worse was taking place in the fields of France. The Germans had taken the war to London and civilians were being mercilessly bombed by Zeppelin airships. But the sight of this was off-putting for the things that would follow. Villa's men fought for a cause and to be shot dead by marauders was a very cruel fate. Gerry and Anatole set about their uncomfortable tasks ransacking the dead men's belongings. They took guns and ammunition, maps and compasses. Anything related to the revolution was of great importance. From the saddlebags belonging to the bandits they discovered bundles of money. American dollars, in the thousands. The temptation to take the money was enormous. But this was tainted money, probably the cash from numerous robberies, neither man had any interest in dead men's money presuming that it was the proceeds of likely murder. Gerry took the dollars and scattered them into the air. Money both men decided they could get cleanly any time. They wanted no part of this.

Then, when all that had been sorted out they turned their attention to the horses. It was clear these had been stolen as well both by the bandits and Villa's rebels. There were definite US Army brands on each of them. Some had obviously been plundered in raids on cavalry barracks. They couldn't take them all back and after picking a good horse to carry some of the things they had salvaged, and once free of saddles, they reluctantly let the rest run free.

The men then mounted their horses together and, with the additional steed and acquisitions, rode quickly to a stream and waterhole. Once the horses were at rest and their water bottles had been filled, they rode up into the hills. It would be a long ride back. The hills were rugged and more like mountain ranges. It was as if the whole of Mexico in all its splendour and grandeur stretched out below them. An orange-brown landscape with cacti dotted along the horizon line was totally devoid of any living creature, man or beast. For a while at least everything seemed peaceful again. But it was a self-delusion for anyone who believed this. Violence and battle could flare up without warning. The revolution was still very much in progress.

Some miles further on from where they had survived the incident they came to an area of huge rocks and boulders. This seemed like an adequate shield from the glaring sun. On approaching them they could see a cave which aroused their curiosity. It seemed like a good place to rest up for the night. There was no doubt that this had been a difficult trail to follow, and riding up steep areas such as this, they had chosen to travel where few horsemen would have attempted. Scouting on horseback for the army was not for the faint hearted. They were on their own, and apart from the elements, they were easy targets for the enemy and any eager opponent. Up here they felt relatively safe. Who would dare ride up these steep inclines other than an eccentric rider. From here they had a clear view of the territory below. It was beautiful but lonely countryside.

The rocks and the landscape they were encountering looked as if it had been pushed up with a seismic force in the manner of an earthquake. It was the highest point they had travelled to in their journey so far. From then on they would ride on a gradually descending trail, as the range tapered downwards to the desert below; then once again they would be at the mercy of bandits and Villa's rebels.

Gerry and Anatole dismounted and started to set up camp for the evening. It was late in the afternoon and still very warm. They would be comfortable here. The rocks and boulders would serve as a protection from both the elements and any other challenges in the unlikely off chance that they found their way there. Anatole took several paces towards the cave and then froze at the sight of something. He stood transfixed as if he had been hypnotised and rooted to the spot. Gerry saw him standing motionless and could immediately see something was very wrong.

"Nat! What is it?" Anatole did not reply. Gerry called out to him again.

"Nat! What is it? Snake?" Gerry grabbed his rifle and moved forward. "Hold on, buddy, I'm coming. Don't move." To his surprise and shock he found Anatole standing over a skeleton with fragments of clothing still visible.

"Why did he have to end up like that?" Anatole asked sadly.

"More to the point who is he?" Gerry put his rifle down and began examining the remains. "And I thought you were facing a rattler!"

This was an eerie find. The discovering of remains at once produced a mystery. Who was this man? What was he doing so high up in a place that was hard to reach? The bones of the skeleton had been bleached white by the fierce Mexican sun. There was no need for clues as to how the man had died. It was plainly obvious. A bullet wound in the temple had clearly done the job. The clothes that barely covered the skeleton had virtually disintegrated into loose fibres also as a result of the harshness of the sun. It was hard to identify if the clothes were a uniform of some sort but the type of material seemed to suggest the man had been a civilian. Several feet away lay a six-gun that was rusting. Gerry picked it up and examined it.

"Looks like the type the good old boys of the Wild West once used," he said, caressing the barrel. He pointed it into the distance and fired. There was no sound. The gun was empty. "I guess this was the murder weapon if it was murder."

"If it was murder? Anatole repeated. "You think it might have been suicide?"

"Maybe." Gerry studied the vicinity for any clues. "I reckon he must have been here for years. What the hell was he doing all the way up here? Let's have a look inside the cave." The two men entered the cave. Before they had gone more than a few feet inside, they found two bags. Gerry knelt down and opened them. "What have we got here then?" He found a couple of textbooks, some maps, a journal and some letters in one. In the other there was another gun, some water bottles and ammunition.

Perhaps it was the sweltering heat, the intensity of the atmosphere, the silence and the rugged location high above the Mexican ranges, but Anatole sensed there was something more to this place. It was as if the rocks, crevices and craggy inclines emitted some sort of spiritual aura. The beaming rays of the sun highlighted strange iridescent colours in the rock formation producing shades and hues that even he, as an artist, would have found difficulty in creating in oil or water colour.

"There's the feel of something sacred about this place," said Anatole and without a hint of craziness in his demeanour, he genuinely felt that spirits of another time were reaching out to him. Gerry didn't reply. He was absorbed in what he had discovered. There was something truly fascinating about the letters and journals he was reading. He stood up and looked at Anatole. His eyes were shining.

"Sacred, you say? All we need to know is in this journal and these letters. Do you know who this guy is? Of course you don't but I'm going to tell you. His name is Professor Bill Kenna. He was a well-respected academic and explorer who went missing about eight years ago. His specialist subject is the Mayan civilisation. Nat, old pal, I think you and I have just made the discovery of the century. Sacred is right. It's hard to believe but in a time long ago, somewhat immeasurable by today's standards, before avalanches, earthquakes, adverse weather conditions, the Mayans lived and worshipped here." He took the professor's letter and began to read. "Listen to this: 'To anyone who makes the discovery of my body and belongings, please read my journal, which I have kept since embarking on my journey to study the culture of the Mayans. My journey of research has taken me throughout Mexico and this now is my final resting place. I have detailed all the events I have lived through as well as my discovering of Mayan and Aztec sites. On the maps in my possession I have placed a cross on each of the places of historic interest. My fine horse, who has served me so well, regrettably became lame and I had to shoot him. I continued my journey on foot until my own health and supplies have diminished to the extent that I have had to take matters into my own hands regarding my own life.'"

"So it was suicide after all, Gerry."

"Yes, according to his own testimony right here in this letter. All the stuff we have here, the maps, his journal… it's a gold mine of information to future explorers." He looked down the full length of the cave. "I get the feeling there's something far more down here." They proceeded to walk and found to their surprise that there wasn't just one cave but a whole labyrinth of them. From above the sun's rays shone through cracks in the rocks creating beams of light that illuminated the caves. Turning into one tunnel they found themselves astonished by the sight of extensive limestone carvings. Anatole and Gerry looked at each other in amazement.

"Holy Jehosophat!" Anatole gasped at the sight of it all. "It's as if we've stepped back in time. These carvings in the rock, I've never seen anything like it before. Back in the States we've got Cherokees, Apaches, Cheyenne, Comanche, Sioux, Mohawks, Kiowa, Shawnee, Blackfoot, Arapaho but I never heard of the Mayans until now."

"The Mayans were an ancient people. They had their own rituals and practices. I read of Bill Kenna's research when he was a young student. He was a professor in Washington. These caves were his last discovery. A fitting tribute to a great man, along with all the other stuff we've accumulated in evidence of our mission. I'll have to hand these letters and journals on to Lieutenant Patton. He can report it so that Professor Kenna's relatives are informed and obviously the location of Mayan sites will be of great significance to the academic world." Gerry sighed in sheer wonderment at it all. "I tell you, Nat, this is some find." Then he suddenly had a brave wave. "Have you got much sketching paper left?"

BRAIN

"Plenty. I made sure I was well stocked up. Hell, I sure have a lot of drawings to take back. The lieutenant will sure be busy studying this lot."

Gerry looked closely at all the Mayan carvings. The scenes depicted were of men wearing masks and headgear together with costumes of armour. In the same scene the men carried weapons adorned in creative designs. The whole mosaic was one of mêlée and confusion, of warring men in battle and sacrifice. It was work of painstaking sculpture portraying a lost civilisation that had once inhabited this lonely humid place. Each carving told a story that was unique to its time yet archaeologists would puzzle and baffle to discover hidden meanings inscribed in every element of their design.

Here in the silence and solitude of the caves the two soldiers stood in awe at the fascinating sight that they were privileged to cast their eyes on. For Anatole his imagination ran wild. The voices of bygone warriors echoed in his ears, and the sculpted figures seemed to come alive and flickered in the rays of light that shone through the crevices. It was as if in modern day life he had entered a zone that took him back thousands of years. Surely they would encounter high priests, warriors and maidens in costume at any moment. The silence in the caves carried an aura with it of things that might have been. Had this area once been a temple of worship to a Mayan god? Could it have been a place where human sacrifice was carried out in homage to a deity that was engrained in an ancient culture? The voices and cries of another age became louder. It was only Gerry who jolted him out of his suspended animation.

"After we've buried our friend, Professor Bill Kenna I suggest you make a few drawings of these scenes here. Unless we've got something to show them no one will believe it. These carvings are works of art that apart from the late Professor I doubt whether anyone has seen them for heaven knows how long." Gerry had put on an air of pretend calm but inside he was bursting with excitement. He could no longer contain himself. "This is history, my friend! And we're part of it! I can just see the headlines in the papers now. *'US Troopers discover remains of Mayan civilisation'*. We might make the front page headlines of the Hearst Press. Not only have we fulfilled our mission, but we have made a major discovery in the archaeology world. That's really something isn't it?"

Anatole could only nod and smile. The two men left the caves and walked out into the blazing sunshine. In all of his life Anatole could only marvel at the amazing experiences that had been thrust upon him. Outside at the entrance to the cave the remains of the distinguished man lay like a marker to the treasures that lay within. His remarkable achievements in uncovering the works of the Mayans would give Professor Kenna a posthumous moment of glory he would never have dreamed of while he was alive.

They buried him early next morning. Small rocks and boulders were mounted on top of each other to signify the location of the grave for future explorers. Neither man could let such an occasion pass by in silence. It was fitting that this learned man should have some sort of Christian burial even if it was conducted on a range high above the Mexican wilderness. Amongst Bill Kenna's belongings they found a Bible. Gerry thumbed through until he found the passage he wanted. With the sun bearing down on the grave beside the entrance to the cave, Gerry began to read the twenty-third psalm. When he had finished the two men stood in silence for a couple of minutes. Then Anatole decided to add a few words of his own.

"When I was a child not long out of Russia, my warm-hearted and much missed mother taught me English. One day she read me a poem by Robert Louis Stevenson. I can't remember all the lines, but there are a few I recall. So I would like to dedicate these to the explorer and gentleman,

Professor Bill Kenna, who we have just buried." Anatole took a deep breath and quoted them word for word.

"This be the verse you grave for me;
Here he lies where he longed to be;
Home is the sailor, home from sea
And the hunter home from the hill."

One day in the not too distant future Professor Kenna would have a dignified memorial service in Washington. The service would be attended by the President of the United States and leading historians. This day was a quiet private service, conducted by Gerry and Anatole on the sacred ground of the Mayans. Once it was over it was business as usual.

"I'll keep a lookout here," said Gerry. "If you can sketch a few pictures of the Mayan sculptures it will be good evidence for when we get back to camp."

Anatole took some papers from his saddlebags and went back into the cave. A peculiar phenomenon of the rocks and boulders was that at different times of the day, depending on the quality of the light, they would change colour. Within the labyrinth of caves this happened inside as well due to the prism of light created by the sun streaming through the gaps above. Anatole sat on a rock within the cave and drew carefully to the best of his ability the carvings before him. In such an unusual setting with the natural light flowing through, he almost felt as if this was his own make believe studio. It felt cooler there than outside. With the right supplies it would have been possible to hide there for a long time. He posed himself the question of how long Professor Kenna had stayed there. It was such a strange and eerie feeling to have made this discovery considering that, apart from Bill Kenna, it was unlikely that anyone else had been here since the Mayans.

Outside, the heat was blistering. Gerry led the horses into the shade of some rocks and boulders. He made sure each one had water and checked their hooves. His genuine love of horses always shone through. Since his own boyhood in Montana, he had always felt comfortable with them. He took his binoculars and looked out at the far off horizon line. In the distance he could see movement of some kind as if a number of men on horseback were approaching; however, his view was temporarily blurred by a shimmering heat haze. He walked along a bit further to try and focus a bit better. Then, he suddenly tripped over something jutting out of the ground. For a moment he lay in the dust and as he picked himself up he caught sight of something. He was stunned beyond belief.

Gerry began to kick the dust and earth away to reveal a chalice beneath the surface. He scrambled around frantically and excitedly. There were limestone slabs with inscriptions and markings clearly visible. To his amazement he realised that the caves they had discovered containing Mayan sculptures were part of a bigger tapestry. More than likely there were the remains of a once thriving city beneath his feet. The ground was too hard to break up. It would take archaeologists, together with skilled men and special equipment, a colossal effort to excavate the site. Whoever could penetrate the surface underneath the ruins would be sure to make a momentous discovery.

He gazed at the chalice. It was probably thousands of years old. In his hands he was holding an historical item that he, as an academic, realised belonged in a museum. On the other hand if he were an unscrupulous profiteer he could put it up for auction and watch the bids soar into orbit. He might possibly become a millionaire. The temptation was enormous but his Catholic sense of guilt prevented him from succumbing. Gerry knew in his heart that the most he could hope for would be a headline or two in the press as one of the discoverers of the Mayan ruins. Back at the army camp he would produce the chalice as proof of their find and let the officers decide what to do next.

The whole discovery had been absolutely breathtaking. To have found these remains of an ancient civilisation by accident so high up was something of a miracle. Over the centuries earthquakes and the upheaval of the earth's surface had completely submerged and covered Mayan buildings that were yet to be rediscovered. Like the fabled city of Atlantis the reality of the structures needed to be separated from the ever-embellished myths. It was possible that the Mayan metropolis had existed on a fault line that had erratically thrown up seismic tremors which had gradually engulfed the ruins. Gerry contemplated just what sort of treasures lay below.

Anatole emerged from the caves with his completed drawings. Once he had placed them together with all his other sketches, he walked over to where Gerry was standing. He could see the slabs and markings through the earth that Gerry had kicked away. Gerry handed him the chalice to examine.

"Evidence of a lost city. We'll take that along with all the other items we've collected. They sent us out to look for Pancho Villa and we discovered a lost city of the Mayans. That's going to be some story to tell, isn't it?"

"I think we've found more than that, Gerry." He was looking out at the horizon line. An army of men on horseback were getting ever near. Gerry picked up his binoculars. His face appeared grave. It was hard to estimate just how many men there were but even from this distance he could see they were well armed. At the very front of the contingent rode one distinctive looking man matching the description of the revolutionary leader. Gerry handed Anatole the binoculars. He could see that they also had cannons in tow.

"Pancho Villa?" asked Anatole.

"It looks that way. Backed by a thousand or so men, I guess, maybe more. Do you realise we're probably the only two American soldiers to set eyes on Villa?"

"Look at them all! If we tried to get close to him we wouldn't stand a chance. No doubt about it. He's a proud looking hombre, that's for sure."

Pancho Villa rode proudly at the head of his own militia. He may have possessed the ability to blend in with the crowd but here now he oozed magnetism and charisma in spades. The scene below was of a formidable band of revolutionaries led by a striking commanding figure. An idea of how strong a rebel army he led could be measured by the time it took for them to pass by. There was no doubt that these men were tough, resilient and a power to be reckoned with.

Gerry and Anatole sat perched on the rocks gazing out at the imposing sight of these men. Through the powerful lens of the binoculars Anatole studied the face of Villa. This man was part of Mexican history. They were all too far away and too many to sketch. It took nearly quarter of an hour for the line of rebels to pass. The two soldiers watched until Pancho Villa and his men had disappeared into the distance. Behind them dust flared up into the air intermingling with the blue of the heat haze.

"I guest that means we've accomplished our mission." Gerry appeared to be philosophical about it. "Lieutenant Patton won't lack for information. We've plenty to show him. Let's go, shall we?"

***

A few days later they arrived back at the camp after a remarkably incident-free return journey. The information they provided was studied assiduously by Lieutenant Patton and his fellow officers. For several hours the military men examined the sketches, maps and possessions that had been brought back for their perusal. The next morning the whole unit headed off in a southerly direction with the firm intention of catching up with Pancho Villa and his men. However, the trail had gone cold and not one American soldier either then or on later patrols ever caught up with him, Villa was to remain elusive for the rest of the American military involvement in Mexico.

Less than a year later in 1917 the Americans finally entered the Great War. The US campaign in Mexico officially came to an end and all the troops were then withdrawn. Soldiers, such as Gerry and Anatole, soon found themselves on the battlefields of France. For Lieutenant Patton, he had a meteoric rise to become a general. His greatest moments of glory would come in the Second World War, when he conducted campaigns in North Africa and Europe in which he found himself in rivalry with Field Marshall Montgomery.

Pancho Villa was destined to never hold public office at all. In 1920 after negotiations for peace by all sides in the Mexican conflict, Villa was granted a pension together with amnesty. He retired to a hacienda in Canutillo but his liberty was to be short lived. In 1923, he was killed while visiting the town of Parral by seven riflemen who fired into his Dodge Roadster. It was never confirmed who ordered the assassination. His legend grew thereafter, improving as the years rolled by.

Professor Bill Kenna's relatives were advised that his remains had been discovered in a remote, rugged area of Southern Mexico. His belongings were returned to his family who decided to donate his journals, maps, letters and the Mayan chalice to a museum in Washington. Gerry and Anatole's involvement in the discovery of this hardly rated a mention in the press. The headlines merely stated that two US soldiers had stumbled upon this find during the course of a patrol.

It was several years later after peace had returned to Mexico that an expedition was mounted to excavate the ruins of the Mayans. For future generations of explorers and travellers, Mexico and Guatemala would remain a source of fascination regarding Mayan history.

After their stint in the Mexican campaign Gerry and Anatole were to experience war with all of its sheer terror and fury in France. Hardly a moment ago it seemed they were in hot pursuit of Pancho Villa. Now they were standing on a boat in New York harbour with many other American troops nicknamed 'Doughboys' bound for the French port of Bordeaux, from where they would travel to the Front. The American forces oozed sublime confidence. '*The Yanks are coming,*' roared the headlines.

So they were, young men from the cities and the mid-west who had hardly been out of their home state let alone to Europe. From the fields of Georgia to Arkansas, from the cattle ranches of Texas to the grapevines of Selinas, from Mississippi to Maine they came.

Anatole felt a great sense of pride that day as he looked at the long line of troops waving to their friends and loved ones. Down below on the docks a band played and people cheered. For a moment the destination and ultimate purpose of his journey was forgotten as he revelled in the patriotism and the fanfare of the occasion. The smiles on the faces of the soldiers were in direct contrast to the sombreness of their mission. Anatole suddenly saw two very familiar faces just a few feet away from him. He knew these men. It couldn't be and then he broke out into a beaming smile. He approached them and without warning they turned around facing him directly. The recognition between them was instantaneous. They were his boyhood friends from way back. Even in uniform they were recognisable.

"Well I'll be…" he gasped. "Jack Clancy and Slugs Mahoney."

"Hiya, buddy!" Slugs exclaimed and he greeted his old friend with a bear hug. Then he put his fists up mockingly the way he did when he was a boxer all those years before. Anatole responded likewise.

"Hullo pal!" Jack Clancy cried. "Who would ever believe it? Our old buddy Nat." They shook hands and slapped each other on the back.

"He's looking good, eh, Jack?" Slugs pointed out, and then with the confidence he had always possessed he added, "But hell he's not as handsome as me!"

"So where the hell have you been all these years?" asked Jack.

"Listen, fellas, I want to hear what you two have been doing." Anatole was genuinely interested. "And then I'll tell you my story. It'll take from here to Bordeaux."

"Before we do that, Nat, we better say goodbye to New York," said Slugs, returning to the rail. The others did the same. Streamers began to break as the boat moved away from the quay. "I never knew New York had so many pretty girls. Nice of them to come and say goodbye to their old pal Slugs!"

"And the rest of us, pal!" Jack added.

It had been a long time since the three of them had last met. They had a lot to catch up on regarding the intervening years.

Twenty-Six

1917

It was raining in Storrington when the car drew up in the early hours at Shervington Manor. Tom Mollomby, the chauffeur, opened the door for Captain Shervington. The look on his face at being home again was one of pure relief. Perhaps the weather was bad and the sky was black but he was home. Away from the bloodstained battlefields of France, there was a peace about this place. He looked up at the unlit house. Inside the son he had never seen was in the nursery. From above, the sound of a baby's cry could be heard. Tom smiled through the rain at the Captain.

"Your son, sir," he said warmly. "It's good to have you back."

"It's good to be back, Tom," Captain Shervington replied and he slapped the chauffeur on his shoulder affectionately before entering the house.

The quiet and peace of the house overwhelmed him. Then, as he gazed up to the top of the staircase, Mariska came into view. She looked shocked for a moment. Then her face broke out into a contagious smile. She came down the stairs and threw her arms around him. Both of them were lost for words. All over the British Isles soldiers home on leave would experience the same emotions with their wives. They just gazed into each others eyes and then kissed.

"Oh darling, I can't believe you're home." It had been so long since they held each other. Finally, she added quietly, "Come and meet your son. Alexander's waiting for you."

They went upstairs to the bedroom. The baby was sitting up in the cot. Alexander looked at the stranger who entered the room and appeared to smile.

"Hullo my beautiful boy," said the captain. The look on his face was one of indescribable joy. He picked the baby up and admired it. A tear formed in his eye. After the unspeakable horror of the war to be here now with Mariska and their son was near nirvana. Mariska moved in towards them. The family were complete.

***

They made love passionately that night. These times of love had to be seized and cherished in wartime as leave was limited and it would soon be time to return to the front. Bernard felt like he was Lord Shervington again, the architect and husband, but soon it would be back to being Captain Shervington, serving officer and fighting soldier in the trenches. After they had made love he lay there in the darkness, listening to the wind howling and the rain hurling itself against the window. The bed felt warm and soft. He stroked Mariska's hair gently. She lay with one arm around him, her head resting against his chest. He had dreamed of times like this when he had been chilled to the bone and soaking wet in the trenches.

Early the next morning when he woke there were two things he wanted to marvel at. He rose and looked at his baby son sleeping. How joyous it was to be a father. It was a privilege to be a father, not a right. It was a blessing, not a burden. He hoped that when baby Alexander grew up he would not have to witness the sights of war that he himself had seen, which would probably stain his memory for the rest of his days.

The next thing he wanted to absorb was the sight of the lush green Sussex Downs. In all of England's countryside he was biased as he felt nowhere else could match its beauty. The rain had stopped now. All the trees and plants seemed to glisten and sparkle with the dripping moisture as it caught the early morning light. He gazed through the window and listened to the sounds of birds making a noise that was much quoted as being the dawn chorus. It was the sound of English wildlife. In the distance, a badger hurried to its sett. A deer came racing out of the undergrowth. For a moment or two at least, he almost forgot about the war he had come from. He could have stayed at the window all day just savouring peacefulness and nature in all its joy.

Eventually after a soak in a hot bath Bernard joined Mariska for breakfast. He was thrilled to be home yet inside he was deeply traumatised, for he had seen things on the battlefield he found it difficult to talk about, even to his wife, who noticed how pensive and withdrawn he had become. His eyes were red from tiredness and long weary punishing days. Moisture formed in his eyes as if he wanted to cry but his stiff English resolve would not allow him to.

"Honey, I know it's been tough for you," Mariska said in a soft, sympathetic voice. Bernard nodded and attempted a half smile. "If you think it would help to talk about it, I am a good listener." Bernard didn't say anything but he leaned across and squeezed her hand gently. "You'll probably find it hard to believe. There were times when the wind blew that I swear I could hear the sounds of battle from across the Channel."

It was the trigger for Bernard to suddenly open up with all the effect of a guilty man in the dock making an unexpected confession. "The noise of the cannons… and the explosions… the rifle fire… the anguished cries of men on both sides… the agonies of the dying, the wounded and the dead. It was all so unimaginable. Yet, when it became real it was more horrifying than any of us soldiers were led to believe." A tear rolled down his check. In his mind's eye, images recapturing the scenes he had been witness to flashed before him. He was visibly shaking. Mariska steadied him, firming her grip on his hand. "It is so difficult to explain to anyone who has not known war in their lifetime, the carnage and the slaughter. This is not like the Boer War or Kitchener's campaign in Sudan or the Zulu wars. On one day twenty thousand men lost their lives in battle." His voice was cold and quiet yet tinged with emotion. "It's not just the warfare. It's the stupidity and arrogance of the officers sending men over the top to certain death. I've seen good men suffering from shellshock who were later shot by firing squads. Their crime? Cowardice! The truth? Night after night bombs went off exploding… and crashing… with shrapnel sprayed all over… and the men were driven to levels of fear where the noise numbed their brains and senses so much that they became gibbering wrecks. Those men weren't cowards! They were heroes! A good stock of working men from places like Accrington Stanley and Chorlton-cum-Hardy. England's youth wasted. Young men who've probably never loved a good woman. Never got drunk on a Saturday night. Never been able to list their ambitions, let alone fulfil them. I've seen men with injuries I wouldn't want to describe to you. Brutally disfigured and maimed by shrapnel. Men who will carry the scars of war both inside and out for the rest of their lives." He paused to wipe his eyes which were filling now with tears, "I'm sorry to burden you with this, Mariska. Very un-British of me to wear my heart on my sleeve."

"If you can't talk about it to your own wife, who can you speak to about it? I understand that there are things you've seen you don't want to bring up in conversation. I won't press you on this. Try to think of better things, Bernard. Think of the time we'll have together after the war with our baby son. There will be beauty again in our lives."

"I still have to go back," Bernard pointed out. "There is a long way to go yet before this chaos ends. Do you know before the war I visited France. I stayed in a chateau in Northern France. The weather was beautiful every day. We sat and drank wine in the sun. It was peaceful, balmy and the last place in the world you would expect a battlefield. Imagine what it was like for me to return to this place with my regiment to find it completely unrecognisable from what it had once been like. Completely ravaged. It was like a completely different country with not a trace or a fragment of what had been." He realised the conversation was becoming terribly downbeat and changed the subject. "I have a week before I return. Is there anything you would like to do?"

"Actually there is. Marie Lloyd is doing a show in London on behalf of the wounded soldiers. Can we go? It's for a good cause. We could get a nurse for the night. Marie Lloyd has been singing in hospitals and factories to support the war cause. It's just one night. The rest of the time you can spend getting to know your son."

"I wouldn't miss it for the world." Bernard was smiling now. "When this is all over I only ever want to see the beauty in this world."

"We will," Mariska reassured him. "It won't last forever."

***

The theatre in London where Marie Lloyd was performing had an audience of service men and women from all over the world. The British troops sat alongside those from Canada, South Africa and the slouch hatted Anzacs. Bernard and Mariska absorbed the atmosphere for these were historic times of which powerful memories were made. In war such moments of happiness ran parallel to the tragic events that would resonate down the years to come. One prominent writer of the day would recall it by saying that it had been the happiest time and the worst of times. A period of comradeship amongst men and folk who, in times of normality, would have had nothing in common. A time when fleeting romances took on a more exaggerated passion in the urgency of the moment. It would create lifelong friendships and loyalties, and marriages between the most unlikely of couples. Such were the strange complexities of war.

Marie Lloyd's entrance on stage was greeted with a huge cheer and a thunderous roar of applause. This chirpy music hall artiste was everybody's darling, always close to the people, and a stage performer who knew how to bring out the smiles in an audience. She launched into a patriotic song straight away called 'Now you've got your khaki on'. Mariska sat spellbound. Back in 1912 when she and Anatole had been touring England in Paul Kapsia's production, they had met Marie Lloyd. How long ago that seemed.

At Shervington Manor the nurse had made up her own bed in the nursery where she would keep watch on baby Alexander. Since the baby's birth, almost a year before, Mariska had not spent any time away from him. This was a rare time for her and Bernard to spend together, and before he went back to war they wanted to make the most of it. The nurse went to the window to draw the curtains and she stopped suddenly at the sight of something far away in the sky. It was a German Zeppelin flying in the direction of London on a bombing mission. The nurse drew a breath and gasped. In a short time innocent people would become victims.

Down at the White Horse public house, the butler, Bobby Grey, was just finishing a tankard of ale when he too saw the Zeppelin through the window. He pulled his coat tight around him and walked out into the main street. The night was cold and clear. Bobby was grim faced. He hoped that a pilot, in the flying corps, would bring down the Zeppelin before it could cause any serious damage and loss of life. Bobby began walking back to Shervington Manor, casting his head over his shoulder every so often to check the progress of the Zeppelin. Soon it completely disappeared from view and submerged into the purple blackness of night.

In the theatre in London Marie Lloyd blazed on stage entertaining the troops with her repertoire of songs which included, 'The boy I love is up in the gallery', 'My old man said follow the van', 'Oh Mr Porter what shall I do?'. It was a happy show despite the circumstances of war. Marie Lloyd had an infectious personality that engendered fun and enthusiasm to her audience. Often the troops would join in with her singing at the top of their voices without any prompting. Then she sang 'Roses of Picardy' and as everyone joined in. The general feeling was that the combined voices were so good it could have been rehearsed beforehand. There are some special times in almost everyone's life which burn on in memory for years afterwards. Hearing a tune or a song popular in its time which, when replayed, could sum up the magic, the atmosphere and the faces of those who were there. For Mariska and Bernard this was one of those times, and the strongest memory of that night would be the immense power of the audience joining in with Marie Lloyd as she sang 'Roses of Picardy'.

Mariska knew the thrill of performing to people hungry for entertainment. But she performed in peacetime and Marie Lloyd was using her great talents to boost the spirits of the people at a time of national crisis. How marvellous it would be, thought Mariska, to be able to raise the morale of the nation through music and song.

There was an absolute rightness about Bernard in uniform. He may have enjoyed the privilege and status of having been a lord but, as a sturdy authoritative captain in the army, he had found the most important role in his life. Here amongst the other servicemen and women he blended in well with the courageous fabric of the nation. In a sense they were all equal in the audience for they were unified in the common cause of the love of their own country, which they were prepared to die for. The battle-scarred, war-weary, injured and the blazingly belligerently brave absorbed the electricity charged performance of the far from shrinking violet, Marie Lloyd, who proved her patriotic credentials with rousing songs that summed up the great British characteristics of good humour, courage without bluster and warmth of spirit.

At the end of the evening Marie Lloyd received ovation after ovation. Then they all stood to sing 'God save the King' before filing out of the theatre into the cold night air. Mariska had thought about calling in to see Marie Lloyd in her dressing room but it was a special time for many soldiers in the audience wanted to meet her. Some would soon be returning to the Front and wanted to meet her and take with them the happy memories of meeting this much loved music hall star.

Outside Bernard and Mariska were greeted by their chauffeur, Tom Mollomby. They were just about to enter the car when there was a massive explosion several streets away. This was followed by another one much closer. A wave of panic swept over the departing theatre goers. Another explosion followed. People in the street began running to take cover in the underground tube train stations. A policeman ran towards them waving his arms wildly.

"Zeppelin! Hurry to the shelters! Now!" he ordered them. The three of them ran with the others to the underground. Up in the sky the fearful presence of the Zeppelin came into view. This airship was capable of causing great damage and just the sight spelt disaster. The theatre and street in front of it had avoided trouble so far, but the bombs were falling randomly seemingly with no specific target in mind. Tom, Bernard and Mariska ran quickly to the underground station and descended the stairs to the platform. A crowd had already accumulated there. More were arriving until they were spaced out along the entire length of the platform.

It was to be a long night. One Zeppelin may have been sighted which created devastation, but the possibility of more of them appearing to cause a widespread assault was a strong one. The people down below were advised not to leave the underground until the following morning when hopefully all would be clear.

They settled down for the night with all the others feeling both cold from the falling temperatures, and with the fear that accompanied such occasions. If they had thought it was going to be a night spent shaking with fear at the sound of the deluge of bombs falling on London it wasn't going to be that simple. The looks on the faces of the young and old may have been that of anguish, but the spirit of the Londoners was never to be underestimated. In the midst of the terror of the Zeppelin raid the people in the underground shelters held together with a mixture of firmness, grace under pressure and good humour. If they had needed a spirit booster it came in the form of Marie Lloyd who suddenly appeared on the platform flanked by a group of admirers and servicemen who had been at the show. She was instantly recognised and applauded.

"Hullo everybody!" she boomed as if she was on the stage of an empire theatre. "We're not going to let them beat us, are we?"

A rich cockney voice from a flat-capped old man roared back at her defiantly. "Not on your bleedin' life, darlin'! We'll show 'em! Cobblers to the bleedin' Hun! London can take it… and survive!"

"That's what I like to hear, luv. Nobody breaks our spirit!" Marie Lloyd cried and no one could doubt the sincerity of this plucky star of the stage. The phrase 'one of us' might have been coined for her. She led them in the singing that night. They sang 'There'll always be an England'. The way their voices resonated the sounds of any bombing would have been drowned out. They also sang 'It's a long way to Tipperary' and everyone young and old joined in.

Bernard had never been an over the top patriot. He loved his country deeply and the thought of an enemy force invading his beloved England appalled him. The Zeppelin's indiscriminate bombing had targeted innocent civilians and not definitive military institutions. He looked around at the ordinary people in the tube station who had been caught up in the night's events. Craggy-faced old timers and the hard living sat with the smooth faced and the tough. The affluent sat with the poverty stricken. Officers and the men in the ranks were seated alongside each other. War had the capacity for breaking down class barriers.

Early the next morning when it was deemed safe to leave the shelters the people began to leave. Tom, Mariska and Bernard walked across to see if the car had survived the night's episode, and miraculously it had and was still intact. Elsewhere the emergency services were busy putting fires out and rescuing people from the damaged buildings. It seemed so cruel and heartless that the innocent peoples of the world should be dragged into the darkness of war and made to suffer. 'London can take it', the old man in the shelter had said. Yes they can, but why should they? That was the real question.

Tom began to drive the Shervington's back home to leafy Sussex on the south coast. A policeman guided them away from the bomb-damaged areas. Firemen and ambulance staff were doing their best in difficult circumstances. Only a short time before some of the buildings had stood for hundreds of years. Now they were reduced to smoking rubble. Bodies were being carried out on stretchers, and the wounded were being attended to by first aiders from the Red Cross and nurses from the Princess Alexandra Hospital. Rain was beginning to fall and the view from the car was somewhat blurred. Every so often flames from a disintegrating building flared up without warning. When this happened the sudden flash combined with smoke tipped Bernard over the edge into a flashback of a battleground. He grimaced and closed his eyes in pain at the memory.

Too many horrors of the battlefield surfaced as he surveyed the wreckage. Bernard started to shake and his eyes brimmed with tears. He leaned forward and put his head in his hands. Mariska did her best to console him. She realised the stark terrible truth that it was not only the ordinary soldiers who suffered from shell shock and battle fatigue, but also the officers too. Bernard was constantly enduring flashbacks of the traumatic events he had participated in. The truth was that he was mentally unfit to return to the front. However, his sense of loyalty and duty overwhelmed any other thoughts he may have had.

At night he would wake up from a nightmare which would return him to a past so real he would jump up looking for a weapon. Then, when he realised it had all been an epic dream, he would stand by the window in the dark night perspiring in anxiety, and shivering with fear. Mariska always did her best on these occasions but she could only hold him so much and try to reassure him that it would soon be over. Bernard knew that once he was back in France he would need to draw on all of his reserves of courage to be strong, positive and able to motivate the men under his command. It was going to be far from easy and he was full of self-doubt now about his own abilities.

During his leave he and Mariska would take gentle walks across the Sussex Downs. Soon this precious time would be over and the future was so uncertain in wartime that Bernard felt every moment had to be enjoyed to the utmost. The greatest pleasure in being home was enhanced by the presence of his baby son. Whatever happened now at least he had the greatest joy in spending time with Alexander. To see his son grow up was the best possible motive to get through these harsh times of war.

Every little thing that Bernard did now he doubly appreciated. Simple things like walking freely and unhindered were a luxury after trench warfare. The walks of his boyhood that he revisited with Mariska took on an extra meaning. There were tracks across the South Downs that he knew by heart. Often paths would be shrouded by bramble blossom, tangle-wood and liana coils which hung from giant ancient trees. Wild flowers and chaotic shrubs proliferated everywhere. The scent of honeysuckle was very apparent. Colourful flora of the continually changing seasons intermittently appeared along the tracks. Animal paw prints were clearly visible in the soft soil of the Downs. On close examination, they were identified as those belonging to the reclusive nocturnal badger, rarely seen except in the night hours.

Sparkling cobwebs gleamed like diamonds as the sunlight forced its way through the undergrowth. Fallen timbers and decayed branches of varying shades of colour including ebony and mahogany were often strewn across pathways. Crunchy leaves fell on to the sodden ones of the previous year,sticking to the footwear of the walkers. On the footpath as they came out to a clearing the irresistible view of Chanctonbury Ring in the distance appeared. With recent heavy rainfall and now sparkling sunshine, it was the deepest shade of green Mariska had ever seen.

The sound of the creatures shuffling through the overgrown bushes was frequent. Grey squirrels raced up trees. A red fox with a huge brush tail appeared up ahead and stood unfazed studying the intruders. Then just as quickly it disappeared into a maze of trees. A tiny hedgehog snuffled its way seeking out edibles. Lone deer suddenly came crashing through the woodland. Surely there must have been all species of animal inhabiting the Downs.

Bird life too was prolific. A heron landed on a turnstile looking keenly about it before stretching its long legs and taking flight to another location. Nearby a colourful pheasant with all the markings of a tropical bird meandered along and flew away suddenly. A flock of birds in the sky flew in an ordered line of formation.

At the top of the Downs Bernard put his arm around Mariska and absorbed the panoramic vista of all that he loved about his home county. Meadows abounded. Fields full of corn shone like gold. Flocks of sheep gathered in near pastures. Cows grazed peacefully. Surely this was God's own country. A turnstile with several pointers indicated just how far other villages were from where they stood. Another pathway led to a lush meadow fringed by bluebells. If he followed this route the two of them would come to a secret spot he had known as a boy high up on the Downs. He had played there often in his childhood years.

Bernard's old hideaway was a disused water mill that had once been a splendidly white building which was now a dilapidated beige structure after years of exposure to the elements. The forces of nature and the progress in the way of distributing water had now rendered this spot redundant. A small weir remained and a stream still flowed. Further down the stream the natural movements of mudslides during periods of heavy rain, and the accumulation of rocks, had created a small waterfall. The water was clear and fresh. Their reflection in the ripples of the stream was a perfect mirror image. Few people knew of its existence except for the more adventurous experienced walkers. Bernard gazed at it in wistful nostalgia for the days when as a boy he had come here with his dog.

They sat down by the cascades and in silence just enjoyed each others company. Mariska put her head on his shoulder and her arm around his back. She wanted to savour the loving presence of her man before something awful happened that might rip him from her life. The orphan girl from the Bronx had always remembered the devastating loss of her own parents at an early age. She dreaded the strong possibility that this cruel war might take away the man she loved.

"When do you think it might end?" Mariska asked softly.

"Soon," Bernard replied hopefully. "Now that the Americans have entered the war with their fighting power, it could be enough to tip the scales in our favour."

"The water looks inviting, Bernard. I should have bought my swim costume."

"I used to swim in there naked when I was a boy." He smiled at the memory of it. "That was a long time ago. Now I've got a little boy of my own. Should anything happen to me and I have to be realistic…"

"Don't speak like that," Mariska quickly interrupted. "It's been such a lovely day."

"I have to. Really! A lot of men are going to the battlefields in France and Belgium knowing it is unlikely they will return. It could happen. I have a will lodged at the solicitors in the high street leaving everything to you and Alexander. I updated it yesterday. Keep a good eye on the Shervington business interests. They are our lifeblood. Send Alexander to a local school. Try and avoid bringing him up with governesses or nannies. I want him to get to know the real world and real people. Too many people from affluent backgrounds isolate themselves from the lives of ordinary working people, often adopting a self assumed superiority that they are automatically better than them when in truth they're often not fit enough to lick their boots. I don't want Alexander growing up like that. Get him to love animals. Not hunt them. I want him to learn about country life, the work of the blacksmith, the wheelwright, the farrier, the chalk pit worker, farming, and all the beauty of country life. Would you do that for our boy's sake if I go down over there? That's all I really want to ask of you."

"If it comes to that," Mariska replied. "But I prefer to think you will return. I came from the Bronx, remember? I know about real people. I was an orphan along with my brother. Show business didn't turn my head; I know where I came from, honey. I know what I have now."

Bernard hugged his wife. "Do you love all this?" he said, sweeping his hand at the beautiful scenery before them."

Mariska kissed him slowly. "This is heaven." Her eyes twinkled with mischief suddenly. "Shall we go for a swim? Like you did when you were a boy?"

He looked at her curiously. Then he decided to remove his clothes and she quickly did the same. In the sunshine, her soft blonde hair caught the light and her firm curvaceous body oozed sensuality. They held hands and entered the water. It was fresh, clean and untainted. Mariska lay back in the water, her body fully exposed in all of its beauty. Bernard relaxed and felt the softness of the water refreshing and revitalising him. Here in this secret spot, hidden deep in the Sussex Downs, they had no inhibitions and were at one with nature.

In this quiet, restful place it was hard to believe there was a terrifying war raging elsewhere. It was as if they had entered the realms of a hidden kingdom like Shangri-La, cocooned from the rest of the world where the brutality of war and devastation was so prevalent. Make the most of this a little voice in Bernard's head had told him. This day is a golden one and must be cherished.

For the first time since he had been home Bernard felt a real sense of peace and tranquillity. There were no sudden noises that jolted his memory taking him back to thoughts of cannons roaring, the sudden fatal consequences of a snipers bullet, or the adrenalin and fear as the men went over the top. A gentle breeze blew over the Downs, ruffling the grass and swaying the trees only slightly. The trickle of the cascade and the ripples of the water took on a melodic rhythm while above them a lone bird squawked. The combined scents of flora, tree bark and wild flowers rose in the air. His spirit was raised and his soul was at rest. Not a single worry entered his mind. Here in the surroundings of lush green and crystal clear water he experienced a sense of total peace both within himself and with the world in general.

Bernard swam towards Mariska and put his arms around her. He held her lovingly. His body was not muscular but firm and taut. Mariska felt soft and sensuous. Just the feel of her breasts and skin against him raised his senses to levels of want and need for her, a desire to be fulfilled, and a deep passionate love for this extraordinary and gifted woman. Her lips were soft and warm. Their kisses were long and sweet. The feel and touch of each other set off waves of deep desire. Her soft blonde hair, the feel of her shoulders and thighs as he ran his hands gently and slowly across her back all set the wheels in motion for her to respond in equal measures of passion. The water soaked into them giving their skin a glistening, sparkling appearance. They emerged from the water and lay down beside the stream. Mariska lay beneath him as he moved over her kissing every part of her slowly, lingering and luxuriating in the warmth of her. She sighed and gasped with excitement and ecstasy as he entered her, throbbing, and moving at a steady rhythmic pace until their desires were both fulfilled. Bernard rolled back and he lay there with her, holding her hand as they lay breathing in and out, absorbing the thrill of the moment and gazing up at a soft blue sky.

It had been one of those joyous days that he didn't want to end. The bliss of love and the countryside had made it almost perfect. They lay there for ages allowing the sun to dry them naturally. When they were ready they dressed and started to walk back to Shervington Manor. Bernard was at ease in the casual clothes he wore, a countryman's hat, a light jacket and trousers, but he dreaded the thought that the following day he would be putting on his uniform again. The peace he had enjoyed today would soon be a distant memory.

***

The next morning he was up early and he felt deep sadness within. Outwardly he didn't show it. After the luxury of a warm bath he put on his uniform again and became Captain Shervington. He and Mariska sat in the nursery with their baby son for a while just playing and laughing happily. Mariska leaned against him and from one side looked into his eyes. There must be no thoughts of finality today she thought. Bernard will return.

Bobby Grey knocked on the door and came in. "The car's ready for you now sir. Mr Mollomby is just bringing it around."

"Thank you Bobby," he responded, and turning to Mariska he added, "This is it. I must go now." He stood and lifted baby Alexander up. "Goodbye, my beautiful boy." It was all too much to bear that he might never see his son again, and he quickly lowered him. The nurse came in and Bernard and Mariska left the room. He shook hands with Bobby. The old man who had been with the family for years was clearly emotional yet he beamed with pride and admiration as Bernard left the house.

Wartime farewells are always immensely difficult occasions. This one was no exception. Outside the house Bernard held Mariska tightly. He gave her one long lasting kiss. Somehow he was too choked up to speak. All he could do was stand there for a moment holding her then he knew he had to go.

Finally he said, "It's time for me to leave. Take care of yourself and our little boy." He turned and entered the car. Tom got into the drivers seat and began driving down into the little village of Storrington.

In later years this village would become the home of three major Hollywood stars who would seek privacy and sanctuary here away from the public spotlight. An African student called Jomo Kenyatta would make his home in the Sandgate area of Storrington during the years of the Second World War. He would work at Linfield's Chesswood Nurseries as a labourer. Eventually he would return to Kenya and rise to become prime minister and later president in 1964. A musical maestro called Sir Arnold Bax would live for some years in the White Horse Inn. But that was all for the future.

Bernard was leaving behind a relatively sleepy agricultural village. From the car he could see the horses pulling ploughs. A shepherd casually walked behind a flock of sheep. There were fields of golden corn. He was leaving all this and his family with a heavy heart. Now he was returning to the turmoil and tragedy of war.

Mariska returned to the nursery and picked up her son. The nurse went home and she was left alone with Alexander. The thought went through her mind that if Bernard didn't return he would live through her son.

It would be a changed world after the war although the modernisation of the nation had already begun. The Suffragette movement had ensured that the role of women in society would be more prominent in future years. Attempts at reducing poverty through the creation of a welfare state by the governments of Asquith and Lloyd George would be made. Increased mechanisation, the innovation of telecommunications and automobile production would create new industries. But there was still almost two years to go before the war would end and the toll it would take on people's lives would come at a terrible cost.

Twenty-Seven

Mrs Price and Bobby Grey sat down in the servant's rest room at Shervington Manor. They were joined by Tom Mollomby who walked into the room carrying a copy of the Daily Mirror. He looked sombre.

"How's the war going?" asked Mrs Price. She was a kindly lady who had worked at the Manor for many years now and was nearing the end of her service there. Outwardly happy with her lot in life, she also had a serious side.

Tom flicked through the paper. "It's all pretty grim stuff. Our troops may have won many battles, but the casualty lists are high."

"My there'll be some celebrations when this lot is all over," Mrs Price replied. "I remember how they rejoiced when Mafeking was relieved, and when the war in Sudan was over. This one will be a good one to forget. A cup of tea Tom? Did the Lord get away alright?"

"Yes please," replied Tom. He sat down at the table. "Yes, the Lord is on his way back to the front. I know you've both been here for many years, long before me. What is the story about the regiment? It seems a family tradition for the Shervingtons."

Bobby Grey leaned forward. "Well the 25th Queens Light Northern Regiment was based in the Northern part of India for generations. You have to go back to the days when Major Gideon Shervington was one of the heroes of Crimea. The next son down the line joined the 25th and so on. I knew Lady Bernadette's husband, Captain Rex. I was a mere lad then of course."

"Quite a few stories circulate about old Rex," said Mrs Price with a smile.

"Oh he was a dashing fellow alright. He and Lady Bernadette in their younger days were the most handsome couple I knew. Lord Bernard's parents were out in India too. Sadly they died of fever quite young, and

Bernard came to live here. The 25th was comprised of lads from Surrey and Sussex mainly, but there were a few outsiders, of course, who came from Scotland and Ireland. They participated in the Boer War. Then they were absorbed into what is now the 7th Service Battalion of the Royal Sussex Regiment, part of Kitchener's New Army. They've been all over this show. The Somme, Arras and a whole lot worse."

There was a pause as Tom thought about what he had just heard. "Do you know something, and I whisper it quietly but the lord is a different man to the one who went away. He's more withdrawn, reticent. The light in his eyes has faded. Believe me I'm an old military man myself. I know the signs from my service in Sudan. When you've been in battle you're never the same man that you were when you went away."

"That's understandable. Our boys have been through hell. Slaughter in the trenches. Look at that catastrophe in the Dardanelles and the loss of life in the British and Australian ranks." Mrs Price was a homely person but she also had strong feelings. She topped up each other's cup of tea. "A lot of young men from round here and Worthing won't be coming home. In the North of England whole towns of youngsters joined up, factory workers who all enlisted together, wiped out. The result? No young men in some towns! This is history in the making and I don't like it. My late husband, Mr Price, his grandfather was at Waterloo. He saw 'Bonie' through his telescope. Can you believe it? Nearly a hundred years on and the nation is at war again. I thought the world had finished with wars."

"Sometimes I yearn for the old days, not only before this war, but before the one with the Boers," said Bobby. "I remember peaceful summer nights. Good times."

"We all do," agreed Mrs Price. "But they're gone forever."

"Shervington Manor was fully staffed in those days. Jimmy Brown, young Jessica, Ravi the young Indian waiter, all gone now sadly. I'll be retiring soon and then it'll be time for new blood to take over." He looked up at the clock. "Well it's time for me to go. I'm off for a tankard of fine Sussex brew and a Welsh Rarebit at the White Horse. I'll see you good folk in the morning."

"Goodnight, Bobby," Mrs Price said with a cheery smile. She and Tom sat in silence. It was nighttime now and Captain Shervington's departure had been a sad note.

"Cheer up, Mrs Price," said Tom. "It can't last much longer. The Americans are in it now. The boys from the Wild West are riding into town."

***

President Woodrow Wilson had never wanted his country to be involved in the war but events had moved at such a pace the inevitable had happened. Major General John Pershing, who had been in command of the Mexican campaign, now found himself appointed to take charge of the American Expeditionary Forces in Europe. In June 1917 the first contingent of American soldiers began arriving in France. Amongst them were Gerry Valentine, Anatole, his old boyhood pals Jake 'Slugs' Mahoney and Jack Clancy. Their reunion aboard the troopship had been a joyous one covering all the years between.

On board they reacquainted each other covering the stories of their lives over steaming hot coffee in the dining room of the ship.

"That is some story!" gasped Slugs on hearing of Anatole's already full life. "I'd even go so far as to say that is the stuff that dreams are made of. You've been through the earthquake in San Francisco and sailed on the *Titanic*! Brother, you've been part of history. The Bronx boy came good, real good!"

"The last time I met you boys you were angling for a career in the boxing ring. What happened? You had real prospects, as I remember."

"Real life set in. That's what happened," Jack replied. "I was working down on the docks by day, fighting by night. Then the dock work got smaller. They took the guys they needed and shut the doors on the rest. Sometimes I might only get two days work a week. How's a fella to get by on two days money? The fight game was getting harder and harder. Sure I could hold my own in the ring but the guys coming up, trying to make a name for themselves, were ambitious: heavy punches and knockouts. A tough boxer called Eddie Breakspeare, who had an unbroken line of wins, took a blow from a young pretender. He went down in the fifth. Never got up again. That was the end of it for me. I decided to get out before the same thing happened to me. I needed work, so what did I do? I did what most Irishmen do in New York: I became a cop, stamping my boots on the precinct. I've never gone hungry since. It's a tough game but it put food on the table. Not a job for the faint hearted. There are some rough boys out there. Now it's a new enemy over there, in the battlefields of France."

"Some place to go for a reunion. What happened to you, Slugs?"

"Ah… you know me, Slugs, old buddy. Bronx kids know how to survive. It's in their instincts. Like Jack I gave the fight game away. I didn't want the world to think the only way I knew how to make a living was by using my fists. No, ol' Slugs is not all brawn and moose-brains. I admit I'm a magnificent-looking guy! Just ask all those pretty girls who came to wave to me at the harbour." He winked at Jack while keeping a straight face. "And I just know I'm going to drive those French ladies wild with desire! But I can't get by on my good looks. So the old man says to me, 'You gotta get a trade, son.' I figure he's right. Yeah… so next thing I know I'm working as a plumber and I'm making out pretty good as a plumber. Everyone needs a plumber. I'm putting in the hours, mending pipes, fixing drains and blockages, and fixing leaks. I'm real busy. Then a new guy with his own plumbing business moves into the neighbourhood. The next thing we know he's stealing our regular customers and slashing his prices by a quarter. He's gradually taking our trade and living away from us. My boss is pretty sore about this. So he goes to see him and they have a truce. The two of them lock horns and decide to combine the two businesses, but the payroll is not big enough for all of us. They arrived at the decision that two guys have got to go. One from each business. Guess what, I'm one of those guys. Ol' Slugs gets the short straw! I'm on the outside looking in. I worked hard. Now I'm pacing the streets to get work. How about that? Some guy tells me the best way to find work is to go down to the newspaper office and check out the job notices on the wall before it goes to print the next day. The next lunchtime after I finished at the firm, I'm heading down the thoroughfare and I asked some swanky dressed gent in a classy outfit that cost more dollar bills than any weekly wage I ever earned, if he can direct me to the *Tribune* office. Sure, he says, I'll be pleased to. That's where he works, this guy tells me. So we're walking down the street having a yarn about this and that, talking about my great love of sport and the state of the world, and of course we're making every lady sigh as we pass them by! And who can blame them we're two of the best looking guys on the street! When I was a plumber many a dame asked me if I'd come back and fix their pipes! I was always happy to oblige. I'm that sort of guy. So, anyway, me and this guy go into the building of the *Tribune* and he says to me come up to the office for a cup of coffee and we'll continue talking. His secretary brings coffee in… wow! She's got a figure with more curves than a cream pastry and just as tasty too. I'm yarning away to the guy about the ball game and my time as a boxer, and how politicians don't get out amongst the people. He says to me, 'I like you, kid. You speak the language of the people. No bull. Straight, upfront, I like that. I'm the editor of the *Tribune*. You've got the job!' I said to him what job? I'm a plumber, I fix toilets and bathrooms. He said to me, 'If you want a job I'll give you one as a reporter. College kids I can get them easy but do they make good reporters? I need a guy who speaks the same language as the stallholder, the fella in the bar next to you and the men at the ball game. I want a guy who, when he writes a piece, will make the reader say he's got a point. I could have said that myself.' So he employed me."

"You never read the *Tribune* then, Nat?" asked Jack.

"Hardly had time to read a paper," replied Anatole.

"Yeah so that's how I became a reporter," Slug continued. "The boss had me cover stories on industry, sport and crime. That was how I met up with Jack again. I went into the station and there's Jack in a cop's uniform. And now we meet up with you again after all these years. Coincidence or fate? It's great to have the old gang back together again. All we've got to do now, fellas, is get through the war and we'll celebrate by tearing up the joint in Paris and New York. Brother we'll make love to a few happy dames believe me!"

Anatole smiled to himself. It was so good to be with his old friends again that going to war was almost forgotten. Slugs was in every sense a good old boy. He was brash, confident, rugged and charismatic. The one time shoeshine boy, boxer, plumber and soldier had a presence about him that oozed the proud American.

Jack Clancy still had a boxer's frame that fitted perfectly into the uniform he wore. His own uncle, who he had been named after, had been a soldier in the British Army. In a way he was following suit. An Irish-American he still spoke in the tones of the country of his birth but his accent and phrases were those of his adopted nation. He wore his uniform proudly.

***

The last time Anatole had been to France was when he and Mariska toured with Paul Kapsia's show in 1911. Six years later he was back with the thousands of other American soldiers. They began arriving in droves at the ports of Brest, Saint Nazaire, La Pallice, and Bordeaux. From there they were transported to the battlefields of the front. If the Americans had thought they were there merely to be supportive of the British and Allied forces, they were wrong. It would be their participation that would ultimately determine the outcome of the war. There would also be a very high casualty rate amongst the Americans.

Anatole was now a sergeant. His service in Mexico had given him the edge on the men who had joined up in 1917. Initially on arrival in France he had expected to go straight into battle. Instead he and Gerry Valentine found themselves at Verdun where they were involved with the training of the incoming troops. Amongst them were his friends Slugs Mahoney and Jack Clancy. He could hardly believe that he had risen to a position of relative authority in such a short time, but war threw up surprising circumstances. There were privates in the US Army who had been Bank Managers in civilian life and labourers who were now officers. Peace loving men became wartime heroes. Street fighters would find they lacked bravado on the battlefield. Such were the intricacies of the bizarre aspects of war.

There was one thing that Anatole learned as he fought offensives across France. Only a fine line existed between so called cowardice and much heralded courage. In any battle there was hardly time to think of either feeling. War seemed to demand instant reflex action. If the enemy advanced the first thought was survival. Even the most frightened men would show bravery without intention in battle. Once the shots were fired and the cannons roared then the only thoughts occupying each man was how to get through and still feel the blood of life pulsating through their veins. No thoughts of cowardice or bravery entered Anatole's head, nor did the prospect of medals hold any glamour for him. In battle and skirmish, day after day, he fought on regardless determined to get home to a peaceful life. His lust for adventure began to wane and in his heart he knew that he had probably done more in his own life than many people could even begin to dream about, but this war with its carnage and slaughter, could never be a happy memory or something to be nostalgic about in future years. It was living on the edge, good men dying for a cause, dead bodies and rotting carcasses, the smell of cannon fire, the permanent scent of death.

Slugs, Jack and Gerry each showed their mettle. For Slugs this was not only about serving with the boys of the American Army and Marine Corps but also sending despatches of war at the front to his editor in New York who had assured him his job would be waiting for him when he returned home to a grateful nation.

Then one day in a forest as a unit of men were pursuing a German patrol Anatole found himself separated from the others. He was nervously running, taking refuge behind a tree every so often. Shots fired from unseen snipers rang out missing him by inches and splintering tree bark. Where were the others when he needed them? Several yards away he saw some German soldiers run through the trees. He turned to look elsewhere and saw more of the enemy approaching. To his absolute horror he realised he was virtually surrounded. The choice before him was to either fight it out, probably to the death, or drop his rifle and risk being captured. Damn it all! He took a hand grenade and threw it towards them. Then he ran quickly, firing at random from his rifle. He wouldn't have known how many men he would have killed in the urgency of those few dangerous moments. This wasn't an act of heroism. It was sheer panic. He found himself running and running until he came to a clearing.

Before him lay burnt out tree trunks and charred earth. The sight he was gazing at bore all the hallmarks of a battle. All across France there were scenes like this. He looked at the stark horror of it for it represented the aftermath of conflict. Behind him there was the sound of people racing through the forest. He turned around and swung his rifle into action. Then he gasped with relief. The first face he saw was Slugs followed by Gerry Valentine and Jack. Then more of the American contingent came bursting through.

"What the hell happened to you all?" Anatole asked in exasperation. "I was on my own back there!"

"We were fighting them off ourselves!" Gerry came back quickly. "The woods were swarming with Germans. We saw them off with a British unit."

"A British unit?" Anatole repeated. "Where are they now?"

"Right here, Sergeant!" a strong English voice boomed at him. From behind, the British soldiers began to emerge. Anatole turned to look at them. An officer in a captain's uniform stood in front of him. The two men looked at each other in amazement.

"Bernard!" The coincidence was remarkable. "I don't believe it! Bernard!"

"Anatole!" He was beside himself with shock. "This is a real surprise."

"You're here, Bernard? I just can't believe it." The two men shook hands. After the initial shock of seeing each other they stood in silence and then broke out into smiles. "Next time you book me on a boat home be a bit more selective in your choice! It's so good to see you... even if it's here. How has this war been for you...? As bad as possible, I guess."

"This has been a stinking dirty, filthy, bloody war." he replied in a cold voice. He looked around as the American and British talked amongst themselves.

"We can't stay long. We have to head off. I have some good news for you – you are an uncle. Mariska gave birth to our son Alexander two years ago."

"Mariska... a mother? How amazing!" He looked across to where his friends from childhood were talking. "Hey Jack... Slugs... over here!" They came across and smiled amiably at Bernard. "Fellas, this is my brother-in-law, Bernard. Jack here was in the orphanage with Mariska and I. Slugs met her a few times. What a place for us to meet up! Mariska's a mother now. How about that?"

Jack shook Bernard's hand. "She was the sweetest kid. My, she grew into a great young lady. When I was in the orphanage she treated me like I was her brother too."

"I'm pleased to meet you, sir," said Slugs. "I've known Jack and Nat here since they were rough and ready guys singing for their supper on New York street corners."

"Well, gentlemen, it's been a great pleasure to meet you." He turned to Anatole quickly. "Before I go I just need to tell you I was home on leave a few months ago. Mariska is fine. What have you been doing? I think she was worried about you."

"Tell her not to worry, Bernard. I was in Hollywood. Then on a Texas oil field, waiting on tables in New York, on army service in Mexico, then here..."

In the distance an explosion took place. This was followed by another one and another. There was the sound of constant rifle fire and the volley of machine guns.

"This is it, gents!" Bernard waved to his men. "Let's go! There's a battle over the ridge. I'll catch up with you before long, Nat… Jack… Slugs. Let's go!"

Without any more hesitation the American and British soldiers began running to participate in the battle that was taking place. Smoke billowed across their faces. The noise of the tumult got louder and louder. A full-scale conflict between the Germans, the Allied French, British and American forces became bloodier by the moment. Through the smoke it was a blurred image of opposing forces undertaking a devastating fight to the death.

The objective was to stop the German advancement from going any further and to take back territory which they occupied. On this particular battleground the combined forces of the British forces, the American Army and Marine Corps, the Australian Imperial Force rallied against the might of the German Army. Despite the strength of the Allies the Germans were highly disciplined. Their firepower and cannons, artillery and sheer numbers made this a monstrous battle for all concerned.

Anatole found himself in the thick of fighting as the Allies and Germans came together, many of them fighting in hand to hand combat. If the Allied Forces lost this battle almost certainly the German Army would take Paris. The smoke at times obscured the figures clashing so it was never quite certain who was rushing forward. There was gas in the air that stung the eyes and face. The mud beneath them was so thick and squelchy that some of the men's boots got stuck and they would have to fight from a standing position. Bullets went past at a rapid rate taking men out in an instant. Men on both sides with bayonets fought like gladiators in a ring. The ground ran red with blood. Men fell quickly into the mud. There were agonising screams. Faces flashed past. Anatole struck out with his bayonet and kept firing. An explosion close by destroyed men and horses in an instant. The horror of body parts being thrown up in all directions was sickening to the extreme. The noise of rifles firing, cannons roaring and people shouting together with random explosions of shells made it an absolute living hell. Anatole rushed forward soaked in perspiration and blood that had sprayed on to his tunic when he had killed men. A bomb exploded near him. Shrapnel splintered everywhere. Something struck him in the legs and head. Then… oblivion.

***

The field hospital was situated in a building that had once been an active village church. Anatole tried to raise himself from his bed. The pain searing through his legs was agonising. There was a bandage wrapped round his head. He felt weak and exhausted. He tried desperately to see what was going on around him. The church was in ruins but amidst the remains miraculously, as if it were indestructible by an act of God, beautiful stained glass windows remained intact. The serene face of Mary looked on over the many casualties within providing a peaceful note to those wounded and dying soldiers.

Stretcherbearers were exceptionally busy bringing in new patients and taking out the dead. He wanted to get up and walk around but there was no movement in his legs. His head was throbbing. The bandage was securely tied around his head and his hair felt matted and sticky. His vision was blurred. Blinking his eyes several times, moisture ran from them. The poor men coming in off the battlefield had all types of injuries. It was clear some of them were half gone already.

Nurses and military doctors were desperately overworked. The sound of men moaning could be heard. Several beds away a man writhed in agony and then suddenly he tried to lift himself, as if he had found a surprise burst of strength. He cried, "Mother!" and then fell back, expiring in an instant. A nurse and doctor rushed to him. The doctor examined him and, on pronouncing him dead, waved to the stretcherbearers who swiftly carried him outside. Men who were alive a moment ago rolled over and their arms went limp. The noise in the hospital was of men giving commands, Nurses consoling patients, military boots hitting the floor, orderlies running backwards and forwards, long agonising cries and howls of pain. The smell of ether and chloroform was overpowering. Anatole's eyes blurred again, but the pain in his legs was so bad it was tears that clouded his vision. He couldn't take much more and he passed out. Perhaps just as well in the circumstances.

When he came too the next day he was woken by the feel of hands. A nurse and doctor were examining him. The nurse was changing his head bandage. The doctor was looking closely at his legs. All around him the scene in the hospital, which the previous day had been one of confusion and chaos, had become more settled now. Nurses and doctors were working hard but under less pressure now. Anatole tried to stretch and to his relief felt some movement in his legs now.

"What year is it, Doctor?" he croaked, more in light relief than anything.

"1918, son!" The doctor gave him a half smile.

"1918! Where did the past years go?" He looked at the doctor seriously. "What happened to me? Am I going to live?"

"Shrapnel, in both your legs. Across your head as well. You've been very lucky. You may not think so now. Your time on active service is over now, I'd say. What did you do in civilian life?"

The nurse adjusted the bandage and sponged Anatole's head. He grimaced slightly. "I was a dancer amongst other things."

The doctor was grim-faced. "I'm sorry to have to tell you this. Your legs are going to take a long time to heal. They'll never be quite the same again. Would you try and move your legs slightly?"

Anatole moved them as much as he could. "You mean I'll never dance again? That's what you're saying, isn't it?"

"To be frank with you, that is the way it looks at this time. You're out of the war too. From here you'll be taken to a hospital on the Isle of Wight and then home. If it's any comfort to you the battle you were in went our way. Rest now. Oh, I almost forgot, there's an English officer outside to see you – Captain Shervington. Are you up to talking to him?"

"Captain Shervington? He got through? Thank God for that. Yes, send him in." He smiled at the doctor and the nurse. "Thank you… for the help."

"We will be back later. In the meantime, rest." The doctor and nurse moved on to the next patient. Anatole lay back and tried to move his legs. They were stiff and it was difficult to even flex his ankles and feet. There were splints and bandages on each one. A vile smelling antiseptic seeped through the bandages. It was clear he was suffering from some form of neuralgia. From now on walking would be difficult, let along hoofing it on a stage. His dancing days had been prematurely concluded.

Bernard entered the hospital. He looked pale and drawn. On sighting Anatole his face lit up and he made his way down the ward. He stopped and looked at the wounds that Anatole had suffered. His face showed deep shock.

"Shrapnel. I don't remember much." Anatole was trying to make light of it. "It's so good to see you, Bernard. I'm relieved you've got through."

"A lot of my men were lost. I've been going round the field hospitals trying to find the missing. The Americans stayed with us to the bitter end. I'm afraid to tell you there was a lot of fatalities in your ranks."

"Slugs…? Jack? Gerry? Do you know if they made it out?"

"I don't know. Believe me it took a lot of effort to find you. At least I can write and tell Mariska you're still alive. What are your plans when you get out of here? The war will be over in a few months hopefully."

"Plans?" Anatole queried. "I never made plans. Life just seems to happen. I'm being transferred to a hospital on the Isle of Wight, and then shipped back home. These injuries ensure I won't be dancing on any stage. I'll probably never walk properly again. Maybe I'll paint pictures by night and wait on tables I guess. You know Paul Kapsia, who put the shows on the road that Mariska and I appeared in, well he was like a second father to us… he died and his pal Sammy Rosen took over the running of the business, music publishing, agent for stars, show producer… boxing matches… everything under the sun. When I get back to New York I might ask him if I could find a way of marketing my pictures in an exhibition. Paul Kapsia did that for me. I sold some. Made a few bucks."

"I've got those pictures you sent us hanging up in Shervington Manor. They were very good. You'll have to visit us sometime."

Anatole knew a visit there would be a while away. His legs which were firmly bandaged and held together by splints would need a great deal of treatment. Apart from the fact that the bones had been broken he was also suffering peripheral neuropathy in them.

"I feel like I've let the others down," he said quietly. "There's a war on out there and I should be out there doing my piece. Not laying here wounded and feeling sorry for myself. Do you know what I mean, Bernard?"

Bernard knew exactly what he meant. For a moment he averted his eyes from Anatole and looked around the hospital at the other wounded soldiers. Inside he was trembling and far worse affected than he ever allowed his English reserve to allow anyone to see.

"You did your bit, Anatole," he said finally. "And… you're still here."

"That's enough about me." Anatole wasn't in the mood to be pitied. What was it Slugs had said years before? Bronx kids don't cry. "How is Mariska?" He really wanted to know more. "Is she enjoying her life… apart from this Goddamn war?"

"She loves it. She's very happy. I had wondered if, after the show business life of glamour, touring America, South America and Europe in better days, if she could ever settle into a life in Sussex. But Mariska has, and we've had happy days together. We love to walk across the Downs."

Anatole was happy to hear that. "Tell her I miss her, Bernard. I want you to tell her that her big brother may be a long way from where she lives, but he's still looking out for her. Tell her, won't you? She's still my kid sister."

"I promise I will." Bernard looked across the ward to where a young soldier was indicating it was time to go. "My driver is here. I'm going to have to leave now." The two men shook hands. "Keep well. If you can survive the San Franciscan earthquake, the *Titanic*, and the campaign in Mexico you can survive these injuries. Promise me you'll never give in."

"Me! Nah! Not me, buddy." Anatole spoke with some bravado. Inside he was feeling deep pain. "Bernard... look out for yourself."

Bernard nodded and smiled. Then he turned and walked off back to the war. Anatole watched him go and then lay back, feeling frustrated and exasperated at what had happened to him. He was out of the war now. The coming months would mean a lot of therapy and difficulty in adjusting to the new set of circumstances that the war had saddled him with. He knew that the physical nerve damage to his legs meant that he would never dance again. His adventurous spirit had waned and he wondered if he could ever feel enthusiastic about life again.

***

For the rest of the war he spent his time at an army hospital in Bembridge on the Isle of Wight. In such a crucial time in the history of the world, Anatole felt a misguided sense of guilt at no longer being able to participate in the war. He could only look on from a distance while the Americans carried out offensives at Saint-Mihiel and Meuse-Argonne. Then, on 11 November 1918, the Armistice was signed. The Great War was over.

Twenty-Eight

In 1918 Mariska gave birth to her second child. This time it was a daughter who, in the absence of Bernard, she named Grace Ekaterina Shervington. Ekaterina as her late mother's name would be a reminder of that gentle lady whose graciousness she had always sought to emulate, hence the first name of Grace. Mariska smiled at the thought of where the baby had been conceived. Grace was to her the original water baby. On that lovely day when she and Bernard had walked across the Downs they had made love after swimming in a stream. Truly the old saying that there must have been something in the water held true on this occasion.

The news that the war was over caused widespread celebration across the land. Lloyd George, the Welsh-born but fervently British Prime Minister, was the hero of the hour. Crowds gathered outside Buckingham Palace. Church Bells rang out the length and breath of Great Britain. Soon the men would be returning home, and life would return to normal. At least that was the theory. The real question was, what was normal? After the tumult and chaos of the last four years, how could the old order of things be restored? The class divisions that had been so prevalent before the war would only continue to serve resentment amongst the people who had so little and the families where young men had lost their lives in defence of their country.

Mariska knew that her husband would be a changed man and she had to prepare herself. How could Bernard ever return to the life he had once known? He had been through so much turmoil in the past few years and witnessed so much horror that he might never be able to find inner peace again.

In order to make his return to civilian life as smooth as possible, Mariska decided to ensure that the Shervington estate's business affairs were all in order. Lady Bernadette had always been a good bookkeeper and meticulous recorder of detail. While her husband had been away at war, Mariska had kept a sharp eye on the details she was provided with by the Shervington family solicitor and business manager, Mr Eric Fielding.

One morning Mariska was working in the study and for a moment she paused to gaze out at the view of the Downs. In the distance she could see the family cook, Mrs Price, out walking with her two grandchildren. Mrs Price was a lovely, warm, true-blue Sussex lady now in her late sixties who doted on her family. She looked happy that day pointing out flowers and trees to her grandchildren. It was a lovely sight to see one generation passing love and teaching to another one. The peace and quiet of a Sussex morning was so intoxicating it was like sampling a fine wine that relaxed a person until they were unaware of anything else that might be happening around them.

All that changed in the swiftness of a moment. To Mrs Price and her grandchildren's surprise, a frightened fox leapt over the fence which separated the Shervington land from the rest of the Downs. Immediately behind came a party of foxhunters and their hounds. One of the riders dismounted and opened a gate. The riders and hounds came bounding through without thought or regard to Mrs Price and her grandchildren.

Mrs Price fell back while avoiding one careless rider who sniggered nastily at her plight. The grandchildren came to her aid quickly. Their distress was further compounded by the children sighting the climax of the hunt as the hounds moved on to the fox. It was a grim sight for a young child to see. Unfortunately it didn't end there. Once the hounds had finished with the fox, they raced towards a small farm where there was a chicken coop. The hounds found a way in and demolished the chickens. A farmer's hard work had been destroyed in a matter of minutes.

From the study window Mariska had been a witness to all this and she shuddered at the less pleasurable aspects of the country that had been laid bare before her. Mariska was very concerned for Mrs Price and upon her return to work would try and obtain an apology for her. The farmer, who had lost his chicken farm livelihood due to the selfishness of the hunters, would also need to be compensated. Her concerns were well justified because the hunt had deviated from its normal course and gone on to Shervington land, which had not given permission for the riders to enter.

Mr Fielding came the next day at her request. He was a slightly built man, distinguished in the field of law and business, and always well spoken. Together they sat in the study pouring over legal documents, account balance sheets and client letters. The world of business was a fascinating one to Mariska. It was also very confusing and she felt happy to have someone to confide in.

"I'm glad you came, Mr Fielding," she said in a genuine manner. "I know it's been quite a formidable task for you to double up as the family solicitor and business manager during my husband's absence at war, but I do appreciate all your efforts. I'm worried about Bernard. He's due to return home any day and I have to tell you in the strictest confidence, the ordeal he's been through may make it hard for him to take the reins again. I don't know whether he will take up architecture again."

"I understand. It's going to be a time of great adjustment for us all."

"Of course… I'm forgetting myself, Mr Fielding." Mariska had realised something. "The news has reached me that you lost your son at the Somme. I realise this is a terribly difficult time for you. My heart and sympathy go out to you."

"It still hurts very much." He was grave for a moment and then reverted to the matter in hand. "Forgive me if we change the subject. You were saying about your husband?"

"Yes. Can you list for me all the businesses the Shervington's have an interest in? Apart from the one's we've talked about this morning, that is."

"Certainly, Lady Shervington. Let's start with the hotel in Cornwall. Obviously with the war it has been quiet but it's still very much a going concern. I honestly feel that this is a good investment to hang on to. The war is over and things will change. People are going to go back to work. The economy is going to be rebuilt. People need holidays. There is no end to its prospects under new management."

"I shall talk about it in depth with Bernard when he returns. Otherwise the boat building business in Belfast is fine, our investment in Alliance Insurance holds good. There's the Findon garden nursery, the Thakeham Brickworks, the stables in West Chiltington, and a small number of fishing vessels."

"Yes. Now that the war is over the English Channel will free for fishing again. All owned by a Shervington holding company." Mr Fielding constantly checked his notes.

"And, of course, Bernard's architectural business will be up and running again. We come to the farming areas. I am right that the three farms we own once back to full strength have something of a future?"

"Indeed but it may take some time. There is a lot to be done."

"I would like to talk to you about an incident concerning one of my staff yesterday. I saw the whole unfortunate episode and I have to say I am very concerned. So concerned I have asked the local constable, John McGovern, to call round this morning as well as the man in charge of the foxhunters, Mr Derek Challenger. Mrs Price, our family cook, as you know, was walking with her grandchildren yesterday on the estate when the chase went across the boundary. In the process Mrs Price was knocked over and sadly the young children saw what happens to the poor fox at the end of the hunt. If that wasn't enough the hounds then went on to destroy a chicken coop, which I might add is a leasehold property on our land. The Shervington family have a stake in that enterprise and the poor man, Mr Montgomery, has spent a great deal of time… years in fact… to build up the business only to have it destroyed in a matter of minutes by these unthinking people who, in pursuit of the fox, were trespassing on our land. Am I right? Looking through all the documents in the study, I cannot find anything that allows them to pursue the hunt on our land."

Mr Fielding was shocked at what he had heard. He leaned forward and adjusted his spectacles. "That would appear to be correct. I am extremely sorry to hear of what happened to Mrs Price. I have known her for a very long time. In fact I sat next to her late husband at school. Mr Montgomery also. He has always been a hardworking man. There are several ways we can approach this. First of all when Constable McGovern arrives we can ask him to press charges. Certainly behaving in a manner that endangers life is a very serious charge. Trespass and hunting on someone else's land is completely unacceptable. Damages to property resulting in someone being deprived of their livelihood demands recompense and compensation in my own estimation. We can also take our own legal action and sue the perpetrators through the courts. On the other hand we could come to a private arrangement between the victims and their assailants"

"Which method do you recommend, Mr Fielding?" Before he could answer there was a knock on the door and Bobby Grey entered. "Sorry to trouble you, m'lady, but Constable McGovern has arrived. Also Mr Challenger from the hunt has just pulled up in his car on the drive."

"Thank you, Bobby. Would you show the constable in here but ask Mr Challenger to wait in the lobby."

"Of course, m'lady."

There was a short silence as they waited for the village policeman to enter the room. In due course Bobby opened the door and Constable McGovern, a ruddy-faced man, thickset and with an authoritative presence, entered the room.

"Good morning, Lady Shervington. Hullo Eric. Nice to see you."

"Please take a seat, Constable," said Mariska. The policeman removed his helmet and sat next to Mr Fielding. "I called Eric here today to talk about the legal procedures regarding the matters we spoke of yesterday."

The constable was quick to respond. "I have spoken to Mrs Price this morning to hear her version of events and I am very concerned at the cavalier attitude of the hunt team towards her and her grandchildren. I have inspected the damage to Mr Montgomery's property. He is very distressed. He has worked very hard on the property, which I understand is leased from the Shervington estate. Is that right, Lady Shervington? Mr Montgomery doesn't own the property outright so it's really yours… or should I say… the Shervington family's. I can press charges. Believe me, you have every right. By rights I should go ahead anyway."

Mariska appeared to be considering her options. She knew the hunt was part of life in the country but she didn't like it. Nor did she like the conduct she had been witness to; however, it was important that in a village some community spirit was maintained even if it meant being courteous whilst inwardly seething.

"Gentlemen, would you allow me to speak with Mr Challenger on his own for a few minutes? I hope you don't think I'm being rude."

"Certainly, Lady Shervington," said Constable McGovern, standing up. "Mr Fielding, shall we adjourn to the room next door?"

"Indeed. May we? We will wait next door and, if it's all right with you, eavesdrop into the conversation. Call us if you need any help."

The two men went into the ante room adjacent to the study. Mariska rang a bell on her desk, which was the signal for Bobby Grey to return. He came as quickly as his ageing legs would allow him to do so.

"Yes, m'lady," he said.

"Mr Challenger. Would you show him in, Bobby?"

"I will, m'lady," he replied. Bobby turned and went downstairs to bring the huntmaster upstairs. Mariska sat pondering over how she would handle this matter in both a delicate and firm manner while, at the same time, being diplomatic and as courteous as possible in such a thorny set of circumstances.

Derek Challenger entered the room ushered in by Bobby. He was a tall, dark-haired man with a thin moustache, who was smartly dressed in a suit and tie. Mr Challenger looked more like a mid-fortyish municipal bank manager than a man who indulged in blood sports. Mariska rose to greet him and stretched out her hand to him for a light handshake. Mr Challenger appeared to study her as if he couldn't quite believe that this young lady had the nerve to beckon him to come to the house.

"Mr Challenger, thank you for coming. We've not met before but first of all I'd like to welcome you to Shervington House. Please take a chair. You have visited this house before, I believe?"

"That is correct," he replied, sitting down in the chair opposite her. "I knew Lady Bernadette and her husband, the late Captain Shervington."

"I see. Did you serve in the 25th Queen's Light Northern Regiment?"

"No, Your Ladyship. That was before my time. I was in the Gloucesters as a young man before going into the insurance industry. I did return to service in the Boer War though."

The formalities once over meant it was time to get down to serious business. "Mr Challenger… I really wish we were meeting under more pleasant conditions. If my husband were here you would be dealing with him. However, as he is yet to be discharged from the army I have had to look after the day-to-day business affairs of the Shervington estate and regrettably I have to deal with the unpleasant situation that arose yesterday. I really would like some sort of explanation from you regarding the conduct of the foxhunt yesterday." A short silence followed as she allowed the words to sink in. Mr Challenger shuffled uncomfortably in his chair. It was plainly obvious that he wasn't used to being called to account and admonished. Least of all by an American Lady who he considered had got lucky by marrying an English Lord. "You do realise the seriousness of the matter, don't you?"

He hesitated before replying and then gritting his teeth he uttered in a low voice, "Well, on behalf of all those involved, I would like to offer an apology and ensure there is no repeat of the incident."

From within the adjacent room Constable McGovern and Mr Fielding looked at each other, wondering what the next response would be.

"Is that it, Mr Challenger?" Mariska asked with an edge to her voice. Anger was beginning to show itself in her eyes. "One of my employees, Mrs Price, was virtually knocked down in front of her grandchildren by an unapologetic huntsman who was seen to laugh at her plight. The young children then had to witness the end of the hunt before the hounds went on a rampage in a chicken coop destroying all of them. A man's livelihood was wrecked in a matter of minutes. Probably a whole year's earnings! The farm is leased from us on our land, I might add, and Mr Montgomery pays us back the rent from his income, which will be non-existent due to this behaviour by the huntsmen. Also, you have no right to continue to hunt on our land! You have not been given permission in writing or verbally to do so! This is not a matter that can be merely dismissed by an apology. If I am reading the expression on your face correctly, you are probably thinking how dare this whipper snapper from the States speak to you in such a manner. Now I think in the name of decency and English fair play, I need something more than a grudging brief apology from you, otherwise I will have no alternative but to start legal proceedings against you. Oh, I know you're not personally to be held responsible for the actions of the individual culprit but you are the man in charge. We have a saying in the USA, going back to the days of the Wild West. If you ride with outlaws you die like outlaws!"

In the ante room Constable McGovern smiled at her eloquence and whispered to Mr Fielding, "She would make a bloody good Sheriff, eh, Eric!"

An icy silence fell over the study. Mr Challenger was quite taken aback. "I am genuinely sorry that things have reached this level, and particularly for Mrs Price and Mr Montgomery. I am embarrassed that this has happened under my watch. I realise the hunt is not universally approved by many people, but we do want to have a good relationship with the community at large."

Mariska looked directly into his eyes and she wasn't sure what to make of this man. He was civil but he was also arrogant and proud. Mr Challenger wasn't used to being spoken to in this matter. At the same time though, to his surprise, he found himself admiring her. This woman in front of him was strong and beautiful. The more she exercised her strength of character, the more beautiful she seemed to become.

"From now on, Mr Challenger, the hunt is banned from this estate. If it happens again I shall instruct the police to instigate proceedings against you for trespass. Your hunt is considered a sport. I don't regard it as such. But in any sport there are winners and losers. Should the fox escape into our land you should consider him the winner and you the loser. I watched everything from this very room yesterday, and I saw the young man open the gate to allow the hunt to continue. That must not happen again. Do I make myself clear?"

"Perfectly, Lady Shervington."

"Are you really genuinely sorry about Mrs Price and her grandchildren? She is a very humble woman with a good heart. Perhaps when we've finished here you would like to come downstairs and apologise to her personally?"

Mr Challenger thought about this for a moment. "Yes I will. I will also try and make amends in some other way."

"Good. Now about the damage to Mr Montgomery's farm, and the loss of his livestock. This is going to cost you more than an apology. I need a legally binding agreement drawn up by the two parties in regard to compensation for loss of earnings. I have an estimate of the damage and the likely amount of money Mr Montgomery would have earned for the forthcoming year. I have based this on previous year's sales." She forwarded a note across the table to Mr Challenger. He blinked his eyes with disbelief at the size of the bill. "If you don't wish to settle this dispute between us, Mr Challenger, there are other alternatives. I can have the police and courts intervene. What do you prefer?"

"I have to say I have never been reprimanded in such a fashion before. Especially by a lady." There was a tone of admiration in the way he spoke. Mariska failed to be impressed. "I really wish we had met socially before and in infinitely happier circumstances."

"That's all very well, and I agree with you there, but we need to come to some sort of outcome. I'm very angry at the whole affair! I'm not here to be mocked or disregarded because I'm a woman or looked at snootily with derision. I want something of substance from you and your hunt colleagues. Now!"

"Very well. I will make arrangements for the hunt members all to contribute to the costs involved. Have your solicitor get in touch with me and we will settle this whole thing out of court."

Mariska stood up and walked across to the door of the study. She opened it slowly revealing Constable McGovern and Eric Fielding sitting outside. "Come in, please, gentleman." She turned back to Mr Challenger. "Let's do it now, shall we? This matter needs urgent attention."

Mr Challenger realised he had been up against a formidable young lady. He was shocked by how skilful she had been yet he was filled with admiration for the way she had conducted herself.

"Good morning, sir," said Constable McGovern walking across the room to shake Mr Challenger's hand. "We were on hand just in case there was some little local difficulty but it seems you have both come to an agreement regarding the incident yesterday. I have to say I am pleased about that otherwise I would have had to charge you and your men individually which would have been a long and laborious task for us all. Can I have an assurance from you... in fact a cast-iron guarantee you and the hunt members will not trespass on the Shervington land again?"

"You have that assurance, Constable," he replied, realising that he had been outwitted on all counts. He looked at Mariska and allowed himself a smile. "You would have made a great Sheriff of Dodge City!"

Mariska let her guard down suddenly. "I didn't survive a New York orphanage and the San Francisco earthquake to be trifled with! Mr Fielding, will you do the honours, sir, and resolve the matter of compensation? Action this day, please, gentlemen!"

"Indeed, Your Ladyship," he responded taking a seat. "Let's get this matter solved."

***

The three men together with Mariska spent the next hour and a half working out a solution. It was handled amicably and politely even though it would cause a severe impact on Derek Challenger's hip pocket nerve. At the suggestion of the Constable it was decided that the route of the hunt would be diverted from now on to avoid the Shervington estate. While Mr Fielding was handling the legalities concerned, Constable McGovern would ensure that the rest of the hunt team got the biggest dressing down they had ever had. True to his word Mr Challenger went down to the kitchen and much to Mrs Price's surprise personally apologised to her. He also went across to see Mr Montgomery together with Mr Fielding to ensure him he would be duly compensated for damage and loss of earnings.

When the business in hand had been completed Mariska escorted Mr

Challenger to his car. Although the manner of their meeting had been a serious one, for some unknown definable reason they had struck up a rapport. Mr Challenger by nature arrogant and haughty had admired Mariska's forthright manner and directness.

"I take it you don't like the hunt?" he asked her

"No I don't approve of hunting," she agreed. "Back in the States my brother and I were part of a dancing act that toured in shows. I was told that Buffalo were being hunted so much they were in danger of becoming extinct. I would hate to see that happen to the fox. I understand hunting for food. I don't understand hunting for hunting's sake. Wherever I have travelled in North and South America, I have always loved to see animals roaming free.

"You have a feel for nature then Lady Shervington?"

"Do you know, Mr Challenger..."

"Derek, please," he insisted. "Unless you want to keep it formal, of course, and in the present circumstances I would understand if you wished to keep it that way. You were saying before I rudely interrupted."

"One of the joys for me as an American living in the English countryside is the nature and the wildlife that I see from the study or when I am out walking with my husband on the Downs. No I don't approve of hunting. I think there is enormous conceit to imagine that the world was created for human beings alone. The animals have a right to the world too. Where I come from in the Bronx you don't see badgers, deer, otters, foxes, squirrels, pheasants, herons and owls as I have been lucky enough to view here. I want my children to grow up loving those creatures. In fact respecting those creatures right to their respective kingdoms. Does that make sense to you?"

Mr Challenger nodded his head gently and looked at her with an expression that was hard to determine if it was sympathy or admiration. In truth he knew that if Mariska had been free she was a woman he would wish to pursue.

"Well your husband will be home soon from the war. I wish you well."

"Thank you," she said softly. Mariska watched him enter his car and drive off. Then she turned towards the house and walked back to where Constable McGovern and Mr Fielding were waiting. Mrs Price was also there with Mr Montgomery who had come across from his farm.

"You handled that extremely well Lady Shervington," said the constable.

"I agree," Mr Fielding added. "I will press Mr Challenger for an early resolution and hopefully this whole episode will be laid to rest."

Mariska turned to Mrs Price and Mr Montgomery. "I am sorry for what you've both been put through. From now on, Mrs Price, I want you to bring your grandchildren here anytime you like, and that includes the main house. This is not a stately home. It's a manor house. I would love to meet them sometime. Having two lovely ones of my own… well who knows? In the future your children and my own might become friends."

Mr Montgomery looked at her with a worried look on his face. "What shall I do now your Ladyship? I've got to virtually start again."

"You can join us all for tea, John, for a start," she replied. "You won't go without. I'll see to that. You'll be paid for your efforts. I'll settle that inside. Gentlemen, and Mrs Price, shall we go inside for some tea?"

***

The next day Mrs Price was enjoying a cup of tea when there was a knock on the door of her cottage. To her surprise she found the members of the hunt standing there with several bouquets of flowers. Mr Challenger gave her a written apology from each of the huntsmen and introduced each man to her. They were desperate to repair their tarnished reputation and eager to let Mrs Price know they were not an arrogant bunch of "Hooray Henrys". Mrs Price invited them in and poured them tea. In that area at least some sort of rapprochement was reached. Mrs Price was far from being a shrinking violet and in a rare moment of temper she gave the men a verbal bruising for exposing her grandchildren to the brutal end of the foxhunt. After she had got that off her chest, she promptly pacified the men by offering them her homemade cupcakes!

Shortly after that Mr Challenger led a delegation of the men from the hunt to repair the damage done to Mr Montgomery's farm. From the study Mariska watched the whole process being carried out. She was unsure herself whether she had felt a sense of accomplishment in obtaining a solution, or if it was in just proving that she wasn't someone to be messed around with. Not many Russian-born Bronx girls became titled English ladies.

The Shervington family driver, Tom Mollomby, took her to inspect the various companies they were associated with as they began to get restarted after the war. It was good to see them operating at full strength. Mariska got to know all the employees by name from foreman to inspector, labourer to manager. She even accompanied a trawler out into the English Channel on one occasion to familiarise herself with the work they performed. In all these areas Mariska was learning and growing with newfound confidence convinced that she could deal with the business matters at any level.

Upon her return to the manor house in Storrington after a busy day inspecting one small company, she went upstairs to the nursery to see her children. The nurse she had employed was very reliable but she was eagerly looking forward to the day when her services were no longer required. Mariska may have come a long way from her roots in the Bronx to become a lady of the manor yet she still yearned to be the kind, gracious parent her own mother, Ekaterina, had been. Alexander and Grace were the joys of her life. Pushing the nursery door open she was totally unprepared for the surprise that awaited her. Bernard was standing in his uniform admiring the children. On seeing Mariska, he broke into a smile and moved towards her with his arms outspread. All he could do was hold her tight and sigh with relief that he was home finally with the woman he loved and his beautiful children. A tear rolled down his face, which was tired and drawn. His eyes had dulled with the pain of what he had been witness to during the last four years of horrific warfare. Mariska could feel his heat beating against her chest and she looked up into his eyes.

"This is our time now," she said softly. "We have the best of days to come, my darling."

Twenty-Nine

Anatole could hardly believe he was back home in New York. He still wore his military uniform and he walked with the aid of a stick. His injuries would ensure that he could never return to the stage as a performer again. He was now thirty-two years of age and, like many other returning soldiers, was wondering what he would do with the rest of his life. Everywhere he looked on the streets there was a sprinkling of uniform. Wounded soldiers were to be seen desperately trying to return to the civilian life they once knew but inside they were changed men, so very different to the youngsters who went away. The war had seen to that.

The Americans may have been considered late arrivals in the war but their contribution, which effectively brought the conflict to an end, came at a catastrophic cost. 116,000 US servicemen died and over 200,000 were injured. At Verdun an American cemetery was created, containing thousands of US soldiers and would remain a monument to their courage.

Unlikely heroes achieved a fame they would never have deliberately sought. A conscientious objector called Alvin York rose to the rank of sergeant and received the Congressional Medal of Honour. Such were the peculiarities of war.

In his first week back in New York Anatole had been to see a show where Al Jolson was appearing. He was a mesmerising performer with a rich singing voice that could generate emotion in every song. Anatole watched Jolson with the eyes of a fellow performer. What a wonderful profession to be in that could provide happiness to the masses. But now by virtue of his wartime injuries it was one that Anatole could never work in again. He could never dance the way he had done in his glory days. To do so might mean a permanent disability and a life spent in a wheelchair. It was a desperately worrying issue. Just how could he make a living without falling into a pattern of drudgery? Was it to be a

268

life spent tablewaiting, washing dishes, doing demeaning work simply to get by?

In his mind he wondered if he could make it as an artist. His paintings had been exhibited and sold by Paul Kapsia before. Perhaps Sammy Rosen might be able to help him out there. In the meantime he needed to earn money quickly to keep the wolf from the door. He left the Jolson show with sadness that night. Anatole had loved the thrill of performing, playing to an appreciative audience and being the centre of attention on stage least. Amongst the repertoire Jolson had performed that night was a song called 'My Mother's Rosary'. He whistled it to himself as he walked out into the night air and the busy streets of New York.

Since returning to America, Anatole had been staying in a boarding house in Brooklyn. He would frequently look out of the window at the city he called home but he realised with dismay he no longer felt this was home any more. Without roots or family here he felt like an expatriate living in No-Man's Land with nowhere to go. He lay in his bed unable to sleep, gazing up at the ceiling. Then weariness would engulf him and he would be lost in a sea of dreams. Suddenly he would find himself back on the battlefield in Northern France and then he would wake shivering with fear yet at the same time covered in perspiration. Nightmares would rock his senses. Worries about how he would make a living combined with the memories of his wartime ordeal threatened to tip him over the edge into depression. Life was too precious to spend time in despair. He knew he had to reach into himself and pull out all the courage and the powers of endurance he possessed.

The next morning he woke in a more positive defiant mood with the steely determination to bury all his demons and make the most of his life. First stop was a visit to his bank to see how he was fixed for funds. It had been two years since he had last stepped inside this building. He walked with a limp to the counter and, on seeing him, the lady cashier noticing his uniform greeted him with a smile.

"Good morning," he said. "I've been on active service in France. I believe my outstanding soldier's pay has been forwarded to my account. Would you check it for me?"

"Of course, sir. What is your name?"

"I'm Anatole Luchenya."

"I need some identification. Can you provide me with some details?"

"Yes, m'am," he replied respectfully and he produced his soldier's pay book, his passport and a copy of his American citizenship document.

The lady cashier took the papers and went into an office where she took out a file in his name. For a moment, she examined it and then went across to a section manager who discussed the contents of it. They both looked up to where Anatole was standing which made him nervous. What on earth were they discussing? Then she returned without the file.

"Would you come through to the office, sir?" she said opening the door to let him in. "The manager would like to talk to you about it."

Why? thought Anatole. He was perplexed. Why did the manager want to talk to him about an account balance, which by his own estimation would not be any more than a couple of hundred dollars. Anatole walked through and the manager stood up to shake his hand.

"Take a seat, Mr Luchenya." Anatole sat down opposite him. "I was at Meuse in France. So I know all about it too. Got back a few weeks ago. You?"

"A week ago."

"How's the injury?" He had noticed Anatole's wound.

"I'm learning to live with it. I don't like it much. I'm trying to get on with my life and forget about battlefields and death. So tell me, Mac, how much have I got, or have you got bad news for me?"

The manager looked at him with a smile. "The name's Sam Mancini, and it's not bad news. Your account has a total of fifteen thousand dollars." He pushed forward a statement. Anatole looked at it in amazement. "I'd say that was pretty good news, wouldn't you, Mr Luchenya?"

"Are you sure this is mine, Mr Mancini?"

Sam Mancini took the file and began to flick through each page. "It says here you were employed as an entertainer through the Paul Kapsia organisation. When Mr Kapsia died, Sammy Rosen, the boxing promoter, took over some aspects of the company. I know, I helped finance some of his projects in the past. He had to pay out some outstanding royalties to Mr Kapsia's performers who toured in his shows. They were paid directly to your account as I see you were away in service in Mexico and France."

"I never knew this but fifteen grand…. The royalties wouldn't be that much. Not that I'm complaining, of course."

"There's more. You worked for a while in San Castillo, Texas, on an oil drilling assignment?"

"How the hell did you get that information?"

"That's because soon after the war began, Joe Donahue and Red Diamond had a big oil strike and formed the DD Oil Corporation. They gave a bonus to their employees. It says here in the notes that you gave a forwarding mail address care of the Kapsia organisation right here in New York. It seems as their oil business took off during the war that Mr Donahue honoured his pledge and remembered his staff. Sammy Rosen deposited the money to your account. In addition the outstanding payments for your army service were also added together with accumulated interest. That's a pretty good welcome home, I would say. If you need any advice the bank is right here for you. Any ideas what you want to do with your future? You've enough to go into business.

"I'm still trying to figure it out," said Anatole. He felt glad to be able to talk to somebody about the pressing problem of work. "I had a real life once as a dancer. As you can probably guess shrapnel in Northern France has put paid to that for the rest of my life. In between show business jobs, I did labouring in the oil field and dishwashing. To tell you the truth I don't know which way to turn. I've also been an artist... sold a few paintings. If I tried that it might be a long journey to get established."

Sam Mancini appeared to consider what Anatole had just told him. He knew the problem his client was facing was shared by returning veterans across the United States. "Tell me, Mr Luchenya, you appear to have very affectionate memories of your life on the stage, would you maybe consider a role behind the scenes?" This aroused Anatole's interest. He looked at Mr Mancini to further expand on what he had just said. "The reason I ask is that this bank has financed a small cinematography firm run by a Mr Andre Aviva. They are located a few streets away from here and were pretty active bringing the news of the war to the folks back home in the picture theatres. I could arrange an introduction for you. Maybe you could start a new life as a cameraman."

This was an interesting proposition. With all his knowhow of the stage and his experience as an extra in Hollywood silent films, this could prove to be a new worthwhile career to embark on. There was no time to waste. Anatole was eager to get started. He went to see Andre Aviva the same day.

***

The office was situated several floors up in a nearby building where Anatole made his way to with a mixture of excitement and trepidation. Clutching the letter of introduction Sam Mancini had given him he took the elevator to the fourth floor. There were reminders of the studios he had worked at in Hollywood. Cameras and lighting equipment were placed around the floor. Reels of film were in cans in open cupboards. A photographic developing laboratory was situated in an annex close to the studio floor. There was a cutting room where film editors and examiners worked studiously on footage.

He found Andre Aviva in a private office and introduced himself. Mr Aviva studied the Letter and smiled. The two indulged in smalltalk for a while then got down to a serious conversation. Andre Aviva was forty-four, a serious-looking man with spectacles who spoke in a quiet voice. He was the son of French immigrants but his accent was that of a well-educated New Yorker.

"I remember you from before the war," he pointed out with a smile. "I was a scene shifter in theatres back in those days. The Dancing Luckies, Nat and Mary. That was you, wasn't it? I remember a great dancer called Jess Reubens."

"Seems a lifetime away now. A different life. The war changed a lot of things. I've been to many places since and in different situations."

"It did for a lot of us. Before the war I was content to build stage sets and put them together. Then I started to study the work of the camera and I thought this is where the future lies. During the war the public were hungry for information. Who could blame them? American sons were losing their lives in boggy battlefields. They wanted the true picture of just what was really going on. That's where the cameraman came in big time. Never before was it so important to record every detail possible. I found myself in London filming Zeppelin attacks. I filmed T. E. Lawrence and General Allenby in Cairo. I was also at Gallipoli and Flanders shooting scenes of events that made history. Constantly, I was moving from place to place. I learned the process of developing film, cutting, splicing and editing. It's a craft that takes time to learn like Engineering or Science or building a car or a construction project. I've learnt… and in fact I'm still learning about projection, camera angles, getting the lights right, focusing and pulling, getting the shots right. Close shots. Long shots. What do you think the essence of a great cameraman is?"

Anatole realised he was being seriously tested and gave the question careful consideration. At last he gave a reply after a few minutes of silence. "I would say getting that history making shot that people will look back on over the ages remembering where they were at the time."

"I wouldn't have phrased it quite like that. A good answer though. It's about capturing the moment. A good cameraman is an observer of life. He is continually focusing on everything that is happening. When the lens of a camera is concentrating on an event... let's say Queen Victoria's Jubilee of 1897, the Gettysburg Reunion in 1913, the inauguration of the President of the United States. It's not just the central characters... the main players of the story, but the looks on the faces of the crowd, the people, their reactions. In the battles of war... and you will know what I am talking about... it may sound cold-hearted and cruel but you have to capture the atmosphere. The fear on men's faces... the urgency and crisis of the moment. The damage to buildings. It's not a job for the fainthearted. There will be times of great terror and there may be moments of great mirth. It's about recording sadness and moments of joy, great sporting occasions, the famous faces of the time: presidents and prime ministers, statesmen, villains, stars of stage and screen, the changing of the seasons. The first blooms in spring as the buds begin to open, the blossoms on the trees and the aftermath of harsh weather conditions such as drought, famine and flood and sun scorched plains; the snow falls that turn drab towns into the chocolate box villages of Victorian-era Christmasses. You have to be alert too for the unexpected. If you were filming in the Himalayas and from out of nowhere the Abominable Snowman made his debut, you would have to be ready to capture his image. Now do you think this industry is one that you could happily work in?"

Anatole's eyes were shining. "This is what I have been looking for. The job sounds so good if I didn't think it was beneath my dignity to do so I would practically beg you for it. Hell yes, I could enjoy this work."

"You don't have to beg for it. I need another team member, but you won't go out on the shoot straight away. Tell me, and I hope you don't mind me asking, but how long before you leg injury fully heals?"

"That's a good question. I have to be honest, Mr Aviva – and I guess you would appreciate honesty – the doctors told me there's no rule. It's up to the individual's constitution. I guess that rules me out as a cameraman."

"Not at all. It just delays it for the time being. That could work to your advantage. You won't be fit enough to start shooting news but from the technical point of filming you can learn all the backroom processes: cutting, editing and developing. Then when you are feeling in much better physical shape, you can start training behind the lens on location. How does that sound? Are you still interested?"

"You bet your bottom dollar I am. This is the best break I've had in years." Anatole was genuinely interested and after agreeing a start date he left the building on a cushion of air. Not only did he have substantial funds in his bank account, but he was now about to embark on a new career and a new chapter in his life. In fact, his whole life since he had left Russia as a child had been a series of very diverse chapters that had been a mixture of personal aim, accident and progress.

For a moment he was so buoyed up by his change of circumstances that he forgot the injury in his leg. He was feeling really enthusiastic. The thought of working in this burgeoning part of the business overwhelmed him. There was a café nearby and he decided to drop in for a while and have a decent meal whilst contemplating his newfound luck. No sooner had he entered the cafe than a policeman and a smart suited man looked up and smiled at him. The policeman was Jack Clancy and the other man was Slugs Mahoney.

They shook hands and laughed and smiled together. "He got through!" Slugs was saying. "Brother, we were worried about you."

It's good to see you, Nat," said Jack. "We really thought you were a goner. Old Slugs and I asked around for you but nobody knew anything. We looked out for your brother-in-law. Never saw him again. Gee it's good to see you, pal. The old team together again. How about that?"

There was one issue troubling Anatole. "Tell me, fellas, what happened to my buddy Gerry Valentine?"

His friends suddenly looked serious. Jack looked towards Slugs, who appeared downcast. He spoke in a low voice. "He didn't make it, Nat." Anatole felt instant sadness. "I'm sorry. He was one of the casualties of that vile war. We were marching down a country lane to meet up with the rest of the guys when we ran into the Hun coming from the other direction. The next thing we know it's *boom boom boom!* Bullets flying around us. Jack and I hit the ground. Then we're running and firing and in physical combat with bayonets. When it was all over… well… we checked out our buddies. Gerry took a bullet real early. That's war for you, Nat."

"That's rough." Anatole took the news badly. "Gerry and I rode over all of Mexico looking for Pancho Villa. He was a courageous fellow. One of the good guys. We even discovered Mayan ruins, did I tell you that?" He paused and then felt compelled to change the subject. "So you guys are back to the old routine then?"

"I'm back on the *Tribune*," Slugs pointed out. "To be fair, even while I was a soldier I was despatching articles back from France and eventually when we crashed through to Berlin in the final days of the war, I had a hefty pay cheque waiting for me and a job to come back to. I was a lucky guy. Luckier than many returning fellas, that's for sure.

"And now I'm back on the precinct," said Jack. "I'm still chasing the bad guys. Only this time I get a coffee break and I get to go home at night. What's your story, pal? Found any work yet?"

"Today, as a matter of fact, guys," Anatole said proudly. "I'm going back to the business I love, this time behind the camera. I've got a job with Andre Aviva's cinematography firm. I begin training tomorrow in the process of filmmaking. I'll be filming news in time. So, boys, we'll be able to meet up from time to time and go to each other's wedding. What do you say, Slugs? Sound good?"

"Hell yes!" said Slugs. "Look at us! Three good-looking guys. The girls in New York will be beating a path to our door."

"Here's to lifelong friends," Jack toasted them with his mug of coffee. The three of them talked for a long time that day. It was afternoon when they had met up and they reminisced and talked of their plans until late in the evening. By the time Anatole got home he felt enthusiastic about life as he once had when he was a young boy who had seen Jess Reubens dance and thought that was the life he wanted.

He remembered the thrill of the time he spent in Hollywood as an extra. It used to amaze him how the interior of a studio could be converted to a palace or a cowboy range. The set designers could come up with original plans that draughtsman would busily create in schematic drawings. Then, the skilled carpenters would go to work reproducing the structures of a backwood cabin, a palace interior, a roman arena; in fact just about anything. Ably assisted by scenic artists, set finishers and props-men, no setting was out of bounds. Make-up Artists could enhance age, or change an actor's appearance totally depending on the requirements of the role. The wardrobe staff could produce costumes and outfits of any era. All the actors had to do was perform in front of the camera. While silent films were yet to give way to talkies, the finished product was a visual feast more reliant on facial expressions and lavish sets. The on screen captions of dialogue told the story.

It was a world Anatole had enjoyed being part of. Meeting the famous films stars of the day had been exciting. Douglas Fairbanks, Mary Pickford, Charlie Chaplin and Fatty Arbuckle, soon to be embroiled in a scandal were all people he had appeared in films with. Soon other stars such as Tom Mix, Pola Negri, Rudolph Valentino, Marion Davies, Theda Bara, Greta Garbo and John Gilbert would light up the screen creating admirers worldwide who would fantasise about them. Now Anatole was going to work as a cameraman filming the realities of the world instead of the fictionalised version as portrayed in Hollywood. He would be interpreting the actions and effects of real people, not role personification. It would be a challenge and more rewarding then he could ever have imagined. *THAN*

***

On his first day at work Andre Aviva arranged for Anatole to view some newsreel footage. In a private viewing room he ran an old report of the Gettysburg Reunion of 1913. In many ways to view the black and white film without the benefit of sound made it more atmospheric and haunting to watch. Andre Aviva carefully stopped the film and ran it to point out how the camera had captured the expressions of these warriors of another age. The Blues and Greys were old men now and once mortal enemies but reunited as fellow Americans. It was a fascinating exercise to learn the rudiments of film making. Andre also ran footage of the war that had just finished.

This made for uncomfortable viewing for Anatole. To see the newsreel footage of the war and battles he had fought in brought it all back to him. There was almost a surreal feel about it. Andre had shown it to him with good intentions in an instructional basis but hadn't realised the effect it would have on a recently returned soldier. Anatole watched avidly but with gritted teeth. It was as if he could feel the atmosphere and every sensation he had experienced as a soldier again. Then he realised that he might possibly have to go into a warzone. God forbid after the nightmare of the Great War that there would be any more such long conflicts to come but a precedent had been set. There could be and would be repercussions with tyrants and despots eager to reclaim territories and invade other countries. Economic chaos in the form of Depressions would also follow, plunging millions around the world into unemployment and poverty. All these events would be recorded faithfully and meticulously by newsreel cameraman and Anatole would find himself at the heart of history in the making.

For the time being, while he was receiving therapy and regular medical examinations for his war injuries, he immersed himself in learning the fundamentals of the film business. He began by studying the process of developing film and the chemical composition of celluloid. The technical aspects were new to him and baffling to someone who had a basic education. However, he persevered with it knowing that in the future he might be required to develop film in some remote location.

Due to his injuries and the slow recovery he did not start training as a cameraman for almost eighteen months. Instead he concentrated on the skills behind the camera. Apart from developing film he learned how to cut and edit with great precision. He studied old film footage of the past twenty years. The great figures of history passed before his eyes: Teddy Roosevelt, Lloyd George, General Pershing, Kitchener, Churchill, Woodrow Wilson. Work was not a chore for Anatole. It was a thrill and an education. Not only was he being paid for something he enjoyed, but he felt that he was now defined as a person by his new career.

Sometimes in his leisure hours Anatole would go to small clubs where jazz musicians played. Even after a long days work Anatole could relax listening to the musicians who played often mournful sounds while glasses clinked in the background and cigarette smoke spiralled in loops. Slugs and Jack would join him occasionally and the three men's friendship became stronger than ever. The appeal of jazz music lay in the varying styles of the musicians. The bands could be big with a mixture of trumpet, piano, saxophone and drums. The music could be just as spellbinding with two musicians. One night in a club a saxophonist and pianist held their audience enthralled for several hours playing a seemingly endless session of haunting music. In the aftermath of the terrible war years work in the film world and music became the focal points of his life.

By the time Anatole moved from the developing laboratory, and the cutting room to becoming a cameraman, prohibition had been enforced in America. It was a time of speakeasies, jazz, loose morals, bootleggers, or as one noted wit wrote 'a period of highly enjoyable bad behaviour.'

The 1920s began to roar into action. People began to work hard and play hard. Along with the rest of Andrew Aviva's team Anatole began to film America as it grew and developed. The documentary and newsreel work he was employed on covered all aspects of American life. His first major job was in covering the elections, which brought Warren Harding to the presidency. Three years later after Harding's tragically early death at fifty-seven the camera team covered the ascension of Calvin Coolidge to the presidency.

Not only did they film the political events of the 'Roaring Twenties' but also the huge industrial changes that put America at the forefront of the world in technological innovation. In between the major films that were being shown at a picture theatre the newsreel documentary brought to the public's attention the changing face of their nation in the twentieth century. For Anatole it was an eye-opener to see the real world in all its forms. In his own life he had lived in the show business environment for much of his career and apart from his brief labouring stints and army service he had been closeted from the physical stresses of industry.

The Aviva camera unit travelled across America in pursuit of the real face of the people. In Pittsburgh they filmed inside a steelworks. The film choreographed the sparkling hot atmosphere as well as the process of producing steel. Andre Aviva decided that it would be difficult to incorporate a number of industries in one documentary. Instead he made the decision to produce a series of short films entitled *America at Work*. These were small educational films that were inserted between the main feature and the second one. Andre realised that after years of war the public craved to be entertained and not educated. So to make the documentary more acceptable to the film-going public, humorous asides were added to the dialogue captions on screen as well as close shots of the workers as if to say: *'These are our people. These are the salt of the earth artisans who work in our industries and create the goods that make America the world's leading manufacturer and innovator'*. The objective of these short films was to show the world just what America could do, and how it could inspire and motivate others to follow suit.

In this the Aviva team were more than just successful. Tele-communications was a burgeoning industry. Since Alexander Graham Bell had first invented the telephone it had become an essential part of every day life. Not just a luxury for the rich but also a must have item in the house. Few members of the general public, apart from the engineers involved, knew of the work that went on inside a telephone exchange. Andre had decided to film how a call was made and the step-by-step process that it went through to reach the other caller. He made a short film which showed a subscriber dialling out a number, which sent pulses down an underground cable or an overhead line to the exchange. Inside the cameraman recorded how the switchgear responded to the pulses. Then another cameraman showed the person who was called answering the phone. The team also filmed the ladies on a very busy switchboard putting long distance and emergency calls through. This short was brief and instructional but it provided an insight into an industry which, in 1920, was still developing. In later years telecommunications would expand with submarine cables, satellites and portable mobile phones which would contain multi-information. At this stage few could see into the future about the far reaching developments of telecommunications.

Construction was playing a big part in the American economy. In the great cities of New York and Chicago new skyscrapers soared towards the heavens. Anatole found himself and the rest of the Aviva team filming in half built buildings. They found filming at great heights a nerve-wracking experience. The wind blew at such a high level and at times it could be so strong that it was an effort to keep the camera firmly held. Anatole concluded that the builders had nerves of steel to work at such heights. They seemed to be pretty *laissez-faire* about safety. In between jobs they would sit on steel girders drinking coffee and eating sandwiches with nothing but a sheer drop of hundreds of feet below them. It made for an interesting photo opportunity. In the captions of dialogue, Andre referred to the architectural, civil, electrical and mechanical aspects that all contributed to the construction of these buildings and how they created work for many Americans.

Anatole enjoyed this work immensely. It was showing him the backbone of the American economy where the life of the ordinary working man was displayed to the cinema-going public. In so many ways it was often a mirror image of the people who sat in the audience and made many realise that whatever their profession it contributed to the American way of life. One short film concentrated on small businesses that were more or less evident on every high street.

Andre was the son of a French grocer and he knew how his father had worked all hours often going out early in the morning and not finishing until late in the evening. In order to get a fair representation of small businesses Andre decided to include the work of the butcher, the delicatessen, the baker, the chemist, the pharmacist and at Anatole's suggestion as an example of the textile industry, the art of tailoring and cutting. He suggested to Andre to film at his father's old tailoring business. ANATOLE   THAT HE

Viktor had died at the premises from a heart attack way back in 1898 but inside it was as if time had stood still. Before filming, Anatole took a walk around the rooms where his father had worked. He didn't tell the proprietor of his own family history relating to this place. For a moment he imagined his father rising from his work bench to greet him. His eyes were moist. He remembered the conversation he had with his father shortly before he died. It was one of the few times he had spoken in depth with his son almost as if he had known his own death was imminent. Even now the resonance of those words had drifted down the span of his years. Anatole and his colleagues filmed the skilled work of the tailors, thanked the owners and then moved on. It was as if he had taken a dramatic step back in time.

The work didn't end once filming had concluded. Often they worked late into the night in the cutting rooms to ensure delivery of the completed short films to the theatres. The series *America at Work* proved to be remarkably successful, well received by critics and the public alike. In years to come these short films would be historically archived and when shown to audiences provided an accurate documentary of life in America in the 1920s. The British cinema would also produce documentaries of a similar nature when the GPO film unit was established. Every day for Anatole and the members of the Aviva team was exciting. A new day brought new locations and an insight into the American way of life.

Andre Aviva had to come up with new ideas to maintain the cinemagoer's interest. He had already struck lucky with filming industry. Now after consultation with his team a unanimous decision was made to make a number of short films that would display America's physical attractions. The series was to be entitled *The Glories of America*. It would be the forerunner of the travel documentary.

Anatole had already travelled the length and breadth of the United States as a dancer. These travel films would take him to the wilder parts of the nation as well as the tourist destinations. How lucky can a guy get? Those were the thoughts that went through his mind so often. He was getting paid to do many of the things that people dreamed of doing.

Thirty

The Glories of America became a long running series that entranced audiences not only at home but throughout the world. There was so much fertile ground for filming that the series ran for several years.

By 1926 Anatole had his own apartment, money in the bank and a very busy lifestyle. He still saw his friends Slugs and Jack round town from time to time but their lives had changed. Jack had married an Irish girl called Miriam a few years before and he was now a father of a girl and boy. Miriam Clancy was a strong-minded girl from Belfast who was a good homemaker and very supportive of Jack. After being orphaned as a child Jack found much happiness in his family. His career was a different matter. Now promoted to the rank of sergeant he had to deal with the rigours of prohibition and the hoods who set up their little empires in New York. Many a cop turned a blind eye to what was virtually an uncontrollable situation. Speakeasies were like garden weeds. Get rid of one and another sprung up elsewhere. Besides if a cop went into a speakeasy the chances were that he would join a judge and a lawyer at the bar anyway. There were plenty of punks on the street that needed arresting. Often a good lead to solving a crime could be found through a contact in the know who may have frequented a speakeasy and the owner might occasionally slip a cash gratuity to a cop to buy his silence. Failing that, the gift of an attractive woman's favours was a strong temptation. The end of prohibition could not come soon enough for Jack. Then it would be back to normal street policing.

Slugs too found himself a bride. Marilyn Law was a brash, sassy, bawdy Brooklyn girl with a heart of gold, a fiery temper when riled and oozing sex appeal, passion and good humour. In short Slugs had found his match. Marilyn was a man's woman. She worked as a secretary and met Slugs in a dance hall one night where they took to the floor and did the most spectacular black bottom anyone could ever remember seeing. They also performed the Charleston pretty magnificently with all the fervour of two passionate lovers in the bedroom. Two daughters followed their marriage. For a man who was so openly masculine in every sense, the birth of these girls brought out the protective instincts in him. Slugs was a man who enjoyed life and embraced every avenue it took him down. This former boxer, plumber and journalist never stopped to analyse life. He got on with it, laughing loudly, living every day to the full, loving his wife and family as much as he could and applying his 'man of the street' appeal to his journalistic writings. He found his niche in writing about industry and business for the Tribune.

On one occasion Slugs and Anatole met up by sheer coincidence when they were both on assignment at Henry Ford's car plant. The Aviva team were filming a short educational clip on the construction of vehicles. It was one of the last industrial filming jobs Anatole was ever to do. The rest of the time the team concentrated on what were truly the glories of America; natural scenery and wildlife.

Perhaps it was the busy lifestyle, but while Slugs and Jack found domestic happiness, Anatole remained steadfastly single. He was so engrossed in his new career, working long hours in different locations that he never found the time to establish a relationship. While Slugs and Jack, despite their own busy careers, found time to spend with their families, life for Anatole was a lonely one. His career took him to the great landscapes of the nation. Amongst the scenes they filmed were Niagara Falls, the Florida Everglades, Monument Valley, the Mojave Desert, the beauties of the mountains and lakes in Oregon which for Anatole was the most picturesque of all the states he had travelled to.

Andre Aviva was sharp enough to realise that scenery by itself may have made for interesting viewing but still pictures by themselves were not enough for cinema audiences. America had an abundance of wildlife. While the cities were a hub of business and commerce, out in the fields, streams, mountains and deserts, God's creatures fought a continual battle of survival against the elements. This became an all-consuming passion for the entire camera team.

While in England his sister, Mariska, had grown to love the nature of the Sussex countryside Anatole found not only great interest in the animal kingdom but also peace. Raised as a hard-bitten New Yorker in the tenements, he now found a love of the filming of animals in the wild. Sometimes in life it seemed that people would find a passion in something that had previously hitherto been alien to them before, but which now to their own astonishment and surprise completely changed their way of thinking.

Away from the rush of the cities, the team of cinematographers would follow the tracks of a mountain lion and record a day in the life of this beautiful but often solitary creature. Anatole had never been so close to such a magnificent beast in all of his life. He smiled to himself as he caught the images of it on film. It was such a beautiful specimen that even a San Franciscan showgirl could not rate comparison. In this he was an expert. He had been close to a number of showgirls in his time. Extremely close!

A family of Grizzly bears playing in the backwoods made compellingly funny viewing, even though they could be dangerous if approached. Yet with the camera focused on them from a safe distance there was something heart warming about the family life of a Grizzly. The mother bear looked after and played with her cubs in the manner of any normal suburban human family. The cubs rolled on their backs and craved for attention. They explored trees and bushes, sniffing out vegetation and looking up in surprise as a flock of birds flew high in the sky above them. Their wondrous world extended to pools and lakes where they would gaze in amazement at their own reflection staring back at them. The cubs would enter the water and as they felt its coolness or warmth, depending on how hot the temperature, their expressions would change. Sometimes the camera would pick up a glint in the eyes of the young cubs like the mirthful joy of a young child. Could animals possibly have a sense of humour like human beings, and know how to laugh? The mother bear would feed the cubs perhaps with fish from streams or another creature of the backwoods. Then at the end of a long day they would go to sleep resting their heads on each other and huddled together for warmth.

In order to capture such scenes of nature it proved to be very painstaking work requiring legendary degrees of patience that men in the cinema world need. That perfect shot, a moment of absolute splendour, a visual image could come and go in an instant. Anatole prided himself on his work. Once he had been a skilful dancer, calculating every intricate step that produced a dazzling display on stage. Now the stage was nature in its basic form. Was it his imagination or did the lens of his camera capture the smile on the mother bears face as her cubs went to sleep against her? Such scenes were the stuff that a cameraman's dreams were made of. His life had a constantly surreal feel about it.

Beavers and raccoons made for fascinating viewing. The beaver was the most industrious and innovative creature animal to watch. In the world of human beings the tradesmen had their tools to shape and manufacture things. Animals had no such luxury. The beaver was a furry animal with a big flat tail and large teeth. They would use their teeth to cut wood and build dams in rivers. The work ethic of these unique animals was something to be seen. It was an amazing sight to see the ingenuity at the way in which beavers worked. By what instinct were they driven to perform in such a way? Did all animals have a language of their own in the strange sounds they made? How did they automatically know how to hunt, how to mate, how to build a dam? Animals were always eternally interesting and fascinating.

The series of films took in the natural habitats of deer and antelope, the breathtaking sight of buffalo on the extensive plains and the multi-coloured bird life who flew above the canyons, crevices, deserts and rivers of the United States. Even before the advent of colour film the scenes in black and white were stunning.

Back in New York Andre Aviva coordinated the cutting and editing of all the films. They had set an agenda for future wildlife documentaries that would continue throughout the following years. The public consumption for the natural delights of their own country would generate calls for preservation of the land and protection for wild animals. National parks would be established housing many endangered species but also by keeping them safe in their own natural environment.

Hollywood had been very impressed by the work of the Aviva team. Andre Aviva had run his unit on an independent basis but the various Hollywood film studios were eager to sign them up on a contract basis. Substantial salaries were offered to each person. Documentary and newsreel work was developing alongside the quality of the feature films. There was a lot of talk about sound being introduced to films and this seemed an ideal time to join a major studio.

However, not all the team were keen to make the move to Hollywood. The offer was made primarily to Andre Aviva to work with cameramen already employed in Hollywood. He would not get to choose his assignments and, as he preferred to be independent, he was reluctant to take up the offer. In order to get a consensus from his team he called a meeting for all the staff to decide their futures.

***

In England, Mariska and Bernard were well aware of Anatole's work in the film industry. They were regular cinemagoers and often took themselves to the Capitol Theatre in Horsham to see the latest movies. The Aviva short films were shown together with the British Newsreels between the main and second features. Anatole had written occasionally keeping his sister informed about his ever changing life.

Mariska felt a sense of pride when she saw her brother's name on the credits far away in England. He never failed to surprise. Her two children were growing up now to appreciate that they had a very talented uncle in the United States. Alexander was eleven and Grace was eight. Even though they were a lord's children, they had been taught that they were no different from other children. Bernard had wanted this from the start and Mariska had been in agreement with him. Why should they be any more privileged than others by virtue of their birthright? They went to a local primary school and played with children whose fathers worked as plasterers, farm workers, painters and decorators. Not in any sense were they isolated from the mainstream of normal life.

Even before the Great War Bernard had developed a social conscience about the working classes and less well off people in society. In this land supposedly 'fit for heroes' the inequalities were so clearly obvious. The working man toiled for a pittance and at times if they clamoured for better pay and conditions they were shouted down by the ruling elite. Using his position in the House of Lords, Bernard became an unlikely but eloquent advocate for an improvement in the lifestyles of the under-privileged. He also spoke strongly in favour of more help for many of the soldiers who had fought in the war, and whose injuries still caused either physical or mental pain in the years that followed.

Another area he pursued was that of the men who had suffered stress on the battlefield. In this he spoke with some experience for he too had suffered shellshock. Men who had been shot by firing squads for alleged cowardice in war often suffered from this trauma of incessant shelling. In latter years, battle fatigue and combat stress were to be freely discussed and recognised as symptoms of war. Despite the efforts of many sincere campaigners to reverse the verdicts of cowardice handed down on those who were then sentenced to death by firing squad, the governments of the day remained adamant on the subject. It was an issue that was being debated well into the twenty-first century when the descendants of those branded cowards approached the governments of Gordon Brown and David Cameron to clear the names of their relatives. But long before, in a climate of patriotism and valour, the officers in war did not recognise such things.

Lord Bernard Shervington was considered something of a maverick. He had friends in high places – the Prince of Wales, for example, who he had met in the London social circle. But he did not seek to use their friendship for his own advantage, although he always expressed his feelings freely and sometimes they were duly noted, usually by an ambitious politician eager to make a name for himself by attachment to a particular cause. In the case of better living standards for the poor, and more concern for the welfare of returning soldiers, left wing firebrands often took up their cause with a passionate zeal.

For the most part Bernard continued to run his architectural business restoring old buildings to their former glory whilst at the same time combining with Mariska to run the other Shervington enterprises. Hard work and a busy life helped him put the awfulness of the war behind him. He was determined that his own children should never see the full effects of warfare in their lifetime.

Nights at the picture houses provided his children with the entertainment any normal family would enjoy. The lovely old Capitol Theatre in Horsham screened the great silent movies of the day together with the newsreels and the documentaries of life at that time. *The Glories of America*, when shown, displayed the breathtaking scope of that vast country. To Bernard it looked intoxicating and appealing. To Mariska it was a reminder of how long she had been away from the land of her formative years.

Sitting in the back of the chauffeur-driven car with Bernard while Tom Mollomby, still a reliable employee after all these years, took the wheel, she smiled at the memory of her musical tours in the United States under the banner of Paul Kapsia's shows.

"Honey, I came here on tour in 1911 and here I am fifteen years later in 1926 still here. What happened to those years?"

The children sat quietly in the back looking at the crowds leaving the Capital Theatre to walk along the rain splattered streets of the attractive Sussex town of Horsham.

"We got married. There was a war… and then we got on with life." He looked at her as if he knew what she was thinking. "Your brother's done well. Those films he made… do they make you feel homesick… nostalgic for America and the life you once had?"

Mariska squeezed his hand. "Not homesick. This is home. But I would like to travel again. To some of those places I went in the States. I would like to go to New York again if just to feel some sort of spiritual closeness to my mother and father. Do you know what I mean? By just being close to where they once lived, and talked, and went about their day-to-day lives, in my mind I could hear their voices again. They left this world too soon." Her eyes were moist. "I would like to see Anatole too. We went through so much together as kids and he's had a hell of a life too. A real rip-roaring adventurous life. No wonder he never ever found time to get married."

"We'll go sometime," Bernard assured her. "I'm sure the children would love to see the scenes their uncle Nat has filmed." In the back of the car Alexander and Grace smiled. "Your mother danced across America once," he added.

"And got caught in an earthquake in San Francisco in 1906 too!" Mariska said with a smile.

Mariska was a business woman and a mother now. She still had fond memories of her years as an entertainer but that was another life ago. In the time she had been married to Bernard he had taken to managing the administrative affairs of the Shervington estate in much the same manner as had Lady Bernadette before her. Both she and Anatole had developed in life in ways that had surprised them. Neither of them had anything more than a minimal education but by a twist of fate, circumstances, luck, and even accident, they had arrived at their present position in life. It could never have been planned.

By the time they got back to Shervington Manor it was late in the evening. They put the children to bed and then relaxed in each other's company for a while. There had been staff changes at the house. Mrs Price had retired, and so too had Bobby Grey who had very sadly died earlier that year. He had been with the family for many years and his loss was mourned by many of the local villagers who loved the cheery old man with the affable manner.

A new housekeeper called Linda Casling had taken up duties in the house. She also acted as a cook having previously worked in top London hotels. A spinster in her forties she had opted for a quiet life in the country.

The butler now was a man who had been a jack-of-all-trades in his life. Ronnie Wiltshire was a fair-haired man also in his forties. A bachelor, he had been a carpenter, a bricklayer, a soldier who had fought at Passchendaele, before, after injuries sustained in the war, going into service in country houses. His new posting to the Shervington household had also brought him love. It soon became obvious he was absolutely smitten with Linda. She too felt exactly the same way.

A new maid came to Shervington Manor. She was a striking young woman in her early twenties with dark hair and a smiling personality. Marilyn Wilce soon became a hardworking and eager to please employee.

In addition a young man of a similar age called Terry Bentley joined the house as a footman. He too became enamoured with his co-worker Marilyn. The general atmosphere had changed at the house to a more youthful feel, with the new staff and the harmonious relationships between them. The world was moving on and so too was Shervington Manor which seemed less stuffy than it had fourteen years before.

Miss Casling brought in a tray with some tea on to Mariska and Bernard in a room that overlooked the Downs. It was late in the evening now but the green contours of the lush rolling Downs could still be clearly seen in the night sky. At the end of a full day they sat quietly enjoying the peace of their own company.

Even after all these years of marriage, Mariska was still passionately in love with Bernard. The man she had married had developed and matured as he had grown older. He had become immensely compassionate towards the battles of society, but also a wise and distinguished businessman. Now forty-seven, his hair had become silver at the sides giving him a real aura of glamour.

Mariska at thirty-six looked more beautiful than she had ever been in her life. She was a fine mother who emphasised that her children should have good manners, a love of animals and the country, and respect for others. Her own character had also developed. It was as if everything that had happened in her marriage had been an education. Once she had been a naïve orphan child who had found a new family through the stage and the applause of the audience. Now with her own, she had never been happier. She embraced the work of the Shervington enterprises which she was constantly learning about. Her love for her husband had never waned and she was as still as passionate about him than when they had first met. Their intimate private life was still as warm as ever.

"With the new staff, the house feels younger," she said quietly. "I do miss dear Mrs Price… and lovely old Bobby too. They were so kind to me."

"Well the whole world moves on. Things change, Mariska. I was very sorry that Bobby didn't have a longer retirement before he died. At least Mrs Price gets time to spend with her grandchildren and in her garden now. We must call in and see her sometime. Perhaps one day next week. We don't want her to think we've forgotten her. After all she was with the Shervington family for forty years."

There was a knock on the door and the new butler, Ronnie Wiltshire, entered the room.

"Sorry to trouble you at this hour, sir," he said.

"Yes, Ronnie. It's no trouble."

"There's a telephone call for you in the lobby."

Bernard stood up. "At this hour? Thank you, Ronnie. I won't be a moment.

He went downstairs and picked up the phone. "Lord Shervington speaking," he said in a serious tone as if he half expected to be dealing with someone in business. The voice he heard speaking to him from the other end of the line shocked him. "You're here! How good to hear you! Well, this is wonderful!"

The conversation went on for several minutes. He was delighted to hear from the man and he knew that Mariska would be too. Bernard returned to the lounge room with a broad smile on his face.

"We have guests coming for dinner tomorrow. It's a surprise." Bernard could hardly contain himself. Mariska looked at him curiously. Could it be royalty? "They will be arriving about eleven o'clock."

Mariska wondered if it would be the Prince of Wales or a show business celebrity. In fact, it was very much better than that.

***

290

At eleven o'clock the next morning Mariska was waiting on edge with excitement. The staff were told to be ready to greet the visitors. From a room at the top of the house she looked out in readiness for an approaching vehicle bringing with it a distinguished guest or so she expected. Bernard had been remarkably coy about who exactly was coming that Sunday morning. Annoyingly so. All sorts of thoughts went through her mind. Then she hedged her bets. If Bernard was happy for her then perhaps it could only be one person.

Mariska looked out of the window. Outside the previous nights heavy rainfall had left the ground moist and the Downs lush, but as the sun began to shine more resplendently the dewdrops sparkled on the trees. The road leading down into the village was virtually empty apart from a morning horse rider who suddenly moved to one side as a vehicle approached. Mariska was on edge as the sound of a motor engine could be heard. Then she relaxed as she saw a small white van driving up. It was obviously not the distinguished guest she was expecting.

How wrong she was! The van came to a halt outside the Shervington Manor House. It seemed ages before the doors opened and out stepped two men. Mariska didn't recognise the first man who stepped out of the driver's seat – it was Andre Aviva, who she had never met. He wore a flat cap, sunglasses and a tweed suit. The man who emerged from the other door wore the hat that a New York businessman might wear and a sports jacket and dark trousers. He also wore sunglasses and Mariska could only see him from the back. He turned around, removed his glasses and looked up at the house. Mariska broke out into a smile. Down below on the drive in front of the house stood Anatole. It was the first time she had seen her brother in fourteen years. He removed his hat and waved it to her. It had been a long time since they had last met.

Anatole gazed up at the house. His sister had done well. It was a long way from their childhood homes in Russia and New York. From within Mariska emerged closely followed by Bernard and the children. He beamed a glorious smile at her and they hugged each other.

"Why didn't you tell me you were coming?" Mariska asked.

"I thought I would surprise you," he replied. "May I introduce you to Andre Aviva, my friend and colleague. We're travelling together on a filming assignment." Mariska and Bernard shook hands with Andre. "You may find this one hell of a coincidence but years ago Andre worked behind the scenes at the State Theatre in New York."

"Is that right?" Mariska gasped in amazement.

"Yes, ma'am. I was a sceneshifter and constructor in the days when you were the Dancing Luckies. I remember Jess Reubens too. Great days!"

"Well, sir, you are most welcome."

"I agree," said Bernard. "Shall we go inside, gentlemen? Oh, Mariska, aren't you forgetting something?" Mariska looked at him in a puzzled expression. "Aren't you going to introduce the children to their uncle?"

Mariska smiled delightedly. She ushered her two children directly in front of her. "Children, meet your Uncle Nat. My brother, Anatole." He promptly shook each child's hand and looked at them with a deep sensitivity. "This is Alexander and Grace... Grace Ekaterina Shervington."

"Ekaterina!" Anatole felt slightly emotional. "After our mother. How goddamn wonderful to meet you both!"

Almost as if in response to royal command, they entered the imposing manor house. Anatole had a strange but warm feeling that Sunday morning. He wasn't sure why himself. Whether it was because he was reunited with Mariska and newly acquainted with his nephew and niece, but as he looked around his surroundings and the rolling Sussex Downs, he felt he had come home.

Thirty-One

It was a real thrill for Anatole to be part of a family once again. He adored his nephew and niece on sight. There was something nice about this new generation who were growing up in this beautiful part of England. The atmosphere of the house was calm, serene and comforting.

Bernard talked to Andre while Mariska showed Anatole around the house. Anatole was surprised to see his old paintings adorning the walls. There were scenes of places he had travelled to in his life: Shanghai paintings, the Chinese countryside, Papua New Guinea, Australia, Nevada, Colorado, Arizona and Texas. There were also pictures of people he had met: a Native American chief, a Chinese lady, and a painting of Edwin Hyde, the convict who lived with an Aboriginal tribe. Then there were old photographs of halcyon days when Mariska and Anatole had danced their way across America. It was as if his past life was being displayed before him.

The two siblings sat down in the study from where the impressive view of the Downs could be seen. Anatole immediately fell in love with the Sussex countryside. He felt eager to explore it for nature.

"Gee it's good to see you, kid." He felt happy to be in her presence once again. "I can't believe it sometimes. My kid sister… a lord's wife… with children of her own… and running businesses. You've done well."

"It's good to see you too, Nat. The children love the films you make with Mr Aviva. But why are you here? What brought you to England after all these years?"

"Well Andre is the boss of the firm and he runs an independent show. Anyway the big boys in Hollywood making the feature films like what they saw in our work and offered Andre a mouth-watering contract to work for them… including all the guys like me, of course. The only stipulation is that he can't pick and choose his assignments. We have to go where the studio sends us. Andre called a meeting of all the staff and some of the boys decided to head for Hollywood anyway. That is effectively the end of Aviva Productions. Andre and I decided we would film in Africa for a while and then go our separate ways."

"Africa. That's exciting stuff. Where will you go when it's all over?"

"Andre will be returning to America… and probably to Hollywood, but for me I'm going it alone. I'm going to base myself in Europe and make films here. In the van outside we've got our own camera equipment and before we go to Africa we want to film the wildlife in this part of the world. We stayed at the White Horse Inn in the village last night. Would we be able to stay here for a few days?"

"We'll be pleased to have you! Oh it's good to see you. The children will be able to get to know you. So, you've definitely left the States then? Never to return?"

"Never say never," he said with a smile. Your little girl is eight. Is that right?"

"Yes. She is the same age as I was when we lost Momma and Pa. I look at her now and I want her to know the love we once received."

"Momma would be so proud of you, Sis."

"And you Nat. How are your friends… I should say our friends, Jack and Jake – or Slugs – wasn't that his nickname?"

"Jack is a cop now, married to an Irish girl, Miriam – a nice girl. They've got a couple of children. Slugs – there's a character for you. Loud personality. He's only got to walk into a room and he can turn it into a party. Would you believe he's a top-rated journalist for the *Tribune* in New York. He writes on science and business. He's called the 'Man of the People' because he writes it as he says it. His wife is Marilyn. She's his equivalent: loud, brash, a real woman in every sense of the word. A real beauty too."

"You never found anyone then in all your travels?"

He winked at her mischievously. "Never had the time."

"Sorry to bring this up," Mariska said suddenly and with concern in her voice. "You never mentioned it in your letters, but Bernard said he met you in France during the war and you were badly wounded. Do they still trouble you? Your wounds?"

"I have some nerve damage in one leg. It comes and goes. The memories of the war haunt me. I get nightmares from time to time. I guess anyone who was in that conflict knows what it was really like. I read somewhere a while back in a journal that someone wrote of the glamour and valour of war! Glamour! Are they kidding! The fields ran red with blood." It was as if a trigger had set something off within him. "War is a horrible experience! Ask the British and Canadians about Passchendaele or the Somme or Flanders. My physical wounds are nothing compared to the mental stain I have of that time. When I got out of that fiasco, I had seen such ugliness and violence and stress under battle that I only wanted to see the beauty in this world and I found it through being a cameraman filming nature. Do you know what I mean, kid? Beautiful women, beautiful scenery, the beauty of animals and beautiful music."

"Bernard has a hard time some days. It all comes flooding back to him if something triggers it off inside. He is very busy though. We both are. I look after the administrative affairs of the Shervington estate and enterprises. Bernard has his architectural work and he speaks in the House of Lords a lot on matters relating to poverty and better conditions for the ordinary working man as well as help for the returned servicemen, particularly those who were traumatised by shell shock. Life is very full."

There was something that Anatole was keen to find out. "I hope the question I'm about to ask doesn't sound out of place." Anatole was being cautious. "You seem to have reached a pretty good plateau in your life. Everything looks swell here for you. The best of houses, a good man for your husband, two great children who are a real credit to you. Are you happy? Is everything you have what you always wanted?"

Mariska smiled ebulliently. "More than I could ever have wished for. Oh, don't get me wrong, Nat. I'm not blasé about my life. I remember my roots. We may have been born Ruskies but we were Bronx-raised Jewish orphan kids who got into show business and saw the world as dancers, and got the kind of opportunities to meet people like Theodore Roosevelt, Marie Lloyd, the Prince of Wales and Sophie Tucker. I'm not kidding myself that I'm a true English lady now. I'm far too streetwise to flatter myself. But I'll tell you this, Nat, I've never felt more at home than I do now. This may well be the best time of my life."

"I'm happy for you, kid." Anatole was genuine in what he was saying and his voice registered sincerity. He cast his eyes towards a photograph on the mantelpiece behind Mariska. "Say, is that an old regimental photo?"

Mariska turned around to look. "Oh that. Sure is. The Shervington's served in the 25th Queens Light Northern Regiment out in India last century. A bit of a family tradition I understand. The regiment was integrated into the Royal Sussex which Bernard served in as you know."

Anatole stood up and walked over to take a close look at the picture. He studied it with great interest. The photograph had been taken back in the 1880s. The soldiers were men of another age in the days when the British Empire was at its peak. They were proud-looking men… perhaps proud of the regiment they served. They were Victorian adventurers who had fought across the wild terrains of the North West Frontier – men with granite chins, bristling moustaches and purposeful characters.

He turned the picture around and on the back he found a caption on the reverse side of the frame. It listed all the names of the prominent soldiers of the regiment then stationed at Fort Valaka in India. They were Colonel Duncan Anderson, Colour Sergeant Harry Chesney V.C. winner, Captain Rex Shervington, Corporal Bill Dunham, Regimental Sergeant Major Sandy Blackshawe, Major Jack Clancy. He almost dropped the frame in sheer amazement at what he had just discovered.

"Mariska! Come and look at this!" Anatole beckoned to her.

She came across immediately. "What am I looking at?" Anatole pointed to the name. "Jack Clancy! Major Jack Clancy! Why, that's the same name as our friend. I've never once in all these years turned the picture over to look at these names."

Anatole pointed to the front row and identified Major Clancy. "That's him, Jack's uncle. Back in New York Jack told me he was named after an uncle who served with the British Army in India. He even told me that it was the 25th Queens Light Northern Regiment. This fine looking major was related to Jack. Hard to believe, isn't it? In those days Ireland was part of the British Isles wasn't it?"

"A lot of the Irish boys probably joined up to escape the poverty back home, I guess," Mariska remarked. "I've lived in this house for fourteen years and never once checked out the names. Well I am goddamned amazed! You turn up and discover this!"

"I wish Jack wasn't beating the precinct right now in New York and was here to see this."

"I might find out if we have another copy and send one to Jack. Do you still have his address?"

"I do, Mariska." He looked round the study. His eyes fell on the array of books on shelves. "Wow, what a great collection!" Anatole was dazzled by the display in front of him. There were the great classics such as the books by Robert Louis Stevenson. Twenty years before, Anatole had visited the home and grave of the author in Samoa. It was one of those memories that seemed surreal. Before him was *Kidnapped*, *The Master of Ballantrae*, *The Strange Case of Dr Jekyll and Mr Hyde*, *Treasure Island*, *Travels with a Donkey in the Cevennes*.

"I remember when Mamma used to read some of those stories to us," Mariska reminded him wistfully.

He smiled at her. The study was a feast for any booklover. There were *Oliver Twist* and *Great Expectations* by Charles Dickens. *Marching to Ava, Buller in Natal, Robinson Crusoe, Lorna Doone, Robin Hood, Pilgrims Progress, Moby Dick*, H G Well's novel of *Kipps* and Rudyard Kipling's *Jungle Book*. Also in evidence were books on poverty and affluence, poetry by Rupert Brooke and Siegfried Sassoon, the science of printing and there was one that instantly fascinated Anatole. It had first been published in 1649 and it went by the title of *Johnson's Arithmetik*. The word 'arithmetik' was now spelt 'arithmetic' in modern day spelling. In fact the spelling throughout the book wouldn't have passed a present day English exam. The word 'decimal' was spelt 'decimall'. With only a basic knowledge of maths, Anatole looked at the theories, tables and quotients spelt 'quotitients' and felt almost privileged to have held this book in his hand. The book was written by a government 'surveigher' not surveyor, for that is how it was spelt by a man called Johnson. What must this distinguished gentleman have been like? In appearance and brainpower he would have been a world away from the books where the study was situated.

Many years later in 2008, a researcher and archivist found a copy of this book which had been gifted to the Worthing Museum and Art Gallery. It promptly took pride of place in the museum's collection of literature.

The study and library at Shervington Manor had a warm, snug cosiness about it. Looking around this room full of good books, photographs of a time gone by in frames, descriptive paintings of family portraits and landscape scenery, memorabilia and huge comfortable armchairs, Anatole concluded that this was a piece of heaven one could easily hibernate to on cold winter's nights.

Mariska reached into a drawer and pulled out some old papers yellowing with age. "Here's something that will interest you, Nat."

"What are they?" he asked taking them

"Old census forms. Look at the occupations of the local people. Apparently Lady Bernadette Shervington used to help some of the locals with their forms and gather them up for study."

The details on the forms made for fascinating reading. "Plasterer, blacksmith, farrier, mole catcher, paperhanger, decorator… Humble professions and good people. This place is steeped in history, Mariska."

Before they could continue their conversation, there was a knock on the door. Ronnie Wiltshire and Terry Bentley entered the room. Each man carried a painting.

"Where would you like these, m'lady?" asked Terry.

Mariska looked at them curiously. "What are these?"

"Paintings, Your Ladyship" Terry replied. "Mr Luchenya asked us to bring them to you from the vehicle outside."

"That's right," Anatole indicated to them to place the paintings by his side. "Thank you, gentlemen." He turned to Mariska. "This is my gift to you."

Mariska looked at each painting. One was a portrait picture copied from a very old photograph. It was of Viktor and Ekaterina standing proudly together and smartly dressed. Their young children, Mariska and Anatole were in front of them. Anatole had painted the picture which had been taken from a photograph of the family at the wedding of Alexander Shezevion and Maria in Leeds back in 1892. Mariska's eyes became moist and a tear rolled down her cheek.

"How wonderful. Thank you, Nat."

"I thought you would like to see our momma and pa watching over you."

Mariska took a look at the other painting. She was mystified. It was a colourful picture of Indian native figures in costumes appearing to look on at villagers of eons ago. They looked as if they were being judged by the three figures who glowed in multicoloured attire against a gold background. It was vivid, intoxicating and spellbinding but nothing like any painting in a public art gallery.

"Well… it's bright and stunning but I have to tell you it's a hell of a mystery. What is it? It's got a sacred feel about it."

"Sacred? That's a pretty good word for it." Anatole was proud of his work as an artist. He liked the idea that it was not an instantly recognisable picture and, if displayed publicly, would probably merit discussion. "These are Mayan gods. When I was in Mexico with the US Army in hot pursuit of Pancho Villa my pal Gerry Valentine and I accidentally stumbled on some old Mayan ruins."

"I remember you mentioning it in your letters. Your discovery made the New York papers, I believe."

"Right. While Gerry and I were there I made sketches of the inside of caves full of Mayan rock carvings. I kept a couple back and I read later that these were of the Mayan gods." He pointed as he spoke. "This one is Chac… the rain god. Next to him is Kinich Ahau… the sun god. And the one here is Ix Chel… the moon goddess. I recreated it in oils. I guess it's a little bit different to the average landscape or still life painting. Do you like it?"

"It's fascinating. An example of just how much distance you've covered. Do you know very much about the Mayans? I know nothing about them."

"Only what my late pal Gerry told me… he died while serving in France… and from what I've read, the Mayans were an ancient civilization who flourished from 250AD for more than 600 years. According to Gerry they studied the movement of the stars, astronomy, mathematics, even calculation and science."

"Even now, brother, you're still learning," Mariska remarked in admiration. "I will treasure these two paintings."

At this point Ronnie Wiltshire returned to the room. "Luncheon is ready, Your Ladyship."

***

"So this is the room King Edward the Seventh and Rudyard Kipling dined in," Anatole stated. They were all seated at a long table in the dining room. It was a far from ostentatious room but, as with throughout the house, there was an historical feel about it. The table had the best silver service and the plates were genuine china with attractive patterns.

"That was in the days when Queen Victoria reigned and Edward was then the Prince of Wales," Bernard pointed out. "I've suggested that Anatole and Andre occupy the lodge house while they are here."

"You'll come to the house for meals of course," said Mariska.

"We'll be pleased to," replied Andre. "If we could use the lodge as a cutting room, we would be most grateful. We intend to do some filming of

English nature. From what I understand the wildlife on the Sussex Downs is pretty prolific. Do you have any tips for us?"

"If you're heading off to Africa soon the Downs might serve as a dress rehearsal on a miniature scale." Bernard was being remarkably modest about an area he loved. "I know it well. I've walked these Downs since I was a boy and it might seem quiet and restful during the daylight hours, but at night it's an animal kingdom when God's creatures come out to play. There are badgers, foxes, squirrels, hedgehogs, deer and feral cats to name but a few. Badgers are nocturnal so you might have to prime your cameras at the ready. I could take you to a sett where you can position your cameras in readiness for the emergence of them at night when they come out to forage for food."

"That would be great!" Andre was enthusiastic. "We will start filming during the day and work through the night. Are you alright with that, Nat?"

"Sure thing. From what I've seen of the countryside round here it's mighty pretty. Maybe we could take in a dairy farm while we're at it and see some of the locals hard at work. I reckon we could get some good footage of English country life here."

Bernard looked keenly interested. "I could take you, gentlemen, tomorrow if you like. I would be very glad to learn how filming is done. I'm always on the lookout for learning new things. You never know one day I might be able to use the technique of filming to record some of the industries we are associated with. There are some interesting old buildings and churches you might be eager to record. Being an architect myself I could give you a lot of background information on them. Would I be able to accompany you tomorrow? May I join you, gentlemen?"

"Of course! We would be delighted to have a third member of the team." Andre was privately pleased. "I like the idea of filming some of the great old buildings in Sussex. One on historical architecture in Sussex, and the other on animal life in the country."

"Sounds great! But by the time we've finished filming, cutting and editing we could be here for a few weeks. A lot depends when you want us to board that boat to Africa, Andre."

"As long as it takes. Remember we're independent film makers. Not part of any corporate structure. It's up to us when and how we work. And let's face it we're pretty good at what we do."

***

The next day the three men set off on their initial filming assignment on the South Downs. There are some fine spring mornings in Sussex when the joy of living permeates through to the very soul of one's being. That feel of an early morning when a slight breeze rustles the grass and the corn in the fields, as the gentle warmth of the sun gives an added impetus to the day. The trees with scented blossoms and the wild flowers of varying colour in shades of lilac and pale red carrying with them their own distinctive perfumery intermingling with the aroma of lush meadows, makes one feel giddy. So it was that day.

The three of them walked up the South Downs carrying the cameras. In the distance a shepherd came towards them with a flock of pristine-looking sheep, who appeared beige against a backdrop of a clear blue sky and emerald green. It made for a great view of Sussex country life and they immediately set their cameras up to capture the scene. The shepherd appeared delighted to be the centre of attention. He beamed them a big smile and doffed his country hat to them. Andre returned the smile too. He knew that every scene of value contributed to the overall quality of a real life documentary.

Further along the track a couple of donkeys in a field looked curiously over a fence. They had trusting eyes and a gentle contentment about them. It was hard not to love such beautiful calm animals. The three men who loved animals each stroked them and made a fuss of the two donkeys. It was clear the donkeys were very much a couple. The male donkey occasionally nuzzled the female. They didn't want for much, just each other's company, food and water, and to be able to graze peacefully and a shelter in inclement weather. The farrier, who attended the horses belonging to the Shervington family, also attended to the donkeys. Their coats were coarser than that of a horse but, nevertheless, were kept well groomed. These gentle animals made for photogenic viewing and after being recorded on camera the men showed their gratitude by feeding them grass from the side of the Downs.

There was an ingenuity about filming an area like the Sussex Downs, for it was not only the animal life that made interesting viewing, but also the plants. Andre had a keen eye for close up shots as well as long distance scenes. He homed his camera lens in on the buds of flowers and blossoms. This displayed how the meandering unplanned character of wild flowers and sprawling trees contributed to a natural mixture of colour.

Further on as the Downs began to rise and curve, almost as if they had been recruited to add more to the view, a Gypsy camp became evident in the distance. This was a godsend to a cameraman. A chance encounter with Gypsies would add even more interest to the film they were making. Their presence in the Downs was totally unexpected.

The Gypsy camp was set back in a field off the main track leading to the top of the Downs. It comprised of a traditional Gypsy caravan that had obviously been lovingly painted in shades of red and white. The wood that it was made of was splintered, cracked and broken in some places giving rise to the number of miles that the caravan had covered. Two heavy-looking horses grazed in the field. A washing line contained ragged-looking well-patched clothes hung between the caravan and a tree. A small makeshift fire was burning and above it was a pan in which a stew of some sort was cooking. On realising that three men carrying filming equipment were approaching them, the Gypsies stopped whatever they were doing and stood in a line eyeing the strangers curiously. They looked on without hostility or humour.

Anatole, Bernard and Andre came closer. "Good morning," said Andre hoping to relax them. "What a beautiful day it is too."

These were Romany Gypsies. They were the original nomadic Gypsies with an air of mystery and a spellbinding romantic legendary aura about them. The attire they wore was colourful, ragged, garish and traditional of their race. They exuded both fascination and magnetism. But there was also the unspoken feeling that their lives were a private space not to be trespassed on. True Gypsies followed their own rules and traditions.

A grey-haired grandmother stood alongside a man in his forties wearing a flat cap. His wife was next to him. A dark-haired young woman with large circular earrings, who was presumably his twenty-something daughter, was barefoot and wore trousers, a light shirt and a bandana, stood with one hand on her hip defiantly. Her brown eyes appeared sensitive and kind. Was it Anatole's imagination or did she give him a second glance as if to deliberately make eye contact and flirt. He didn't mind in the slightest. One thing about her made him ponder. What would this attractive, slightly grubby, tomboyish girl look like with beauty treatment, a coiffured hairstyle and womanly clothes? All the Gypsies seemed to have an inbuilt tan that indicated their overseas origins. A couple of young children, a girl and boy both of single digit age, stood in front of the family group.

"Sir, may we film you and your family?" Andre asked pushing his luck fully contemplating that they may refuse to participate.

The man looked at each member of his family as if to silently ask their permission. The grandmother beckoned him to come over and whispered something in his ear. He did the same to her and saw her nod her head in agreement. A faint smile played around his lips.

"Of course," he replied in a voice with an indefinable accent. "Will you pay us something? We are humble people who move around the countryside?" Andre reached into his pockets and proffered the man several pound notes. He took them and winked at the family. "I am Roget. This is my mother Elena, my wife Marguerite, my young children Patrick and Alida" Then with a sweep of his hand he introduced the last remaining member of the family. "This is my eldest daughter, Trevilla."

"I can dance!" she proudly announced and, grabbing a tambourine from the caravan, she gave the men an impromptu display of gypsy dancing. Trevilla was lithe and sexual with eyes that flashed degrees of flirtation and humour. "I am good! Huh?"

"Very good!" said Anatole. "I used to dance myself. Watch this!" He broke out into his old vaudevillian hoofing style. Trevilla watched with fascination and amusement.

"Hey we make a team, huh!" Trevilla stood with both arms outspread from her hips, threw her head back and laughed. It was a loud infectious bawdy laugh from someone who loved life. "Maybe you come back later at suppertime tonight and I change into something different and you film me dancing. I can do better if you want."

"You can count on it, honey," Andre replied. Trevilla eyed up Anatole as if she was seriously assessing his eligibility. "Now ladies and gentlemen I'll set these cameras up and we'll record how you Gypsies go about your daily chores."

Bernard turned to Anatole with a smile. "I think that young lady has taken a bit of a fancy to you, old son."

***

They filmed the Gypsies for a couple of hours and spent time talking to them before continuing their walk. Usually very private people they found the Americans and Bernard easy to talk to. The Gypsy family knew obviously what cameras were used for but admitted none of them had ever been to a picture theatre in their lives. They were sadly grubby people who washed in streams and boiled water over a fire that was used in a tin bath they carried. The family worked as casual labourers, often picking vegetables in garden nurseries and farms. They were under-nourished but dined vociferously on rabbit stews, any pheasants they caught and anything edible they could cadge, beg or find. The caravan wasn't always big enough for them all to sleep in and on warm nights some would take their slumbers outside. Usually Trevilla would be one of them for she loved to lay back and gaze up at the stars like a bright-eyed child in wonderment at all the untold secrets the celestial bodies high above contained. She had one burning desire, that was to share these nights with a man whose own passions reflected those she had that raged within her. Anatole quietly considered that in another life Trevilla, the sparkling Gypsy girl, would have made a very seductive Tango dancing partner.

The next filming stop the three men made was at a dairy farm halfway up the Downs. An obliging farmer gave them permission to film the cows at milking time. In truth he was really quite flattered that his trade could be considered important enough to be featured in a cinema film. He was proud of his work that his farm carried out in making cheese and butter as well as delicious milk.

In the milking sheds a number of farmhands squeezed cow's udders while Anatole and Andre focussed the cameras on the method. Bernard took notes for the script that would accompany the documentary. At the back of the sheds sat several anxious cats all eagerly waiting for samples of warm milk that the farmhands gave to them in small dishes. The cameras swung towards them for this was of interest too. My, how the cats enjoyed their daily treat! On finishing their milk, the cats licked their lips and blinked their eyes in cat ecstasy. They all began to lick their paws and wash themselves almost as if a film director had ordered them to do so. It made for charming viewing as if human beings had been invited to a cat's tea party. There are few animals as photogenic as those that are members of the cat family with their whiskers like antennas, their tiny noses scenting every flower and shrub, and their curious natures regularly stretching their nine lives.

Finally the team arrived at the top of the Downs and Bernard took them to a spot where he knew a badger sett existed. It was hard to discern at first because the sett wasn't clearly visible as it was shrouded by a clump of trees. When they came to it, badger tracks could be seen embedded in the ground. It was quiet and peaceful without a sound. At night time it would become a badger's playground.

"This is it, gents," Bernard pointed to the entrance of the sett. "I know it looks empty now but it will be a hive of activity after twilight. The badgers are sensitive to the presence of human beings and other animals of the forest so I suggest that the cameras be set up at a clear distance, well hidden from view. That is a few hours away yet."

"Well we have an invitation to see Trevilla, the Gypsy girl, dance before all of that," Andre pointed out. "We might as well get that on film and then return here later this evening."

***

At the Gypsy camp, as the day turned to night, a small controlled fire was burning. Roget and his family were finishing the evening meal when the team returned. Trevilla emerged from within the caravan. Compared to how she looked earlier her whole demeanour had taken on a very different appearance. It was obvious she had washed and scrubbed herself perhaps to impress. Her change of clothes gave her an image more in keeping with that of a professional flamenco dancer. Inside she was feeling thrilled to be the centre of male attention if only by the rarity of being filmed by cameramen. In truth she was a natural exhibitionist without inhibitions. A genuine wild child if ever there was one.

Trevilla was barefoot. Her dress was short enough to reveal a pair of dancing legs honed by long periods of practice. Dancing was her passion, hobby and part of her tradition. She swirled around at high speed and then performed the most outlandish, provocative moves playing to the camera lens perfectly. Anatole could see that she, in her own way, was teasing him. It had the desired effect. He was captivated. If Paul Kapsia had still been alive he would almost certainly have wanted to sign her to one of his shows. She didn't disappoint. The Gypsy girl was wildly entertaining and charismatic.

Andre focused his camera on the rest of the Gypsies who sat by the warmth of the fire totally ignoring the cameras as if they weren't there. Trevilla rattled her tambourine and danced around the fire as it crackled and sparkled, and sprayed embers into the night sky. Her eyes twinkled with variations of smouldering passion and unrestrained laughter. When she had finished and the cameras stopped rolling she threw back her head and laughed loudly. Casting a look directly at Anatole's face close up, she winked.

"I like you! You like me, eh!" Trevilla was mischievous and playful. She shook her tambourine at him and blew him a kiss. "I be your sweetheart, eh. How you like that?"

Bernard intervened, quickly glancing at his pocket watch. "Gentlemen, we better get back up the Downs and set the cameras up. The badgers will be waiting for us."

The men said their farewells and thanked them, moving quickly back up the track. Anatole turned around just once to see Trevilla standing watching them go. She stood with one hand on her hip and gave him the brightest of smiles. He returned the compliment and doffed his hat.

What was it about this Gypsy girl that so entranced him? Her sparky, effervescent larger than life personality seemed so out of contrast with the placid nature of the Sussex Downs. In his life Anatole had met and made love to beautiful women across the world. He had shared love with showgirls, dancers and women of a free and easy nature, but it had always been him who had been the pursuer and wooer.

Trevilla wore no make-up or cosmetics. She obviously cut her own hair. Her clothes were little more than patched up rags yet there was something beautiful and charismatic about her.

When the men had moved off at a safe distance, Trevilla followed them. Every so often she hid behind a bush or a tree watching the direction they headed. Her curiosity had got the better of her.

Thirty-Two

The badger sett was quiet when the camera team arrived. At a space of approximately seventy-five yards Bernard, Anatole and Andre positioned their cameras behind some bushes so that the lens was just poking out. Up above in a navy blue sky the presence of a full moon ensured they had additional light like the effect of a spotlight on the undergrowth.

There was a sudden ghostly cry that broke the deathly silence of the night. Andre, acting instinctively in an urgent reflex action, pointed the lens at a tree. His camera immediately captured the sight of a blue owl with emerald green eyes that shone in the darkness. It stared directly back into the camera lens and moved its head from side to side, trying to determine just what this strange object was that protruded from the bushes. Then another noise from behind the men caused it alarm, and the owl quickly disappeared into the night.

Trevilla suddenly made an appearance in the background without the men being aware of her presence. She hid behind some trees and watched with curiosity as the men waited patiently for the stars of their nature film to make their debut. The essence of a good naturalist cameraman is patience and an instant response to the unexpected sighting.

All of a sudden there was a muffled sound of something scraping earth in the sett. The full moon acted like a torch and an animals head could be seen ascending from the sett. For Anatole and Andre it was their first sighting of a badger. Animals never ceased to fascinate. They had seen beavers and raccoons in the United States but the badger was unique with a white head and two wide black stripes on it. The cameras were now focused firmly on the sett as the first one came into view. There was a pause between its emergence and the arrival of the rest of the sett. They were the size of dogs and they began to scurry around digging their claws deep into the ground in a bid to find something edible to eat.

To witness the nocturnal world of the badgers was as if to cross over to a parallel universe where creatures reigned supreme. The badger was playful, rough, loveable to look at but apt to fight back viciously when cornered, energetic, predatory, timid, feisty and in a strange way highly entertaining to watch. They had their own territory centred in and around their sett. Seldom did they venture too far away from it, except if they were feeling adventurous and desperately hungry if food couldn't be found in their immediate vicinity. The claws of a badger were strong and while they were being filmed one of them climbed a tree.

It all made for a fascinating window on the world of the badger. Few people ever saw a badger. Such is the reclusive nature of the animal. For Trevilla who was no stranger to camping in out of the way places, it was a new experience for her to see badgers close up even if it meant several steps well hidden behind the cameramen. Once her curiosity had been satisfied she turned around and walked back down the Downs. Trevilla was by nature inquisitive. The arrival of the camera team had aroused her interest in the work that they did.

For this Gypsy girl she had never really known about life beyond the confines of the one in which she existed. In all of her twenty-seven years she had lived as a roving Gypsy, travelling with her family across Southern England in a dilapidated caravan. Home comforts were alien to her. All she had ever known was casual farming work. A brief marriage in her teens to a fellow Gypsy had ended in widowhood barely a year later. The unfortunate man had been working temporarily as a hod carrier on a building site when a wall had collapsed on him, crushing him to death.

Soon after Trevilla returned to the family fold and continued on with travelling. She yearned to break free of the life of a Gypsy. There were times when, although Trevilla was proud of her Romany heritage, she felt that it wasn't her destiny to continue on with this way of life. Trevilla was a firecracker, a passion-filled woman with burning desires, oodles of latent energy, an unleashed sexual tension, a bubbling personality, an unrestrained exhibitive nature especially when dancing, and a curious mind as to how she might fit into the rest of the world.

The arrival of the cameramen had provided her with a short interlude as to the many opportunities and experiences that lay out there in the wider world. Trevilla was eager to grasp them at all costs. She wanted love; loud, unbridled laughter; to taste warmth and friendship; she wanted to dance wildly and provocatively; to sip from the goblet of life and savour it like a fine wine sending ecstatic waves to the palate and tongue. She wanted to warm her body in the summer glow of the sun and swim in cool waters that would seep into the pores of her skin and cleanse the soul. Here on earth she wanted a heavenly paradise.

Rarely did she ever speak to people beyond her family circle and those who she worked with in occasional farming work. Her knowledge of the real world was limited because of her Gypsy family's isolation. Trevilla's eyes had fallen on Anatole and for some reason that even she was at a loss to understand, she felt herself drawn to him in the manner of iron filings to a magnet. She wanted desperately to speak to him and learn more about the world from which, in so many ways, she felt excluded.

The night was clear with stars evident in the country sky. Trevilla looked up at them and thought how much she wanted to change her way of life. She felt optimistic that Anatole might be able to help her.

On finishing their filming work for the night, Andre, Anatole and Bernard quietly stopped what they were doing and made their way back to the house. The film of the badgers in their natural habitat was one that the camera team felt would appeal to lovers of nature and the British countryside. They returned to Shervington Manor in the early hours happy with the work they had accomplished. It was one of the joys of being a cameraman that when filming nature they invariably caught the sights and sounds of animals that the vast majority of the general public were never privileged to witness. To see badgers at play was a tremendous thrill to any animal lover.

***

Despite only having a few hours' sleep, Anatole was up early the next morning. Immediately after breakfast he decided to go for a short walk up the Downs. He had fallen in love with its tranquillity and the sheer beauty of the view of the surrounding countryside.

Gazing down at the rectangular gold and green fields he absorbed the freshness of the air and could feel a peacefulness within him. It was the silence that soothed him broken only by a breeze rustling the trees or the squawks of birds flying in formation above or the bleating of sheep in the distance. A man could be very happy living here. Anatole had been all over the world. He thought back to what he had seen: Mayan temples, Aboriginal corroborees, South American palaces, Pacific Islands, the American prairies. There were few places as beautiful as the Sussex Downs.

He carried on walking and he realised the Gypsy camp was not far away. Before he got there he was aware of the lone figure sitting on a fence in the near distance. At first glance it looked like a little girl lost sitting there swinging her bare legs backwards and forwards. On approaching her Anatole could see that it was Trevilla. She looked up and gave him a smile of delight.

"You come to see me, eh?" It was difficult to tell whether she was being serious or not. "I attract you, huh? I sensed you were coming."

"Beautiful, isn't it?" Anatole asked with a sweep of his hand, indicating at the wide panoramic vista that lay below their vantage point. "I just love it here. This is the England I always dreamed of. Meadows and green fields. Thatched roofed houses."

"Where you from?" Trevilla inquired.

Anatole jumped up beside her on the fence. "Recently America. Originally from Russia. My parents took my sister and I to New York when we were very young. I'm an American citizen. I served with the American army in Mexico and France. I've also travelled the world but right now there's no place I would rather be than this leafy green county."

"My ancestors came from Europe. I am a Romany Gypsy," Trevilla pointed out. "Are you married?"

"No. I have been to China. I have been in San Francisco, Sydney and Samoa, but I have never been married."

Trevilla was really curious now. "How come you never marry? You not like women, huh? You are good-looking man. I thought maybe some woman snare you, eh. She make you her husband."

"I just never got round to it." He was honest about that. "I love women… and I have loved women… without regret. My life was chaotic and unsettled. It still is."

"Maybe you learn to love me, huh!" She laughed loudly. "I am good woman, eh! I am good lover! Very passionate! How about that? I make good wife and mother of beautiful babies." She laughed in between sentences, leaving Anatole wondering if she was wildly optimistic or being humorous. Then a sad look appeared on her face and she spoke with a trace of sadness in her voice. "I was married once… for less than a year. I was young, only eighteen. He was young. He died, you know."

"I am sorry. It must have been very hard for you. I have lost family too." Anatole looked at her sensitively. "Do you want to talk about it?"

"We Gypsies marry young. My parents… they marry when they are only seventeen. I am born one year later. I am twenty-seven now." Anatole did some swift mental arithmetic and calculated that her parents Roget and Marguerite were forty-five now. "So I marry my husband… Cazare… he is good man. Same age as me. He work hard on the buildings but he die when wall collapsed on him. I still miss him. But I think I marry again one day. I find good man one day. Not Gypsy though. I want to settle in one place and have family. Fine family. Boys and girls. I want to live in nice house, maybe a farm. Work hard on farm, with goats. I love goats. Have goat's milk, goat's cheese. And when I am not working and looking after children, I want a good life, to wear nice clothes, to take a warm bath every day, let warm water run over me and use soap that smells nice, that smells like flowers in garden. I want to wash my hair in shampoo; I want to be real lady, drink wine occasionally, talk to people, lots of people! Not just Gypsy people. I want to hear music, dance, sleep in nice warm bed and wake up and walk amongst the flowers." She stopped expanding on her dreams and aspirations for a moment. In the pause she turned and looked at him directly into his eyes as if she was trying to see into his soul. It was almost as if she was waiting for him to kiss her. He didn't take the bait. "You think I am silly Gypsy girl, eh, I bet?"

"No, I think you're a woman with dreams and desires, the same as any other. You speak with real ambition. You are pretty too."

"You not think I am beautiful, huh? Well I am beautiful in here." She pointed to her heart. "The next man who loves me will find out just how beautiful I am. I care for my own family. I have great love to give."

"I didn't say you weren't beautiful," Anatole protested quietly. "And I think you have beauty within."

Trevilla gave him a shy smile. "I have temper too! I speak without thinking sometimes."

"I have the same problem myself!" Anatole assured her. "I've not met Gypsies before. You are the first Gypsy girl I have ever met. It seems you follow tradition… marry by tradition… follow the same sort of life that your parents led. I understand that. I am Jewish. There are certain traditions people of my faith follow. It doesn't hurt to dare to be different." Then he added as an afterthought. "It doesn't hurt to dream either."

Trevilla gave him a studying look. "Have you lived all your dreams?" She took one of his hands and ran her fingers down the palm. "I see you are a man who has had a past, a good past. But your hand lines say that you have hit trouble from time to time. I like your voice. I sense in your voice that you are a good man. I don't understand why you never married though. Maybe there was some girl you loved but you didn't get her love back, I don't know, you do. Are your parents still alive?"

"Long gone. When I was twelve both parents died."

"You are a lonely man, eh?" Anatole nodded and smiled. Trevilla gripped his hand as if they were lovers. "I like to see you again. Where you go next? Maybe you take me?" She laughed loudly again. "I good traveller."

Always Trevilla spoke in a halting accent of an unknown origin. Perhaps it was the fact that her parents and grandmother who were genuine Europeans only spoke English in short broken ways too. Trevilla had never really broken beyond her family circle to improve her knowledge of the English language. Her schooling had only been spasmodic to say the least.

"Why would you want to go with me?" Anatole asked, wondering whether she was being serious. "I am going far away to Africa to film the animals. I will be away for many months. Besides, I am forty years of age. Much older than you. We're from completely different cultures too."

"I could love you," she replied in a whisper. Then in a soft sincere voice she added gently, "Will you love me? Give me much love and affection. I give all my love to you." Without waiting for an answer she put her arms around him and gave him a long passionate kiss. Anatole enjoyed the kiss and prolonged the pleasure but he had been genuinely taken aback by surprise. "Love is a beautiful thing. Love is good." Trevilla put her hand on his face. "I bet no woman ever kiss you like that, huh!" She leapt down from the fence and gripped both his hands, and looked right into his eyes. "I have to go now with my family to work on farm. Pick vegetables. Will you come and see me again? Please say yes. I feel something good for you. I think you feel something for me, huh!"

Anatole was wary of committing himself. His pending trip to Africa was his 'get-out clause'. "I have to go too. I have work to do. We are here for a little while yet." He stepped down from the fence and looked at her square on. Close up she appeared more vulnerable than the brash woman she came across in speech and mannerisms. This time it was his turn to surprise her. He took her in his arms and kissed her. Finally he said to her, "You're right. I do feel something for you. I will see you again when I get the chance."

Trevilla smiled at him like the cat that got the cream. She stood watching him walk back down to the village. The warmth of the early morning sunshine seemed to up the temperature or was it her own feisty spirits that were soaring? The world suddenly looked that much brighter to her.

Anatole felt good about himself too. Always in his life it seemed that he lived to expect the unexpected. Now to his surprise he had a budding romance with Trevilla the Gypsy girl. He looked forward to a possible liaison with her but for the next few days he had a busy filming schedule.

On Bernard's advice Andre had decided that he and Anatole would film a number of stately homes and castles. They filmed Amberley Castle, Windsor Castle, Buckingham Palace, Arundel Castle, Woburn Abbey, Dover Castle, and also the homes of famous people such as Rudyard Kipling and Baroness Orczy. The opulence and grandeur of these residences of splendour was in stark contrast to the real world of the General Strike that had taken place in May that year. It was clear on these filming assignments that class distinction and the gap between rich and poor was part of the fabric that wove the garment of the British way of life.

Their film work was always assiduous. Both men were conscientious with an eye for detail and relevance in every carefully framed shot. From the ornate paintings to the stone masonry of each antique building the camera recorded everything. Anatole in particular felt it was a privilege to film both interior and exterior visages of such important historic buildings. His work was his admission ticket.

They filmed the Royal Pavilion in Brighton. This building was the outstanding set piece in Brighton which visitors from far and wide came to see. For Andre and Anatole it was a joy to film such an exotic and unusual structure which seemed strangely out of place in this seaside resort. It's very shape looked as if it had been uprooted from Rajasthan and transplanted against a backdrop of Regency and Victorian terraces. In its heyday it had been the magnificent seaside residence of King George IV with an exterior resembling Indian minarets and an interior décor of Chinese influence. Old masterpieces on the wall depicted the cuisine that the occupants would have dined on in bygone ages notably Swan which was in the modern era, a protected species.

The entire assignment was over in a matter of weeks. Andre had been informed of a developing studio in Ealing near London. He decided that they would take the cans of film there and begin the cutting and editing process. Also both Anatole and Andre had transferred funds to the London banks in a bid to support themselves whilst they journeyed to Africa. Andre had scheduled a meeting with some film finance moneymen in London as well as conferring with a British cinema company for distribution rights to picture houses throughout the British Isles.

In the meantime Anatole wanted to spend precious moments with his sister and his niece and nephew. He also planned to make time for Trevilla. There was something about her that was so alluring; he couldn't possibly not see her again. Sometimes the attraction between man and woman can be a thing of great beauty. It can also be dangerous and intoxicating. Beneath the feistiness, Trevilla was in fact quite vulnerable.

The love he had for his sister's children was something wonderful to behold. It was a good feeling to savour family life after years of single living. The children, although seemingly privileged, displayed a delightful sense of naivety and a firm sense instilled in them that they were no better or worse than anyone. They loved to ask their newly discovered Uncle Nat about his own childhood with their mother and his travels. He would sit and talk to them for hours. In a way it was as if he was reliving part of his own lost childhood by spending time with them. He realised how much he had missed by not becoming a father himself.

They were an extremely busy family who in the light of modern life probably did not spend as much time together as they would have liked. Bernard was overseeing a number of Architectural projects as well as being a regular speaker in the House of Lords on matters relating to the poverty that engulfed much of the population at that time. Mariska audited the various Shervington companies and carried out administrative matters. Anatole together with his colleague Andre was busy filming. It would not be long before they both departed for Africa.

Time was precious. Bernard took Mariska and the children to Worthing with Anatole one afternoon. There was a fun fair by the beach that day. The children wanted to try everything out. Bernard, as protective as any could be, went on a carousel with the children. From one side Mariska and Anatole smiled at the happiness of everyone at the fun fare. It was an amusing sight to see a peer of the realm enjoying all the various rides with his son and daughter. In the stuffy snobbish self-serving, self-important House of Lords, Bernard Shervington was a surprisingly down to earth man who bore no comparison to his learned colleagues.

"Does this place remind you of anywhere?" Anatole asked Mariska.

"Coney Island." She smiled at him. "Bet that surprised you."

"Good to know you haven't forgotten your roots. Do you think you and Bernard will ever go to New York?"

"We've talked about it but I think not now, especially as you no longer live there. In fact, we're thinking of making big changes in our life. Bernard's interested in the film business now and so am I."

This came as something of a surprise to Anatole. He thought that the Shervington's were fully occupied with the businesses they ran.

"Well that's a stunner for me. Was it the trip to film the badgers that got him interested? He seemed to enjoy it very much."

"Sure was. If it wasn't for the children, Bernard would have joined you on safari. So would I. We love the work you did on *The Glories of America*. One of the things I love about this country is the animals. With my background in show business and Bernard's enthusiasm about breaking into filming nature we would both like your advice and help."

"I'll be happy to do this sis," Anatole genuinely meant it. "Maybe when I get back from Africa we can all work together on a project."

"I will look forward to that." She smiled at Bernard and the children on the fairground rides. "We're winding down on some of our business affairs. Selling off a few things we have shares in and the idea of a small independent company filming various things is quite appealing. We would really like to give it a go." Then she changed the subject quickly. "Say, let's pretend we're young Bronx kids and go for a ride on the carousel."

***

The enjoyed themselves that day. Happiness was spending time as a family. So much of Anatole's life had been spent as a solitary traveller. The warm blanket of family life was something he didn't take for granted. Knowing that his life was always unpredictable and soon he would be thrust into the unknown, he savoured every minute of the time he spent with Mariska and the children. It was truly sublime happiness for him.

Worthing was soaked in sunshine and the warm weather seemed to reflect in the people's faces. How different the old buildings, the Dome Theatre, the pebbly beaches and the pier looked when the sun shone. One thing that Anatole concluded was that the English were a cheery lot who got on with life regardless of the fact that their country had been bled white by the Great War. All Anatole could see that day were smiles and happiness, proud parents with laughing children trying out all the rides available at the fair. Couples walked hand in hand along Marine Parade. Families sat on the beach with ice cream cones and toffee apples. Men went paddling in the sea wearing handkerchiefs on their heads and their trousers rolled up above their knees. Such were the eccentricities of the English.

Children and parents rode the dodgems or took the mystery rides with a spooky atmosphere where a luminous skeleton would suddenly appear and shock, or a ghostly apparition suddenly came into view. There were walls of mirrors which when gazing into would produce a comical and distorted appearance to the eye of the beholder. It was all such fun that Anatole considered he enjoyed it even more than the children! At the age of forty he unleashed the child within him that he had never really been due to the sad circumstances of his own early life. Bernard and Mariska shelved all the frontispiece of maturity and inhibition to try everything at the fairground, much to the sheer delight of the children. Happiness in a life of work and struggle was often a fleeting thing. Today had been a joyous one.

Anatole liked the English very much. After the hell for leather, go-getting attitudes of the Americans, he found many aspects of the British way of life to be very favourable. To his astonishment he found he wasn't missing America at all. The presence of family members here added extra warmth to his stay in England. The thought went through his mind that on his return from Africa he might consider a life for himself here.

***

While Andre was busy in London, Anatole had several days spare. He decided to make use of this time and meet up with Trevilla. He had wanted to meet this fascinating yet naïve but also curiously ambitious woman again. They found a pleasant spot on the Sussex Downs. It was peaceful, so restful that it was soothing just to sit there in the long grass and feel totally relaxed. They both lay on the grass absorbing the view of the villages down below and soaking themselves in the sunshine.

The normally talkative Trevilla seemed a little quieter today. Whether it was the balmy sunshine or not was debateable. She leaned across and kissed him. There was a certain look about her suggesting she wanted to say something and was unsure of the words to use.

Finally she said almost tearfully, "I am leaving here soon. My family is moving on. I have to go with them."

Anatole looked surprised. He had expected to leave her first. Not the other way around. "Why? You are a grown woman. Surely you could find work on a local farm round here. You're a young lady in your twenties. Is that what you want? To go with them?"

"I cannot disrespect my family. The life of a roving Gypsy family is not like the normal life of someone who works in a village or a town. My father is the head of his family. I have no husband. Where would I go on my own? What would I do? When I was married to my dear Cazare we had such plans. He wanted to settle in one place. Then came the accident and my poor lovely Cazare was taken from me so I once again sought the shelter of my family. You understand me, huh? The family… they go to my father's old friend for work… Henry Chester of Chester Farm in Yalding in Kent. I have younger brother and sister who need me. There is my mother too and my grandmother… all need looking after. We Gypsies believe in strong family… together… loyal… help one another. But now I meet you." A tear formed in one eye. "You fascinate me. You are… so… so interesting. I never met a man like you who has done so much and been everywhere. I learn from you. You know… different things about life and animals. I want to know more. I want to learn so much more about life that I will fly like a bird in the sky."

Up above them with sheer coincidence a flock of birds flew in formation. The sky was a clear but mild blue. Trevilla looked upwards as if she suddenly wanted to sprout wings and fly away from her predicament.

"I am going soon as well," Anatole said quietly. "Is there something I can do for you before we part company?"

"I have never been for a meal in a café or to a picture theatre. Would you take me? I want to see a film. I want to dine like a real lady in a restaurant and be served by waiters. Would you do that for me?" Her eyes were shining with enthusiasm. "Oh, please take me! I will be your lady for the night. We will hold hands and walk together like lovers do. I have wanted that for so long. I will be a fine lady for you and you can be my fine gentleman. But I need clothes. I would like to take a warm bath where you live now and wear perfume. Let me be your lady. Buy me clothes! Dress me as your lady."

"Anything else?" Anatole couldn't believe the length of her wish list.

"I want to dance… with you. I want to feel your arms around me holding me as if we are lovers. I want you to bring the passion out in me! Make me feel like a woman who needs love. Make me feel… as if I am loved! I am a woman of great desire who wants to be a lady not just a Gypsy girl crawling around in the fields picking vegetables. In here," she pointed to her heart, "the beat of my heart ticks for you. I am a lover. I am a dancer. I have zest, energy, passion… I am… what is it the French say… formidable! Look at this beautiful countryside. This is our world. I want the world to know that I lived here. We could take it by storm you and I. Hey, I read your fortune!" She grabbed one of his hands and studied his palm with interest, scrutinising every line as if she was a stockbroker studying shares. "Oh yes! You are lover too! You enjoy love, eh! Very much, I think. Your lifeline tells me you embrace life and seek out the new."

Anatole was sceptical of her observations even though she was right to a certain extent but he just smiled at her affectionately and kept his opinions to himself.

"Tomorrow I am going to take you shopping to buy you some nice clothes and shoes. I'll pay for you to have your hair done and then you can take that warm bath with soap and shampoo. Then I am going to take you to lunch and to the picture theatre in the afternoon. How does that sound?"

"Just wonderful, Anatole!"

"I would say you'll scrub up nicely after a good bath and new clothes."

She put her arms around him and kissed him. "For you I will be a beautiful scrubber."

Anatole almost broke into laughter at her misuse of the word scrubber.

"Let's just say you'll be a beautiful lady… a beautiful Gypsy lady."

Thirty-Three

Andre was busy in London touring his documentary films to distributors for national release. There was a ready market for his films back in the United States where his reputation stretched as far as Hollywood. He was also seeking additional funds for his journey to Africa. Attempting to build on his work with the series *The Glories of America*, which had been shown to great acclaim from British cinema goers, he was showing his latest work to a specially selected group.

In a private viewing room several executives and a top London impresario called Arthur Burnside sat transfixed to the film displayed on the screen before them. It was proved more interesting by the fact that the films had been made from an American visitor's point of view for the audiences back home in the States unacquainted to the British way of life. The castles and historic buildings had been beautifully filmed showing all aspects of interior and exterior designs. Undoubtedly the real stars of the two documentaries were the badgers. Rarely seen by the general public the on-screen debut of these enigmatic creatures was an entertainment in itself. At times it was like watching a children's party in the animal world where the occupants ran wild.

But there was one star who absolutely captivated the invited audience. It was Trevilla. Truly that day an unsuspecting, unintentional star was born. The men in the audience were captivated by her mesmerising charismatic performance. In the small viewing room upon the screen she blazed and crackled with her virtuoso dancing performance. What seemed like a well-rehearsed provocative dance routine was, in fact, a spontaneous burst of unleashed energy that filled the screen in the manner of great Hollywood and London stage stars whose very uninhibited personalities made them shine like beacons in the dark of night.

Arthur Burnside was particularly enamoured. He was a well-dressed, grey-haired distinguished-looking man who held his cigar like a prop. His eyes sparkled at the sight of this fabulous woman and her dancing prowess. She was just what he was looking for to appear in one of his shows. After years of producing shows an impresario develops the knowhow to spot star potential and so it was with Arthur Burnside. Once he had set eyes on Trevilla he knew she was a showstopper. He had to sign her up at all costs. This girl had the whole star studded package.

The film executives shook hands with Andre at the end of the preview and assured him of their financial backing as well as definite bookings on the same bill as major films. His independent film work would appear in cinemas midway between the leading moving and the second feature. He had established a rapport with the British Film Industry.

Shortly afterwards the impresario approached Andre in the foyer of the theatre. Arthur Burnside's very motive was that of a man intent on finding this girl who he was convinced would prove to be a major talent if nurtured correctly. Long before becoming an impresario Arthur himself had been a performer. He had started in the music hall tradition in the years of Queen Victoria's reign. His story was a typical tale of rags to riches. Born in the Elephant and Castle in London's East End, he graduated to the West End via the stage where he had performed as a singer, dancer, actor, clown and comedian. Arthur had worked with many of the greats: Dan Leno, George Robey, Malcolm Scott, Marie Lloyd, Vesta Tilley and Sir Harry Lauder. He had known them all at one time. Now as a producer he had restaged Gilbert and Sullivan operas, Ivor Novello musicals, Vaudeville shows from the United States, comedy plays and revues. By coincidence Arthur was currently casting for a musical show about Gypsies. He could not have been more delighted to find an authentic one in Trevilla who could add not only genuine talent but undoubtedly sex appeal and charisma too.

"Arthur Burnside's the name," he said, stretching his hand out to Andre for a strong handshake. "I admire your work, Mr Aviva. We haven't been introduced but I'm very prominent in theatrical circles here in London. I've staged plays and musicals. I have investment in some picture houses where your films have been screened. Rest assured while I have influence, your work will be displayed."

"Thank you, sir. I appreciate your confidence." Andre was no slouch in judging people's sincerity, however. He posed a leading question to

Arthur. "Which of my films did you enjoy the most?" Andre had seriously underestimated Arthur, who proved to be more knowledgeable than he realised.

"I enjoyed the newsreels of your presidential elections as well as the reports you made during the war particularly of Lawrence of Arabia, and the series *America at Work* was a great advert for your nation. I think Henry Ford will be grateful for your promotion of the automobile industry. *The Glories of America*... well if you show this too often to our people they'll be leaving these shores in droves for the warmer climes of the good old USA. I toured there myself in my performing days in a minstrel show back in the nineties. By God they were good days. Wine, women and lots of songs! You do your nation proud in producing scenes of the great stretch of land that is an unknown quantity to much of the population here.

"I'm impressed, sir. You're obviously very well acquainted with what my team has produced for many years."

"I am, Mr Aviva. I make it my business to keep abreast of change in our industry and to watch out for star quality in every shape and form. Tell me, have you agreed contracts and money with the gentlemen here? There is something you can do to help me."

"Certainly. I will be going back to the south coast when terms, distribution and dates are sorted out. With my colleague, I will then be heading off to film in Africa. What was it you wanted me to help you out with?"

"I'm putting a show on in the West End about Gypsies. That girl dancing in the rural scene, she's just what I need. A blazing firecracker. I want to sign her. Can you tell me what agency you hired her from? I can use her in any number of shows I've got lined up.

"Agency?" Andre gave a slight laugh at the assumption that he had hired a Gypsy dancer. "Whatever gave you the idea that I signed her from an agency? She's a complete natural. We were out walking along the South Downs and happened to encounter a Gypsy camp. I asked them if they wouldn't mind if we filmed them... and for a few of your English Pounds, they agreed. The young lady even offered to dance for us. They pick vegetables for a living. That's about as far away from the London stage as you could possibly get. That young lady has never been near a theatre or an agency in her life. She told us she has never seen a film in a picture house.

Oh my, she's never heard of Charlie Chaplin or Mabel Normand. She's a complete innocent as far as show business is concerned."

"The more you tell me the more I like the sound of her. I could make this girl a star. I've got a set of Gypsy musicians playing hot jazz. If she can spin round and rattle her tambourine she could add real sparkle to the show. In my time I've seen all sorts and believe me she's got it. If she's as naïve and humble as you describe, I could open up a whole new world for her."

Andre smiled at Arthur Burnside's enthusiasm for his potential protégé. "I wouldn't exactly say she was naïve and humble. In fact I would say she was quite extrovert. When we aimed the cameras on her she was pretty wild and uninhibited. I guest she enjoyed having an audience. Her life as a travelling Gypsy may have been pretty restrictive."

"What's she like close up?"

"Grubby." Andre replied honestly. "Rough round the edges. Beauty treatment wouldn't go a miss. She knows she's a woman though. She flirted like mad with my colleague. Her name is Trevilla."

"Trevilla, eh? I want to meet her – where do I find her?"

***

Trevilla relaxed in the bath of the Lodge House at Shervington Manor. Oh what sheer bliss to luxuriate in warm water with real soap and shampoo instead of a bucket wash or a dip in a stream. Her hair and body felt sparkling clean. She had liked the freshness of good toothpaste; she had brushed every corner of her mouth so much that her teeth, tongue and palate felt like mint.

She stood up in the bath and the water dripped down her naked body. In the mirror Trevilla studied herself and admired her own figure. Only her late husband, Cazare, had seen her in the nude. A thought flashed through her mind. Why keep it all to herself? It was a body worth sharing. She felt like being cheeky that morning.

Anatole was already nicely washed and scrubbed. He sat at the other end of the Lodge House wearing a nice suit and tie. That very same morning he had taken her shopping and bought her some nice clothes together with some good shoes. An expensive exercise! He felt like a modern day Professor Higgins trying to transform Eliza Doolittle. His efforts would not go unrewarded. Something made him turn around and, to his surprise, Trevilla stood naked with a cheeky smile playing around her mouth.

It would not have been an understatement to say that in every sense he could have adequately risen to the occasion had he allowed lust to override his self-discipline. He stood up to face her and put his hands on her shoulders.

"I think you really need to put something on," he said without a flicker of embarrassment and he turned to a small table from which he took a tiny bottle. "Try this perfume." Trevilla took it. "Then when you've applied it, you can put those expensive clothes on I bought you this morning and we'll go out for lunch. I'll wait outside while you change."

Anatole winked at this lusciously tempting woman and then, without warning, he slapped her bottom sharply. Far from being offended, she did her now familiar routine of throwing her head back and laughing out loudly. If there was anything she liked more than to tease, it was to get back a surprise response.

Outside the Lodge House, Tom Mollomby arrived in the Shervington family car, a shiny new Bentley, highly polished and exuding an image of flashiness and expense. Anatole stood by the car waiting for his date. Finally Trevilla emerged. Both Tom and Anatole blinked their eyes in disbelief. The transformation was staggering. It was as if a servant girl had entered a palace and left as a princess. Surely this wasn't the same bawdy dazzler who had first entranced him at the Gypsy camp on the South Downs but it was. Trevilla looked like a classic beauty. The clothes Anatole had bought her fitted like a glove. In a long flowing cream dress, a matching jacket and a hat, she looked every inch the lady she had always dreamed of being. Tom could not resist smiling broadly. Then before he got carried away he opened the door and held it for Trevilla. She had never known this type of courtesy.

"Well it's your day today, Trevilla." Anatole said proudly. "Enjoy it."

"I fully intend to," she replied. In her own mind she was going to speak and think like a real lady today. At least that was what she meant to do but she failed to realise that even well brought up ladies can harbour amorous thoughts and be mischievous. "Where are we going first?"

"I've been recommended somewhere special in Horsham." Anatole got in beside her. "Today you are my lady and I am your gentleman."

From the window of her study in Shervington Manor Mariska stood with Bernard looking out. "Let's hope he doesn't end up in Shanghai," she joked.

"I hope so too," said Bernard. "I want to learn more about the work of the cameraman." In the room behind him were his latest acquisitions he had purchased in a bid to learn this trade. He had bought some wooden de Brie cameras complete with tripods and lenses. "He might be going soon when Mr Aviva gets back from London. I want to start using those. I'm going to be pretty busy soon myself. Next week I'm going to make a major speech in the House of Lords about poverty and the victims of shell shock. Will you come with me?"

"Of course, darling," she replied. "On a more lighter note, you haven't forgotten we're taking the children to the Circus in Parham Park next Saturday?"

"Not at all," he said with a smile. He knew that the arrival of the Circus in the village was always a fun filled occasion that brought a lot of joy to the locals.

***

The 'something special' that Anatole took Trevilla for lunch that day was Chesney's Teashop in Horsham. Once it had been a basic café at the front of a warehouse importing tea from India and Ceylon. Harry Chesney had turned it into a popular venue for meals frequented by well to do ladies and gentlemen in Horsham. The atmosphere inside was one of olde-worlde charm with plush candelabra on shiny mahogany tables. Potted plants and mini palm trees were allotted around the room. The carpet was beautifully patterned. On the walls the same pictures that had hung there for years displayed India in the great days of the Raj.

Trevilla had never been anywhere like this before. When she and Anatole had walked in, Trevilla was almost thrown off balance by the opulence of her surroundings. Such was her charisma and unabashed natural beauty that it seemed as if every man and woman looked up in admiration of her. She smiled back pleasantly at them. The waiters were immediately subservient to her every need. *Is this how the rich lived normally?* she thought. To dress well and dine on roast chicken, succulent vegetables followed by gateaux and drink tea from Darjeeling was to taste a lifestyle light years away from anything she could have ever imagined. In fact it was

324

only a beginning to massive changes in her life that would soon envelop her. Winds of change would soon blow through her life.

"Do you feel like a real lady now?" Anatole asked her gently.

"I am still Trevilla the Gypsy girl," she replied, "but I feel I am in another world." She leaned forward and whispered to him. "The men are so smart and handsome here. The ladies are so beautiful. They have been to school and learned many things of which I know so little. How could I ever be such a fine lady?"

Anatole touched her hand gently. "A true lady doesn't have to wear the finest of clothes, Trevilla, or live in a world where money is no object. A lady is what you are inside, the way you behave, the courtesy and respect you show others. That is what distinguishes a lady from a woman. My mother was a lady yet she never wore a cut of cloth that any of the fine people wear here. It's the beauty in your soul that counts. I believe a beautiful soul makes a beautiful person. You spoke to me the other day about your loyalty to your family, the strong bonds that tie you to your family roots and traditions. I admire your compassion – a ladylike compassion."

"You understand me well," she stated and her eyes softened towards him.

"I sense that, beneath that bravado and brash confidence of yours, there is a woman yearning for love, who is vulnerable and feels they are living a life in the shadows."

Trevilla looked at him in near amazement. How was it possible that this dark-haired Jewish man, who had led such a cosmopolitan life, was able to see deep into her mind.

"I like you, Anatole," she said, softly taking his hand in hers across the table. "You are my gentleman."

Their conversation paused briefly. In the background on a small stage in the restaurant a young lady began to play a harp. It was an angelic sound that only helped to reinforce Trevilla's belief that she was in heaven. The tune was soft and soothing. It was instantly recognisable as 'Greensleeves'. While it was being played the buzz of conversation and the clinking of crockery faded away as the diners stopped to listen. Trevilla's eyes were shining. She looked deep into Anatole's eyes and smiled. It was a lover's smile. Her attraction to him had been instantaneous from the start. Everything seemed so utterly blissful to her this day.

Here in the restaurant, which sold itself short by retaining the name of a tearoom, the atmosphere was luxurious and intimate. Trevilla was experiencing the simple joys of good food, good company and beautiful music. She gazed around at the other well-dressed patrons. For the first time in her life she abandoned any feelings of inferiority she may have had about herself. So what if she scratched vegetables for a living and lived in a Gypsy caravan? When she wore good clothes she was the equal to any woman in here.

"Why did you stop being a dancer?" she asked him, ever more curious about this man who constantly fascinated her.

"War injuries when I was a soldier," he admitted. "I can still hoof it up a bit but not like when I was a young man."

"What was it like to be famous?"

"I was never what you might call famous. Well-known, perhaps. Fame is a phoney anyway. I danced because I loved it. Not for the money or the fame. When my sister and I formed a dancing duo we did it because we loved the profession. It took us all over the world. We even performed at the theatre in this town many years ago. We were orphans and the stage became our home."

"Where is home for you now?" Trevilla's unidentifiable European accent always made the way she asked the simplest of questions sound exotic.

"I really don't know." Anatole said very gently. "I'm going on assignment to Africa and then maybe I'll come back here or Paris. I loved Paris years ago. That would be a good base. I guess I've reached a crossroads in my life. Do you know the big house, Shervington Manor?" Trevilla nodded. "Well my sister lives there. She married Lord Bernard Shervington. It's possible I could live in the Lodge House from time to time."

Trevilla looked amazed. "So if my family didn't go to Yalding I would be able to see you." It was clear she had deep feelings for him although Anatole was unsure about the chemistry between them. "You could teach me so much." Then she became open with her thoughts and expansive as if she had found her soul mate to confess all to. "I always dreamed that life could be like this," she swept her hand around to indicate the affluent atmosphere of the restaurant, "and that there was something I was waiting for. Something that would change my life. Take me into a new life. Do you know what it is like to be a Gypsy? No! You are a good man but you would not understand. It is about life on the open road.

Constantly travelling. Always doing what the rest of the family wants and you follow the rules the father sets. Your friends are few. The family is everything. Yet if you want to fly like a bird on your own to make your own life, it is difficult. I try to tell my mother and father that I love them so much, but I also tell them I have to live the life of my own choosing… my own choice!… and they feel upset that I do not want to follow the traditions they have done. I try to explain I have a spirit within me and one day I will let that spirit be free. Meeting you has been so wonderful. Eating good food here, dressing like this makes me feel so good about myself that I am not just a woman – I am a person. Today I have tasted gateaux. I did not know what gateaux was, but I will eat plenty more in my life I am sure. I have loved this day so much."

"And it's far from over yet. When we've finished here we will go to the picture house to see a film. Then tonight we are going to a theatre in Brighton. This will remain a surprise!"

A waiter came round to their table and offered her another piece of gateaux which she took with delight. Anatole was enjoying seeing the pleasure on Trevilla's face. She may have been a passionate woman in one sense but there was also something of a child about her too. Anatole may have fascinated Trevilla but she too fascinated him. It was as if two contrasting people of entirely different backgrounds had found a person they could be constantly interested in. They would never be bored with each other.

The young lady playing the harp began a new piece of music that added to the atmosphere of the restaurant. It was an excerpt from Tchaikovsky's 'Swan Lake', which was both soothing and haunting. Such beautiful music enhanced the occasion for Trevilla. She had never heard classical music before and it added to her education as to the wider world outside of her Gypsy lifestyle. It was both an irony and coincidence that the young lady harpist had chosen this particular piece of music. Anatole's surprise for Trevilla that evening was to take her to see the ballet of 'Swan Lake' in Brighton.

When they left Chesney's Teashop they walked into the centre of Horsham by the town's bandstand where a crowd had gathered to watch some musicians playing in full throe. A band of the Royal Sussex Regiment were playing a number of well-known tunes that resonated with the crowd. They listened to 'The Minstrel Boy', 'Mademoiselle from Armentieres' and

'It's a Long Way To Tipperary'. Trevilla walked arm in arm with Anatole in the way she had hoped, giving people the impression that they were lovers. They stood together and she gently swayed to the music, tapping one foot in time with the rhythm. How she enjoyed the music and the occasion! She felt as if she had emerged from her Gypsy existence to the glittering sunlight of a new life.

The sound of good music always has the power and magic to transform an occasion or an event of particular significance so that a tune would be automatically associated with it for ever more. Trevilla was to hear a lot of music that day. In her cream coloured outfit, matching hat and with her hair peeking out she looked absolutely ravishing in the crowd. No one could possibly have thought on looking at her that this elegant lady with an appreciative ear for this splendid music was in reality a tomboy, who had spent many nights sleeping under the stars and getting her hands dirty in the fields.

Anatole felt proud to be with her. She received many admiring looks from other men that day. In the space of a morning and an early afternoon Trevilla had heard the beauty of a classical harpist and the rich, rousing foot-tapping sounds of a military band. Oh what a joy good music can be! It filled her heart and soul with pleasure. The sun was shining. She wore good clothes and had dined well. Her companion was a good man. The day was just getting better and better. They were off to see a film now.

The next part of the day was a totally new experience for Trevilla. It would have been hard to believe for any normal person but, at twenty-seven, Trevilla had never been to a picture theatre as they were called then. The famous names of the cinema such as Charlie Chaplin, Harold Lloyd and Theda Bara meant absolutely nothing to her.

When they entered the Capitol Theatre the elegance of the interior entranced her. It was as if she was a child again wide-eyed with excitement at the new world that lay before her. Compared to many theatres, the Capitol was cosy and well designed. Locals might have nicknamed the cinema the 'Fleapit' but it was far from being so. It was an old-time theatre that had housed many shows.

The seats varied in price. The four-penny seats at the front were nicknamed the 'neckbreakers'. The middle seats with a more comfortable view were 9d. Anatole decided that for Trevilla's first visit to a cinema she was worthy of a balcony seat. These cost 1s 3d which were considered above the 'hoi-polloi', a humorous term used to describe the 'ordinary' people rather than the more affluent members of society.

Trevilla and Anatole took their seats in the balcony and gazed down towards the screen. Behind the brass rail and flaming red curtains, there were a group of musicians ready to play the accompaniment to the scenes of the silent movie about to be shown. The cinema was packed out for the afternoon matinee. It was a special showing on that day. The film had been originally released in 1921 but was now being shown again in tribute to the lead actor who had recently died.

Then the houselights dimmed. The curtains drew back. The musicians began to play some exciting music that hinted the film was set in an exotic location. Trevilla gripped Anatole's hand in excitement. For the first time in her life she was about to view a film. The audience seemed to draw breath as the film began. The thrill of the movie was that it would take the audience to a location on screen they were never likely to go to in real life. The hero of the film would be an impossibly handsome man while the heroine would be desirable, breathtakingly beautiful and out of reach to ordinary men.

The movie was *The Sheik* and its star was the recently deceased Rudolph Valentino. The setting of the film took place on the golden sands of the North African desert. Its story was one of smouldering passion and lust that set female hearts pounding. The sheik abducts an English woman and concentrates his desire on her. Ably played by the Italian-born Valentino, his intense looks towards her left no one in any doubt as to his intentions. Some of the ladies in the audience came close to swooning at the sight of this man's dark handsome features and the seduction he had in mind.

Trevilla watched the movie with a real surge of excitement and her own desires were stimulated at the thought of a man taking a woman in such a manner to make love to her. The lady concerned seemed powerless to resist the charms of such an individual. The music for the scenes was played dramatically as the melodrama progressed. Without sound the movie seemed to be more effective, leaving the audience's imagination to run wild at the drama between the two main characters in the story.

During the time Anatole had been an extra in Hollywood, Valentino had yet to make his mark. His meteoric rise and early death at the early age of thirty-one had created a mass outbreak of mourning around the world.

Such was the power of Hollywood studios; an Italian drifter had become the object of women's desires across the globe.

Trevilla's eyes shone. She was genuinely enthralled about everything she saw before her on screen as well as the atmosphere of the cinema. The stunning desert scenes and the plot of forbidden love between an Arab Sheik and a titled English lady belonged to another world which she knew nothing of. On seeing the film her eagerness, enthusiasm and quest for a more exciting life sought to increase her ambition. Sitting there in the privileged position on the balcony of a country town cinema, she knew her life would change somehow. Destiny, fate or force of hand ensured that it would.

The whole cinematic experience left her bubbling inside with joy and pleasure. There was a wider world outside she wanted to be part of even if it meant breaking the mould of her own family traditions.

Outside on the streets of Horsham the crowds of the cinema poured out, all talking about the film they had seen which would go down in history as one of the legendary silent romantic dramas. Trevilla held Anatole's hand as they left the cinema. Her happiness was contagious. It seemed to Anatole that the more Trevilla smiled the more beautiful she looked.

"I am so happy! I enjoyed it so much!" She kissed his cheek in quick gratitude. "That was so exciting. The sheik... what a handsome man!" Then she laughed suddenly and her eyes became mischievous. "Not as handsome as you, of course!" She still felt thrilled about the film. "Did they really go all the way to the desert in Africa to make that film?"

"Looks that way, but I'd hazard a guess it was made in and around Hollywood." At that precise moment Tom Mollomby arrived in the Bentley outside of the cinema. "Here we are, young lady. Well we're off to the theatre in Brighton tonight. Before that we are going to have high tea at the Grand Hotel on the seafront at Brighton."

"High tea?" Trevilla didn't know what that meant. "Sounds nice."

Tom opened the door for her. She entered as a middle-aged couple passed by. The man indicated the car with his eyes to his wife.

"Alright for some, eh? Lord and lady so and so!"

Trevilla heard the remark and put her head out of the window. "I'm not lady so and so! I'm a Gypsy and I live in a caravan!"

Her response brought a smile to the faces of Tom and Anatole. The man who was passing by looked to the heavens in disbelief.

"Some caravan! And I'm Rudolph Valentino!"

Anatole got into the car beside Trevilla and held her hand gently. She smiled back warmly at him.

***

Trevilla's day seemed to be full of delightful surprises. High tea at the plush Grand Hotel in Brighton was another one. She and Anatole sat at a table centrally located in the middle of the dining room. There was a small orchestra playing where the musicians were all nicely turned out in evening wear. They were adept at playing anything the diners could dance to, be it a Waltz or a foxtrot. It was not a frenetic or busy atmosphere; but slow, unhurried and peaceful. A high tea was a reminder to some of the elderly, well-travelled customers of a time in another place, perhaps an old colonial outpost on a rubber plantation in Malaya or a Tea plantation in India, where such customs were observed as a virtual ritual down the ages.

People watching was something Trevilla enjoyed, not only was she fascinated by the faces and characteristics of the customers around here, but also by the accents and contents of their conversations. Some people seemed stilted and rigid while others were gregarious with loud laughter that carried across the tables sometimes making her smile. On this day amongst different people in different venues she felt she was amid real life, a participant, not an outsider looking in, or isolated in an existence where she laboured in the fields and lived in a draughty caravan. This was life! This was living! And my goodness how she savoured it!

Her beauty was evident here too. The cream outfit she wore was the perfect match with her inherited dark skin and hair. Men would often pause in conversation to look at her while other women, probably curious about her origins, would study her. Trevilla had definitive film star looks and a sparkling personality to match. In another age she could have been elevated to the goddess like pantheons of beauty containing such luminaries as Lily Langtree, Ava Gardner and Elizabeth Taylor. Anatole and Trevilla sat enjoying the high tea which was more like a feast than a snack between main meals. They had a choice of assorted sandwiches to work through. These comprised of either Salmon, Cream Cheese, Chicken, prawn or fish paste. After this they then moved on to a Devonshire cream tea and scones, butter, clotted cream and jam together with a pot of Earl Grey tea.

It was all very swish even for a travel connoisseur like Anatole who had sat in the hotel dining rooms of the world. The British had customs, style and grace in so many areas of life that set them apart and set standards that other nations would follow.

When Trevilla was happy her eyes shone and for a girl who had never been to a dentist she had a beautiful smile that revealed fine white teeth. Her eyes shone a lot that day. She watched the graceful dancers on the floor and knew it would only be a matter of time before she could coerce Anatole into joining them.

"Do you think I could paint a picture of you sometime this week?" Anatole asked out of the blue. "I have another string to my bow. I am an artist as well. When we go our separate ways, I would like to have a picture of you to remember our time together."

"Of course you can paint my picture," she replied looking at the dancers and then turned to face him directly. "Must we go… our separate ways?"

"I have to go to Africa to film. You know that." It was clear to Anatole that he was finding himself drawn into a relationship he had never deliberately sought. "Let's enjoy this day. We will talk about it in depth later. Meanwhile, I would be failing my duties as a gentleman if I didn't ask you to dance. Will you?"

Trevilla needed no prompting. She stood up and took his hand. They joined the afternoon dancers. While some of those on the floor displayed their skilled footwork, Trevilla was happy to relax in Anatole's arms and glide around the dance floor. The orchestra played a romantic tune that befitted the atmosphere of the Grand Hotel. It was a tune that could have been played in Victorian times but didn't date today. The composer had exactly that in mind. To create a tune that set the mood for lovers.

When they returned to their table the two of them were happy to sit back and relax, comfortable in each other's company. Anatole found himself in the position of having fallen in love with a girl he could never ever imagine he would find himself with. The old maxim of 'you don't choose who you fall in love with' certainly applied to him. It surprised him. He hadn't thought he was capable of falling in love with anyone until now. Soon he would be leaving this lovely part of the world to go to Africa and he knew his departure would break Trevilla's heart.

"I love to dance," Trevilla said, suddenly breaking Anatole's chain of thought. "When I was a little girl in Europe, I remember a time when we were in Hungary and Gypsies from all over came together in the fields we camped at. I was six. Everybody danced." Trevilla was suddenly serious and looking back at a spellbinding childhood memory. Anatole became interested. He was keen to know more of her history. "I sat with my mother and father in the fields. I remember a fire burning. The Romani danced around it with their tambourines and the dresses of all colours kept swirling until it was one great flash of colour… like a rainbow in the sky… it became faster and faster. Other Gypsies joined in. They held hands and danced wildly. Oh Anatole, my darling, it was so wonderful I tell you now! I felt so thrilled and excited. Gypsy musicians from all over played their instruments. Someone played the sitar. Another man played the Balalaika. Oh, the instruments they had! The trumpet too! Castanets. A drum to beat. I remember it so well. A lady danced like they do in Spain. I forget what it is called. I don't read too good. But I watch… and I am gone. You know what it is?"

"Flamenco," replied Anatole. "Spanish folk music and dance."

"That's right," agreed Trevilla. "Flamenco. I try to dance that. One day someone will teach me. I am told that day was a Gypsy festival. One that was an accident, huh! Everyone came together by chance. From Spain… from Turkey… Albania… Russia. And you know something else, Anatole? You think Gypsy dancing is all swirling and playing the Tambourine? Well I tell you this – Gypsy dancing is different. It can be graceful like a swan gliding on a lake, or it can be like belly dancing. It can be like all types of dancing together… slow and graceful… then it can be fast and wild. You will never be bored when a Gypsy dances! That is where I first saw that dancing is beautiful… it is a feeling… a feeling that goes through your whole body. You want to dance because you are full of energy and it makes your spirit soar! And when I dance, I feel alive! Alive! That is right huh! I tell you now. Dancing brings happiness and joy!"

Trevilla was exhilarated at the thought of that day long ago. She savoured the memory. It was all so clear in her mind the magic of that occasion. She remembered much but only through the eyes of a child. In truth that night could be analysed for its true content. Essentially Gypsies were an ethnic minority, often persecuted, much misunderstood and maligned for the supposed sin of being a nomadic dispossessed race of people. They trailed across Europe seeking a safe haven and all manner of Gypsies had come together. A gathering of Gypsies sought to combine their culture and find the promised land of their dreams.

The night of the Great Gypsy Festival had taken place in 1899. They had indeed come from Russia, Albania, Austria and the Balkans as well. All of them had demonstrated their particular skills in dance relative to the country of their origin. The Russian Gypsies were the most vibrant and energetic of all the dancers. They were real extroverts and showmen who would clap over their bodies and legs to the beat. It became infectious to all who were there that night.

Trevilla had been carried away by the memory. She turned to Anatole who could see that she had drifted away to another time. This unpredictable woman could show many varying sides to her personality that ensured she would be hard to fathom but always an interesting companion. The orchestra had played music that entranced her. Not only did she love to dance but she listened to music with a keen ear unable to ascertain whether it was classical, traditional or just the popular appeal of the time. They had sat quietly for a few minutes as the orchestra had played in the Palm Court tradition. Her grip on Anatole's hand had not softened. She could not believe herself any more than he could of their deep feeling for each other.

"This has been one of the most wonderful days of my life, Anatole. I feel as if I have been blessed today. I feel as if I have tasted the joy of life itself. Good food, good music, and you, my darling." There was real sincerity in her voice. "The Gypsy girl that I am has been treated like a lady. It is so good for a woman to feel that way. You understand what I am saying, huh?" Anatole nodded. "The music I have heard today is like the music in my soul. It has made me so happy I will hear it in my dreams tonight if ever I will find a way of going to sleep while I am still so thrilled. Do you know what kind of music I like? I will tell you, my fine friend. I love music that is so tender and sweet, so warm and beautiful that it is like the gentle trickle of a waterfall or the flow of a mountain stream; or that it makes me think of a blue summer sky over the green of the Sussex Downs when birds fly high above. The music that brings to mind two lovers holding hands, and how deeply they feel for each other. The music that makes me think of an island far away where the sun shines and there are palm trees with coconuts and happy people smiling… happy dark-skinned people who live a simple life yet they are filled with the joy of living life… loving life itself! Yes, I love music that touches my heart and makes me cry. Cry with bliss and happiness. Cry with emotion. Then there is the kind of music like the harp strings that I can listen to, close my eyes and feel it in my soul. So much so that I become part of the music. I am the tune that is being played and the emotions and feelings of that tune are my emotions and my thoughts and love of where I am and who I am with. You are part of that music, Anatole. The music of my spirit and soul."

This time is was Anatole's eyes which were shining. For once in his life he felt truly lost for words. Trevilla who had little schooling or basic education had expressed herself eloquently and spiritually in a way that surprised him. This down to earth girl, who had been an agricultural labourer for much of her life, had the capacity to put her views across with all the passion of someone of a scholastic nature. She was enigmatic but revealing, brash but vulnerable, a strong personality yet sensitive. Trevilla was that rare package of a woman, a bundle of contradictions: baffling, infuriating, passionate, loving and at times uncannily psychic. The type of woman a man would be lucky to meet once in a lifetime.

"Let's have one more dance and then we'll make our way to the theatre." Anatole took her hand and guided her out onto the dance floor. This time they danced like a newly married couple at their wedding reception. The music was slow, sentimental and lush, where the violin and cello seemed to blend perfectly together. Anatole looked down into Trevilla's face. Her eyes were closed and she was smiling. Anatole thought about what she had just said. Was she feeling the music in her soul and mentally absorbing herself into the lush paradisiacal strings of the nirvana of the moment?

This fascinating enthralling woman brought out all the manly instincts in him. In one sense he wanted to protect her while in another he wanted to shower love and passion on her. Then she opened her eyes and laughed gently.

"I am a little girl again exploring a whole new world." The child-woman once again came to the fore. She kissed him quickly on the lips. "Shall we go to the theatre?" I am ready for the next surprise."

***

The next surprise for Trevilla was a trip to the theatre to see a ballet. They walked through the streets of Brighton in the early evening. Anatole kept her in suspense right up until they approached the entrance of the theatre.

It was clear to Trevilla that this really was going to be a special evening for they were surrounded by the glitterati and elite of Brighton.

They had come to see a ballet performed by a visiting Russian troupe. The ballet was Tchaikovsky's 'Swan Lake'. Anatole had decided that if anyone was going to the ballet for the first time 'Swan Lake' was the best introduction to that art form.

Once again their seats were high up and from their vantage point Trevilla would be able to see the beauty of the ballet very clearly. Right from the very beginning she was totally captivated. 'Swan Lake' managed to encapsulate the finest aspects of ballet with its colourful costumes and fairytale story. It was virtually timeless in that it would entertain audiences down the ages.

Trevilla had one distinct disadvantage. She did not know the story and being semi-literate could not read the programme. However, Anatole told her the basic story line and she was able to enjoy the visual feast of the ballet. The spectacle of seeing a ballet for the first time was an experience never to be forgotten. Each separate act brought a delight to the spectator of intricate and skilful ballet moves, lush settings and beautifully designed costumes. Every ballerina seemed to possess a suppleness and agility that came from extensive practice resulting in a breathtaking display of dancing.

In the first act the setting was 'The Garden of Prince Siegfried's Castle'. Swans make an appearance in flight above Prince Siegfried setting the stage for what is to come. The ladies in crowns and multi-coloured robes were dazzling to look at. What an entertainment for Trevilla this was proving to be! In act two the dancing in 'The Lakeside by Moonlight' was so graceful and moving to watch that it moved Trevilla so much a tear rolled from her eye.

Anatole wasn't sure where this emotion came from. Was it a tear of happiness unlikely as that may seem? Was it a tear that came from watching something so immensely moving and artistic that it moved her? By the time Act Four came and with it the scene where 'True Love is Triumphant', Trevilla was smiling yet shedding a tear at the same time. The applause was inevitably rapturous and the performers received a standing ovation.

The music of Tchaikovsky would be ringing in Trevilla's ears for the rest of the evening. Totally beautiful days are rare in anyone's life; when they do come they are cherished long in memory, for decades perhaps. Trevilla didn't know it then but her life would change dramatically soon.

It had been a busy day for the chauffeur too. Tom had been graciously lent to them by Bernard and Mariska. He was ready and waiting for them as they left the theatre. Anatole and Trevilla entered the car and immediately held hands. If it were at all possible to feel two emotions at the same time then Trevilla was experiencing this. She felt both sad and happy. Sad that such a beautiful day was coming to an end and in all likelihood her time with Anatole too. Yet she also felt blissfully happy in a way she had not felt since her brief marriage to Cazare. Happy to have lived such a near-perfect day, and to have tasted the good things that life can offer, while feeling the warmth of kindness and love.

"I will remember this day all my life, Anatole," she said in a quiet emotional voice barely above a whisper. "You have bought this Gypsy girl so much happiness today. The ballet was so wonderful – I didn't want it to end. The music and the dancing was so good that I felt it touching my heart and I cried… this Gypsy girl cried because… because it was so beautiful. Thank you, my darling. I hope I have been the lady to your gentleman. Was I a lady today, huh? Tell me, please! Have I been a lady?"

"You are a lady, Trevilla. Make no mistake, you are a lady."

***

Tom drove them back to Storrington. Several times Trevilla kissed Anatole and sat with her arms around him. She felt safe with him. The thought of him not being there in her life worried her. She had grown attached to him to such an extent that she saw in him all the traits of mentor, tutor, protector, friend and lover.

When they arrived back at the village Anatole escorted Trevilla to her caravan on the Downs as the Bentley was unable to drive up the narrow lane. It was near midnight but the night sky was so clear the moon seemed to be hovering over the Sussex Downs like a lantern guiding their way. The craters and crevices looked visible. It hung there as if to mark the end of a perfect day for Trevilla.

At the place where the Gypsy caravan was situated the smouldering embers of a small, carefully controlled fire crackled and sparkled in the night sky. Trevilla took both his hands and looked into his eyes.

"I don't think I will ever have a more wonderful day in my life," she said. "Even the moon has come out for us." Trevilla laughed. Her happiness was evident. "I thought my world had died when I lost my lovely Cazare but I know now there is much more out there. I would like to see more of the world you have shown me today."

Anatole took her in his arms and kissed her, making it last. He held her tightly and then kissed her again.

"There's a circus on at Parham House next Saturday. Why don't you come? Bring all your family with you?"

"I will talk to them. That is something else I have never been to. A circus… I will have seen everything then!" Once again she tossed her head back and laughed. "Will I see clowns and elephants maybe?"

"And I will paint your picture too one day this week." He rubbed her arm gently. "I must go. Thank you for being my companion… my lady today."

"And thank you for being my gentleman."

He gave her a smile, turned round and walked back down. Trevilla looked up at the night sky and stretched her arms. She still felt like dancing. The euphoria she felt prevented her from feeling tired. In fact she felt so ecstatic she thought that it would be hard to sleep that night. A happy smile crossed her face as she remembered the dancers on that night long ago in Hungary, who had performed around a similar fire to the one burning now by the Gypsy caravan.

How she had loved the ballet that night. For a few moments she tried to dance like a ballerina. She tried to balance herself and attempted a pirouette only to fall over causing her to laugh at her plight. The dance routine of a ballerina had fascinated her. Trevilla stretched her arms and legs out to try and recreate the dance movements she had been witness to in 'Swan Lake'. Then she gave up and walked towards the fire.

The sight of it reminded her of those colourful Gypsies she had seen in Hungary, seemingly dancing impromptu without rehearsal. In her mind she could hear the beat and rhythm of a potpourri of musical instruments from all sections of the European Gypsy community. Trevilla clapped her hands and began to dance around the fire. She was sprightly and energetic, twirling and spinning.

From within the caravan her parents, Roget and Marguerite, together with her younger brother and sister, Patric and Alida emerged. They all had a bemused look on their faces. Trevilla stretched out her hands and indicated she wanted them to join her in dance. They instantly responded.

Each held hands and began to dance in a ring round the fire while her grandmother, Elena, looked on in awe.

Halfway down the path on the Downs, Anatole turned to look back at the full moon. It looked so close Anatole felt that with one bound he could leap onto the surface and explore the areas known as the Sea of Tranquillity and the Sea of Serenity. Then to his astonishment beneath the backdrop of an ultra blue moon and a matching night sky he saw the little family group dancing. They were dark silhouettes highlighted by the lunar beams of far away. It was as if a special dance show had been staged on the Sussex Downs purely for his own entertainment.

Thirty-Four

Arthur Burnside was a hugely entertaining man. He had a permanent laugh in his voice, a generally happy nature and a constantly smiling face. Down to earth and friendly, he was the son of a Covent Garden market stall holder. While still a child in Queen Victoria's time he had sung on the streets to supplement the family income with a few extra pennies. His rise from the lower echelons of society to becoming a top London impresario was the stuff of legends and worthy of a play in itself.

He had been spotted singing outside a music hall by the entertainer Dan Leno and introduced to the world of the stage which he had embraced. From there he began his career by sweeping the stage and shifting scenery, to performing as a juvenile actor. He had sung, danced and been a wise cracking joke teller with a mischievous face and a wicked sense of humour. With determination and a sympathetic bank manager, he had built up an international theatrical agency, developing along the way, a shrewd knack of being a potential star spotter.

Wearing tweed suits, colourful bow ties and holding a cigar as a prop which was rarely smoked, he looked every inch the larger than life colourful impresario. In fact it was a carefully designed masquerade for he was very much the epitome of the 'common man' at home with everyone from tram conductors to wharf labourers. This masked a businessman who knew a sure-fire winner when he saw one. From the moment he saw Trevilla the Gypsy girl on screen in Andre and Anatol's documentary he knew she was a box office star in the making whatever her background.

Andre had jokingly offered Arthur a lift in the van used to transport the film equipment. He imagined that a wealthy man like Arthur would have opted for his own chauffeur driven vehicle. In fact Arthur, despite his apparent affluence, had no airs or pretensions and happily took up the offer.

He was a good companion and raconteur who entertained Andre all the way down to Sussex with many theatrical stories of performers he had known. It didn't seem to matter to Arthur that he only had a one-man audience in Andre, he joked and regaled in the way only a well honed entertainer could.

"Are you sure the Shervingtons will be all right with me coming to meet them, Mr Aviva?"

"I rang them last night, sir. They're very happy to meet you."

"I'm looking forward to meeting them too. From what you've told me about the family they sound interesting. I must say I'm enjoying the ride in this van. It reminds me of a song one of our great music hall entertainers used to sing. Have you heard of Marie Lloyd?"

"Yes, sir. I have. I believe she was the people's favourite."

"That's right. She was indeed. She used to sing a song called 'My Old Man said Follow the Van'. Have you heard it?"

"Can't say I have, Mr Burnside."

Arthur was a born entertainer. It was just the opportunity he was looking for. "You've not heard it? This great old music hall song? Oh my! Let me sing it for you!"

Andre looked to the heavens quickly. In addition to stories of old stars of long ago and endless anecdotes, Arthur also told continuous jokes that he had once used in his routine. Now he started to sing 'My Old Man' at the top of his voice. For Andre it was like being the only person in the audience at a Royal Variety performance.

***

Trevilla had been patient that early afternoon. She had finished work early in the fields to meet Anatole who had decided to paint her portrait. For the picture she had reverted to wearing traditional Gypsy clothes. She posed as still as her normally infectious nature would allow while perched precariously on a wooden fence overlooking the Downs. It was a picture Anatole would treasure all his life.

She wore a red beaded necklace, a light blue patterned top with long sleeves and wide cuffs, a beige waist scarf and a long colourful, multi-layered pleated skirt. With the green of the Downs in the background, and an English light blue sky in the background, it made for a good picture. It managed to capture the essence and magic of Gypsy mystique.

"You can come and look at it now," said Anatole looking out from behind the easel.

Trevilla gratefully stepped down from the fence and walked across the grass in her bare feet to take a curious look at her painted image. On seeing the picture, her eyes widened with childlike amazement.

"Do you like it?" Anatole asked, hoping eagerly that she would.

"Is that really me? Do I really look like that?"

"You don't like the painting, I guess," Anatole assumed incorrectly.

"It just looks so… unlike I thought I looked. You make me look so different to how I imagined. I look better than I think that I do. More… am I allowed to say beautiful?"

"Of course. In years to come I will look at this and remember you, Trevilla. The enchanting Gypsy girl I met on the Sussex Downs." Trevilla's eyes seem to melt. Anatole stood up and embraced her. "I've been everywhere but right now this place is the most beautiful I have ever seen. I never expected or imagined that I would grow to love someone like you, so different to anyone I have met before. Mr Burnside, the London impresario, is waiting at the house for you. He's going to offer you a job as a dancer in one of his shows. This is a new opportunity for you. I will be going to Africa next week and won't be back for some time."

"You speak as if we will never see each other again," Trevilla said sounding downcast.

"You must not think like that," Anatole pointed out. "Another thing I must add right now, my sister Lady Shervington is offering your parents the chance to run a small holding on the estate. If things don't work out for you as a dancer the farm will be there for you all to fall back on. How does that sound?"

Trevilla looked astounded. "I am ready to meet Mr Burnside now."

Anatole removed the picture from the easel. "Let's go."

***

Back at the house Andre and Arthur Burnside were in a hugely entertaining mood. Mariska and Bernard found Mr Burnside to be in every sense of the word a truly larger than life character. Such was the charisma of Arthur Burnside that he held court in the centre of the lounge room as if he was performing solo at an Empire theatre.

When Anatole and Trevilla arrived at the house a window upstairs was open and they could hear laughing. From within Roget and Marguerite emerged. Roget wore a broad smile.

"Mrs Shervington has asked me if we would stay on and run a small holding. We have agreed."

"Oh father!" Trevilla hugged him. "That is such good news."

Marguerite turned to Anatole. "We know Trevilla wants to dance in Mr Burnside's shows. She may be grown up but she is still our little girl. Will you ask Mr Burnside to look after her and make sure she is safe?" Then she added with a mischievous smile that indicated she was well aware of the relationship between Trevilla and Anatole. "Until you return."

"I give you my word," said Anatole. He meant it too. For years he had hung on to his single status and he had fought against falling in love with Trevilla, but he had finally succumbed. On his return from Africa he thought that he would seriously consider a future with Trevilla.

It was the first time in her life that she had ever entered a house like this before. Trevilla looked around her like a child entering a magical sweetshop. The portrait pictures of the Shervington military ancestry seemed so real she almost imagined a white-bearded general would step out from the frame and salute her. Marble elephants and Indian carvings adorned mantelpieces and shelves. Old sepia photographs of Sikhs and Maharajahs appeared on different corners. It was a world within a world. They ascended the stairs and came to the doors of the huge lounge room where from within Trevilla could hear laughter and conversation. Anatole gently pushed the door open. The occupants could be seen clearly. All at once they stopped their frivolity and stood in smiling silence as Anatole and Trevilla entered the room.

Trevilla was a natural uninhibited extrovert who had no fear of the crowd or of being a spectacle but for some reason even she was at a loss to calculate the sight of her new audience unnerved her. Arthur Burnside stood in the centre of the room flanked on one side by Mariska, Bernard, Alexander and Grace, and on the other by Andre who stood next to a move camera he had set up close by.

"My what a spectacular filly you are, my dear!" Arthur exclaimed, and his face lit up as if a beam of godly light had fallen on him from the heavens above. "Thank you so much for coming." He moved forward and shook her hand lightly. Then he turned to Anatole and shook his hand. "So, you're Mr Luchenya. I've heard a great deal about you, sir. Along with your sister, Mariska, you were one half of the Dancing Luckies, I believe. You both bedazzled audiences from Baltimore to Broadway, Miami to Manchester, Toronto to Tunbridge Wells! How very nice to meet you both. Of course I'm an old stager myself, you know. I've done everything on stage from sweeping it to dying on it!"

"Oh everyone's died on stage including us, eh, Mariska! May I introduce Trevilla to you all."

"You're very welcome, Trevilla," Mariska said, moving forward to greet her. Given the disparity of their ages and their different background it was amazing that in some ways there were similarities in their characters. Both were charismatic. Both were showstoppers. They would undoubtedly get on well.

Bernard too was unaffected by her presence. "Welcome to the house, young lady." The word 'lady' made Trevilla smile for she had always wanted to be considered just that.

The children looked up at Trevilla in curiosity. Her natural Gypsy attire, dark hair and laughing eyes made her the most unique-looking person in the room. A moment ago it had been Arthur Burnside – once known as 'Laughing Arthur' in his stage performing days – who had dominated the room by his sheer magnetism. Now it was Trevilla in her garish clothes who became the focal point of the room just by being there. *Such natural stage presence*, thought Arthur. She was destined for stardom. No doubt about it.

"Well, Trevilla, Mr Aviva here has shown me film footage of you dancing on the Sussex Downs. I have to say I'm mighty impressed. I stage musicals and theatrical productions in London. I have a show going into rehearsal soon, a musical about Gypsy dancers. I can arrange accommodation for you to stay in a flat with other lady dancers while you begin rehearsals. If you want to sign with me – and I hope you will for it's a chance in a lifetime – I'll pay you £25 a week to begin with. If the show is a success, I'll double the wage to £50 a week. The show may even go on tour to other big cities. Even overseas if we can get bookings. What do you say? Do you want to take up a big opportunity?"

"That sounds grand, Mr Burnside. I say yes, yes, yes!" Trevilla sparkled. She threw her head back and laughed happily. Then without inhibition she twirled and span in the centre of the room. Everyone watched as this fascinating woman danced.

Arthur eyed up the piano in the corner and with a laugh in his voice said, "Someone play! Let's have a party!"

Andre at once responded and began to play a rhapsody that befitted the occasion. It was something haunting and continental. Trevilla performed to the tune while Bernard looked on, bemused that the normally staid lounge room had suddenly become a centre for entertainment. When Andre had finished playing everyone clapped spontaneously. Bernard left the room briefly to call out to Terry Bentley and Marilyn Wilce to bring drinks and sandwiches to the room for the guests. If they were going to have a party it might as well be a good one.

Arthur was delighted that Trevilla was going to sign with him. Her little display of dancing had convinced him of her value to his future shows. He approached her to doubly ensure that she would take up the options he was offering her.

"My chauffeur is coming down from London on Monday to collect me. If you're ready, I could take you in the car. Would you be prepared to come up with me then? We could get you sorted in a place of lodging and you can begin rehearsals immediately."

"So soon!" she said, surprised at the speed in which her life was about to change. Quickly she glanced across at Anatole who smiled at her. "Okay, we go Monday."

"I believe Lady Shervington has offered your parents work on an attached farm here. So you'll have somewhere to come home to. I understand there's a circus in the village on Saturday and that you and your family are going. Well, all of us here are going too. I love circuses."

"You were a clown once in the music hall weren't you, Mr Burnside?" asked Bernard, who had rejoined the group. "Amongst many other talents, I believe."

"My word! I was on the same bill in Whitechapel with a young fellow called Barney Barnato. He became a big shot in South Africa you know. Went on to make his fortune in diamond mining. Such are the mixed fortunes of people's lives." He paused in mid conversation to sample a chicken and prawn sandwich that Marilyn Wilce had brought to them on a platter. He called out to Anatole who stood by the piano with Andre. "Mr Luchenya, how about a song from your vaudeville days?"

Anatole nodded in agreement and then told Andre the name of the song he was going to sing. Andre started to play and the room went quiet. All eyes were suddenly directed towards Anatole and Andre. With a small attentive and intimate audience, Anatole began to sing 'My Mother's Rosary'. With only the spartan accompaniment of the piano, Anatole performed this moving song in a rich clear voice enunciating every word and phrase beautifully. A little bit of emotion was clearly evident in his voice as he sang and thought of his own Russian mother, Ekaterina. When he sang it was more of a performance in the manner of Jolson acting out the words with a tear formed in his eye as he looked up at the portrait painting of Viktor and Ekaterina that sat above the fireplace.

The small audience were spellbound. It had been so long since he had performed that he had forgotten just what a thrill it was to be an entertainer. Downstairs the staff Ronnie Wilshire, Linda Casling, Terry Bentley and Marilyn Wilce all stopped their kitchen and serving duties just to listen to the warm timbre of Anatole's expressive voice that carried around the house.

Trevilla looked on, thrilled by Anatole's performing ability. For Mariska it brought back memories of a time of her life that had been so spectacular and exciting that no matter how long she lived or wherever she went, nothing could top those wonderful days. Arthur looked on beaming with sheer delight. The old showman was moved to the point of tears. Oh how much he loved his job in show business. It had brought him into contact with fantastic entertaining people of all sorts who had considerably enhanced the fruits of his life. At the end of the song everyone applauded and that included the staff downstairs.

This time it was Mariska who decided to make her own contribution to the party. She whispered into the ear of Andre who smiled at the mention of the tune. Over twenty years before when he had been a young stagehand in a New York theatre he had seen Anatole and Mariska perform to this tune. Mariska beckoned Anatole to come across.

Andre began to play the tune of 'Lenora' that had been heard in a thousand or so western saloons. Anatole remembered it so clearly. Years ago it had been one of the first tunes the Dancing Luckies had performed to. In that role Mariska had played the part of a shy young woman who Anatole attempted to woo. The pair began to recreate that act of long ago. Despite Anatole's war injuries he was still able to dance, mock proposing while Mariska pretended to be shy and coy and imitated ballet steps. All the years fell away. The brother and sister of Russian birth and heritage were once again the New York kids destined for stardom and adventure. Suddenly they were youngsters again.

They saw stars in their eyes and in their own minds were transported back to an early twentieth century audience at the State Theatre in New York. Here in this manor house in Storrington in leafy green Sussex, the vaudevillians performed as if Paul Kapsia was indicating that President Theodore Roosevelt was in the audience. From downstairs the staff came quietly upstairs with more food and drink for the guests. They took the opportunity to view the little show with great interest. None of them had ever seen anything like this before.

Trevilla was not made to feel as if she didn't belong there. On the contrary she was made to feel welcome. This was her farewell party too and she had mixed emotions that day. The man she loved was sailing to Africa the following week and she would be leaving her own much cherished family to begin a career on stage in London. Something was saying to her to enjoy this time. Today was close to perfect.

The entertainment went on for a long time. Once started it was like a fast moving West End show. Everyone got in the act. Bernard recited 'The Green Eye of the Yellow God' while Andre played a tune with Indian overtones in the background. Totally unprompted Trevilla and Mariska began to dance behind him, their movements recreating Indian maidens performing traditionally.

The old showman, Arthur Burnside, was thoroughly enjoying himself. He felt half inclined to sign everybody up! There was no doubt that in his time Arthur had been one of the greats in music hall. With his thumbs in his lapels he recited 'Gunga Din' and he played to the gallery as only a seasoned performer knows how to, casting his eyes at everyone, smiling wickedly and contorting his face with good humour. Once again Andre played a tune with a suggestion of India in its notes while Trevilla and Mariska danced with gently swaying movements and hand gesticulation.

At the end of the evening Bernard invited the staff upstairs to join the little group and toast those who were soon to depart. It was an unexpected happy impromptu gathering, almost a finale in fact, with a sixth sense telling all who attended that things were about to change. Some would never meet again.

"Would you charge your glasses please ladies and gentlemen," Bernard boomed out. Ronnie Wilshire and Terry Bentley immediately uncorked Champagne bottles. Everyone including the servants were given glasses. "Ladies and gentlemen, this is a very special and in some ways also a sad occasion. It has been a great pleasure to welcome to this house my brother-in-law, Anatole, who I last saw when we were soldiers in the Great War and we met purely by chance in a wood in France. Anatole, we have loved having you here as well as your friend and colleague, Andre. We wish you both well on your filming assignment to Africa." He turned to face Arthur. "Mr Burnside… sir. We've only just met you for the first time but you've given us a right royal music hall performance in the tradition of Dan Leno and the great George Robey."

"I should do!" interrupted Arthur. "They taught me!"

"And we have loved your company, sir! You are leaving on Monday, taking your new star, Trevilla, with you. Trevilla, your magnetism and presence here has made a great impression on us all… and one man in particular, I know." He winked at Anatole, who did the same. "We wish you well in your new career on stage and assure you that your parents and brothers and sister, who will be working and living on the adjacent farm, will be looked after. That's it. The only thing left is for me to do is to say this. Would you please raise your glasses and toast this happy gathering."

Everyone clinked their glasses and toasted each other. Then Andre returned to the piano and began to play 'Auld Lang Syne'. Automatically, all the people sang. Mariska had a premonition that there was something final about this day. She absorbed the moment for posterity as she sang. Across the room Anatole smiled at her. It seemed that her often wild and unpredictable brother had been tamed by the love of a Gypsy girl. One thing felt certain though that night. Every so often in people's lives there were defining moments when it really felt as if a new chapter was about to begin. Somehow the refrains of 'Auld Lang Syne' as sung that night were farewelling an old life and ushering in a new one.

***

The following Saturday the whole group of them went to the circus at Parham Park. Trevilla was accompanied by her parents, grandmother, brother and sister. They all sat happily with Anatole, Andre and Arthur.

This time there was a surprise omission: Mariska and Bernard weren't with them. They were in fact both behind cameras filming their own documentary, although their children were with Anatole.

At another side of the big top Mariska and Bernard were busy starting their new careers in the film industry by recording the activities of the circus. While they had plenty of other enterprises to support them this was a whole new venture. It was one they hoped would eventually develop into something spectacular.

The circus gave them plenty to film. It was entertainment on a grand scale which never failed to thrill, excite, amuse and surprise audiences of all ages. There was the ringmaster, the polished professional master of the entire show. He looked like a man who couldn't believe his luck that he had such an enjoyable job. His larger than life personality boomed and echoed around all corners of the big top with all the aplomb of a Shakespearian actor conquering the role of Hamlet.

For Trevilla it was the first time in her life that she had ever seen all the sights and spectacle of a circus. She sat enthralled by the endless parade of acrobats, trapeze artists, clowns and animals that passed before her. Her parents, grandmother, her younger brother and sister sat together, a happy family group, while Arthur Burnside, Andre, Anatole and his niece and nephew were alongside them savouring this happy time.

It was strange for Anatole to look across to Mariska and Bernard behind their cameras filming their first documentary beginning with the thrills of the circus in Parham Park. They had ventured into this new project with great enthusiasm spurred on by the achievements of Andre Aviva who had been an equally enthusiastic guide. It would take them a while to learn all the tricks of the trade including developing, cutting and editing, but on that day they learned not only to focus on the performers but also the people who matter the most. The audience. It seemed that all the villagers were there. No matter what grade of work they carried out they laughed at the mirthful antics of the clowns, thrilled to the high wire artistes and marvelled at the animals in close proximity. There was something for everyone of all ages.

Mariska focused on Anatole and everyone around him. Recorded on film it was a scene she would often replay in future years. After an absence of fourteen years, she had finally met her brother again. The camera recorded a lot of images that afternoon but for Mariska the scene of that happy little group all laughing together and enjoying the entertainment seemed to sum up the joy of living.

***

The following Monday, Arthur Burnside's chauffeur duly turned up just after lunchtime. He had driven down in a very impressive Rolls Royce, which was a clear indication of how wealthy Arthur had become in his career. Arthur had been a house guest at the Shervington home and being a true gentleman he went around and shook hands with everyone including the staff.

"I'm very grateful to you for your hospitality, Lord and Lady Shervington," he said to them in the lounge room. "I've enjoyed my stay here and meeting you all."

"It's been our pleasure, sir," replied Bernard. "I hope we will remain friends."

"Indeed. When you've finished making your film bring a copy to me, and if you need any editing work, I can arrange that for you together with distribution to the film theatres, royalty payments as such. I will be happy to act as an agent for you."

"That will be wonderful," Mariska said with delight. Her appetite for filmmaking had increased, and she wanted a break from the Shervington business enterprises.

Arthur turned to Andre and Anatole. "Gentlemen, it's been a pleasure. Be sure to keep in touch." He shook their hands. "I hope we meet again soon."

Terry Bentley knocked on the door and entered. He looked towards Bernard. "Good afternoon sir. Miss Trevilla and her family are waiting downstairs. Miss Trevilla said she is ready to leave now. She has asked if she could speak with Mr Anatole before she goes."

"I won't be long, Mr Burnside," Anatole assured him.

"Take as long as you like," said Arthur with a smile.

Anatole left the room quickly and went downstairs to the lobby. Trevilla was standing alone while her family waited outside. To Anatole's surprise she was wearing the outfit he had bought her for her special day out. For some reason she looked more beautiful that day than he had seen her previously. In a strange way he also thought that this normally supremely confident young woman seemed vulnerable that day. Was it some sort of sixth sense that told him she was nervous about her departure for the London stage?

"I wanted to see you," she said softly.

"And I you," Anatole responded. There was no one else in the lobby and they were alone with the freedom to say what was in their heart without the embarrassment of anyone hearing.

"You know we Gypsies have some sort of psychic sense. Something tells me we may not see each other again. I fear for you, Anatole, going to Africa. I worry something might happen to you. When I was younger I lost my lovely husband, Cazare. You are the man I love. I do not want to lose you too. I want to be your bride one day. Do you understand me? Do you hear what I am saying, Anatole?"

"You must not worry about me," Anatole said emphatically. "This trip to Africa is nothing. I've been through a war and survived that. Besides, you've got a lot to look forward to, Trevilla. You're going to be a dancer in a stage show in London. Aren't you thrilled?"

Unusually Trevilla looked lost for words. Her response was to move forward, put her arms around him and kiss him. They both luxuriated in the passion of the moment. Anatole held her tightly. He stroked her hair gently, looked deeply into her eyes and then kissed her again. He really didn't want to let her go but he took his hands away from her slowly.

"This is goodbye then," Trevilla said softly. Before Anatole could say anything Arthur Burnside appeared at the top of the stairs.

"Are you ready to go, my dear?" he asked.

"I am," Trevilla replied. She took one last look at Anatole and smiled warmly at him. Then she turned and walked outside to where her family stood patiently.

Arthur put his hand on Anatole's shoulder. "She'll be all right," he reassured him. "We'll look after her." He then left the house.

Trevilla hugged each member of her family. She didn't look back at the house. Anatole watched as she and Arthur entered the Rolls Royce. The car engine started up and the chauffeur began to drive away slowly. Trevilla's family waved to her.

Anatole suddenly felt a deep sadness within him. He had not ever intended to fall in love with anyone but it had happened so unexpectedly with a fascinating woman he would never have chosen in normal circumstances. There was an alarming feeling within him, a premonition perhaps that he would never see Trevilla again. He realised with dismay that her presence in his life had brought him a joy he had not previously known. The Rolls Royce gradually disappeared from view and he lowered his head in sadness.

In the car Trevilla looked out at the Sussex Downs. Part of her felt excitement at the new experiences to come but the sudden change in her circumstances made her question if this was really what she wanted. She thought of Anatole and their romance. Would they ever have a future? A tear rolled from her eye.

Thirty-Five

Several days after Trevilla's departure Andre and Anatole found themselves on the deck of a ship in Southampton, which would shortly sail to Africa. The stage was set for a filming assignment which would take them the length and breadth of the 'Dark Continent' as it was so often referred to.

The adventurous spirit that had driven Anatole since childhood was beginning to wane. He had enjoyed his stay in the beautiful county of Sussex. In fact he had fallen in love with it. He had loved the pristine rolling green of the Sussex Downs, the rustic lanes, the old cottages and churches dating back centuries. There was so much about it that made him feel at ease there.

Perhaps it was the quiet of a peaceful sunny Sunday morning broken only by the sound of the church bells in the village. It could have been a combination of things; the scent of hay bales and the fresh meadows, the clean air with a breeze blowing the faint aromas of flowers, the proliferation of wildlife that he had been privileged to see and record on film in his working capacity as a cine-cameraman.

But after drifting around the world and the sharp frenetic pace of New York, the small relatively unknown, unspoilt village of Storrington felt like home because of the presence of his sister, Mariska, there. Her family was his family. He loved his niece and nephew enormously. Lord Bernard Shervington with his articulate, dignified and authoritative manner had seemed an unlikely suitor for Mariska with her show business background. However, it had been a great match and Anatole had warmed to him very much.

Anatole had liked the Sussex people who he felt had a different accent to Londoners. The true Sussex accent had a softer burr that instantly separated them from their counterparts in other counties. That was one of the things that puzzled Anatole about the British Isles. How was it possible that even though English was the common language that as a person went from one county to another in the space of a few miles, the accents would vary widely.

When he returned from his cinematic jaunt to Africa he felt sure that he would continue his career in England. He looked out at Southampton Docks. Mariska, Bernard and their two children waved to them. There were streamers running between the ship and the wharf which began to stretch and break as it moved out to sea. A military band on the dockside played the traditional South African song 'Sarie Marais'. It was a moving send off for this proud ship of the Union Castle Line which was bound for the ports of South Africa.

Mariska watched as the ship sailed out into the English Channel. A breeze blew up slightly ruffling her hair and bringing moisture to her eyes. She looked up at Bernard who could almost read her mind. He was intuitive enough to realise that Anatole and Andre were undertaking a very exciting, but probably also dangerous, assignment.

"I know," said Bernard sympathetically. "We have our own work now to do in filming wildlife."

***

The following evening they returned to the Sussex Downs. This time their objective was to film the natural habitat of the wild fox. The husband and wife team ever eager to widen their horizons were in the infancy of their new careers. They walked up winding paths and lanes they had traversed many times before. At night on the Downs the clear visibility of the moon acted like a torch light to them as they sought a suitable spot to film from.

Since boyhood days Bernard had explored every part of the Downs. He knew exactly where to find badgers in their setts, squirrels in their dreys and foxes in their lairs. He also knew that the animals of the woodland had acutely sharp hearing and an extra-sensory perception for the stealthy predator. To capture their way of life on film would require extraordinary patience and perseverance. The chances were that they would have to sit still and quiet for hours before the sight of the fox came into view.

The Downs held many a secret. From a distance they looked lush green and bushy. Once entered the vast woodland had many alcoves, niches and openings that revealed views and sights of the hidden world of nature. The ground beneath them bore the paw prints of foxes, and Bernard instantly knew he had found a suitable spot to make his observations on camera. It was simply a case of waiting.

In the early hours of the morning when both were beginning to fall asleep behind their cameras, there was a sound like a banshee wailing that permeated through the night air. Instantaneously they moved to the cameras and started focusing quickly. The same ice cold cry rent forth once again. This time Mariska identified the owner of the cry. It was a vixen crying for its mate. Then by its lair the enchanting sight of the vixen's cubs came into view. They played and frolicked in the relative safety of this very secluded spot, totally unaware they were being watched. Then all of a sudden they stopped playing and sprung up in surprise as if something unexpected was approaching. Even at such a young and innocent age the animal acumen was sharp.

Mariska was concerned just in case a human hunter was nearing them. She was on the brink of jumping up when into the view of her camera lens came a dog fox carrying the night's kill, which was obviously a pheasant. He dropped it from his mouth and the entire family, including the vixen, moved forward to enjoy a feast. Every now and then as if subconsciously aware they were being filmed, one of the animals would look up almost directly into the lens of the camera. They were bright-eyed, energetic and fun to watch.

Neither Mariska nor Bernard dared to move from their secluded spot for fear of making a noise that would scare the stars of their show away. Eventually the fox family finished their meal, played together and quietly disappeared to the relative safety of their lairs. It had been a long night but they had successfully completed another part of their filming assignment. They felt a tremendous sense of satisfaction at what they had achieved. It was their first efforts and had been an enjoyable experience.

Before they returned to the real world of running the Shervington enterprises, including Bernard's architectural business, they wanted to film one more aspect of country life. They found it in the iconic figure of every rural community, the village blacksmith. Poems had been written about this man, often portraying him as a soft-hearted, muscular yokel, working in a constantly hot atmosphere with burning sparks and the fierce heat of the forge. The mental image they had of this man, a preconceived picture it would have to be said, was of the toughest, strongest male in the village who got on with his tasks in virtual solitude.

In fact the village blacksmith they decided to film was an anachronism of traditional old time values. He was a gentleman. The word gentle could have been aptly applied to this man in every aspect. He was softly spoken with a warm smile, an old-time Sussex man of gentle manners, hardworking in his chosen trade, physically well built and with a love of the horses he served. While he fitted their horseshoes he spoke to them in a soft reassuring voice as if they were his long-time friends.

The scene in the blacksmith's place of work was something befitting the time and era of his occupation's greatest importance, for the age of the motorcar had taken precedence over the physical power of the horse. It was clear he was a real animal lover and they would always hold a special place in his heart. Not only horses but dogs and cats too.

The cameras began to roll. Far from being a sweltering workshop it was a place of space and light with a wide entrance where doors on either side were flung open and observers on the street could see the industry within from the street, Huge oak beams criss-crossed the ceilings and provided supports on the walls. Several horseshoes hung from the beams above providing a clear identification of the mainstay of the Blacksmith's work. On the stone floor a section of a massive tree stump supported an anvil. In the background there was a flame-red furnace in the manner of old that had probably remained unchanged since the previous century. From an oak beam traversing the ceiling a young cat, making the transition from kitten to curious feline, sat looking down at the scene below. Another cat, presumably the mother, a happy-looking tabby with a shiny coat sat quite contentedly with a cockerspaniel watching the blacksmith at work. The most important guest however was a serene chestnut mare for whom the blacksmith was making special horseshoes. The horse watched silently, rather in the manner of a human customer waiting inside the cobbler's special workroom while their best pair of shoes was being suitably re-heeled. The blacksmith talked to the horse who seemed to respond by raising its head up and down. It was a lovely fetching scene of one aspect of country life.

Bernard and Mariska's newsreel documentary was fast becoming detailed, varying and interesting for the viewing public. Buoyed up and very enthusiastic about what they had achieved so far, they decided to film something else that was close to the heart of the British.

For many people the steam train had a certain magic about it while others thought of them as smoky noisy engines that never arrived on time. But in fact they were highly photogenic. Bernard rightly assumed that in time these engines would be replaced by more advanced electricity driven trains, and that a documentary made now would prove to be of great historical value in future years.

They set to work filming the majesty of the trains that ran in the South Coast of England in the Sussex area. The small branch lines that extended to the remote rural villages were of particular interest to them. One day a future government would render sweeping cuts and these lines would be closed down leaving only a memory of rickety train stations and chugging, clanking steam engines. In fact the train stations that the Shervington's filmed at were often well kept by proud staff who added flowers in baskets and pots to adorn the platform.

It was a good documentary well thought out, that in years to come would show the Britain of another age between the wars. They decided if they were going to film the magnificence of these old steam trains, they needed to concentrate on the technical aspects of how they were actually driven by both mechanism and driver. An explanation of the two types of train engines used seemed to be a good introduction to the supposed magic of the steam railways.

Bernard and Mariska subsequently filmed a train driven by an Atlantic engine comprising four big driving wheels. Then they filmed the Pacific engine which had four smaller wheels in front of six driving wheels and two smaller ones behind.

Having a deep technical knowledge Bernard then decided to film how a steam train is powered. In fact this was almost another story in itself for steam engines were essentially the basis of the industrial revolution. The inventors of the steam engine, James Watt and Thomas Newcomen could not have imagined the far-reaching uses of their creation, which would power industry on a widespread basis. This included boats, factory plants and locomotives.

Bernard filmed the process of a steam engine beginning to work. It started with coal being burnt in a furnace surrounded by water, which created steam. This steam that was confined in a cylinder was pushed by a piston linked to wheels by rods. These turned the straight thrust of a piston into a rotary motion that effectively drove the wheels of the locomotive forward. Ordinarily to the normal viewing public this aspect may have been boring, but in the context of an historical cinematic document, it was worth its weight in gold.

Their completed work encompassed the filming of a circus, a family of foxes, the work of the village blacksmith, and the steam railways of the rural South of England. It was something of a tour de force for two budding film enthusiasts who were basically amateurs but, even at this early stage of their new careers, their ambitions had been fired by this new experience. In due course when they had attended to their own business interests, they would take the film to Arthur Burnside at his London office where it would be edited and then distributed to cinema theatres. While there they would also look up Trevilla to see how their newfound Gypsy friend was getting on in the world of dance.

Life went on normally otherwise. Mariska adored her two children, Alexander and Grace, who she made sure were never forgotten or lacked love and affection. Always she would play with them, talk to them, and walk out proudly with them. In her role as a business administrator, she kept a sharp eye on the books of each company they were involved with, auditing and reconciling figures to the finest detail. For hours at a stretch she would work hard in her study looking out at the beauty of the Sussex Downs from time to time in between pouring over reports. She knew in her heart that business no longer held interest to her. Mariska knew her forte and her future was in filming wildlife.

Bernard sat at a desk in his office in Horsham. In his role as an architect he had several restoration projects that he was working on. One was the refurbishment of a once great theatre in Surrey that had fallen into a seemingly irretrievable condition. His task was to restore it to its days of divine glory. He and several draughtsmen worked tirelessly on the project to bring the theatre into the modern age without losing the charm and ambience it had once contained in the days when such performers as Marie Lloyd and Vesta Tilley had trod the boards. His work schedule was particularly heavy.

If that wasn't enough he also travelled to London on a regular basis to speak out on behalf of the poverty stricken masses especially the returned servicemen of the Great War who he considered had been forgotten. He campaigned too for the unfortunate shellshocked soldiers who had been executed during the war for alleged cowardice. His speeches in the House of Lords resonated and crackled with an anger he was unaware that he contained within him. He was a passionate speaker who truly believed in the causes he fought for.

But now he added a new cause to his list. He became a firm campaigner on behalf of animals. In this he was encouraged by Mariska, who had grown to love the natural wildlife of the English countryside. In short, Mariska and Bernard as a couple with their shared interests, unlike some couples who grew apart, grew together forever developing their enthusiasm to tackle new fields.

In London they took their completed film to Arthur Burnside who studied it in a private viewing room. He was always amiable, a lover of life, and a great raconteur, but Arthur was a professional who wanted near perfection from those he employed in his theatres. Mariska and Bernard weren't professional cinematographers in the sense that Andre and Anatole were but they were keen to learn more. Arthur took them under his wing and assigned a film editor to their project. He edited their work without too much being taken out and together they added subtitles to each scene for the audience to read. It was a joy for them to watch their first efforts.

Their first documentary was called 'The Pleasures of Country Life'. At Arthur's offices in the Strand, a private viewing was arranged. For both of them it was a thrill to see their work on screen. The scenes of the circus at Parham Park were particularly entertaining to watch. There on screen were Anatole and Trevilla amongst the audience. In future years it was a scene she would often replay.

They went to see Trevilla in her debut on the London stage. Trevilla's parents and her younger siblings came along too. A curious and unusual friendship had developed between the Gypsy children and Alexander and Grace. Their backgrounds, traditions and lifestyles were worlds apart but it made no difference. They all became friends who would grow up not to be prejudiced or biased and in turn would learn from each other.

Arthur sat with them at the theatre in Drury Lane. The venue brought back memories for Mariska. When Paul Kapsia had brought them all to England they had played at this marvellous theatre back in 1911. Was it really fifteen yeas ago she pondered? Paul Kapsia… now there was a name to conjure with. If Anatole hadn't met him on a warm Saturday afternoon in New York in 1898 Mariska would never have begun a career in show business that had taken her around the world and introduced her to her husband. It was curious how often in life a chance meeting, an accident of fate or a coincidence could generate a lifestyle and the manner in which one lives. It is easy to plan the pattern of one's future life; to pretend to be the author and manager of the years ahead. But in reality there was a lot of truth in that old saying 'you can have your plans but the gods laugh'. Someone once told Mariska that 'Life is a series of unplanned events, accidents and unpredictable circumstances that dictate the course of the years'.

So too had that been the course for the events that occurred in the life of Trevilla. It was as if the hand of fate had plucked Trevilla from the relative obscurity of her Gypsy lifestyle to the glamour and hypo charged accelerated heart beating speed rush of the London stage. Mariska remembered what it was like to perform to a packed house with an audience of hundreds of faces all concentrating on her as she went through a blazing well-rehearsed act of song and dance against a colourful backdrop on stage. A sense of nervous excitement and energy pulsates through the veins of a performer as they begin to act. Then there is the worry that if it is good today, reaping standing ovation and critical acclaim, can the performance tomorrow be even better? Such were, and are, the insecurities of a performer.

Trevilla was soon to know all the feelings and emotions associated with the stage. Normally she was a girl who knew no fear but from the side of the stage as she gazed out at the audience she felt a mixture of adrenalin and fright at the imposing sight of the people who had come to see the show. For months she had rehearsed with the rest of the cast under the strict guidance of an esteemed choreographer. He was noted for his attention to details and trained them hard and harshly like a Sergeant Major drilling raw recruits. But the end result was the proof of the pudding. It was a highly professional show that harnessed together the finest talents possible with the infusion of new blood.

Arthur was beaming a huge smile. This was his show. Normally his status as a top impresario in London theatrical circles merited him a balcony seat. But on this occasion he preferred to sit in the main seats with Mariska, Bernard, their children, Trevilla's parents, grandmother and siblings, who were beside themselves with excitement at the thought of seeing a member of their family on stage. Arthur looked around in the audience and found himself waving to other well known figures. Amongst them were Noel Coward, Ivor Novello, his old mentor George Robey and George Bernard Shaw. He thought to himself that the audience was almost as impressive as the cast.

Then after waiting for what seemed like an age, the orchestra began to strike up the music. The houselights dimmed. The stage curtains drew back to reveal a colourful backdrop. There was a collective hush and the story began to unfold.

'The Prince and the Gypsy Girl' was a simple story on a similar theme to many stories before and since. A prince of a European country in the early part of the twentieth century tells his advisers he is not up to the job of becoming king until he meets and mingles with the ordinary populous. It was a musical and, in between ordinary dialogue, the young man sang with a powerful and emotional voice. The young prince is struggling with his conscience that he lives a sheltered protected life while there are many people of his nation living in poverty. He resolves to get out and about amongst the ordinary people; however, he disguises himself as an ordinary man travelling the road and meets people in markets, and down and outs who he offers charity to. Unbeknown to him he is being watched by the leader of a gang of robbers. When Prince Augustus takes to the open road he is set upon by these robbers, all his belongings are taken and he is left for dead. The music is dramatic and reaches a crescendo.

In the act that follows the Prince wakes up to find himself in a Gypsy camp where he is brought back to good health. The Gypsy's do not know he is the prince who will one day inherit the crown and become king. To them he is just a fellow traveller who they have found at the side of the road. He is shown the traditions of the Gypsy's and treated as if he is one of their own. It is the first time in his life he feels free of the responsibilities of his office and royal status. He enjoys the simple pleasures of their lifestyle and falls in love with a vivacious and dynamic Gypsy girl called Saffron who in turn is equally infatuated with him. Prince Augustus knows that their love affair can never be for one day soon he must return to his royal duties.

In time a search party from the palace finds the Prince and his identity is revealed to the Gypsies. Saffron is heartbroken but for years afterwards she will cherish the memory of their time together. The Prince becomes a wise and just king who also cherishes the golden times they spent together. The music, songs, drama and settings, ensured that it was a colourful musical audiences would love. Such was the variation on a well-worn theme of musicals before and since that it didn't really matter. The dazzling display of all types of Gypsy dancing introduced audiences to the previously undiscovered delights of their artistry. To many it was a display of an unknown culture.

The role of Saffron called for a great deal of dancing and a strong singing voice. It was played to near perfection by Trevilla who surprised not only her family with her crystal clear strong voice, but also Mariska and Bernard who had been unaware of her vocal talents and range. Arthur smiled the most though. From the first moment he had seen her on the film documentary Andre had shown him, he knew she was a genuine star in the making. With singing training and a disciplined choreographer Trevilla had proved her potential and shone like the light of a chandelier in her debut performance. At the end of the musical the audience in the Drury Lane Theatre gave the cast a standing ovation.

"I knew she was good! I didn't know she was outstanding!" Arthur exclaimed as he stood and clapped along with the rest of them. He winked at George Robey and smiled at Noel Coward.

Afterwards the whole group of them made their way to Trevilla's dressing room. She hugged each and every one of them, particularly her family. There were tears in her eyes yet she was smiling with a happiness that was contagious.

"We're all so proud of you, Trevilla," Mariska said with a genuine warmth. She really was thrilled for her. In Trevilla she could see the elements of the young girl embarking on a stage career she herself had once, so long ago in the theatres of the United States.

"I am just an ordinary Gypsy girl. A few months ago, I picked vegetables. Tonight I have been a performer on stage in a musical. I just cannot believe it! I never planned any of this. It was as if something picked me up and shook me. Do you believe in fate, Mariska?"

"I don't know. I believe in life. I believe if you are given a chance you have to work to justify it. This is only the beginning of it for you. There will be many first nights for you. Times of excitement, new music, new songs, different places, different people. Oh, you have such great moments to come! Take the opportunities Trevilla and enjoy everything that comes your way. Never feel guilty about all the good things you taste in life now and never take it for granted either. Anatole and I never did."

That was the cue Trevilla had been waiting for. "How is Anatole? Have you heard from him?"

"Yes. He's in South West Africa filming at the moment."

***

Anatole had written from all the places he had visited. The Union Castle Liner had docked first of all in Madeira. The island was sunny, colourful and warm. Andre and Anatole had dined at Reid's Palace, the best hotel then on the island that overlooked Funchal. They sat sampling a Madeira rum, while enjoying a delicious seafood meal looking out at the Atlantic Ocean and the adjacent sub-tropical gardens. It had been established by William Reid who had arrived in Madeira as a fourteen-year-old cabin boy. Through a mixture of hard work, shrewd investment and good business sense, Reid had become a successful wine trader and hotel builder. Reid's Palace was truly the icing on the cake. It had been designed by George Somers Clarke, an innovative architect and Egyptologist who had been the creator of the Shepheard Hotel in Cairo. In later years Reid's Palace would play host to such luminaries as Edward VIII, Lloyd George, George Bernard Shaw and Winston Churchill.

From Madeira the ship sailed down to Cape Town, South Africa, where Anatole and Andre disembarked to film their long assignment. Sailing into Cape Town for the first time and seeing Table Mountain soaring into the clouds was a magical experience even for a seasoned traveller like Anatole. 'The fairest cape of them all' was the gateway to the epic stretch of the Dark Continent. There was so much to explore and distance to cover. It was hard to discern but the beating heart of Africa held mysteries that had entranced explorers over the centuries.

Anatole soon fell under its bewitching spell. In a life that had taken him from Russia to England, the United States, China, Australia, South America, Mexico and Europe, this was to be the ultimate travel experience. From the very start of their arrival the pair became aware of glorious African sunsets, panoramic vistas, a red sun against clear night skies and white flocks of birds flying in symmetrical formation.

South Africa was a pot-pourri of colourful scenery and fascinating history of war and confrontation. They filmed in and around the Drakensberg Mountains. Then they moved on to the battlefields of Isandlwana and Rorke's Drift. It was hard to imagine that this area of quiet beauty and silence echoed a history when the landscape had run red with the blood of English soldiers and Zulu warriors. Rorke's Drift had passed into history as a scene of great heroism when on the 22nd and 23rd January 1879 approximately 150 British troops managed to successfully defend the garrison against a massive onslaught by 4000 Zulu warriors. Eleven Victoria Crosses were awarded for gallantry. When they had finished filming Anatole and Andre stood in silent memoriam visualising the events that had taken place nearly fifty years before. What must it have been like with the noise and the fearful slaughter between the two opposing forces? The silence held many secrets.

Their original intention had been to film the wildlife but there was so much more that was of interest that they decided to widen their horizons even more. The scars of the Boer War still hung over the nation. They interviewed two surviving former Boer commandos who told them of their own experiences. It was interesting to hear their perspective on that conflict and it was clear that these tough hardy Boer veterans still harboured much bitterness about that time. In particular they were incensed by the prison camps the British military had introduced to house Boer prisoners and families. The result of which was that thousands of innocent people including children had died from disease in squalid uncomfortable conditions. They spoke too of the rape of women that had taken place in the incident of war. For Anatole and Andre, two war-hardened veterans, it was a harsh reminder that all the victims of huge international military struggles are not necessarily found only on the battlefield but in the villages, the towns and the homesteads. Women in war often paid a very high price for the gung-ho zeal of their political masters eager to establish their own chapter in history at any cost

They filmed at Mafeking and Spelonken, which were steeped in history. In the years that had passed since the siege of Mafeking, time and progress had changed the original visage of the place to the extent that only ghosts of a distance past remained. It would have been the same for any veteran returning to the battlefields of France. The once muddy trenches had become lush green, enriched with vegetation, whereas once cannon fire roared and the spent ammunition cartridges had spilled out from the soldier's rifles, only history books and the survivors of the campaigns remained to tell the story of what had once been.

The whole of Southern Africa was a cinematic goldmine for filmmakers. It had once been a land of great adventure and promise. Vastly untapped mineral resources and the addictive lure of gold had brought about a huge influx of Kopje Wallopers and diggers all eager to unearth discoveries that would make them rich beyond their wildest dreams. A knockabout Jewish east end of London boy, Barney Barnato, once dubbed the Whitechapel Clown proved he was no novice in the Goldfields. He went on to become a millionaire of a vast empire in South Africa before his untimely death at the age of forty-four after falling overboard on a sea voyage from Cape Town to England. His exploits quickly passed into legend.

Anatole and Andre has been so overcome by the abundance of history, commercialism and breathtaking beautiful scenery of South Africa, that they had almost forgotten what they had really come to film. Wildlife. There was so much filming material available they had to continually restock with reels obtained from studios in Cape Town. But oh! – the wildlife could not be missed! It was such a privilege to be able to film close up to the beauties of the African bush. The heartbeat quickened at the sight of the great creatures of Africa, elephants, zebras, hippopotamus, lions, leopards, antelopes, ostriches and white rhino, all strutted the stage of God's own landscape. They were the performers participating in a natural unscripted story of their own world of survival and exploration of their surroundings.

The more they filmed the animals in their natural habitat the more they became aware of the communication that exists between them. Not only that but also the signs of great love indicated by the care and attention that one creature lavished on another. Truly the animal kingdom had its realms, rules, warning signs, while at the same time, its protective instincts and emotions too. Anatole gained some spiritual insight into his wildlife observations. God created the world not solely for the whims of the human beings but to accommodate the great families of beasts in the wilderness.

It became clear to them that while human beings were gifted with speech they did not possess the supernatural capacity to read other's mind. Animals in a herd, however, could somehow convey telepathy to others if they felt threatened or alarmed. A sudden storm, brush fire or the approach of a ravenously hungry predatory creature could signal emergency to a single animal who would generate the warning signs to the rest of the herd, culminating in a frantic stampede to an area of safety. Then as sure as night follows day, the reason for their getaway stampede would emerge into view be it a lion, a fearful electrical storm bringing with it great claps of thunder and torrential rain, or the type of brush fire that would spread murderously ensnaring everything in its path.

Filming lions in a family group was both rewarding and touching. The lioness, truly a beautiful and maternal creature, softened her eager eyes at the sight of her adorable playful cubs. Returning from a hunt with her kill and the food for her family she would grunt and roar to tell her cubs that the evening meal was here.

The affection existing between a family of lions was heart warming, even to non-animal lovers. One of the great privileges of being a wildlife cameraman for Anatole and Andrew was to witness sights such as this. Beneath the trees on the veldt, a proud lioness relaxed with her cubs. This normally fearless and dangerous creature had a look of immense love on her face. Her feelings were reciprocated by the cubs that huddled together with her. Animal love on full display was a touching sight.

Throughout their filming they soon learned how to determine the disparity in ages of Lions. The young lion was easily identifiable by the lack of mane. The older lion had a look of maturity and some romantics would say a sense of wisdom about it like a king dispensing wise advice to its subjects. Yet this was a king of the animal kingdom with a fully-grown mane, a magnificent beast with a flourish and presence that made it a fascinating mesmerising creature to watch. The boys from New York never ceased to marvel at their luck in their choice of career that had given them such opportunities as this. How could anyone not want to thank God for the chance to see all the best of African wildlife.

During a break from filming Anatole and Andre decided to go to Johannesburg to do some cutting and editing on the footage they had so far. They tried hard not to be self-satisfied by their efforts and good fortune in filming wildlife but in truth, they were tremendously thrilled.

For anyone filming animals in their natural habitat, surprises would abound. How could anyone top the sight of the great beasts of the jungle? The answer was simple. Go and film the great beasts of the desert. They were given a pointer in this direction by a German settler from South West

Africa who they met in a hotel bar in Johannesburg. He told them of the untold story and mysteries of the land which one day would be called Namibia.

They had been sitting at a table in the bar pouring over maps working out what the next stage of their journey would be, unaware that a slouch hatted man in a safari suit was listening keenly to their conversation. Anatole spoke of travelling north to Rhodesia while Andre preferred the idea of filming in the Sahara Desert. The two men talked about it in depth and also considered the other different countries in between. Unable to reach a compromise they sipped on their beer for a few minutes. The slouch-hatted man approached them and without being invited, sat down at their table.

"Gentlemen, may I join you for one moment?" he asked. "My name is Joss Von Vuren. I couldn't help but overhear your conversation. You are cameramen filming the great animals of Africa… eh?"

"That's the general idea," Andre replied, a little annoyed at the man's intrusion. "And your line of work, sir?"

"Horses. Trading, training and grooming."

"You've knocked around Africa a bit?" Anatole asked. One of the great joys of travelling was in meeting different people of all professions.

"You could say that," Von Vuren answered. "I didn't mean to be rude, gentlemen, by butting in. I heard you discussing where to film next. There is plenty in Africa to film but do you know South West Africa has many widely unknown beauties to discover?"

"Such as…?" Andre was curious.

"Such as Fish River Canyon, my friend! Dramatic landscape. It would look good on film. Even better when you are there! The Kalahari Desert, the Namib Desert, the dunes of Sossusvei, Sesriem Canyon. You would be amazed to see the animals there and the conditions that they survive under."

"Well, you've convinced me," Anatole said with a smile. "Whether I can convince my colleague here is another thing. Tell me, what is your history, Mr Von Vuren?"

"My history? I came from Germany before the war and I decided to try my luck in South West Africa. I wanted to go somewhere different and unusual. I had worked on the railways but my first love… apart from women of course…is and has always been horses. I went to work for a former officer of the Kaiser and horse lover who owned a 50,000 hectare farm on the edge of Namib."

"Who was this guy? Anybody famous?" Andre was curious as to where this conversation was leading.

"His name was Baron Hans Heinrich Von Wolf. He imported mares and stallions from Germany. Beautiful horses, my friend. Proud animals. They lived and survived in the harshest of weather conditions. The heat on the Namib is intolerable. The scenery may be beautiful but the landscape needed hardy creatures to survive."

"This sounds more and more interesting." Andre leaned forward now.

Von Vuren continued. "In 1908 German colonialists built a railway across the Namibian Desert Believe me, it was a job for coolie labour but the end result was magnificent. However, steam engines that cross the harshest terrain are like those of the animal kingdom and the human being. What do they all need? They need water! Steam engines especially. In a place called Garub, my countrymen dug a well. In order to supply the well, ground water flowed through pipes approximately sixteen feet below the surface. So subsequently Garub eventually became a fully fledged station."

"But what point are you making here?" Anatole asked impatiently, eager to cut a long story short.

"The point I am making here, my American friend, is—"

"Russian-born, but what the hell? Go on!"

"In 1915 when the world war raged that I wanted no part of, the South African armies moved into South West Africa and brought the German rule to an end. Then when the war ended the soldiers of the South Africa forces left the Garub and also, without respect to their very existence, these magnificent horses. But these horses were smart, my friends! Never underestimate the intelligence and capacity of a horse. They never strayed far from the waterhole. When the rare shower falls on the desert of Namibia the green shoots and vegetation seems to spring up overnight providing food and some nourishment for them as well. Now eight years after the end of the war these horses not only survived but now they have descendants. Young foals born into a hostile climate and environment, play like children in the glowing sunlight. Believe me gentlemen it is one of the most touching, emotional and breathtaking sights you will ever see of the survival of these horses. I have seen it many a time but I am still awed by it all and I am not an easy man to impress. I am one of life's great cynics

– a hardened city man, some might say cold – yet the thrill of it brings moisture to my eyes. Film it; record it for the sake of the historical context of the age; take it to your audience."

Andre's eyes were shining with enthusiasm. He had been fired up by the way Joss Von Vuren had spoken. He looked across at Anatole who was smiling back at him. They both knew that South West Africa would be their next destination.

"Well, Nat, I guess there's no argument there. Looks as if we'll be following Mr Von Vuren's advice here. We'll get the reels of film we've made so far sent off to Mr Burnside in London, and he can send the cheques for our work to the bank in Cape Town. We'll head off to the Namib within the next week." Anatole nodded in agreement and then Andre turned to the German horse trader "It's a great idea, Mr Von Vuren. What would you recommend as our starting point? How best may we travel to see these horses and the other destinations you mentioned?"

Joss Von Vuren seemed to swell with pride. "I am glad you see fit to take my advice gentlemen. May I suggest you commence your journey in Windhoek? I have a contact there, a man with a balloon service. He or one of his compatriots will fly you to wherever you choose. Across the dunes and the canyons. To where the horses play."

"This could be one hell of an assignment, Andre." Anatole was enthusiastic.

"Unknown to many cinemagoers I would guess. What do you think?"

Andre replied without hesitation. "Let's go for it."

***

The trip across Namibia to see the miracle horses was to prove that there was always something worth filming even in the remotest of places. Anatole and Andre followed Joss Von Vuren's advice and hired a balloon to take them across this hostile, harsh and very hot environment where it seemed unlikely that any living creature could possibly survive. From the safety of their balloon they filmed canyons, desert and a rugged landscape that seemed to belong to the surface of a yet to be discovered planet. Their aerial shots of this part of Africa would almost certainly thrill the cinema going masses.

The balloon master who knew the territory well and had mapped the landscape to pinpoint precision landed fairly close to a spot that had been designated as a waterhole. Clearly it was a case of patience and waiting for the right moment. The two cinematographers were surprised to be informed of the life that existed in the harshness of the Namib Desert. An amazing little beetle managed to stay alive from an unusual source of moisture. The coastal fog created a condensation that the beetle caught on its wings and then absorbed the water through its mouth. Truly there was magic in nature for every creature was either gifted with a penchant for survival or created its own method of self-sufficiency.

How did an antelope called the Oryx survive in such blistering heat? It was as if a scientist had designed its special brain network of pulsating veins that gave it immunity against the force of nature. Then there were the springbok and the ostriches who raced across the horizon line like dancers on a stage teasing an audience. The question could be asked. Was it survival of the fittest or was it survival of the most gifted with intuition?

After several hours of keeping cool and carefully consuming their supply of water their patience was rewarded in abundance. Through the desert haze intermingled with the great power of the sun and the scenic landscape colours of red-brown, orange and yellow, there came the most enchanting sight any student of the cinematic arts would relish. The rumble of wild horses hooves could be heard and then the magnificence of their very majesty came into view. Beautiful proud horses throwing their heads back as if in joyous laughter at the sheer delight of living where others could not, galloped and played before them like a family on a picnic outing. The cameras began to roll and the horses seemed to participate as if they were re-enacting a scene like skilled performers in an epic film. They were photogenic and graceful to watch.

One by one the horses would go to the water well situated on barren dry land where a hot wind blew and they would quench their thirst. The vegetation was sparse. It was clear that this well, that had remained untouched since the German colonialists had left, was the magnet that existed now as the life force for the miracle horses of the Namib. Young foals followed their mothers to their secret water well like children being shown how to navigate their own way in the world. It was all so beautiful, touching and sentimental that it could create tears in the eyes of the cameramen or looks of great excitement.

When the film was completed the three men boarded the balloon and took off in the direction of Windhoek. Anatole's eyes were shining. This had been a glittering assignment that the produce of which, when shown on screen back home, would surely enthral many armchair travellers. Andre noticed the delight on his colleague's face.

"Never knew that a wilderness could yield such beauty," he said with a smile. "Shall we head for the Congo next, then Kenya?

"Congo?" Anatole thought about it. Then he nodded his head in approval. "I'm loving every minute of this. Yep. Sure. Let's head for the Congo and make Kenya our last stop."

They were both buoyed up by what the next assignment would hold. Beneath the balloon the desert sands glowed iridescently.

Thirty-Six

The boys in New York still talked about their old buddy Nat whenever they met up. However they led such busy lives with the pace of their careers, and the demands of their families, that they didn't meet up as often as they would have liked. Both eager to know if the other had news of Nat they arranged to meet at Carlo Sparizi's coffee lounge. They both knew that a push out panel inside was the secret entrance to Sparizi's Speakeasy. It was immaterial anyway. Some of Sparizi's best customers were policeman and judges.

Jack sat down at a table in the corner of the café he usually occupied, and sipped from a mug of coffee. He was conspicuous in his police uniform even though on the other side of the wall all sorts of illegal activity took place. Whenever he entered Sparizi's coffee house it was an unwritten rule that neither he nor any companion he was with would ever pay for anything. Sparizi paid Jack a certain amount from time to time to buy his silence about the alternative side of his business. Jack knew he shouldn't take the money but hell! Half the cops from his precinct drowned their sorrows in there. He wasn't about to bust up their party and, besides, most of his colleagues were on the take too. The money made him a dishonest cop yet he considered it a perk of someone else's dishonesty.

His deep sense of Catholic guilt hung over him. He felt that he must go to confession sometime and expose his secrets to Father O'Casey. Jack wouldn't do that tonight. Father O'Casey had been spotted by him with a ravishing blonde dressed to the hilt and entering Sparizi's Speakeasy. *Well it takes all sorts!* Besides Jack was past caring. He had, in consultation with his Belfast-born wife Miriam, made a momentous decision which would have far-reaching consequences.

Since returning from the war Jack had risen through the ranks of the New York police force. He had tangled and tussled with hoods, corrupt cops and politicians with dirty vices and open palms for filthy money, well spoken erudite gangsters posing with false respectability and easy charm. Every aspect of low life had crossed his path and now he was yearning for something new. Something peaceful. Somewhere peaceful and that was when his thoughts turned to the land of his birth. Ireland, the emerald isle. He wanted to go home.

Eventually after what seemed ages of carrying out his favourite hobby… sitting on his backside people watching… Slugs entered. My what a smart, rugged tough-looking guy Jake Mahoney had become,. With a smile that displayed pearly white teeth in walked the big guy, the renowned reporter and sports loving man about town. It was as if everyone recognised him. He shook hands with people and acknowledged others with a ready smile.

"Hiya buddie!" he said with delight as he espied Jack in the usual corner. He caught sight of a passing waiter. "Two coffees, friend. Put a dash of rum in mine, will you?"

"It is prohibition, senor," said the Cuban waiter.

"Sure I know that, pal! So what the hell? Tell that to the guys on the other side of the panel."

The waiter smiled. "Rum in your coffee, sir. Of course."

"You never change, do you, Slugs?" Jack grinned. "I'm going to miss you, old friend."

"What do you mean, you're going to miss me, pal? Are you planning on going somewhere soon?"

Jack then gave him the breathtaking news of his pending departure. "It's been a long time since I landed on these shores as a kid with my parents. But we've decided to make a move. That is the family, all of us. We're going home to Ireland."

"Gee! That's floored me! Wow! More than that rocket punch that almost put me out of the fight business back in '04 when you and I had that bout."

"I remember it well. Two New York Irish kids eager to prove themselves a real tough guy, yet the best of friends. Miriam feels about it the same way. We both want to go home to Ireland."

"Ireland? Hell, buddy, most Irishmen are booking steam tickets to America and Australia and building the railways in England. Sure, they all love Ireland as long as they can sing about it in Chicago, Boston or New York. Look at the police force here. It's filled with Murphy's, O'Donnells,

O'Connors, and the construction industry practically relies on big burly Irish bricklayers and hod carriers fresh off the boat from County Cork, Galway, Dublin and Belfast. What about the troubles there too? It's only a few years since the boys in the Black and Tan marched with their Lewis guns through the streets of Dublin." He paused as the waiter returned with the two coffees, one of which distinctly gave out the aroma of rum. Slugs winked at the man and carried on talking. "Why the sudden rush, Jack? I'm your old friend from days when we were kids. You love the city and the people. I know you had a bad time as a kid with your old man being bumped off in a bar room brawl, and your ma going so early but you made good here. A great wife, great kids. The police force gave you an interesting life and a good living. What's the big secret? I know you better than that."

"No wonder you're a top notch reporter, Slugs. You've got a snout like an anteater. Well I'll tell you…" He looked around cautiously as if there may have been a casual eavesdropper lurking in the background. "There's a web of corruption about to break in the police force… and when it blows it's going to be big. I know all the names and I've not been chaste either. The people here pay me to ignore what's going on behind that wall… and I've taken the money."

Slugs pretended to be serious for a moment and tut-tutted like a disapproving school teacher. "So you're a hardworking… corrupt… cop that picks up a tip like a French waiter in a boarding house in Bordeaux." He broke out into a broad grin and let out a laugh. "Welcome to the party, buddy! You think I didn't know that! If they rounded up every cop who took a gratuity and a free drink… cheers" He raised his coffee and rum to his lips… "There'd be no guy policing the precinct. Jack… listen… we go back a long way and good buddies will always be honest with each other. They'll tell the other guy the truth and things they don't want to hear. We're Brooklyn and Bronx. Is this what you really want? To go back to a land of poverty compared to big bucks here, hamburgers and steaks. Prohibition won't last. Then when it's over the hoods… well they'll go legal. It won't be as much fun though. But nobody will notice. We'll be hard at work trying to make an honest buck. What would you do back in Ireland?"

Jack shifted in his chair and leaned across the table. "I'll miss you, Slugs. Y'know, pal, all I see in my life as a cop is the down at heel grimy side of life, the street punk, the hood, the worst side of life. The tears of a victim's family, the corpse of someone who once had blood pumping through his veins and felt emotions like the rest of us, the robber stuffing his pockets with the money of a guy who sweated buckets to make that dough for his family. The fraud, the cheat, the swindler, the domestic argument that went wrong and ended in blood, the bar room brawl… like the one my father got into when I was a kid that left me and my ma struggling, and caused her early death ensuring I grew up in an orphanage. These things hang hard in the memory. I'm in my forties and I want to see the beauty of life. Not the slush. Not the mire. I want clean air and good company. Get my meaning, old pal?"

"The old gang is breaking up, I guess. Nat's over there in Africa making films about wild animals. His sweet kid sister, Mariska, is an English lady living in a manor house in England. What's the destiny for you then? No more police work for you, I guess. You made that pretty clear."

"I just want to be an ordinary Joe, honest Jack. The guy in the crowd you don't notice. Invisible to the masses. But a pillar of strength and wisdom to my wife and kids. The way I figure things these days is that a man's character is not measured by his status or his prestige or the role that he holds in society. A man doesn't have to be a president or a police commissioner or a major player in a corporate structure to be a great man or a role model to his kids. He can work at the most humble profession, a carpenter, dig the roads, or mend the pipes…"

"I know I was a plumber once, Jack, and if the newspaper trade ever ejects old Slugs out onto his butt into the street, I'll be sure as hell fixing sinks, baths and toilets again. I know where I come from. I know my roots. I've got this far and I'm still going to keep moving. The editor of the *Tribune* wants a correspondent to go to London for a couple of years. Guess what? The guys asks me! He says to me, 'Slugs, you've got a big mouth, a big heart, a belly full of confidence, and the butt of a buffalo. How about shifting that butt to London and report back on parliament, business, sport and what's going on in the social quarter and royalty.' So I said to the editor, 'Are you sure you've got the right guy?' He nods his head and says, 'Sure as I'll ever be.' So I'm considering the offer. Imagine it! Me… fancy pants in fancy land. Reckon I'll cut a swell? Like I said I am weighing up my options. It's decision time for me too, old pal."

"My cousin in the south of Ireland has a farm. He said we would be welcome to stay. I could work there a while, maybe get a job on the railways, a port perhaps. My wife says I should try and get a job with the Garda."

"What's that? What's... the Garda?"

Jack smiled. "The Irish police. Before you say anything... I know. But that's different policing. I would be a novelty sure. A true New York Irish cop serving in the Irish police force. No prohibition, no city hell, country life. I guess by going home I would be near my mother, in spirit. I've family there, cousins, an aunt, people who knew my ma. It wouldn't be like being a serving member of the New York police force. I'd be a country cop. We'd both be near our families."

Slugs finished his coffee and appeared to be thinking over what his friend had just said. "When do you go?"

"Two weeks' time."

"That soon!"

"Will you come and see us off at the docks, Slugs?"

His friend normally exuberant, enthusiastic and a laughing happy man suddenly took on the air of a downcast fellow who could feel a huge chapter closing in his life.

"Of course I will, pal, my old pal, my best pal. The kid on the street who sang 'I'll Take you Home Katherine'. You sang it on that street corner back in 1898 I guess. An ode to your mother you were about to lose." The big man with the big voice and the big personality wiped away a tear. "Beneath this facade there lurks a sentimental soul. I'm just as sentimental as the next guy who picks up a puppy dog and loves it, or swells with pride at the sight of his newborn kid. Sure we might have been cocky young kids pretending to be tough kids. It took a war for us to prove how tough we were and we sure as hell went through some rugged times on the battlefields in France and Belgium, eh, Jack?"

"That we did, Slugs. And you know while we are in the mood of sentimental memories, do you know the biggest lesson I learned in life?" Slugs waited for Jack to elaborate. "A tough guy doesn't tell the world he's tough. He wades through life raining off the blows and punches that are inflicted upon him. He never goes purposely looking for a fight. He defends his honour, his principles and his family. A tough guy gets up in the morning, kisses his wife, hugs his children, and goes to work each day walking through the storms of life and the sudden bolt of lightning that strikes, and he pushes the mugs to one side like Moses parting the waves to allow the Israelites to walk through. You and me, pal... and let's not forget our old buddy, Nat, out there in the African bush somewhere... we're cut from the same cloth and we're the great ones, the survivors the ones who emerge from the dark shadows we all have in our past and head for the sunlight of the future. That's all we can do, pal. And you know what? At the end of our days when we get to sum it all up we'll be saying we tried. If a guy doesn't try in life… even if he fails… like the aspiring boxer I once was until you knocked me out after the best fight many had seen in all their days What's the point? A guy's gotta try. Real hard. We sure did, old buddy. We showed them how!"

***

When Slugs returned home that evening he was feeling sad, but he was also seriously considering his career as a newspaper man in New York. The offer of being a correspondent in London held some mouth-watering possibilities. He thought to himself that every so often in a man's life he needs a challenge, to be tested in a new environment and to keep learning.

He took his time going home that night. For some reason he wanted to absorb the atmosphere of his home city. It dawned on him that a person could live in a city all their life and just pass through without ever knowing it or understanding the mixture of people who inhabit it. For all intents and purposes Slugs was a New Yorker through and through. But in truth he was a second-generation American. His Irish ancestry could be traced back as far as his great grandfather who for some now apparently minor misdemeanour of stealing pigs from a neighbours farm was transported to a penal colony in New South Wales where he subsequently died at a relatively young age. Slug's own grandparents left their home in Cork and headed for the new world where their children were born. Jake 'Slugs' Mahoney never took on the pretensions of being an Irishman, for as far as he was concerned he was a true blue New Yorker, almost as if he was the citizen of an independent nation within the United States. This he considered a fair description. After all, anyone he met from the United Kingdom never spoke of themselves as British. They were always Scottish, Irish, English and Welsh. Some Americans liked to assert themselves as a Texan, Californian, New Englander or a Floridian as if they were more proud of their home state rather than their full nationality

New York at night buzzed with life, anticipation, loud voices and a tough, brash manner of people going forward who were not given to sentiment or nostalgia. The city was booming not only in the increase of population and the influx of European migrants, as well as the African-Americans, who sought out work and better living conditions than they had previously been used to. But also in the amount of work that was going on in the city. Construction was booming, skyscrapers were soaring; the most famous of these were the Empire State Building and the Chrysler Building that seemed to be a pointer to the growing wealth and prosperity of the city that would one day be nicknamed the Big Apple.

Slugs smiled to himself. Funny how when a person is about to leave a place they have lived in all their life, some things that were previously taken for granted suddenly seem to take a glow about them.

It was late when Slugs got home. The first thing he did as soon as he entered the house was to check on his two daughters sleeping peacefully. Due to his heavy workload he hardly spent any time with them and he realised they really needed a great deal more attention. He loved being a father. For him family meant everything.

Marilyn was in the kitchen preparing a meal for him and she looked up at him beaming a glorious smile. Their passion for each other remained undimmed.

"My how lucky can a guy get? What a good-looking woman you are," he said with a laugh in his voice.

They greeted each other like lovers who had been apart for months and, instead of the quick husband and wife kiss, they held each other tight indulging in a long, passionate embrace.

"What's that for?" Marilyn asked, as if she didn't know the answer.

"Old Slugs loves ya, babe," he said. Then he sat down and pulled her down onto his lap. "I want to ask you something and if you say no I'll understand."

"Sounds serious," she said, looking concerned.

"How would you like to go travelling, honey? Jack and his family are moving to Ireland in a fortnight's time." Marilyn's eyes widened with surprise. "Yep. That's right. He's going back after all these years."

"Wow!" she exclaimed. "That's a big step."

"The old gang is breaking up. The boys are moving on. The editor has offered me a post in London as correspondent for the *Tribune*. It's not just London but I would be covering what's going on in Europe as well. The assignment is for two years, maybe longer. It includes a house in London where we can bring the kids up. I've thought about it and it would be a chance to expand my career and show you a bit of the world. What say you, Marilyn?"

She looked puzzled at the suggestion and rose from his lap to put the evening meal on the table. They both sat in silence for the moment.

Then Marilyn said, "Our kid will be born an Englishman then?"

Slugs nearly choked on his meal. "A… kid! You mean you're expecting?" Marilyn nodded and smiled proudly. Slugs stood up and moved across to her hug her. "Oh, babe, I'm so proud of you! How could a sassy dame like you ever get hitched to a big moose like me? How lucky can a guy get?"

"Sure let's go to London if that's what you want. What with our folks long gone and no ties, let's go travelling, Jake. London! Wow! I fancy having an English son. I'm sure this one's going to be a boy just like his father!"

"I wouldn't wish that on anyone! A boy. A son of ours. Wow! That would be great. Hell, this is great news. Mind if I open a bottle to celebrate?"

"Not at all. I'll have a small one too."

Slugs was beside himself with happiness. When he was happy he was contagious. He practically danced around the table with joy. When he had poured the drinks he raised his glass to hers in a toast.

"To us, Marilyn."

"No!" Marilyn was a strong woman who could be a match for Slugs in any department, including the bedroom. "To Jack, Miriam and their family. May our decisions to leave this country be the right one for all of us … including the one that's coming."

"I'll drink to that." After he had taken sip he leaned across the table and kissed her. "You know, honey, I reckon we're lucky. Ole Slugs is lucky. To have you and our sweet kids." He stretched his hand across the table and held hers gently. "For most folk when they marry they never know if it's going to work out or not. I love my sport but I'm no great shakes on horse racing. The odds of us are five hundred to one, I reckon, us being the strong no nonsense characters we are, but you know something, I reckon we'll always be okay together. Sure I know some people think I'm Jake Mahoney, the blockhead from the Bronx, who goes through life without a heart but they're wrong. I might have the nickname Slugs from my punch-drunk pugilistic days, but in my heart and soul you and the kids are what I live for. You're my reason for living, you know."

"I know. We've had a good life so far. I like the idea of living in London.

Walks through the parks with the kids, Buckingham Palace, Big Ben, Old Father Thames… isn't that the song the limeys sing? We might even see the king and queen. How about that? My family… the Law family who came over from Scotland a few generations ago. We might be able to trace our ancestry. Go back to the places of our roots."

"That's a possibility." Slugs smiled at the prospect. "The Mahoney's came from Cork. My great grandfather got himself transported to Australia for his sins. I might have family back there in Ireland I might not even know about. And…! And we could look up old Jack if we go across to Ireland from England. We may not have seen the last of the old son of a gun at all!"

"Don't forget Nat either. He might turn up in England too. Didn't you say his sister is married to an English lord some place down the south coast of the green country."

"In the county of Sussex. Some village called Storrington surrounded by green countryside, meadows and Downs so I am told. We've got a lot to look forward to. I'll tell the boss tomorrow. We're going to London!"

Thirty-Seven

Jack Clancy made the most of his last days in New York. He absorbed every sight and sound that made this vast metropolis tick. The changes that had occurred since he was a boy had been remarkable and he felt that as the city had grown so too had he. The city was dynamic with construction, finance and retail igniting the economy. The signs were everywhere. Smart suited office workers rushing to work and meetings. No one seemed to walk at an even pace. *Why does everyone rush in New York?* he asked himself. Eagerness to make money? Or was it eagerness to make something of life and never to waste a valuable day of life?

Once he had been the son of poor Irish emigrants, Sean and Kathleen Clancy, who had come to this country with high hopes and enthusiasm only to find heartbreak, tragedy and early deaths.

Jack could only vaguely remember his first years in Ireland. Sean was wild and handsome but wilful and irresponsible. Highly likeable and fun to be with. He would carry young Jack on his shoulders as he walked the country lanes and beaches of Southern Ireland.

Kathleen was in every sense of the imagination a typical Irish girl, evoking all the qualities that a man would associate with her background. She was warm, demure, trusting, loyal, a good homemaker but like many naïve women she had married the wrong man. Her instincts about Sean had been wrong. Within months of marrying and getting pregnant she found him an inveterate drinker capable of cruelty both physically and mentally. The marriage was difficult and both decided that a huge change by immigrating to America might repair the damage.

Jack was only five years old when the family undertook the long sea voyage to New York. Even now as he stood by the side of the New York docks in late 1927 in his police uniform savouring his last days of the force, the memories came flooding back to him. Right from the beginning

381

of those early days he had held a protective instinct towards his mother often standing in between his parents during Sean's drunken rages. Those terrible memories haunted Jack. He remembered the night Sean stormed out of their apartment in a drunken state and headed for a city bar. Sean didn't return home that night. The police called round the next day to tell Kathleen and Jack that Sean had gone into a bar, dallied with a married woman whose husband had the mother of all brawls with him. During the fight that followed the man had drawn a knife and stabbed Sean to death. The man and his wife disappeared and were never brought to justice.

For Jack and Kathleen their life thereafter was scared by the terror of this incident. His mother's early death propelled him into the orphanage. Tears rolled from the eyes of this hardened cop who stared out at the docks from where he and his family would sail to Ireland very soon. Perhaps his character had emanated from that unhappy childhood. He had channelled his anger and aggression first of all in the boxing ring then into his police career where he had been no stranger to back alley brawls and underhand tactics. His memories haunted him and taunted him it seemed. He had a troubled past.

In the last fortnight of his service with the New York police force he decided to reacquaint himself with places of his past life. In the course of his beat he stood outside the tenement block he had once lived in with his mother. Jack looked up at the crumbling edifice and for a moment he was lost in thought. It was as if the voice of his mother spoke to him from another age.

"We're on our own now, Jack, yourz father's gone. We have to help each other," Kathleen was saying on the day that Sean Clancy had been laid to rest in his early thirties. "Whatever your father did, he didn't deserve to die in such a manner." She broke off from what she was saying and began to cry. "I'm sorry."

Jack who was only seven rushed to his mother's side. She in turn held him tight. They found themselves crying in each other's arms.

"It's alright, Ma. I'm here," he said, emotion trembling in his voice. "We'll be all right. I'll help you."

***

All that had been thirty-four years before. Jack realised how much he had loved his Irish mother. When he thought about her he remembered how hard her life had been and how much she had suffered at the hands of his father. Kathleen had shown grace under pressure and loved her son enormously. Her tragic death from stomach cancer at the age of thirty-four broke his heart and even now at the age of forty-one if he thought too deeply about her difficult, tragic life his eyes were capable of welling up with tears.

In a strange way he thought that by moving his family back to Ireland he would become closer to her again in spirit at least. He wondered what it was in his subconscious that had prompted this pending move. There were a number of reasons. The first was that over the years he had come to realise he really didn't like himself that much. His career in the police force had hardened his character and on the street in his line of duty the job had brought out the aggressive side of his nature. One of his greatest fears was that he would turn into a replica of his violent father. He wanted to suppress this side of his character and be more like his mother.

***

The only way Jack felt he could achieve this was by completely changing his environment, his career and lifestyle.

He had other concerns too. City life and the pressure of his job was taking its toll on his health and family life. The more he thought about it, he felt absolutely certain that he was doing the right thing.

During those last days in the police force he took a walk around the Irish, Jewish and Italian quarters. He was an old, streetwise cop who knew every street, alleyway and block on the precinct. People knew and trusted him. He was, after all, one of their own. In the course of his work he had consoled a victim's family, and on the other side of the coin when a family member had been arrested he would see that the wife and children, or parents, of the offender, were helped should they need assistance. It was a rocky road that he travelled, straddling both sides of the law. The one black mark on his career was the curse of the speakeasy. The temptation of easy money and free service was one that he had succumbed to. There had been times that when he had been threatened by a vicious thug in a back alley, or on a scrap of wasteland, he had proven himself to be a match in brutal retaliation. This was a side of his character he wanted to be rid of. In Ireland he was determined that he would be a new man – a peaceful, private man.

The word had got around the streets that he was going. Old friends would stop to shake hands and wish him well. People of all backgrounds who he had helped including a criminal's family acknowledged him. In one sense, the Irishness in him gave way to a sense of regret of leaving the streets of familiarity but in another the thrill of moving away from the world of crime to one of a more peaceful nature spurred him on.

On his last day in the New York police force he went around headquarters farewelling many colleagues he had worked with before and after the war. When he entered a busy office or the recreation room where some officers were playing snooker, there would be sudden quiet before tumultuous applause and a cascade of good wishes. Then in the early evening as he walked out of the building as an ordinary civilian, he joined the cities commuting masses shed of the responsibility of law enforcement. For the first time in years including his army service he no longer wore a uniform. In his own words he was an 'ordinary Joe'. Just a face in the crowd, invisible to the population, a fleeting figure, a face that flashed past those waiting for buses and trams. Someone nobody knew or cared about. He was Jack Clancy, ordinary guy, husband and father. It was a strange feeling walking through the crowds as an ordinary civilian. In one sense he was free of a difficult past and in another he was in limbo, going from one chapter of life to the next. For the first time since he had made the decision to leave, doubt entered his mind. He began to wonder if he was doing right by his wife and children. Was he being selfish or just behaving rashly? Only time would tell now. Miriam had been initially enthusiastic. Would she have her own doubts now? It was all such a terrible gamble that might not work.

Jack entered their small house a while later. It had all the appearance of a family in transit. It was no longer warm and welcoming. All of their belongings had been packed in boxes and cases ready to be taken down to the docks the next day. Miriam sat at a table with their seven-year-old son, Jasper, and six-year-old daughter, Annabella. His eyes lit up at the sight of them. They were his *raison d'être* for living.

Miriam and Jack came from different parts of Ireland. While Jack had come from County Wexford in the Republic of Ireland, Miriam had arrived from Belfast in the province of Ulster, which still remained in the

United Kingdom. Their accents were considerably different in the way that a Yorkshire man's was from a Londoner, or a Texan's from a Bostonian. They had met at a welcome home party for servicemen shortly after the end of hostilities when she had been a nurse for the Red Cross. Miriam was dark-haired, curvy and spoke with a slightly husky voice that echoed sensuous tones and which had grown men on their knees. Jack was to say in many a conversation that when he heard Miriam speak behind him he fell instantly in love with the voice, and when he turned around he was bedazzled by the face of the owner.

Ireland's war of independence had been a particularly bloody campaign, with the IRA inflicting much damage to the opposing British forces. The result of the war gave Ireland independent rule, except for Ulster, where the situation remained unstable for generations to come. It wasn't until the advent of Tony Blair's Labour government in 1997 that significant proceedings took place resulting in the Good Friday peace agreement.

Miriam had one older brother who had decided not to go to America when the whole family had emigrated and he in turn, to escape the Irish troubles, had taken himself to Wales. He had settled near Whitebrook in Monmouthshire where he ran a grocery business by day and also became the popular landlord of a thatched roof pub called the Barley Mow. If all went well, Miriam hoped to catch up with her brother whom she had not seen since she had arrived in New York aged eight with her late mother and in 1900.

"How was your last day on the force?" she asked, rising from her chair to kiss him. The children stood up and Jack acknowledged them both. He tousled his son's hair and kissed his daughter on the cheek.

"Kinda sad," he replied sitting down. The children went into another room to play with hoops. He was glad because he wanted to have a private talk with his wife. "Am I doing the right thing by you and the kids?"

Miriam poured Jack a cup of coffee. "I'd be lying if I said I didn't have my doubts," she admitted. "But I know there comes a time in everyone's life when a change might be the right thing. Do you know, Jack, I was thinking hard today about life in general. Harder than I've ever thought. Like you, as a kid, I came here with my parents. I've lived here all my life really apart from that time in Ireland and when I was a nurse in France during the war. This city is full of migrants: Italians, Greeks, Polish, Russian, Irish, Scots, Limeys and French. Every nationality you can lay your mind too. And you know what? All my life in New York I've always felt like a long-term visitor, as if I'm looking in from the outside – a migrant kid although I'm thirty-five now, and I received an education here, trained as a nurse, married and our children are born Americans. After all these years I still have that sense of belonging elsewhere. Maybe it's because I still have blood relations in Belfast and an aunt and uncle in Donegal not to mention my only brother who didn't come with the family to America back in 1900 when he was eighteen. He crossed the water to Wales, to Monmouthshire where he still lives. I've got a brother and I don't even know him. He's done pretty well too, runs two businesses: a grocers shop and a pub. Can you believe after twenty-seven years here I still feel a stranger? People hear my accent and still ask if I'm newly arrived. Some people say you can never go back to your roots. Well, I disagree. Maybe that's why I think this is a good move. I'll support you all the way Jack come hell and high water. Life is about taking chances and doing things."

Jack smiled at her. Any self doubt he had evaporated in the space of an instant. Instead of being filled with apprehension he was now bubbling with enthusiasm.

***

At the docks Slugs and his family came as he promised to say goodbye to his old friend. The ship would shortly sail to Dublin, Belfast and then Liverpool in the North of England. On board were many returning Irish families and Americans going to the old country of their ancestors. It was only a little over a week across the sea to Ireland but it was really a lifetime away.

The wind blue and there was a chill in the air. The eyes of the Mahoney and Clancy families were wet with tears. It was an emotional morning for all of them. They hugged, kissed and embraced. Then Jack shook hands with Slugs. In the next instant, Jack and Miriam, together with their children, were walking up the gangplank to board the ship. Jack would never return to America again. That part of his life was over. Soon after the ship sailed out of New York, accompanied by the strains of music played by a military band on the dockside. The tune they played was 'I'll Take You Home Kathleen'. Slugs waved his hat to the Clancy family and then held it to his chest. On board the ship Jack did exactly the same. He remembered how glad he was to see New York harbour when he had come home after the turmoil of the Great War. Now he had seen it for the last time.

***

Just a few weeks later Slugs and his family sailed for Southampton in southern England, where they would take the train to London. It wasn't a final farewell for Slugs. This was the opening chapter of a new career as an international correspondent; one that would bring him great prestige and distinction as truly a man of the people able to talk to prime ministers and factory workers alike. Over the next twenty years, Slugs would return to America from time to time but for him and his family this would be a permanent move to Europe.

***

Returning home to Ireland was an emotional experience for Jack and Miriam. The voyage across the Atlantic Ocean had been a pleasant time for them meeting and making new friends amongst the passengers, and participating in shipboard activities.

Ten days after leaving New York the first sight of their home country came into view. Shrouded in mist a grey coastline was just barely visible. It didn't matter that they had to strain to see it. This was home, the country both had left in the previous century. Some of the passengers swore that they could scent heather in the air. A couple of early morning fishermen in a small boat waved to them from a rocky cove. Even though it was a cold grey morning for some reason Jack and Miriam felt a great sense of warmth as the ship sailed around the Irish coastline. Ireland had always seemed to each of them like a mythical green land in the mists of time like a dream they had in a fitful nights sleep. Now it was there before them, composite and solid. Beyond the coastline lay their roots of ancestry. Their children looked out anxiously at the shore. For them America was all they had ever known in their short lives, and this was something totally new to them. This was their first experience of travel.

The circumference of the coastline took them to Dun Laoghaire where they disembarked for Dublin. Jack had been there as a child but they were faded, blurred memories. The city he and his family saw now was one of a strange beauty steeped in a tragic past. The time of the 'troubles' as it was so often referred to was never far from conversation, but the people quietly got on with their lives and for much part were polite and charming especially to the Clancy clan who were greeted more as Irish-Americans than returning citizens.

They stayed in a small hotel by the river Liffie. From there they did a walking tour around Dublin. They looked at the gracious old buildings such as Four Courts, the great university and the post office where Irish rebels had been in an infamous siege with the British Army. This was a city that evoked the influential names of the past: Eamonn De Valera, Michael Collins, Parnell and Oscar Wilde. Yet it did not rest on its laurels. O'Connel Street was filled with businessmen all rushing to work to contribute to the commerce of this country, which was largely seen as an agricultural economy. In Phoenix Park, on the only sunny day in the grey misty week they spent in Dublin, the family had a picnic. Nearby on a park bench a couple of rotund priests were heard to discuss in heated conversation the merits of the sports of Gaelic football and hurling. An old lady in a shawl fed the birds and muttered to them as if they were friends she regularly met up with.

From Dublin they travelled north to Belfast to meet Miriam's relatives. To her absolute delight, apart from cousins, aunts and uncles, her ninety-three-year-old grandfather was still alive. He had outlived her own parents and, although sad at their relatively early deaths, he was beside himself with the joy of meeting his American-raised granddaughter. Tears of joy filled his eyes as he met Miriam, for in his own words, she was the spitting image of her mother, his own late beloved daughter. The whole family had a wonderful get together with much singing, dancing, joke-telling, reminiscences, laughter and smiles all around. Jack felt instantly at home with his in-law family. The children loved their relatives who made them feel loved and wanted.

Miriam had an aunt and uncle in Donegal that they went to meet. The Clancy family stayed with them at an old white stone thatched roof cottage by the sea. The house was humble like its owners and sparsely furnished yet this too was a place of warmth, laughter and compassion. It was only a short way from the rocky coast and they spent many happy hours exploring the coves and inlets. Sometimes they would walk the long sandy beaches and run quickly when huge foamy waves came crashing in suddenly.

The newness of it all and the rural scenes made Jack feel as if he had returned to a different country from the one of his past but he loved it. The final thrill for him was to travel down south and take up residence in County Wexford.

They arrived late one afternoon at the farm owned by Jack's cousin. The motorbus dropped them at a stop a hundred yards or so from the farm and they walked the remaining distance to the house passing golden fields and lush meadow.

At the farmhouse there was no one about. They stood outside looking at it. Jack Clancy was not a man given to sentiment, at least not in public; however his steely resolve began to break and in his mind he visualised his mother, Kathleen, in this very area when she was a young eligible woman and he knew that he too had once trod the very soil that lay before him. He had left here a boy who knew nothing of the world, and had now returned as a man with the wisdom of Solomon. He once again in his imagination heard the words of his mother.

"Ireland. I often think about it. The green countryside and the farms." Jack could feel his emotions rising as he remembered what she had said. "There were lovely empty beaches I used to walk when I was a girl. I used to love listening to the roll of the waves and the sea crashing down on the beach. The fishermen were always out early. I was happy then. Happy there in my home village with my mother and father, sisters and brothers. The fields were deep green. It's not called the Emerald Isle for nothing, you know. Oh… and I just loved the country lanes, seeing the people at their doorways and smiling as I walked past."

The door of the farmhouse opened slowly. Jack looked anxiously waiting. Then a man in a flat cap, with a pipe in one hand and a pint of dark beer in the other, emerged from within. He stood peacefully contemplating the world.

"That's him," said Jack to Miriam in a voice barely above a whisper. "That's my cousin Padraic."

From behind another man came into view. He also held a pint mug, occasionally taking a sip and indulging in good humour with Padraic. Miriam could hardly believe her eyes. She broke out into a smile.

"My God! It's my brother, Seamus! How did he know we were coming? I didn't write to him."

Jack kissed her on the cheek quickly. "I cabled him from Dublin. He must have caught the first boat over from Wales."

The two men at the farm suddenly realised who the visitors were. Padraic turned back to the door and called out to the occupants inside. The wives of both men came into view. Then a white-haired old lady with a stooped man holding a stick also came out.

"Oh I don't believe it!" Jack gasped quietly. "It's my Aunt Rosie and Uncle Rory." Before he had finished his sentence another white-haired couple came out of the house. "Oh… my it's my mother's elder sister, Aunt Fionnulla, and her husband, Uncle Dan."

The emotion for Jack was too much. He found himself in the position of smiling through his tears of joy. Both families moved forward to hug, embrace and welcome the Clancy's home from New York. It was a joyous reunion that Jack had never known before in his life. The thrill of seeing his blood relatives again was overwhelming.

Inside the farmhouse trinkets and photographs adorned oak-beamed shelves. Amongst them were pictures of Kathleen and Sean on their wedding day which he had never seen before. The house was humble and snug. In fact Jack began to think that everything about his background was humble. It was a mirror reflection of his own late mother and he liked that feeling of being back in the fold.

All of his relatives who had gathered there that day were beside themselves with joy at the long lost son returning home from America. He was to all concerned the orphaned son of Kathleen and Sean who had been a longshoreman, boxer, soldier and policeman on the toughest streets of New York. He had quite a story to tell and all of his family members listened to his story with fascination. They too had stores to tell of the events that had happened in Ireland while he had been away. Their party went on all night. Again, as with other reunions, there was laughter, some tears but not too many, much story telling with humorous embellishment, plenty of blarney and some emotion. To his Irish relatives Jack was a charismatic legendary figure, larger than life personality but the truth of it was that for most of his life he had felt like an exile. From some long forgotten writer his pen had inscribed the words 'you can never go home again' perhaps meaning that the past is a different country of places and faces that have all moved on and changed beyond recognition to which, when the prodigal son returns, he finds he is a stranger amongst once familiar things. Not so with Jack. He may have had faded, blurred memories of his early childhood here but he felt at home in the warm bosom of the family. That night as he sat with his relatives he looked at their warm craggy faces and bright smiles. In his heart he knew he had made the right decision. Jack Clancy had come home.

The next morning Jack rose early. He and his cousin Padraic took a walk to a nearby beach. The waves crashed down on pristine sand, a wind with a hint of ice blew and seagulls squawked above. Out on the very choppy waters Jack saw a sight he had not seen since childhood. There were lobster potters bravely battling the elements. It was all so peaceful though and Jack and Padraic found a suitable spot to sit down for a while. He tried to imagine Kathleen and Sean courting in this place well over forty years before.

Padraic understood Jack's long silences as he gazed at everything before him. Jack was wondering where all the years had gone. The reality of being here again in this lush green but often troubled land still seemed like a dream he was yet to wake up from.

"A great pity my mother never made it back with me after…" Jack broke off still unable or unwilling to talk about his father's demise. "My mother always spoke of this place as if it were a heaven of some kind. My God it's good to be home!"

"Ireland may be a heaven to you right now and I wouldn't disagree on that score but living here is not easy. Good jobs are scarce to find, employment is hard. Pay is low if you are lucky enough to have a job. Have you got any plans, Jack? You can work with me on the farm for a while if you want to."

"I appreciate that, Paddy. The first thing I must do is get the children to school. Then when our belongings arrive from the docks we must move to a place of our own. I sold my house in New York so we're fine there." He changed the subject. "I can't believe I'm really here! All those years in America, away from everyone. Then last night after nearly forty years, I am sitting amongst aunts and uncles, cousins, nephews and nieces. I'm looking at this beach where I played as a child. It's where my mother and father walked once. You know what happened to my father, I guess?"

Paddy looked serious. "Yes we know about Sean. His family were bereft. I know you had a hard time after Kathleen died, and you were in the orphanage. We didn't want to bring the subject up. Besides, hopefully now that you're home with the family these will be better times for you."

"I hope so too," Jack said quietly. "You know this is a beautiful place but

I can't sit here all day. There's a life to be led. Would you be able to run me into town so I can get my bearings and look for work?"

"It'll be my pleasure, Jack." A thought crossed his mind. "There's a pub in town called the Limerick Castle. They're looking for a new landlord. You wouldn't fancy the job, would you?"

"Now there's a thought." Jack smiled at the prospect. "After prohibition in America I'd become a pub Landlord in Ireland! How about you show me the place and I'll give it some thought?"

***

Later that day Padraic and Jack rode into town in a small horse-drawn carriage. They passed through some beautiful countryside of meadows and fields, full of sheep and cows. Workers in the field would wave their caps and politely acknowledge them. The sun came out soaking everything in splendid light enhancing the green and the blossoms. Jack smiled to himself. He was loving every minute of being home. How could he have been away from this lovely land for so long? All the years of pounding the beat of the great metropolis of New York seemed now to belong to another age.

The town of Dromana was something out of a child's picture book. It was comprised of olde worlde buildings, cobbled streets, a picturesque church and right slap bang in the centre of the town stood the public house. The Limerick Castle was obviously the focal point where the local populous got together to enjoy gossip, singing, frivolity and glasses of the darkest beer with a rich, creamy foam on top.

"Come on," urged Padraic. "I'll introduce you to the landlord, Tommy Mulligan. He's a great character and fine fellow."

The two men entered this fine looking establishment. Outside the main street of the town was to all intents hardly busy. A few horse-drawn vehicles passed by which would not have been out of place in the wild west of the 1880s. A bull-nosed Morris shook and shuddered down the street. People seemed to be standing around talking in shop doorways. Truly the pace of life here was so slow that in contrast to the rush and chaos of New York's busy routine, it was as if the world had stood still here and remained in a timeless zone.

Inside the Limerick Castle it was full of oak beams and trinkets. There were pictures of sportsmen on the wall together with a large portrait of Eamonn de Valera situated above the fireplace. The various drinkers situated around the main saloon looked up as Padraic entered with a stranger in their midst. The regulars, who knew everyone by name, looked curiously at Jack who acknowledged them with a smile. Who was this well built stranger? Tommy Mulligan, the Landlord, emerged from behind the bar. He was a thick set man with a ruddy face and broad smile. He looked every inch the Rugby player he had been in a former life before he had become a pub Landlord.

"Padraic, my fine friend!" he boomed. "And who is this gentleman?"

"Jack Clancy is the name." Jack was quick to introduce himself to Tommy and shook his hand with a vice like grip. At the mention of the name Clancy several of the drinkers in the bar turned their heads to look at him.

"Jack's my cousin home from America," Padraic proudly announced.

"So you would be Kathleen and Sean's boy?" Tommy exclaimed. "By the saints! I knew your parents well when we were wee children. Welcome home, Jack!"

At this point various customers stood up and came across to meet him. Some had known the Clancy family from way back and there were warm handshakes and smiles all around. Jack didn't know any of them but in a strange way it was as if he had known them all of his life. They gathered round to hear his story and to tell them a few of their own.

Jack went to work with Tommy Mulligan the next day. Tommy was a good employer who trained Jack in all the fundamentals of managing a public house. It wasn't a career move that Jack had even remotely considered but with the scarcity of good employment in Ireland and with a family to look after it was a responsibility he embraced with open arms. Tommy was soon to leave the pub to take up a job with the brewery and he wanted to know that the Limerick Castle was in good hands. Jack found this job to be everything he needed.

Unlike his previous job as a New York policeman, he never felt threatened or under pressure from external and internal forces. He became the new Landlord and settled right in as if he had been doing the job all of his life. His children started at a local school while his wife Miriam found work as a nurse. They bought a small cottage nearby which became a peaceful family home. The garden was filled literally with roses and all manner of flowers and a vegetable patch. At night when they lay in their beds they could hear the sound of the sea and the waves rolling onto the nearby beaches. It was all so different to the life they had known across the water.

To walk again in the footsteps of his ancestors and to still have relatives close by gave him a feeling of security. Jack felt no nostalgia for his New York days. Much of it seemed from a distance to be a rough and tumble existence from which the Clancy family had extricated itself. He occasionally read the national papers and thumbed through for articles about what was going on in America. It was more out of curiosity than any feeing of yearning for the land which had been his home for so long.

He looked around the countryside and the people. Everything felt right. Ireland may have been a troubled country that had been through a turbulent period during the War of Independence and the Irish Civil War of 1922–1923 but there were no signs of conflict evident there. It was the sort of place Jack felt that he would be happy to grow old in. He pictured himself as an old man in a rocking chair looking out towards the ocean with a pint of Guinness occasionally taking a sip and contemplating the sum total of his life. The orphan kid had come home.

Thirty-Eight

Slugs and his family happily took in the sights of London. Apart from his army service in war torn Europe he had never been to England before and as with every new experience in his life he tackled things head on. There was never a day in his life that he didn't appreciate how a chance meeting with the editor of the Tribune had transformed his life taking him from being an every day plumber to a man of the people journalist.

London held many fascinations for Slugs. He was a big American in every sense of the word big. Not a man who was easily impressed, he found endless inspiration in the never ending attractions and activities of the greatest city in the world. He took his family around the Museum of the Natural History, Science, and the Victoria and Albert, constantly marvelling at the exhibits on display. His family took picnics in Hyde Park, St James and Kensington Gardens where they were photographed by the statue of J. M. Barrie's greatest creation, *Peter Pan*. There was never a free moment that the Mahoney family did not utilise whether it was a visit to Buckingham Palace or the British Museum.

The *Tribune* had arranged accommodation for them at a house the newspaper owned in Ealing Green. It had the feel of an English village set amongst the London suburbs. The house was a warm cosy Victorian semi detached building with the greenest of lawns and a multi-coloured flowerbed. Their children went to St John's Primary in West Ealing while Marilyn found a job as a secretary with the local newspaper, the Middlesex County Times. The family would often go across the road from Ealing Green to Walpole Park, which became a peaceful haven for them all.

At his office in Fleet Street, Slugs, as the representative for the *Tribune* in London, always had a colossal workload to contend with. His editor in New York required daily despatches. Slugs couldn't wait for news to happen. He knew early on in his career that a good journalist can devise a story by asking questions of public figures and turning their replies into fully blown articles. Subsequently he interviewed Lloyd George, Ramsay MacDonald and Stanley Baldwin. He found these three leading political figures impressive but not messianic in the way that American presidents were. The thing that puzzled him the most was that the reward for an elected President of the United States was a tenure of residence in the grandeur of the White House. For his efforts in winning an election the British Prime Minister got to live in a back street terrace at No. 10 Downing Street, which looked and felt draughty, damp, and in urgent need of redecoration. Hardly a piece of prime real estate for a national leader. More like a downgrade to a lesser residence!

Slugs liked the English. He liked their honesty, good manners, sense of humour and their 'mustn't grumble' attitude, even when they were caught without umbrellas in a sudden downpour of rain. His assignments took him into the business houses of the City of London and to the manufacturing industries of the Midlands and the North of England. Another thing he loved about the British way of life was their immense enjoyment of sport. There was something for everybody. The thrill of the great game of soccer in misty stadiums with a full capacity of spectators cheering for their home teams, Rugby League and Union football where well built players attempted to outflank and outwit the opposing side running, dodging and weaving with great energy. Slugs who had once been an aspiring boxer was amazed at the strength of the British pugilists who could more than hold their own in round after round of often punishing blows. He was to learn that many British boxers came from the tough backgrounds of the East End of London and the Welsh coal mining communities. There was much to admire about the British in business, sport, commerce, law and even in the simplicity of the lives of the salt of the earth artisans who went about their lives looking after their families, and often working long hours for pittance wages.

There were many sunny days to come on Ealing Green for Slugs and his family. Life was opening up new dimensions for all of them. He finally found the time to get in touch with the Shervingtons of Storrington, who suggested he might like to see Anatole's girlfriend, Trevilla, in her show *The Prince and the Gypsy Girl*.

At Drury Lane, Slugs and his family met up with Mariska and Bernard. It was a happy reunion for all concerned. Although Bernard had met him in France during the war, Mariska had not seen Slugs for nearly twenty-five years since the days of their New York childhood. She was thrilled to meet the big guy and his brash sexy wife, Marilyn, who she adored. Before the show the four of them went out to dinner at a nearby restaurant oozing class, good service and a menu of meals that offered satisfaction. It was also downright expensive.

"So Mr Mahoney, how are you finding living in London?" asked Bernard, genuinely interested.

"Well sir, I have to say it's one hell of a city. Marilyn and I are proud that our next baby is going to be born right here in London town."

Mariska basked in their happiness. "How wonderful for you both! Congratulations! You're as American as Mount Rushmore, and you're going to have an English… well whatever… boy perhaps."

"After our two beautiful girls I feel sure this one's going to be a boy," Marilyn said with a laugh in her voice.

"We think it's great," Slugs affirmed. "You know I had a few ideas about what we were coming to in England. I have to say it's like trying to predict the score in the ballgame. You just never know what the other side has to offer. And I've been mightily impressed by this country. This is a gutsy hardworking polite place where the ordinary guy, whether he's swabbing the pavements or delegating behind a desk, gets on with it. Mustn't grumble, they say! Why the hell not? They work hard enough for dough they have to stretch to breaking limit like an elastic band in a pair of bloomers! But hell baby, I don't see a revolution coming. I don't see no fighting in the streets… except after a good night in a pub. The people live to work and they smile. Even the poor people smile. Ole Slugs knows how to work hard but as sure as hell Ole Slugs knows how to have a good time too. That's why I like this place. We both just love the big museums… eh, Marilyn?"

"I just love the Victoria and Albert Museum. Wow what a piece of history! Those costumes and paintings give you a real feel for times gone by in British life. Our daughters are amazed at the prehistoric skeletons in the Natural History Museum. We love the parks too. Oh the London parks! They're just gorgeous. Hyde Park, Kew Gardens, Hampton Court. Even where we live in Ealing Green there's beautiful Walpole Park close by. There's so much to see in London, I think we could live here all our lives and never get to see everything."

The restaurant was busy that afternoon with pre-theatre goers. It was run by an Italian who had established himself as one of the leading figures in London's cafe society. Albert Santini had come from Naples at the turn of the century and was now something of a much celebrated maître-di.

"There's something captivating about London," continued Marilyn. "I thought New York had it all, and more, but here it's like we're always walking in the footsteps of history, Slugs has interviewed no end of people here. The prime minister too."

Slugs was enjoying every moment of his life. He looked happy and felt at home with the Shervingtons.

"Looking at you now, Mariska, I can hardly believe you were the same kid back in the Bronx. So long ago now. Before I got to know you, Nat and Jack as friends, I used to see your family together some days. I was just the kid that passed you by in the street. I remember when I was delivering papers before school I'd see your pa going off to work at the crack of dawn and coming home on the late bus. Sometimes I'd see you all together. Your mother was a sweet kind a lady. And here you are now a real lady married to an English Lord. If we'd all been horses at the starting gates no one would have ever predicted how we would have ended up on the last lap of the race."

"You've done pretty well yourself, Slugs," Mariska reminded him. "Once a plumber, now an international journalist. Not bad for a hot-headed kid who got the nickname Slugs because he was known in the neighbourhood as a slugger."

"That was me in another life," he said with a smile nostalgic at the memory. "I had the mentality of a moose back then. I thought that in life like our parents, you just got by each week. You looked forward to Saturday night for a drink and a dance. Then you got back to the office and that was it. I thought I'd try and make money in the ring only to get done in by better, more eager, more capable fighters, who were mean and tough, and took no prisoners. They delivered knock out punches that sometimes did considerable damage to their opponents, and often put them permanently out of the fight game. Well when I got out of plumbing and into the newspaper business I thought to myself that the key to life is not only enjoyment of life, but employment of life. It's doing the most you can with whatever cards, good or bad, life deals you. Life's about learning. Ole Slugs is always learning. Meeting all kinds of people. Reporting about different industries. I've seen the tough conditions the miners work in. The steel workers sweltering away in hot as hell workplaces, the sparks flying round like comets in the solar system, the ship builders on the Clyde, the market traders in Covent Garden, the butchers at the Smithfield meat market, the flower sellers outside the main train stations – I've learned from them all. I've met the main political leaders, sat in Downing Street interviewing the prime minister. What a place for a national leader! Gee, I've seen better real estate in the Bronx! I've been to stately homes and seen the slums. I tell you this, friends, life is a continuous learning experience and I mean to see it all and, as a journalist on the *Tribune*, report back as I see it to the readers in the States."

Bernard and Mariska were impressed by Slugs. He had a way with words and always put his thoughts across in a straight and direct way. He had been an unlikely candidate to be a journalist of renown alongside other famous writers who had been university educated. It was precisely his ordinary guy image and the fact, unlike other esteemed journalists of the public school background, he never thought of himself as a cut above anyone. He was always everybody's pal and their equal whatever their status.

A trio of musicians suddenly struck up a tune and wandered around the tables playing any requests the customers had. It added something to the atmosphere of this prestigious restaurant. In the far corner the owner, Albert Santini, nodded his approval to the head waiter. Business had been good that day.

They moved on to Drury Lane shortly after. Mariska and Bernard had seen The Prince and the Gypsy Girl on it's opening night. Months on, and it was still playing to packed houses. So successful had it been that Arthur Burnside had negotiated with an American impresario to take the show across the water for a run on Broadway. The J. C. Williamson Theatre Group in Australia had also expressed an interest in the show being staged out there. For its unexpected star, Trevilla, it would take her to far away places she could never, ever, have imagined herself in.

Slugs and Marilyn, who were seeing their first West End show, enjoyed it immensely. Trevilla's performances got better and better as time moved on. She had grown into the role and was mesmeric every time. There were some performers who worked hard to become a star while others simply had the attributes and charisma that marked them out as natural recipients of stardom. Trevilla had become an unexpected star. All of her latent energy and passion she channelled into her nightly performances. Combined with her blatant sex appeal, which hitherto she had herself underestimated, she sparkled and crackled on stage. It was as if a light surrounded her when she danced across the stage or sang a solo with real expression and emotion. That indefinable quality of being a star had transformed her from being an agricultural labourer to a true West End performer, who had newspaper reporters scrambling to write her rags to riches life story. It was truly the stuff that dreams were made of.

Hollywood stars such as Douglas Fairbanks, Mary Pickford and Charlie Chaplin, on their visits to London, had seen the show. The king and queen had also seen the show and gone backstage to meet the cast. Although exactly what this serious royal couple actually thought of the show was never known. Their visit to see the performers had been more of a courtesy call rather than royal protocol.

The Shervingtons, together with Slugs and his wife, went to see Trevilla in her dressing room. Arthur Burnside was also there too, revelling in the success of his protégé. While the occasion was a happy reunion, Trevilla seemed strangely quiet despite smiling constantly. Mariska seemed to sense this and she approached her.

"How is my family?" Trevilla asked gently.

"They are fine. Missing you, of course."

"And the horses?" Trevilla was referring to the two trusty horses that had pulled the family caravan since the earliest days of her childhood. Despite the change in her fortunes and lifestyle there was much about her old life that she missed.

Mariska smiled. She knew how much Trevilla loved the horses. "They are fine. Enjoying their retirement in a lovely big field with a warm stable, a farrier and loving care from their owners… your family and our staff."

"That is good to know." She looked around the dressing room as the others chatted happily amongst themselves. "I will come down soon before the show goes to America. I can't believe I am going on tour there."

From behind them Arthur joined in the conversation. "When the show finishes its run here in a month's time, it's New York bound."

"A month's time?" Trevilla was astounded. "That soon?"

"That's right," Arthur was beaming with delight, totally oblivious to the fact his normally confident protégé was unusually nervous. "Furthermore, I had lunch with a Hollywood producer this week. He thinks that *The*

Prince and the Gypsy Girl could transfer to the big screen. In the absence of sound they can produce it as a drama using the original cast. The world is really opening up for you Trevilla. A lot has happened since Nat and Andre discovered you on the South Downs." While Trevilla was absorbing the breathtaking news, Arthur turned to Mariska quickly. "That reminds me, Lady Shervington, I received several reels of film from Nat and Andre last week of their adventurous exploits in darkest Africa… except that it's not so dark. It looks sunny and bright. My team ran it in our projection rooms and the films are great. The scenes of wildlife and tropical jungle will have our audiences craving for more. I only wish we could film it in colour and have sound. That will come in time, I'm sure."

"Where are they now?" Mariska was always fascinated by the different chapters in her brother's life.

"The Congo, I believe. Then they will move on to Kenya before coming home."

"Coming home!" Trevilla perked up with excitement.

"Yes. That's right."

Trevilla threw back her head and laughed. "I will ask Anatole to marry me when he returns! I won't wait for him to propose to me! He will be tired and ready for home life after his long journey. What do you think about that, Mariska?"

"You'll have to ask him, Trevilla. If he's happy then I'm happy."

Arthur had a twinkle of amusement in his eyes. "All sounds very good, young lady, and I wish you well if that's what you want but they won't be back for a few months and the show will be off to America. If the Hollywood deal goes through for the film we'll all be heading off to sunny California. Then the J. C. Williamson Theatre Group in Australia want to stage the show out there. It's going to be a very busy time for you my dear. We could be away for over a year." He looked at her with a hint of sympathy. "I understand that heady flush of love. I shouldn't get carried away just yet. You might find yourself choosing between a career and marriage."

"I once had to make that choice," pointed out Mariska. "I had enjoyed a great career that had taken me across the United States, Europe and South America. Yours is just beginning."

At this point the conversation was saved from becoming too deeply serious when Slugs and Marilyn came across to introduce themselves to

Trevilla. Their colourful and entertaining personalities entranced Trevilla and she was soon happily laughing in their company.

***

A month later the show closed in a spectacular finale after a year-long run at the Drury Lane Theatre. One week after the show's closure, the excited cast of the *Prince and the Gypsy Girl* sailed for New York. For Trevilla this was an experience that was truly beyond her wildest dreams. Frequently she would ask herself how a mere Gypsy girl, who lived in a rickety old caravan on the Sussex Downs, had picked vegetables in the fields and wore grubby hand-me-downs, was now a lady who wore perfume, beautiful clothes and was a stage show headliner who found herself on a luxury liner bound for America. Was all this really happening to her? Was she about to wake up from a dream? Did she really go from being anonymous to a position of theatrical fame?

Trevilla was learning that it is impossible to predict the outcome of one's life. She had never planned for any of this. Her chance meeting with Andre and Anatole had been a miracle encounter that had taken her from a rural life to places she had never dreamed.

Anatole had told Trevilla much about his upbringing in New York. She was not only excited to see this great city but curious to see it from the point of view of tracing Anatole and Mariska's footsteps. By coincidence, the show *The Prince and the Gypsy Girl* made its New York premiere at the State Theatre where Anatole and Mariska, using their stage name of Nat and Mary Lucky, had made their debut in the world of show business. It was an irony of life that while they had gravitated across the water to Europe, Trevilla had gone the other way to America.

The show was popular with audiences. The tunes and costumes were mesmeric, and the performances were electrifying – they had to be. New York theatre critics were hard-nosed, unsparing and could make or break the duration of a show. The cast rehearsed and rehearsed, even when the previously night's show had gone extremely well. There was absolutely no room for complacency as far as Arthur Burnside was concerned. This show had to be one of the biggest hits on the New York stage so that it had a chance to be transferred to the Hollywood screen.

Trevilla put her heart and soul into every performance. Her voice grew stronger and with the able tuition of a singing coach, she learned to sustain her notes and put emotion into every phrase. She was fit and glowed with good health. Her dance movements were provocative and sexual, leaving men in the audience excited and breathless. At night her dressing room would be bombarded with flowers from would-be admirers, but her heart still belonged to Anatole, who was far away filming in the depths of the Congo. Her own heart ached for him; she wished that Anatole could be here to watch her perform on his home turf, and theatre he had started his own career in.

Oh, how she loved New York! During her breaks from performances she and other cast members would explore all the main attractions. They went to the top of the tallest skyscrapers, saw the Statue of Liberty, Central Park, and went on the Staten Island ferry. With the high wages she was earning, Trevilla went on a shopping spree at the biggest department stores, buying presents for her family back home and beautiful clothes for herself. *This is life*, she thought. This was the world she had always dreamed of. Suddenly it was as if there were no boundaries anymore. For the first time in her life Trevilla felt she could do anything and go anywhere. Her appetite for travel had been well and truly whetted too.

In the Bronx, Trevilla strode the streets where Anatole and Mariska had once been children. She tried to envisage the man she loved with his parents and sister in a time gone by. Anatole's journey in life had been a long one too.

Trevilla was always learning and absorbing everything around her. The world was opening up before her. To be in America was a dream that she thought she would never wake up from. It was cosmopolitan, with all manner of races – colourful and rumbustious. Even though she was loving every minute of it she was curious about Anatole. Where was he now? Just where had his adventurous life taken him?

Thirty-Nine

In all of his world travels since he had left Russia as a little boy, there had been nowhere that had fascinated and intrigued Anatole as much as the continent of Africa. Apart from the diverse wildlife, which was every cameraman's dream, filming the land was constantly mysterious with surprises around every corner. Not only in its diverse scenery, but also in its tribal races with their customs, traditions and distinctive markings.

Andre and Anatole were equally enthusiastic about everything they saw in their journey across Africa. There was so much to see that they were frightened to miss anything. Their cameras were constantly primed to catch the chance sight of something unusual and striking. It may have been the cascades of a waterfall with creamy white foam set against the backdrop of a vivid blue African sky. The sight of lions soaking themselves in a river. Zebras and giraffes making their way across the plains. The sight of a gorilla emerging from the jungle. The miracle horses of Namib.

They got through reels and reels of film. There was really so much to see that Andre estimated they could spend the next ten years in the Dark Continent and still be able to make endless documentaries to keep cinemagoers enthralled. In a sense they were wild safari cinematographer pioneers. The film industry was still young and they were setting the precedent for the wildlife camera teams that would come later. In the 1930s a Belgian film maker, Armand Denis, and his glamorous wife, Leila Roosevelt Denis, made *Wheels across Africa*. This covered much territory previously unseen and unknown by cinema audiences. A few years later an American millionaire, Lawrence Copley Thaw, and his wife, Peggy, made similar films of India at the height of the Raj, and from Cairo to the Cape. They were much better equipped than the two lone cameramen filming at random. Armand and Leila Denis as with Lawrence Thaw travelled in convoys of well-planned expeditions.

The forests and mountains of the Congo could not be travelled without a great deal of preparation. Anatole and Andre had arrived thinking that this would be an easy terrain to cross and they now had to rethink their strategy. They realised that they would need a strong dependable vehicle to travel through the Congo as well as a substantial supply of food and water. All this had to be arranged and in the city of Stanleyville they found everything they needed.

Even before they had attempted to film the vast areas of the Congo containing all kinds of wildlife they realised that Stanleyville was a small city and trading post in comparison to the great capitals of Europe was well worth extra footage. It was named after the Victorian adventurer and journalist, Henry Morton Stanley, who had famously discovered the whereabouts of Dr Livingstone. It had been founded as a trading post for King Leopold II of Belgium in 1883. Belgian immigration gradually expanded its economy, transferring it from a fledgling town to a thriving city.

This was the initial introduction to Andre and Anatole's documentary of the Congo. The real work would begin when they travelled to Albert National Park. This was a colossal reserve of almost two million acres, established in 1925 by King Albert of Belgium several years before. It contained rugged difficult scenery to traverse but the abundance of wildlife that lived within its boundaries were truly God's own creatures.

At their hotel in Stanleyville, the two men sat at a bar the night before they began their expedition. It was strange but after working together for so long Anatole realised he knew very little about Andre. He had always found Andre to be studious, painstaking in every detail about filming, but often going to places impulsively. His private life was not so much guarded, but never mentioned. The hotel bar was filled with travellers, traders, safari-suited men who spoke in different languages thus illustrating how the Congo was a draw card for people of all nationalities.

"Is this our last port of call, Andre?" Anatole asked. "In all our travels through Africa we've shot about 40,000 feet of film. We've sent reels and reels of film to Arthur Burnside in London, enough to provide short films on Africa in between the main movies for a couple of years."

"I guess you're right. If we carried on filming in Africa in every part of the continent, we'll never get back. Besides, Mr Burnside is footing the payroll. We need to wrap this one up and get back to London. He may not want us to continue, in which case, I'll head back to America."

"You've never said, and I've never braved to intrude on your privacy, especially considering you were my employer. Do you have family, Andre?"

Andre was slow to respond but when he did he seemed pleased to be able to talk about it. "I have a daughter who lives with my late wife's parents in New York. My own parents have long since passed on. She's a great girl. Studying hard. I'm very proud of her. I see her from time to time. When I get back I must try and spend more time with her." He paused to think of her. "What about you? I know you have your sister and family. That girl, Trevilla, seems passionate about you. Are you going to marry her?"

"I've thought about it," he replied. In fact, Anatole had done a great deal more than just think about it. He had wrestled with his conscience whether to ask Trevilla before she had gone to London. In the end he decided Trevilla needed to find out if a show business career was what she really wanted. "She's a star now on stage. Things have changed."

Andre finished his drink and looked around at the people in the bar. "I'm going to turn in now. Don't forget we've got a meeting with the Belgian district commissioner tomorrow at nine for things to look out for. Then we'll leave soon after. See you tomorrow."

"Good night, Andre." He rose and left the bar leaving Anatole nursing a half empty glass of beer. For a moment he sat there thinking of his girlfriend and then he quietly said her name. "Trevilla."

***

On stage in New York Trevilla and the rest of the cast of *The Prince and the Gypsy* seemed to improve with every performance. The original score of the show had been enhanced as new songs had been added by local writers. There was one song that had become the high spot of the show. This had been specially written for Trevilla who gave it everything she could. In the show Saffron, the Gypsy girl, finally discovers the man she loves, who she thought to be a handsome vagabond, is in fact the Prince and heir to the throne of the European country they live in. When it is revealed who he is and the Prince returns to take up his royal duties, Saffron is left broken hearted. In the show Trevilla performs the number 'The Day I Lost My Man' written by an up and coming New York songwriter. It was irony that when Trevilla sang this song on stage, with emotion resonating in her voice and genuine tears spilling from her eyes, she was thinking of the two men she had loved the most in her life. Her young husband, Cazare, who had died so tragically, and Anatole far away in Africa. Trevilla sang to great acclaim. Backstage Al Jolson, Sophie Tucker, Rudy Vallee, Joan Crawford and Tallulah Bankhead, all called by to offer their congratulations. In future years her showstopper number 'The Day I Lost My Man' would become her theme tune in the same way that 'Some of These Days' would always be associated with the legendary vaudevillian, Sophie Tucker.

***

Anatole was deep in thought at the bar that night. It had become quite noisy with loud conversation, and somebody was playing a tune from the latest dance craze in Paris on a piano that had seen better days. Not that it mattered as the crowd clapped and cheered along, but Anatole was oblivious to it all. He was thinking of Trevilla. He remembered one night when she came to him a few days before her departure to begin a stage career in London.

***

Rain fell heavily one night in Sussex. Anatole was asleep in the guesthouse lodge of Shervington Manor, but the wind, lightning and torrential rain woke him up. He rose from his bed and looked out of the window. To his amazement he saw Trevilla standing beneath the eaves of the main house and on espying Anatole she ran towards the lodge. Immediately Anatole opened the door and let her in.

"Trevilla! What are you doing? It's three-thirty in the morning! And look at the weather girl!"

"Where is Andre? Are you alone?" She looked around her nervously.

"Yes, Andre is in London. He's coming back sometime tomorrow." Anatole took her coat and threw her a towel. Even soaked from the rain Trevilla still managed to look strangely beautiful. "What is it? What's the matter?"

Trevilla dried herself. For a moment she did not reply. The she pushed the towel to one side and walked close to him. So close in fact she was staring into his eyes. Without saying anything she put her arms around him and kissed him. Anatole responded with equal passion.

"Won't you love me Anatole?" Trevilla whispered. "Must you go far away to Africa? I don't want you to go."

Anatole did not reply. He kissed her once again, luxuriantly and lavishing. Then he picked her up like a groom to his bride on their wedding night, and carried her into the bedroom. Amidst the flickering shadows of swaying trees in the storm outside, and the sudden lightning flashes that with each bolt momentarily turned night into day, they made love with real passion, energy and emotion. Neither gave quarter to the other, they wanted love. Lots of it. Each gave way to the latent desires they had for each other as if they might never have the opportunity to do so again. Trevilla was wild and uninhibited. Her lips were like wine, intoxicating and warm. She wrapped her arms and long legs around him and ran her hands up and down his back, and through his hair. Not only did she kiss his lips, but so too did she kiss his entire body. Anatole responded likewise. Frequently Trevilla would rise above him and take her pleasure before Anatole twisted her over and thrust repeatedly while kissing and licking her breasts, her neck and earlobes, while she smiled in ecstasy and sighed with the greatest delight. When they had exhausted themselves, they sat naked with their arms and legs around each other. Their hearts were pulsating in such an excited and continuous rhythm it was as if they were joined together by their union of love. Anatole gazed deep into Trevilla's eyes as a tear rolled from them. He wasn't sure whether it was a tear of joy or one of sadness. The sudden flashes of lightning illuminated Trevilla's face. It was a face flowing with love and warmth.

***

He remembered that night so well. A few days later Trevilla was on her way to London. For Anatole it was a loss that he had never had to comprehend before. The power of real love had befallen him. In the bar that night he savoured the memory of it. If he was never to fall in love again, he had at least tasted the greatest love of his life and he would always cherish in memory. It was would be hard for him to ever look at a woman now without making a comparison to Trevilla.

He sipped the remains of his drink and decided to get a breath of fresh air outside. Through the maze of travellers and customers of all nationalities, the exhibitionist dancers moving in time to the discordant jangle of piano playing, Anatole strode out in to the street. Some young African women walked past; he was fascinated by their intricately woven hairstyles. There was beauty in this land, in its peoples, its animals and scenery, yet it was also a place scarred by leprosy. The Congo not only attracted men of trade and commerce, chancers and gamblers, explorers and hunters, but also those of the medical profession who came to offer their services to the ill and diseased. In whatever capacity they came, the Congo represented a great challenge often seemingly insurmountable.

The next day Andre and Anatole met up with the Belgian district commissioner who they informed of their travel plans. When he learned of the filming tasks they hoped to achieve he was only too happy to help them for, as he saw it, their work would promote the interests of the Congo. His knowledge of the African wildlife and native tribes was inexhaustible. It was not only clear that this man knew the Congo intensely but he had an enormous love of the land.

Andre and Anatole studied the map of the Parc National Albert that the commissioner had provided. Thick forest abounded between the high mountains of Bishoke, Mikeno and Kartsimbi. The district commissioner made it absolutely clear that to enter the extensive undergrowth would be folly for it was fraught with the danger of encountering rampaging and angry gorillas. Both men knew that despite being virtually forbidden from entering this area their devil may care attitude would almost certainly attempt to film within the jungle. It mattered not so much that they endangered their own lives, but that there was a wealth of animal life teeming inside that jungle that once recorded on film would entertain and surprise the cinema going masses.

Later that day they set off on their journey. It proved to be very unpredictable, difficult and far more exhausting than they had anticipated. The vehicle they hired could only go so far and often they would have to leave it while they crossed some rugged terrain on foot to film some wildlife. They found getting close ups of some animals to be an enormously difficult task. It was dangerous but the element of risk was part of the job specification of a camcraman.

They both had a great love of elephants. These magnificent, big-eared animals were strong and imposing, yet there was also an innate gentleness about them. Andre and Anatole had set up their cameras behind some trees and bushes, waiting patiently for the opportunity to film them at close range. In this they were rewarded handsomely as a large elephant and its baby came through the jungle. They rolled the cameras as the elephants moved slowly through the undergrowth. Each man filmed nervously. They were fearful that if the mother elephant caught sight of them it might suddenly charge at them instinctively as if they were potential predators. African elephants could be temperamental.

In fact is was as if the mother elephant was educating its young in the ways of finding food for its survival. It scented flowers and bushes as it lumbered along. The baby elephant did exactly the same. It looked up at its mother as if to be inspired and devoured exactly the same foliage. The elephants seemed to scent everything. Then every so often the mother elephant would stop in its search for food, flick its enormous ears back as if it's acute sense of hearing had picked up that some other creature was in the vicinity. Both men froze in their tracks. It was clear the elephant was aware of their presence, perhaps by scent or the rhythm of the cameras in motion. The mother elephant began to move towards the trees and bushes where Anatole and Andre had positioned their cameras.

Andre nodded to Anatole to move back. Anatole started to move back slowly with one camera. Andre continued filming but reached into his safari jacked and pulled out a handgun. Instead of moving away Andre moved out from behind his vantage point and virtually moved forward almost in open defiance of this beautiful animal. He moved the camera and adjusted the lens so that he managed to obtain a close-up of the elephant. It appeared perplexed by the man with the camera and instead of charging it stood motionless like a monument in the wilds of Africa. Andre at once saw that this elephant had a sad demeanour yet sensitive eyes and a peaceful tranquil nature. Then just as quickly as the elephant had picked up on the scent of the two human beings, it turned suddenly. Several other elephants came into view.

Their arrival signalled to Andre and Anatole it was the moment to quickly move away. Both men hurried off as the two elephants rejoined the main herd.

"That was a close one, Nat," Andre said with a sigh of relief. "Let's get the hell out of here."

However, that was not the end of the situation they had just encountered. The two men moved swiftly away from the elephants with more haste than speed. They were soaked through with nervous perspiration due to the tension and the uncomfortable sticky humidity. Their hearts were pounding and their nerves on edge when as they emerged from a clump of trees they found themselves facing the magnificence and fierce grandeur of a lion. To Andre's surprise, Anatole acted with courageous instinct and under imminent threat of attack by the lion; he placed the camera directly in front of it and began filming. It roared and snarled, and moved forward as if it was about to pounce. Andre again took his handgun out as if he was ready to shoot. Then once again divine intervention and providence came to the rescue.

From within the vast forest area came the sound of thundering limbs hitting the ground with real force. The elephant herd were stampeding and rampaging. Andre and Anatole immediately took cover to one side. Now both men were filming with real enthusiasm for before them they captured the visual feast of a herd of elephants charging past and the greatness of the lion quickly retreating into the distance as dust swirled and trees and vegetation were crushed under foot. So strong was the impact of the stampede that the ground felt as if it was vibrating and that a centrifugal force had been created sending Anatole and Andre backwards. They quickly rose to their feet and left hurriedly.

When the tumult was over the African scenery suddenly took on a strange hush. But as the two men began to walk away the squark of birds and the sound of animals crying and howling in the distance could be heard. It took a long time to return to their vehicle which gratefully had been out of the path of the stampede. Quickly and quietly with their valuable cargo of film, they began to drive away.

They knew precisely where they were going. The area was off limits to them. The Belgian authorities had strictly forbidden them not to enter the deep forest area. It was reputedly teeming with gorilla life within its dense undergrowth; however, Andre and Anatole were determined to flout convention and authority in order to get stunning footage of the gorillas in their natural habitat despite the risks involved. Andre assured Anatole that great cameramen like journalists of renown would always defy rules to get the best stories.

This section of the trip had been more carefully planned than their previous excursions. They made sure they had enough provisions to see them through the difficult weeks ahead. Andre had also found a supplier who furnished him at great cost with two handguns and ammunition in order to confront any emergency situations. The density of the forest was an obstacle that was going to be difficult to overcome. Carrying their cameras and packs on their backs was exhausting.

They were determined to film gorillas in the wild. It was a foolhardy assignment. The gorillas were known to attack and they ran the constant risk of a surprise assault. Every so often they had to pause for rest. The undergrowth was sticky and muddy. Both men were beginning to wonder if this trek through the jungle would be beneficial in the end. After several days and nights they had yet to encounter a gorilla. Around them life proliferated in many other forms. Nocturnal animals of the night made all kids of noises ensuring that sleep patterns would be constantly disturbed.

For the two men concerned they felt that this was going to be an increasingly fruitless expedition. At their makeshift camp one night they sat contemplating whether to continue. To film gorillas in the wild would be the icing on the cake and the successful conclusion of months and months of recording animal life on the African continent. Reluctantly they decided that the next day they would begin their return journey and start planning their departure from Africa for Europe.

Then the next morning in the early hours, as the sun began to rise and the jungle began to spring with life, strange sounds began to carry alerting Anatole and Andre that something was happening in the nearby vicinity. Without saying anything they set their cameras up and prepared themselves. Andre armed himself with one of the two handguns and tossed the other one to Anatole. It was rightly assumed that if a dangerous life-threatening situation arose they wouldn't hesitate to use it.

They pushed their cameras forward and slowly at a snail's pace. Somewhere in the distance the sounds of grunting and groaning could be heard but by the different tones of each noise it could have been surely perceived as a two-way animal conversation. Simultaneously the sound of tree bark and branches being broken rent forth into the air. This was surely what they were waiting for and what a sight it was too! A few hundred yards ahead of them, partially concealed by the foliage that fell across the view like a half-drawn lace curtain, were a family of gorillas. For all intents and purposes, it was as if the gorilla troop were building a residence! At one side an elderly-looking gorilla, possibly the grandfather of the group, watched as the other members of the family made settings in the trees with the branches they had broken. Every so often the grandfather gorilla jumped up and down, swung his long arms together as if he was applauding, leapt up and swung between the trees. The gorillas varied in height and dimension as in any normal human family. On average they were around about five foot or more with extraordinary long arms that when stretched to full span must have been a staggering seven foot across from the end of one arm to the other. They were powerfully built too with a surprising amount of strength, ferocity, and forceful in their movements.

Anatole and Andre were transfixed by the sight before them. The temptation to move their cameras forward for even closer shots was enormous but to do so would almost certainly run the risk of them becoming apparent to the gorillas. If they knew they were being spied on only a guess could be hazarded as to what their reaction could be. Andre motioned for them to start moving back slowly. They had done everything they had set out to do. All they had to do was leave as quietly as they have arrived. They began the long journey back constantly looking over their shoulder, and all around, in case some predatory animal leapt out at them. The nearer they got to leaving the thick undergrowth, the broader their smiles became at the thought that they had achieved almost everything they had set out to do since arriving in Africa almost a year ago.

"We've done it!" Anatole said with a beaming smile. "We've filmed the impossible." He was so happy he was almost skipping with joy. "Wait 'til Mr Burnside sees this film. He'll be ecstatic!"

"Others will follow now to make films here," Andre said enthusiastically. "We've really started something now."

***

By the time they got back to Stanleyville, they were still patting themselves on the back at having filmed so many marvellous scenes of animals the length and breadth of Africa. The whole experience had been breathtaking for both men and they sat in the bar of their hotel summing up everything that had happened. They both knew that the trip had changed them from being merely wildlife cameramen to men believing in conservation and preservation of all animals in the wild before they become extinct.

The bar was as usual filled with travellers, hunters and a mixed clientele of people of all nationalities. A pianist played a haunting melody in the background that seemed to sum up the atmosphere of a warm humid night in the Congo. It was the type of tune that if it was played in a smoky London pub, or a bar in New York, would conjure up images of far away places, swaying palms in a tropical sunset, and exotic women with long eyelashes and mysterious eyes, usually wearing tight colourful saris or white dresses in the glorious sunlight.

"This has been one of the greatest trips of my life, Andre." Anatole's eyes were moist. "Look at the hunters here." He pointed across to a group of safari-outfitted men. "All the creatures we have seen are God's children too. Why do they hunt such noble animals for pleasure… so-called pleasure? We should be doing all we can to protect the wildlife of Africa. Look what happened in our country America with the shooting of thousands of buffalo."

"That is something you could ask your brother-in-law, Lord Shervington, to speak out against in the House of Lords. Your brother-in-law fights for causes, I understand? The plight of former servicemen I believe."

"I will mention it when we get back." He looked at the dancers and the drinkers in the bar and then turned to face Andre square on. "What next for you, Andre? Would you like to return? We've covered a lot but there is so much more to film. I want to come back. I love Africa."

"I've got commitments to honour in America and I want to see my daughter. I guess this is the last post for both of us as far as our working partnership but never say never. I just want to say it's been a great pleasure to work with you, Nat. We've achieved a lot between us."

"The pleasure's mine, Andre. I will always be grateful that you gave me these opportunities after the war."

They paused to take a sip of their drinks. The music changed to a tune that seemed familiar to Anatole. A French-Creole singer with a larger than life personality stood by the piano and started to sing 'Some of These Days', the old Sophie Tucker tune. Hearing it here in the Congo brought a smile to the faces of Anatole and Andre for it brought back memories of their show business days in New York a long time ago. Andre and Anatole raised their glasses in a toast to each other. Turning to look at the very receptive audience in the bar the singer's voice had a particular earthy resonance about it that had them all spellbound. 'Some of These Days', the title seemed apt to Anatole. He put his own personal interpretation on the phrase. *Some of these days are like the finest wine,* he thought, *to be sipped and devoured.* For the taste of the splendour of fine days filled with love and achievement to linger on in the memory. For the taste of a great love to be retained long after the impact of those first thrilling moments, leading to the constant joy, is suddenly extinguished by the passing of time, or the course of natural events. Some of these days, some were fine, some were sad, some were good, some were bad, that is the course of life. Anatole drifted away and visualised the great Sophie Tucker singing the same song on a New York stage.

In the lobby of the hotel the man at the reception called out to them both as they entered. "Gentlemen! A message came from the district commissioner today. He wants to see you both at his office at nine o'clock tomorrow morning."

Andre looked at Anatole concerned. "I wonder what he wants to see us for. Sounds ominous."

***

The next morning they both promptly turned up at the Belgian district commissioner's office. They were shown into his colonial office full of maps on the wall, a world globe, charts, reference books, mahogany furniture and potted plants placed strategically around the room. Above his desk hung a portrait picture of King Albert of Belgium. The room was hot but it was cooled by a tropical fan that swished backwards and forwards thus ensuring the interior was kept at a tranquil moderate temperature.

The commissioner was in no mood for niceties. He sat quietly shuffling through some papers, deliberately keeping the men waiting. Somewhere in his fifties he was tanned with dark hair and wore glasses that made him look studious. Then after a few minutes of an earth-shattering silence he leaned forward.

"Gentlemen, you were told not to enter the thick woodland where the gorillas dwell!" How on earth did he find out the two men thought? Oh yes, you were seen by an aerial cartographer! Do you realise the danger you put yourselves in? Say something had happened to you both. No one would have known you were there. It was irresponsible to say the least!"

Andre was the first to respond to the man's genuine anger. It was plainly obvious that the Commissioner did not like his authority demeaned.

415

"Sir, with due respect, I have faced greater danger before. So too has my colleague who has never been far from danger all his life. I was a war cameraman. During the Great War I filmed in all the major battlefields of Europe, including your home country Belgium and the Middle East."

"That's very commendable of you, Mr Aviva, but the point I am making is you were specifically told not to go there. By rights I should confiscate the film you have. Those animals can get quite vicious, you know."

"You have no jurisdiction to do that," Andre pointed out. "Besides, won't you be harming your cause by not letting the outside world see just what the Congo has to offer?"

The commissioner looked stern but then appeared to soften in mood. "You must understand that I have great responsibility for all expeditions and travellers in this region. Their safety is paramount. I value my position here and I value my reputation. I won't quibble about the film you have. I agree that all the filming you have done so far will be of enormous advantage to informing the world about the Congo. Now, gentlemen, have you concluded all your filming activities? If there is anything I can do to help you please let me know and please keep me informed as to what your plans might be."

Anatole and Andre quickly looked at each other as if waiting for the other to agree to continue their filming expeditions. It was Andre who always took the lead. He suddenly had a brainwave.

"Sir, you made mention of the fact that we were spotted by an aerial cartographer." The commissioner nodded. "I take it you are speaking of an aircraft that was used in the Great War with a pilot at the front and a cockpit at the rear where a gunner would have been positioned?"

"That is correct. Did you have something in mind, Mr Aviva?"

"One of my many assignments during the war was to fly in aircraft like that and film the battlefields from above."

"Sounds dangerous work, my friend."

"Oh, it was but it brought home to the people the true scale of the war and the devastating effects it had on once peaceful places and how their homes and centuries old buildings and monuments had been destroyed. It would be good to do some aerial filming here."

The commissioner second guessed him. "You would like me to put a plane at your disposal to film the areas you were unable to penetrate? I can arrange that for you, or for both of you?"

"Just one of us, Commissioner." He turned to Anatole. "This will be our swan song here. Shall we toss a coin for it, Nat?"

"Why not?" Anatole produced a coin. "Okay, call."

"Heads, of course," Andre replied with a smile. Anatole flipped the coin. The commissioner watched with amusement as the coin landed on his desk. Both men leaned forward as the coin revealed its face. "Tails! You are the lucky guy, eh, Nat, that gets to film from the air. Mr Commissioner, sir, would you organise that aircraft for my friend and colleague here?"

***

At a remote airfield some distance from Stanleyville Anatole was introduced to a Belgian pilot who had joined the Royal Flying Corp in Britain during the Great War. He specialised in reconnaissance missions for the Congolese authorities as well as flying surveyors and anthropologists to difficult to reach places. His knowledge of the difficult terrain was unsurpassed. The two men shook hands, established a good rapport between them and then fixed a camera within the aircraft for aerial filming. They prepared themselves to fly over some of the dense areas of undergrowth in a bid to film wildlife.

Andre watched perhaps with a sense of envy as the aircraft took off. The whole project in Africa had been one of nervous excitement and unpredictability. Here in the Congo there was an intense beauty, mystery and magic combined with a sense of danger that made it an irresistible draw card for the more adventurous of traveller.

Tropical rainforest covered a vast area of the Congo. It was so dense with tall trees of various species crammed tightly together that it was difficult for sunlight to permeate through. Flying across it, the view below was of unbroken forest beneath which animal life no doubt proliferated and prospered but remained well concealed. The Belgian pilot skilfully guided the plane down low in order that Anatole might, with a little bit of luck, just possibly film some sort of wildlife. All Anatole could find to film was the lushness and green of endless forest as far as the eye could see. Where were the fabled creatures of Africa?

In the years he had been working as a cinematographer he had developed an eye for the long shot or a colourful landscape in the manner that an accomplished artist managed to achieve on canvas Without any animals or birdlife in the immediate vicinity he concentrated his camera lens on the resonant deep blue of the African sky, the light and shade of the colourful trees and foliage, and the fuselage of the world war fighter plane that had obviously seen better days and was so shaky in flight it felt as if it had been tied together by string.

The plane had obviously been ready for the defence of Africa if the Kaiser's forces had any intention of taking over the territory during the Great War. Now it was a rickety, noisy erstwhile rustbucket that the pilot and passenger placed the safety of their lives in during every flight. Even at a relatively high altitude the air felt sticky and humid. Only the breeze the plane created, as it soared through the sky, cooled things down.

Down below in the undergrowth a steamy vapour rose from the forest. How on earth did anything live in such torrid conditions? What on earth lived there beneath the darkness of such overcrowded chaotic vegetation, and the masses of trees that grew into each other? Anatole kept a vigil with his camera in case of a sighting of something unexpected. He didn't have long to wait. Suddenly the pilot was pointing down eagerly. The sight below was one of sheer delight which brought a smile to Anatole's face.

At the top of some trees chimpanzees swung and played like seasoned performers putting on a display for the viewing public. They were like naughty children running amok amongst the trees, it made for beautiful viewing. Just a few minutes of film was about all that he could manage before the sound of the low flying aircraft frightened the chimpanzees away. They quickly vanished into the mysterious depths of the forest.

The aircraft flew higher and higher until they were well clear of the endless trees below. Anatole concentrated on the view convinced now they wouldn't find anything else to film. He gazed out at the rolling contours of the Congo. Time and time again he would ask himself, *How did one guy get so lucky to see everything he had in his lifetime?* He was just getting carried away by his thoughts of grandeur when his face felt as if it was being stung by wet pellets. In the space of a few minutes a violent storm had broken out. There were startling red flashes that lit up the sky like flames soaring high from a brushfire. Thunder cracked; lightning, with terrifying yellow streaks, seemed to fire backwards and forwards in the direct path of the plane while a deluge of rain poured down on Anatole and the pilot. Then there was a colossal clap of thunder and a lightning bolt that seemed to pass through the fuselage of the aircraft.

The plane spiralled out of control. Flames shot up across all parts of the aircraft. Then the plane exploded. Fragments of the aircraft were thrown in all directions. The storm raged furiously with all the wrath and ire of a tempest of biblical proportions. The debris of the aircraft and all its contents rained down on the forest.

Forty

Mariska stood gazing out of the study window towards the Sussex Downs. She clutched the telegram in disbelief that Andre had sent her from Stanleyville informing her of Anatole's disappearance. Although his body or that of the pilot's had never been recovered, she couldn't even begin to use the word death. It was all too final, not yet confirmed. Surely there must be hope that he would be found, that somehow he, who had been through so many dangerous situations, had survived. It seemed highly unlikely but she knew her brother. He had great instincts for survival.

Bernard entered the room and stood behind her, placing his hands on her shoulders. He had already read the contents of the telegram and was very saddened. Over the years he had grown immensely fond of his brother-in-law, and also admired his adventurous spirit and versatility. He genuinely liked him.

"He loved the South Downs," Mariska said softly. "He was happy here."

"I know." Bernard's response was equally muted. "I've sent telegrams to Mr Mahoney. I rang his office in London, he's currently visiting Ireland. I believe he'll be going to see Jack Clancy at his home in Southern Ireland. I sent a telegram to Mr Burnside in New York but the show's cast, including Trevilla, have moved on to Los Angeles. He'll let her know. She'll take it hard I bet."

"Trevilla will be broken-hearted." Mariska wiped a tear away. "Nat is still alive. He must be – Nat's a survivor. He got through the earthquake in 'Frisco!"

"We can't get too much hope up." Bernard tried to be gentle with her. "But we have to be realistic. This was a tough assignment he took. He knew the risks."

***

In Ireland, Slugs had travelled from Dublin to the town where Jack lived. It was raining hard when Slugs walked through Dromana looking for the Limerick Castle Public House. Eventually he found it. The pub wasn't open for business but in a bid to get out of the pouring rain, he hammered hard on the door. Neither had met up since leaving America, it was to be a surprise meeting. Slugs had been on assignment in Dublin and on a whim had decided to visit Jack. Just minutes before he had left his hotel in Dublin a clerk had given him a telegram telling him of Anatole's presumed death in Africa. He was bereft at the thought of his boyhood friend lost forever; however, there was still nothing final yet. His body was yet to be found. There was still hope. Faint hope – but there was hope.

Jack was cleaning glasses and preparing everything ready for the first customers when he heard the hammering on the door. He was used to impatient customers by now, especially those that couldn't get through the day without that first drink. In the time he had been the proprietor of the Limerick Castle he had developed a reputation as an amiable and good-humoured landlord. He didn't want to ruin things and very grudgingly went to the door expecting to see a dishevelled local eager for the shelter of the pub and a glass of black gold.

He opened the door slowly and his jaw dropped at the sight of Slugs standing there in the pouring rain. The water dripped off Slugs' hat. He smiled broadly at Jack, the big guy from New York stood there large as life.

"Hiya, buddie!" he exclaimed. "How about an Irish Stout for your old friend?"

The two men embraced and found it hard to hold back their joy at seeing each other again. It had only been two years since all three had departed the shores of America. Now it was almost 1929 the year that the stock market would crash ushering in the Great Depression. All those things were far from their minds as they sat at the bar of the pub catching up on each other's news. There was great sadness too. What had happened to their boyhood friend Nat?

"So what brought you over to Ireland then, old friend?" asked Jack, topping up Slugs glass with the black Irish gold. "Did London ask you to go?"

"The newspaper sent me. And by the way I love London. You ought to come over for a visit sometime. I was sent here to write a review on

Ireland's progress since the troubles. I could not come here without catching up on you. I'm only sorry I came with the news about Nat."

Jack was too hardened by his years as a New York policeman on the toughest beats to show too much emotion but his lip quivered slightly and there were clear signs of unwept tears in his eyes. He remembered only too well the time he had spent in the orphanage where Anatole and Mariska had become like a brother and sister to him. They were family to him.

"What do you think happened to our old friend out there in the jungles of Africa?" He asked. "Do you think there's any hope he'll be found alive?"

Slugs was equally downcast. "No. None of us are immortal, old pal. I'd kinda like to think he survived. Sure, old Nat survived being shanghaied to China. He got through the San Francisco earthquake, managed to survive the sinking of the *Titanic*, the Mexican War, the Great War and God knows what else. But I don't think he survived this. I reckon he bought it this time. The plane exploded into smithereens. I can't bear to think about it either buddie. Let's drink to his memory Jack. The guy that really lived a life."

"He'd like that. Boy, did he do some mileage. To Nat." They both clinked their beer glasses as the rain hurtled down outside.

***

In Los Angeles Trevilla and the rest of the cast of *The Prince and the Gypsy Girl* had transferred to a Hollywood studio to make a silent dramatic movie of the stage version which had been so favourably received. Under the watchful eye of Arthur Burnside, the one-time stage musical became a drama which in terms of silent movies, being without sound or songs, lost much of its momentum but in other ways it gained in that it was a compulsive, romantic story to become engrossed in.

It was an irony that barely a year before Anatole had taken Trevilla to a cinema in Horsham, Sussex for the first time in her life to see a film called the Sheik starring the late lamented Rudolph Valentino. Now by a series of twists and turns of fate, Trevilla was starring in her own film which constantly amazed her.

Arthur's delight at seeing his own stage production turned into a film was only hampered by the news about Anatole who, in the telegram he received from Andre, was still at this stage 'declared missing, presumed dead'. He had been asked if he would inform Trevilla. Arthur was full aware of the relationship that existed between the two and he was worried about the effect it would have on Trevilla. He walked to the studio lot where from the sidelines he watched her perform in a key scene of the film under the guidance of a well-established director. She was a professional. No doubt about it. In her role as the Gypsy girl who wins a prince's heart she was an extrovert, an exhibitionist and could perform without inhibitions or embarrassment.

When the scene was completed Trevilla looked across the studio to see Arthur standing there. It was almost as if Trevilla sensed by the look on Arthur's face that he had bad news. She walked over to him. Her Gypsy sense of perception told her that it could only be Anatole.

"You've finished for the day, Trevilla?" Arthur asked her. She nodded that she had. "Let's go for a drive to the beach. I have some news for you."

***

Shortly afterwards they drove to Santa Monica Beach. Trevilla had guessed beforehand about the news that was to come. She sat silently as they drove to the beach that had become her favourite since arriving in California. Everything had gone so well up 'til now. It had all been so wonderful and uplifting. Good things rarely last. There is always some sort of blow that brings people back down to earth.

Arthur wasn't quite sure why he had chosen Santa Monica beach to talk to Trevilla about Anatole's disappearance in Africa. Perhaps because a crowded studio full of props cameramen, scene shifters and extras was not the kind of environment to break tragic news to a person. Trevilla may have been naïve in some respects about the ways of the world although, like a cat curious about every new highway before her, she was also tough from her years of Gypsy travels and the loss of her husband.

The waves crashed down on the golden sands of Santa Monica as Arthur and Trevilla walked along. California oozed the good life and it was surely a place where dreams could be realised; however, for Trevilla the shattering news had suddenly clouded the sunshine and she felt the sudden urgency to go home.

"Why do all the good men go so soon?" she asked, stopping to look out towards the huge surf rolling in from the Pacific.

"That's a question I asked myself when my son didn't come home from the war." Trevilla turned sharply. Arthur had never spoken of any family. She had always assumed him to be a happy-go-lucky wealthy bachelor with more love for the theatre than family. "Oh yes I had a son. He was only twenty-one. Died somewhere in No-Man's Land. His mother was American you know. As fine a woman as they came. I met her when I was touring in a minstrel show back in 1890. A real beauty! By God she was! Breathtakingly beautiful. She was a dancer in Connecticut when I first saw her. High-kicking long legs with a great smile. I always think she died of a broken heart when our son died."

Trevilla stopped for a moment. She paused to ask him a question that seemed to be at a tangent to their conversation. "Have you had a good life, Mr Burnside?"

"I don't really analyse it." He replied, somewhat surprised by the question. "I get on with it but then I've got plenty to get on with. I've been working since I was twelve. Why do you ask Trevilla?"

There was s silence for a moment or two broken only by the rolling waves. "I have lost two good men in my life." Tears began to roll from her eyes. "Why should I feel such pain? First my lovely Cazare and then Anatole. I am only a simple Gypsy girl. I never looked for much, except to be loved! Why am I being punished for loving someone?" She put her hands over her face for a moment and then turned away to wipe away her tears. "I don't want to be here! I don't fit in here. This is not my world."

Arthur was very concerned about her. He tried to reassure her. "My dear, don't distress yourself." He gripped her shoulders fleetingly. "I understand the pain you've been through. I lost a beautiful wife and son too. In any life there is an element of pain and happiness, some of it more than the other. It's not possible to live a life without experiencing tragedy of some sort. You must ask yourself this too. You say you don't want to be here, that you don't fit in, and this is not your world, but it sounds like the tragedy of the moment is obscuring your reasoning. You've enjoyed it pretty much so far. Every night you've worked hard and been paid well for it. Enough to be able to provide for your family back home. This film is almost completed. What do you want to do? Go back to living in a caravan on the South Downs and picking radishes and turnips for a living? No, of course you don't! Life goes on. You have to move on We all do. Am I making sense to you Trevilla? And you've got talent too. Bucket loads of it. You don't want to waste your potential, do you?"

"No you are right, Mr Burnside." Trevilla started to take control of herself. "It's just so painful right now. My mind is everywhere."

In some ways Arthur had always been something of a father figure to all of the performers, and staff he employed. Although Trevilla was a grown woman he could see in her all the naivety of a little girl lost. He felt very protective and had indeed promised her father, Roget, that he would look after her. He sought to put things into perspective.

"You are still young, Trevilla. But if you dwell on everything that goes wrong in life you would never go forward. You would never want to take risks or explore new things and places and make new friends. Believe me, for you in the future, there will be times of splendour. One day you will look back and think of those splendid memories."

"Those splendid memories." Trevilla repeated the words. "I shall remember those words. I will try to know this splendour but I am hurting badly today."

They began to walk again. "Tomorrow you must get on with things. Finish the film and give it your best efforts. When the film is over we have more work as you know. The cast will be sailing to Sydney to begin the tour of Australia. The J. C. Williamson theatre organisation will be staging the show in every major city out there. I will be with you all managing the production. It should be a wonderful tour. We will be sailing from Los Angeles to Hawaii and then across the Pacific. I'm looking forward to it."

"Have you been there before?" Trevilla asked curiously.

"No. It is an unknown quantity to me. I believe they're building a bridge over Sydney harbour. We'll drive back now." They walked up the beach to where the car was parked. Santa Monica beach was filled with swimmers and sunbathers. It looked glorious in the sunshine. Arthur smiled at her. He could see that she appeared to be in better spirits. "There is one thing that has always puzzled me about you. Where does your name come from?"

For the first time that afternoon she smiled. "I am an Hungarian Gypsy girl true, but my mother had an aunt and uncle who travelled to England and lived in their caravan in Cornwall near a place called Trevilla. My mother liked the name so much she decided to call her first born baby the name of Trevilla. So that is how I got the name."

Arthur rose to the occasion. "So, if your aunt had gone to live in Leighton Buzzard or Tunbridge Wells, you might have been named after those towns."

"I think I prefer Trevilla," she said with a wry smile.

They drove away and on the surface Trevilla seemed to be putting on a brave face. In reality she was broken-hearted and as she looked out of the car window floods of tears spilled from her eyes.

***

The film version of *The Prince and the Gypsy Girl* was completed just over five weeks later. Trevilla had decided with a heavy heart to perform the scenes to the absolute best of her ability. The story was about the loss of a great love when the prince's real identity is revealed and he returned to his own people leaving behind a devastated Gypsy girl called Saffron. It mirrored the true-life situation to a certain extent of the love between Trevilla and Anatole, and in her performances on screen the tears she shed were real. Critics and studio bosses found her acting realistic, not realising Trevilla's real life emotions were coming through in her performances. None of the studio bigwigs or other actors who watched her with such sheer unbridled admiration knew of the pain she was carrying within her. The word was out amongst the top agents in Hollywood that Trevilla was a star in the making. They were all keen to sign her, each trying to outbid the other.

Trevilla's story was the stuff of dreams that Hollywood absolutely loved. The rags to riches story of a Gypsy girl plucked from obscurity to stardom on the West End stage and then the bright lights of Broadway before going on to star in one of the last great silent movies of Hollywood. With her charismatic presence and her dancing skills combined with a laughing personality and strong natural singing voice she would surely be a hit in the era of the 'talkies' that was soon to arrive. Al Jolson was soon to star in the first talking picture, *The Jazz Singer*, and from then on the distinctive voices of actors and actresses would earmark them and, in some cases, typecast them for stardom.

According to the publicity statements of Trevilla's work, she was never groomed for stardom. They lied unintentionally. By virtue of the fact she was a Gypsy girl living in a caravan on the South Downs of the Sussex countryside, and scraping a poor income as a vegetable picker her discovery during the filming of a documentary by Andre Aviva was all the more extraordinary.

In an age when Hollywood often invented fictitious backgrounds for some of their major stars, Trevilla's life story needed no embellishment. It was pure gold and Hollywood loved it. Many of the stars who followed on in the 1930s grew to such prominence they were almost considered to be more than mortal. But up on screen they represented an image that many American cinema goes could identify with. The strong character of Clark Gable equally at home as a working man or soldier of fortune; the tough but fair Henry Fonda, who projected 'Americanism' in every situation; the hell for leather pioneering visage of John Wayne who would automatically assume the mantle of leadership by example; the cynical and worldly-wise Humphrey Bogart trusting no one and always coolly acting with integrity.

The 1950s would see the arrival of the rebellious, always compelling Marlon Brando; the non-conformist sincere man of conviction in Montgomery Clift. and James Dean's wild singular unpredictable loner that depicted the complexity of the wilderness of youth. Such were the diversities of the male image in Hollywood films in its glory days.

The female stars were of a mixed breed of foreign and homegrown talent. Greta Garbo, Marlene Dietrich, Theda Bara, Ingrid Bergman, Pola Negri, Hedy Lamarr, Lili Damita, Annabella, all set men's hearts beating and their pulses racing. Their ability to fill the screen with radiance and expression made European women seem unattainable and mysterious, giving them an even more attractive aura. There were many other beautiful and desirable women who combined talent, charisma and whatever the magical ingredient was that elevated them from such varied careers as a copy typist, a model, a club singer or a hat check girl, to become a goddess of the screen. In the years that followed women such as Jean Harlow, Claudette Colbert, Myrna Loy, Grace Kelly, Lauren Bacall, Gene Tierney, Linda Darnell, Maureen O'Hara, Ava Gardner all became synonymous in the pantheons of the film star goddesses who would inspire such bountiful worship.

It was a world that was totally alien to Trevilla. Performing had come naturally to her. She never considered fame to be important. It was the love of appearing before an audience that really thrilled her. The huge salary she earned was merely to her at least a means of looking after her family back home. She was puzzled that in Hollywood beauty and glamour at that time, more so than talent seemed to be a prerequisite for a successful career. If there was anything Trevilla had loved more about her newfound way of life then it was the opportunity to travel. This was a real bonus in her life.

At one stage Trevilla had never considered a life beyond the Sussex Downs. The thrill of sailing across the sea to America was one she would never forget nor the first view of New York from the deck of a ship. She was like a wide-eyed child when she boarded a train to take her to Los Angeles with the rest of the cast to work in Hollywood. California was a dream destination for her. Endless sunshine, orange groves, golden beaches, happy confident people, high-rolling surf, everything that created the perfect image of Lotus land.

Now she was sailing to Australia, a place she knew nothing about. Arthur Burnside was hoping that the excitement and adventure of this tour would go some way at least in helping her to overcome the loss of Anatole. The J. C. Williamson group were a great contributing force in promoting the interests of Australian theatre. They were arranging to stage *The Prince and the Gypsy Girl* in the grand old theatres of Hobart, Perth, Adelaide, Melbourne, Brisbane and Sydney. Lovely old theatres with names such as Her Majesties, the Tivoli and the palace would soon be bursting at the seams with audiences eager to see the show. James Cassius Williamson and his wife, Maggie Moore, had come to Australia from American in 1874 to star in the play Struck Oil which, ironically, they had found through a Californian miner. They had become the powerhouse of Australian theatre and their work had generated through the ages to the present day.

Along with the rest of the cast, Trevilla would always remember the wonderful hot sunny morning when the ship they were travelling on entered the heads of the Sydney Harbour. There before them in 1929 the famous Harbour Bridge was still under construction and it would not be until 1932 that it would be fully completed and opened. Made by the British firm Harvey, Bradford and Toyer, it would become part of the spectacular backdrop of one of the most beautiful harbours in the world. Twenty-three years before Anatole had sailed into this very harbour on his way back to America after having been shanghaied to China.

Now it was the starting point for a long gruelling theatrical tour in a young brash country still trying to discover its national identity. Trevilla's world was constantly expanding and deep in her heart she knew it was all a direct result of her meeting Anatole just over a year before. It had been a rollercoaster ride since then.

***

Mariska tried hard to continue with her life. It wasn't easy. She totally lacked enthusiasm for anything. Until she finally knew what had happened to her brother she could only live in a permanent state of anxiety. It would be impossible to even mourn his loss. Apart from looking after her children she spent much of the time working on the financial journals that showed the rise and fall of the Shervington family business interests. Bernard was busy with his Architectural business and attending the House of Lords whenever there were important issues to be discussed. Life somehow went on.

Andre Aviva stopped over upon his return from the Congo. He spent a few days as a guest of the Shervingtons before returning to New York. It was a deep mystery to him regarding the disappearance of the aircraft. Andre could only explain how he had waited at a remote airfield in the Congo for Anatole's return. Hours and hours he had waited until the lustrous blue African sky had turned pitch-black, illuminated only by the haphazard sprinkling of stars. The aircraft should have returned within a couple of hours. Andre feared the worst possible outcome. A search party organised by the Belgian commissioner went out the next day only to return a week later having discovered the charred burnt out fragmented remains of the plane strewn in all directions. So badly destroyed was the aircraft that it was impossible to tell if there were any human remains. The torrential rain and violence of this fearful storm had also eroded much of the material.

With an extremely heavy heart and grief for his friend, Andre had reluctantly left the Congo. He also felt great sadness for the Belgian pilot who left behind him a Congolese wife and son. In the study of Shervington Manor as he recounted the story to Mariska and Bernard, he found himself breaking up with emotion. Normally a quietly authoritative, studious and resilient man, he had been deeply affected by the events in the Congo; however, in the light of this apparent tragedy he vowed that it would not deter him from further adventures. To continue would be the greatest tribute to his friend, Anatole, and once he arrived home in New York he started to plan his next assignment. He invited the Shervingtons to join him on it.

There was the matter of sorting out Anatole's affairs that was left to Mariska to deal with. When Anatole had sailed to England he had considered the move to be a permanent one. Subsequently he had transferred all his financial assets to an English bank. All the money he had earned in England and Africa had accumulated and remained untouched. Mariska sought advice from the Shervington family solicitor. Eric Fielding had long helped the Shervingtons and as well as being an astute legal adviser, he had also doubled up as their business manager. He had sadly died in recent years, but the firm of Fielding Solicitors had continued under the shrewd guidance of a very capable man called David Stuart-Wright. He was grey-haired, distinguished looking and spoke in a soft honey warm voice. The two of them sat in the study looking through legal papers and documents.

"I appreciate all the work you have done for us since Mr Fielding died. It was very good of you to come to the house to help me with all details regarding the Shervington enterprises. Would you be happy to continue on as our business manager? We would like to retain your services."

"I would be more than happy, Lady Mariska. In fact the firm would consider it an honour. I believe from our records Lady Bernadette was dealing with the Fielding Solicitors back in Queen Victoria's day. It's a long association and I hope under our stewardship it will continue. All the books seem to be in order and as far as the various leases on property where your firms are located, and existing hire agreements for plant and machinery are concerned, we will renegotiate all contracts for you. There was another matter you wished me to discuss with you regarding your late brother."

"Yes, that is right, Mr Stuart-Wright. The term you have just used – My late brother. Well, nobody knows. Andre Aviva, who was my brother's colleague on filming assignments in Africa, recently visited us and he tells me there were only remnants of the aircraft found in the Congo, but absolutely no indication of what happened to Anatole and the pilot. I know the plane apparently exploded and that doesn't leave anything to the imagination but there's not even been a trace that explains the situation. At the moment all of Anatole's savings and earnings from his work paid by the film company and Arthur Burnside's management organisation are sitting in a London bank. What is your advice?"

Mr Stuart-Wright pondered over this issue. "It's something of a Marie Celeste mystery, isn't it? For the moment at least I will cease to refer to your brother as late. That was a mistake on my part and I apologise for it. In any legal matters and documentation, it may be better if we speak or write of him in terms of fate unknown. Hopefully we will know something shortly. I will write to the authorities in the Congo to ask them to pursue this mystery. Should you hear anything first you will let me know, won't you?"

"Of course. Do you mind if I ask you one other thing? I loved my brother very much. We were kids... Russian Jewish kids... who were taken to New York by our parents escaping persecution and then we became orphans when they both died. We both made our own way in life since then as dancers on stage. He had a varied life. He was an extra in Hollywood films, drilled for oil, washed dishes and waited on tables, a soldier during the Mexican War and in the Great War, and a cinematographer. He took risks all of his life. Now I am to all intents and purposes a business woman looking after all the Shervington companies. My husband and I have also made our own films about the British way of life and we are planning to do more with Anatole's colleague, Mr Aviva, sometime in the future. I live in hope of Anatole's return but if nothing is heard from him again, what is the statutory period before he is officially declared dead?"

"I wish I could be more encouraging, Lady Mariska. If I was to say I am sure he will turn up, I would be offering false optimism. In the case of the absence of a body it may be a case of waiting for years. Perhaps as many as seven."

"As many as seven?" Mariska was genuinely surprised.

"Yes. I am afraid so. Unless a judge rules otherwise for some exemplary reason. I agree it's a long time to live with the presumption of death or the expectation that somehow and somewhere he is still alive."

Mariska put her head in her hands more out of frustration than grief.

"It's the not knowing of what happened to him that is so painful. Not only for me but for his lady friend, Trevilla, too."

"Where is she at the moment? Trevilla is the dancing Gypsy girl, I believe."

"Well she's on a stage tour. Trevilla appeared in a show in New York which then transferred to Hollywood. Now she's on the other side of the world. Trevilla and the rest of the cast are somewhere in Australia."

Mariska gazed out at the Downs from the study window. For a brief moment she envied Trevilla whose career was blossoming and taking her to new pastures. The thrill of performing to new audiences around the world was something that those who worked in the profession never completely got out of their system.

"If there's nothing else?" David Stuart-Wright rose from his chair and politely shook her hand. "I will be in touch."

"And so will I, should I hear anything," Mariska said, forcing a smile.

David Stuart-Wright left the room quietly. Mariska walked across to a world globe in the corner of the room. She examined first the Congo and then turned the globe around until Australia came into view. What was it like for Trevilla to be so far away she wondered?

Forty-One

If America had been an eye opener to Trevilla, Australia was to prove even more so. Upon landfall the cast and crew had been largely unprepared for it, some thinking that it was a place that combined British tradition and American style energy. Trevilla knew virtually nothing about the land and she was at times delighted, shocked and surprised by what she saw.

The tour opened in Sydney and would move right across the length and breadth of the country. She had never seen a sky so deeply blue in all of her life nor felt the power of such resplendent sunshine. The old architectural style of some of the colonial buildings such as the New South Wales parliament, the great University of Sydney and the grandeur of Martin Place, seemed to belong to the Victoria era of England rather than the roaring twenties of twentieth-century Australia.

The accents, slang and vernacular together with their brash, confident, speak as you find nature, took a while for the show's cast to get used to. They were to find, as many did before and after, that the up-front attitudes of the nation as a whole marked an innate kindliness and warmth. Even the style of humour of the Australians was bewildering at first. One night during the run of the show in Melbourne, Trevilla and some of the cast went to a theatre to see a local comedian nicknamed 'Mo'. His real name was Roy Rene and he had a manner of telling a joke or speaking a phrase in such a way his audience would fall about laughing. He would howl across the stage, 'The barmaid and the butcher! I'll down ya like a tack! Strike me lucky, matey! You little trimmerrrr!' None of the lines seemed particularly funny but the mirth and jollity was in the delivery. Trevilla didn't understand a word of it but laughted out loud at Mo's way of coming across to the audience.

Sometimes in the late afternoons, Trevilla and her companions would gaze into the window of a public house. Truly what she saw in the interior of a pub was a vision of hell or a front seat at Dante's Inferno. The 'six o'clock swill' was a sight awash with beer being drunk at a frantic pace as if they were trying to break records for downing ale. At six o'clock, the pubs closed and the men spilled out on the streets in a drunken haze. Trevilla thought to herself that in Europe people drank for pleasure. In Australia they drank alcohol as if it was a job of work. It would be many years before civilised drinking hours were introduced which would end the almost traditional six o'clock swill.

There were glorious moments when Trevilla would enjoy some of the scenic best that Australia had to offer; a trip out to the Blue Mountains or a swim in the surf of Sydney's golden beaches such as Bondi, Avalon and Manly. In Melbourne there were days out in the Dandenong Ranges or to see the stunning rock formation The Twelve Apostles. All the time Trevilla was savouring her new adventures and absorbing the moment with a photographic and retentive memory so that she could tell her family back home of the sights she had seen.

In a public place if Trevilla was speaking to one of her fellow actors, her loud laughing manner and distinctive accent would arouse the curiosity of people close by. Australia at that time was a raw nation still unacquainted by the various languages, dialects and accents of the cosmopolitan Europe. They were friendly with the Anglo Saxon and Celtic familiarity of the lands from which so many of their ancestors had originated; however, they were suspicious and wary of strangers in their midst; the people they considered to be alien to their way of life who wore long dark coats, kaftans, or the attire of rural European country folk. In later years mass immigration, integration and mixed marriages would change the very nature of the population so that the surname of many Australians would indicate the nation that their ancestors had been born in. From the 1940s the assisted passage scheme would bring over a million British migrants to settle there but they were not the only ones who sought a new life in a country that was still growing and developing. Italians, Greeks, refugees from war-torn Europe would come to live there. Australia was young and naïve yet it would become a prosperous nation of full employment, a lifestyle that served up the good life in a place that had not yet been torn apart by political or civil strife. It was warm, open and exciting.

Trevilla and the cast of *The Prince and the Gypsy Girl* felt privileged if not blessed that their thespian occupation had taken them first to America and then Australia. The price of their ticket had been to perform to audiences. Arthur Burnside, a born showman, had heard that audiences in Australia gave no quarter and my how he made them perform as if it was their last night on earth! They performed so well that some of the cast including Trevilla over reached themselves and everywhere they went across the 'Lucky Country' the audiences whether at the Tivoli, Her Majesties or some obscure theatre in an outback town, would cheer wildly. Not easy for a country that was not easily impressed.

Across the Nullarbour plain on the way to their last shows in Perth, Trevilla looked at railway workers carrying out construction on a new gauge line. It was 106 degrees in the shade and the heat was scorching. Big, well-built, healthy-looking men laboured in these extreme conditions. Trevilla who was far from being a shrinking violet, thought to herself that this was not a country for the faint-hearted. But she loved it and felt thrilled to be there although she was eager to return home and see her family.

***

Jack was a hardworking publican at all times in his little haven in Ireland. He was a popular landlord and was treated as something of a character with his American background. He wasn't a man who looked back too much. His tough upbringing aroused no nostalgia.

After all, his wild and domestically violent father had been murdered and his dear mother had tragically died young from cancer, thus propelling him to the same orphanage that Anatole and Mariska had found themselves in. It was because of this that Jack considered the pair of them to be almost family to him. Jack was saddened by the apparent demise of Anatole. He carried on regardless, trying to be good humoured and cherishing Miriam and their children.

One night a local villager came in with an accordion and another man decided to play the piano that sat in the corner of the saloon bar. Jack drank his milk stout and for some reason even he couldn't fathom why he began to sing. The song was 'The Minstrel Boy' and from behind the bar he felt like the kid who sang on the street corners of New York to bring home extra money for his mother. His voice resonated across the pub as he sang this traditional Irish song. All of the drinkers in The Limerick Castle stopped their conversation and banter to listen to Jack singing this emotional song to the accompaniment of the accordion and piano. It was spellbinding to see this former hardened New York cop sing in a strong voice with moisture in his eyes. He was singing for his lost boyhood friend with whom he had been through so much of the fortunes of life; nobody there knew that, of course. When he had finished the song he turned around and raised his glass of stout towards a photograph set in a frame. It was of him, Anatole and Slugs in their army uniforms. He smiled at the memory of it.

***

Six months later Slugs was working late at the London office of The *Tribune* in Fleet Street. For the folks back home in the United States he was writing up his observations on the British way of life in his usual man of the people style. His articles were well received on the other side of the pond, which amused and entertained the Americans with details of the eccentricities in their eyes of the British. Slugs wrote on a number of subjects. They included the nation's genuine love of sport, which he shared. In the time he and his family had lived at Ealing Green Slugs and had become a supporter of the local football team, Brentford, whose ground he regularly attended. He was also a great admirer of Rugby League, which he compared to Grid Iron football. On his trips to the North of England he would always make a point of seeing a match if teams such as St Helens, Crewe or Wigan were playing. The tennis finals at Wimbledon were something he enjoyed watching and writing about. Years later Slugs was proud to say he had been a potential star spotter, and had tipped Fred Perry as a future Wimbledon Champion, which he won three times in a row, in 1934, 1935 and 1936. By coincidence, although Manchester born, Fred Perry had been educated at Ealing Grammar School, a stone's throw from where Slugs lived.

Slugs, who had begun his journalistic career as something of a journeyman writer, had blossomed and grown in his profession. Early on in New York the editor of the *Tribune* had told him that, apart from a love of the English language, the greatest skill of a journalist was in the power of observation. The articles that he despatched to the United States never lacked detail. He was painstaking in his description of even the basic things.

One article he wrote was of the British love of shopping, how they bought their goods in the corner shop or big department stores such as Harrods, Woolworths, Selfridges or from Barrow boys in Petticoat Lane.

He wrote about quaint English villages in the Cotswolds, the Sussex market towns and the lovely agricultural areas of Kent, known as the Garden of England. He was working late that night when a story broke that was to be one of the highlights of his career. His secretary, a pleasant young lady called Valerie Smith, knocked on the door and entered.

"Sir, I was just about to go home when a telegram came for you. Do you want to read it now or shall you have time tomorrow. I know you're busy."

Slugs turned around. "What does it say Val?"

"It's about your friend Anatole Luchenya, the gentleman who went missing in the Congo." Slugs immediately stood up. Valerie continued. "He's been found."

"They've found his remains?" Slugs pre-empted her.

"No, sir. They've found him. He's still alive."

"My God!" Slugs almost snatched the telegram from her hand. He read it and then a broad smile stretched across his face. "The old son of a gun! He's beaten the grim reaper again!" He was so delighted he roared with laughter. "So help me the guy's got wings on his feet!"

Valerie smiled too for she was well aware of their friendship. "It's quite a story, isn't it, sir?"

"It's a modern-day Stanley finding Livingstone! It's like Robinson Crusoe being discovered on his tropical island. It's like Long John Silver turning up and buying a round at the Admiral Benbow Inn. What a great story! He's my goddam pal as well! I want you to ring the Shervingtons now and send telegrams to Jack Clancy in Ireland and Arthur Burnside in Australia. Oh, and another thing, honey. Book me on the first available steamship to the Congo. Get the *Tribune*'s photographer on the phone tonight. Tell him he's going to the Congo too. Book him on the same ship. Valerie, we have ourselves one hell of a great story!"

"Yes sir!" Valerie left the office and immediately begun the process of informing the various people. The telegrams weren't sent out until the following morning. For all the recipients the news was amazing and they greeted it with disbelief.

The Shervingtons were in the lounge with their children when the telephone call came. Terry Bentley, the footman, had taken the call and eagerly came into the room beaming a broad smile. It was a very happy day for him already. He had recently married the lusciously beautiful maid of the house, Marilyn Wilce, and that very morning she had announced her pregnancy to him.

"Sir, you really must come to the phone now. It's Mr Mahoney's secretary, Valerie Smith, ringing from New York *Tribune*'s office in London. It's grand news, sir, it really is!" He was beside himself with excitement. "By the way sir my wife, Marilyn, and I are expecting."

"I'll come straight away, Terry," said Bernard. "Congratulations, young man. Give my best wishes to your lovely wife." He took the phone and answered. "Valerie, is it? Mr Mahoney's secretary? Yes, this is Lord Bernard Shervington. My footman says it's grand news!" He listened carefully as she recounted what had happened. He almost dropped the phone in amazement. "Anatole! I can hardly believe it. Alive! After all this time? What absolutely marvellous news!" He continued listening. Then he broke out into a smile as happiness at the news followed after the surprise. "Thank you for letting me know. Tell Mr Mahoney I'm grateful to him for informing us and wish him a safe trip to the Congo. Keep in touch with any further news. Good night, Valerie."

For a moment Bernard stood by the phone hardly able to speak. He just could not believe that his brother-in-law had yet again survived another of his skirmishes with death. Perhaps the real question was how had he survived? Bernard walked back into the lounge and Mariska looked up at him noticing the quizzical look on his face.

"What is it, darling?" she could see he was smiling broadly.

"It's your brother, Mariska, Anatole. He's still alive!"

***

Trevilla was in Perth, Western Australia. It was the final night of an extensive tour that had taken the cast of *The Prince and the Gypsy Girl* backwards and forwards across the vast continent of this sunburnt country. *'I love a sunburnt country. A land of sweeping plains. Of ragged mountain ranges. Of droughts and flooding rains. I love her far horizons.'* So went the lines of Dorothea McKellar's famous poem 'My Country' that Trevilla heard recited in the Botanic Hotel in Adelaide one night. It was strange to Trevilla that for such a masculine country Dorothea McKellar referred to 'her far horizons'. Surely Australia, which boasted rugged sheep shearers, the six o'clock swill, Jackeroos on cattle drives, the tough sports of Rugby and Rules football, could only have been a 'he'. But Trevilla didn't debate it. She loved her 'far horizons' too.

Now the tour was coming to an end, and after a few days of well-deserved rest the entire cast would board a ship in Fremantle and sail for home. The last show of the tour was at Her Majesty's theatre in Perth. It would have been a much-vaunted phrase to say the show had been a runaway success on its Australian tour, but there was really no other way to describe it. Just before Trevilla went on stage, Arthur Burnside came to see her ostensibly to wish her luck on her final performance not that she needed it. By now after only two years since her discovery she performed and sang with unbridled passion. Offers of further stage work, films in Britain and Hollywood had been pouring in.

Arthur Burnside was a true gentleman in the way he looked after all the performers in his stable. His kindness, courtesy and general encouragement to each of them as both a manager and figure was rewarded with great loyalty. Arthur was of the people. Born in humble circumstances by virtue of his work ethic he was a working-class gentleman who behaved better than many men with a background of privilege. He was especially fond of Trevilla in the manner of a father's concern for his daughter. He knew that she had never chosen this profession. To a certain extent it had chosen her through a manner of luck and good fortune. If it had been difficult for him to tell her about Anatole's apparent demise, it was going to be a thrill to tell her of his certain survival. Arthur knocked on the door of her dressing room and she let him in.

"My dear, I've just called by to wish you tremendous luck in your show tonight. This is it now. In a few days' time we'll all be sailing from Fremantle docks. I want to thank you from the bottom of my heart for the enormous effort you have made in not only this tour but in America too. There are many opportunities to come for you and I will offer you guidance and advice wherever possible."

"Thank you, Arthur." Trevilla was genuinely touched. "So much has happened to me in the last two years, it is a dream. Hey, Arthur, I have even learned to speak better, eh?" I don't say huh so often!"

"You have progressed in leaps and bounds. The girl on the South Downs has become a truly talented lady now. A lady in private, a lady on stage. And what a lady! We are all so proud of you."

Trevilla laughed. It was the laugh of the old Trevilla. The girl who had watched Anatole hoof it up on the South Downs like an old-time vaudeville artist. She had stood with her hands on her hips and had tossed her head back and laughed in sheer delight.

"A lady? I have always wanted to be a lady. To be thought of as a lady!"

"You are now. But like me, a boy from the East End, never forget where you came from and never, ever, get above yourself. We are mere mortals working in an environment of talent, music, colourful shows but in truth we are no different to a Smithfield Market butcher or a Covent Garden florist or a Hatton garden jeweller. The Aussies have loved this show. The takings have been superb. My dear there is one thing I want you to do tonight. Go out there and give the Aussies the best show they will ever see in their lives. Give them the best performance in your life. You have every reason to. Especially now."

Trevilla did not understand the last part of Arthur's kind words and looked at him curiously.

"Oh yes, my dear, I have wonderful news for you. Your friend… indeed may I say our friend, Anatole, has been found alive."

"He is alive!" Trevilla was astounded. Her big expressive eyes looked as if they didn't know whether to shine with delight or burst into tears. "How? When? Where is he?"

"I don't know the full details yet. I was forwarded a telegram from his friend the journalist, Mr Mahoney, that Anatole had been found in the Congo and that it is quite a story. Mr Mahoney I understand, from a later telegram I received from Lord Shervington, is en route to the Congo as we speak. In six weeks' time when the boat we are travelling on returns home and you go to Sussex to see your family he may well be there waiting for you."

Trevilla laughed and cried at the same time. It was a touching sight that for one moment made Arthur feel as if he wanted to cry too. She leaned across and hugged him.

"I am lost for words," she said. "I will sing my heart out tonight!"

***

Trevilla did indeed sing her heart out that night. The whole cast had never been more finely tuned and enthusiastic as they were that night in Her Majesty's Theatre, Perth, Western Australia. It had been a long exhaustive tour with extended seasons in all of the major cities and record-breaking box office takings. The tour had gone on for many months and all the cast were looking forward to returning home. They were all equally enthusiastic that they wanted the tour to end on a high note and take home their very fond memories of an exciting tour.

When it came to Trevilla's show stopper song 'The Day I Lost My Man' she went to the centre of the stage and belted out the number with great expression, poignancy and with the happiness and emotion trembling in her voice, whilst at the same time with tears rolling from her eyes. Her rendition of the song earned her a standing ovation. At the end of the show the entire cast had numerous curtain calls and ovations. The cast returned the compliment by lining up from one end of the stage to the other and singing a specially rehearsed song that the audience could join in. The song was 'Waltzing Matilda'. It was a fitting end to a spectacular tour down under ending on a very happy note for all concerned.

After a few days' rest in the beautiful city of Perth, perhaps Australia's best-kept secret, Arthur Burnside and the entire cast boarded a boat in Fremantle and sailed for home. This too was another great experience for Trevilla. The route home from Western Australia took her to such exotic destinations as Colombo in Ceylon, Bombay, Aden, through the Red Sea, the Suez Canal, Egypt, Naples, Marseilles, finally arriving at Tilbury Docks in England.

***

Slugs duly arrived in the Congo. Time after time Jake Mahoney would pinch himself. How on earth did this big guy, a former boxer and New York plumber, find himself in a career as an international journalist going on assignments to places like Africa. Never ever did Jake take anything ever for granted in this life. He may have been nicknamed Slugs by his friends for his youthful pugilism but he was forever embracing every new experience and learning like a university-educated intellectual with an insatiable thirst for knowledge. Here he was in the Congo. The hot, sweltering, colourful Congo. He strode through the markets and the streets in Stanleyville to where he knew his old friend Anatole would be staying.

He felt a real surge of excitement going through him. It was as if he was trembling with the thrill inside him at being here and meeting his old pal who had one hell of a story to recount to him. Boy, was he a lucky guy? In the hotel that seemed to be full of indistinguishable foreign accents and exotic women mingling with travellers, explorers, chancers, conmen, handsome devils who were outrageously good looking and servants in pristine white uniforms, Slugs checked in. Somewhere in the lobby he knew he would find his friend.

An impeccably polite servant took his case to his room where Slugs immediately bathed and donned a white suit, and broad panama hat more in keeping with the climate of the Congo than his double-breasted suit from Saville Row. Slugs had not seen Anatole since their New York days and in his mind he had considered the visual scenario of what their first meeting after so long would be like. The story of Stanley's meeting with Doctor Livingstone flashed through his mind. It seemed pretty low-key for Stanley, an America correspondent, to merely say after what must have been a treacherous and merciless journey through the terror of so called darkest Africa, 'Doctor Livingstone, I presume'. Was it embroidered or deliberately played down for journalistic reasons? Whatever the reason the worlds 'Doctor Livingstone, I presume' made the front pages of the world's press in the way that the phrase 'one small step for man, a giant leap for mankind' did in 1969 when Neil Armstrong became the first man to walk on the moon.

This event wasn't quite in the same league but Slugs was sure to milk it for all that it was worth. After all, the guy was his friend from the old days. He walked downstairs to the bar. It was absolutely filled with people of all nationalities while a French band played a jazz number in the background. No sign of Anatole. He was on edge with nervous tension. Where could he be?

The Belgian commissioner had told Slugs that Anatole was staying here before his impending departure. Slugs ordered a beer. He was so hot and excited he sank a half without batting an eyelid. He promptly ordered another. Through the crowded bar a grey-haired Catholic priest came up beside him. *Funny place to give a sermon*, thought Slugs. The bar seemed to be full of amply bosomed, dazzling predatory women with figures, and looks that would grace the screens of Hollywood films. By God, if he was still single, Slugs thought, how easy it would be to cut a swathe through these ladies and still come up gasping for more. Then he thought of his wife, Marilyn, his two daughters and recently born son back in London. No one could put a price on the love he had for his own glorious family.

"Oi'll be having a nice cold beer," said the priest in a voice that sounded like a grossly exaggerated Irish accent.

"Of course, Father Flanagan," replied the Congolese barman.

"Call me Father Ray. No need to stand on ceremony," the priest assured him. "And I'll be ordering another one for my friend here."

Slugs glanced sideways to see who the man's drinking partner was. Maybe the priest was conducting an illicit affair with one of the glamorous women in the bar! Now that would be a story for the British Sunday papers, which thrived on scandal. No such luck! A man with a suntanned, rugged sunburned countenance, appeared beside him and sipped from the beer turning to look at the women in the bar and giving them a wink and a smile. He looked every inch the cosmopolitan traveller and man of the world he was now. It was Anatole.

He turned to Father Flanagan and said, "Gee, isn't it great to be alive?"

"You wouldn't be dead for quids, eh?" agreed the Father.

Slugs leaned across the bar. "You can bet your ass on that, buddy boy!"

Anatole almost spilt his beer. The last person he ever expected to see in these parts was Slugs. The two men gave each other a bear hug while Father Flanagan looked on with a mixture of surprise and admiration for their show of brotherly love.

"Saints preserve us!" he exclaimed. "You fellows are not strangers then! You've obviously met before!"

Forty-Two

It was a warm and humid morning when Slugs and Anatole sat down together on wicker chairs in the shaded veranda of the hotel in Stanleyville. The previous night they had embraced as old friends and enjoyed several beers together, which in the perspiring heat had assuaged their thirst, but not made them the slightest bit drunk in the least. Perhaps they had been too high on the mere pleasure at just being alive. Slugs in a broad hat and white suit into which his strong body frame fitted, looked every inch the Hollywood version of an American reporter of renown and legend. Anatole had all the characteristics of the well-heeled traveller who had been everywhere and seen it all. The night before he had not wanted to talk about what had happened when the plane had blown up in mid-air over the Congo. Today was different. He was going to reveal all to Slugs who was not only keen to know to satisfy his own curiosity, but also for professional reasons as this was the best scoop story he would ever get.

"So old buddy, are you up to talking about it? I know it may not be easy for you. If you don't, I'll understand." He had said that earnestly because he remained intensely loyal to his old friend. However, in his heart because of the nature of this story of adventure and survival, he, in his capacity as a hard-nosed reporter in the dubious newspaper circulation war, desperately wanted a blow by blow description for the *Tribune* in New York. He knew the scoop would enhance his reputation, his worldwide status as a reporter and probably increase his salary triple-fold. Yet at the same time, Slugs, for personal and altruistic reasons, was prepared to set aside the story if it meant endangering his long-standing, much-valued friendship with Anatole.

He breathed a sigh of relief when Anatole finally decided to answer. "Yes I'll talk about it. I guess for your readers it will be something of a back from the dead story."

"Nat, if you don't want it reported I won't write a word of it. It will be just between you and I. That's a gold plated, copper bottomed promise. We go back too far and you know me too well. I'm Slugs the big guy… and the big guy always keeps his word."

"I know. You're my pal along with Jack." Anatole smiled at him. "Let's get going then." Slugs took up a note pad and pen. "Where do you want to start?"

"Tell me how you survived the plane explosion and what happened to the unfortunate pilot."

Anatole looked pensive for a moment. It was obvious his narrow and somewhat miraculous escape had made him feel circumspect about that particular occasion in conversation. After a short pause he began to narrate the story.

"This is what happened when the violent storm broke…"

***

SERE
SEARING

Red flashes, the colour of soaring forest fires lit up the sky with terrifying effect in front of the faltering aircraft. The plane carrying Anatole and the Belgian pilot was spluttering and stalling as extremely heavy tropical rain poured down with the speed, ferocity and impact of flood waters bursting riverbanks. Terrifyingly loud, eardrum-shattering thunder resonated from all directions as if its volume was being broadcast from strategically placed loudspeakers. Bright yellow lightning streaked backwards and forwards like dangerous killer beams from futuristic electrical weaponry giving no quarter to their hunted doomed prey. One of these lightning bolts found its victim when it struck the fuselage of the aircraft immediately igniting it.

Anatole wasn't quite sure just what happened next. In an instant to avoid the smoke and flames he had leapt up from his seat and found himself hurtling from the aircraft as it exploded above him, disintegrating into pieces. He must have been two or three hundred feet above the densely thick forests as he plunged to certain death. At least that was how it seemed. In the space of what only seemed to be a few seconds he was crashing into the tightly crammed trees below. They were so heavily entwined together, the effect as he thudded against them, could have been likened to that of landing on a trampoline. He found himself ricocheting across the tops of the trees like a thrown pebble skimming across the surface of water. Then suddenly tree branches broke beneath him and he was falling between leaves, vines and lianas to come landing down on a flooded and muddy jungle floor. The water from the storm had created rivulets that swept him along until he found the strength to hold onto a tree trunk. He held on for about a minute until with horror he saw a gruesome looking snake slithering down the trunk towards him. At once he let go and allowed himself to be taken away by the flood waters. The streams had suddenly converged and became fast-flowing cascades of water. Such was the strength of the current he could not fight against it.

It was a near miracle that he had survived the fall, which, had it not been for the remarkable density of the trees, would almost certainly have been fatal. Now battered, bruised, scratched and exhausted, he vainly waved his arms around to keep his head above water. The more the rain fell, the more the forest became flooded. Very little light penetrated the trees and Anatole felt as if he was swimming in an underground tunnel. The thunder continued and the noise was comparable to that of a mythical dragon of legend or a prehistoric dinosaur in full rage.

He was close to giving up and letting fate take its natural course. The power of the growing and developing waterflow was so strong that it sapped virtually all Anatole's strength. The deluge of torrential rain which managed to permeate the trees came down on him like the pressure of a waterfall. Then, up ahead of him came his saviour in the form of a long strong branch hanging over the water. Mustering all of the strength he could find he heaved himself up and grabbed the branch as the flow of the water took him closer. The branch was strong but very slippery from the rain and he almost lost his grip. With all his might he swung his legs up and wrapped them round the tree. Then he started to manoeuvre himself along the branch until he could get to the main trunk of the tree. He wedged himself into the alcove between the branch and trunk. All he could do was hang on for dear life until the storm abated. He had no idea of how long he was there for, but the storm suddenly seemed to stop as quickly as it had started.

Anatole just rested for some considerable time. He lay back against the tree and in the steaming temperatures to his surprise he found himself shivering. It wasn't because he was cold. He was feeling the after effects of shock. It was no surprise. He had seen the pilot blown to smithereens. He had fallen several hundred feet without a parachute and only survived because of the density of the trees breaking his plunge like a trampoline. Then he had struggled in flood water until he had reached this resting place.

He was faced with the prospect of trekking through the dark forests of the Congo, not knowing which direction to take, and if his choice would lead him into more danger. During the Great War his experiences had been harrowing and apart from his escape from the *Titanic* he had never been so close to death before. He wasn't sure what to do next. For a moment he listened to the sounds of the forest. It was springing to life again after the storm. He could hear the squawk of birds and the fluttering of wings as they soared through openings in the trees in a bid to escape to the freedom of the wide African sky now that the storm had ceased. Somewhere out of sight chimpanzees chattered in their own unique language like villagers at an English market day. An elephant let out a tremendous cry, which could either have been interpreted as a roar to assert its superiority, independence and sheer relief as having survived so foul a storm or a call to arms to other elephants in the forest that it was time to gather together like a small army and move off in the direction of their own choosing. There were grunts and growls of creatures impossible to define in the undergrowth. The dormant insect population resurrected itself from various places of sanctuary and buzzed, and sung together like magical choristers in a world known only to themselves. The forest held not only its dangers but its charms too.

The flood waters had receded and been absorbed into the ground. The result was that steamy gaseous vapours rose through the bottlenecks of the undergrowth combining the scents of tropical flora and fauna together with the pungent smell of something like an open sewer. Anatole knew he could not remain there in the faint hope that a search party would eventually find him. He had to brave the dangers and elements of the jungle. His path was not going to be an easy one. The heavy, muddy surface of his journey ahead was a treacherous one and virtually impassable. It was a risky one too. The various creatures of the locale could bite him, eat him, sting him or trample him underfoot. His choice of demise was a wide selection. He thought to himself that he had not fallen out of an exploding aircraft and survived flood waters to be nourishment for some starving creature. Besides if he were to survive he would have to find some way of obtaining moisture to drink and easily obtainable edibles to supplement his energy from the mysterious land he had been jettisoned into and to which he was now exclusively privy to witness in all of its glory and secrecy.

Anatole began the descent from the huge tree to something akin to as firm a ground he could find to begin the slow perilous trek to some sort of civilisation. From the remote spot he found himself in civilisation seemed to be in another stratosphere. He broke off a firm branch and used it as a stick to support himself on the long directionless journey he had before him. The walk was extremely difficult at first. The muddy surface made it hard for him to maintain his footing. It was not so much a slow walk but rather more a slow-motion trudge in difficult terrain.

The heat was asphyxiating and every few feet that he moved he found himself covered in perspiration. In addition to this his whole body ached. He conceded that it had been a miracle to have fallen so far without incurring any broken bones or physical injury. He had no idea of what time it was, although by the light that streamed through the tops of the trees in the dark forest, he assumed that it must still be daylight. Even so, there was a particularly eerie feel about the dense woodland he walked through. It was as if he expected some wild creature or a hostile native to leap out and attack him in a terrifying instant. He felt constantly on edge, full of nervous tension in the same way he had endured on the horrific battlefields of France in the Great War.

Some of the trees were spiky and untouchable, for they were sharp enough to bring forth blood. Others oozed sap. Close up, the sap had a sour, acrid smell about it that gave a clear indication that it was probably poisonous. Not only were there predatory animals to contend with but plant life that was hostile in its very existence. He could not have chosen a worse environment to have been marooned in without food, water and something to defend himself from whatever sought to attack him. Anatole knew his chances of survival in such harsh conditions were slim. He was determined that he would not give up without a fight and if his energies were low he felt sure his spirit would carry him onwards.

For some considerable time he trudged through the forest. It was teeming with life but it was not clearly visible. To some extent it seemed as if the animals, perhaps wary of the human stranger in their midst, were keeping a safe distance. Then to his surprise and genuine astonishment, a hundred yards or so ahead of him he saw some very agile chimpanzees swinging from tree to tree. Several of them with frustration clearly etched on their faces were attempting to break open the bark on the trees. What on earth were they doing? It soon became clear as the bark fell away. The bees had pollinated the tree and, once opened up, the chimpanzees seemed very much to reflect the very characteristics and expressions of human beings. Their delight in tasting the sweetness of honey was like that of the smile of a human who had just achieved success in his or her favourite pastime.

Anatole carried on with his journey slowly but exhaustingly. The pangs of thirst were beginning to take their toll on him. He was perspiring so much in the sticky heat that he felt as if he was constantly walking through a laundrette. Pretty soon he would be so weak he wouldn't be able to carry on. If he couldn't find anything to drink or wet his mouth he faced the danger of delirium and severe dehydration. Then he saw an immediate answer to his predicament. The trees were dripping with rainwater which soaked the leaves. He at once stepped up to an overhanging branch and supped the water by cupping his hands over the leaves. The water seemed to explode within him as he absorbed each mouthful. The temptation was to drink as much as he possibly could but to do so might have caused him to bring it straight up. Every little bit of sustenance gave him a small amount of energy to keep his walking up. He continued his journey until the light dimmed considerably and he realised with utter dismay that night had fallen.

There was nothing else he could do but rest for a while on some soft earth by the base of a tree and sit there half asleep-half alert in case any nocturnal creatures suddenly assumed he was theirs for the taking. The strange animal and bird noises that he listened to were a clear indication that the jungle doesn't close down for the night. Like a cabaret in Havana or Rio de Janeiro, it was still pretty much a case of business as usual. Anatole closed his eyes for a quarter of an hour, then opened them again and did so right throughout the night until the morning when the rays of the sun began to filter through the gaps in the trees. He was just mentally congratulating himself that he had survived the night when the sound resembling drums being beaten vigorously could be heard. Except they were not drums. He knew exactly what it was. The ground shook, trees and bushes swayed, great bellowing cries could be heard: huge, marauding elephants were heading his way. He desperately tried to scramble up the tree.

Within a minute or so of Anatole climbing a very slippery treetrunk to a suitably safe vantage point, he watched a herd of forest elephants follow each other tail by tail until they had all but disappeared into the density of the trees. He concluded that somewhere perhaps not too far away there would be light and space for elephants are intelligent creatures who, according to legend and myth, do not forget. Almost certainly they would be heading for the elephant watering hole.

This assumption gave his spirits a boost. If he could persevere it would only be a matter of time before he would find something civilised like his own personal Shangri-la. Quickly he came down from the tree and was just about to follow the elephant trail when his eyes froze with fear as he heard an animal grunting behind a clump of bushes. He grabbed a broken tree branch and prepared to swing it hard. From behind the bushes a fierce-looking gorilla appeared and with its tremendously long arms began beating its chest. Then it roared up and down, grunting and groaning loudly before charging at Anatole. The sheer force and energy of the gorilla was frightening. The animal came at him and just as Anatole went to wield the branch at him quickly, it turned around and scampered away. It repeated this several times as if it was playing with him. Close up Anatole found himself looking into the face of the gorilla from a distance of no more than a few feet away.

Then to his surprise the gorilla stopped its display of fury and rage. It sunk down on all fours as if some unseen force had pacified it and slowly it meandered towards Anatole, whose grip on his makeshift weapon of a tree branch suddenly eased. Was it a false dawn? Was the gorilla lulling him into a false sense of security before showing him how devious it could be before launching into a rampaging attack on him? The gorilla appeared to be studying him, moving its head from side to side and projecting it forward like a woman about to kiss a man. For such an obviously fierce creature it had, strangely, sympathetic eyes. In one sense its initial behaviour had been like that of a demonstratively angry child on its first day at school eager to show its rebellious naughty side. In another it was showing the signs of maturity belonging to the child who had now settled down peacefully and was eager to learn. Anatole felt wary at the animal's rapprochement towards him for he feared it would suddenly change its temperament and lash out with hostility. But to his genuine amazement it ignored him and wandered away into the undergrowth.

Truly the animal kingdom never ceased to astonish in all of its patterns of unpredictable behaviour. Such were the thrills and dangers of the jungle.

Anatole continued his long and seemingly directionless journey. He had not realised the density and interminable length of the forest. Days turned into nights. He took sips of moisture from leaves. Rested beneath trees. He found nourishment from berries and some edible fruit. His energies were terribly depleted, his strength completely sapped, and his fortitude in the face of so many lost days and nights in the jungle had gone. Delirious, faint and exhausted he staggered on semi-comatose before collapsing on the ground. For a split second before passing out he was certain he had seen a gap in the trees ahead and real sunlight streaming onto an open expanse of land. He eyes closed and exhaustion overwhelmed him leaving him without physical or mental incentive to carry on. He drifted into a sleep of images and wild imaginings.

Once again he was a child in the snows of Russia. Then he was in New York. He was a young boy with his parents. He was listening to the soft love filled voice of his mother and the wise counsel of his father. An image of his sister, Mariska, greeting him with relief in San Francisco after the earthquake flashed through his mind. Trevilla, the Gypsy girl, who had brought love into his heart and soul was standing on the South Downs of Sussex, her arms outstretched from her hips tossing her head back and laughing out loud. Oh that unmistakeable laugh! Then the sound of raging elephants roared.

He woke up in a fright. There before him was a clearing. He didn't have strength in his legs to stand. All he could do was lay there. To his surprise he had emerged from the treacherous forest and lay on the edge facing vast space, bright sunlight and a wide deep blue sky beneath which elephants played like children. By the heavens above he had encountered an elephant playground. He watched as two elephants appeared to be wrestling. It was in fact the mating season and the elephants were battling over the females. He watched for a few moments fascinated and enthralled through a haze of blurred eyes like a sleepy child allowed into this magical kingdom. However, the exhaustion and the heat began to overwhelm him. His energies were so low that no matter how he tried to stay alert his lack of physical strength gave him no power to rise. He drifted into visions of a world moving from glorious Technicolor into faded black and white images, then oblivion. He lay motionless on the ground, his heart and pulse still maintaining a rhythm but death's door would not be far away.

In fact he lay there for some time before wet moisture began to stream over his face and he began to revive. Someone was giving him something to drink. There were faces milling around him in the haze of heat and his own exhaustion. He barely had any strength in him to speak let alone get to his feet.

Who were these people? At first glance he began to discern that he was surrounded by African children. At least that was what he thought. He was somewhere else too. Someone gave him some more water that he gratefully absorbed. Finally, he found a little bit of energy to raise himself. There was something strange about the children who surrounded him. They weren't children at all. For a moment he felt as if he was in some sort of dreamland full of miniature adults; a black African native tribe with most of them about four feet in height. He felt like Gulliver in the Land of Lilliput. The people were the Pygmies of the Congolese rainforest. Somehow they had carried Anatole to the relative safety of their own makeshift settlements under the canopy of the interwoven trees that provided a certain amount of protection from the elements. Their huts were shaped like straw domes and were constructed from tree branches and thick leaves pasted together.

Anatole knew that they spoke in their own language and dialect. He listened intently and nodded with thanks, and smiled at them. The men had bows and arrows. The women had baskets on their backs. They were for the most part amiable and apparently peaceful, lacking any hostility to this stranger they had found; however, they did not smile. If anything their facial expressions were those of concern. These people were the Mbuti Pygmies. One woman came forward and offered him some sort of meat. He took it out of politeness. It was obviously some sort of game. He didn't question what it was. After days of lack of nourishment, he ate it. His malnourished body nearly exploded as he took in this food of substance. A man then offered him something else. It was a splendid tasty and sticky form of broken tree bark that he licked and swallowed. It was honey. Considering the monkeys and apes both practised the same habits of prising open tree bark and taking the honey, Anatole considered that in the depths of the jungle it must have been a life-saving – life giving – and life-preserving necessity in these parts.

He nodded with thanks to the Pygmies and tried to smile. But he felt dizzy again, his vision blurred and he felt as if he was fading out of this world. The strain of the past weeks of trekking through the Congo forest had taken its toll on him.

**

Anatole opened his eyes slowly. He felt different. Then he realised he felt washed and clean. He was lying in a bed, a civilised bed with clean sheets and pillows. There was movement and murmuring around him. He looked to his left and right. There were other beds with patients being attended to by nurses. There were also a couple of nuns close by. It was obviously a hospital. A slight breeze blew down the ward. It was the first time in weeks that Anatole had felt cooler after a lengthy time soaked in perspiration in the stifling humidity of the Congo.

At the end of the ward there appeared a smiling, grey-haired priest. He spoke to several of the patients and the nursing sisters for a few minutes. The man had a caring and reassuring nature about him. Then one of the nurses pointed down towards Anatole. The nurse had a very familiar look about her as if he had seen her before somewhere, but he could not place just where though. Both the priest and the nurse came down towards him and stood by the bed.

"Good morning," the priest said amiably. "Father Ray Flanagan. Pleased to meet you."

Anatole shook his hand. "An Irishman? You fellows get everywhere!

"Sure that we do," Father Flanagan replied with a laugh in his voice. "If you went to the North Pole you would find a Catholic priest preaching a sermon to the polar bears. When I was a wee young lad my father said go forth unto the arable pastures of our green land and multiply thine seed. So I became a priest and ended up in the Congo."

"Where am I, Father Flanagan? How did I get here?"

"You're at the Karobush station hospital on the banks of the Congo River and you were delivered here courtesy of the Mbuti tribe. The Pygmies, that is. You were in a very bad way, old fellow. We have a question for you. Take as long as you like in answering it."

"What is that, Father?"

"Who the bloody hell are you?"

"I'm Anatole Luchenya," he replied, coughing slightly.

"How in God's name did you get out there in the wilds?"

The nurse answered for him in a soft, cultured American voice. "You are the cameraman whose aircraft went missing, aren't you?"

"That's right," Anatole murmured.

"You're very lucky to be alive, Mr Luchenya," said the nurse. "I'm afraid they found the remains of the pilot. A search party went out looking for you. Are you up to telling us what happened?"

"I haven't the energy to talk about it now. I'm very sorry about the pilot. He seemed a nice guy. He had a Congolese wife and child. Tragic for them."

There was a short silence which the nurse brought to an end. "You're quite a survivor, aren't you, Mr Luchenya, or should I say, Nat Lucky?"

For a moment he looked at the nurse, frantically trying to unscramble the potpourri of mixed memories of his fascinating life. No matter how hard he tried he just could not work out where he had seen her before. He was about to be both pleasantly surprised and shocked.

"Nat Lucky was my stage name when I was in vaudeville back in the States. Believe me, honey, I've not used that name for years."

"I know," smiled the nurse. "You don't remember me, do you? You took me out on a date once... and what a date! It was in San Francisco back in 1906. We went to see Caruso at the Grand Opera House. Then you took me to an Italian restaurant. That was the night of the great earthquake."

"My God!" Anatole looked at her and smiled. "I remember! I really do." He racked his memory. "Your name... was Jane?" She nodded that it was. "And you came from a place called... I forget... somewhere near Lake Winnipesaukee... how about that?"

Father Flanagan looked on and smiled. "Well, Mr Luchenya, your memory is still pretty lucid as the doctors will no doubt be delighted to know. You two will no doubt have a lot of catching up to do but, in the meantime, try and get plenty of rest."

"We'll be back later... Nat," said the nurse. "The doctors will be down to see you in a few minutes. We'll catch up. Good to see you again... after twenty-three years!"

Anatole smiled at her and lay back. How good it felt to be clean again and to be in a real bed. He could not believe that he had just been talking to a girl he had once known in what seemed to be a different lifetime in a place far away.

***

Slugs had been writing down everything that Anatole had told him. He looked up from his notepad to see tears in his friend's eyes. This seemed to be the right moment to take a break. Almost as a sign that this was the right thing to do a hotel waiter banged a gong to inform the guests it was time for the midday meal. Slugs was eager to sample the local cuisine.

"What's the food like here, old buddy?" asked Slugs.

Anatole wiped his eyes. "Sorry about the moisture, must be onions in the air." His sense of humour hadn't deserted him. "The food? Oh it's interesting. I know you'll like it! My old pal Slugs will eat anything as long as you don't know what it is 'til afterwards!"

"Sounds about right," Slugs agreed. "How about we continue after lunch?"

Forty-Three

It was well into the afternoon when Slugs and Anatole resumed their session on the veranda of the hotel in Stanleyville. During the course of their delicious, somewhat elongated lunch the two men talked about all things that old friends do when they get together after a long time apart. Now it was back to business and the interview.

"This girl, Jane, that you knew in San Francisco all those years ago… what was it like meeting her again?"

***

The grounds of the Karobush station hospital were filled with a kaleidoscope of multi-coloured African flowers and lush green palms gently swaying in a slight breeze. A stunning deep blue sky and a radiant tropical sun only served to illuminate everything in the purest light, enhancing every vivid colour and feature of the hospital and gardens where patients sat recuperating.

One of those patients was Anatole. He felt so overwhelmed that after his ordeal he had survived the most impossible circumstances. The nurse, Jane Galyer, was now a forty-two-year-old woman who despite her prim starched uniform, still retained much of her earlier youthful attractiveness that had entranced Anatole all those years before. They sat together in the sunshine while other patients and nurses passed by them, some of whom were obviously exercising after amputation and operation. Others just soaked up the sun and sat in peace.

"I often wondered if you survived the earthquake," said Anatole.

"So did I," replied Jane. "For a few years, anyway, until one night a group of us from medical school in Pittsburgh went to the theatre and there you were up on stage as one of the Dancing Luckies."

"It all seems a long time ago now. I'm a cameraman now, filming wildlife. Tell me, how did you end up here?"

"I married an American doctor who specialised in tropical diseases, so we came here. He works in another wing of the hospital. Every now and then we are sent to a leper camp to help out there. Perhaps when you are well enough you might like to see the work that we do. We also go to other villages to check on the local people's general health. Malaria is a big problem and leprosy is a harsh reality. Poor diet and malnutrition is all too common too. There is a lot to be done for the health of the population."

Anatole was impressed by the lady's genuine commitment to her chosen profession. "I would like to see that sometime."

"Father Flanagan often accompanies us on these trips, to add some moral and spiritual guidance as well as helping out in any capacity that he may be able to do. I will make arrangements with him for you to come with us. Tell me... did you ever get married?"

"No," replied Anatole, although he added wishfully. "There is someone in England I'm considering asking."

"Is that where you live now? In that cold, grey land?"

"Cold and grey?" Anatole was genuinely surprised. "I don't find it cold and grey. At least not where my sister lives. She married an English lord and lives in Sussex. I found it lush green and the people were cheerful and for the most part good natured. I'm not sure where I live now. I'll go with the job. I may never go back to the States, I haven't a reason to. Do you know, Jane, I find Africa spellbinding? It's like being hypnotised and entering a world that once into, holds you and fascinates. It's like the magic of finding a beautiful woman with great magnetic beauty and warmth in her soul and heart that makes a man never want to let go. I've found what I've been looking for all my life: purpose and real ambition. To work for the protection of the African animals, to film them and take it to the world and tell the hunters and the ivory merchants to , and the wildlife soldiers of fortune, preserve and protect these animals, for like the Buffalo on the great plains of the wild Indian country of America, they may become extinct one day. I want to film the African people, the tribes, the customs, however contrasting, hideous or cultural, in the hope that the other nations of the world can help and civilise them without losing their basic character and identity. I guess I'm all fired up with enthusiasm. I survived falling out of an aircraft at three hundred feet. I feel like I can go anywhere and do anything."

"You'll find some things less to your liking, Nat," Jane was swift to point out. "Of course, there's beauty here. But there is an ugliness in its diseases, and some customs which are medieval and need drastic change. I believe those changes will come with medical advances, the proliferation of the Christian influence, and the natural progress of history."

"I'm sure they will. It's good to see you again after all these years. So, after the San Francisco earthquake you were at Medical School in Pittsburgh. Then what happened next?"

"I was nursing at a hospital in New York. When the war came I volunteered for service in France…"

"I was there too," interrupted Anatole. "And wounded."

"Yes, I was a nurse there and then back home again where I married my doctor husband. We went to London – oh yes, cold and grey London, but magnificent in the summer. I worked at Guys Hospital while my husband did research in tropical diseases, which eventually led to us being in the Congo." She looked at her watch. "I must go now, duty calls. You must rest and get better now. We'll organise those visits for you to see the work that we do."

Anatole smiled at her and watched as she walked away. He relaxed and sat back in the sunshine. The whole African experience had been something that could never ever be surpassed in his life for its breathless excitement, enchantment and the constant anticipated danger that always added impetus to the adventure.

***

Slugs signalled to a passing waiter for two glasses of beer. He put down his pen and notepad. His friend, Anatole, silently reflected on all that had happened. Finally he spoke again.

"Father Flanagan and I went to leper camps where I saw how devastating that disease is to the peoples of Africa. Far worse than I ever imagined. I saw tribalism, malnutrition, impoverishment on a widespread scale. I helped out as an orderly in the hospital for several months until I felt it was the right time to move on. I'm ready now to go back to England. I hope this is a good story for your readers, Slugs."

"To coin a phrase, it's a bobby dazzler! The story about a guy who escapes from an exploding aircraft and falls several hundred feet without a parachute to land on his ass in darkest Africa, and to trek through the Congo forests with dangerous creatures all around only to be rescued by Pygmies, and to be taken to recover in a bush hospital… well I mean… that's a story, pal! That's a rip-roaring knock 'em out, knock 'em dead, ripping son of a bitch yarn – better than any Wild West saga! It's about survival in the extreme and I love it! Believe me, I love it! The question is, will you? I'm quite prepared to let it go if it means endangering our friendship. Are you sure, old pal? The readers will love this story."

"Go ahead, Slugs. And that's final. After we've had a few belts in the bar how about we book our passage back on a boat to England."

"Sure thing, buddy. Anything else?"

Anatole thought for a moment and looked up with a smile. "Let's cable Jack in Ireland and Andre in New York. Tell them to come over to England. Not just for my arrival but for a very special occasion."

Slugs looked at him curiously. "What's the occasion then?"

Anatole came back as quick as a flash. "I've been single too long. I've sailed too close to the wind. If Trevilla still wants me I'm going to ask her to marry me."

At this point the waiter returned and placed two beers on the table. Slugs looked on in amazement. Then the two men picked up their glasses of beer and, without saying anything, clinked them together. They each took a sip of the cold beer and sat in silence for a few moments. A broad smile appeared on Slugs' face and then he let out a laugh of real happiness for his friend.

"Hell, buddy," he began, leaning forward and slapping Anatole on the shoulder, "this calls for one hell of a celebration!"

***

Jack Clancy stood behind the bar of the Limerick Castle pub in Dromana. In his hand he held the telegram telling him of Anatole's plans. He smiled happily too that day. His old boyhood friend who had been through so many adventurous exploits was finally going to settle into the warmth and sense of belonging in marriage. Jack had been told of Trevilla, although he was yet to meet her. From what he had been informed, he gathered that life with her would never be dull or just plain conventional. She was a talented, exciting, amorous and unpredictable woman. Just right for an equally unpredictable man in Anatole, who in his own way was a death-defying roving adventurer.

He turned around and picked the phone up. It rang and at the other end and Miriam answered. He told her the news about Anatole and then added for emphasis, "Start packing our bags. We're going to a wedding in England!" A wedding for his old friend. It all seemed so wonderful.

The bar was unusually quiet that night. There were always instruments in the Limerick Castle ready to be picked up and played at a moment's notice by some of the talented amateurs who sipped their milk stouts and gossiped about gossip and blarneyed about blarney. Jack was feeling buoyant and happy. What better way to celebrate than with a song.

"Gentlemen! You're all very quiet tonight. Will you join me in a song? One of my old pals is getting married and I want to sing! I know that much. Singing is good for the spirit and food for the soul. Let's sing!"

Some of the regulars moved into position taking up the vacant instruments that always were placed near the bar. They included an accordion, an old piano, a banjo and a violin.

"What'll it be, Jack?" One of the regular drinkers asked as he picked up the accordion.

"How about the 'Black Velvet Band'? And let's sing so loud it'll take the slabs of the tombstones in the cemetery!"

"Now what would you want to disturb my old grandfather for in the cemetery?" asked one man dryly. "He's only just got to sleep. He was always an insomniac in life."

"How old was he when he died?" asked Jack out of curiosity.

The man replied, "Oh he was a mere youngster when he died. There's no telling what he could have achieved. He'd nine children with my old granny and it's rumoured he may have had a bit of practice and produce with some of the local colleens ~~women~~ before and after the marriage. Poor man. He was a mere ninety-seven years of age! I miss his words of wisdom and many women mourn the measure of the man!"

"Ninety-seven huh!" said Jack in amusement. "What did he die of?"

"Oh, he was doing an Irish jig on a tavern table with a frisky bumptious lass and he collapsed with a heart attack. The tavern table did too. It was beyond repair. He died laughing, you know. The priest came to read him the last rites as he lay in bed. The poor old priest got his cassock caught in the door and slid over and broke his leg. He tried to get up and fell head first into the lass's bosoms. My poor old grandfather laughed his way to heaven! He laughed so loud it caused an earthquake they felt in Dublin."

"It's a great story! If it's not true, it should be. C'mon let's sing!" Jack started to sing and soon all the customers joined in. The words resonated throughout the Limerick Castle pub that night.

> *'Her eyes they shone like diamonds*
> *I thought her the queen of the land*
> *And her hair it hung over her shoulder*
> *Tied up with a black velvet band.'*

When Trevilla arrived back in England from her year long tour of America and Australia, the boat had docked at Tilbury on a very rainy night. The whole trip had been at times exciting, exhausting and exhilarating; so many countries, people, performances and pleasures had given her memories she would treasure for however long she lived. She had loved the experiences she had in visiting the glittering cities of America, and the 'newness' of Australia, its raw naivety and apparent unscarred youthfulness. Yet the moment she and the rest of the cast, as well as a proud Arthur Burnside beaming like a father at the sight of his first-born, saw the luminous White Cliffs of Dover on a black, rain-filled night from the deck of the liner, they all felt that wonderful sense of being back home in the 'Old Country'.

The last part of the voyage took them past the North Foreland, Shoebury, and then on to Tilbury Dock. The sun may not have been shining but the incredible thrill of having been so far away and coming home to see family and friends again was simply divine. Home! England! London accents, Bovril and Marmite, Lyons Cafes, red London double-decker buses, cocoa, trolly buses that sparked electricity as they went round corners, barmaids who repeated the orders in a boisterous pub on a Saturday night, "Arf a pint was it dear?" and cricketers in resplendent whites on the village green. These were things they missed the most about England. Even in the pouring rain it looked welcoming.

Trevilla went straight down to Sussex on the train to see her family. They were very happy working hard on their small holding on the Shervington family estate. It was everything they had ever dreamed of. After years of living a roving life to be finally settled in their own farm on the South Downs of Sussex was a dream come true for them. They knew living there was a mutual arrangement between them and the Shervingtons, but they worked hard to justify their good fortune. Amongst the crops they grew and lovingly tended were parsnips, turnips, asparagus, beetroot, tomatoes, podded peas, swedes, potatoes, mint, runner beans, cabbages, lettuce, carrots, celery, as well as looking after the orchard trees that yielded a fine crop of apples and pears. They also grew rhubarb and strawberries, and picked bags of blackberries, which ensured tasty puddings for many of the local folk who bought them on market day. Roget had been asked by the Shervingtons if he could experiment on a spare patch of land, the possibility of growing hops for the beer working men liked to sup. In short this part of the Shervington enterprises was not only traditional but innovative too.

There was no doubt that Trevilla loved the South Downs. Just the sight of the lush green rolling contours again was like a glimpse of heaven. She may have travelled the world and performed to audiences of all descriptions but to once again scent the perfumed breezy air of the Downs meant that she was truly home. Her family were absolutely delighted to see their incredibly charismatic daughter who, as Arthur Burnside had advised, had not forgotten her beginnings. Neither did she take on airs or graces and only spoke with real amazement at the course her colourful life had taken her. Always she was passionate, boisterous, enthusiastic, energetic and excited about life. Trevilla was genuinely interested in her parents' new farming venture and momentarily forgot she was a bona fide dancer and entertainer. She could not resist getting her hands dirty to work on the farm. This was only temporary of course because Arthur Burnside and Hollywood would soon contact her for new shows and film contracts in her career.

Trevilla was not only thrilled to see her family but also the old horse who had drawn the caravan for years. One day she went to see her old friend in the field by the Shervington estate. It was enjoying a well-deserved retirement being cared for by the farrier. Then she went down to stroke it and talk to it in a way only a mistress can to her pet. The horse wasn't lonely. The Shervingtons had taken in a stray donkey from a redundant farm, given it some loving care and put it into the same field where it became a happy and peaceful companion to the horse. Mariska was there and the two women greeted each other warmly. They had both once occupied different worlds but now by virtue of their shared show business experiences they had far more in common than both had previously realised. Mariska was quick to note a new understated sophistication in Trevilla.

"Thank you for looking after my family, Mariska," Trevilla said. "And thank you for looking after my old friend Dobbin the horse. He is my faithful friend… aren't you?" She stroked the horse. "I see you have found him a new friend to play with. A lovely donkey."

"Yes, he came from a nearby farm that closed down. He looks happy here. You're comfortable in the farm with your family, are you?"

"After many hotels around the world, to be home with my family is so good. Oh, Mariska, I have seen so much! The excitement of being on stage and filming in Los Angeles and the hot dry heat of Australia… I never ever dreamed I could do such things and see such places! It is as if I have dreamed it all. Did you ever feel such things when you and Anatole danced on stage across the world or is it just me, the Gypsy girl, who thought such a life was an impossible dream?"

"Not at all, Trevilla." Mariska smiled at the younger lady's enthusiasm for her new life. "There was never a minute of my stage career that I did no appreciate. We were poor Russian orphan kids in New York who got one hell of a lucky break. It was great while it lasted. I wouldn't have missed it for the world."

"Mr Burnside has another show in London he wants me to do and then I have been offered a part in another film in Hollywood. I'm going to make the most of my time here. How is Anatole? When is he coming home? I miss him so much."

"Oh, I almost forget to tell you," Mariska said suddenly and she appeared to be looking over Trevilla's shoulder at a pathway leading from the South Downs to the main house. "Anatole's friends Jack Clancy and Slugs have arrived for a short visit. They're up at the house staying in the guest rooms. They're here with their wives."

"I like Mr Slugs. He is like me! Loud and fun." Trevilla let out that old familiar laugh. "I've heard a lot about Jack too. Oh, I can't wait to see Anatole. I love him so much!"

"Do you?" Mariska asked. She broke out into a broad smile. "Then why don't you tell him? Now!"

"Now?" Trevilla was puzzled until she realised that Mariska was looking past her towards the South Downs pathway.

She turned around and saw a man slowly approaching them. She couldn't believe her eyes. Then she spoke in a voice barely above a whisper. "Anatole!" It was all the more mesmerising for above the Downs a rainbow of deep resplendent shades of colours provided a welcoming arch for Anatole's return.

He suddenly stopped at a distance of about a hundred yards or so away from her. It was as if he had returned from the dead after having been reported missing in the Congo. He stood there gazing at her. What a sight for his weary eyes! At once he could see how much more beautiful and confident she looked now after her long tour. His admiration for her was mutually returned for Trevilla could see in him everything she respected in a man, including resilience and the quality of endurance that ensured he would always bounce back no matter whatever the obstacle. Anatole looked smart too. He wore a sports jacket and tie, his hair was smoothed back, his eyes sparkled and he smiled the broadest smile he had ever given anyone in his life. His heart quickened and his pulse raced. The next thing they knew both were running towards each other and there on the Sussex Downs they held each other as if there was no tomorrow and kissed passionately. Words somehow seemed inadequate for on that occasion conversation and explanation was unnecessary. To hold each other and savour their deep love was joy in itself.

Mariska turned and walked back to the house. She was quite overcome with emotion too. Her brother and Slugs had only arrived back from the Congo the night before and she was still getting used to the fact that Anatole was back home again. Now he had been reunited with Trevilla, the one true love of his life; the fabulous Gypsy girl who had won his heart.

From the window of the study of Shervington Manor, Bernard, Jack and Slugs all looked on at the sight of Trevilla and Anatole in the distance reaffirming their love for each other. It was a moving moment for Jack. Anatole had been like a brother to him from the days when they sang on the street in New York and found themselves in the same orphanage. A tear rolled down his cheek.

Slugs noticed the expression and tears on Jack's face. He put his hand on his friend's shoulder and said, "We're sentimental old sons' of a gun, aren't we?"

"It's the Irishness in you," Bernard pointed out.

"No," Jack answered softly. "The kid we grew up with has found himself one hell of a dame to love. Eh, Slugs! Big guy!"

"Sure, old buddy," said Slugs. "The old team is back together again. Who would ever believe it?"

Forty-Four

A fortnight later Trevilla and Anatole were married at Caxton Hall. The difference in their respective faiths and origins meant that they could not marry in a church but it made no difference to them. They were in love… truly, madly in love… and the ceremony may have been simple but the love they felt for each other was lavish and exhilarating; beautiful in every context.

It was the first sunny day in a week of downpours which felt as if it had been ordered by a higher authority. Their happiness was absolutely contagious; they made a sparkling couple rivalling any royal couple or towering echelons of society. Trevilla wore a cream outfit and a huge floppy hat. Anyone seeing her with such glamorous film star looks would never have thought that such an exotic woman was a Gypsy by birth, tradition and nature, who had once scrambled in the dirt making a living by picking cabbages and nurturing mangel-wurzels. She had finally got her man and she was ecstatic.

Anatole wore a beautiful double-breasted dark blue suit and bow tie. At forty-three he cut a dashing figure and had a real magnetism about him that was hard to define. He had thought that he would always remain the eternal bachelor but now he had surrendered the single life to be happily captured and captivated by Trevilla. Perhaps now it seemed that marriage would curb his nomadic wandering adventurous ways.

Not a bit of it! They were no ordinary suburban couple who would sit by the fireplace at home in Greenford or Ruislip. Their exciting and demanding careers meant that life would always be challenging and never remotely dull.

Both were, by virtue, family-orientated people. Their separate faiths and backgrounds dictated and upheld strong family values. They were also shrewd enough to know that the opportunities afforded by their wonderful careers had to be taken now and the benefits enjoyed to their utmost because such things were once in a lifetime gifts from God that could dissolve at any time. However, they were committed to having their own family and children would surely follow through.

They posed proudly on the steps of Caxton Hall as photographers from the national press snapped eagerly, as did their friends, family and Trevilla's fellow cast members from her recent tour. How amazing it was that a Gypsy girl and a Russian émigré had come so far that their wedding was headline news.

Slugs felt proud. He had got his international scoop, making him the envy of his fellow journalists. And what a scoop. Not only had he got the edge on the big boys of Fleet Street, but his story had hit the stands from New York to Sydney. It was the stuff of legend how Anatole had plunged several hundred feet from the burning wreckage on an aircraft and lived to tell the tale of his survival in the Congo undergrowth, his rescue by a tribe of Pygmies and return to England. Then to top it all, a truly happy ending to this story of adventure in darkest Africa with his marriage to Trevilla, the current darling of the theatrical world. Now that was a story!

Needless to say it was made even more fascinating by the fact that Anatole's life had encompassed so much. He was, after all, the poor Russian Jewish boy who had been orphaned in New York. Yet he had gone on to form a vaudevillian dance act with his sister that had knocked the socks of audiences right across North and South America as well as playing to packed houses in Europe. In his private life he had been shanghaied to China, returned via Australia and the islands of the Pacific Ocean only to get caught up in the 1906 San Francisco earthquake. If that wasn't enough he had returned from a tour of Europe aboard the *Titanic* and survived its sinking. He had then worked as a Hollywood film extra, an oil driller, a waiter, a soldier in the Mexican Revolution and the Great War, before becoming a cinematographer.

The whole story of his life was incredulous. Certain sections of the press dubbed Anatole a 'Larger than Life' character but in truth he was just a fellow who had lived life like a game of chance.

Lord Bernard Shervington had been delighted to have been chosen as Anatole's best man. It had been a deliberate but well thought out choice by Anatole in order to avoid offence to Jack and Slugs, who he loved like brothers. Amongst the guests was Arthur Burnside, always beaming, always happy but today particularly. He was thrilled to see his young protégé Trevilla so happy. From his own vast music hall and stage experience he understood the insecurities of performers in the theatrical world. He had no doubt though that theirs was a perfect – if rather unusual – match.

Andre Aviva had taken passage from New York on the first available vessel. For him, personally, this was an incredibly happy day. To see Anatole again who he had thought lost and dead in the Congo was wonderful beyond words. It was made even more happier by the fact that his friend was marrying the wonderful and quirky Trevilla, truly a prize for any man. After all Trevilla was in the prime of her life now. With an insatiable quest for all of life's new experiences, a heightened sexuality and a total awareness of it together with deep feelings of love and loyalty to Anatole and her own family, she would bring brightness and happiness to all those who came into contact with her.

Bernard and Mariska's children, Alexander now aged fourteen and Grace who was eleven, happily mingled with Trevilla's proud family. Her father, Roget, could hardly believe the turn of events that had propelled his vegetable picker and precocious daughter to be the centre of attention at a London society wedding. Trevilla's grandmother Elena, her mother and her siblings, Patric and Alida, all posed happily together for a stunning family photograph. Stunning indeed. How remarkable how beautiful clothes could transform a family used to wearing often ragged attire, to an appearance of elegance and affluence.

The boys from New York, Jack and Slugs, also posed alongside the happy couple, together with their wives and children. Slugs' wife held their recently born son – a true Englishman, they would say in later years – and it was truly smiles all around. Oh but the happiness was contagious amongst all who were there! No one was forgotten when the photographs were taken either. Arthur Burnside, the old showman, stood amongst them all as if this had been another of his West End spectacular box office runaway shows. Andre Aviva, a normally shy man, basked in the limelight of his friend and colleague's apparent resurrection from the dead to a rebirth, and a reigniting of his own exciting life. Trevilla was to say later that night to Anatole that it had been such a wonderful day could they do it all again the following week!

The wedding reception was held at a function room in the splendour of Claridges. The guests poured in. It was actually a ballroom that had been converted to accommodate the entourage of Trevilla's family and friends together with the cast members of *The Prince and the Gypsy Girl*, plus Anatole's friends and family. All the tables were set for the 'scrumptious sumptuous' wedding breakfast with Trevilla's family and Anatole, Bernard, Mariska and their children seated at the top. However, Anatole and Trevilla were to make a special entrance when all the guests were seated. Arthur Burnside had organised a band who sat at the ready for when the guests would surely take to the floor. The musicians wore white tuxedos and bow ties. There would be a few surprises. 'This was no ordinary wedding.'

When the guests were all seated at the reception, in the traditional long-standing manner of indicating quiet, Bernard took a glass and tapped on a spoon several times. He stood up to command everyone's attention. A surprise had been organised. Jack Clancy walked over to the band and stood by the microphone.

"Ladies and gentlemen," Bernard began. "Would you please welcome… Mr and Mrs Anatole and Trevilla Luchenya!"

Through the open doors they appeared holding hands and in a theatrical manner they bowed to all and sundry before they walked out into the middle of the ballroom smiling. The band began to play and Jack Clancy sang in a rich strong voice 'Oh How We Danced on the Night We Were Wed'. This was the cue for Anatole and Trevilla to take to the floor and dance like the true professionals they were. There was beauty in the way they danced. It was slow and graceful, like two courting swans in a crystal-clear lake. They seemed never to stop smiling and savouring every happy moment on their wedding day.

Bernard was professional to his boot heels that night, not only carrying out his duties as best man, but also as a master of ceremonies. After all the speeches and the meal had been eaten Bernard was keen to use the talents of several of the guests there. It wasn't only a wedding reception but also an off the cuff cabaret.

"Ladies and gentlemen," he boomed confidently to all guests, thoroughly enjoying his moment of fame even if addressing a slightly different audience to the one he normally had in the House of Lords. "Mr Arthur Burnside, veteran of music hall of an age gone by and now theatre impresario is with us. Give him a round of applause." The guests applauded him and like a true professional Arthur stood up and bowed. "While you are on your feet, Arthur, how about giving us a display of your dancing prowess. I happen to know you do a mean Charleston."

Arthur responded happily. "It will be a pleasure, Lord Shervington." He looked towards the band and walked towards them. "Boys, you know what to do. Start up the music!"

Immediately Arthur surprised everyone be doing the Charleston. He had obviously rehearsed this routine privately but for an elderly man he showed that he had still the energy and enthusiasm to perform such a vigorous dance. Everyone stood up and gave the old stager a standing ovation. He obviously enjoyed this moment in the limelight and was determined to make the most of it. He had a quick word in the ear of the bandleader who was seen to tell his musicians the name of the number in Arthur's routine. It was a very popular tune of the time.

This time a smiling Arthur performed a song called 'Ballin' the Jack'. Complete with dance movements and the magnetic and mischievous facial expressions of the wise cracking performer he had once been, he showed why he had once been dubbed as the 'old stager'. He knew how to make them laugh, make them cry and make them sigh. It was so good that everyone was joining in imitating the dance and singing along. He did the 'Lambeth Walk' too.

Everyone looked so incredibly happy that night. Sublime happiness is truly the nirvana of human emotions, rarely experienced, seldom witnessed, but when seen and privileged to have been surrounded by the participant takes away a memory of El Dorado proportions, they will keep returning to for the rest of their days.

There were so many images that were caught on film that night by the specially hired photographer as well as a movie camera recording the reception. Andre Aviva had arranged for the entire day to be filmed. With his knack of anticipating a special time in history he thought that perhaps the happy couple would quite rightly want to look back and relive the joyous day of their marriage.

Slugs and Marilyn virtually stole the show at one point. They asked the bandleader if he would play a request for them. The big guy certainly had no inhibitions about taking to the floor with Marilyn and showing he was no slouch when it came to dancing. He and his wife showed the others how to dance the Blackbottom. They were promptly joined by Bernard and

Mariska, Jack and Miriam, and it was impossible to resist too for Anatole and Trevilla. Even Arthur Burnside got into the act dragging a cast member out who was energetic and enjoying every minute too.

Few wedding receptions ever had such a dazzling array of talent on display. It was as if everyone was celebrating the great feeling of simply being alive. The band then played a good old fashioned 'Knees up Mother Brown'. Just about everybody who had an ounce of energy and zest in their soul took to the floor. It was a night in Claridges when the floor shook and the walls vibrated.

Just when it seemed the night couldn't get any better than Slugs, Jack and Anatole moved to the microphone in front of the band. Anatole stood in the centre flanked by his two best friends. He stooped slightly forward to speak to the guests.

"I just want to say that this has been the happiest day of my life and to thank Trevilla for becoming my wife. The love I feel for her today is beyond words. Thank you darling." This drew a huge applause from all the guests. "I have married a wonderful woman and I love her with all my heart." From the dance floor Trevilla blew him a kiss. "I also want to pay tribute to my wonderful sister, Mariska. Once upon a time she and I toured the world as the Dancing Luckies. Tonight on the dance floor right here the Dancing Luckies were reunited." This drew more applause. "I'm a hell of a lucky guy. Lost in the Congo only to return and now I am a married man. Boy was someone up in the skies looking after me! I want to thank my friends and colleagues, Arthur and Andre down there. I don't know what Arthur has for breakfast but boy do I want a big helping to be as fit as him!" It was Arthur who laughed the loudest. "For Andre my colleague and friend, I want to say an enormous thanks for taking me on in the cine-camera business. If we hadn't come to Europe I would never have met Trevilla. Nor would I have seen the great thrills of Africa."

"It was a pleasure, Nat," Andre called back to him. "We'll do it again soon. This is a great day for you. You deserve it."

"Thanks, Andre," Anatole replied, and it was easy to see he was becoming quite emotional now. "This is a great day in so many respects. My brother-in-law, Bernard, is doing a steadfast job tonight as best man. Bernard is a great guy and a real compassionate battler for the poor of this country. Would you all give him a huge round of applause, ladies and gentlemen."

The audience responded as requested. Bernard looked quite touched by the gesture. Perhaps even a little bit embarrassed but he smiled back, and Mariska and the children looked at him adoringly.

"Finally, before I have one last dance with my wife before we leave tonight…" Anatole's voice faltered slightly. "You'll see beside me my two best pals. We're true New Yorkers. Sure Jack may have been born in Ireland and I was born in Russia, and our buddy, Slugs the big guy… is of Irish stock… yessir two Micks and a Ruskie… but we came up the hard way on the streets of New York. Jack and I… well we were in the same orphanage with my kid sister, Mariska. We made a living singing on the streets. Later on, Jack, Slugs and I fought in the battlefields of France before returning to the challenges of civilian life. Now we're together again, all three of us married men. The three of us are going to sing a number that I hope you'll enjoy listening to as much as we're going to enjoy singing."

The bandleader knew exactly what the song was. He gave the cue to his fellow musicians. The boys from New York began to sing. The song was called 'Heart of My Heart'.

'When we were kids on the corner of the street
We were rough'n ready, guys
But oh how we could harmonise
"Heart of My Heart" meant friends were dearer then
Too bad we had to part
I know a tear would glisten
If once more I could listen
To that gang that sang "Heart of My Heart"
C'mon now, Let's everybody sing!
"Heart of My Heart", I love that melody
"Heart of My Heart" brings back a memory.'

The song was heart-warming and sentimental. The applause was loud and on conclusion of the song Slugs, Jack and Anatole all shook hands, gave each other hugs of friendship and stood there smiling. Then Jack and Slugs returned to their chairs alongside their families at the reception table. Everyone else did too except for Anatole, who walked across to Trevilla and took her hand. She took his and they moved to the centre of the dance floor, eagerly watched by everybody.

Then they took up position. The band immediately launched into a stunning Latin American rendition that set the scene to allow them to dance the Tango. What is it about the sensuous, dazzling, and seductive movements of the Tango that so bewitches and fascinates the onlooker? Different people could put varied interpretations on the theme of the dance. Was it a dance of seduction? Was it a dance of passion? Whatever the mystery behind the creation of this most iconic dance, when performed by two people genuinely in love, it had a pure indefinable magic that made for the most compelling viewing. Love and warmth oozed through the very fibres of Anatole and Trevilla's being. Their eyes shone with the optimum of love each had for the other. The movements of their separate bodies mirrored the other in a symmetrical fashion as the pulse of a warm and deeply passionate love flowed through them like the powerful current of a fast-flowing river. It was mesmeric, enchanting, entrancing and to the guests at the wedding it felt as if they were travellers who had arrived at some celestial destination belonging to a fairy tale myth that only they were privileged to behold. The dance finished with the suddenness of one awakening from a dream that took the person from a land of nymphs and spirits of Greek and Roman mythology to the one of reality but in better condition to face the rigours of the reality of the natural world. A crescendo of applause erupted. Anatole and Trevilla held hands and bowed to the wedding guests; this had been the grand finale for their wedding day. It would have been true to say, as with many seasoned performers, they knew how to bow out, leaving the audience craving for more. Their smiles of a glorious happiness and bliss were a signal that Anatole and Trevilla's wonderful wedding day had come to an end.

***

Before they left for their honeymoon in Venice they returned to Shervington Manor. The South Downs of Sussex had always been a special place for Anatole and Trevilla. They knew however unpredictable their lives or the world may be, the Downs would always be a place of peace and tranquillity for them. The summer sunshine seemed to enhance the green and the wild flowers that swayed in a gentle breeze as they walked along their favourite pathways. It was as if a mysterious voice spoke in the breeze to the happy couple welcoming the newlyweds back to the place they had first met. The birds twittered and buzzed in the leafy green trees. Sheep bleated in fields far below. The scent of golden cornfields and blossoms rose to greet them.

Hand in hand they walked until they arrived at a spot at the very top of the Downs. Dressed only in casual clothes they were completely relaxed. Happy in each other's company and in love, they felt the world and all its opportunities lay before them. Trevilla was so happy now that she was finally married to the man she would remain passionately in love with and fascinated by for the rest of her life. She was so full of energy and passion that her state of being could be compared to a fizzy bottle of champagne on New Year's Eve. Once shaken and uncorked the bubbles would quickly rise to the surface and shower everyone. Her personality could explode but always with joy and pleasant to taste like a champagne of a fine vintage.

The view from the top of the South Downs was very clear and distinct that day. Anatole and Trevilla leaned against a wooden fence and gazed out at the panorama. It was so clear that they could see the blue of the English Channel and faintly in the distance the coastline of the Isle of Wight. They stood in silence admiring the view for a few moments. Anatole turned to look with adoration into the eyes of his bride who put her arms around him. She kissed him with a deep passion.

"Happy is the man who finds a true friend in his wife," Anatole said very quietly. Trevilla looked at him curiously. He was quick to reassure her. "Just a phrase I heard somewhere."

Trevilla gripped his hand tightly. "Do you think we will be all right, my darling?"

"Of course," Anatole replied. "We will be fine, Trevilla. Life will be good for both of us... and the children we will have." Trevilla's eyes lit up and she beamed a happy smile at the thought of having her own family. Anatole turned to look at the green and gold meadows and pastures that lay beneath them far below their vantage point. "I have seen the world in all its glorious colours but to me there is no greater beauty than the South Downs. This is our place, Trevilla. This is where it all began for us. There will be new times now for us to come."

"Mr Burnside said to me that in the future there will be times of splendour." Trevilla remembered the conversation clearly. "He also said one day I will look back and think of those splendid memories. You have many of those, don't you?"

Anatole's eyes shone as he thought back over the years of his life since he had left Russia as a little boy. A cavalcade of people, personalities and faraway places, as well as the history he had been part of flashed through his mind. There was a certain grandeur about it all.

"Splendid indeed!" Anatole said with a flourish. "Hell yes! Let's get out there and make a few more."

Trevilla took his hand and they began to walk across the top of the South Downs. The sun shone brightly for them that day.